ATAPI SORCERESS

by

MARGARET GREGORY

TAT Publishing

Also by Margaret Gregory

TYMOREAN TRUST SERIES:

Book 1 - Power Rising
Book 2 - Great Ones
Book 3 - The Return to Earth
Book 4 – Earth Mission

ATAPI SORCERESS SERIES:

Book 1- The Wild One

THE THIRD GENERATION SERIES

Wanda: From Bad to Worse

ATAPI SORCERESS

CHAPTER 1 - Koenig and Kaer - POV

Koenig, High Minister of the Kimh, scowled when the first words of the report registered in his mind.

"There is still no sign of Jai Cassidy." He recognised the precise handwriting of his youngest son, Kaer, and thumped the pages onto the table in front of him.

An extremely rude curse came to mind, but he did not utter it. How had that abominable hybrid managed to escape again? The chit was little more than a child, and an alien at that. Jenha Mosellan had a lot to answer for, allowing it to discover it had sorcerous talents and to learn how to cross planes. If it could move instantly from place to distant place, it could be anywhere.

While he hoped the hybrid would lose itself somewhere in the darkness between planes, it had proved so far to be skilled enough to avoid that fate. Somehow it had known of the Atapi's sacred rock and gone there. It had also known of that mountain glade and the waterfall. What other places did it know of?

His hand reached for a crystal glass; he touched it to his lips and realised that it was empty. A silent figure drifted to his side before he could fling the offending glass at the tapestry covered wall. He hadn't noticed the servant enter the room.

Koenig glanced at the white tunic-clad servant as she filled his glass from a crystal carafe and did not turn her eyes to look at him. He nodded his thanks, not concerned that the figure did not see it. These new servants were silent, discreet and never intruded on his concentration. It almost seemed that they could anticipate his needs, even read his thoughts. Right then, he craved the calming effect of the fruity smelling ruby drink. Someone had trained this servant well.

"Have my son, Kaer, summoned," Koenig directed. The silent figure nodded and retreated.

He gave the servant no further thought as he read his son's report, then stood to stretch his muscles and straighten his official robes. The long purple open front tunic, trimmed with white fur, was impressive, but it tended to twist around him as he worked.

He crossed to the window where the morning sun shone into the room, warming it to a comfortable temperature. The activity of the Kumatan guards patrolling the gardens of the Royal Palace was ordered, unhurried – as it should be. In contrast, thinking of Jai Cassidy, the human-Atapi hybrid from that alien world called Earth, was like hearing a blowfly buzzing around his head – an unpredictable, chaotic element. Surely the Traegers could find the female child. It would have to approach a town to get food – probably steal it.

While waiting for his son to appear, Koenig paced his office until the colourful geometric pattern of the tapestry on the wall caught his attention. The shapes represented order, problems neatly solved. The hybrid was like a tear in the fabric that let order unravel. In spite of this, his body reacted to the design, and he began to relax as he recalled the first mantra for calm.

Koenig was a man of middle years and had been High Minister for almost two decades. He still looked to be in vigorous good health, though the demands of his position kept him inside too much and allowed little time for exercise. Like all his kind, his hair was white blond, his eyes purplish blue and his skin faintly luminescent. He would not show the depredations of age on his hawk-like features for many years yet.

A gentle chime announced a visitor, and Koenig strode back to his official table to seat himself before calling out permission to enter. Kaer had arrived with satisfactory promptness, and his bow of greeting was precisely correct.

Koenig scrutinised his son's appearance in an instant and found nothing to criticise. His dark blue formal robes were impeccable, his hair once again neatly trimmed – a vast improvement from the previous week when he had returned from that alien world.

"So you have still not recovered that hybrid," Koenig challenged as Kaer approached to the accepted distance for an audience with the High Minister. "It has been a week already."

Kaer stood three paces away from the table as protocol demanded. His face flushed to a faint mauve. "No, Father," he admitted, keeping his voice controlled. "As I wrote in my report, a thorough search was made in the area where Traeger Pentan was found. We found traces of Jai Cassidy and a child there, and between the waterfall and the river, but no tracks leaving the area. The tracker guards even followed the river downstream until it got too deep and turbulent to walk in and found no signs they left that way. A cave behind the waterfall showed signs of having been occupied, but nothing was found there. The Traegers believe she has crossed planes to somewhere as yet unknown."

Koenig grunted with displeasure. "So she has Mosellan's son with her. He must be found. We cannot allow him to remain with her." He noticed the tight, almost rebellious expression on his youngest son's face. "Ensure that the Traegers and guards keep looking. Have them check out the area where Stacion Ansuni used to live. Since the hybrid killed him, that land is hers now, isn't it?"

"Father, Jai Cassidy is human, and born on Earth. How could she know of it?"

"How did she know of that pagan monolith in the desert? How did she know of that waterfall area?"

It was a good question, Kaer decided. "She had an artefact from her mother…"

"More likely a power relic stolen from Stacion Ansuni," Koenig countered. "Atapi females can't make power relics. She doesn't have that any more, does she?"

"No, Traeger Pentan took it from her."

Koenig gave his son a sharp look. "Notify the regional garrisons to look out for them as well. Who knows where they are now. However, they will have to try to get food somehow – so have them look out for reports of stolen food or clothing."

"Yes, Father," Kaer responded obediently.

"That hybrid must be found," Koenig emphasised. "Part Atapi, part human – what a horrible mixture. Humans, I have heard, are a violent lot."

"Not all humans," Kaer felt compelled to object. "The war finished soon after the Traegers started opposing Stacion Ansuni. I have little doubt that he was a contributing factor to that conflict. Anyway, Jai Cassidy is not like that."

"You are still naïve, Kaer. That hybrid put four Kumatan guards in the infirmary – all on her own. If you call that peaceful and honourable…"

"She was provoked!" Kaer interrupted, realising instantly that he had breached protocol. He snapped his mouth shut, seeing his father's expression tighten.

"I think your objectivity is still confused," Koenig remarked, using a tone meant to soothe his son. "Perhaps you are correct, but when she is brought here, the Counsellors can assess her."

He stared at his son until Kaer nodded acquiescence. Then he slid another report in front of him.

"Pentan. The mind healers have recommended his retirement. He is no longer a Traeger. He requires permanent supervision," Koenig informed his son. "And Mosellan. The counsellors say that he needs an extended period of counselling, and possibly retraining, before he will be allowed to resume his duties. That hybrid has corrupted two senior Traegers and is probably corrupting Mosellan's son. Two eminent Traeger bloodlines – destroyed. That hybrid could not have contrived to help the Atapi more."

"Father, I do not share your impression of Jai Cassidy. The Atapi on Earth wanted her dead. She has little love for them and Pentan brought his condition on himself," Kaer stated, but he knew his father would disagree.

"If that hybrid can move herself using Atapi sorcery, who knows what else she can do. I want her here, muzzled," Koenig pronounced. The subtle luminance of his skin increased, betraying the intensity of his desire. "And if I decide you are being less than conscientious about finding her…" He glanced at his son, noticing the rigid posture and flushed face. "I see that you don't agree, but allowing that hybrid to run loose is criminal. She can't possibly know how to get food without stealing it. This is for her wellbeing too."

His voice was no gentler when he added, "I think that being on that barbaric planet has affected you. I will arrange counselling sessions for everyone who spent time there."

When the flush faded from his son's face, Koenig went on implacably, "Finding that human pollutant is your priority. I cannot risk losing any more Traegers, we need every one we have. The Atapi are causing so much trouble these days. Did you hear how they have killed and barbarically dismembered several groups of off-world engineers? I cannot allow any further atrocities, or we will have that Selkrit Councillor insisting on compensation or withdrawing his people. If either happens, it will set back Korvu's progress by decades."

Kaer nodded. "I understand, Father," he replied meekly. He didn't ask why his father seemed to be blaming Jai Cassidy for trouble that had happened on Korvu before she'd even arrived. "I will speak to the Traegers in charge of the search."

"If you get the slightest hint of where she is, I want you to get the Traegers there as fast as you can," Koenig told him, before waving his hand in a shooing motion.

Kaer didn't linger. He was relieved to be dismissed and wanted to be well away from his father's office and the observant guards outside the door.

Once he was alone, except for the calm faces in the portraits on the passage wall, he unfastened the front of the archaically styled formal robes and considered removing the outer tunic. His gut was in tight knots and he made an effort to calm himself and the unvoiced resentments swirling in his mind.

He was an adult, twenty years old – not an untutored child. He didn't need another lecture on objectivity. His father might be High Minister, but he was wrong. His advisors were wrong. Jai Cassidy had honour and was not like the male Atapi sorcerers. The advisors had not been on Earth. Their conclusions were based on two things – that Jai Cassidy was half Atapi, and when the Traegers first arrived on Earth, the people there were doing their best to kill each other.

Without consciously thinking about it, Kaer headed back towards his suite. He had left the administrative wing of the palace, with its impressive décor of white stone and polished wood floors, and headed to the wing where the family of the High Minister lived. Here the walls were hung with tapestries and the floor carpeted with woven wool mats.

His thoughts were still roiling, going over the conversation with his father. It would be no use debating the issue of Jai Cassidy with him, but there had to be a way to convince him that she was not evil.

As for the atrocities that his father had referred to, they had to stop. He had read a report about them and it had shocked and sickened him. The attacks had been unprovoked, or so it seemed, but then if the alien engineers had strayed into Atapi territory, that would have been provocation enough. What he did not understand was why the off-world engineers had been that far from where their work was to be done. From what he had heard since returning to Korvu, the power stations and irrigation systems they were to build needed to be near the Kumatan and Kimh towns.

On the subject of Jai Cassidy, he didn't feel the same certainty. Yes, he would continue to have Kumatan guards looking out for her, but he did not agree with his father that she should be arbitrarily neutralised, nor that she should be used against the Atapi. She didn't deserve to be treated like she was disposable. Even so, he knew that his father would never get her to think like the Kimh or the Kumatan, though Jenha Mosellan had done a masterful job already towards civilising her. One thing was sure; he needed to get his mind straight about her before the counsellors broached the subject with him, or else they might find out that he knew how Jai Cassidy had vanished.

Kaer then wondered if his father had noticed the Atapi that were housed near the palace. The idea intrigued him. He had heard that those Atapi now considered Jai Cassidy as their leader, their sorcerer.

Jenha Mosellan had rescued them, promised them sanctuary, and so they would have it. The odd thing was that since they had arrived, just over a week ago, they had shown no sign of the barbaric behaviour that everyone seemed to expect of them. What that meant he didn't know. Perhaps if he spoke to Ellhi Mosellan, she might be able to tell him something. He certainly could not ask her husband just now.

Kaer considered the idea. Yes, he should visit her. She had lost her sister to Stacion Ansuni, the now dead renegade sorcerer, not long before they returned from Earth. Now, her son Jahni was missing and Jai Cassidy, her friend and co-consort, was being hunted like a traitor – not to mention that her husband had been taken from her and placed into seclusion by the Counsellors. She would need a friend that knew some of what she had experienced away from Korvu.

I felt the onset of labour and I was ready for what was to occur. Jahni, son of my Kumatan mentor and consort, Jenha Mosellan, knew what I would need of him, but the hardest part was still mine.

It was late evening and above me, the stars were beginning to appear as bright points of light in the clear night sky and the first of Korvu's two moons had risen. While I could, I kept walking around, trying to hurry the birth. When the contractions grew more urgent, I returned to the cave, passing along the narrow path behind the waterfall. Once there, I lay down on a mattress of soft ferns and let their gentle scent, and the sound of tumbling water, relax me. Nearby, the little fire was burning low, keeping off the evening chill.

In the seven months since I had come to Korvu, I had become attuned to its aura and the truth was, I felt more at home here than I had ever felt on Earth. As my labour pains became more frequent and more intense, I felt the aura damping the pain. This land had accepted me, and it was waiting to recognise my child.

Jahni stayed by me, giving me drinks, wiping my face and rubbing my back. He kept the fire going so that the water in the clay pot stayed warm. He was little more than a child himself, but he was wiser and more intelligent than his eleven years suggested.

We had often talked about what his Kumatan tutors had taught him and what I had learnt growing up on Earth. It was sometimes hilarious, the interpretations his people had placed on various human behaviours. He learnt from me about growing up on a farm. I learnt about the everyday life of a Traegers family. The more I learnt, the less I doubted the rightness of keeping him from the Kimh. However, he was a child of an old and talented Kumatan bloodline, and they would want to train him as they had trained his father. They would want him to be a Traeger, a slave master. They would expect rigid obedience to their Nuath, the ethical code they lived by.

Jenha, the father of my child, was more than just a 'yes man' of the Kimh. He had vision and compassion. He had seen me as a wild, half-human, half-Atapi brat before I even knew what I was. He sensed my power before I knew I had any. He had taught me self-discipline, allowed me to prove I had honour, and that I wasn't an Atapi abomination to be killed on sight.

I spared a thought for him. The Kimh, leaders of Korvu and the superiors of the Kumatan, had stripped his rank from him because of me. They thought I had corrupted his mind. I knew better. The Kimh were stagnating, their minds closed to new ideas.

After many hours, a much stronger contraction brought my mind back to the present. Another followed, and another. With them, I pushed – eager for my child to be born. With a rush, that part was over.

I breathed in gasps as Jahni lifted my child onto soft animal skins, and then he did as I had instructed him. He knotted the umbilical cord and cut it with our one knife. Even as he dealt with those things, my child gave one sharp cry, followed by a sound closer to a laugh.

"I have a brother," Jahni told me. He was almost crying. So was I.

Jahni handed the child to me, and I felt his tiny face but could barely make out his features in the flickering light of the fire's embers. Dawn was not far off and I was impatient to see his face clearly.

Jahni held the child again, now loosely wrapped in a small blanket of joined skins, as the rest of the birth process occurred. I lay for a while, recovering my strength. Then I went and cleaned myself by standing under the waterfall. I redressed in my well-worn but clean human type clothes and took my child, washed him gently with the warm water and let him nuzzle and suckle for a while.

"What will you name him?" Jahni asked, still awed by the tiny boy.

I thought of names from Earth, and none seemed right. Then one came into my mind. "Mikha," I said aloud, and I liked its sound.

I heard Jahni draw in a deep breath. "That is a good name. It means mighty warrior. But it's funny."

"Why?"

"The Mikha in the legends was Atapi."

I shared the joke. "Well, he has that blood too. It will serve to remind your kin of what he is."

"Why would you want that?" Jahni asked.

"Because I cannot look after him. Your father and mother can keep him safe and protected."

"And what of me?" Jahni sounded hurt.

"It is time that you returned too. Your father and mother will have missed you, sorely."

Jahni looked away from me, towards the cave entrance and the lightening sky beyond the waterfall. "Will you be coming back too?"

"No."

"But why? Don't you want to be with Mikha?"

"Of course I do, with all my heart. It's just that if I go back, I won't be free to act. Your kin don't trust me."

"What could be more important? You are Mikha's mother."

I didn't say that I thought the Kimh might not let me look after Mikha, even if I did go to the place where the Kimh lived.

"Your mother will love him like he was her own, and he is your father's son too."

"And what about me? You are making me go back. Can't I stay with you?"

"Jahni, I don't want you in danger any more than I want Mikha to be harmed. But I need you to go with him. I want you to be his most important friend," I explained. "You can teach him about me."

"But I could help you."

"If you go with Mikha, you will be helping me. Truly."

I was glad it was still dull in the cave, for Jahni could not see the tears I felt swelling in my eyes at the thought of sending Mikha away. My heart and mind were at war. I knew what I had to do would be dangerous and I didn't want anything bad to happen to the innocent child I had nurtured to life. The sense of urgency, to start doing what I must, was building within me.

Jahni slumped down nearby. I sensed that he would do as I asked. "What are you going to do?"

"I have to convince the Atapi sorcerers to change. If I have to, I will fight every damn one of them," I told him bluntly. "Then, when I have their attention, if not their respect, I intend to move them and their tribes to this plane, where no Kimh or Kumatan can persecute them."

"By sorcery!" Jahni exclaimed, afraid for me.

"Yes, but my kind," I said, implying a great difference. "The Kimh and Kumatan who don't know me, expect me to be like Stacion Ansuni and will want to lock me up… study me like a fascinating new insect – because of my mixed blood. I don't think they care if the Atapi die out or kill each other. If I bring the Atapi to this plane, where they won't be bothered, they will have a chance to thrive."

"But the Atapi like fighting each other, as well as the Kumatan," Jahni said. "Papan said so."

"Yeah, that's part of what I need to change." I tried to make that statement sound simple. "But on this plane, which the Kumatan and Kimh don't know about and have never been to…" I mentally crossed my fingers. "They can spread out and have no need to fight each other."

Jahni subsided. I detached Mikha from my breast and wrapped him in the fur, my finger gently tracing the shape of his face.

"I don't want to go back," Jahni blurted. "If I do, the Kimh will want to train me as a Traeger. Then I will have to act against you."

I chuckled. He was correct in that thought. However… "Two things, my young and very good friend. I said I would move the Atapi to this plane, so they won't be found and having been in my corrupting company for so long, do you really think you'd still be a good Traeger candidate?"

"No," Jahni said after a moment. "But what if they try to make me hate you?"

"Will you?"

"Of course not!"

"Exactly. You know me. They don't. That is why I want you to go with Mikha and be a wise advisor to our mighty warrior. Tell him about me, and don't let him be taught to hate me. Teach him his Kumatan heritage, and when he is older, he can seek me out to learn the rest of it."

"I will do that for you, Jai," Jahni promised after thinking for a time. "But what if they decide to hunt you down?"

"It is a risk," I admitted. "But they will have to find me first."

I moved Mikha so that he snuggled next to my chest, and pulled a larger fur blanket around us both.

"Your father once implied to me that there must have been a reason that there were three races on Korvu. My mother saw the Atapi as Korvu's defenders."

"But the Kimh call the Atapi vermin, and say that they are little more than savages," Jahni said, repeating what his earlier teachers had told him.

"True, but that is why my mother created me. She wasn't free to act, but I am. I will have to change that attitude too."

In the brightening light, I saw Jahni shrug. It was his way of dropping a subject. "How soon must I go?" he asked instead.

I held Mikha more closely. I meant to go this morning, once I had recovered, but…

Now that I held my child, my precious creation, I couldn't bear to leave him yet.

"Soon," I said finally, fighting a very real feeling of needing to move on. Had my mother had even this much time with me? I concentrated on Mikha, sent to his mind all my love, all my pride, and I hoped he would sense it on some level and remember.

The light was increasing and I adored the face of my son for a long time. His face was as red as any human newborn, but he had the pale skin and ethnic bone structure of the Kumatan, and the slightly protruding eyes and black hair that were a characteristic of the Atapi. I decided, after looking at Jahni and then back to Mikha, that my son's skin was slightly darker than Jahni's – perhaps it was a touch of the brown skin pigment from the Atapi genes. I handed Mikha to Jahni and went to pack my few things in a bag made from woven vines.

I returned, and said abruptly, "Walk with me."

I had reminded Jahni of his duty to his parents and given him my trust. He would never be as much of a rebel as I was; he didn't have two disparate cultures warring in his soul.

Jahni held Mikha as I walked us all back to the place and plane where we had first arrived, the plane where the Kimh and Kumatan existed.

"I must go now," I told Jahni. "Lord Kaer will come. He might be Kimh, but you can trust him."

Jahni tried to reach out to hold me, but I walked again, taking three steps to another place. Even as I used sorcery to transfer myself to a distant place, using a vision given to me by Jenha Mosellan, I sensed Kaer arriving and finding Jahni and my son. Simply thinking at him had been enough. I had been put in his charge; he knew my mind. Even after seven months without contact, he reacted in an instant. The Kimh really wanted me in their control. I wondered if they feared me, or the Atapi, that much.

The visual memory I had chosen was of a hilltop vegetated by low scrubby bushes, which grew from cracks in the rock. Compared to the lush forest area near the waterfall, it was barren, but it suited me. Turning around, I could see into the distance in all directions. There was not the faintest sign of a town or a remote habitat of people anywhere.

My almost defiant words to Jahni seemed little more than bravado now I was alone. The truth was - I had no idea how I was going to start, let alone achieve my intention.

The rock reflected heat up at me and it was invitingly warm. I sat, still tired from the long night and from Mikha's birth. In this place, the sun was near zenith. I had left the waterfall at dawn, so this place was a very long way from where I had left Jahni and Mikha.

The thought of my son nearly undid me. Tears threatened to pour from my eyes, and my skin where Mikha had briefly nuzzled felt tight and painful.

"You did the right thing," I told myself aloud. "You can't have a baby around when you intend to poke sticks at sorcerers."

That was as apt a description as any for what I intended to do. There was no way for me to plan ahead. I was a stranger to Korvu, unfamiliar with its ways and customs. If I were to convince the sorcerers to change, and to listen to me, I would have to deal with whatever situation arose. I would be limited if I had to protect a precious innocent.

Sitting with the warm sun on my back, I felt my energy returning. I would need all I could get. It amused me for a while to pretend that each of the scrubby bushes was a sorcerer, kneeling in homage to me.

"The queen of all I survey," I said, as the phrase came to my mind.

I laughed wryly at my folly. If Stacion Ansuni, the late and not lamented renegade sorcerer was any example, trying to change the attitude of the Korvu sorcerers was not going to be easy – though if the knowledge my mother had instilled in me was true, I had to.

Stacion, as powerful and depraved as he had been, had underestimated me – and he was dust now. He had been thoroughly blind in not seeing that my mother was a sorceress. When he started to realise that I was - it was too late.

My mother had left me a metal box, carved with runes that had been a trigger for powerful mind memories. More than that, I think part of her essence remained tied to it as well, for when Stacion had sensed the power in the box and reached out to wrest it from me, some force took over my body. I heard my mother's voice in my head, speaking a ritual that disempowered him and I am sure that she used me to kill him.

I think my mother, or part of her, was still with me. I don't know if this had been since receiving the box, or if it had always been so. Certainly, I had always been different to my father's other children. My father, and various other authority figures, had called me a brat or a delinquent because I had never wanted to act the way they thought I should. Not one of them had convinced me to 'toe the line'. All they had achieved was to spur me on to greater lengths to outwit them.

At least I had a very good idea of how the local sorcerers would react to me, but I needed their cooperation, even if it was reluctant. Without it, the tribes would die out. As things were now, the tribes were dying out anyway.

My mind suddenly recalled the aftermath of Stacion's death. His warriors had returned to the Atapi village and killed every one – old males, females, and young ones, even the tiniest of the whelps. I am sure they were commanded to do this by Stacion, and perhaps it was in the belief that the tribe were better dead than enslaved by the Kumatan, or me… though Stacion would never have thought I would better him.

The only ones to survive were the ones Jenha Mosellan had captured less than an hour before Stacion died.

I hadn't thought of those Atapi since I had arrived on Korvu. They considered me their sorcerer. The Kimh said I was responsible for them and I had promised to protect them. So far, I had left them to be protected by Jenha's pledge to them. I wondered how they were faring, and decided I really should find a way to check on them.

Faces hovered in my mind; the rounded brown Atapi faces of the few of the tribe I had actually spoken to before coming to Korvu. One was a brown-faced, white haired elder woman.

"Jai-devil?" One of the faces seemed to turn to me and speak, and I heard the words in my head. "Are you well? We have seen your son. He is beautiful."

I was startled at hearing the voice, and answered aloud, not just in my mind.

"Already? They let you near him?"

I heard a chuckle. "Yes. Two of us work in the suite of Kaer."

"I did not think the Kimh would allow Atapi servants," I thought back.

Again a chuckle. "They only see what they expect, Jai-devil. And we have practiced being perfect imitations of perfect Kumatan servants."

"I see. You are very clever."

"It is you who suggested the way," the old woman in my mind told me. "Is there more that you wish us to do?"

"Keep my son safe," I thought at once. If this two-way thinking was reliable, they could do a lot more. "And be my eyes and my ears there. Remember what you learn, but don't risk yourselves."

"We do that already. We have learnt to be next to invisible," the woman chuckled again. "We also watch those that you care for – the former Traeger, his consort, and now his elder son as well."

"Bless you," I thought, infusing it with my gratitude. "All of you are well?"

"Yes, Jai-devil. It is as you told us. We have an area that is for us, and we are left in peace. The males do what they can – the Kumatan half expect them to fight, or act like wild men when in our true shape. They are blind to us when we shape their form. They can't conceive that…"

"What?"

"That you are like no devil we have ever heard of. Your ideas are different, and we are different because of how you lead us. We have power over the humanoids here because of that. If we don't act as we once did, they don't see us. My son, Teregan, is training with the Kumatan guards, and they do not realise he is Atapi."

I finally recalled the name for the face I saw in my mind.

"Farcine, you are a wise and wicked old woman," I chuckled, letting my mind go blank and the contact fade. Then I stood up and stretched. Speaking to Farcine had reminded me that I wasn't without weapons in the confrontations I planned. I knew things about sorcery, even if I had little experience using it, and I had my wits, along with the advantage of unpredictability. All had served me well so far – I should not begin to doubt them now.

Well, I had to start, and the best place to go was the Rock of Arkor. The sorcerers would sense my presence in their sacred place and come to me.

CHAPTER 4 – The tribe of Con Ansuni - POV

The near naked brown-skinned child wriggled from his mother's grasp and scuttled to join a group of older children. His mother hissed softly for him to return. The other mothers shared a smile and a shrug.

"Cassia, the boy is Atapi. None take well to restrictions once they can walk. It is like trying to change the weather."

"He is only three summers old." Cassia tried to keep her worry hidden and seem more grown up than her sixteen summers.

"He will come to no harm with the other boys." Opia, an older Atapi woman with black hair greying to white, consoled her. She had twelve children – the two youngest had potential for sorcery.

Cassia allowed her worries to ease, but her brown eyes followed her son as he trotted off after a group of pretend hunters who had long sticks to imitate spears.

The females talked around their fire long after all the children had gone to bed. Most waited for their mates, who were off talking around their own fire. Some listened to the bragging of the men, but did not grow worried by the talk of the signs of Kumatan strangers found on the edges of the tribe's land. No strangers had ever penetrated the sacred precincts of the tribe whilst under sorcerer Con Ansuni's protection.

Cassia had never seen a Kumatan, the pale pink-skinned humanoids who were the enemies of her people. She had seen sketches in the sand, and heard that their features were more pointed than her own rounded ones. Her mate, in all the years he'd patrolled the borders of their territory, had never seen them either. His father had once seen a group of Kumatan riding horses, but that had been from a distance. Though they were enemies, Con Ansuni decreed that they would not hunt them, so long as they did not come into tribal territory.

Cassia checked her sleeping child before undressing and joining her mate, Tesla, in the sleeping furs. Josai, her mate's first wife, slept apart from them. She was too egg heavy for any bedsports. Josai's three children were also sound asleep.

As the sun rose, Josai and Cassia awoke. They pulled on the simple rough spun cotton tunics they wore by day, and went to join the other females to prepare the communal breakfast. More slowly, the children began to emerge; they did not bother with clothes like those that their parents wore. The men, clad only in leather or cloth leggings, emerged last from their caves or mud dwellings.

Cassia only noticed her son's absence when he did not come to her for his breakfast. She went into her cave to see if he still slept, but found his furs empty. Not too perturbed, she went to speak to Josai.

"My Toki hasn't come for breakfast either," she remarked. "I expect Luka is with him. They won't be far. Toki never misses a chance for food. If we don't see them, we will look for them when breakfast is over."

The fires were out and the great kettles and dishes washed and returned to the community cave when Josai and Cassia went out. Other females were also leaving to gather food and hunt small game for the evening meal. Each group knew to look out for the boys.

"Toki likes the waterfall," Josai commented. "We will go that way."

Cassia nodded, but somehow felt they would not find them there. She felt a sense of dread.

The waterfall was deep in the tribal territory, and was a sacred place where Con Ansuni taught promising male children and warriors were initiated. Females could go near there to collect water and hunt, but not during the ceremonies.

Mindful of their duties, Josai and Cassia, hunted and gathered as they went. They followed no set path, for the small animals avoided the well-used trails. As a result, their woven shoulder sacks contained several rodent creatures, and some wild land grains. Once they reached the river, they paused to gather some of the water grains and then followed the river upstream. When they neared the waterfall, they spread out to search for the tracks of the two small boys.

Cassia, crossing one of the lesser trails let out a yell of elation. "I see tracks. I think they were going to the cave behind the fall."

Josai heard her; she had come out onto the main trail and was already trotting through the trees towards the river. "Wait!" she called to Cassia. "There are other tracks here."

Cassia, when she saw her friend through the trees, stopped and ran back to see where Josai pointed. There were odd marks on the main trail.

"What kind of creature made those?" Cassia stared at the huge and unfamiliar oval shaped tracks.

"Boots," Josai said with a snarl. "Tesla told me once that Kumatan wear boots that make marks like that."

Josai took out her hunting knife and gestured for Cassia to do the same.

"What are boots?" Cassia asked.

"Hard leather things that cover their feet," Josai told her.

Cassia glanced at her own bare feet. "Why would they do that?

Josai shrugged.

Both females grew apprehensive as the boot tracks reached the secondary trail and began to follow the tracks of the small Atapi feet.

"Can you smell something strange?" Cassia asked in a very quiet whisper.

Josai nodded. The trees grew close to the trail, and they often had to brush them aside – some of the smaller branches they came to had been broken.

"Is it Kumatan stench?" Cassia asked.

"No. Tesla says they smell a bit like the Poskai tree. This smell is an affront to the nose. It is foul."

The females began continued to follow the marks on the ground as the trail twisted through the trees, until a stronger breeze blew brought the smell of smoke and cooking meat to their nostrils. Josai, leading the way, indicated to stop.

Cassia whimpered when she saw what Josai had seen. A few steps ahead was a pool of purplish blood that had soaked into the light coloured dust. From that spot, the boot prints were dragging something and purplish blood marked the trail winding through the trees. A single set of childish prints continued. Josai held Cassia to prevent her from rushing ahead.

"We must warn Con Ansuni, and bring warriors," Josai murmured. She knew that Luka was dead and her Toki possibly was too. She knew her son's footprints were the ones that went on. "They must know of this. If Kumatan or some other creatures have come this far into our land and done this…"

Cassia nodded, anger rising in her breast.

Atapi females were never made warriors as that life could be dangerous and all females were precious. They were needed to bear children to strengthen the tribe. Yet, they were still warriors even as much as the men, but in a different way.

"It was Luka the bastard took, wasn't it?" Cassia asked, stifling a howl of grief.

Josai nodded. "Yes, for Toki has one toe bent out on his right foot. His tracks go on. I think Luka fell behind him.

You go back," Josai urged. "I will watch." She was equally determined to avenge the outrage done to her mate's children, but right now, Cassia could run faster.

Without consciously choosing, Cassia went into stealth mode and raced back to the tribe's camp, using trees, bushes and dips in the ground as cover. Anger and fear made her run faster and kept her alert.

She ran directly for the tall mud building that stood alone on the far side of the communal clearing. Her mind was focussed on her errand and the urgent need to speak to Con Ansuni. She was almost at the wood framed opening when two warriors stepped into her path, grabbing her and jerking her to a stop. One released her and brought his spear up to block her way.

"What are you trying to do, woman? The sorcerer will see no one until he has finished the morning devotions."

Cassia struggled free, and then stood catching her breath until she could speak. These two warriors were both older than her mate. They had metal tips on their spears, not flaked rock like Tesla, and their hide vests were decorated with intricate swirls made by pointed rocks.

"My son is dead! Killed near the waterfall. Josai and I saw boot tracks and smelt something foul, and smoke was coming from the cave."

The stance of the warriors stiffened. They sniffed the air and then circled Cassia, sniffing her. As some of the intruders smell had been brushed onto the trees, some had been transferred to her as she pushed past those same branches.

"You will come with us," the elder of the warriors ordered her.

Cassia watched the warrior push aside the door made from lengths of hanging vine. The first warrior entered. She felt a moment of fear as she was pushed after him. Only now did she stop to think that a woman did not usually enter the sorcerer's private abode unless chosen to mate with him. Moments before she had been prepared to force her way in, but now her mind realised the possible consequences. She trembled.

The space she entered was like an empty cave, with an alcove that showed the top of some stone stairs rising from below ground. Only some hanging woven mats decorated the walls.

The warriors escorted her down the steps cut from sandstone. Tiny fires inside fist-sized crystals lighted the way. When the steps ended, they walked along a narrow curved passage and then the light grew brighter as they approached the wide entrance of a large cave.

Cassia was pushed into the opening. Her eyes went immediately to the altar lit by two flames rising from clay bowls. Before it stood Con Ansuni, magnificently nude, wings flared out behind him, long slender tail rising and curling at his neck. The tiny scales on his brown skin glistened in the candle light. His arms were raised towards the figure carved into the wall behind the altar. The figure was a pregnant winged Atapi – Larcia.

Sensing the presence of others, the sorcerer turned slowly, anger pulsing from him. Cassia shrank back, too frightened even to look away from him.

"This woman has news that you must hear, Magnificent One." The elder of the warriors bowed to his sorcerer.

"Speak, woman!" Con Ansuni demanded. "I will judge if it is worthy of the intrusion."

Cassia tried to speak clearly, but her words tumbled over themselves.

"Silence!" Con Ansuni demanded. He had caught enough odd words to know this matter was something serious. The woman was rightly terrified of him, but he needed to hear her out. He took a breath and thought of peace and harmony. In a gentler voice, he said, "Speak again, young one."

Now, Cassia found she could talk freely, and did so, not hiding her anger, fear and loathing.

As had the warriors, the sorcerer sniffed her, and scented the faint odour that he did not recognise.

He spoke to his warriors. "We hunt! Be ready." Then to Cassia he said, "Lead us, worthy mate of Tesla."

Cassia stood straighter. "I will lead you, Magnificent One, unworthy though I am. My son is dead. I did not protect him."

"A warrior's life is dangerous. Your son was a warrior, even if young. He warned us of a danger to the tribe. Help me dress, woman!"

Cassia looked for the sorcerer's hunter's garb, and as she did for her mate, she brought them to him. He donned the furred hopper-skin leggings that clung to his legs and would protect him from thorny bushes. The neckpiece of bone, skin and crystals was the sign of his position. She was blushing a deep purple, sensing the male power he exuded. It was a relief to her when he took up his weapons and walked up the stairs, expecting her to follow in his wake.

His warriors, about eighty males ranging in age from adolescent to very old, were quivering with eagerness when Con Ansuni emerged from the mud hut. He glanced at Cassia, who took off at a trot, Tesla right behind her.

When Cassia reached the place where they had first found the boys' tracks, she stopped and the warriors fanned out. Tesla told his mate, "Go back! Wait!"

Emotions warred inside Cassia, and rooted her to the spot.

"Go!" Tesla raised his fist in warning. Cassia obeyed, retracing the trail at a trot. When out of sight, she slowed. She knew it was wrong for a female to be a part of a hunt such as she had unleashed, but her heart cried out for revenge. A while later, Josai joined her.

"The bastard will not escape," she hissed at Cassia. "He is still within the cave."

"You saw him?" Cassia asked. She listened to Josai describe a creature, its face hidden within a cowled robe, eating a haunch of meat. She felt faint, and no longer heard Josai's voice. The desire to howl in grief rose in her throat, but she stifled it. Instead, she began to run back towards the village – forcing Josai to run faster to keep up.

The other females gathered around Josai and Cassia as soon as they returned. The sense of danger had spread to them when the warriors had gathered in force and run off. Now the forty grown females heard what had happened. The older children, only twenty of them, listened – wide eyed and scared.

One by one, the females sent their children to hide in their caves or excavated holes and slung their hunting knives from a loop on a waist sash. The instinct for trouble had brought them all back to the village from their hunting forays. If the heart-place of the tribe was attacked while the warriors were away, all the females and the few old men now patrolling the village would fight. Without anyone directing them, each woman took a position outside their homes and watched for trouble.

A procession of twelve warriors, led by Con Ansuni, trotted back to the village. Two pairs of warriors bore the ends of poles with prisoners slung from them. Two more individuals carried child-sized wrapped bundles and others carried things that were not identifiable. The remaining warriors surrounded the group, their eyes roving from side to side.

The procession stopped in the centre of the village. The pole bearers took the prisoners, still trussed like animal carcasses but now moaning softly, into the ground level of the mud house. Those carrying unidentifiable objects went there as well.

The two warriors carrying the wrapped bundles, one of whom was Tesla, carried them to Cassia and Josai. Con Ansuni led them. "I share your grief," he said gently to the two females.

Cassia turned to face him, dragging her eyes from the last sight of the prisoners, and the blue blood seeping from cuts all over their bodies. She murmured the ritual reply, feeling the need to howl in grief.

"Prepare your sons for a warrior's honour," Con Ansuni told the grieving mothers.

Cassia managed to nod as she took one little bundle from Jostu, Tesla's brother. Josai took the one from Tesla, managing to control her face.

The men withdrew and the females clustered around, having collected cloth, water and the blessed sacred oils.

"A warrior's tribute," Josai said in wonder, awed by the honour granted to her child.

Cassia didn't share her sentiment. With her dead child in her arms, she knew what she would find. As a group, the females retreated into Tesla's cave. When the small bodies were unwrapped, all that remained of them, the howling began in earnest.

Though handling her son's butchered remains was sheer torture, Cassia forced herself to do as the old mothers directed. The front of Luka's head was untouched, the back was crushed, and his last expression was of terror. His torso had been hung like slaughtered horsemeat, and all that remained of his limbs were bones bearing traces of charred flesh. She could see teeth marks on one arm where some flesh remained.

Josai also worked woodenly, though her son was less damaged. Toki had died from some kind of arrow or dart, a shot perfectly placed for the heart. The intruders had skilfully butchered his body and hung it for the blood to drain out, but on all parts, the flesh had not been touched. While the funeral preparations were underway, the females howled out their grief.

At last, the bodies were placed in a semblance of repose, wrapped in cloths seeped in the sacred oils, and each was placed on a litter big enough for a fully-grown male. Warriors entered the cave then, led by Tesla and Jostu. The litters were carried outside the group approached the door to the Sorcerer's hut.

Con Ansuni emerged, clad in a robe of very fine woven hopper fur that was dyed a brilliant shade of crimson. It draped over his furled wings, hiding them from view, and the sleeves hung from his wrists. He was chanting in a very low tone, and as the litter bearers approached, his voice became louder.

The dark doorway of the hut began to glow with mystical brilliance and then the sorcerer led the litter bearers and Tesla into the light.

Cassia saw the light fade, and knew her child would be laid to his rest in the care of Larcia at the sacred Rock of Arkor. Then her world went black.

The howling quietened as the females helped the grieving mothers back into their cave. They placed Cassia on her bed and covered her with a fur. They made and offered Josai a drink of bark tea. For the rest of the day, the females kept company together, the grief howling slowly quietening.

The warriors did not return, but the females knew they were scouring the tribal lands for any other traces of the intruders.

When the sun began to rise the following day, and the tribe began to emerge from their caves and holes to kindle the sunrise fire, Con Ansuni stood waiting behind a small wooden altar. He wore a warm fur robe over his hunting attire, but he threw that aside as the males began to assemble in front of him. Next to the altar was a small fire, consisting of glowing embers.

The females stayed back, but their noses, like those of the males, were quivering, smelling the odour emanating from the grisly bluish flesh on the wooden altar.

When all eyes were on him, Con Ansuni began to voice a chant that seemed to take in the anger of his tribe and gain power. The tribe heard him invoke the protection of the powers that created all life on Korvu, and then promise vengeance and retribution on the creatures that had defiled the sacred cave of the tribe.

He switched to the sorcerer's secret language and his chant became louder. He lifted the flesh from the small altar, and those who watched saw that he held two hands that oozed blue blood, not the natural purple blood of the Atapi. With a loud shout, Con Ansuni flicked the hands into the small fire, followed by a small hide sack that burst on contact with the fire. The flames suddenly shot high into the air, and the increased heat forced the tribesfolk back. The sorcerer remained where he was, watching the flames, until they finally died down. He gave another shout, when he saw that no trace of flesh or bone remained. He took it as an omen that they would see the end of all the evil invaders.

Con Ansuni stalked the perimeter of the village, wings half spread and his mind alert for thoughts from his warriors. He feared that more of the alien creatures had penetrated his land and, if they had, he wanted to know. More than that, he wanted to learn about them so he could ensure that no more came.

The two prisoners that they had caught refused to answer questions. It was possible the vile creatures had not understood their captors. They had died not from their wounds, but from swallowing poison that had been secreted in their mouths. That smell, like the body odour of the aliens, was imprinted in his memory.

He still hoped the bodies might still tell him something. He had left them on a rock altar below, in a state in which decay would not touch them, and with only a hand missing from each.

When his warriors reported to him, he would consider all they had learnt and he himself knew of them. Then perhaps he should spread a warning about them to the other tribes through his mental link with the other sorcerers.

Con snarled to himself, thinking cynically that perhaps other sorcerers already knew and had not bothered or considered a warning necessary. These days, most of the other sorcerers were as wary of talking to each other as they were about going near the Kumatan.

It was wrong, he snarled again. The sizes of the tribes were diminishing. The sorcerers really needed to pool all knowledge and bloodlines – yet the sorcerer-devils leading the tribes were jealously guarding all of their blood, lest another sorcerer take them away. To a point, he shared that fear. His tribe was small, only a hundred and forty adults, but two thirds of those were warriors. Not all of those warriors would be able to mate as there were only forty adult females, and some of those were too old for breeding.

Traditionally, the best warriors could have more than one mate. Perhaps he should insist that females without children from their mate should service another warrior. However, should he do so, there would be resistance. It was one thing for the sorcerer to show interest in a male's mate – an honour in fact – but quite another for another male, no matter how honoured the warrior was.

Con smiled at the thought of trying to mate with every female not currently with egg. It might be pleasant, but his time was not just for pleasure.

The mind of one of his warriors impinged on his, not in words, but in a need for him to come to him. Con felt along his neckpiece of beads for the crystal that was bespelled to extend his mind link with his warriors. He spoke a word of magic, recognised the mind of Jostu and then saw what he was seeing. He walked forward three steps, vanishing from the village and arriving moments later between Jostu and the unidentifiable artefact that he had found.

The peculiar object had to be alien, for nothing in his memory resembled this round bubble of metal that tapered to a narrow tail. He wondered what the small metal cross at the end was for, or why there was a much larger metal cross balancing horizontally on top of the bubble. The structure below was obviously to stop it rolling over.

"It reeks of those vile creatures we caught," Jostu reported. "It is not alive, but there is some clear stuff at the big end where you can see its guts."

Con nodded, seeing all that for himself, and sensing no kind of life. It reeked of wrongness – the stench of the aliens and other acrid odours for which he had no name.

"It is nothing that belongs on our world," he pronounced, moving closer to touch the thing. In size, it was smaller than a dwelling, but big enough for two creatures the size of the prisoners to sit in. He reached up and touched the upper cross. It moved, revolving at a point on the roof.

There were odd depressions on the side of the thing, and he adjusted the shape of his hands to mimic those of the prisoners. He explored the depressions, and a door opened. A blast of reeking air rushed out. He drew a breath of cleaner air and looked in past the door.

Inside, there was a seat attached to the floor. This was covered in what felt like some kind of scraped pelt, though of no creature he had ever seen. A table, or altar, was under the clear stuff, and this had strange objects, that felt like hard mushrooms, embedded in it. A metal stick protruded from the floor.

Jostu had ventured closer, following his sorcerer. He looked behind the seat and without going in, he pulled several paper wrapped packages out.

"Master? What are these?"

Con glanced at the bundles. "Open them."

From the first, smaller bundles fell out. Jostu tore one of those apart and found them to contain a brownish paste. He sniffed it and passed them over. Con flicked his tongue at it the odd substance.

"Not poison. Food perhaps, though I doubt it ever had life."

"I would not eat such stuff," Jostu stated.

"Nor I," Con agreed. "Not while I can hunt and forage."

Jostu's eyes widened in anger. "Those who had this thought our children were animals – are they in league with the Kumatan who call us such?"

"The Kumatan would not kill our children," Con pronounced.

The second bundle contained clothing of an unfamiliar style and strange fabrics.

"Much finer than any cloth that I have seen," Jostu commented. "Our prisoners were wearing coarsely woven fabrics when we found them."

"I think they were more than they wanted to seem," Con murmured, as he studied the scene around the odd artefact and made up his mind. "Jostu, take all the loose things back to the village. I will bring others here to hide this thing. The cave by the mountain should be big enough. The metal, if we can get at it, is too valuable to waste, and I have no desire for any alien creature to have it back. Nor will I share it with other tribes."

The sun was low in the sky when the last pieces of the alien artefact had been cleared away. Only when he was sure no traces remained, did Con Ansuni return to the village.

As the evening grew darker, the day's warrior scouts returned and the night scouts went out. Con Ansuni heard of tracks being found at many places along the river. A few warriors brought in odd scraps, like the wrappings from the paste bundles. Others had seen ash from fires and the bones of cooked rodents.

These were traces of the alien intruders, nothing more. It was unsettling, but he did not need to tell his warriors to be alert. The death of the children had raised a lust to kill in all the males, including himself.

Darkness fell, and Con retreated to his temple – to the carving of Larcia. The alien remains were on low makeshift tables to one side, guarded by the Ancient One. He squatted in contemplation, receptive to any wisdom that she might impart. Since he had set her likeness in his temple, he sometimes thought she spoke to him.

He heard no whispered words about the intruders, but the sense of needing to warn the other tribes grew in intensity. The urge to go to the

Rock of Arkor was equally strong. He dressed in his most impressive finery and gathered his weapons.

As he prepared to walk across planes to the sacred meeting ground, his mind received an outraged message from the Old One, the oldest and most powerful sorcerer.

"An intruder desecrates the Rock!"

Con Ansuni wasted no more time; he walked the three steps from his temple, through the twisting darkness to the join the Old One at the Rock of Arkor. His mind was filled with the fear that this intruder was another of the profane creatures who had invaded his lands and killed his children.

The Old One noted his prompt arrival with a snarl like grin of approval. Together, they walked the two miles from the standard arrival point towards the Rock. One by one, other sorcerers arrived and trotted fast to catch up with them.

Con made mention of the child-killing intruder, and he sensed the Old One's anger.

"There have been others of that blood," the Old One said. "After the first, they are killed on sight. Strange that you did not find them sooner."

"I agree." Con refused to accept censure or the implication of incompetence. "What did those first ones do?"

He meant, "How were they noticed?"

"They were stealing our hidden treasures," the Old One snarled. "The first ones were sent back to be a lesson."

The lesson had obviously been ignored. "Should more come to my lands, they will learn to fear the name Atapi," Con Ansuni said fiercely.

The Old One growled approval.

Con added, "Though I wish to know where they came from."

"No doubt, since they consider us animals, they are known to the Kumatan or those who think themselves noble," the Old One snarled.

The pair now had six others with them, and one of these asked, "Might this intruder be another such as Con Ansuni speaks of?"

The Old One ignored the question. "We will draw the intruder to us, and we will see."

Using the light reflecting from Korvu's larger moon, which was near full, they found the tracks of small feet, wearing foot-covering similar to that used by the Kumatan and not unlike those of the blue-blood strangers.

"I have seen the likes of these tracks before," a gaunt, white-haired sorcerer told the company. "Three seasons ago. Now, as then, they head towards a fissure in the Rock."

The Old One hissed at the memory. "Yes, that creature was dangerous and I want it. Recall how it summoned our enemies and escaped. Go and see where the tracks go this time."

The sorcerer ran off, following the tracks. He went right up to the rock and felt over the surface before returning at a slower trot. "The tracks go into the Rock, but I cannot see a cave."

"We will not waste our energy searching for the way in – we will draw the creature to us and it will pay for its disrespect for our sacred place. We will begin, and when the slothful members of our elite arrive, they can join in."

Con Ansuni joined the circle, sitting down and linking hands with two other sorcerers and voicing the chant for the ritual of summoning. In the part of his mind that he kept private, he thought back to that earlier time and the very brief glimpse he'd had of the two intruders before they vanished. He would be wary in case there were two this time as well. He wondered anew how a stranger, someone who was not a sorcerer, could find a cave and stay hidden in the Rock. Surely the aura here would revile and reveal such a one.

A very old memory tickled Con's mind – a fleeting image of his sister that he stifled immediately. To think of her now would risk him sharing her aberrant ways with his brethren. Nevertheless, his sister, a female and not a sorcerer, had claimed to have done just that. It couldn't be her though, for she was far removed, on some distant world, with Stacion, his sire.

A faint thought was aired to the group mind. "There are tame Atapi at the Kimh palace."

Con Ansuni's mind caught the thought to consider later, and then tightened his own concentration on the ritual of summoning. The thought must have come from a less experienced mind, though if that mind had caught his own thought; it was one to be wary of.

More and more sorcerers arrived until all were present. The power of the summoning grew with each addition, but the intruder stayed hidden.

The Old One gave the command to circle, and the eddy of power grew to a whirlwind. Finally, as the second moon rose, the Old One ignited a fire. In its light, they saw the small figure of the intruder emerge and begin to walk towards the circle. The circling sorcerers slowed their motion but the speed of the whirlwind continued to increase. The two sorcerers nearest the Rock parted to let the intruder move between them and the whirlwind sucked her inside.

The wind slowed, allowing the dust to settle, but power still imprisoned the intruder. All that the sorcerers could see was that the short creature was not in a trance as expected, but alert and wary.

Con Ansuni looked at her – for it was definitely a female, and she was definitely not Atapi. His indrawn breath was of shock, but it was masked by the hiss of anger as the others saw what he had.

Bad enough that it was female and resembled the pale skinned Kumatan, but it had power and was alien. However, the most unacceptable and inflammatory aspect was that it carried something only known through ancient legends – the golden sword of the ancient sorceress, Larcia.

Con listened to the outraged thoughts of the other nineteen sorcerers, but contributed nothing. Instead, he concentrated on an elusive mind touch that he had sensed. He should mention it, for seemed that none of the others had sensed it – perhaps they were too full of anger.

Perhaps he had imagined it? Just as it must be imagination that the creature trapped within the circle resembled how his sister had looked when she shaped the Kumatan. Dangerous, his mind warned him. He must not let that idea be sensed by the others. He must not let thoughts of his sister influence him now. This was not her.

Yet there was defiance there…this creature knew things…

The Rock of Arkor was a huge reddish monolith, an island mountain, huge and long, even when I was still half a mile away. It was magnificent, with the brilliant afternoon sun shining on it.

When I had come here first, having broken free of the Traegers bringing me to Korvu, I had been too weak to appreciate it. The next morning, when I had rested, I had needed to disappear quickly.

Now it seemed to be drawing me to it with a subtle hint of power. As I drew closer, it seemed to be welcoming me. I knew what I sensed was empathy. It was the same power that had recognised me, far away in the mountains, and it was now welcoming me home. I began to run.

When I was close enough, I could see the cave where Jahni and I had sheltered before – my mother's 'dreaming place'. I slowed back to a walk, and stopped to look around, before I entered the cave. A long way behind me, I sensed the arrival of an Atapi sorcerer. He felt to me much like Stacion Ansuni had felt – powerful and lacking empathy. Still, there was a difference. This arrival was full of the aura of Korvu; Stak – to use his secret name - had been full of stolen life energies.

I wondered what that sorcerer had sensed of me. Perhaps it was the part of me that was alien to this place. As I watched him come closer, following my footprints, he was sniffing the air and looking around. I don't think he saw me.

Another sorcerer, and a third joined him. I moved into the opening of the cave, and saw more arrivals. They were all following my trail, but did they realise that I had walked there from a place far away? That I had crossed planes, the way they could, to get here?

I sat within the arch of the rock passage and watched one of the sorcerers run up to the rock and feel the air in front of me as if rock existed there. His agitation was obvious in the twitching of his tail and the flicking of his wings. He turned and trotted off, but at a less confident pace.

A smile formed on my face. It seemed that this cave was more completely hidden from them now than it had been on my first arrival. Stranger to Korvu I might be, but this cave was mine. The magic that protected it was not, it came from the power that had recognised and accepted me. I felt that I had passed some test.

Feeling secure, I stood and walked deeper into the cave, remembering what I knew of it. I went unerringly to the stretch of wall where water trickled down into a small pool, overflowed and sank back into the sandy floor. I cupped my hands and gathered water to drink – it tasted pure and cool.

Then I went to the shelf, just around from the entry passageway. When I had climbed onto it, my fingers felt for the runes inscribed there. Once again, I traced the runes with my fingers and, at the last one, felt the meaning forced into my mind. "The dreaming place of Jai Ansuni." This had been my mother's secret place when she was learning sorcery. Now it was mine.

I hopped down and explored the cave again. I found the short passage with its carpet of old manure. I guessed it had been used as a privy. I continued circling, using the light that come from the evening light outside to see by. Back at the passage to the outside, I turned and faced the centre of the cave. One part of the wall, where the light did not touch, seemed to be glowing.

Odd! It almost looked like the back of the cave was now further back into the rock. Intrigued by what I thought was an illusion, I moved to feel the wall and found myself going past where the wall had just been and stepping into a well-lit chamber. I could not see the light source. The rock itself must have been glowing. The dazzle before me eased, and I saw rock steps going up to a rock altar.

I couldn't see the top, only the side where runes were inscribed. I thought I should have understood them.

I went closer, walking warily up the first two steps, and then going one more to see what was on the altar. At first, it looked like a dark, formless bundle. As the light increased again, I saw it was the miraculously preserved body of an Atapi, dressed in barbaric splendour. The fabric was rich velvet, threaded through with strands of precious gold, silver and copper.

I studied the features and realised that, despite the wings folded beneath it, this Atapi was female.

A glow, brighter still than the ambient glow, formed around the head of the figure. It looked like a crown of golden light. Alongside the figure, a second glow took on the aspect of a glowing golden sword.

"Larcia!" I said aloud. I moved closer. This woman was an ancient legend. My mother had mentioned her when the magic of her legacy spoke to me... yet I had the sense that there was still a faint flicker of life in the body before me. Was it possible?

I felt myself being held where I stood, and seemed to feel a presence moving around, studying me. I watched the ancient lined face and saw the eyes flick open. I could move again and without thinking, I went to where I could look into the deep purple eyes. The depth of power there awed me.

Those eyes seemed to look right into me, down to the depths of my soul. I felt a presence in my mind and it was as if my mind gave up images of my whole life, from when I had first opened my newborn eyes to see my mother's sad face and felt all her love pour into me.

In that moment, I realised that some essence of my mother remained within me, possessed me. I should have realised that. Her essence had filled the box she had made and given to my father to keep for me. It was her voice that I had heard telling me of what I was and what I had to master. It was she who asked my permission to use my body to kill Stak, the sorcerer Stacion Ansuni, back on my distant home world of Earth.

"You are the one!" The ancient, quavering voice of Larcia spoke into my mind. "You are the one that I knew would come to inherit my sword and my crown."

I felt a compulsion to grab the sword. Feeling that urge, I instinctively resisted.

"What use is a sword to me when I can't use it?" I said aloud. I spoke in Atapi, even though that is not my native tongue.

The feeling of compulsion stopped. The ancient face smiled. Once again, I had the sense I was being tested, and had passed.

"It is a symbol of power, a conduit to the aura of Korvu. You will need it for your quest," the ancient one said.

"My quest?" I asked. What could this ancient relic know about what I intended?

"Young one, I know you are a stranger here, but I know what you are. Your mother chose well when she created you. You delight me with your passion and compassion."

"How could you know what I intend to do? I thought you would swat me for wanting to wrap those sorcerers up in their own twisted sorcery."

"A quaint description, but appropriate." The ancient one seemed to smile again. "They have grown away from the old ways – the ways your mother learnt from me. These new ways destroy the natural balance and make enemies of those who should be our equals and bring ruin on all the tribes."

"Am I stupid or arrogant to think I can actually beat them all?" I found myself asking. "Just because I outfoxed Stak?"

"Young one, you are the first in thousands of years to know the truth and have the freedom to act. You have already made the choice to change the way things are. If I was much younger, I would be there with you, but I can no longer exist away from this cave. Take the sword, use it to cut through illusion and find the truth. With it, I will be with you. You may return when you have won."

I suddenly felt the weight of the responsibility I had taken on. "Do you have any advice for me?" I asked.

I felt Larcia laugh gently. "If you are willing to take it, child, do what you have already determined. Fight them by their own rules, and win."

"Yeah, and hope that they know when I have won," I muttered, more to myself.

"They will, you will," Larcia promised, though she did not explain. "Use what your mother taught you."

I nodded. That was obvious, but the trouble was that I didn't know how to use all the knowledge my mother had crammed into my head.

"That is also your strength," Larcia told me, as the glow in the cavern faded and with it the 'presence' on the altar. All that remained was the golden sword. I left it there and went to see what the sorcerers were doing outside.

I watched the circle of ten winged sorcerers sitting in the moonlight, facing inwards and chanting some ritual. I wondered what they intended, and allowed myself to sense the power around me. It felt like a breeze blowing on my back. I guessed they were trying to compel me to go out to them. I wanted to laugh at their puny efforts. If the combined will of ten sorcerer devils couldn't bring me out, they would have to call on more of them.

Was I that strong? Or was Larcia protecting me?

By the second moonrise there were twenty sorcerers circling around a fire not far from the Rock. The chanting had not let up since they had started. I was beginning to feel the pull towards them. I was going to have to face them and convince them not to kill me on sight. Not only that, I must not let them gain control of me or my 'quest' would be over at the beginning.

I stopped resisting and let my feet carry me out of the cave. In my hands was the golden sword – I could feel it, but not see it. It had appeared in front of me when I began to walk towards the entrance of the cave. I would have refused it again, as I had left it on the altar, but I had wanted something to get their attention, and to make them think twice about killing me. Perhaps the sight of the sword would do that.

Once I set foot out of the cave, the strength of the summoning ritual increased sharply. I felt like I was walking with my back to a strong breeze. My emergence was noted. The sorcerers stopped circling, but the power was still there, and as I drew closer, I could make out a whirlwind around the fire. They all thought I had succumbed to their ritual, but I had not. The combined will of these Atapi-devils was strong indeed, but as I had done on Earth when I resisted the will of Stak, I was determined not to give in to them. They had no conception of my contrary and stubborn human nature.

Two sorcerers moved to make an opening in their circle. The inward pull continued, and I imagined myself as a queen being greeted by her subjects. The whirlwind sucked me in rather than flinging me around, and now the firelight illuminated me. I saw the Atapi faces lit by the flames, becoming clearer as dust settled out of the wind. I turned slowly, glancing at each of them, noticing differences.

There was definitely nothing wrong with their eyesight, for there was a united hiss of anger. I didn't need to read their thoughts; I knew what they would be thinking.

One, that I was a female, even if I was dressed like a male. Two, that I was humanoid, not Atapi. Three, I was on their sacred ground without an invitation. Four – I was carrying what could only be the legendary golden sword of the she-devil, Larcia. The darn thing had started glowing as soon as I had neared the fire.

Well, I had their attention – and they thought they had me imprisoned in their circle of power. I was content to leave it like that until I figured out how they were going to react. It was protecting me as well as keeping me in that spot.

I needed to know what they planned to do next, so I relaxed a part of my mind and listened to their thoughts. They had no idea that I could do that, and if I didn't think at them, they wouldn't figure it out.

What I sensed was that the sorcerers shared a communal pool of knowledge, and they had quickly determined that I was neither Kumatan, nor Kimh, since I was lacking any of the distinctive features of both of those races. I was humanoid like those races and not, as far as they could tell, Atapi in changed form. But then they didn't believe that option possible. To these arrogant know-alls, only sorcerers could change shape, and not even the junior devils without tribes would shape a female. None of them had heard of Atapi-alien hybrids either, and that surprised me. Stak had known – or maybe that was another perversion he had instigated. I had been told that hybrids like me were killed at birth. Some of that idea must have reached the minds, for I felt some of them shudder at the idea of Atapi mating with other races.

I picked up on the idea that had I been an Atapi female, my life would have ended right then, but I wasn't. Had I been a Kumatan, a Traeger, the only others that could 'cross planes' as they had decided I had done – I would have been tortured and then killed for the sacrilege of being there. But Traegers were males – I was not.

Their noses were sniffing like hounds on a scent – confirming that I was of no race they knew. I sensed in their minds a kind of alien, one that killed Atapi children and ate them as meat, and stole the treasures of Korvu. Lucky for me, I did not smell like those aliens.

Failing to put a name to what I was, they decided that I was a blasphemy of some kind, and I could not be allowed to keep an artefact that rightfully belonged to the male descendants of Larcia.

Oh, right, I thought to myself. I had doubts they could succeed in taking the sword away from me since the damn thing followed me, but if it came to an argument, which of them had the most right to it? Larcia was a she-devil!

While the Atapi sorcerers continued to seethe and argue about what to do, other than killing me and being done with me, I allowed my amusement free rein as I drew power from their imprisoning wall and changed it into protection for me.

Eventually they noticed, and the wall suddenly vanished. Their thoughts stopped on one single thought – I was a female and I had just proved I was something of a sorceress.

"Took you long enough to figure it out," I muttered in my native Earth English.

CHAPTER 7 – Jai Cassidy – POV

One of the sorcerers used his mind to reach out to bind my mind to his. I let him form his binding and gloat at the ease of his capture. Then I walked forward three small steps and broke the binding. It was only then that the sorcerers realised that I was not there because of their magic.

Their combined anger was a palpable force as twenty sets of eyes glared at me, and some had produced long knives from under their robes. They were infuriated because I was a female and I had broken a binding that should have held a fully trained sorcerer.

Next, I sensed their combined will trying to force a way into my mind. The effect was like the sudden onset of a blinding headache. I countered it by filling my mind with a load of useless human trivia – like the inane chattering of a dozen bored women. Half a minute of that, and they abruptly stopped trying to overcome my mind. The cessation of the headache enabled me to sense someone sneaking up behind me. I spun around to confront the sorcerer that had crept up close.

He was a young one – I could tell because he had removed his fancy robes, and what I could see of his wings indicated that they were not yet fully formed. I didn't underestimate him, because if he was in this group he must be one of the elite sorcerers with a tribe of his own. Still, I did not sense an immediate threat from him.

"Who are you?" he demanded.

I understood him and answered in Atapi. "I am Jai."

"How do you come to be here and what are you?" he demanded.

I chose to change the order of the questions to answer them.

"I was born on Earth. I am daughter of Jai, who was daughter of Stacion Ansuni. My father was of Earth. I am here because those who followed him to Earth would not leave me there."

That statement created mutterings of anger. From their thoughts I learnt that Stacion had been dishonoured and having him for a grand sire was not a favourable recommendation.

"And what was the fate of the tribe of Stacion Ansuni, abomination?" a harsh voice demanded.

"Stacion, your former peer – also known as Stak- is dead!" I told them flatly. "He underestimated me."

They listened to my warning and didn't believe me.

"And his tribe?" the harsh voice insisted.

"Most were killed by his warriors," I told them, not trying to hide my anger and sorrow. "Some were rescued by Traeger Mosellan and returned here."

I sensed a mixture of reactions to that. Some felt the warriors deserved praise for denying me the lives of the people of those tribes, and some felt relief that I did not have control of them. Oddly, there was a faint sense of sorrow from within the combined mind. I heard a thought that they knew of the Atapi living at the Kimh palace – ones they referred to as 'neutered'.

Hard on the end of that thought, I stated, "They serve me."

My words had the effect of a thunderclap. I might just as well have said straight out that I was a sorcerer-devil too. I definitely had their antagonistic attention. Every one of them now had a weapon in their hands.

The oldest of the sorcerers walked up to me and demanded, "Let me touch you!"

I held up the sword so that the fire light glittered off it and stated, "NO."

After a pause to let my refusal sink in, I added, "I will have your name first." The Old One hissed in anger and gestured to the younger one to withdraw back to the circle.

There the twenty sorcerers joined in a conference of minds. They were considering killing me because they, like Stak, considered me to be an abomination. I was half Atapi and half something else and should have been strangled at birth.

One mind spoke against killing me. "It is not responsible for its birth, or for being here. It has power and we need to know how that can be, and it has as good as told us that it killed Stacion."

A mind voice that sounded like the Old One snarled, "Something that you failed to do!"

The young sorcerer walked forward again. "I will take the knowledge from the abomination's mind," I understood him to say, "If you are all too weak to try."

Oh, he is an arrogant one, I thought.

The Old One growled at the younger sorcerer, then turned to me. "You will tell us everything we want to know, abomination."

He stayed back and I let the young one come closer, but when he reached a hand out towards my face I stepped back.

There was a quiet murmur of both amusement and anger.

"Why don't you try asking nicely?" I asked in Atapi.

The young sorcerer jerked as if I had insulted him. He hop-flew towards me and reached again. I was an abomination, lower than scum, lucky to exist – he would take what he wanted.

I ducked under his arm and spun around, keeping my eyes on him.

"I was willing to talk to you," I said casually. "Now, I am not!"

"You will tell us everything," the young sorcerer insisted.

"Make me," I taunted. Then my mouth spoke words I had not planned to say. "And if you can't – I will have your name!"

He took a step back. "You are not one of us," he tried to insist. "You are a thief and an abomination. I will take that sword from you and you will feel only agony. You will talk to make it stop."

Again my mouth spoke words without me thinking them first. "I accept your challenge."

I was aware of movement amongst the other sorcerers, and I dared a quick glance at them. The firelight glinted off knives, but they were now lowered, and the wielders were backing off.

Distancing themselves from the challenge, were they? In case I won, I wondered.

As the young sorcerer stooped into a fighting crouch, and began to circle around me, I decided that I had already won the first round. My challenge had been accepted, as though I were indeed one of them. The others would not interfere yet, I warned myself.

For now, it was me versus the arrogant whelp. No doubt the others were hoping that he'd win, and none of them thought I had a chance, but they definitely didn't like the idea that I might.

They had no idea that I had watched some mock fights between the Atapi guards in the colony back on Earth, and that I already had an idea of their combat technique. Those Atapi hadn't even been warriors though, and I knew from Stak that sorcerers had their own tricks. I would have to watch for them.

I copied my opponent's crouch, imitating his moves; I saw his wings opening as if he were preparing to lift. I backed off two paces, earning a mutter of contempt but giving myself a better view of the space I had to work in. I noticed that the circle of sorcerers had widened to give us more room.

I studied my opponent; he had a height and weight advantage as well as longer arms. If he chose to fly, if he could fly, I would be at a disadvantage. I saw his arms change form slightly to be suitable for grappling.

My advantage would have to be in speed, in being unpredictable and knowing things they didn't expect me to know. For now, he would be expecting me to fight like he did from having seen me imitate his moves. I still had the golden sword in my hand, but I knew that it wasn't the kind of weapon it looked to be. Still, it made it look as though I was intending to attack, even though my best tactic was defence and in letting this fool make mistakes.

I waited for my opponent to make his move, but he was still studying me and muttering the things he planned to do to me. Nothing I hadn't heard before, and rather simplistic compared to what Stak had started to do.

The other sorcerers began a monotonous chant, and I began to feel a little lightheaded.

"Oh, no you don't," I thought to myself.

They were trying to make me weaker. I sensed the energy of the aura of Korvu, and began to feel it flowing into me like a cool breeze, replacing the energy being drawn from me.

My opponent began to rise onto his toes, preparing to spring. I was ready for him.

When he moved his wings, still small compared to Stak's, and leapt for me, he covered more distance than I expected. I rolled free at the last instant, his wings rubbing my shirt as he failed in his attempt to entrap and smother me. I was on my feet again before he realised he had missed.

He spun around and saw me ready for him, sword held in front of me. This time, he strode forward as if he intended to wrest the sword from me, but disappeared on the second step.

As soon as he vanished I spun around, guessing he would reappear behind me. He did, but in the moment between arriving and turning around to grab me, I kicked him in the behind. It had little physical effect, but I infuriated him.

He snarled in fury and reached to grab my neck. I stepped back two paces and stopped, stilling every movement of my body, including breathing, and thought, "Don't let him see me."

I felt the aura rise up to surround me.

The reaction of my opponent was almost comical. It was as if I had indeed become invisible. He spun around, expecting me to have imitated his trick, but I was not there. He walked off a few paces, looking for me. The other sorcerers were muttering angrily, thinking I had escaped.

I needed room to try something, and I used the pregnant pause in the fight to think it through carefully. I would only get one chance. When my opponent stopped in one place, with his back to me, I moved forward. The movement broke the illusion of invisibility, and although the others had spotted me and yowled a warning, it was too late. I walked two steps forward, having my destination, and what I would see, firmly in mind, and imagined the third step.

This was my version of a flying leap, and I had used it once before with great success. I rematerialized above and behind my opponent, looking down at him. He had no time to avoid me, and my full weight landed on his head and shoulders. He fell like a stunned ox.

Into my mind came a name – Inrak. I didn't get it from his mind, but from the Rock – from Larcia. She had given this whelp his secret name, and now I had proof that I had won.

When the sorcerer began to struggle to try to dislodge my weight, I whispered that one word in his ear and the struggles stopped.

Along with his name, I learnt that he was the youngest of the full rated sorcerer-devils. I could have chosen to humiliate him further, but that wasn't my intention. I wanted their respect and acceptance, eventually.

I rolled off the defeated sorcerer and stood to face the others, turning to glance at each of them. They glanced from me to my opponent, who now stared at the ground. He made a gesture that I took to be a ritual sign of accepting defeat.

"I have won in honourable challenge," I stated, using words put into my head by Larcia. I looked at each of the sorcerers in turn, trying to judge if any were going to dispute that claim. All seemed to be thinking that I had been lucky, and I could never defeat them. My second victory – they each wanted to prove that point.

Advice came into my mind that I wanted to argue against. My immediate revulsion was countered by a feeling of needing to trust Larcia.

I spoke loudly and clearly. "It is necessary for you to know what I am. I will submit to an examination by Inrak."

Nineteen male voices growled in anger – they had finally realised that I needed to be taken as a serious threat.

The oldest gestured impatiently for Inrak to begin. I knew what he was thinking; he could learn all about me and gain an advantage against me – and indeed, I sensed the combined minds linked to Inrak, so they would know everything the younger sorcerer learnt.

That my mind was also part of that group mind was further proof – to me – that I belonged amongst them.

I tried to relax. These sorcerers still saw only a human, an alien, an abomination. They were yet to be convinced of my Atapi heritage – in spite of my claims. There was a lingering conviction that I was some kind of Kumatan trick. They also did not believe that I had killed Stak, or could have survived him.

With my mind thinking only of the need for them to know what I was, I tolerated Inrak's touch. Prior to this, my experiences with full-blooded Atapi males had been unpleasant at best, agony at worst. Inrak's touch only roused revulsion. The massed mind wished me ill, but didn't sense my mind watching theirs.

Inrak began by touching my fingertips, feeling them quite gently. His mind observed images of things that my hands had touched. As most of this was from Earth, I was aware that the Atapi found much that was incomprehensible. Inrak moved to touch my hand – some of the flashing images now involved the Kumatan – people and places from their Earth colony. Since some of the images showed me in trouble with them, the voyeurs gloated.

As Inrak moved his fingers up my arm, he reached the point where I had once worn a slave band. A ghostly glow appeared there, and it was clear enough for Inrak to read the meaning of the inscribed glyphs. Then I felt the pressure of the massed mind, pressing on Inrak's mind, to strangle me.

To the watching minds that understood what Inrak read, it was proof that I had power like their own. They knew that even the Kumatan had recognised that fact, but they had kept me alive. They concluded that I was in league with their enemies. I let no trace of my thoughts mingle with theirs. I had no wish for them to learn how I had escaped the Kumatan.

Inrak was confused when he reached the rolled up shirt sleeves. The clothing was Earth made, and unlike anything the Atapi were wearing, and felt alien to them. My glances at the sorcerers had told me some were wearing robes, others merely wore sleeveless vests – just enough for me to ignore the fact that were otherwise nude. Here on their sacred land they felt no compulsion to wear clothing to pay lip service to the humanoid races.

Hiding the fact that I disliked the idea, I shrugged Inrak off so I could free my shirt from my overalls and then pull it off. I had nothing under the shirt, and to my relief Inrak seemed unmoved by the sight and continued his feeling of the flesh of my arm.

His touch awoke ghostly red glows where Stak had once touched me with hands like glowing brands. The injuries had long healed, but the memory of them was still in my flesh.

Some of the minds recognised the ritual Stak had used. Others realised that this was something they needed to learn. They all wondered how I, a weak female, had survived.

The examination continued, revealing further injuries from Atapi and Kumatan weapons. When Inrak reached my waist, I shed the rest of my clothes. The minds thought that my form was not too different from that of the Kumatan.

Inrak was in no way roused by my human nudity, but did seem to enjoy probing even my private places. I simply met his gaze expressionlessly. He learnt that I had borne a child, but not who had sired it. He continued until he reached my feet. When he straightened and reached out to touch my head, I stopped him with a brief command, "No."

It was not my intention to let them into my mind.

Inrak stepped away from me, and I challenged the watchers.

"Inrak has examined me. You all know I have a human father and, as I said, my mother was Atapi. How else could I have the same power as you?"

"You are an abomination. Your mother was an abomination," the oldest Atapi declaimed.

"I've been called worse names than that," I told him intently. "Along with bastard, traitor and sorceress. My grandsire sought to kill me for what I am. He failed, and he died. My mother is dead and no names can hurt her now. I am like her – a sorceress. If I am as you claim, an abomination – then why did I receive this golden sword from the altar of Larcia? Why was it that none of you were welcome there?"

Mentioning Larcia unsettled them. Most seemed to have a primal fear of even mentioning her name.

An irreverent thought occurred to me. Even these fierce sorcerer devils must have been dominated by their mothers once. To prove it, I announced, "I am a sorceress, and before I am finished, I am going to have the name of every one of you."

Oh, yes, that definitely enraged them. Every one of the other nineteen sorcerers were already thinking of ways to kill me and prove to me that I wasn't invincible.

None dared ignore the implied challenge, lest their fellows thought them a weak coward. None of them wanted a female to get the better of them, or to even think I might be the reincarnation of the fabled she-devil, Larcia. Now they knew that I was of the blood of Stak, a powerful sorcerer before he had been dishonoured and disempowered.

The next challenge came immediately. Another rash young sorcerer trying to prove how clever he was.

"I challenge you to a test of healing!"

"I accept the challenge," I responded formally. This Atapi expected me to become helpless, easy prey. He didn't realise I could sense his thinking. He meant 'self-healing', and he believed he could heal himself faster than I could, then kill me when I was still helpless.

My challenger gave me no warning that we were about to be grabbed from behind. I felt two pairs of hands suddenly on me; one snapping the bone in my left forearm before I had even begun to think of struggling. The other reached for a burning stick and tapped it against my leg, giving me a deep burn. The first then took delight in using his hunting knife to give me a deep gash in my side. The tormentors moved out of reach.

I didn't scream. Having been on the receiving end of Stak's tortures, I'd had practice in holding them in. I took a deep breath and drew on the aura. Meanwhile, my challenger had been treated in exactly the same way so as to test his endurance, and I realised that I was feeling his pain as well as my own. To distract myself from it, I filled my mind with the memory of the exquisite pain of childbirth and sent that at my challenger. I heard a faint sound escape from his stoically sealed lips.

The aura was surrounding me, as it had done during Mikha's birth. I welcomed it and used it to see my condition. The knife wound hurt least, but it was bleeding dangerously. It looked to be a clean cut, and it had reached no vital organs. Already it was starting to heal. I summoned heat to my fingers and cauterised it.

The burn on my leg was still fiercely hot, but my body concentrated cold in that area, quickly equalising the temperature before blisters began to form.

The broken bone in the forearm was a different matter. I felt over the area, using the aura to dull most of the pain. It was a nasty break. I turned my attention inward, while remaining aware of my challenger. I could sense the location of bone splinters in my arm and, by fingertip massage, I moved them back to the main bone. The two ends of the bone needed to be put back together, but to do that, my arm needed to be stretched but I could not change the dimensions of my arm as my opponent was doing. He was grin-snarling because he realised I was bound in my current form. Certainly, he had more practice changing his shape, but even though he had re-joined the bone, it was not yet strong enough for him to use. It gave me time.

I told myself that the bone had originally met and it should again. What my opponent didn't know was that I could make slight changes in the dimensions of my body. I tried that, but it was not enough.

A moment of panic stopped me thinking. I imagined the sorcerer catching me like this, helpless, and my stubbornness took over. I took a deep breath and let ideas flick through my head. It actually felt like I was hearing the voice of a healer. Perhaps I was.

I could not change shape, and if stretching my arm slightly was not enough, I might be able to selectively alter the density of it. I pictured the bone shrinking inward, becoming dense. For the skin and flesh, I imagined it becoming lighter, stretchier, expanding. In this way, I made my arm seem longer as I massaged the ends of the bone into position. I relaxed my concentration and my arm regained its normal dimensions.

The pain was tremendous, and I felt I was about to pass out. I drew on the aura for energy, and thought at it, "Make my arm as it was."

I felt a tingling itching in the arm as the aura worked to return my arm to wellness. The pain receded, and I spared more attention for my opponent. He had quickly dealt with his other injuries, faster than I had, but now he was passively waiting for his broken bone to heal.

That was what I had done when the Atapi on Earth had failed to kill me. Thanks to the knowledge my mother had bequeathed to me, I now knew better.

As soon as my arm healed enough to take some strain, though while the inflamed flesh was still painful, I leapt at my opponent and knocked him off balance. I hurt his injured arm further, judging from the slightest of grimaces. I held him down with my 'broken' arm. He struggled futilely, and I glanced at the other sorcerers. They did not want to accept this proof of my victory, for they all snarled angrily, but it was too late. I now knew my opponent's name.

"Sastek," I whispered and his struggles ceased. "I have won," I announced loudly.

Through my touch, I still felt Sastek's pain. He was healing faster than I had done on Earth, but not as fast as I had here by calling on the aura. On his behalf, I summoned more of the aura and directed it at his pain until I felt it ease. He was surprised at my treatment.

I let Sastek scramble to his feet. Into the group mind, he thought, "She healed me!"

There was consternation amongst the other minds. Only Inrak and Sastek stayed neutral. They were lowest in the order of seniority amongst the sorcerer-devils, and acknowledged that I now ranked above them. From the thoughts of the others, I knew it would be a vicious fight to the top.

While the eighteen higher ranked sorcerers discussed me, I sat with my back to the fire. The circle of sorcerers had re-joined, with the two defeated ones outside. I watched the half circle in front of me, and hoped they did not all decide to rush me.

When some conclusion had been reached, they began the tuneless sub-vocal chanting. I felt no effect from it, and decided they were simply summoning power. I did the same without the 'noise'.

Two sorcerers broke from the circle and approached me. Their minds were empty, and I wondered if they suspected I could share the group mind and intended to give me no warning of their intention. They vanished.

I felt a disturbance in the aura immediately behind me – between the fire and me. I knew I could not rise and turn quickly enough to face them. So I waited, and commented as if to myself, "Two on one – it seems that Atapi sorcerers have no honour – or they have realised that individually they are no match for me."

My shoulders were taken in a harsh grip, one by each sorcerer. A force flowed through me, seeming to hold me to the ground. I saw no sense in struggling when the force changed to dragging me to my feet. I exerted my own will, and where their hands touched me, their hands stuck.

"You will fight," my captors told me.

I did not expect to be dragged backwards onto the fire. I felt the heat of the flames on my skin, and was glad that I had not re-dressed.

I sensed their surprise when my captors realised that the fire wasn't touching me. I was backed by power, like those who thought they held me. I could endure the heat as long as they both could.

When this became obvious to them, one of the two used his free hand to draw out a small pouch and throw it into the fire. The leather of the pouch burnt and the contents blazed up like a magnesium flare.

My eyes were blinded by the brilliance. I somehow knew that the Atapi eyes wouldn't be affected as much. Perhaps it was because mine were blue, and theirs were dark brown. So they wanted me to fight blind – hardly fair, especially with two to one odds.

I released the two who held me before they had even realised I had, and twisted free, punching one and kicking the other where I hoped Atapi males would hurt most. I had the sudden sense that those two were not the only ones in on this. I sensed danger and turned trying to locate it.

The flickering flames, that cast constantly varying shadows, confused my perception. It made it hard to see shadows or silhouettes that might be other sorcerers sneaking up on me. However, fire obeys natural laws, and the knowledge of fire was in my mind – I made the fire die down and go out. That it was now dark made no difference to me – and little to my opponents. I could see in the dark in shades of orange – the heat emanations of the sorcerers and the ground.

Now I could sense others near me. I could sense the pain of the two I had hurt and I found their crouching shapes to my left. Yet I could also feel intense hatred, being directed at me from my right. When I made no move towards any of them, they must have assumed that I could not see them, for the two crouching shapes stood up, and then all four began circling me – and not one of them made a sound. They began to move in to attack, from four directions. I suddenly sprinted three steps towards the slight gap between two of the presences. They moved to stop me, but I vanished from their sight, earning a growl of outrage. I only moved to a point between their circle and the outer circle of sorcerers. If I went beyond the outer circle, I would be deemed a coward and these four sorcerers, no, there were six now – would win.

I froze in a crouched position, ready to move if any of the six came too close. I was invisible, not incorporeal.

All six had knives out. This was turning into the unfunny game of 'hunt the human'. I still had the golden sword, not glowing now or it would have betrayed me. It was giving me the picture of the six hunters, in spite of the after-glare in my eyes.

There was a whispering in my mind, becoming louder. It was angry, but impotent to act. It was not the sorcerers, but Larcia, and she was incensed by the six to one odds. I had not even accepted this challenge officially. Snippets of knowledge came into my mind, hints of how each of the six usually fought. I saw patterns to their movements – they were each predictable.

I stood up, and the illusion of invisibility vanished. All six spotted me immediately, and came at me individually, making random attacks whenever they saw their way clear between their fellows. That was to my advantage. I let Larcia guide me, and my movements became instinctive as I ducked, jumped, twirled and rolled, sometimes stopping sharply, before moving quickly, or diving under knives – whatever I needed to do to foil the next attack. It wasn't all Larcia – she showed me the next attack, and where I needed to go, and I went.

The six thwarted sorcerers were getting enraged, even more intent on killing me, and I knew I could not keep avoiding them all night even with the aura to draw on. I had no weapon I could use to disable or disarm them.

Finally I recalled a trick that Stak had used on me. He had bound my mind, drawn it and me into that dark place between planes. My mother's teachings had mentioned that the power to bind minds also had the potential to break such bindings. As I continued to move instinctively, I considered how Stak had done it. Trouble was, I couldn't remember. He had made me unconscious first. Damn.

I recalled how I had broken free – and how I had escaped the Traeger who brought me from Earth to Korvu.

Yes! That was it. It wasn't much different to moving someone else across planes. I would have to be touching them to do it, though.

My opponents were continuously moving, following their individual patterns of motion. When the next one came at me, I ducked under his arm, twisted to grab it and then walked two steps before releasing him. He had thought he was simply moving to dislodge me.

On the third step I turned, knowing exactly where the other five sorcerers were. I had a momentary advantage as they had lost sight of me. I grabbed at a second and pushed him forward. He stumbled two steps and joined the first in the weird twisting darkness between planes. Now two minds cursed me.

The other four were glancing everywhere, looking for me, looking for the missing two. One of them spotted me and raced forward to stab or slash me. I moved aside, grabbed his weapon hand and used his momentum to bind his mind and drag him into the darkness, too.

The last three were wary now, realising what I had done. They had no intention of being easy prey, and were keeping a little more distance from me. I tried my trick on the next one into rushing me, but he laughed and snapped my binding before I could banish him. He whispered vile insults into my ears, and cursed when he felt me twist his knife from him.

I skipped back and was aware that he and one of the others had drawn a second weapon – in each case, a metal rod that looked like the force whips that I had seen used by the Kumatan on Atapi slaves. I'd had one used on me before, and it had disabled me for a short time. I couldn't afford to have them use it on me now.

The three remaining challengers were circling me again. I judged the distances and dived for the largest gap, intending to try again to touch and drag them into the darkness. I only just managed to stop before touching one of two suddenly glowing beams of light emanating from the metal rods. I didn't have time to move backwards before both beams swung at me.

I felt my body jerk as though I had been struck by lightning. Nauseating images, evoked when I had overheard when my brothers talking of a lightning victim, stuck in my mind.

"NO!" I thought I yelled. I was not going to die! I was not!

I dug my fingers into the ground and repeated to myself, "I am not going to die."

While the beams stayed on me, my body kept jerking and a third beam joined the first two. I heard the three sorcerers laughing at my agony. I heard Larcia snarling too, and then a force flowed from the ground back through to me, neutralising the power of the beams and protecting me.

My body stopped jerking, and the sorcerers thought I was dead, but they kept the beams on me as if trying to burn me as well. They were still laughing and enjoying their perceived victory.

The other sorcerers were drawing nearer when I felt Larcia release control of the counter flow. Pure energy flowed through me still, but now it also flowed back along the beams. The spell-created energy created within the rods was a perversion of the natural aura. It was neutralised in a concussion of power and the rods disintegrated in the hands of the wielders.

The three nearest sorcerers, the ones that had wielded the rod like weapons, were blasted backwards, and fell unconscious. The sorcerers that were standing beyond them were pushed away. I was under the blast and felt the pure energy replacing all I had lost in the fighting.

When I stood up, my vision was also back to normal. I turned and looked towards the oldest sorcerer, directing my words to him.

"You can collect these six of your inferiors at your leisure. If you haven't gathered them by morning, I will have conquered six more challengers," I said defiantly.

The Old One strode forward and examined the fallen ones. He didn't ask about the others.

"I do not accept your challenge to redeem them," the Old One snarled. "I am forced to accept that you have powers that no woman has had for thousands of years, but you are still a piece of excrescence that presumes to be a sorcerer. And weak! Why did you not kill them?"

"It is not my intention to further weaken the Atapi tribes," I told him, trying to make him believe it. "Nor is my motive revenge. I want the loyalty of all the sorcerers."

"Never!" he snarled. "I will never bow to a woman."

"I don't intend to usurp your authority," I tried to begin to explain.

"No? Then is it your intention to die?" he hissed.

"I would rather talk to you, tell you…"

"Talk is a coward's weapon. Cowards die."

He was not intent on reason.

"I will await your challenge," I said to end the discussion.

He growled and gestured to the other sorcerers. They all seemed to walk towards me, but after two steps they had all vanished.

I wanted to collapse with relief, but I stayed standing in case this was another trick, still sensing danger. I allowed my empathy to examine the danger and felt it was different to the anger and malice of the sorcerers. What was receiving, now, was a sense of determination. Then the answer came into my mind.

"Kumatan! They dare to come here?" That came from Larcia.

I wasn't sure what the Kumatan intended, but I didn't want them to find me, and it wasn't my intention to give them the three unconscious sorcerers. I could only think of one thing to do. I crouched down and dragged one onto my shoulder. I thought of the cave and walked three small steps forward crossing the distance to the rock by passing through the darkness between planes rather than try to carry the dead weight across the twenty yards. I dropped the sorcerer in a heap next to the entrance and went back for the next.

With the third one, I envisioned the cave inside the rock, intending to arrive within it. On the third step, I felt like I had run into a rock wall rather than passing through the illusion of one as I had expected. I bounced off it, and my nose felt like it was broken. I felt Larcia's anger for having tried to bring a male sorcerer, one who perverted the aura, into her cave.

"Damn it!" I swore, thinking at that incorporeal mind. "I will not let them be taken by the Kumatan. I know what will happen if I did."

"They are weak and unworthy," Larcia snarled into my mind.

"Maybe," I agreed. "But if they are taken by the Kumatan they will try to escape, and will be killed. There are only twenty sorcerer-devils now. The Atapi as a race can't afford to lose six tribal leaders, nor even three. I want to change them, not weaken their tribes to extinction. I can't take over the protection of their tribes' folk – I can't even protect those who look to me now."

Suddenly, the cave was open to me again, and I dragged the three sorcerers inside. I made one last dash out to get my clothes, and then saw the fiery torches in the distance, coming fast and accompanied by thundering hooves.

I returned to the cave and checked my victims. I did not think any of those three would rouse yet. The other three, those trapped in the darkness between planes, were still impotently cursing me.

I dressed and went to get a drink from the water wall. I filled my cupped hands with water and splashed my face, rubbing water over my arms and legs. It made me feel fresher, and a little less like wanting to sleep.

I ignored the approaching Kumatan, confident that they would not see this cave. I did not know who was in the group of riders, but if Kaer, my one time 'guardian', or Jenha, my mentor and consort, were with them, either of them might glimpse my surroundings through my mind and learn I was 'consorting' with Atapi sorcerers. I didn't want the Kimh or Kumatan to realise that yet.

So I sat and watched for signs that my challengers might wake before dawn. It was possible that the three in the cave might wake up, or one of the other three might figure out how to free themselves. If any did, I would have to fight them all over again.

Inrak and Sastek, the first two defeated challengers, had gone with the others, and I was glad that the approaching Kumatan had scared them all off. Not that those other sorcerers would admit to being scared off or wanting to avoid taking me on.

Larcia's sword lay on the dust beside me, as if I had put it there. I had stopped holding it when they had speared me with those rods of energy. I had also forgotten it while I was dragging the three sorcerers here – yet it had followed me here as if on an invisible string, always ready to my hand.

"This sword would rouse less comment if it was in a sheath on my waist, like the Kumatan wear them," I spoke to myself. Larcia had been silent since letting me in with these males. The sword moved by itself to hang from my side. "Thank you," I ventured, speaking into the silence.

I shrugged to myself. I considered that having Larcia's sword still meant she wasn't completely disillusioned with me. But what did she expect? I wasn't my mother, who had at least grown up knowing some Atapi niceties. I was human. I had to do things the way I knew.

I fought off sleep by drawing up a trickle of power from the aura. I began to think over the night's events and considered myself lucky to have survived. The first two sorcerers had been young and overconfident. The next six had perhaps not expected so much of me. Those who had merely watched had had a chance to evaluate my strengths and look for weaknesses. Each one wanted me dead. Whatever the next one tried would be worse.

However, I had done it. I had prevailed against eight of the sorcerer devils – all trained to be tough and ruthless.

I know Larcia had helped me a bit; it was hard to say how much. She had told me that I had to fight them using their own rules, but I doubted that their rules included having help from ancient sorceresses.

"It does not!" the voice of Larcia spoke in my head. Nothing more, just that.

I considered what she meant, and why she had helped me anyway. There was the fact that I was her means to try to change those arrogant sorcerers. I was also the only one who believed the need for that, and had the power to do it.

"You are still an ignorant whelp," Larcia muttered.

Well, yes, I knew that. I was going to have to prove myself to her.

So why did she help? If I wasn't good enough, I was of no use to her.

I chuckled at one idea that occurred to me. If those sorcerers refused to believe in Larcia, they wouldn't believe me if I said I had help from her.

"Quaint notion, human whelp," Larcia growled. "They needed a lesson, and a warning. If they heed the warning, they might learn new ways and become stronger. They have become their own worst enemies. As for honour… they have forgotten what the word means. Six of them to one small female. They will be less arrogant in the morning."

I decided not to arouse the ancient one any further, and effectively spent the rest of the night alone.

At dawn, while the Kumatan still scoured the rock and the land around it, I woke the three unconscious Atapi by whispering their secret names.

"Khonak, Drek, Tsik."

They sprang up, looked around and glared at me.

"I won in honourable challenge," I told them formally, not saying that six to one odds wasn't fair by my standards. "The other sorcerers have retreated. Kumatan are searching the area around the Rock. It would be wise if you went back to your tribes."

"Where are we?" Drek demanded.

"Safe within the Rock," I said. "I did not hate you enough to leave you to the Kumatan."

Khonak glanced towards the opening and hissed.

All three bowed fractionally to me, and walked from my sight. I guessed that would be the only acknowledgement that I would get from them of my victory.

The other three were a different matter. The tone of their curses had come to be like the wailing of frightened children. I walked two steps into the blackness and called them by their secret names. Like drowning sailors, they came and clung to me, and I walked them back into the cave. They bowed low to me.

In my mind, I heard Larcia's caustic comments about cowards and weaklings. I admitted to myself that I had not intended to break them. I wanted them strong and confident, able to protect their tribes, but willing to listen to me.

"I won in honourable challenge," I stated formally. None of them disputed that. "I commend you on your courage and strength," I went on, trying to rouse them back to confidence. Inspiration occurred to me. "Had you been less strong – you would not be standing here. You would be mindless idiots."

They were not far off it now. "You all deserve to know how to counter that trick I pulled on you."

I felt their anger stirring at the thought that I had tricked them. Good.

"Should you be caught that way again, all you need to do is think of a place in the real world, and image yourself walking there."

I saw three fierce grins, as they assimilated the knowledge and realised that I had taught them something that was totally unknown to their fellow sorcerers. Naturally, they would not pass the knowledge on.

"Go!" I told them, and was relieved when they did. I wondered when they would realise that I hadn't told them how to trap people in that blackness.

I finally felt able to sleep, and curled up on the sandy ground with no fear of any of those six returning. Larcia did not want them in her cavern, and she had proved to me that she could stop anyone she chose from   entering.

CHAPTER 9 - Con Ansuni –POV

Con Ansuni heard the Old One's order to retreat, but requested in turn, a chance to talk. The Old One was his grandsire, who might have ways to understand this female who was proving to be a strong opponent and clever too. It was hard to judge just how much power she had, since she did not use it the way all sorcerers were taught.

Was she really, as she claimed, his sister's child? A human? Did that mean his sister was still alive – perhaps with those at the palace?

His surge of hope quickly faded. No – if she had come back, he would have known. However, if that female was her child, in human form, with a human father…? Con shuddered.

His sire might have enjoyed degrading women of Kumatan birth, but he did not. The women that his sire had used had ended up dying. Atapi seed was like poison to them – they preferred death to being alive afterward. Was it the same with human seed in Atapi females? No, of course not – if that female was indeed his sister's child. He let his mind consider possibilities, but he had no knowledge to work on.

While the other sorcerers returned directly to their own lands, Con was still keeping pace with the Old One. By mutual agreement, they went to a cave on the far side of the Rock.

"How can an Atapi woman birth a human child?" Con asked the Old One. "I have never heard of such a combination."

The Old One spat on the ground. "Nor I. Humans I know not. It looks like Kumatan, but they don't dare breed with us."

"It can't be a fake. We all felt it draw on the aura, and it speaks our language and knows things that no Kumatan could know."

The Old One snarled in abhorrent agreement. "It is an abomination, no doubt created by the dishonoured one. The mother must have been bound into the form of a human and forced to bear human seed, though I cannot see what use it would be. The mother would die birthing it, if she survived that long. As for the whelp, it knows little of true sorcery but much of trickery."

Con moved away from the old sorcerer. He sensed that the Old One, who was pacing the cave, was still consumed by roaring anger and determined to swat that 'piece of excrescence that presumed to be a sorcerer'.

While his back was turned, the Old One chose to leave, and vanished between one step and the next. Now Con began to sense the Kumatan rapidly approaching, in overwhelming numbers.

When Con decided to return to his lands, he chose to arrive on the outer boundary. He wanted to think, undistracted by the demands of his rank.

He sat on a rock outcrop and felt a cool night breeze caressing his face as he allowed old memories to surface. At the Rock of Arkor, other sorcerers might've sensed his thoughts, but alone on his land with no one close, he could think of his sister.

He alone knew of her skill. Her power had been greater than his own. She could have been a sorcerer if she had been male. Had his sire, Stacion, known of her power, she would have been marked for death.

Jai, his womb mate, had been accepted at the Rock of Arkor – in his eyes, that did make her a sorcerer. Had Stacion finally discovered her secret? Had he challenged and beaten her? Had he forced the vile mating on her – knowing she would die? He couldn't disbelieve it.

Yet that female creature, his sister's child, had claimed to have killed Stacion. Incredible, if it were true. He could sooner believe that the Traeger had killed his sire.

How long ago was it that Stacion had dragged his sister and those who remained of his tribe to that distant world? Too long to remember.

And those tame Atapi at the palace, saved by Traeger Mosellan the female had said, were once of Stacion's tribe.

Traeger Mosellan had gone after Stacion and so had his son, Jenha. Saving Atapi was something his quixotic friend Jenha might do, not his Traeger father.

The female said the Atapi at the palace served her – rank heresy. They should have chosen to die rather than be slaves to the Kumatan and the Kimh.

Then Con Ansuni had the thought; if that intruder female calling herself Jai, had actually been his sister Jai, would it have shocked him? Yes, for she had more sense than to openly announce what she was. Stacion need only command her mind and she would have walked to her death. However, she had pledged to kill him, and he had deserved killing.

Con gave thought to the Atapi at the palace – the ones that the Old One disparaged with the epithet 'the neutered ones'. In the mind of the old sorcerer, they were nothing. Con tried to feel equally detached, but he could not. His tribe had split from Stacion's and usually that meant a severing of ties. Those at the palace might still have kin ties to his tribe for not all who had chosen to stay with his sire had done so through loyalty to Stacion Ansuni.

Some, Con knew, had shifted loyalty to him, but stayed with Stacion. Not because they had any respect left for his sire, but out of loyalty to his sister, and to help contain his sire's excesses. If there were old ones at the palace, with kin ties to his tribe, it might mean a way for him to find out more about the neutered ones. He pursued the intriguing idea. As a sorcerer, blooded to his tribe, he could if he chose to, use the 'sorcerer's over-mind' to read the thoughts of anyone in his tribe. It required a blood connection. If one of his could reach one of those… there was an outside chance.

But… had he really touched the mind of that female? If there was no blood connection, how would it be possible? His memory then dragged up a picture of his sister when she had shaped into Kumatan form, and he compared it to the female intruder. Everything he was thinking settled into truth. The intruder was who she claimed to be. No imposter could have touched Larcia's sword and lived. He had noticed, if others had not, that she did not always carry the sword – it moved with her.

The question of how she had come to be paled into insignificance if the ancient one, Larcia, accepted her. Now Con accepted the fact that he had tried to ignore: the female was as much of a sorcerer as his sister had been. If the Old One was not so blinded by fury, or if that creature had been male, the Old One would have apprenticed it to him fast. If only so he could control that raw natural talent.

Con considered doing just that, and decided he'd have no hope of keeping her controlled. But he would not underestimate her as his fellow sorcerers had. Their arrogance and rage had defeated them. That thought worried him. What would happen to the three unconscious sorcerers? The Kumatan would take them if they found them. Did the female want them dead?

The answer came at once. No. Hadn't she finished the healing of Sastek? But did she know the Kumatan were coming? Did that worry her? He dared not go back to see what happened. With six sorcerers indisposed, three of them in the open, he dared not risk himself. The threat posed by the blue blood aliens was too constant. At least he knew that the female did not have blue blood.

Some instinct told him that the female did not mean harm to the Atapi any more than his sister had wished it.

No, he would definitely not underestimate her. She had already defeated two sorcerers, and possibly six more. Even if they all now hated her, she had earned a position in the ranks of sorcerers.

He wondered what she would do next. If she was like other sorcerers, intent on advancing in rank, she would fight the lesser ones first… or they would try to kill her first. How would she find them now? Never mind, he decided. Personally, he was in no rush to meet her again. He would let the lower ranked sorcerers try to stop her first. He could wait. And instead of sleeping, he would go to his altar to Larcia and strengthen himself.

Koenig looked up from his desk when the Kumatan guard knocked and entered. The guard, clad in the dark blue all in one suit, bowed and waited for the High Minister to gesture for him to speak. With the Kimh leader were five of his sons.

"High Minister, Councillor Auglan from Selkrit wishes an audience with you," the guard announced.

"Bring him in," Koenig agreed.

He gestured for two of his sons to move. Kaer, as youngest, moved first, and moved back towards the side wall. His oldest brother, Malachi, moved next, since he had been occupying the most comfortable of the guest chairs. The other three merely stood up and moved a few steps back.

"We will finish this business later," Koenig told his sons, glancing at each of them. "Malachi, Kaer, stay. The rest of you get back to your duties."

The three who were dismissed waited politely for the Councillor to enter and then quietly departed.

"How may I help you, Councillor?" Koenig invited, gesturing to the chair Malachi had vacated. He did not miss the clouded face of the Galactic Council representative. The caped stranger had a face with a bluish tinge, revealed now, as a gesture of equals instead of cowled.

Auglan glanced at the two younger men as if questioning the need for their presence.

"Councillor, may I present two of my sons, and assistants – Malachi and Kaer."

As the introductions were made, each of the younger Kimh bowed slightly to the visitor. Auglan carefully seated himself, twisted slightly to keep the younger men in his side vision.

"High Minister Koenig, I have come to protest your security measures. They are totally inadequate."

Koenig's expression became severe. "You have had problems here – within the palace?" he asked politely.

"Not within the palace," Auglan spoke with repressed anger. "Two of my men were flying over those wild lands, where the position is perfect for one of the power stations we are to build for you. They were forced down and we have not heard from them. We have sent another team to look for them – they found lots of blood and many footprints. I insist you do something about those lizard creatures. I was assured that the area was not polluted by them."

Koenig did not change his expression. "Councillor, you were advised to take a Traeger with you on such explorations. They are trained to handle our wild savages. Where were your people ambushed?"

"In that forest area, north of your city of Elkar." Auglan managed to control a snarl.

Koenig spoke to Kaer. "Have a Traeger attend me."

Kaer nodded and retreated to speak to one of the door guards, just outside of the office.

Auglan continued, "There have been too many incidents like this – even when your Traegers claim the area is safe. If you cannot exterminate these savages – I will be forced to bring in those who can!"

"That will not be necessary, Councillor. I will ensure that a Traeger remains with you at all times."

Auglan's face twitched as if this was an unwelcome suggestion. "I did not want to impose on their valuable time." He didn't sound gracious.

"It is their duty, Councillor," Koenig explained.

Traeger Ambrose arrived and introduced himself to the Councillor. He listened to the report repeated by Auglan and requested clarification of the details.

"Elkar," he mused. "That must be a new group. We have had no tribes daring to be that close to a town for over forty years. With your leave, High Minister, I will lead a squad there to seek out the barbarians and get them to move on."

Koenig waved a dismissal and returned his attention to his guest. "Should your teams require to venture out again, please arrange an escort. We have no desire for harm to come to you and your specialists. It is unfortunate, but we still do have trouble with our wild men, even if their numbers are diminishing."

"I will insist my teams are armed," Auglan stated as a warning.

Koenig made no comment. Kaer, stirring from against the wall, did. "Councillor, if I may offer some advice." He spoke with impeccable courtesy. Auglan nodded stiffly. "We have no desire to exterminate our wild men. We have negotiated with them to remain on their own lands. Since then, conflicts have been minimal and incidents have been settled on a tribe-by-tribe basis. Should an incident of mass deaths occur, I fear that the inter-tribe feuding will be put aside and the tribes will unite to fight against their enemies."

An expression of some emotion passed across Auglan's face. He rose and said, "I will await the report of your Traeger." He nodded, cursorily and departed.

"He is not happy," Malachi commented.

"I felt he wished to remove all Atapi," Kaer spoke evenly. "Even though they are barbarians, do we have the right to allow them to be killed?"

"If they are murderers, should we allow them to bring harm to guests who are working to help improve our world?" Malachi countered.

"No, of course not! That is why a Traeger should over see their explorations and working sites," Kaer insisted. "We know the Atapi and have agreements with them. The Atapi know the agreed penalties for breaking them. The aliens may have provoked them, quite innocently."

"The Councillor was correct in saying it would be a monopolisation of our Traegers, to need to have them constantly with our guests," Koenig said with emphasis.

"If I were him," Kaer began carefully. "I would insist on such company, considering how he mentioned all the incidents. It occurs to me to wonder if they do not wish to be overseen."

"You have some odd notions, little brother," Malachi teased. "Our agreement with Auglan specified where they could go and where to avoid. The first incident was unfortunate, as the weather forced their flying craft over Atapi lands. I don't condone the situation. The Atapi should have escorted them off their land, not butchered them. There is no doubt that they were killed by Atapi."

"And I have no doubt that the other incidents were Atapi savagery," Koenig stressed.

"We found no evidence to prove that," Kaer insisted. "And in several instances, we only have the Councillor's word that teams went missing. Traegers searched the locations and found no wreckage or any evidence they had been there."

"The Atapi may have scavenged any artefacts," Malachi murmured.

"Not if the craft were not on Atapi lands," Kaer contested.

"What are you implying, Kaer?" Koenig demanded.

"Father, I only wish to be sure that the true facts guide our decisions. That is what I have been taught."

Koenig waved his hand as if accepting that. He changed the subject.

"Malachi, what was that alarm about last night? The one that sent all the Traegers off in a hurry?"

"Apparently it was a gathering of Atapi sorcerers," Malachi reported. "The Traegers believed they were working some major ritual. They were gone by the time the Traegers rode in."

"I wonder what they are up to now. Could it be that hybrid stirring them up?" Koenig said, glancing at Kaer.

"Her tracks were found there," Malachi added.

Kaer flushed a darker shade of purple. "If she was there, Father, you probably won't need to worry about her for long. I cannot see her surviving the combined might of the tribes."

"That would neatly solve the problem," Malachi commented. "What about your other one? Did you get much sleep last night?"

"Enough, Malachi!" Koenig said sharply. "With three daughters already, and another baby due, you should have more consideration."

Malachi merely grinned.

Kaer managed to answer without snapping at his brother. "Aniki asked Ellhi Mosellan over. Jahni settled then, and between them, Mikha settled."

"How do you find the boy, Jahni?" Koenig asked, intently.

"At the moment, I would say he was confused and lost. After all, he was born on Earth, and since being here he has lived in the wild. It will take time for him to learn how we live here," Kaer explained.

"That may be," Koenig agreed. "But I have approved you as guardian to both of Mosellan's sons. I want Jahni seen by the counsellors to assess his suitability for Traeger training. I fear, however, that his unconventional early learning, and his exposure to that hybrid, will make him ineligible. Do your best to rectify that. The Mosellan line has always bred strong Traegers."

"I will, Father," Kaer promised. He knew the appointment was an honour, but he had doubts about his ability to succeed.

Koenig waved his sons out, and sat back to consider the matters just discussed. The ever-unobtrusive servant, eyes demurely downcast, glided over and filled his glass with ruby liquid. Koenig had the passing thought that she must have entered when his sons left.

He gave the servant no more thought, and she smiled and retreated. She had been there all through the meetings, and no one had seen her. She retained the memory of everything discussed, and approved of the attitude of the High Minister's youngest son.

Kaer returned to his suite in the royal palace and found a scene of pandemonium. A baby, Mikha, he recognised by his tone, was bawling. His own daughter, two-year-old Kelhi, was adding her distress. Jahni was yelling at the top of his voice. At a lower volume, Aniki and Ellhi were trying to settle the disturbance.

"Silence!" Kaer felt the command bellow from him, and surprised himself.

Some of the noise ceased. Mikha kept screaming, while Kelhi subsided to a whimper and ran to her mother. Jahni made to dash past Kaer.

"Jahni!" Kaer said in a quieter but nonetheless cautionary voice. "You will go to your room and wait for me."

The boy looked rebellious but, after studying Kaer's face, he turned and obeyed.

"What is going on here?" Kaer asked, looking at his wife who was on the brink of tears.

"Mikha won't settle, Lord Kaer," Ellhi said, still holding Jai's squalling son. "He has been fed; he is dry and does not seem to be ill."

"Have a medic come and look at him," Kaer directed, and his wife went to obey. Kelhi released her mother, and came to cling to Kaer's leg.

"My Lord," Ellhi asked boldly, though respectfully. "Mikha is my husband's son. Could he not come and see his child?"

Kaer seemed to relax a bit. "I had planned to arrange that," he admitted ruefully. "Until other matters held my attention. Do you think this little hellion will listen to a Traeger?"

Ellhi answered boldly. "He tamed Mikha's mother."

Kaer found a faint smile. "Then I wish him success. Has Mikha stopped crying at all?"

"Only when he has exhausted himself," Ellhi told him.

Kaer now understood his wife's distress. "With all that crying, he is probably thirsty," Kaer suggested, feeling out of his depth. Fatherhood was still new to him.

Ellhi considered his suggestion and summoned the Kumatan woman being paid to be wet-nurse for Mikha. The woman arrived before the medic, took her charge and went to sit on a comfortable couch. She put Mikha to her breast, tutting at the screaming child that he would milk her dry, wanting to be fed every hour. She managed to interest him in the nipple offered and silence fell.

Kaer lifted his two-year old daughter, and asked quietly, "Were you upset for him, little one?"

Little Kelhi nodded. "Mik hungry."

Kaer glanced at Mikha suckling vigorously, and agreed. "Seems he was. Are you hungry too, little one?"

Kelhi giggled. "No, Aunt Ellhi made me biscuits."

Kaer tickled her chin. "What say you come with me when I speak to Grand-da?"

His daughter tightened her grip, content to be with him. She hugged him as she looked at the framed pictures on the walls of the passages in the Royal Palace. As yet, they made no sense to her; they were just part of the way things looked.

Koenig called for him to enter, turning from his contemplation of one of the meditation tapestries. He smiled, seeing his son with his granddaughter.

"Father, I came to ask permission for Jenha Mosellan to be allowed to see his son."

Kaer expected opposition, and was surprised when Koenig only said, "Speak to Lord Eamon. He is overseeing Mosellan."

"Thank you, Father," Kaer acknowledged and withdrew promptly.

He waited until he was away from his father's office, and the guards outside it before muttering aloud, "I think you bewitched him, Little One. I didn't think he would agree. Don't you think Mikha's Da should see him?"

"Yes," Kelhi agreed.

"Well, let's hope you can charm my uncle, too," Kaer murmured.

Finding his uncle was a little more difficult, but when he approached him in his work space in the House of Contemplation, Lord Eamon agreed to the request immediately.

"Of course Jenha should see his son. I will arrange it, and I think I would like to meet the little marvel for myself."

Kaer gave a rueful smile. "The only marvel I want to see is for Mikha to settle. For a child who is less than a week old, he has huge lungs."

Eamon chuckled. "He will settle," he assured Kaer. "You go back, I will follow."

The medic had arrived in Kaer's absence and was observing the baby feeding. He glanced up at Kaer's entrance. "From here, I can't see a problem with him," he said. "He's feeding well."

Aniki spoke up as she went to disengage Kelhi from her husband. "That might settle him for a short time, but then he begins yelling again. He's feeding every hour. I really think he needs a second wet-nurse."

The medic considered that. "When he is finished, I will examine him. He is Jenha Mosellan's son?"

Kaer nodded. "His mother is Jai Cassidy. Half human, half Atapi."

The medic's mouth formed an 'o' of surprise. "Human? I have not heard of them."

"They are much like us in form," Kaer commented. "Jai looks like us, not like the Atapi. It seems that humans are similar enough to the Kumatan to breed with."

"Apparently," the medic considered. He made no comment on this obvious violation of the cross-species mating taboo that he had always considered a wise policy. "I understood that Kumatan and Atapi are not compatible. However, that is irrelevant now. This little man looks strong. If I had to give an opinion, I would say he is not getting all he needs from Tokay's milk. I will look into a supplement for him."

A gasp of pleasure escaped from Ellhi, and she ran to embrace her husband when she saw him being escorted in. The medic pretended not to notice and Kaer looked away. Meanwhile, Lord Eamon approached the now gurgling infant and took him from the nurse.

"Well now," Eamon said, tickling the boy. "What's all this fuss you've been making? Not a good way to meet your father."

Mikha gave the start of a squall. Eamon ignored the warning, and took Mikha over to Jenha Mosellan.

"I think this one will make your life interesting," Eamon commented to Jenha. He studied the former Traeger's expression as he took and held his son for the first time.

"Yes," Jenha agreed, studying the tiny features, the big blue eyes, the dark hair and the faintly tinted skin.

The baby snuggled into him, seemed to sigh and fell asleep.

"He knows you, husband," Ellhi whispered, still keeping close to Jenha.

"And Jai? Is she well?" Jenha asked of Kaer.

Jahni heard his father's voice and raced from his room, reaching and clinging to his father before Kaer was aware of him.

"Jahni, I told you to wait in your room," Kaer said quietly.

"I want my father," Jahni yelled.

Jenha Mosellan used his free hand to disengage his elder son. "Jahni, Lord Kaer is your guardian for now. I expect you to obey him. Go back to your room. I will talk to you there."

Jahni gave his father a mutinous look, betrayed by his eyes brimming with tears, but he obeyed.

"He is confused," Kaer said quietly to Jenha when the boy had gone, slamming the door behind him.

Jenha did not comment on that, or ask why his son could not stay with his mother. He knew. As his status as Traeger was suspended, and his objectivity and obedience to the Kimh in question, he was not considered a fit guardian for a potentially Traeger-gifted child. At least Kaer was allowing Ellhi to be near him.

"I have the medic here to examine Mikha," Kaer went on. "I think, while he does that, we do need to talk to Jahni."

Jenha nodded and handed Mikha to the medic. He whispered something in Ellhi's ear, and then followed Kaer.

Ellhi watched him go with clouded eyes. It hurt her to see him so disgraced. She hoped, though, that he could get Jahni to accept his new life.

In the small bedroom, Kaer kept back while Jenha moved to the bed where Jahni had hidden his head to hide his tears. The trembling of his body betrayed him.

"Jahni?" Jenha said quietly. The boy threw himself at his father, still crying. Jenha placed an arm around him and gently rocked him, as Kaer had done with his daughter many a time.

When the shaking finally eased, Jenha spoke quietly. "I am very happy that you are back at home again."

"I want to be with Jai, too," Jahni admitted in a whisper.

Jenha made no answer to that, aware that he had to guard his thoughts. He simply hugged his son more tightly for a moment, in a wordless gesture of understanding.

Keeping his voice even, Jenha asked, "What did you learn while you were away?"

Jahni calmed as he told his father of his new skills of hunting and fishing, making clay pots and all the other things he had done to survive in the wilds.

"And I helped Jai when Mikha was born," he said with pride.

"Jai was lucky to have your help," Jenha praised him. "She is well?"

Jahni nodded. "I didn't want to leave her, but she wanted me to stay with Mikha. I promised. But why can't we stay with you now?"

Jenha kept his emotions well controlled. "There are important things I must do," he explained. "I have been away from Korvu for a long time, and there are aspects of a Traeger's training that I missed by going there as a child. I am learning those things now."

"Will I have to learn them too?" Jahni asked, remembering things Jai had said to him.

Jenha did not give a direct answer. He deeply hoped not, but he could not admit that or even think of it.

"What you need to learn now is your place on Korvu," Jenha said tactfully. "Your mother and I tried to teach you before we returned here, but much of that teaching was more suited to Earth. The ways are different here. It is a great honour that you and Mikha are to be guided by a son of the High Minister. Until I have completed my training, he will be your guardian and you must obey him as I would expect you to obey me. Do you understand?"

Jahni nodded solemnly.

"I am pleased," Jenha told him. "It is my wish that you learn what he can teach you. I want you to remember that Lord Kaer is of the Kimh. On Korvu, they are to be obeyed. He is also a good and fair person, who will do his very best by you."

Jahni's expression betrayed his uncertainty. He had heard of the Kimh and they scared him. Jenha sensed that.

"I cannot think of a better guardian for you," Jenha stressed, hiding the fact that he was in no position to agree or disagree with the choice. "And you will be able to see your mother often."

Janhi calmed.

"Is there anything you want to add, Lord Kaer?" Jenha asked.

"Not at this time," Kaer decided. "Jahni, why don't you see if my daughter left any of your mother's biscuits?"

Jahni brightened, seeming to realise his guardian was not about to punish him for his rudeness.

Kaer waited for the door to close behind Jahni before speaking again.

"The medic thinks that Kumatan milk is not enough for Mikha. What is your thought?"

Jenha considered if the question was yet another test.

"We cannot provide him with human milk," Jenha answered obliquely, testing his understanding of the reason for Kaer's question.

"That is not the only missing element," Kaer said, appearing to look past Jenha.

"There is a solution to that problem," Jenha ventured.

"Then I require you to see to it," Kaer directed, sounding like one of his elders. "With your utmost discretion. My father is aware of Mikha's uniqueness and wishes it to be nourished."

Kaer met Jenha's eyes, and saw there that the former Traeger understood how the High Minister's directive was to be interpreted.

"Yes, Lord Kaer. I will attend to that as soon as I am finished here."

"One more thing," Kaer said, once again not looking directly at Jenha. "My brother reported a major disturbance in the aura at the Rock of Arkor. He says it was consistent with the working of a major ritual. The tracks of Jai Cassidy were also found there."

"I doubt the sorcerers will accept her as one of them," Jenha murmured.

Kaer made no comment for a moment. When he spoke his next question, it was in a formal tone, requiring a direct answer. "Jai Cassidy has such power?"

"Yes, Lord Kaer. She does, as did her mother."

"Explain!"

Jenha was obliged to answer. "Jai Ansuni had power equal to any male sorcerer. Stacion never saw it. She never used her power in the way the male sorcerers do. She was foremost a healer. It is her learning that Jai Cassidy has inherited."

Again, Kaer did not verbalise his thoughts. Jenha's words melded too well with his own instincts.

"The Atapi in that compound call Jai their leader. How can that be?" Kaer asked, because it was a point he did not understand.

"By right of blood and by right of conquest. Stacion died by her hand," Jenha told him. "Beyond that, it has never happened before."

"Perhaps that is why those Atapi are so different," Kaer mused aloud, then closed his mouth. He then nodded as if coming to a decision, but he kept it to himself. "We should return." He gestured to the outer room.

They returned to hear the medic saying, "I can find nothing wrong with the lad. I think he just needs a dietary supplement, and more frequent feeding for a time."

The medic nodded to Kaer.

"I am pleased to hear Mikha is well," Kaer acknowledged. "However, I think I will find a second nurse capable of feeding the boy, as well as assisting in his care. Aniki is looking worn out with him already. It makes me wonder if all babies with Atapi blood are like this."

Ellhi edged back to her husband. "Are you well?" she asked, infusing it with a wealth of meaning.

"I am, Ellhi," he whispered back. "I am finding my way again, and you, dear one, need to train a new nurse for Jai's son."

"Ask Farcine for Teresa," Ellhi whispered back, understanding what he didn't say.

"You are as wise as ever, dear one," Jenha said softly as he saw Kaer's gesture for him to leave.

"I'll expect the supplement details soon," Kaer instructed, and dismissed the Kumatan medic.

As Kaer began to walk to the door of the suite, Lord Eamon excused himself from Aniki's company.

"Kaer, I expect you will escort Jenha back to the meditation rooms when you are finished here. I would like a word with both of you."

Kaer stiffened, sensing the mild rebuke in his uncle's tone. He relaxed marginally when Eamon added, "There is no need to rush. A father must have time to enjoy his new son."

Ellhi relaxed too, sensing kindness from the Kimh Lord. She moved back to her husband, and joined him in looking at the sleeping Mikha.

Kaer let Lord Eamon out of the suite, and Aniki came and snuggled into him. "I hope you are not displeased with me, husband."

Kaer relaxed his controlled façade to kiss the top of her head. "No, of course not. Things will settle down."

Aniki sighed. "I hope you can find a nurse who can handle that mongrel child. He will not listen to me."

"I will," Kaer promised. "But please do not let my father hear you call Mikha a mongrel. He has mixed blood, yes, but my father is very interested in his welfare."

"I'm sorry," Aniki apologised at once. "It is just that I am so tired."

Kaer hugged her tighter. "You should go and rest while it is still quiet. I will ask Ellhi to watch him for a time."

Aniki said, "I will, I think." She pulled away from Kaer, went and spoke to Ellhi who gave her a nod and a smile as an answer.

Kaer watched her go into their sleeping chamber, and reflected that his wife was little more than a child herself – only eighteen. She had been a mother at sixteen. He had been her age now when he had become a father.

Kaer controlled his expression again when he left his suite to escort Jenha Mosellan back to the House of Contemplation. He had an intended detour on his way, and wished no one to question him.

Jenha had once again raised the hood of his robe, and followed the expected half step behind the Kimh.

"It amazes me how neat they keep this," Kaer murmured as they approached the Atapi compound.

"Perhaps they are not as uncivilised and unteachable as some of your elders think," Jenha dared to suggest.

"One day I will discuss that with you," Kaer promised.

At the perimeter fence, Kaer waited. An Atapi woman, showing age by the whitening of her hair, came to greet them and bowed in respect to Kaer, then nodded in recognition to Jenha.

"You honour us, Lord, and you as well, consort of Jai-devil."

Jenha silently wished she had not phrased it that way. As far as the Kimh were concerned, that relationship was dissolved. Still, Kaer would not have understood the words spoken in Atapi.

Kaer gestured for Jenha to respond.

"Greetings, Farcine. I see you are well. I have heard of the excellent service that you and your kin are providing at the palace."

Farcine bowed faintly, accepting the praise directed at her fellow tribes people. "We obey Jai–devil in all things," Farcine murmured.

"Then perhaps my request will be well received," Jenha told her. "The son of Jai-devil is here in the palace, in the care of Lord Kaer. His wife is but a child herself, and I believe Atapi children can be quite…" he searched for a tactful adjective.

"Aggravating?" Farcine suggested with a faint smile. "You are correct, honoured one. What do you wish us to do for Jai-devil?"

Jenha spoke directly. "I think the milk of those of my blood is not enough for him. Nor, I think, is Kaer's young wife wise enough to deal with such a child as Mikha."

Farcine nodded. "I have seen the young warrior. His name suits him. Honoured one, I offer Teresa as a nurse for him. Her son is old enough to be weaned. I also offer myself. I have raised four strong sons of my own."

Jenha tilted hid head sideways, approving her offer. "My senior consort predicted your selection," Jenha smiled. "She will explain what is required."

"She teaches us well," Farcine commented.

Jenha nodded and turned to leave, but then had a thought. "If you are able to offer advice to Jai-devil, suggest she should not take a bigger bite than she can chew."

Farcine bowed again to Kaer, and turned to return inside the Atapi dwelling place.

Without comment, Kaer resumed walking, heading now for the House of Contemplation.

"Do not put yourself in the way of questions for my sake," Jenha murmured a reminder to the younger man.

Kaer did not look at Jenha when he replied. "I did what was needed."

Jenha was reminded of a time in his youth when his sister had explained the concept of 'tacit silence' – when knowledge held by two people need not be mentioned or thought of.

It seemed that way now, with Kaer and himself. And the lingering resentment he'd felt, when he had been told that his son would become a ward of the Kimh, vanished. Kaer was not as inflexible as his kin. That was well.

CHAPTER12 – Atapi Servants - POV

After his busy day, Koenig retired for the night. He was grateful for the solitude of his private chamber. He was so tired that he fell into a deep sleep within moments.

Two of his servants padded into the High Minister's office and began the nightly task of putting it to rights. Today, there were two broken glasses to remove from the base of the wall, five books from beside the desk, and one wall tapestry to re-hang.

One reached the chair where the councillor from Selkrit had sat. She suddenly leant down and sniffed. Her hackles rose and she hissed. The second servant came over and copied her action.

Here was a smell that their minds recognised as danger, evil. They did not consider how they knew, even though it was the first time they had encountered it.

Two more servants arrived, summoned by the empathy they all shared. The newcomers, day servants, repeated the sniffed inspection of the chair.

"The one who is a councillor," one said very softly. "Not Kumatan, not Kimh – outsider."

These servants were still learning their new environment.

"Smell is of those who kill children."

There was a combined hiss. The older servant had more to say. "Yes, this was one of that kind. He wants to kill Atapi because his kind trespassed onto Atapi land to steal from us and died."

None of them thought that wrong. "They keep trying to steal from us," the older one went on. She sniffed again. "This one was frightened."

"Of us?" one of the younger ones asked.

"Our distant brethren," the elder corrected.

The other day servant, who had been unobtrusively present during the Councillor's meeting, added her thoughts. "He should have accepted the offer of a slave-master."

The elder snarled, "They don't try to steal when a slave-master is with them."

One of the first two, younger than the newcomers, said, "I do not like how they show up in places far from here – have they a need to?"

The elder considered concepts still foreign to her. "They are to make 'power stations' and 'irrigation systems' – whatever they are." She used words in Kumatan as there were none in the Atapi language. "The people here consider this important. These scavengers have convinced the ones here that they wish to help them. I do not think so."

The four conferred, then stood quiet for a long moment.
"It has been decided that strangers such as this, without slave-master observation, be killed on sight," the elder said. The others knew she had blood kin in a distant Atapi tribe, and could sometimes learn things from their minds.
"We promised Jai-devil we would watch for the welfare of the High Minister," she summed up. "We will add our protection to that of his Kumatan guards."
They all nodded. The two elder day servants agreed to go and watch the sleeping High Minister until the night servants finished their assigned duties   and   could   take   over.

After sleeping for many hours, I awoke in the late afternoon. I was immediately aware that the Kumatan were still scouring the area, actively hunting for Atapi sorcerers. Their presence was like an itch on my skin.

I had no desire to show myself, though I did wonder if Jenha was with them. I hoped he had seen his son.

Perhaps it was my thought of my son, and of Farcine having seen him, that formed the link. I began to hear Farcine in my mind.

"Jai-devil, what do you wish?"

"To know that you are well, and that my son is well," I admitted.

"Mikha is well, and has been ruling the nursery in Lord Kaer's domain," Farcine chuckled. "It seems that the milk of the Kumatan is too weak for your whelp's appetite. His father has arranged for an Atapi nurse, and along with Teresa's milk he will learn respect from me. He is too much for Lord Kaer's young wife, but I know how to manage an Atapi whelp."

I had to smile, and wonder what I had been like at that age.

"And how is his father?" I thought, feeling awkward about asking.

"Will I tell him that you are well?" Farcine asked. "He was concerned that you were attempting more than you could manage."

"A tactful way of warning me against annoying male sorcerers," I told her. "Sweet of him, but the warning is a long time too late. I annoy them by existing, and so far that has been to my advantage. I am well."

"I will spread the word. Everyone will be pleased," Farcine assured me.

"The Kumatan are at the Rock, seeking the sorcerers," I mentioned.

Farcine commented in turn, "We have heard that the Traegers are seeking Atapi who killed some alien engineers."

I recalled mention of aliens in the minds of the sorcerers, and repeated some of what I understood, in turn I sensed Farcine's anger.

"We had heard of the child killers," her mind thought was a hiss. "One came and spoke to the High Minister. His kind are to build 'power stations' and 'irrigation systems' for the Kimh."

Farcine did not understand the words, but I did and I wondered about them.

Why did Korvu need power stations? That suggested a higher level of mechanisation than I thought Korvu had. Perhaps I had a false idea; I hadn't exactly been travelling around since I had come here.

Irrigation systems could be a benefit, but surely they didn't need power. On my father's farm, it had been a matter of channelling water from the river.

I mentally shrugged. "I can't worry about such things right now, but I can't see why those alien builders must go so far from Kumatan and Kimh towns. If they went onto Atapi lands... I would not trust their actions and motives."

"Then we won't either," Farcine told me. "You said they had blue blood, and not purple like us?"

"Exactly, and not red like me and the Kumatan," I added.

"Perhaps that is why they smell so vile," Farcine commented. "We will continue to listen."

I broke the link, and considered that the Kumatan here might leave soon, if they had pressing duties elsewhere.

I felt the ancient one, Larcia, stirring in my mind.

"Aliens," she hissed. "Still they try to rob our lands…"

"They've been here before?" I asked in my mind, and images flashed through my head. Most were only glimpses of caped and cowled creatures.

"We frightened them away, but new ones come. They are like a rash." The 'we' Larcia mentioned I took to be the Atapi.

"So far, we have prevailed," I ventured to think.

"They are testing us, testing our strength," Larcia told me. "They have the measure of the so-called leaders of Korvu who are blind to the truth. Those aliens cannot blind us – they are blights on the aura. But we are not as strong as we were. The aliens feed the phobia of the leaders against us and they hunt us now. Our tribes are diminishing in size and strength. One day we will not be able to fight these aliens."

"What can we do?" I asked, but I was beginning to have an idea.

"We must teach the sorcerers the old ways, the forgotten ways. Only then will our strength grow. Once there were hundreds of tribes, not just the twenty who came here. If they all worked together we still might prevail, but it seems the tribes shun each other and have grown isolated, insular. It should not be that way." There was a trace of anger and impotence in her voice.

"They certainly seem united in wanting to kill me," I thought back to the previous night.

"They fear change – even change for the better, but do not realise that over the years they have changed for the worse. Someone must show them what is better. You are that one!"

I didn't need Larcia to stress the point. "I already figured that out, but are you sure they will listen to me, even if I do beat them all?"

"You must make them listen," Larcia said, unequivocally. "Only united in purpose, with sorcerers working together, can we protect the land and make the tribes flourish."

I had to agree, but now it seemed that the sorcerers were just as likely to fight Kimh and Kumatan, or each other, as they were an alien enemy.

I sighed. I couldn't see those arrogant sorcerers changing their minds in any time short of a century or two.

"Sit, child, and I will tell you how things should be," Larcia directed me.

How long I sat, enthralled by the information Larcia shared with me, I didn't know. But during that time, I learnt a great deal about my mother and what she had been like.

Larcia expanded on the knowledge that I had absorbed from the metal box bequeathed to me by my mother. I began to see and understand how the tribes had changed over time. It gave me further insight into the thought processes of the males. At one point, I had commented that it would take many human lifetimes to learn all I needed to know. From Larcia, I received the sense that I would have a very long life.

From Larcia's memories, and the memories of generations of sorcerers, I began to have a sense of a pattern in the alien interference. A sense of urgency grew within me – the fear that we would not be ready when they finally decided to attack. I had to start now, I had to be ready. The Atapi had to be ready. Larcia thought little of the humanoid races when it came to protecting Korvu.

"Jai."

"My queen?"

"There is no more time to linger here. The Kumatan will continue searching until they are sure the sorcerers will not return. You must go to the tribes of the devils and challenge them one by one on their home ground. There they will fight alone. Only here will they fight together and they will not return here until this sacred ground is purified."

I saw the sense in her advice. "How will I know where to go?" I asked.

"Take my sword. Through it I can guide you."

"I will, my queen," I promised. I stood up and glanced around. "I am ready."

An image of a clearing near a river came into my mind and I recognised it as one from when I'd absorbed the aura from my mother's metal box – although that version of the image had been in daylight, and this one was when it was coming on dusk.

Larcia expected me to go, and expected me to win. I walked three steps, holding that image in my mind and I was there.

I went, half expecting to meet the sorcerer on the instant of my arrival. Instead, the area was quiet. I slowly looked around, and smelt smoke and meat cooking as I did. That warned me that I was not far away from the dwellings of the Atapi tribe.

I would need to be cautious. I did not think that I needed to go and immediately declare my challenge. If I could first look around and get a feel for the land here, it would be to my advantage.

Not far away from the cleared area was a waterfall for I could hear the sound of water splashing on rocks. I followed the sound, to the source, and thought I could make out a cave behind it. It was very like the place where I had waited for Mikha to be born. I took that as a good omen. I could not stay out in the open much longer, for I expected the sorcerer to sense me soon. I began to move towards the waterfall hoping that the sound of water would cover any sound I made, but knowing that it would also hide the sounds of anyone hunting me. I kept glancing around, and when I reached the river and needed to wade it to reach the cave, I moved as carefully as possible.

From the mouth of the cave I had patches of clear sight, as the water did not fall in a solid sheet. It seemed I had entered just in time, for I had glimpses of Atapi warriors stalking around the edge of the clearing, looking intently in every direction. In here the aura was very strong, and I drew on it to hide myself.

Too late, I thought of my footprints in the sandy soil.

"Idiot," I told myself. Then I quickly thought through the few rituals I knew and chanted words to summon wind, imagining a breeze that smoothed the ground and blew leaves and plant litter over my footprints.

Rather than stopping it abruptly, I gradually decreased the strength of the breeze back to nothing.

Even by doing that, I had still caught the attention of the Atapi. The skulking warriors withdrew into the trees and stood watching, looking towards the waterfall. If I had to read their attitude, I would guess they were either spooked or suspicious. When dark fell, I sensed them beginning to move closer.

Some of Stak's warriors had been very good at tracking me. I had to assume these warriors were, too. I drew on more of the aura to ensure I was invisible.

The warriors scoured the area for over an hour, but what I thought was odd was that they never crossed the river to check the cave. They looked this way often, as if they knew or suspected that I was there. I wondered if they would summon their sorcerer. If they did, I would have to go out and face him – or I would lose.

I really didn't want to fight in the dark on strange ground. That would give the sorcerer the advantage of belonging here, and darkness.

Part of my attention moved from watching the warriors, to feeling I was not alone in the cave. It was the same sort of itching on my neck as I'd had when I had first sensed my grandsire. What if this was the sorcerer's lair and I had just walked into it like a stupid rabbit? Maybe that was why the warriors didn't enter?

At that thought, I brought my full attention to inside the cave. The walls, I now noted, were glowing faintly and I felt something stirring in the aura. According to my eyes, there was no one else in the cave – but every other sense was telling me that there was. I heard faint rustling noises, like a breeze blowing leaves, and the breeze felt distinctly chill. My nose smelt a scent not unlike Atapi, but much fainter along with a musty dead odour.

I wanted to run out of this cave, but I didn't dare. I knew what was waiting for me outside and, if this was a ploy of the sorcerer, running meant losing.

"FILTH, EXCRESENCE, ALIEN DESPOILER!" The words roared into my head with the force like that of the thundering steam trains I had seen on Earth. Then a force, stronger than a gale, blew me against a wall and pinned me like a butterfly.

"Where are you?" I shouted, not caring if my voice carried outside. "Show yourself!"

Something in me was not surprised when a cloud of white vapour, eerily unaffected by the wind, seemed to solidify, but only to a point.

The thundering stream of insults and vile accusations continued in my head. They were all variations of what I had heard before – except for the one about being a tribe killer.

"If this is all you can do," I said, very deliberately, "It isn't even enough to make me want to kick your head in. You aren't alive anyway."

The mental bellowing stopped, creating a silence as loud as the voice had been. Instead I began to hear a buzzing like from a blowfly sized mosquito. Something bit the hand that I could not move off the wall.

The insect noise stopped, and the silence now was more unnerving that the sense of being watched.

The voice when it came again was a whisper. "Jai… Ansuni?"

I was startled. The voice was almost reverent.

"No," I answered just as softly. "She was my mother."

The force holding me to the wall eased to nothing. I was able to breath properly again.

"You are like her, but alien too. What are you?"

"I was born on Earth… where Stak went," I began, only to be interrupted by an angry hissing. I spoke louder. "She created me so I could kill Stak… he's dead."

Why I phrased it like that, I don't know, and it wasn't Larcia who whispered his name to me.

"Loschak, you can rest now… if you want," something caused me to say.

"No!" he hissed. "The evil ones have returned."

"Evil ones?" I asked.

"Tribe killers, child killers. I stay!"

The feeling of another presence vanished abruptly, and just as suddenly, I wanted to sit down. I leant against the rock wall and drew on the aura, with no intention of going to sleep.

CHAPTER 14 – Jai Cassidy – POV

A toe, nudging my side, woke me. When I tried to react and stand up, I couldn't. My arms and legs were tied to something, and I was spread eagled on the ground with Korvu's hot sun blazing down on me. At least I didn't have to stare into the sun; my eyes were closed and they felt like they were weighted with slimy ooze.

"Awake, I see," said a voice that reminded me of Stak. The words were accompanied by another prod.

I tried to form a retort, but no sound rewarded my effort and I really couldn't think due to a pounding headache.

I felt a soft scaly hand force my mouth open, and then a stream of liquid almost choked me when I tried to drink. It was probably water, but it had a strong mineral taste.

"Why did you come here?" The voice speaking Atapi was now deceptively mild.

"I was sent," I said, which was true enough. It occurred to me that until I could get free, provoking a challenge was a very stupid idea.

"For what reason?" The voice was still mild, but I did not doubt that the speaker was capable of violence. A thought came into my mind of dismembered bodies.

"Larcia sent me," I claimed.

"Larcia is a myth," the voice claimed. "If you expect me to believe that, then you should never have been let out without a keeper. Larcia has been dead countless generations. If she still lived, she would not let a Kumatan spy live."

"I'm not Kumatan!"

"No?" I felt something slice my arm. "Red blood, pale skin, and some of them can stir up the aura. Do you know what I am allowed to do to spies who try to corrupt my lands?"

"Let them go?" I suggested before he began to describe any punitive actions. I heard sniggers from multiple throats.

"Unfortunately, killing them is not allowed. But we are allowed to accompany them until they are off our land and leave them suitable chastened." The voice seemed casual about the matter. "But, since you are not Kumatan, those restraints don't apply – do they, little sorceress? What I can do to aliens is far worse."

The other watchers snarled in anticipation. I couldn't control a shudder.

"You are wise to be afraid, little fool. My warriors captured you with ease. And did you not realise that to neutralise a sorcerer, one only needs to bind his limbs and blind him… or her?"

I started to feel itchy as ants began to crawl all over me, and there was I could do nothing about it. No, there was something I could do, and I didn't need fancy arm gestures to do it. I drew on the aura and told the ants that I was not food. It worked. The itches stopped. The strength of the aura either scorched or they had fled.

There was a sense of amused discovery in my mind. I decided I must be sharing something of the sorcerer's mind. I kept my own thoughts still.

"Why are you here?" I was asked again, and this time the voice meant to command me.

I kept my mouth stubbornly shut and said nothing.

I had no warning of the clenched hand that hit my face below the left eye, but I smelt a whiff of Atapi sweat.

"Afraid to challenge me, little sorceress?" the voice taunted me, and I had confirmation that the voice belonged to the sorcerer of the tribe I had sensed.

"No. Release me and…"

"I don't think so," the voice said with thoughtful menace. "I think you would make a useful slave, once you are tamed."

"Never!" I tried to shout, but only a hoarse snarl came out. I recalled visions of the hanging Atapi bodies on Earth who had tried to control me.

I knew this sorcerer sensed the images when I felt another punch to my face.

"I know what you claim to be, human." The sorcerer was no longer trying to hide his malice. "You are not a worthy opponent. You are in my power, and helpless."

"You don't know my secret name," I taunted, making him think. Possibly, any other sorcerer caught as easily as I had been would have yielded his secret name.

"No," he admitted thoughtfully. "Then perhaps there is more to you."

One of the other voices spoke up. "Master, if it is alien… aliens eat our children."

The sorcerer moved, and I heard the rustle of his wings. "This is not one of those," the sorcerer said, stopping the background muttering. "It has red blood and claims to be the child of Jai Ansuni."

There was a united yowl from the warriors. I sensed more amusement in the mind of the sorcerer.

"Master, let us teach this weak female a lesson for its presumption."

There was a long pause before the sorcerer spoke. I guessed he was studying me, but this time his thoughts were not obvious.

"Leave it for now. See if it drops its presumption by morning. Do not presume it will be still weak, or that it is helpless. After all, it got this far into our land without being seen."

"Is it really a sorceress?" a warrior asked.

"So it claims," the sorcerer confirmed.

"Why do you let it live, Master?"

"To study it, learn from it, use it," the sorcerer said casually.

"Presumption." A gruffer sounding voice spat out the word. "I say that the weakest of my warriors could tie it in knots."

The sorcerer chuckled. "That might be amusing to watch. In the morning, we can see if that is true. If it truly plans to challenge me, it must first prove itself a worthy opponent. Maintain a guard here, and continue your patrols. I have no wish for one of the evil ones to deprive me of my pleasure."

By evening, my face and exposed skin felt like it was severely sunburnt. That was in spite of my efforts to keep my skin cool. The headache from the morning, probably the result of what ever had knocked me out, had eased. I was beginning to be able to think again, and I tried to figure out how they had captured me, and how to get free.

I had dozed off and on during the day, waking when I was poked by the guards who wanted to see if I was still alive. Evening came, bringing a cool breeze and a change of guards. I only knew that the sorcerer had returned too when I heard him challenging the day guards.

Some of the day guards had been young, and thought it fun to poke me with a sword tip or knife. They had laughed when I told them to stop it, and more when I threatened to tie them in knots as soon as I got free. They'd gone off then, not guiltily, but as if they expected to be censured. I'd then had to divert the trickle of the aura that I could draw on to heal the cuts.

The sorcerer spoke to the senior warrior and, from his comments, I knew he went off to speak to the other warriors.

I sensed that for a moment I was unobserved. Now the sun had gone, I used the trickle of aura to try to return flexibility to the bindings on my wrists and to adjust the thickness of my arms. I managed, finally, to pull my hands free and wasted no time clearing the ooze from my eyes before sitting up to try to free my ankles.

I was grabbed from behind before I finished. "Going somewhere, carrion?"

Carrion? Well, at least it was a change from being called 'vermin'.

A flash of power finished the job of freeing my feet. My captor hauled me upright.

"You're early," I said rudely, directing the comment at the sorcerer, not the warrior holding me. "You weren't meant to be back until morning." The Atapi in front of me had his wings furled, and was clad only in black leather leggings. I saw his tail-tip twitching from side to side behind his head – an involuntary sign of his annoyance.

"And where would you have been then, carrion?"

I addressed my answer to the sorcerer, ignoring the warrior. "I was going to stay here until you stopped being so cowardly and accepted my challenge."

The sorcerer merely laughed at me and his wings rustled, unfurling behind him. The warrior spun me around and gave me a forceful thwack across my face.

"Enough," the sorcerer said mildly, but he did not condemn the warrior for his action. The annoying bastard was beginning to irritate me. He was supposed to challenge me.

"You are so weak as to be beneath my notice," I was told, but the sorcerer was watching for my reaction.

"Coward, you won't fight me because you are afraid I will win." Two could play at insults.

I did sense a surge of anger at by belittling of him in front of his tribe. He controlled it well, and no trace of it was betrayed in his voice, only some humour.

"My Chief Warrior believes that his weakest warriors could still tie you in knots. I believe him."

"If you mean those insufferable puppies who thought it funny to poke me with their toy swords all day – I'll sweep this clearing with them," I retorted.

The sorcerer turned from me and looked over the day guards who had assembled there. He finally turned back to me.

"Yes, I think it is fitting that you should try. Show me you are not a weak and squeamish female." His tone suggested that he thought I was. He'd hit my anger switch.

The sorcerer gestured to one of the young warriors, and the Chief Warrior released me. I couldn't see the puppy's expression but, from the way he approached, I guessed he knew he was being punished. He had his sword pointing at me, as if he expected me to rush him. The Chief Warrior said sharply that he was not to use his sword, since I was unarmed. The young warrior carefully placed in on the ground, all the while watching me.

The sorcerer and the Chief Warrior stepped back.

Judging from the height of my first opponent, I knew he was little more than a child. My anger cooled, but not my desire to teach him a lesson.

Back on Earth, when I had been a prisoner, I had seen young Atapi males having mock fights. This one watched me and when I didn't move to attack him, he sprang into a run. If he expected me to stay there and be pummelled, he discovered his mistake when I simply held him off with a firm grip on his forehead. Try as he would, his arms were just too short to reach me, and bashing my arms did not force me to release him. The Chief Warrior cuffed him free and gave him a demeaning job to do until morning.

The second warrior gave me no warning. He jumped onto my back and tried to choke me. I fell backwards, elbowed him unexpectedly in both sides and used command voice on him to "release me." His hands obeyed, but as he wriggled free he immediately tried to punch me. I caught one arm and twisted it as I stood up. He could not move, or he would have dislocated his shoulder. Once again, the Chief Warrior cuffed my opponent and set him a detested task.

The third tormentor was an arrogant one, and he tried to make me angrier. A good tactic, except that he amused me. I began to realise that while I was proving myself, I was also giving these young puppies a lesson.

"If you want to piss me off," I told the arrogant one, "you will have to think of better insults." I then began to use some of the choice insults that other Atapi had used on me. I found his anger switch.His style was more like the fighting style of my brothers, and I finished that one with a knee in his delicate place – enough to hurt, not to damage.

This time, the sorcerer rebuked the would-be warrior. "You will sand polish rocks for the next three days. Go and begin."

Whatever that involved was definitely not a treat. The young warrior's indrawn breath, which suggested he was about to object, earned him a solid thwack from the Chief Warrior.

The fourth one was more cautious, but he made the mistake of assuming I'd fight like he did – as if it were a supervised match of skills. One, I don't follow rules, and two, I had never learnt his. I soon had him breaking his own rules and he ended up receiving a hard swat on his rear that caused him to yelp. The old warrior sent him off in disgrace too.

I wondered how many more I had to fight. When I tried to draw on the aura to refresh my energies, I found I couldn't. I didn't know what was blocking me, but it had to be the sorcerer's doing. If he wanted me to fail, I damn well would not give him that satisfaction.

The next one was older, and his expression was more like an Atapi leer.

"My sire told me how to handle Kumatan women," he claimed. His technique would have been dirty if I hadn't anticipated his grip between my legs, one he'd intended to be painful. I got him instead.

"Really?" I commented as he was writhing on the ground, clutching his man-bits. "My brothers taught me to handle males like you. My Human brothers."

The Chief Warrior grabbed that one by his neck and tossed him aside, with a promise of a worse punishment to come.

The sixth and last of the puppies had my measure and saw the feral light in my eyes. He was terrified of me, and refused the challenge.

"Knots, was it?" I snarled at the Chief Warrior.

The sorcerer spoke in his infuriatingly calm tone. "You have not finished with this one." He meant the puppy now trembling in the old warrior's grip.

"Do with him what you think appropriate. I don't intend to attack one who is obviously a child. At least he has learnt not to poke swords at sleeping scorpions."

That one did not escape punishment. He received a severe cuffing from the Chief Warrior and was sent to stand guard near the waterfall cave for the rest of the night.

I sensed that all those young warriors had been punished for tormenting me when they were meant to be guarding me.

The sorcerer gestured for the Chief Warrior and the day guards to depart, and for the night guards to start their patrols. I took the chance to get my breath. This sorcerer was not acting like any of the others I had challenged and that was making me wary.

"Have you learnt that same lesson?" the sorcerer asked me.

I knew what he meant, and kept my mouth shut. The answer was no, and even Jenha Mosellan had not managed that. I still managed to ask for trouble.

The sorcerer must have read my mind. "I thought not," he murmured. Then after a moment, he asked, "Why did Loschak not disembowel you?"

"He's a ghost," I said.

"I know," the sorcerer admitted. "And he rouses when there is a disturbance in the aura. That was when I came to investigate. I sent warriors in to get you – they slip beneath his notice. Sorcerers and aliens do not. I tend to leave him quiescent."

"Coward," I muttered.

"I see no purpose in fighting him. He serves a purpose for me by being there. And you haven't answered my question."

"He decided he liked me," I said.

"You are an aggravating creature."

Nothing new in that statement, I thought.

The sorcerer went on. "The last two aliens that made the mistake of hiding in that cave came out looking like sword targets."

A voice in my head advised, "Tell him, child."

I stopped being smart-mouthed and told him what happened in the cave – the appearance of the apparition, the bite by the buzzing thing, him knowing my mother, my telling him who I was, and that Stak was dead.

The sorcerer went tense, but nodded. He deigned to explain to me, "The nameless one weakened Loschak in a battle that neither won, so much so that he had no strength to defend his tribe from an alien party. Those aliens killed warriors, women and whelps, and even him, though he fought to the end of his strength and beyond."

I wanted to ask a question, and hoped that this sorcerer might answer it. "How does that relate to his awe of my mother?"

He paused. "Jai Ansuni hated the nameless one with a passion that matched his own. She promised to kill him if no sorcerer did."

I had the feeling that there was a lot more that he didn't say.

"Did you know her?" I asked. "My mother?"

I didn't think he was going to answer that.

"Some," he admitted finally. "Enough to disbelieve your claim that you killed the nameless one."

"He underestimated me," I said, omitting my belief that it had not been me that controlled the knife that killed him.

"A mistake that I will not make," he promised me. "I still do not believe it."

"Please yourself. The damn Kimh and their tame Traegers all believe I did. I still had the bloody knife in my hand when they found me."

"If that is true, they would have kept you controlled until they retrained your mind," the sorcerer told me.

"I didn't give them the chance," I boasted. "Besides, they had second thoughts about interfering with a human, though they should have been grateful that the bastard was dead and they could all come home."

"So, why are you here?"

"They had third thoughts," I said sourly.

"And then?"

"I made them think again!"

That caused a snarled laugh.

"Why don't you challenge me?" I asked.

"I don't have to challenge you," he claimed, confusing me.

"Won't they think you are a coward if you don't?"

He didn't react to that. Instead, he began to walk off. Since I still wanted an answer, I followed.

"You could go and challenge the Old One, if you were so minded," this sorcerer told me. "If you won, you would have your insane wish and rank over all of us. Of course, after you won, every other sorcerer would want to challenge you for the position."

"I'm not ready for the Old One yet." That I knew in my very bones.

"Then you are not completely lacking in wits," he told me. "Have you learnt anything from me yet?"

I thought that an odd question. "Only that you are the first Atapi sorcerer that didn't want to kill me on sight."

There was a malicious chuckle echoing in my mind. Somehow, I was missing a point here.

I felt the sorcerer trying to command me when he said, "You will come to the village with me and stay where I put you."

Just to show him that his command voice didn't work on me, I stopped walking until he noticed. He kept walking, but called back to me, "Or you can stay out here, where those other aliens might be wandering still, and risk my warriors finding you again. If you like being staked out in the sun…"

Damn him! I don't trust 'nice' from an Atapi sorcerer.

"Tomorrow, I will define the terms of my challenge, since it is the only way I will be rid of you."

I followed him then. I was getting edgy with waiting.

CHAPTER 15 – Jai Cassidy – POV

While following behind the sorcerer, no one seemed to be aware of me, though his tribe's folk all regarded him with deference as he passed. He stopped outside a cave that was more of an opening in a small hill.

"You may sleep here," he told me.

I took the invitation and went in, when I turned to see if he was following, I saw the sorcerer take something from a pocket in his robes and drop it in the door opening. It glowed for a moment before going dark.

The cave was dark except for a faint glow emanating from the walls. It had no comforts, only a convenient hole, that I found by locating the source of a particularly putrid smell. I was tired, hungry, thirsty and sore, and wondered if the generosity of this sorcerer extended to food and drink.

I heard him outside, calling out two names. The first to arrive, a warrior, was given orders to guard the cave entrance, while the other, a female, was told to bring me some food and water.

The sorcerer called me a guest, but I am sure they all thought he meant prisoner. When the female returned with a sack of liquid and a platter with food, the warrior forced me to the back of the cave at spear point, and the woman glanced at me with what seemed like terror. I sat down at the back of the cave and thought of peace and gentle thoughts. It didn't seem to help.

After they had gone, I returned to the entrance of the cave and watched the activity of the tribe. The females, whelps and warriors gradually returned to their caves, holes or whatever they called their homes.

I finally approached the food and ate it cautiously. I couldn't help feeling that there was danger around, but I kept telling myself to keep out of it as it didn't feel directed at me. For a while after eating, I watched the guard stroll back and forward, and the warriors who were patrolling around the village.

After a while I allowed myself to doze, although I was waking at the slightest hint of movement or sound. One sound I recognised, and I was so surprised to hear it that I ran out of the cave and looked skyward. I had only heard a helicopter once, back on Earth, but the sound was unmistakable even if this one was quieter. To prove my deduction, a dark shape flew over the village, and its general outline and behaviour agreed with my memory.

As I watched the direction to which the helicopter had gone, I was trying to think what such a machine was doing on Korvu.

My attention was abruptly diverted when I felt a solid blow on my shoulder. I was knocked to the ground and that shoulder was too numb to help me push back up. I would have stayed down, except a sharp voice from an angry warrior caused me to roll, just avoiding another blow that was meant to kill me. I needed no other warning to go into full survival mode.

I hadn't exerted myself with the 'puppies' that I had fought earlier, as I hadn't wanted to seriously hurt them. I had no such restraints now against this murderous maniac. I found all of my senses heightened by the need to fight for my life. I realised that, in spite of the darkness, I could see my opponent as clearly as if it were day.

The manic warrior grew angry, and then enraged, when I kept diving under his attacks, or rolling just ahead of them. His emotions were totally uncontrolled, and he seemed to be beyond reason. I wished I knew why.

More by luck than skill, he landed another solid blow; I felt the bone in my left leg break. There had been no rhythm or pattern in his attack, and now my leg slowed me. I couldn't run or stand and jarring the leg was agony. He came back at me again, intending to finish me. I blocked the blow aimed at my head with one arm and used my free hand to yank on the carved branch he was using as a bludgeon. He fell on me, pinning me down. I felt him reaching for another weapon, and struggled against the scaly hand he used to hold my face down. While my mind and strength was focused, he stuck a knife in my side. As I felt myself blacking out, I reached for the aura and commanded, "Do not kill."

One tiny part of my mind was aware of the warrior being dragged off me and flung aside. I expected a similar fate, but I was left where I was. Not far off, I heard females wailing, and closer there was moaning. I had a pounding headache and it was made worse by the resounding roar of, "SILENCE".

It made the wailing females go silent. The moaning sound stopped too – I realised that it had been my moaning, and I had been too weak to resist the command. I forced one eye open. I was on my side and could see the knife sticking out of me.

Damn it! I was not going to pass out again.

"Josai! Cassia!" the sorcerer roared.

One of the now silent females rose and approached the sorcerer, bowing low and staying that way. A second approached timidly from a group of silent watchers.

"Take your mate, and make sure he is fit to answer questions immediately after sun-greeting. If he is not, I will send him off my land."

Before he turned his attention to me, the sorcerer retrieved the stone he had dropped earlier in the entrance to the cave and studied it.

A really old looking female with white hair and a younger one approached the sorcerer, each carrying a burning torch. Neither exuded the fear I sensed from everyone else. The old one spoke softly to the sorcerer, and some of the sorcerer's anger drained off, but not all. He gave orders to the two females and stalked off.

He'd spoken quietly, but I heard the sorcerer say, "… she is too persistent to die and she can heal fast given a chance. See to it that she can answer questions by sun-greeting. Treat her in my outer chamber. I have no time for sleeping with intruders about my land. Send Cassia to me when she is finished with Tesla."

The females lifted me gently, breaking my connection to the ground and the aura. I did black out then.

I re-awoke in a chamber that was well lit by candles and decorated by fabric hangings. I was lying on a pile of soft furs and I amused myself by thinking I might be lying on the sorcerer's own bed. After further consideration, I decided that I didn't like that idea. When I tried to move and to sit up, firm but gentle hands held me down.

"Lie still," a female voice ordered in a no nonsense tone. I sensed no threat from either female, rather the opposite. I could feel them using the aura, which was particularly strong in this cave.

The younger of the two females walked into my view, carefully carrying a small clay pot. "Keep hold of this, Kumatan," she told me, as she put my hands around it.

"I'm not…" I was about to correct them and say I was Human, but I realised that the pot felt like a concentration of the aura.

"You have a nasty fracture," the old woman told me. "We have set the leg, but you must not move. Soon I will have a soothing salve ready and it will help you heal."

"I can heal myself," I told them.

"So our sorcerer said. But bones take a while when they are as bad as this. We must have you ready and able to stand by sun-greeting."

I recalled that my attacker, Tesla, was also to be functional by then.

"Why did Tesla attack me?" I asked, hoping one of the females would tell me.

The younger finally decided to speak. "I cannot say for sure, but outsiders killed his children, butchered them like animals and ate their flesh. You are an outsider, Kumatan."

"I am more outsider than that," I admitted. "I'm Human; I wasn't born on this world."

"Yet you can use the aura," the younger pointed out without seeming to be afraid of me.

"Oh, I'm half-Atapi, but for all that, I can't change form like all the rest of you."

"The only female I know who could change shape was my friend Jai Ansuni. Is it true that you are her child?"

"Yes," I admitted without elaboration.

"The salve is ready, Bernea," the older woman said.

"You are called Jai as well. Is your mother still alive?" Bernea asked.

"No, she died from birthing me."

"What of her friend, Suzi Mosellan. The Kumatan?"

"I never heard of her. I only met Jenha Mosellan. He stopped Stak killing me."

I sensed a reaction to that reference, but Bernea covered it by instructing me, "It is important now that you lie still. Applying the salve may hurt a bit. You can draw on the power of the aura by holding the pot. It is a minor power relic I can use when healing."

I felt the salve going on. At first it simply numbed the sore places, but then I felt heat seeping into me. I wondered if Tesla was being treated as well.

My thoughts drifted to why this sorcerer would insist that I be healed. Surely, being injured, I would be easier to defeat? Stak would not have hesitated. The heat from the candles and the salve made me drowsy, and I dozed off to sleep.

Bernea woke me gently, simply by touching my arm and saying my name. When I opened my eyes, she said, "It's nearly dawn."

I moved, noticing that only a few candles were still lit. When I tried to stand up, I realised most of my pain was gone. The leg was tender, and

Bernea supported me as I stood, but it held my weight and I could walk to the earthen pot that served a necessary purpose.

There was no sign that the sorcerer had returned, and this was a relief. I hadn't forgotten that he had promised to set the terms of challenge. To my mind, it was an odd way of doing it. The other sorcerers had given me no time to prepare or any warning of their challenges. Perhaps he wanted to torture my imagination?

Then there was this business about the sun-greeting ceremony. Why did I have to be there for what I guessed was a matter to do with tribal discipline?

Bernea disappeared and returned with a round bowl of a milky liquid and a kind of heavy bread spread with an aromatic smelling paste. It made me realise I was starving, and I didn't let myself think about what I was eating. I had finished the milky drink, and decided I liked the odd taste. When Bernea told me it was mare's milk, my human upbringing almost made my stomach rebel.

An old warrior, not the Chief, came to fetch me. I wanted to glance at Bernea for reassurance, but that would have been a sign of weakness. I did sense her following a few paces behind me, but she stayed at the entrance to the cave, while I continued out into the pale pre-dawn light.

It looked to me like all the adult males, and near adult males, were present, but I was sure some were patrolling. I was led to a place to one side of the gathering, and many eyes followed my progress.

Once there, I didn't try to hide my interest in my surroundings. The large clearing was surrounded by trees, and there was enough light to see the females watching from amongst them. I assumed their homes were amongst the trees.

My eyes returned to a rough rock altar, set within the clearing. The sorcerer stood there, standing with his back to the gathering, looking at the direction of the slowly rising sun. He was only wearing the briefest of privacy covering. His wings unfurled from his back and rustled open – they were easily the size of Stak's.

More movement caught my eye. Tesla was escorted out by two warriors and taken to stand behind the sorcerer. He was left to stand alone.

The attention of all the males, even Tesla, was on the sorcerer as he spoke in a chanting tone. I tried to understand his words, but they must have been on a different dialect to the one I knew. My attention drifted as the males responded to parts of this dawn ritual. When the voices stopped, the silence seemed more intense. I had been hearing a background of birds, chirping at the dawn, and even they were now silent.

The sorcerer turned suddenly and stared at Tesla, who trembled slightly before straightening to look back at the sorcerer. I didn't wonder why, as I could sense the sorcerer's anger. It was enough to make me feel like trembling myself, and I was thankful that I hadn't provoked him this far yesterday.

"Tesla, son of Aretas, you attacked, unprovoked, a female who was under your guard. You dishonoured yourself and this tribe. What is your reason for this?"

Tesla seemed to be trying to speak, but without sound emerging.

"Speak!" the sorcerer demanded.

"I… can offer nothing, Majestic One. I do not recall my actions, but I have been told of them. I do not know why I acted."

To his credit, Tesla stood straight, met the eyes of the sorcerer and, even knowing that he was to be punished, did not disgrace himself by trying to beg for forgiveness or slinking away.

The sorcerer gestured towards me. My escort, who had stayed behind me, now pushed me forward.

The sorcerer turned his attention to me but, although his gaze was intent, his anger was not with me – this time. "As the victim, have you anything you would say?" he asked me.

I glanced at the warrior, and considered what I was sensing from him. "I don't think you should think of him too harshly," I said, doubting he would actually listen to me. "He's grieving, deeply. I heard his children were killed by some aliens."

"And how should that excuse him?" asked the sorcerer, determined not to agree with me.

"Yeah, well, I would prefer to be a Human – and as far as you lot are concerned, that's another type of alien. I heard that alien helicopter go over, too, and I think your warrior reacted to the threat."

Tesla turned his head fractionally – amazed, I think, that I spoke in his favour.

The sorcerer did not look at me when he spoke again.

"One who was a guest of this tribe was ill-treated by this warrior. He failed his duty, lost control of his mind and self. A warrior must be in control at all times." The sorcerer glanced at all of his warriors, and the young males before continuing. "Tesla, son of Aretas, for beating a guest under my protection you will receive five lashes. For failing as a warrior, you forfeit the honour of a second wife. Cassia will be in my keeping until another warrior proves worthy of a mate."

Tesla trembled, expecting worse.

"In addition, you will be exiled from the village until I see fit to allow your return. Be thankful that I do not exile you from my lands and that your victim chose to speak in your favour. The tribe needs all its warriors, with these vile aliens intruding everywhere. Until I say otherwise, you will patrol the outer boundary and fend for yourself."

The sorcerer turned to me. "You say you are a sorceress, therefore it is your right to punish this male for his treatment of you."

"You already passed the judgement," I responded. What did he expect me to do? Punch him?

The sorcerer gestured to the warrior next to me. The warrior drew out a rod-like weapon and held it out to me. I recognised what this one did, and wanted nothing to do with it.

"No," I said clearly.

In my mind I heard a malicious chuckle – and then the words, "Weak, you are."

I felt my face turning red, and hoped none of these Atapi knew what a blush meant.

The warrior moved from my side and proceeded to use the force whip with efficient impartiality. I wished I had not been so squeamish, for I would not have wielded it so forcefully. And I wished I dared look away, but if I had, I would have been seen as weaker still in the eyes of this sorcerer. He was watching my reactions as well as the punishment of the warrior.

I moved uneasily, trying not to betray the fact that I was feeling some of Tesla's pain. The sorcerer walked to Tesla, who'd stoically kept on his feet. He then took his arm, dragged him forward three steps and vanished. I assumed he was carrying out the exile part of the sentence.

Within moments, he was back, sending the warriors and others back to their normal duties. He gestured to two warriors and ordered them to bring Cassia to his cave.

I watched the quietly howling female being half-dragged across the open space until the sorcerer came forward, blocking my view. He was close enough that I instinctively moved back. I felt his attention, like a pressure on my mind. I thought of human trivia, and heard a snarl.

"Are all humans so squeamish?" he accused me. "Or did you think that Tesla was beneath your notice? Or that I was too harsh? Or do you like being beaten?"

A voice in my head warned me not to interfere in tribal justice. As usual, I ignored the advice.

"Tesla needed help, not punishment," I said, ignoring the other questions.

The sorcerer snarled and slapped the side of my head. I reacted by hitting back, only he grabbed my arm before I connected.

"Perhaps I should give him to you as a mate. You deserve each other," the sorcerer insulted me. "A brainless warrior and a brainless whelp who thinks she knows better than everyone."

I felt him casually twisting my arm, and I was considering kicking him where he was hardly protected. He pushed me away and I spun around, expecting an attack.

"Weak!" he said again. "Weak of body, weak of mind. It was trickery, not skill, that let you win against those lesser devils. The others will not be defeated so easily."

"Why should you care?" I demanded.

"Care? Beating you will have no value except to rid this world of an annoyance. Go from here and pick a fight with someone with time to spare. I have none."

"If you won't fight me, you must be a coward," I said.

He snarled. "If it is a fight you want…" He stopped speaking and adopted a listening pose. "You will have it later."

With that, he grabbed my arm and led me forward. Suddenly I was within a rock chamber. The sorcerer was gone again before I'd fully realised it.

"Don't try to leave," he said in my mind, "or my devil wind will kill you."

"Damn you!" I thought back, and heard only that horrid malicious laugh.

The rock chamber wasn't dark; the walls glowed faintly, and showed me it was circular. The rock looked smooth and there was no sign of a door.

"Illusion," I muttered, and I moved closer to the wall to see if I could feel the doorway. As my fingers were just about to touch the wall, I felt a tingle of warning. I drew back for a moment and considered it, but decided to try again.

I felt pressure and a stinging in my fingertips. I looked and saw two fingers had lost layers of skin. The bleeding stopped quickly. I now knew what the sorcerer meant by his devil wind. I wouldn't be able to break the illusion that way.

I thought of trying the sword, and I invoked it by drawing it from its invisible sheath. I willed it to glow brightly and used its light to look for the door. It was meant to show me the truth, but still no door. I touched the sword to the wall, and it was wrenched from my hand and flung behind me.

A memory surfaced in my mind of the wind that Stak had once used to confine me. This had to be something similar, acting as a boundary in the cavern, and honed to razor sharpness. If there was a door, it was hidden by the wind, not by illusion.

I sat down in the centre of the chamber next to the sword, and cursed myself for being a fool. Hadn't I been the one who had distrusted 'nice' from a sorcerer, the one who'd expected no warning from a sorcerer when they decided to challenge me? This could be his challenge now, and I had walked into it like a lamb.

If I couldn't get out of here, I would lose. I who was human, fighting a war I'd provoked – I had a duty to escape... somehow.

CHAPTER 16 – Jai Cassidy - POV

I tried to cross planes to escape; after all, the sorcerer had walked me here that way. There was just enough room to pace three steps across. I thought of the clearing I had just left, and walked forward – but on the second step, instead of the twisting blackness, I felt myself thrown against something hard.

When my head stopped spinning, I realised I was flat on my back, and still in the circular cavern. When I had recovered enough to think, I was annoyed, but grateful that these spinning walls were not also closing in on me. It meant I had time to think of options.

When Stak had tried something similar to this back on Earth, I had been wearing slave bands and they had helped negate the wind. Here, I had tried the sword, but it had no effect since the wind was real and not an illusion.

I was already beginning to dislike the small space. I was not like most Atapi who liked caves and holes. To pretend I was elsewhere, I closed my eyes and recalled every bit of sorcery lore I had absorbed from my mother's box. What few ideas that gave me didn't work. I could still not get past that wind.

For a time I rested, but my mind was not still. If I couldn't escape physically, I had an idea of how to take my mind out of the enclosed place. I stood and walked two paces, and stopped. This time I wasn't picturing a place I wanted to go. If there was any way for a watcher to see me in that cell, he would see my body fading in and out of visibility. My mind was in the dark void between planes, and on Earth I had discovered that this place did not have to be without sensation. Now, as then, I saw visions summoned by my thoughts.

Annoyance had been replaced by curiosity. I had seen some of the Atapi village on Earth and I wondered how this sorcerer's tribe compared. That triggered a view of the village from the aspect of a bird, if a bird could hover in one place.

For mid-morning, it looked too quiet. There were no young whelps running around. I guessed that whatever had happened to cause the sorcerer to go off abruptly had required all but the very oldest warriors to deal with it. I watched several females moving about, but they seemed like hunters, wary and watchful. They seemed to be guarding the centre of the village, whilst the old warriors were patrolling the edge.

Idly, I watched two old females stride off purposefully towards a grove of trees. As they approached, wind rustled the leaves of the trees and their hands moved to hover over the handles of their wicked-looking hunting knives.

I wondered what was in the grove, and my mental view changed. I felt a surge of grief, and saw a shape huddled between two small mounds. On each mound was a newly planted sapling, surrounded by a ring of stones and childish treasures.

The females went to the huddled shape and helped another woman to her feet, gently urging her to come away. I recognised Tesla's first mate. I had heard about the children, and felt Larcia stirring in my mind – in protest.

Then I began to wonder where the males had gone, and I seemed to go higher. The view now seemed more like a map, but with Atapi ants moving purposefully. After watching for a while, I saw that the warriors were circling an area. At the question in my mind, I saw their quarry.

At first glimpse, the cowled figures reminded me of humans. I wondered if they were Kumatan. Two figures were using little picks to examine pieces of rock in a small blind canyon, oblivious to the approaching danger. I almost tried to warn them, but one turned and tossed back his cowl to better study a rock sample. They could not be Kumatan – the face was clearly alien, even to me. At my mental wish, my view drew closer. A chill of dread and a mental whisper went through me as Larcia hissed, "These are the enemy."

The bluish tinge to their skin that had first attracted my attention was the most obvious difference. The facial structure was also more angular and more elongated than that of a human. Ridges of bone were evident under the skin above the eyes. The skin on the cheeks was tightly stretched, and did not have the rounding effect of cheeks. The fingers holding the rock were longer than a human's and were pointed at the tips, like a cat's claw. Their eyes, while rounded, had a slight triangular shape. There could be no mistaking these creatures for human, Kumatan, or even an Atapi shaping a Kumatan.

I wondered what it was about this canyon that interested the aliens so much. The place, from my view, seemed to be no more than sandstone rock.

Their tapping and chipping lost my interest, but I did wonder where they had come from. My view shifted, moving slowly so I could look for signs of a camp or their base. My mind was drawn to a stand of trees nearby. At first I couldn't see why, but a breeze ruffled something below my view, and made it look like the ground was moving. Finally I made out an oddly mottled sheet of some fabric strung between some tree branches. I wanted to see below, and my view approached the place from nearer ground level. I saw a dump of rubbish to one side, a pile of rocks near a trickle of water from a small spring, a lean-to structure, a fireplace and another stretched piece of fabric over a pile of boxes.

The camp was deserted, so I let my mind move the view to look around. The breeze came again and ruffled the trees as I looked in their direction. I caught a glint of sunlight off a shiny surface, and wondered what it could be.

I willed my view closer and it moved through the trees to where I saw what did indeed look like a small helicopter. So this is where that flying thing from last night had gone.

While I studied the mind image, I felt another mind impinging on mine. Anger surged there, and then I felt my body being gripped by the scruff and dragged.

I fell to my knees, realising that I was out of that enclosed cave in the village, but before I could stand and look around, a powerful fist punched me backwards. I found myself looking up at the enraged Atapi sorcerer. I tried to scrabble backwards, away from him.

"I should let the evil ones have you," he snarled, stalking closer. "You seem to have a wish to die."

From out of the ground, vine-like roots protruded. They grew quickly in length and wrapped themselves around my legs, arms and torso, then tightened. The sorcerer turned and stalked away.

I glanced along my body. Only one hand was free and I imaged Larcia's sword in it. Where the sword touched the vines, they seemed to snap. As real as it felt, the vines were merely illusions.

I freed myself and called after the sorcerer, "That was hardly a worthy challenge, Cotek."

He continued to walk away as if my defeating him meant nothing.

In my mind, I heard, "Go and let my fellow sorcerers kill you. I've had enough of your aggravation. Now that you have my name, there is no reason for you to stay."

I looked around, and had no idea where I was on Cotek's land.

"Larcia?" I asked in my mind, tentatively.

There was nothing tentative in the mental mind-lashing I received from the ancient one. She listed all my mistakes and the many times I was lucky to have survived. Clearly, and with hurtful precision, she described what any of the other male sorcerers would have done to me — had they had me in those positions. I quailed, and felt like I had survived each torture.

When I felt like scavenger droppings, Larcia let up.

"Where do I go next?" I asked meekly.

The mental voice fell silent, but it was to give more weight to what she had said.

"You know Cotek's name, but you have not defeated him. You have alienated him when you need his support. He cannot, and will not help you with later challenges, but when you reach the pre-eminent position, you will need it. You have not yet learnt his most important secret."

"What must I do, my queen?" I asked.

"Win his loyalty," my mind was told.

"How?"

That question went unanswered. I sighed. I would have to figure that out for myself.

I sat where I was and thought how different Cotek was to Stak. Cotek was tolerating me when his fellows would not. He had said he wanted to use me, learn from me. I had assumed he wanted to learn my weaknesses, and perhaps he did, but it wasn't just that. He was a confident sorcerer, respected by his tribe — look at how they had all accepted his judgement this morning. Even Tesla had accepted his punishment, and if I felt sorry for any male Atapi it was Tesla. He had been stripped of a wife, and sent out to be not quite shunned — all because he was distracted by grief.

"Larcia? Can you show me where Tesla is?" I asked with a small polite thought.

I received a vision, but nothing else. I walked to where I saw the tracks of a lone Atapi. On arriving at that distant place, I followed the footprints until I found Tesla standing rigidly, with teeth clenched.

He heard me approach, even though I had intended silence. He spun around with his weapon ready. I stopped just out of its reach. He glared at me, but made no attempt to approach closer or to speak.

"I came to apologise for being the cause of your disgrace," I said — me, who had never apologised before.

For a long time, I didn't think he understood. "Why?" he frowned. "I am dishonoured. You will be punished for talking to me."

"Yeah, but… he's already mad at me anyway."

He lowered his weapon to a less aggressive angle. "You spoke up for me, to him. I did not expect that."

"I don't know that I helped," I said.

"I could have been exiled from the tribe, and from its lands," Tesla said. "I could have been deprived of both Josai and Cassia. You could have stayed silent. Still I am dishonoured, and I don't know why I attacked you."

"I think I do," I said softly. "You may be a warrior, but you are also a father. One who has lost two sons in a way that no one should suffer, and one your young ones did not deserve. You need time to grieve."

"I am a warrior," he insisted.

"And a father," I iterated. "Females have the outlet of crying. And you feel you cannot, because you are a warrior. I think the sorcerer was kind to send you here."

He snarled at me, not agreeing.

I stood my ground. "I do, because here, no one is around. No one will hear you howl out your grief. Last night, it was the aliens' flying machine that made you forget, and I was there, an alien too, though of a different kind. You acted as a warrior, but grief had blinded you. I forgive you, Tesla."

I turned to leave, but I heard a shaky, "Stay?" I turned back.

"Will you…?" Tesla tried to ask what he wanted.

"I will howl with you, warrior," I agreed, knowing this was what he wanted.

The tenseness left Tesla, as I did my best to imitate the howling. After a time, Tesla stopped and bowed slightly to me. "Are you a healer?" he asked.

"Not really. I just see things differently. Now you can be a warrior again, and regain your honour."

"And you?" he asked me.

"I am going to have to risk aggravating your sorcerer a bit more," I said, but then I had a totally scurrilous idea. "Are you meant to stay unseen, or just be seen to be doing your duty?"

"Since this morning, and until now, I did not want to be seen," Tesla admitted. "But I still have a duty, and now I am not afraid to be pitied."

"Good, because I know where some of those aliens are camping."

Tesla's eyes lit, but he said, "I am not to join the hunt."

"The others are circling the aliens. The camp is deserted and their flying thing is there. I would watch it so they cannot use it to escape."

Tesla's snarl rivalled Con Ansuni's.

"May I hunt with you? You need not consider me a female," I asked.

He nodded, and trotted off in the direction I pointed. I needed to run very hard to keep him in sight, but every now and then Tesla stopped, restraining the comments on the tip of his tongue. He was treating me as a fellow warrior – almost.

When we neared the camp, he accepted my warning for silence, and I led him to the side of the helicopter furthest from the camp. We stopped and I pointed. Tesla hissed when he saw the machine.

"It is not alive like an animal," I told him. "It needs one of the aliens to make it move, to rise and to fly. I don't know how they do that, or why it flies without falling, but I do know that those pieces that form a cross…" I crossed my forearms to show what I meant. "Must spin very fast to do it. Can you think of a way to tie them up?"

"Vines," Tesla said at once. "I know where some grow near here."

"I'll watch," I offered.

The machine was 'dead' and I saw no aliens around it, but my view wasn't the best. Some forgotten sense of prudence stopped me from creeping closer. Armed Atapi warriors were hunting these vermin. I was not armed and I did not wish to spook these aliens.

I tried to do what I had before, and sought to see from above. I watched the two aliens I had seen earlier. From their actions, I realised they were prospecting – and, from the intensity of their concentration, they had found something of value to them. They chipped off small rocks, measured them, weighed them on a spring scale and sat them on a box.

I could sense when one of the Atapi warriors had cut the tracks of these aliens. Now, the Atapi were between the creatures and the spring they used for water, and were circling to cut them off from their camp. Some split off from the main hunting party to find the camp.

Once again, I shifted my bird's eye view to judge where the Atapi were, but now I could not see them. Yes, I realised – Cotek was cloaking them with the aura.

Tesla returned, dragging several long vines. He looked at me now for guidance. I squatted to clear a patch of sandy dirt and began to draw pictures. I pointed to a part of my sketch, and then to the same part on the helicopter. Then, using my crude drawings, I explained what I thought might work.

Tesla snarl-grinned and began to tie loops at the ends of the vine. Then he stood, ready to throw the loop over the blades, perfectly confident of his ability to get it there. He waited for my signal to throw it.

My mind returned to the aliens in the canyon, still ecstatically unaware of the trouble approaching. I knew, even if I couldn't see, that Cotek was approaching them, and his warriors were creeping down the sheer canyon walls to come up from behind them.

When all were ready, Cotek allowed himself to be seen approaching. The aliens dropped the rocks they were examining and drew knives from under their robes. Both aliens glanced around, as if to confirm that this Atapi lizard man was alone.

"Arrogant bastards," I thought.

They charged Cotek, with expressions displaying their intent to kill. The sorcerer stood firm, seemingly unarmed, until they were nearly on him. Then, from out of nowhere, he drew a sword and slashed, knocking the knife from one and inflicting a nasty gash on another. I could read Cotek's expression now – he was deadly intent. These aliens had invaded his land, were stealing its treasures, and their kind had killed two of his tribe's children.

He stepped back, and the uninjured alien dived for his knife. His attempt was easily blocked, and I wondered why Cotek did not simply finish them by sword or magic. I decided he was testing them as he had tested me. He was learning their tactics and fighting methods.

When he began to circle them, I felt the aura stirring. The aliens watched him now with wary respect, waiting for a chance to attack again, unaware of the ritual he was performing.

I felt the aliens' terror as their bodies froze into immobility. I felt the terror escalate when they saw dozens of warriors racing at them from all directions.

Cotek was restrained as the blood lust of the warriors was allowed free rein. I seemed to be watching now through Cotek's eyes – when I would have turned away, I felt him hold my mind there. I had to watch the sickening spectacle of the warriors hacking at the aliens, who lost their flesh piece by piece to the swords of the warriors.

I felt Tesla grip my arm, and I wrenched my mind free. He was pointing to the helicopter, and the blades were beginning to turn slowly, as if they were warming up. He had his vine lasso ready, and I nodded. I only just realised that there must have been an alien in the machine all the time that we were watching.

I had not expected the loop to snag a rotor, but it weighted the vine enough for it to drop between two of the blades. I heard the change in the whine of the motor as the vine added drag.

Tesla threw a second vine with equal success, putting this one across a diagonal gap. Already, the first vine was being wound around the axle of the blades. Surely the alien was aware of the motor straining. Would he come out and check? Tesla had his spear ready if he did.

I risked checking where Cotek was, and felt him seize control of my sight and use it to look around. He betrayed nothing when he saw Tesla with me.

"Why?" he queried, noticing the vines.

"So it won't fly," I thought back. "There must be one of them inside."

Thus warned, Cotek and his warriors approached. Some were carrying the carcasses of the prospectors. No doubt the globs of gore that remained in the canyon would be scavenged by the wild dogs.

Cotek appeared and approached the helicopter. He sent the carcasses, magically, to where the door was on the side nearest us.

Once again, I felt the aura stirring, and this time I felt the chant in my head. I recognised the ritual; he was trying to make the occupant come out. I waited to see if it would work on the alien mind.

The helicopter was trying to lift. The engine whine increased in pitch, before slowing. I almost grinned, as Tesla was doing, except I realised that the helicopter was turning its front end towards Cotek. I saw, through his eyes, a long metal tube protruding from the front.

"Down!" I yelled mentally. Cotek hit the ground and sent the command to his warriors.

"What?" Cotek demanded of me, but seconds later he understood as a stream of bullets flew over him.

The helicopter was spinning on the ground now, spewing bullets in a full circle around it. Perhaps I was the only one to sense Cotek's uncertainty in how to deal with this threat.

"Use your wind," I told him mentally.

He did not acknowledge me, but I felt the aura stirring yet again and the air begin to move, to circle faster and faster, and saw the dust begin to rise and swirl. The raised dust began to circle around the helicopter and spiral more tightly.

I heard the motor whine urgently, and began to smell something acrid and unfamiliar. The gun was still firing its lethal stream, and it seemed the machine was slowly lifting. I didn't think it would be able to fly, but if it tilted slightly, the bullets might hit the prone Atapi.

I did not consider it strange to add my will to Cotek's ritual. The wind spun faster, and shrank further. Cotek tried to hide the sense that it was still not enough. The 'wrongness' about the alien machine was still extremely powerful. I thought to call on Larcia, but my mind rebelled. Instead I thought of Loschak. I reached out to his ghostly aura and his ghostly but powerful will joined to Cotek too. The difference was immediate. Cotek's skill, Loschak's centuries of experience, and my sneaky humanity all worked together.

Cotek warned his warriors to retreat, but his concentrating was on the helicopter.

I heard a high pitched scream, which I guessed was a metallic screech as the devil wind sheared off pieces of metal and sent them flying in all directions. I smelt something that was like the fuel used in cars back on Earth. Moments later, there was a massive explosion and a fireball rose within the whirling wind, forcing black smoke into the sky.

I withdrew from Cotek's mind and felt a satiated Loschak slip away, drawn back to his cave. The whirlwind slowed, continuing to draw smoke upward. The fire was still fiercely hot.

I approached Cotek, very cautiously. "If you remove the air, the fire will go out."

"Water kills fires," he replied tersely.

"Um, not liquid fuel ones," I said, trying to sound very meek. "Every Human knows that."

Cotek accepted my suggestion, and the column of black smoke thinned and dispersed. When the air stilled, a twisted blackened mess of molten metal and plastic settled to the ground. The occupant would be hard to find in the mess.

The warriors began an ululation of triumph. Cotek allowed it for a time, and then told them to remove all traces of the invaders. The wreckage would be allowed to cool first – but nothing was to be left to indicate that anyone had ever been in the canyon or the camp.

Cotek turned his gaze to Tesla and said curtly, "Continue your patrol, warrior."

Tesla straightened and trotted off. He must still complete his punishment, but he had been commended for his part. He was still a warrior. Cotek turned his gaze on me and said nothing.

CHAPTER 17 – Jai Cassidy – POV

"Deben, Litok," Cotek spoke aloud, raising one arm as he did.

Moments later, two figures materialised in front of him and bowed a greeting.

"Father," each one acknowledged. They both eyed the scene of the battle, and sniffed the unfamiliar smells.

"Deben, you will supervise the removal of all things that do not belong here, as well as what is yonder where these invaders camped and in the blind canyon where they were chipping rocks. Be thorough – the Kumatan will react to the use of sorcery here. I cannot say how long they will be."

Deben ran off, seemingly competent for the task.

"Litok, this is Jai Cassidy. Go with her back to the village and see that she is treated as an honoured guest until I am finished here."

"Couldn't I help you, Father?" Litok dared to ask.

"There is no need," Cotek said, not angered. "However, I do need someone to assure the others that she is my guest. Since you know how well she can fight, perhaps she can teach you some useful tricks. That way I won't find all my resting warriors unfit to work."

Litok seemed to stand taller.

Listening to Cotek give orders to his child, I realised he was also giving me an oblique warning not to cause trouble for this innocent child. He was also shrewd, he'd figured out that I didn't like hurting others, particularly youngsters. This time, though, I was not sorry to be sent away, which was what Cotek was doing. I think he must have realised that I had no intention of leaving his village until I had learnt more from him.

I wondered at his attitude. I was not sure if he was treating me like a sorcerer who'd defeated him – one he had no right to ask favours – or someone he had no desire to allow to be involved further in the affairs of his tribe.

I did wonder what the Kumatan might do if they came. They would want Cotek to explain what he had been doing. So I let Litok lead me to an ornate wooden hut structure, the same one where I had seen Tesla's young wife taken. I had thoughts of talking to her but, when we entered, the single room was empty.

"I will bring you some food and drink," Litok said, bowing to me. He turned and trotted from the hut, taking his task seriously.

I tried to follow him outside, but a force stopped me. "Tricked," I muttered, annoyed.

When Litok returned with a tray of things, he passed straight through without taking a hand off the tray.

"I tried to get out, but I can't. Is there a reason for that?" I asked.

"It's only a warding," Litok said, innocently frank. "Father has it there because he does not let just anyone in here. You will not be bothered here."

I couldn't cross planes to get out of there either, I bet myself. Cotek was really rubbing in my ignorance. I decided to test my limits and asked, "Later, would you show me around the village?"

"Yes. Will you teach me those fight tricks?" Litok asked daringly.

"Okay. But some are not nice tricks. They are for enemies not friends."

It was early afternoon by now, so after I ate, I was ready for Litok to show me around. I noted that the females all sent their whelps into their dwellings when they saw me. I wished they wouldn't.

For amusement, I did teach Litok some of my fighting tricks. He took me to a secluded clearing where we could practise, and I found him to be a fast learner. After I tired of that, I used the aura to refresh my energies, and that seemed to wake up some old sorcery. I felt something nearby, pulling on me. Litok seemed unaffected.

Instinctively, I felt for Larcia's sword. It was still following me like it was sheathed. I located the source of the pull. It was a small outcropping of rock, with many broken off pieces piled on it like a cairn and roughly cemented together. When I touched it, it crumbled. I heard Litok's sudden indrawn breath. He stared at the crumbled cairn, horrified.

"It's old," I said. "Whatever held the rocks together has probably eroded over time."

"Father will be angry," Litok predicted. "That is the foundation cairn."

I wondered if I could fix it, so I gathered the pieces and began assembling them like a jigsaw of rock. Amongst the fragments, I found a highly polished pebble of a dark purple hue. When I picked it up, I felt the strength of the aura in the inch round stone. I also felt an emotional response, but I knew that did not come from me. Litok suddenly ran off, and I felt myself lifted by the neck. I really hated that!

"Cotek," I greeted him.

"You agitate my village, endanger my lands and disturb my mind when I have too many other concerns. Is it your only function to anger everyone you meet?" he growled. "Is it not enough that I accept your claim to be a sorceress? Must you also try to completely dominate me? If so, you will fail, for you are merely a lucky whelp. Those you still must face – if you intend to persist in your aberrant scheme – will not be so generous, and will still try to kill you. And you are abysmally ignorant of the depths of your ignorance."

At the anger in his voice, I felt a shiver of fear. He was not Stak but, at that moment, he reminded me of him.

My hand reached down to Larcia's sword. I was suddenly dropped. When I spun around, Cotek was staring at the sword, which was glowing.

"Go back to the hut. I will join you as soon as I have warned the tribe we are leaving."

"To go where?" I asked.

"That is not your concern."

I held out the polished stone. "I was going to repair the cairn. This was in it. It was pulling me here."

Cotek's face betrayed a flash of emotion and then returned to being inscrutable. "Keep it," he said before stalking off.

Litok returned, watched his sire warily, and dared to grab my hand and pull. I went with him, still trying to interpret the undercurrents in that last exchange with Cotek. Indeed, there were things I needed to know.

Litok left me in the hut, passing in and out without trouble – unlike me. There was nothing in this hut to occupy my mind, so I sat down on the floor mat and let my mind wander.

Once again I found the air view of the village. I saw Cotek standing and people running to him. I watched for a while, as people were sent off on their tasks, returning with things that Cotek showed his tribe. I lost interest in whatever he was doing, and wondered at the anomaly of an ornate hut in the midst of people who dwelt in caves and excavated holes.

I moved on to wonder where Tesla's young wife had gone from here. The visions that came into my mind were of darkness, but gradually I began to make out shadows and a faint glow. In this vision, I was descending a sandstone staircase. I hadn't gone far when the light grew brighter, and as I descended further I came to the opening of a cave that was vaulted and quite large.

My eye was drawn to an altar, surrounded by a myriad of lit candles. On that altar was a pile of something, unrecognisable in the flickering shadow. I had no interest in looking closer, but my point of vision moved to a hovering view over the altar.

I managed to view the hacked body without feeling sick. It had been roughly human in shape. I wondered if it were Kumatan. Then my view moved to where I could see dark blue stains on the light brown cape the body had been loosely wrapped in.

"Child killer," Larcia hissed in my mind. If I had any doubts about who was giving me these odd air views, they vanished.

My view moved back to the steps, I seemed to go lower still, deeper into the… would have said Earth… into Korvu. Then another chamber appeared, one that was decorated in barbaric splendour. There were hanging furs from animals I had never seen before, and ornaments in gold, silver and copper. More furs covered the ground, and I saw a low table set with candles. The table was in front of an alcove. I thought surely that this must be the lair of Cotek. As such, it really didn't interest me. Even though I stood still, my view moved around in a circle, stopped at the steps going down. I had the feeling those steps led to the chamber that Cotek guarded with his devil wind.

My view was dragged back to the upper chamber with the mangled body. In my mind, I sensed Larcia and her outrage at what this alien had done. Some primal anger moved in my mind. I translated the feeling into things I knew. On Earth, the Kumatan might have treated Atapi like slaves and called them barbaric animals, and sometimes killed them, but never to eat. Even Stak at his vilest, had never treated Kumatan as food. These blue blood aliens must have come from some other world, like Earth or Korvu. Had they heard Atapi called animals and thought it was okay to kill and eat them? Would they treat Kumatan the same?

I spotted bundles of odd things about that altar. None were clear. I felt Larcia's hiss of frustration.

"My queen?" I questioned.

"Go there and look at those things. I must know more of these infesting insects."

My immediate thought was, "How?"

"There will be a pass through from above, if you can't find the steps," Larcia told me, as my view returned abruptly to the hut at ground level.

I stood up to look at the hanging furs. Under the third one, I saw the stairs and started to walk down. On the second step, I felt a familiar twisting, and I thought of the upper chamber I had seen. On the third step I was there.

I smelt the reek of dead meat at once, and almost threw up. Larcia snarled at my weakness and I mastered the impulse. Fortunately, Larcia was interested in the items on the floor and I could stay away from the grisly remains. She examined, through my eyes, everything I picked up.

"The aura around these is vile," Larcia hissed. "Surely they mean this world no good."

"Some of these things are almost familiar, from Earth though, not here," I said.

How long I spent there, I don't know, but I suddenly felt Larcia's attention switch elsewhere.

"Go deeper!" she ordered me.

I really didn't like underground places but I went down the steps to the lower chamber, thankful for the faint glow of the walls. The barbarically splendid chamber opened out before me. It was well lit by the candles and I hoped there was a flow of fresh air.

My feet appreciated the softness of the furs on the floor of the cave. My shoes were next to useless now, but still slightly better than bare feet. I could look around more easily than I had in Larcia's vision. The metal ornaments glittered in the candle light – drawing my attention to them. They were of no creatures that I recognised and I did not touch them.

Being in that chamber was unsettling. I did not think Cotek would appreciate my presence. But Larcia had said to come here, but I still didn't know why, so I moved further in to look in the alcove.

Directly behind the candle filled table was a golden statue of a winged Atapi female. It was magnificent, and I did not need to discern the crown and sword to know who it represented.

"Larcia," I breathed.

I sensed a stirring of power and saw that one of the statue's arms was reaching out, but not to me. I heard a soft whisper in my mind. "Be at peace, my child. Let my daughter help you."

When I looked in the same direction as the eyes of the statue, I realised that I was not alone in the chamber. A female Atapi was kneeling at the base of the statue with her head touching the ground. I could not tell if she was praying or wanting to hide.

When I moved closer, she heard me and straightened up. I saw a look of terror on her face that increased when she saw I looked humanoid. She carefully got to her feet and began to inch away from me.

Her face, when the light fell on her, looked bruised and contused. Her expression became wide-eyed and rigid when she identified me as the one her mate had attacked. This was Cassia.

"Don't hurt me," she begged.

"Why should I?" I said quietly. "You've done me no harm, and Larcia called you her child."

"You know of Larcia?" this woman, barely more than a child, breathed incredulously.

I glanced at the statue. "Yes, my mother spoke of her."

Then Cassia realised what Larcia had said to her. "She called you daughter."

"Hmm," I agreed, seeing Cassia's face take on an expression of awe.

"What are you?" she asked.

I grinned wryly. "That depends on who you are talking to," I commented. "I have been called everything from abomination to she-devil."

The woman's eyes widened further. "Can you bring my child back?"

In that moment, I shared her anguish, grief and pain. It struck me then, that she, like I, had empathy. I shook my head, Earth style, and then realised she would not understand the gesture.

"No," I said gently, sitting down on the fur and patting a spot beside me. "Not even Larcia can to that."

I felt the anguish overwhelm her and I ached to comfort her. I doubted that she would like to be hugged. Something I had heard years back came to my mind and I rephrased it.

"Perhaps your son's warrior spirit could be reborn in another child."

I meant it to be a comforting thought, but she snarled at me.

"I am not worthy to be a mother. I let my child go into danger and die. My mate struck me down and told me I was…"

I did not think that this child deserved to be called the things I had been called.

"Did he beat you?" I asked her. She looked away from me.

"I'm sorry," I said, finding I meant it. I reached out and took her hand. She flinched, and then realised I meant her no harm.

"Your mate was grieving, but as a warrior he had no way of expressing it without seeming to display weakness at this troubling time for the tribe. He shouldn't have blamed you."

"But he is disgraced, sent away. I am no longer his mate. He lost status because of me, because I let his son die."

I recalled what I had seen of the young Atapi on Earth. They were not 'good' children. An octopus would have its tentacles full with one.

"How could you know that your brave young warrior would meet such an unknown peril? You couldn't. He was doing nothing different to other young males of his age. The fault is not yours, nor your mate's, or your leader's. Has anyone but Tesla told you it is?"

"No," she had to admit.

"Tesla disobeyed your leader's instructions," I told her. "By my mere presence – being human and alien – I provoked him beyond control. I have had that effect on a lot of people. He was punished for failing his duty."

Cassia looked away from me, and pulled her hand free. I wasn't helping her very much, I thought.

"I don't hate Tesla for what he did," I said softly. "I could see what drove him to attack me and I told him I forgave him."

"You spoke to him?" Cassia turned back to me. "He was sent away. No one is allowed to help him."

"No one told me that," I shrugged. "I think your sorcerer is giving him time to grieve and to prove he is still a warrior. Your tribe needs every warrior."

Cassia seemed to relax a little. "I should have known my son was in trouble. I should not have let him out."

"It is natural to feel that way, particularly as you care so much, and you feel your mate's pain with your own. Is that why you came here – to ask Larcia for help?"

"No, but when I saw her here, I begged her to help my mate and I wanted my child back."

"What of yourself?" I asked.

"I'm not worthy to be a mother or a mate," Cassia said. "Why else would esteemed Con Ansuni bring me here but to punish me or sacrifice me to Larcia?"

I didn't have an answer to that – my mind was struck witless. Con Ansuni! Whelp of Stak, Stacion Ansuni, and sibling to my mother!

I recalled the remark the old sorcerer had made to one of the others, back at the Rock of Arkor. One had spoken out against merely killing me, suggested learning more about the one who claimed to have killed Stak. The mind voice had told that one, "Something you failed to do."

My mind filled with questions, but I now knew some possible reasons why Larcia had sent me to Cotek's lands first, and why he hadn't instantly tried to kill me. It was either because I was his sister's child, or because he, like my mother, thought in different ways to the other sorcerers. It might have also been because he believed in Larcia and the ancient ways.

"I deserve to be beaten, too," Cassia was saying.

"I don't think he will do that," I found myself saying. "He's not like the other sorcerers. If he has an altar to Larcia, then he…"

I stopped, realising that I didn't know what it meant. I only had half ideas in my head – I was in no position to say what he'd do.

"He's not like the other sorcerers," I repeated. "If he was, then I wouldn't be here now. Every other sorcerer thinks I am an abomination that should have been strangled at birth."

"Why?" Cassia asked me. I could almost hear her wondering what crimes I'd committed.

"Because I am an alien, and I had an Atapi mother and a human father, and I inherited great power for sorcery and I am a female."

"Alien? Like those who killed Luka?"

"Alien, yes, but like them — NO! I don't know what they are, but it isn't human." I shuddered just thinking of them.

"You don't look Atapi. You look Kumatan. What is your name?" Cassia asked.

"Jai Cassidy."

Cassia liked it because it was like her name.

"Cassidy is from my human father, Jai for my mother," I said.

"I did not think such a thing was possible," Cassia marvelled. "I have never heard of such a thing."

"It is not allowed because the Atapi woman dies giving birth to such a mixed… child."

Cassia and I were both startled when we heard Cotek's voice. She scrambled around to abase herself at his feet, as she had been at the base of Larcia's statue.

I moved and stood between him and Cassia, staring at him. Cotek was now dressed in a richly decorated robe that hid most of his wings and tail. I was closer than I liked being to an Atapi sorcerer, but since I had sort of defeated him, he returned my stare.

"And when they turn out like you, Jai Cassidy," he said, "it is surprising that they survive each day. Did Stacion make her mate with a human?"

His tone betrayed hatred of his sire. I shook my head and mentally said, "No."

Cassia heard the anger and thought it was directed at her.

"She-devil, I do not deserve to be protected," Cassia protested, still keeping her head down.

"You have every right," I snapped at her, still watching Cotek. I demanded of him, "What are you going to do with her? You took her from her mate — was that to punish her, as well as Tesla?"

Cotek reached out and punched my face again. "You will keep out of my affairs, Jai Cassidy. How I rule my tribe is no concern of yours."

I pretended my face wasn't throbbing. "You can't punish her, it isn't fair!" I realised that I was risking another punch.

Cotek glared at me, and then relaxed slightly. "Your mother grew up knowing life was not fair," he told me. "Life isn't if you are Atapi. If you haven't learnt that, Human, you have led a sheltered life. If you intend to continue with what you have started, you will learn…"

I stared and didn't react to what sounded like a curse.

"Cassia is to be my mate," Cotek told me, as if that should settle the matter.

I was still coming to terms with the idea of this sorcerer being, by Earth standards, my uncle. However, hearing him state he was going to mate with another male's mate went against all I had been taught as a human – quite in keeping with my opinion of Atapi sorcerers, though.

"Does she get a choice?" I demanded.

I sensed movement. Cassia had straightened and was standing up.

"Esteemed One, that is an honour I am not worthy of."

Since I had been trying to convince her of her worth, I didn't want to argue with her.

I shook my head again, "Obviously he thinks you are, Cassia," I told her. My mind however still recoiled at the idea.

Cotek spoke to my mind. "As tribal sorcerer, I have the right to choose whoever I want as a mate – to strengthen my tribe. It is not a punishment. I am not like my sire, as you also pointed out. And I must thank you for easing her fears. I did not want to fight her."

"You sound almost civilised," I thought back.

"Perhaps you will explain to her why I chose her," Cotek suggested.

"Why?"

"She seems to listen to you," he said. I guessed Cassia had been too upset for logic before.

I turned to her. "Cassia, it is like I said. Your tribe needs strong warriors. Your Luka was strong and brave and fearless, even though he was young. That is why Con chose you."

"What if I whelp a girl?" she asked, trying to read Cotek's inscrutable expression.

"Another child of Larcia," I said as if awed. "Then there would be another strong woman to breed strong warriors. Perhaps you will have a child who will be a sorcerer." Then, I added silently, "Like me."

Cassia put her hand in mine. "She-devil, thank you for your wisdom."

"Chosen One, go to Bernea, and tell her I sent you to help her," Cotek instructed Cassia.

Cassia bowed and ran off to obey, probably so Cotek wouldn't change his mind.

"She-devil," Cotek said, tasting the title in his mind. "Whatever gave her that idea?"

"I did," I admitted. "Someone called me that."

"Is that so?" Cotek murmured. "Who?"

"Stak."

Cotek snorted softly. "Then it was not meant as a compliment. Did you aggravate him as much as you do me?"

"More. I didn't like him, since he was trying to kill me."

Cotek was silent for a time, his mind unreadable. "Is he really dead?"

"Oh, yes," I said with satisfaction.

"How?"

"My mother bequeathed me a metal box. My father kept it for me. When I got it, I already knew I was an abomination by Stak's standards. The box taught me things, magic things. It exuded power. Stak sensed it on me, and reached for it. In the moment when we were both touching it, some force took me over. I held the knife, but I think it was my mother that killed him."

"And my womb mate?" Cotek asked.

"Dead. I thought you knew that, uncle."

Womb-mate? I thought very privately. Con and my mother were twins?

"I guess you would rather it had been her returning, not me arriving," I said quietly, without my usual belligerence.

"It cannot be," Cotek said, calmly enough. "And you are here. Still, I would rather it wasn't known that you are in fact related to me."

"Isn't it a bit late?" I asked. "I told all the sorcerers who my mother was."

"My sire always attested that when my mother laid two eggs within minutes of each other, that Jai was not from his seed," Cotek explained. "He had my mother killed for lying with another male when she was his."

"He was daft to believe that," I said, annoyed.

"He was believed, and so all her life she was not acknowledged and no male would have her. Once he forced her to mate with a captured sorcerer, in the hope she would whelp a child he could use to destroy that other tribe. Was it like that with your father?"

"No," I said, trying to explain. "She created me. I don't fully understand why, or if it came to that, why she chose my father. It was something about – I would be protected until I was old enough to look after myself. It was only by accident that the Atapi there found out about me."

"Perhaps it was because she was not free to act, and could not draw on the aura. Certainly Stak knew she hated him and would never let her close enough to endanger him."

"Well he certainly underestimated me," I claimed.

"He underestimated your mother. Jai promised to kill him if I did not. And yes, I wish she were alive."

In that moment, I felt that I really had kin on Korvu, but Cotek's mood returned to business.

"I felt you looking at the alien's things. Did they tell you anything?"

"Not really. Some things remind me of things on Earth, but nothing was familiar," I explained.

"You recognised the flying things," Cotek reminded me.

"Yeah, I saw something like that on Earth once. I think it was looking for me. Some big fat local bigwig set the police on me."

Cotek didn't understand me – 'police' had no local equivalent. I explained it as best I could in Atapi terms.

"You see this guy had grabbed me – wanted to make me his whore. That's means a female that he could let males mate with. I wasn't interested, so I kicked him in his man bits and ran away. But because he was filthy rich, he could get people to do things for him, so he got people to look for me. Some of those people had access to a helicopter. Didn't help him though. Mind you, that creep turned out to be Atapi. Maybe a sorcerer, too. Jenha fixed him. He called himself Lammond."

Cotek growled. I sensed he was pleased. "Lancho, my sibling. He was like my sire – arrogant and living for reprehensible pleasures."

I considered that might be another reason why Stak hated me.

Cotek threw off his cloak and stalked the room. I thought it safe to ask questions. "What were those creatures, at the canyon?"

I listened as he told me all he knew including the details of what had happened to the children. It was far worse that what I had already heard. I wanted to be sick. "They must be known to the Kumatan and their masters," Cotek growled.

I agreed. "Yes, but I cannot believe that they are aware of the true nature of those aliens. The Kimh have all those high and mighty moral views. I will ask to see if any of my friends at the palace know anything."

"Friends? Kumatan, Kimh or the tame Atapi?" Cotek's tone held a trace of anger.

"I have no intention of coming to the attention of the first two groups for now. They would try to stop me…"

"Intelligent of them," Cotek snarled. He was still ambivalent about my powers. Then his eyes seemed caught by something at my side. I looked down and saw that Larcia's sword was glowing.

"Not intelligent, ignorant. There are things I must do for the good of the Atapi."

"I'd like to hear what they are," Cotek challenged.

"There is no time now," I hedged. "I have to prove myself first."

Cotek snarled an agreement. "So… you mean the tame Atapi."

"Did you know those of Stak's tribe?" I asked.

Cotek growled. "My tribe split from his. We did not wish to follow Stak's reckless and foolish beliefs. He was a traitor and an arrogant fool."

"I wouldn't have put it quite so politely," I commented. "Those 'tame' Atapi are all that are left. I inherited them – the rest died."

"At Kumatan hands?" Cotek snarled, expecting a positive answer.

"No, the Kumatan saved those. Stak's warriors killed the rest – males, females and whelps."

There was no mistaking Cotek's anger. "Then I owe respect to the Traeger who acted with honour. Was it Jellarn Mosellan?"

"Huh? Jenha," I corrected. "He was the only Traeger when I encountered the Kumatan."

"Yes, I would have expected that of Jenha." Cotek seemed to be remembering things. "So those Atapi at the palace…"

"Serve me, like I said. And by serving the Kumatan, they are protected, which I cannot do for them. They are my eyes and ears in the palace. They are showing the so-called civilised races that they are not barbarians."

"She-devil," Cotek growled. "My chosen mate is correct in commending your wisdom."

"Hardly wisdom," I had to admit. "More likely my sneaky, devious, contrary human half. I'm not much older than that woman-child who was here."

Cotek snarl-grinned. "Then you are a worthy whelp of my sister. If you find out things from your tribe, will you share them with me?"

I nodded. "I would like to learn more about my mother."

"There is a lot I might share, but later. I will say that Stak never saw the potential in my womb-mate, but I think that Larcia shielded her. While I learnt to be a sorcerer from my sire, she learnt from Larcia. We taught each other."

"So you challenged him?" I assumed.

"No, he challenged me. I was much your age and far from ready. Your mother helped me, but if that had been discovered, Stak would have won. Traegers sensed the battle and came in large numbers. Stak decided to flee and used an artefact to take him where he went. He completely drained his land to do it, and it is only now recovering."

I sensed a presence approaching and identified it as Litok. Cotek acknowledged him and heard his report.

"Everyone is assembled in the grove, father."

"I will come," Cotek said, and he reached for his cloak. Litok dashed off. "Come and help me make the pass through. I have learnt that working with another makes my magic stronger."

"I think that is one thing I must teach the other sorcerers," I decided, but kept the idea to myself. To Cotek, I said, "I will work with you."

Even though it was very early in the morning, Dahl Malachi greeted the Selkrit Councillor with the poise learnt from his father. He'd been training to be Koenig's heir since he was first put in lessons. Kaer stood behind him, to the left of his brother's chair, feeling very much like a servant just then. They were in Koenig's official office.

"Councillor Auglan, my father sends his apologies. He is held up in a meeting of extreme importance."

"My business is extremely important," Auglan insisted, his face turning a deeper shade of blue. "I have proof – irrefutable proof – that those lizard men are barbaric murderers. I can show you…"

He was clutching a case.

"I would be most interested, Councillor," Malachi said. He gestured for Auglan to be seated, but the man stayed on his feet.

"If I may," Auglan requested, "I will set up this projector to show you what was observed."

Without waiting for permission, Auglan placed his case on the desk, pushing a pile of files out of the way.

Malachi decided not to make an issue of the rudeness, for he was interested in what Auglan was doing, and trying to look like he knew what it was.

Kaer moved to have a better view of the Councillor's actions. First, Auglan took some kind of scroll from the case and attached it to an odd framework so the flat fabric stayed in a vertical position. Then he lifted out a smaller box with a round tube at one end and positioned this facing the fabric. On top of this box were raised squares.

"I am not familiar with this…" Kaer sought for a word, "… technology."

Kaer glanced at his older brother, who gestured for the Selkrit Councillor to explain.

"It is a projector of images of things that have happened," he explained to them. "It records the images so they can be watched many times."

"Thank you, Councillor," Kaer said politely.

Kaer knew that his brother had no more idea of this technology than he did himself. However, in the interests of maintaining dignity and power, and being the lower ranked representative, he admitted his ignorance.

Both Malachi and Kaer were impressed by the moving pictures that showed two Selkrit engineers examining rock samples in a canyon.

"Where is Traeger Ambrose during this time?" Kaer asked pointedly.

"When you have seen all of this film, you will agree that he is probably dead, too." Auglan sounded righteously angry. "These men are testing rocks so that we can determine the correct way to begin building the power station control structure. The waterfall nearby is ideal for a hydro-electric generator."

The film rolled on. "We did not edit it, so please keep watching. There! See! The lizard man just appeared."

There was a jump in the picture. Auglan waved it off. "Sometimes there is a glitch in the feed to the ship. But look, the lizard begins attacking unprovoked. And he does something here – he's still moving, circling around, but my men can't move. And here, dozens of lizards appear."

Auglan said nothing as the Atapi began hacking at the two Selkrit men. Instead, he watched the horrified expressions of the Kimh. The Atapi that Kaer knew to be the sorcerer halted the carnage and sent the warriors off. They returned with two litters for the fallen corpses.

"Those lizard vermin must be exterminated or I will withdraw my engineers, which will delay project completion," Auglan threatened.

Malachi looked suitably severe. "I will ensure that my father hears of this."

"There's more," Auglan revealed. He pressed the raised squares again as he looked at a tiny screen, and then a different view was on the screen.

"One guard remained in our air vehicle. He received no warning of the attack on the engineers, or the attack on himself. This was started when he sent an emergency signal. You will see that there are ropes or something over the rotors of our air vehicle. He was alerted when a fault signal activated."

Malachi nodded, as if understanding all the implications.

"Am I to understand," Kaer began, glancing at his brother, "that those ropes, vines I think, prevent it from flying?"

"Yes, yes," Auglan said, annoyed at the interruption. "If the rotors can't turn, the craft can't lift. A clear indication of ill intent." Then, a bit later, "There! That lizard again," Auglan pointed.

The flying vehicle was turning its front to the Atapi, who suddenly fell flat.

"The pilot fired a warning burst," Auglan explained, without apology. There was another jump in the film and it suddenly showed the air vehicle spinning around. Then dust began swirling around and rising.

"I don't know what is happening here," Auglan claimed. "The flyer's rotors are not spinning, so the dust is not being caused by them."

Soon it was visibly obvious that parts of the flyer were breaking off and flying in all directions. Then the film showed a massive explosion, with flame contained in a circular area and then thick black smoke. The fire was soon dampened and a molten mess lay where the flyer had been.

Kaer spotted the short dark haired figure near the sorcerer. "Jai," was all he said, but Malachi heard him.

"I know that lizard destroyed our flyer," Auglan insisted, thumping on the table. "Do you know how?"

"Sorcery," Malachi said curtly. "Councillor, you are correct and this matter will be dealt with harshly. Do you have the location of where your men were working?"

"It is in the same area that your Traeger deemed clear after the last atrocity," Auglan snarled.

"Councillor, would you please wait here while I go and speak to my father? I will have refreshments brought in for you," Malachi requested. He gestured to Kaer to follow him out.

"I do not understand how they obtained such amazing moving pictures," Malachi admitted to his brother when they were well away from the High Minister's office. "I would have thought them trickery, except for one detail."

"Jai Cassidy," Kaer agreed. "Father will want to see those pictures for himself."

"Yes, and there will be no doubt that this sorcerer is dangerous and must be dealt with. I wonder if the Traegers know which one he is," Malachi pondered.

"I am concerned by seeing Jai Cassidy friendly with him," Kaer remarked.

"Seems she had you and Mosellan fooled, little brother. You will have to work harder to find her."

"No doubt," Kaer agreed, keeping his other thoughts to himself. His father was going to be livid. "I wonder if this is related to the matter the Traegers are buzzing about."

"Which Traeger went there last time?" Malachi asked. "We will need him to provide the location."

Kaer paused before answering. "It was Traeger Ambrose."

Malachi uttered a mild oath. "I have no wish to be indebted further to that Councillor. Who else has knowledge of that area?"

"We should ask the senior Traeger," Kaer suggested.

The High Minister was annoyed at Malachi's intrusion until he heard Jai Cassidy mentioned. Then his face darkened from mauve to purple as he turned on his youngest son.

"This is your failure. If you had not let her go, she would not be stirring up trouble now."

Kaer hid his anger at the rebuke. "Father, I do not think she had a part in the deaths we were shown."

"NO?" Koenig roared. "She is consorting with a sorcerer. None of them can be trusted. I will see this visual proof for myself. Solomon, come with me. I want you to identify this sorcerer if you can. I want him brought here and made to explain his actions. Bring Mosellan with you, too. He claims he can control that abominable hybrid. He must prove it to me, if he wants to regain his position."

Koenig stalked out, accompanied by Malachi and Senior Traeger Solomon.

Kaer stood back, and when the others were out of the room, he gestured to one of the unobtrusive servants.

"Please arrange a soothing beverage for the High Minister," he requested.

The woman nodded and trotted off. A short distance away, she paused and spoke in a low voice to a second woman, and then continued on her errand. The second woman found a reason to speak to Farcine, who in turn ensured that all of Jai's tribe knew of the events that had been discussed, and then tried to reach Jai to warn her.

Jenha Mosellan was in the middle of a meditation exercise when Kaer was announced. He bowed, as did all the young Traeger trainees. Kaer gestured to him to move away from the youngsters and informed the supervisor that the High Minister had requested Mosellan's presence.

On the way to join up with Koenig, Kaer explained all that had been happening.

"I have no doubt that Jai Cassidy agitated the sorcerers at Arkor," Jenha said softly. "If she is indeed in this marvellous picture record –

then she held her own there. I am surprised that she was seen with a sorcerer in a friendly position. Most of the sorcerers – like Stak – would want to kill her.”

“Do you think she would be a party to killing?” Kaer asked Jenha.

“Like you, I think not,” Jenha said first. “Could you tell me once more, the circumstances?”

Kaer spoke again, and Jenha stayed silent. He did not want to believe that Jai had changed so drastically.

“You will be asked to find her,” Kaer warned.

“I see,” Jenha murmured. “I will do as I am bid.”

“Take me back quickly,” Kaer instructed.

Jenha took his arm and ‘walked’ him back to the palace door.

The moving picture record was just finishing as they arrived. Koenig insisted that they both watch it from the start.

“I don’t know how you could choose to be near that vile hybrid, Mosellan. You are lucky that it did not kill you in your sleep. Gullible, that’s what you were. I want that hybrid here, neutralised. You will bring her to me, Mosellan. You claim you can control her – do it and prove your loyalty to me.”

“As you wish, High Minister,” Jenha bowed, agreeing to obey.

“Solomon,” Koenig said, turning his attention to the senior Traeger. “Who is that sorcerer?”

“High Minister, that one is young. I do not know him.”

Malachi asked a question. “Who took over Stak’s tribe when he disappeared?”

Kaer spoke up. “He took his tribe with him. Is that not true, Mosellan?”

Jenha had not time to form his answer when Koenig accused, “Your father was involved in that, wasn’t he?”

“Yes, High Minister. However, not all Stak’s tribe went with him. His son split the tribe up before he challenged his sire.”

“Do you recognise that sorcerer, Mosellan?” Koenig demanded.

“Yes, High Minister, I do,” Jenha admitted.

“Well?” Koenig prompted impatiently.

“It is Con Ansuni,” Jenha said, hiding his regret at having to betray one who he had once called a friend. Still, he had only been a boy then, and so had Con Ansuni.

“Ansuni!” Solomon exclaimed. “Stacion’s whelp?”

"Like sire, like whelp," Koenig stated as if the conclusion was inevitable. "We must not let him become as bad as his sire. Who did you say that hybrid claimed for a mother, Mosellan?"

Jenha betrayed nothing as he answered, "Jai Ansuni."

Koenig stared for a moment. "Well, it begins to show its true colours. Bring that hybrid and Stacion's whelp here."

Councillor Auglan, sitting back and ignored by the ruling hierarchy of Korvu, was pleased with his efforts. It seemed, finally, that the weak-willed Kimh would move to destroy the creepy, unpredictable and murderous lizard folk. Then his teams could do their tasks without hindrance, without suspicion of the gullible Kimh. He excused himself from the discussion.

Solomon requested permission to organise the delegation to go to speak to Con Ansuni.

Jenha Mosellan, standing quietly, recognised that the group that had gathered was a hunting party. The squad of Kumatan guards and senior Traegers were preparing for a vicious fight. None of them believed that Con Ansuni or Jai Cassidy would calmly give themselves up to the Kumatan for questioning.

He was sure that Jai Cassidy would not. She had no reason to trust any Traeger, except for himself. He did not know her opinion of the Kimh, except that they had insisted she come to Korvu. As for Con Ansuni, he was not like his sire. The younger Con had made friends with Jenha's younger self. He might think other Traegers were like Jenha – unless he recalled how the Traegers had treated Stacion.

"None of us has had cause to go to these lands Con Ansuni has claimed. According to our records, those lands were shunned for over two hundred years. Consensus has been reached that our best and only option is to trace Jai Cassidy," Solomon told Jenha. Then he asked, "Can you find her?"

Finally, the question he had been expecting and dreading was asked.

Jenha bowed to the senior Traeger, and said quietly, "Yes."

"Excellent." Solomon gripped Jenha's shoulders in an encouraging and satisfied reaction. "As soon as you have a reference, I will come through and bring the others through."

Solomon turned and gave orders to the group, and then he turned back to observe Jenha.

Jenha needed to take a series of deep breaths to calm himself. He thought of Jai, and allowed himself to recall how he felt about her. He and Ellhi had brought Jai in to create a triumvir, a three-way relationship. The Kimh had ruled the relationship null and void. Still, the love, desire and other complex emotions had not gone away, in spite of the efforts of the Kimh counsellors, and in spite of the passage of nine months without contact with Jai.

To have any chance of regaining the rank he deserved he had to betray that love, and show nothing of how much it tore at his heart to do so. All he could do was hold onto his belief that Jai was not a barbaric murderer, and that she needed to come and clear her name. He must hide his fear that his superiors would not let her free again if she came.

He closed his eyes and sought for the unique mind of Jai Cassidy. Kaer moved up behind him, providing his unspoken support and encouragement.

When I awoke from sleep next morning, I felt Farcine calling to me. I was startled, and my hand instinctively moved to touch Larcia's sword.

"What do you want?" I mentally asked Farcine as I thought of her face.

"Jai-devil, the Traegers and their guards are preparing to hunt for you and Con Ansuni. They are calling you murderers and are insisting that you be found and brought here. The High Minister is most adamant."

"How can they think that of me?"

"Some alien, a blue-tinged one, had pictures of what was done – a picture of you," Farcine reported, but she did not understand what had been described to her and could not understand Jai's questions about it.

"Your warning is timely. Continue to watch that alien, and any others of his kind around the palace. I do not think he should be trusted, because those who came here were thieves and would have killed us if they were able. Was there more?"

Farcine was not one to avoid difficulties. "Mikha's father must find you. He has no choice. And they say that a Traeger has been killed, too."

I felt my heart contract at hearing that Jenha had to betray me. I abruptly ended the link.

I left the empty cave I had slept in and went to tell Con the part that affected him. "The Kimh are sending Traegers in force to find us. Somehow, those aliens had the means to make pictures of what happened here. They will be out for blood."

"Jenha Mosellan is honourable," Con said, surprising me. "I will talk to him."

"Since returning here, Jenha Mosellan has been treated for Atapi contamination. He was stripped of his rank and his superiors still do not trust his loyalty. He cannot help us, but must find me. I have to leave here. So must you – to get your tribe away."

"He knows you well enough to locate you?" Con asked.

"Yeah. He is the father of my son," I admitted, and I shocked him.

Then Con snarl grinned, but only briefly. "Can you block him?"

"For a time," I said, but I wasn't sure. "You should go. No, wait. I also heard from my tribe that they believe a Traeger was killed – by us."

Con snarled, and his attention seemed to go elsewhere. He seemed to be looking into the distance somewhere. I added a thought to Larcia, "We need to find if the Traeger is alive or dead, and where he is."

In my mind I heard, "What importance is he? His kind will capture you. I will not allow it."

I thought back at Larcia, "That's good, because I don't want to be caught by them. However, my mother believed that the three races were once equal. I assume she learnt that from you. If that is so, this Traeger's life is as important as that of an Atapi."

Larcia sent a wordless sense of approval.

Con snarled, and hissed. "He is alive, barely. In a cave, hidden amongst trees, north of the blind canyon." I wonder if Larcia had helped him.

"Can you give me the image?" I asked. A picture formed in my head and I memorised it.

"Go!" I urged Con. "I will lead the hunters away from here. I doubt they can find you without me."

Con gestured for me to go first. I belatedly realised that he might wish to protect the new village site from discovery, so I wasted no time on polite farewells.

I 'walked' to the location Con had given me, but no caves were visible. I walked slowly, trying to sense an injured Kumatan. It was then that I began to feel the pull on my mind and body, and knew Jenha was seeking me. Resisting it was torture, but I wanted to find the Traeger before Jenha found me.

If I had a chance to help the man, it would show my good intentions. With growing urgency, I recalled Con's picture of the cave, positioned myself so I faced it, and walked forward.

The cave was more of a hole in the ground, and I saw it just before I would have fallen into it. That it was the right cave was confirmed by the faint moaning coming from within. There seemed no obvious way in, so I guessed that the aliens had knocked him out and tossed him in. I wondered if they knew that the Atapi liked holes and caves, and if they had done this to throw more suspicion onto them. My other question was – had they expected him to die?

I was not Atapi enough to like underground places, but I started to climb down. There was a slight slant, and the way in was narrow enough that I could brace myself against the roof as my feet edged down the rock.

I felt Larcia's sword touch my leg, and I thought of light. I wanted to see where I was going and avoid landing on the injured Traeger. Once again, I seemed to see a faint glow coming from the rock itself. When I was almost to the bottom, I saw the man and dropped down beside him. He was feverish and in pain – one touch on his skin told me that. I felt carefully along his limbs and found broken bones in all of them. His breathing was shallow, as if his chest had been crushed, too. I had initially thought to get him up to the surface, but I realised now that if I tried I could kill him.

Some of my mother's lore entered my head. She had been a healer as well as a sorceress, and I needed to heal this man at least a little.

"Call his brothers," Larcia advised me. "Is the one you lust for not calling you?"

Did she have to remind me? For just a fraction of a second, my mental shield against Jenha slipped. That was all it took, and I knew Jenha had the mental image to 'walk' here. I tried to forget that and think only of the hurt I was trying to heal.

The aliens had erred in putting the Traeger down here. The hole was rich with the aura, and even if the Traegers did not know how to draw on it, this injured one was being sustained by it.

I knew when Jenha arrived. His mental calling increased abruptly. I fought old habits to run to him. I did not have that luxury now. How long would it take the Kumatan to find this hole? It didn't matter. I would use the aura to help this Traeger for as long as I could.

I didn't move my position, even when I heard scrabbling noises from the entrance. What I did do was take the stone I had found in the cairn from my pocket, and slipped it into a pocket of the injured man's clothes. The power in that stone would continue to help him when I could not.

I was grabbed roughly and pulled to my feet. In terse clipped phrases, I was warned to do nothing, make no moves or gestures, and only do what they directed.

"We have her," one of these Kumatan guards called up. I felt the tug of Jenha's nearness suddenly cease. I was both relieved and bereft.

"He has fractures on both arms and legs," I warned the two guards as one of them was about to touch the injured Traeger. "I have tried to heal his chest, but he is dehydrated and feverish."

"He doesn't need your kind of help," the man examining the Traeger spoke sharply.

I stared at that one impassively. He stood up and aimed a rod like weapon at me. I wasn't sure what it would do if activated.

"Climb up the path and don't try any tricks."

I did consider just 'walking' away, and wondered how these two would stop me if I did. The answer to the last was standing at the entrance, watching me. I still didn't know exactly what Traegers were capable of, and how they worked, but they were not underestimating me. For once, prudence made me obedient. Besides, I wanted to see Jenha. The Traeger grabbed my arm as soon as I reached him, and dragged me the rest of the way.

Once outside, the first face I saw was Jenha's. Our eyes met, and I saw there the pain he hid – the pain of having to betray me. What he saw on my face, I don't know. His mind, though, was totally controlled. I envied him that ability, but I knew this was not easy on him. Not at all.

As soon as I was clear of the hole, others who were probably medics went down. I was dragged to where Kaer stood with another man I didn't know. I guessed, though, that he was another Traeger. Jenha stayed back and did not try to approach me. I deliberately looked away from Kaer as he reached me.

"Jai, where is the sorcerer Con Ansuni?" Kaer asked.

"Why do you want to know?" I answered, still looking away, as if having no interest in talking to them.

My face was forced around.

"Look at your betters when they talk to you," the Traeger hissed at me. "You will address Lord Kaer with respect."

Kaer ignored my rudeness and explained, "He must come with us to answer questions on his actions here."

"He has not been here," I said, speaking literally.

The Traeger holding me gripped harder. The one with Kaer looked angry. "We know he's been here – nearby at a canyon and near a camp of our allies, where he and his warriors killed three…"

"And are you going to bring those vile blue aliens to task for their deeds, too?" I interrupted, rudely.

"That is hardly possible if they are dead!"

"Solomon," Kaer said quietly. That Traeger subsided. "Our allies are helping us to build…"

"I don't care what they have tricked you into believing they are doing," I interrupted again. "But if those blue aliens are dead, they won't be killing, cooking and eating Atapi children," I said, and deliberately relayed the images I had received to the minds of Kaer and the Traegers. "Which they did, no doubt, because they heard the Atapi being called animals."

Traeger Solomon looked sick. "Show me proof," he demanded.

I stared back at him, saying nothing, because I wanted to give Con enough time to protect his village. Instead I said, "If they're dead, they will no longer be stealing the treasures from the soil of Korvu."

"What makes you think that, you ignorant creature?" Solomon demanded. "The Selkrit engineers are being paid to build power stations and irrigation systems."

I almost admitted that I knew what they were meant to be doing.

"In a dead end canyon of arid sandstone, at least five miles from the nearest river?" I said scornfully. "And heavens knows how far from one of your towns? I don't think so!"

"And what would you know, human?" Solomon demanded.

"More than you, I bet. Do you even know what an irrigation system is?" I challenged.

"It is important for the progress of Korvu," he blustered.

"Irrigation is bringing water from a river to water crop fields," I told him. "And power stations are more economical placed near your city, and if they are hydroelectric plants they need a river to generate power. No! They found something of great value in that canyon. Why else would they draw knives and attack, and intend to kill a lone Atapi?"

"That is a lie," Solomon almost yelled. I thought he needed some work on his self-control. "The Atapi attacked first," he insisted. "And then the warriors hacked them to death."

"How can you possibly claim to be so damn sure of that?" I challenged. "If they are all dead as you claimed, who told you so many damn lies?"

Kaer stopped Solomon replying. "It is the truth we seek, Jai. Will you help us find out the truth?"

I shook my head in a human gesture that only Jenha really recognised and understood.

The injured Traeger was emerging from the hole, on a stretcher carried by the two guards.

Solomon looked vacant for a moment, and then a third Traeger appeared for long enough to 'walk' the medics and the patient back to the palace of the Kimh.

"Jai," Kaer spoke to me in a quiet voice. "Will you come with us, of your own will?"

"No. I can't. I have things to do for the Atapi and for Korvu," I said evenly. At least Kaer was being polite.

"You are not in a position to refuse," Solomon told me, finally deciding to apply slave bands on my arms. "Denying our polite request is to take a provocative attitude."

"What's that in English?" I asked sarcastically.

Jenha answered that. "You are provoking trouble for yourself." Did I sense a tenuous wisp of amusement there?

"Thank you," I said to Jenha, but I returned my attention to Solomon. "It should please you to know that there are still eleven sorcerers who will totally agree with you, so you and they have something in common."

Kaer intercepted the outburst Solomon was about to make by putting his hand on Solomon's arm.

"Jai, we are not making an arbitrary request. And I do understand that there are matters that you are not aware of. For years now, we have had a treaty with the Atapi, regarding people intruding across recognised borders. Con Ansuni has broken that agreement."

"And your precious engineers?" I asked, belligerently. "Who invited them onto Atapi lands? And aren't you intruding here and now with armed guards? Did you even listen to what I said? No, you ignored that and insist I come with you – using threats…" I pointed to the slave bands. "Threats may work to keep the Atapi animals in line, but getting their cooperation would be better. Except to do that you'd have to change, and so would they."

"So you, a human, are going to do all that?" Solomon sneered.

"Yes!" I promised him.

"A human," Solomon repeated.

"I have a unique viewpoint. I can see the virtues and flaws on both sides. And I am not like the male sorcerers."

I finally sensed Con's "all away" thought.

"I'm sorry, Jai, but we can't let you stir up the Atapi," Kaer told me.

He really was sorry, I felt, so I nodded as if agreeing.

"Very well," I said, more politely. "You should check the grave grove of Con's tribe." I gave the picture to Jenha, as I had seen it, with Josai crying over her child's grave. "Please disturb it as little as possible."

I saw Solomon start to move as if ready to go to that grove.

"Con Ansuni?" Kaer reminded me.

I sighed, as if in resignation. "I last saw him in the village. It is not far from the grove. But if you really seek the truth, you should go to that blind canyon and the clearing near the spring." I gave the images clearly, sure that no evidence remained.

"Solomon." The Traeger holding me drew attention to Larcia's sword. I already knew it was glowing, for I could feel the pull of Larcia on my mind.

I was ready when the bands sprang open. I stepped forward, half-saluted Jenha and Kaer, gave Solomon my best 'catch me if you can' look, and disappeared. Not that I went far – just away from them.

From my new vantage point, I could tell that Solomon was looking angrily at Jenha, who was in turn standing calmly. In my mind, I was aware of him saying what I took to be, "I did exactly what you asked of me. You did not ask me questions about Jai Cassidy, nor did you request me to offer suggestions."

Jenha wanted me to hear that. He wanted me to know he was not my enemy.

I flicked a brief thought back at him, just recognition of his continued concern for me. It was all he could do to help me. He knew I was no killer, and knew what I intended. I hoped he knew I had already overcome nine challenges.

I felt a flick in return – sort of "well done and be careful."

I hoped that he would erase this bit of subtle rebellion from his mind before his next session with the Kimh counsellors.

Dahl Malachi intercepted Kaer on his return late in the morning, as he was walking along the main hall. He saw at once that his youngest brother was agitated, even though he was doing a reasonable job of hiding it.

"Do I take it that you didn't find the hybrid?" Malachi asked.

"We found her," Kaer corrected.

"And?"

"She got away, somehow," Kaer admitted stiffly.

"How did it happen?" Malachi asked, moving to shepherd his brother into a small entertaining room so they could talk privately. The main hall was too public.

"Was Solomon prepared?" Malachi continued the question, as he half perched on the table in there.

"Yes," Kaer reported, choosing to grip the back of an upholstered chair. "And Traeger Marin had hold of her. Solomon had even put on the restraints without Jai trying to avoid them. But when she decided to leave, the bands simply snapped open and Traeger Marin lost his grip. Before any of the guards or the Traegers could react, she was gone."

"I see," Malachi murmured. "What could have been done better?" He wasn't saying that their father would be very annoyed.

Kaer risked being open about his thoughts. "Father should never have insisted that she come here, to Korvu."

"She has Atapi blood. We could not leave her on Earth to terrorise the humans. She might have become like Stacion Ansuni," Malachi insisted. "The humans have no protection against a sorcerer."

"She is nothing like him," Kaer stated. "Once Stacion and his two apprentices were dead, there would have been no one to teach her sorcery. And Stacion was trying to kill her, not teach her."

"That is what Jenha Mosellan said," Malachi pointed out.

Kaer heard the unspoken innuendo – that Jenha Mosellan's detachment was suspect. Why else was he undergoing re-training?

"In the short time I was on Earth," Kaer spoke carefully. "I did not encounter any other humans to compare her with – but she was never violent. She might have been stubborn, uncooperative, opinionated, and rude, but she respected Jenha Mosellan and obeyed him without resentment."

"What are you trying to say?" Malachi asked.

"You cannot expect a human to obey us unquestioningly. They are alien."

"Alien, yes, but what I have heard of humans from those who were on Earth too, is that humans don't hold life as sacred as we do," Malachi instructed his brother.

"I think Jai does," Kaer calmly disagreed. "She was with Traeger Absolom when Jenha located her."

"I heard he was found in a critical condition," Malachi confirmed.

Kaer added, betraying some resentment. "And Solomon would have it that Jai was responsible for his condition. I do not agree."

"Then why did she not stay and tell us so?" Malachi asked reasonably.

"No doubt because she rightfully believes that we would curtail her freedom and not see past the fact that she is alien and Atapi."

"You explained why she should come here," Malachi asked for confirmation.

"Yes of course, but she said she could not because she had things to do for the Atapi and for Korvu."

"I don't like the sound of that," Malachi admitted.

Before Kaer could form a suitable reply, there was a knock on the door, and Malachi gave permission for the servant to enter. The servant, a young Kumatan male, bowed; Malachi was, after all, the High Minister's heir.

"Sir, the High Minister has requested a report on the capture of the hybrid."

Malachi was aware of Kaer taking deep, calming breaths.

"Have Traeger Solomon await us outside the council chamber," Malachi directed the servant.

When they were alone again, Malachi spoke to his brother, "I understand your reluctance to speak to father. This won't sit well with him."

"I am aware of that," Kaer admitted, having managed to quell his agitation. "I guess if it soothes him to rant at me, I should let him."

Malachi stood up from his perch on the table. "He can hardly blame you for her escape," he pointed out. "That was Solomon's job. And you did try to make her understand what was reasonable and polite. Did she disrespect Jenha Mosellan? I thought you said she respected him."

"Mosellan did exactly as Solomon asked him to do. He located Jai," Kaer kept his voice even. He did not mention the personal cost that Jenha had borne in obeying that command. He had seen the tiny signs in

Jenha's expression, and the open longing in Jai's. What his father had ordered was a cruel torment. Jenha had obeyed, to his own credit.

"Perhaps it is as well that Solomon was in charge," Malachi said.

For a moment, Kaer thought his brother was revealing sensitivity to Jenha's situation, but then his brother said, "Mosellan is still too close to that hybrid. Did he ask her to come with you?"

"Jenha was not asked to try to persuade her," Kaer stated. "Solomon considered his methods adequate."

"Do you think she would have agreed if Mosellan had asked?"

The truth was, "No."

"There, you see, Jai Cassidy is a dangerous and unpredictable influence. Since she came out of hiding there has been a sharp increase in activity from the Atapi sorcerers. She needs to be neutralised."

Kaer knew he hadn't convinced his brother, and his father would be even more obdurate. But neither of them would convince him that Jai Cassidy was dangerous.

"We'd better get this meeting with Father over with," Malachi said decisively. "Though I think I should organise a soothing draught for him or he might work himself into another seizure."

Traeger Solomon was waiting for them outside the Council Chamber. He followed Malachi and Kaer into the room.

Malachi glanced around, noting the identity of all the seated members. He was relieved that there was only Korvu Council Members, and no off-world Galactic Councillors present. This business did not concern off-worlders. He then proceeded to approach his father, who was already seated in the central chair of the arc shaped council table that was set at a higher level than the other tables. The places on either side of the High Minister were filling as the other Elders arrived.

One of the white clad servants was bringing in refreshments. Malachi detoured to speak to her and make his request. He watched her leave, though none of the other councillors seemed to notice her.

Koenig called the Council to order, and the last few of the Kimh took their places. Malachi took the seat to the right of his father and Kaer sat at a table below.

"Traeger Solomon," Koenig addressed the Senior Traeger. "Where is the hybrid?"

"High Minister, we were unable to contain her. She had an artefact with her that enabled her to overcome the slave bands and escape."

"Are you sure Mosellan didn't help her?" Koenig demanded. "Have him brought here. I have questions for him."

Solomon gestured to one of the council servants, and passed on the request. "High Minister, Subni-traeger Mosellan followed my instructions exactly. He found the female, and took us directly there. He had no opportunity to approach her."

"What was the artefact, Solomon?" Koenig demanded. "How did you not know about it?"

"High Minister, the first I knew of it was when it began to glow, and that was just before the bands snapped open. Mosellan had no knowledge of it either."

Koenig drummed his fingers on the table. "I want every available guard and Traeger looking for that hybrid and Stacion Ansuni's whelp."

"Yes, High Minister," Solomon promised. "One positive result came from the events. We have found Traeger Absolom. He is alive, but had been badly treated."

"Tell me!" Koenig snapped.

"We found him in the underground cave where Jai Cassidy was hiding. She boasted to the guards what his injuries were."

Kaer stood up and gestured for permission to speak. Koenig nodded.

"There is no evidence to indicate that Jai Cassidy was responsible for Absolom's injuries. It is my contention that she was trying to heal him, and warned the guards of his injuries so they would not make them worse. The medics found bruising on his chest that was closer to healed than the bruises elsewhere. They were concerned, at first, that he had lung damage."

"Have you evidence of that, Kaer?" one of the Elder councillors asked.

"As none of us were there, no, but I do not believe that it was Jai's intention to be caught. I do believe she stayed to help Absolom, and could have escaped while the guards were approaching."

"High Minister, that hole was hard to find. She may have expected us to fail to find it," Solomon countered.

"What are you implying, Traeger Solomon?" Koenig asked.

"It seems to be proof of Councillor Auglan's claim that the Atapi wish to drive away his teams. It can only be so the Traeger could not report on their actions in killing the Selkrit engineers."

Kaer, still standing, protested. "Father, Jai Cassidy is a short, slight female. Absolom is an experienced Traeger. She might have potential for sorcery, but no male would train her. She could not have overcome Absolom.”

“You forget yourself, Kaer,” Koenig said glaring at his son. “Recall that the hybrid and Ansuni’s whelp were working together.”

Solomon made a waving gesture to indicate that he wanted to speak. Koenig turned his attention away from his youngest son.

“The hybrid made accusations against the Selkrit engineers, and insisted we question them. Impossible of course, since they are dead. When I demanded proof of her claims, she told us of the canyon where Ansuni attacked the two geologists. She called me a liar when I said Ansuni attacked first. She implied that the Selkrit were stealing from the canyon. It is sandstone there with nothing of value in it.”

Koenig believed the evidence that he had seen in the moving picture record. “Intended misdirection,” he pronounced. “Kaer, do you have more to say?”

Kaer bowed slightly, “I informed Jai Cassidy of our treaty with the Atapi, as I am sure she had no knowledge of it. She made the point that there is no treaty between Atapi and the engineers. Our agreement with the Atapi does not give us permission to allow others onto their tribal lands. I believe this matter should be clarified or we will be allowing more Selkrit to be endangered.”

Several councillors nodded and turned to discuss the point with their neighbours. Koenig allowed the discussion to continue whilst he challenged Kaer. “Did you insist the hybrid come here to explain her view to us?”

“I asked her to help us find out the truth,” Kaer stated.

“And?” Koenig insisted.

“She told me she could not, that there were things she had to do for the Atapi and for Korvu.” Kaer told the truth, as was demanded in the council chamber, even though he knew it would be disbelieved and the meaning misread.

Koenig banged his fist. “Yes! Stirring those Atapi devils into a fury!” he accused.

“I do not think that is her intent, Father,” Kaer insisted.

“And what do you think her intent is?” Koenig asked in a voice that was almost a snarl. “If you know her so well.”

“To bring about a change in the attitude of the Atapi,” Kaer suggested. “Please recall that Subni-traeger Mosellan had the means to control her on Earth and the ability to enforce the lessons.”

"Mosellan's training was most irregular. I cannot accept that as a recommendation."

A messenger entered, a young Kimh male. He brought a message to the High Minister, and then retreated. While Koenig was reading the content, Jenha Mosellan slipped into the room and came to stand next to Solomon.

Koenig put the message on the table in front of him and demanded, "Any word on the Ansuni whelp?"

"Father, Jai Cassidy told us where she had last seen Con Ansuni. The site of his village was deserted. She also told us where there was proof of Selkrit crimes. We found nothing conclusive in the canyon or at the site of the whirlwind that destroyed the flying craft. Examination, and exhumation of an area she called the grave-grove revealed small Atapi bones, charred and with the flesh missing."

"Those Atapi devils probably did that themselves to make it look like the Selkrit were responsible," Koenig declared.

Kaer closed his mouth on the comment that came into his mind. His father was acting oddly. It was as if he did not want to consider that the Atapi may be civilised and honourable.

Koenig instead turned his attention to challenging Jenha Mosellan.

"Kaer tells me that you trained the hybrid."

"Yes, High Minister," Jenha admitted calmly. "On Earth she learnt honourable behaviour, and was no friend to the Atapi. She was an important part of neutralising one of Stacion's apprentices and, as you are aware, was responsible for his death."

"Then how to you explain this intention of hers to change the attitude of the Atapi?" Koenig challenged further.

"It will not endear her to the sorcerers, but I believe she is stubborn enough and contrary enough to do it. That does assume that she survives challenging the remaining devils," Jenha spoke calmly. "The sword we observed is a relic from the time of Larcia, the one called she-devil. In that time, the sorcerers used their power differently. To have that relic, it indicates that it was given to her by Larcia."

"What utter rubbish," Koenig started. Then he lost composure completely and swore vile oaths.

Several nearby councillors began to rise to speak, as Koenig finally recalled himself.

"Even if that statement has logic," Koenig said more calmly, "The myth of Larcia is over a thousand years old. How did you learn of it?"

Jenha maintained an unruffled calm. "Before my father Jellarn went off after Stacion, he requested that I check old records on a number of matters. That is one piece of information that came to light."

"What else did you find?" Koenig insisted.

Malachi rose and requested permission to speak.

"Father, we are straying from the matter in hand," Malachi reminded his father. "If you recall, Councillor Auglan requested a report of our investigation."

"Yes, thank you," Koenig accepted the polite reminder, though he really preferred to not have to deal with the man. "The matter is not yet clear or resolved," Koenig summarised. "I open the meeting for questions and recommendations. Mosellan, you are excused."

The other twelve councillors were able to air their thoughts and clarify matters in their own minds. Koenig gave every indication of listening to their discussions.

His brother, Lord Eamon, insisted that the Selkrit engineers, who were prepared to undertake important works for Korvu, were not to be endangered. Did not the Nuath say that all life is sacred? And life from different worlds was to be cherished?

Koenig agreed with that, but not with Eamon's further insistence that Jai Cassidy, the Earth human, should receive the same consideration. He whispered to Eamon, "When that unholy mixture of two races is causing more Atapi uprising than its Atapi grandsire? Oh, didn't you know that? That hybrid is the child of one of Stacion's female whelps."

"This one that was born away from here and brought here at your insistence," Eamon reminded him. "What did you hope to do for her?"

"Protect the innocents of Earth from misused sorcery," Koenig hissed. "I did not intend it to risk itself running loose on a strange world. She was to be a guest here."

"Guest," Eamon nodded. "An Atapi…?" he asked suggestively.

"One that hated its kind," Koenig said. "I hoped to learn ways to… change the Atapi."

"Which I believe she claims to be trying to do," Eamon pointed out. "Perhaps you should let her…"

"No," Koenig refused.

"Why?" Eamon probed.

"Because I was wrong! It is beginning to show its true colours, and I will not have innocents in this world endangered by stirred up Atapi. Nor will I have our plans for power and irrigation, which will improve thousands of lives, being abandoned because of that hybrid."

Eamon backed down from his probing. He was satisfied that his brother had considered the greater picture, as well as the lesser.

Koenig rang a small bell in front of him and the discussions stopped. "I have considered all the opinions expressed here and the following actions will be taken."

The unobtrusive scribe, seated at one end of the council table, was ready to take notes.

"I cannot condone, or stand by and let the Atapi kill guests to our world. No matter if the guests strayed into tribal lands by accident or not. We will bring the issue to the Atapi sorcerers and insist that the guilty ones be brought before this council."

There was a murmuring at that. It was an ideal first step. It would give the Atapi the chance to state their case.

"Until we can ensure the safety of those who are to work for Korvu's future, we must insist that all the Selkrit teams return from the field. I will pledge them quarters here, in the palace, as reimbursement for lost time. No time penalty will accrue for this delay."

That was unanimously approved.

"Traeger Solomon," Koenig went on. "I stress the importance of bringing Jai Cassidy here to explain her intentions to us and to have her to hear our concerns. Please use all due courtesy and any means possible to do so. If she should prove to be reluctant, you will ensure that she realises the importance of this matter. I will not be pleased with a refusal. Similar action should be taken in the case of Con Ansuni. Secure quarters should be arranged to protect him from possible recrimination."

Koenig indicated that Solomon could leave. The Senior Traeger bowed and obeyed.

"Please invite Councillor Auglan in as you go out," Koenig called out. Solomon bowed again.

Councillor Auglan strode into the council room with a self-important strut. He was clad in clothing that imitated the look of the high-ranking Kimh, and knew that it made him seem to be like them. He came forward and bowed in front of Koenig, with the correct degree of deference and a cynical smirk. "High Minister Koenig," he greeted.

"Thank you for coming, Councillor," said Malachi, acknowledging the greeting on behalf of his father. Koenig was sipping the drink in front of him.

Auglan studied the High Minister and decided he looked unwell.

Malachi continued. "We have considered the problems that your people are having. In each instance, your people have trespassed onto Atapi tribal lands. In past years we have maintained peace by treating those lands as off limits. The Atapi are not permitted off their lands and we do not trespass onto them."

"Nothing like that was mentioned to me," Auglan acted innocently accusatory.

Malachi countered that smoothly. "We examined the sites that you requested to visit. All were safely away from tribal lands."

"Then your backward technology is useless," Auglan stated. "If you truly want the most efficient power stations and irrigation systems we can provide, we need to have the most efficient sites. Clear out the lizards, then. Move them to other lands."

Koenig, feeling the effect of the soothing drink, listened without reaction.

Malachi hid his anger at the man's behaviour. Galactic Councillor or not, if he continued in this belligerent manner he would be evicted from the council room.

"Councillor, relocating the Atapi is not an option," Malachi stated.

"Then what are you collyflowers going to do?" Auglan demanded.

Lord Eamon rose from his seat and spoke. "Councillor, this Council has behaviour standards that all who attend must follow. Your belligerent manner is unacceptable. If you do not modify your tone, you will be asked to leave."

Auglan's face turned deep blue, but he controlled himself.

"What is the council's decision?" he managed to say politely. He glared at Koenig, as if wanting to insist that the High Minister answer his question.

Koenig chose to speak, silencing Malachi with a hand flick gesture.

"I will not permit your people to be endangered," he stated flatly. "You will recall all of your people until we have renegotiated aspects of the contract we have with you… please do not interrupt… you have indicated that there are very efficient sites located on Atapi lands. To ensure the safety of your people, we must negotiate safe passage for them and convince the Atapi of the benefits to them. To arrange this, I need a complete list of these locations you refer to. I also require a list of all locations where you have teams so that a Traeger and guard detail can be sent out to provide protection for them."

"This will take time and cost me money, paying men to be idle," Auglan threatened. "The cost of our services will have to be increased."

Malachi spoke up, "The agreed cost was for evaluation, erection and completion as a whole. The time frame was not specified. Your teams will be guests of the Kimh until it is safe to resume work."

Auglan visibly tightened his mouth. "Very well, I accept your offer of accommodation for my teams. I will arrange their recall and provide the list." He didn't sound pleased. "May I ask if that Atapi murderer has been apprehended yet?"

"The sorcerer has been identified and I have people searching for him. His village, when we went there, was found deserted," Koenig reported.

"You will have to do better than that," Auglan warned. "The Galactic Council looks poorly on races that allow the torture and murder of other races."

Koenig's face went a deeper shade of purple, and when he spoke his voice was barely controlled.

"That is why, Councillor, we advise the withdrawal of your teams until the danger is over and why we use negotiation, not force, to mediate."

Auglan spoke quickly, "High Minister, I mean no disrespect to the Kimh or Korvu. It is those murderous lizard men that I refer to. I understand your ethical concerns about simply killing them, but the Galactic Council can assist in relocating them to another world where they will be free to act as they wish."

Jenha Mosellan had not left the council chamber. He had simply taken a seat at the rear of the room. He stood now, requesting permission to speak. Koenig was still glaring at Auglan, so Malachi gave him permission.

"Esteemed Council members," Jenha spoke correctly. "Any notion of removing Atapi from Korvu will be a grave mistake."

Koenig swung around. "Mosellan, you have no say here! If the Atapi were moved where no other races exist – they can only practice their barbaric rites on each other. It is actually a suggestion worth considering."

Jenha sat down, recognising that Koenig was not receptive to reason.

Koenig turned back to Auglan. "My son, Caseon, will oversee the recall and provide security for their return and see to suitable accommodation."

Caseon rose and walked to Auglan, and began to escort him out.

"I will be reporting this to the Galactic Council, High Minister," Auglan said over his shoulder, and trying to sound helpful, not threatening as was closer to the truth. "Some of my teams will probably prefer to return to our ship. I will get them to produce aerial maps of proposed dam and power station sites. High Minister, could you organise to give me copies of your latest area maps so that I can compare them?"

Koenig waved a hand in agreement. Auglan turned and stalked from the room, causing Caseon to speed up to match his pace. With firm control, Auglan kept his muttering in his mind. He was angry at Koenig for outmanoeuvring him, but elated at the success of his counter move. He had aerial photos of the terrain of Korvu, but getting maps made from the ground by locals was a priceless advantage.

As soon as Auglan was gone, Koenig announced, "Council will adjourn until tomorrow."

Kaer rose to leave, but Koenig caught his eye as he gestured to Jenha Mosellan. Kaer walked towards the council table, noticing that Malachi and Lord Eamon were lingering with his father. As he drew near, Koenig abruptly threw his half-filled glass across the room and rose to his feet.

"I think I am correct in thinking that the hybrid has found one sorcerer who will teach her," Koenig roared at his youngest son who was only three feet away from him. He shared the glance of antipathy with Mosellan.

"If both of you had done your jobs correctly, this matter would not have degenerated to one human-Atapi causing a potentially deadly and inflammatory situation," Koenig vented his frustration. He added, speaking to Jenha, "You failed to deliver her here. Now we have her provoking sorcerers and enraging them to a killing frenzy. It seems that all we can hope for is for one of the sorcerers to succeed."

"Father," Kaer protested, trying to maintain calm. "It was Traeger Pentan who disrupted the transfer in bringing Jai Cassidy here, not Subni-traeger Mosellan."

"Irrelevant," Koenig dismissed that. "She should have died birthing the whelp he gave her."

Jenha had to work hard to control his reaction of shock and dismay – more so when Koenig went on. "Her grandsire was one of the vilest creatures ever whelped. His whelp is going the same way, and she is in league with him. Must we fear that her whelp will grow up and kill us in our beds?"

"Father!" Kaer's voice was sharp. "Mikha is a babe! He will not grow up to be a sorcerer – he will learn the Nuath as we did."

"Brother," Lord Eamon interrupted smoothly. "We will find and question both Con Ansuni and Jai Cassidy. Surely the important problem now is to negotiate with the Atapi tribal leaders to enable the projects to go ahead."

"In their present mood?" Koenig growled. "At least no more of our Selkrit guests will be harmed. No – we must remove the influence of the hybrid and let those devils settle down. How it galls me that she is holding our population to ransom – stopping important projects."

The High Minister noticed a young messenger hovering nervously. "Yes? What is it?"

The messenger, wearing the uniform of a Kumatan Guard–cadet, passed the written message to Koenig and quickly retreated. Koenig read the message and then flung it away, angered because it was too light to fling effectively. Malachi leant over and retrieved the message, all the time watching his father warily.

Eamon poured more of the drink from the flask on the table into a different glass. "Brother, have a few sips of this," he suggested. He was alarmed by the odd colour of his brother's face.

Koenig batted the proffered drink away.

"Con Ansuni and Jai Cassidy were spotted on Stacion's lands when a disturbance was traced there. Two, then one, wind whirls were observed. When the Kumatan approached, both winds and Atapi disappeared," Koenig roared.

Then his face went from deep purple to greyish and he collapsed.

Eamon was the first to crouch down and feel for a pulse. "Malachi, call for a medic. Jenha, I know your healing skills are impressive – can you help him?"

Without hesitation, Jenha knelt beside the High Minister, and first checked his heartbeat, and then began a soft vocalisation, which focussed his power and began to regulate and slow Koenig's heartbeat, and to induce sleep.

When the expression on Koenig's face relaxed, Jenha's vocalisation changed, as did the appearance of his eyes. Eamon was used to that effect and only wondered what Jenha was sensing.

Jenha murmured to Eamon, so only the Kimh elder heard. "It would be wise to take a specimen of blood to check for poisons. And to check all he eats and drinks."

Eamon thought for a moment. "Our medics will tell us if it is an Atapi poison."

Jenha said softly, "It may be an unknown substance."

Eamon murmured in return, "When the High Minister is resting, I think I would like to hear why you do not believe it is Atapi work."

"Yes, Lord," Jenha agreed, keeping his expression neutral, and eyes averted.

Kaer watched as two medics checked his father and prepared a stretcher to move him. Malachi came across to stand with him.

"I suggest you get some rest while you can," Malachi advised his brother. "Eamon and the medics will watch him."

"Yes," Kaer agreed, keeping his answer short. None of what was passing through his head was polite, pleasant, or wise to speak of. "I'll clean up here," he offered. "I will bring the paperwork to you, will I?"

"Yes, that will be best," Malachi agreed with a sigh. He was going to have to substitute for his father until he was better. "Don't worry about the glass shards, the servants will clean up`."

Kaer nodded. He hadn't even thought of doing that. He waited until his brother strode out before walking to the council bench, and the central place reserved for the High Minister.

On top of the pile of brief reports was the message he had received during the meeting. Kaer knew, since he was not a councillor, that reading those reports was neither polite nor correct, but this time he did not resist. He picked it up and read the terse report.

"The rock samples from the canyon are sandstone, but contain traces of an unidentified metal." It was signed by Dendar, a scientist Kaer knew well.

Kaer experienced a sense of vindication – Jai Cassidy had been correct. Then he had to quell a sense of injustice. His father had chosen to withhold the information. He was not willing to admit that Jai Cassidy might be concerned for more than the Atapi.

Pushing aside the thoughts and accepting them, Kaer collected Koenig's papers and the carefully noted council decisions from the scribe's desk. With these in hand, he went to find Malachi, who would probably be in their father's office.

Kaer was surprised to find the office empty, but then he heard voices coming from the adjoining room. Malachi was there, in the library, talking quietly to Caseon. The Selkrit Councillor was studying maps set out on a wide table and making notes.

Kaer noticed the otherwise ignored white-clad servant standing quietly, waiting for orders. From his vantage point, it seemed to him that the woman was watching the Selkrit intently. While she was unaware of his scrutiny, Kaer studied the woman's face and decided it was similar to the faces of the two extra nurses that came to help tend Mikha. He realised that this woman was Atapi. He made the decision to keep the information to himself.

Malachi noticed him and came over.

"The papers are on Father's desk," Kaer reported. Malachi gripped his shoulder in a gesture of thanks.

"If you don't need me, may I leave?" Kaer asked. Protocol demanded that he request permission to leave, since Malachi was now Acting High Minister.

His brother waved him out, ignoring the correct protocol, because his attention was elsewhere.

On the way to his suite, Kaer slowed his pace to give himself time to think. He recalled that many of the servants he had seen lately were alike – and did not have the racial bone structure of the Kumatan. Then he asked himself, why are the Atapi taking so much interest in the affairs of the Kimh? That was immediately followed by the question of how the Atapi females could shape the Kumatan so well. He understood that ability was a trait of the sorcerers, not the untalented ones.

He felt a momentary qualm to turning a blind eye to what he'd known. If he was wrong about Jai Cassidy, then he was wrong about her tribe, and he could be endangering all within the palace. But was he wrong? Was Jenha's suggestion of poison true, or had it happened because his father hated Jai Cassidy?

Kaer shuddered. Hated was a strong word, and if his father hated Jai Cassidy, his mind was losing its control. Kaer squashed that thought. It was unworthy of him to think such a thing of his father.

He reached his own suite and allowed the Kumatan guard stationed outside the door to open it for him. It seemed that Malachi had not wasted time in increasing the security within the palace. Was it because he suspected the Atapi of something? Was it to protect the Selkrit from the Atapi or, the powers forbid, protect the Kimh from the Selkrit? Perhaps it was only in the belief that Con Ansuni and Jai Cassidy would be found quickly.

He didn't know anything of Con Ansuni, since the Traegers knew very little, but he would wager that Jenha did. That would be something he would ask the former Traeger, and soon. As for Jai Cassidy, he was sure that she would only be caught when it suited her purpose, and only for that long.

The scene in his quarters was so normal and peaceful that it soothed his mind. He could not see Aniki, so she had probably gone to rest. She was pregnant again and tired easily. The Kumatan nurse was not in sight and was either resting or off washing the clothing that she struggled to keep on Mikha. Kaer smiled, thinking of the boy who was gurgling happily (half undressed again) and enjoying the attention of Kelhi and Jahni.

Farcine and Ellhi were watching the children and talking quietly. Certainly, since Farcine had come to help with Mikha, the boy was quieter. The fact that Ellhi, who had much reason to dislike the Atapi, was happily talking to Farcine gave Kaer a sense of reassurance. She was from a Traeger bloodline too, and she would sense if there was danger. The females both turned at the same time, aware of his presence. Both bowed with the correct degree of respect for one of his rank. Kaer let Ellhi report to him of the important events of their day so far. She confirmed that Aniki had retired for a few hours rest, and told him the children would shortly be bathed and put to bed.

Kaer met Farcine's eyes and asked Ellhi if he could speak to her helper. Asking was a politeness, no more, and both knew it was more of a command. He gestured for Farcine to follow him to the small room he used as a private retreat.

Farcine watched as Kaer seated himself in a comfortable chair.

She bowed to him and asked, "Have I displeased you, Lord?"

Kaer looked up at her, surprised by the question. "No, not at all. I can see the improvement in Mikha since you have been here."

"Thank you, Lord. All young males soon learn to heed the Eldest Mother."

Kaer had already sensed the truth of that. "Farcine, I wish to learn from you." He was fully aware of the things his kin would think if they found out about his intended conversation.

"I have given you my service, Lord Kaer," Farcine assured him.

"Second only to Jai Cassidy," Kaer asked, watching his servant's reaction.

Farcine bowed to acknowledge that.

"I see you have other Atapi throughout the palace," Kaer said, seeing Farcine's 'Kumatan' expression change to one of surprise.

"Does this anger you, Lord?" Farcine asked. Kaer waved the question aside.

"Since no Kimh gave you orders, I will assume it is at the request of Jai Cassidy. What did she ask you to do?"

Farcine answered honestly. "To protect those she cared about – you, Lord Kaer, your father, Mikha, Jahni, Ellhi and her consort."

Kaer nodded. "Why my father, when he shows no compassion for Jai Cassidy?"

"It was not my place to question her orders, Lord."

Kaer thought on that. "Why, then, was there one of you in the library?" Kaer expected to hear that it was chance, and the Kumatan servant master had ordered it.

"Jai-devil also asked that we observe Galactic Councillor Auglan," Farcine admitted.

"Really?" Kaer hid his surprise. 'Observe', he'd noted, not 'protect'. He had sensed that Jai did not trust the Selkrit, but how had she sent instructions to Farcine? Accept that she had, Kaer told himself, and assume details of this talk would be passed back.

"In view of what you have told me," Kaer began, choosing his words carefully, "Jai's consort has suggested we check my father's food for poison. He was taken ill a short time ago."

Farcine looked at him intently. "Lord, one of us always tests his food and drink. Theona is a healer who can detect such things. Do you wish to talk to her?"

Kaer waved his hand. "I was unaware of that service." He fought a short battle in his mind to maintain impartiality. He still had a duty to represent Jai Cassidy, and that meant to keep his mind open to her needs, manner and viewpoint. He had developed a wary respect for her. But the fact she was part Atapi, and the memories of centuries of Atapi atrocities didn't just get forgotten.

"I trust Jenha Mosellan's instinct," Kaer said.

He was surprised again when Farcine said, "Jai Ansuni was a powerful healer, and I think she may have taught him a little."

Kaer accepted this deliberate revelation as a reminder that Jai Cassidy was Jai Ansuni's child, even if she was Stacion's grandchild.

Farcine spoke unprompted. "Lord, I thank you for your trust."

"What do you mean?" Kaer asked sharply.

"I had expected you to… ask us… if we had poisoned him." Farcine lowered her eyes.

"I cannot deny that it would be the first thought of many, if Atapi were allowed in the palace," Kaer said, implying to Farcine that he had not mentioned his knowledge to others.

"Would they not also suspect anyone else who does not belong here?" Farcine asked. "Visitors and guests?"

Kaer looked more intently at Farcine. "Are you suggesting Galactic Councillor Auglan?" The Selkrit councillor was the only guest at the moment. "I cannot see a reason for him to act in a dishonourable way. His people and mine have valuable agreements."

"I do not know him," Farcine said tactfully. "But until the council meeting, he was nowhere near the High Minister." That relieved Kaer of a very impolite thought. Farcine went on to say, "However, this morning, Lady Deandra invited the High Minister to taste samples of exotic delicacies brought by traders. They all seemed harmless, but being alien…"

Kaer straightened. Lady Deandra had also been taken ill – ill, as a euphemism for 'hysterical'. He decided he had learnt enough.

"Please accept my thanks for loyal service," he told Farcine. "And pass on to Jai Cassidy my concerns for her continued wellbeing, and the message that I must do as I am directed. I need to bring her here."

Farcine inclined her head in a gesture that reminded him of Jai Cassidy.

Kaer dismissed her, and waited for some moments in quiet thought before leaving his quarters to speak to the medics and the Kumatan guard leader.

Councillor Auglan pretended not to hear the conversation between the two who were the offspring of the high fool, Koenig. It pleased him that the High Minister, who had looked quite ill, had collapsed. He was even more pleased that it appeared to be another in a series of seizures.

For a moment, he forgot his annoyance at having to agree to have his actions and those of his men overseen, and for having to provide details that were of no business of the Kimh. He couldn't refuse to comply, as that would prejudice the case he planned to put before his fellow Galactic Councillors.

He could, however, simply neglect to tell them everything. It was just so very inconvenient that some of the richest ores were on lands polluted by the lizards. He could get around his presence in those places, so far, by claiming poor maps, lack of information and so on. Getting back there would be more difficult, especially if those lizards wouldn't negotiate because some human vermin was agitating them.

No – on further consideration, he could use that to his advantage. That human had no more right to be on those lands than he did. And, if he recalled correctly, humans had not yet advanced enough to go into space. That human's planet was probably closed and proscribed. He would have to learn more about the circumstances there and why she'd been brought to this planet.

Auglan was aware of the elder of Koenig's sons departing, and was not surprised to hear the other address him.

"Councillor, I will need to advise the servants to prepare guest rooms. Would you be able to provide the number of people we must prepare for?"

All graciousness, Auglan replied, "As soon as I can, Lord. I will need to return to my shuttle at the spaceport to contact my ship. I do not wish to strain your generosity. I will advise my ship to be ready for most of them to return. I will keep the senior members here."

Caseon decided that was reasonable and began to ask for the other details Koenig wanted. He kept in mind to instruct the guard leader to assign guards to accompany Auglan back to his shuttle – not that he expected trouble from the Atapi this close to the palace.

Two very junior Kumatan guards followed Councillor Auglan as he walked out into the noon sunlight to the transport departure point outside the palace. When the Selkrit stepped up into the carriage, the same guards hopped up onto a standing place behind him.

"The space port," Auglan directed. The driver of the horses was a very old Kumatan with thinning white hair and skin withered by being outdoors so much. The man climbed onto his seat, took up the reins and flicked the rumps of the animals to get them moving.

Auglan sat and seethed at being escorted, and at this tediously slow mode of transport.

The area set aside for the spaceport was well away from the palace and the surrounding town, so that its ugly starkness was hidden in a dip between hills. It was to keep the few regular off-world trader clans where they could be overseen, and not have them landing just anywhere and scorching the ground down to bare rock.

Auglan gritted his teeth at the rough ride over unmade roads. He inwardly cursed the slow speed, and the lack of comforts and technology on this mineral rich planet.

"Gullible rulers," he sneered to himself. "So parochial, so ineffective. How much more proof did they need before deciding to exterminate the lizard vermin? Couldn't they see that the lizards were preventing work on their projects by interfering in ours?" Auglan thought more venomously.

He thought back to his abortive meeting with Koenig. He was still angry with the man's insistence on having the teams recalled, and forbidding further excursions until the trouble was settled. He seethed, even though Koenig had only withdrawn teams from the areas where the lizards had been seen. The backward yokel rulers had no means to check the other areas. What they didn't know about wasn't an issue. But those other areas were of minor value. The areas of richest deposits had all been plagued by lizards.

Well, if Koenig would not act decisively, he would. As a Galactic Councillor, he would place an official complaint with the Galactic Council. He would protest the lack of control by the rulers here over those lizards. He would mention how some of the lizards had escaped, gone to that human planet and terrorised the population there – proof that the lizards were dangerous.

Then he could mention how the rulers of Korvu had brought some female away from that world, and how that creature was stirring the lizards up and making them even more vicious.

He'd insist that Koenig round up all the lizards, neutralise their devils – good name for them – and also round up this female. Which of course, the High Fool wouldn't because of their so called ethical beliefs. So, since the Selkrit had a contract to build power stations for the Kimh, and they couldn't if the lizards were killing the teams…

Yes, that should do the trick. He knew exactly how to word things to get the council's attention.

Next thing, he would have to call his ship – still in orbit – and ensure that they watched the remaining teams. Better yet, get his captain to send down some of the idle layabouts to be guards for the teams.

He was not going to let his million galactic credit scheme be negated. The idiots of this world did not need the metals and technological minerals.

Auglan climbed from the carriage with relief as soon as it stopped at the very edge of the port area. He straightened his robes and strode confidently into the port building. He told the two Kumatan guards that he would re-join them in a while, and they should wait near the carriage. Once he was sure they were not going to follow him, he went to show his identification to the port guards so that he could get access to the area where his shuttle was parked. Had he bothered to glance back again, he would have seen that one of the young guards was not by the carriage.

Teregan, one of those guards, told his partner that he had an urgent call of nature to attend to, and walked in the direction he had seen Auglan go. Once in the building, he slipped out of sight and looked for another figure to shape. He saw a floor sweeper and followed him into the room where he put his broom away. The fellow did not know what happened then. Teregan made him sleep, and set about becoming like the sweeper. He borrowed the man's ID card, since he had observed that to move freely here such a thing was needed. Finally, he picked up the broom and emerged from the room. He walked confidently towards the door leading out to the parked ships.

No one paid him any attention, and so no one noticed that the sweeper's eyes had become larger and now bulged slightly. The guard at the gate merely glanced at the ID and waved him through.

Teregan grinned when no one could see him. He hadn't quite mastered that facial expression of the Kumatan yet. Still, his skill at shaping the humanoids was much valued by his mother, the Elder Mother of Jai-devil's tribe. Not even his partner guard guessed he was actually Atapi.

Trotting openly, Teregan moved to keep the Councillor in his sight, but made it appear as if he had no interest in the alien. The big Atapi eyes had much better side vision that the humanoid races realised. So when the blue-skinned alien disappeared into one of the odd metallic caves, Teregan moved to circle that ship and to approach it unseen. He would act as if he was searching for something.

Two traders, of some other alien kind, called a greeting to him. He waved back as he had seen Kumatan do. Instead of continuing on, the traders approached him.

"Near those ones you should not be," one trader said in appalling Kumatan.

Teregan glanced at the blue alien's cave. "Them?" he queried.

"Steal from your back your clothes they would," the other said. "From them, profit we don't."

"Oh," Teregan pretended surprise. "Have you met a lot of them? I have not."

"Those muck moles everywhere are," the first complained. "Even places where no one is. Traces you see, of them."

"Odd thing to know," Teregan commented. "I thought you only trade to towns."

The traders laughed. "Profit better where competition is not. Go we do, to tiny places. We see those moles. Signs of them, even there. Rob us they would if we fight not better."

Teregan nodded. "Still, find a lost pecki I must. Have you seen it?"

Both said, "No," and went on their way. Teregan went back to his pretend search, and gradually approached the metal cave. All the while, he was trying not to breathe in the metallic stench.

Close to the blue alien's cave, there were a lot of the shiny black scavenger beetles with their distinctive stench. Teregan glanced around and saw the piles of rubbish dumped on the ground – no wonder the beetles were around here. These aliens left rubbish everywhere if the traders spoke the truth. Considering this with disgust, Teregan muttered a chant that his mother had taught him, to discourage the beetles from biting him. He hoped it would still work in this alien smelling place, from which the aura had almost fully fled.

He had not seen the insects until a full turn of the seasons ago. Earth, where he had been whelped, did not have them. When he had first arrived, he'd seen one and prodded it with his finger and it had bitten him. He had yelped, and his finger had swollen up. He had been lucky that his mother had recalled the cure and he had not died. After that, he had learnt what to do if he was bitten again.

Teregan wondered what the blue alien would do if the beetles got into his metal cave. He imagined a stream of them going into the cave – flying and crawling. He grinned when he saw it happening.

It sounded like a ground tremor was affecting the metal cave. Something heavy was stomping inside, and suddenly the blue alien was running out of the opening, glancing around for anyone in sight. Teregan turned quickly and pretended to be obliviously sweeping.

"Hey! You!" Auglan yelled.

Teregan ignored the call until it was repeated. He began looking for the speaker and appeared to notice the alien. He trotted over with his broom and bowed as if he were addressing one of the Kimh.

"Lord, do you require me?" Teregan asked.

"There is a plague of black insects in my ship. How can I get them out?" Auglan demanded. "Insects like those there."

"Nasty things," Teregan agreed. "I try to sweep out?" he asked.

Auglan gestured for Teregan to go in.

With hidden glee, Teregan began to sweep the beetles out, knowing that he would irritate them, and they would squirt their stench everywhere. He would tolerate the abominable smell if it made the alien uncomfortable. When the smell was strong enough, he pictured the beetles fleeing out the door, and some finding the cape of the alien a good place to go. He was emerging from the metal cave when Auglan gave a piercing shriek, and began to flick beetles off his cape.

"Lord? Were you bit?" Teregan asked deferentially.

"Yes, on my hand. You must take me to a healer, immediately." Auglan demanded, trying not to shriek again.

"Lord, no time." Teregan drew a small knife and grabbed Auglan's hand. "Must remove venom right away. In blood it can make you sick to death."

Auglan made a futile attempt to free his hand, but he turned a sickly grey when he saw how his hand was swelling. He almost fell down when Teregan made a cut across the bite, and squeezed it so the wound bled blood and venom. He made no sound as Teregan sucked on the cut and spat blood, until nothing more came out. The taste of the venom was not as vile as the revolting blue coloured blood.

"Best you see healer now, Lord," Teregan advised when the swelling began to go down. "You might still be little sick."

Auglan was unable to think. The shock of the beetles entering his ship, then the bite, and the treatment was so unexpected. He felt weak and sweaty. He never gave a thought to the chance that the menial Kumatan might get sick from sucking the venom.

"I help you, Lord," Teregan offered, trying to pull Auglan back to the big building.

"No, wait. Fetch those boxes over there." Auglan pointed to some things he had dropped by the cave opening.

Teregan bristled at being ordered around like a servant, but he went and fetched the unidentifiable bundles. He had the strangest idea that they contained something deadly.

"Carry them for me," Auglan ordered. "Do you know where the radio tower is?"

"No, Lord," Teregan had to admit. "All I am is sweeper."

"Never mind, I know it. Help me back to the building."

Teregan was beginning to regret his keenness, but when the alien had to rush into what he knew to be the excrement dump, his humour improved. He wondered if the need was due to fear or the beetle bite.

Auglan made an effort to maintain his pose of importance when he neared the tower. In Teregan's opinion, he failed for the excrement stink lingered on him. Still, the Kumatan probably wouldn't notice.

Before Auglan entered the tower, he said, "Go find my two escorts – useless young palace guards – and tell them to have my conveyance ready."

Teregan bowed and turned to leave. Once again, he had the odd idea in his head that this alien was planning something bad for the Atapi. "Should've let him die," he thought maliciously.

"The boxes, imbecile," Auglan said nastily.

Teregan realised he still had the boxes and handed them over and bowed.

Once out of Auglan's view, he trotted quickly back to the sweeper's little room, replaced the borrowed broom and ID and reshaped his Kumatan shape. Then he trotted off to find his guard partner to pass on Auglan's command, but not the alien's indisposition.

They were waiting at the carriage when Auglan approached, talking to a Kumatan official.

"Lord, I can arrange to have your ship smoked to kill any beetles still there. There is no need for a Traeger to come."

"I was promised protection," Auglan argued, and angry because he was feeling quite ill. "I insist on a Traeger checking my ship. You must tell your servants to clean up the rubbish they dumped near my shuttle. It is disgraceful, and it must have attracted those… things. If I return, and the mess is not gone, I will report it to the Kimh."

Auglan felt momentarily better when the official cringed and promised it would be done, insisting there was no need to bother the Kimh with such trifles.

As soon as Auglan had seated himself in the carriage, Teregan and his partner hopped up onto the rear standing place, and the cart moved off. From there Teregan could see the neat bandage on Auglan's hand, and the beads of sweat on the man's neck.

The afternoon sun was getting low to the horizon when the carriage returned to the palace. Carrying his odd bundles, Auglan went straight to the guest quarters he had been assigned. He was relieved when only one of his guards escorted him there and did not try to come in.

As soon as there was no one to observe him, Auglan took out a small, palm-sized weapon. He proceeded to check every nook and cupboard in the sparsely furnished room, ready to laser any bugs he found. His relief at finding none brought some colour back to his face, but he still felt sick, and went to sit back down in the comfortable chair. His hand was still stinging from the ministrations of that menial Kumatan idiot, but he ignored it by thinking on his plans.

Firstly, the Kimh High Minister would not be a hindrance much longer. Tonight, or the next, he would have a fatal seizure. His successor, that arrogant child, would have to deal with the Galactic Officers coming to deal with his complaint. He would not have the experience to stand up to their pressure. They would insist on taking charge of the human annoyance and rounding up the lizards for questioning.

Then his teams, so far untroubled, would keep working. The ones that the Kimh knew about, plus one or two others, would not be idle for long. He now knew exactly where the lizard men were, and he could send in covert troops to kill them. He also knew where the natives of Korvu had identified common ores. More importantly for his future plans, he knew where he could locate secret bases. This world with its unworldly, gullible rulers was ripe for his plucking. No one, man or animal, would stop him.

Meanwhile, Teregan had slipped away to the Atapi compound as soon as he was dismissed by the guard master. He changed back into his own shape and rolled on a patch of thick grass in an attempt to take the stench of the spaceport off his skin. Since it was now night, he knew his mother would be back from the palace. He had a lot to tell her.

Farcine listened to her son's report, chuckling at his description of the alien's discomfort. She actually felt kindly towards the disgusting stench-beetles for the first time in her long life. Then she went to prepare a potion for her son.

"Yuck, that's disgusting," Teregan spluttered.

"You may be lucky, you precocious whelp," she told him sternly. "The venom is destroyed in your stomach. This will counter any that was absorbed on the way down. It was just as well that you helped that alien, for you had no right to endanger him. You will have to answer to Jai-devil for that!"

Teregan still remembered Stacion Ansuni when he was in a rage, and shrank in size.

"I bless Larcia that Stacion did not train you," Farcine said, aware of her son's reaction and thought. Her own thoughts were on the need for a strong teacher to take Teregan in hand. She had no doubt of his sorcerer potential, but Jai-devil had no time to train him.

"That alien is planning something," Teregan suddenly blurted. "He is not being honest with the Kimh."

Farcine tried to find out more, but her whelp did not understand what he had seen, or the significance of what he claimed the alien to be thinking. For a brief moment, she considered approaching the consort of Jai-devil about her son. A Traeger could control the sorcery growing in him, but it might be forever. If that was so, she would have no means of learning hidden things about the alien that Jai-devil distrusted.

Instead, she stood Teregan in front of her and addressed him with the full authority of her position as Eldest Mother. She warned him of the dangers he faced if he played with the aura to make it obey his whims.

"We live here, serving the Kimh and the Kumatan, in return for safety. If they decide you are using sorcery, they will not consider your age, or innocence – only that. They will take you away and stop you using what is natural to you. They will think no further that that that you have the blood of Stacion Ansuni in you."

Her warning had the desired effect. Her son was not a fool.

"I will pass on what you learnt to Jai-devil."

Teregan took that to mean that his mother would also tell her how he had learnt it. He slunk away to his bed hole.

I had not expected to see Con Ansuni again, but I appeared in front of him with Larcia in my mind telling me to ask him to teach me his 'wind'. When our eyes met, I grinned wryly and bowed slightly.

"The Traeger is off your land, alive," I told him. "I suggested that they check the grove, and where the aliens were. Do you think them capable of reading the story in each place?"

Con flicked his wings in a gesture I did not recognise, but I took it to be like a shrug.

"Was Jenha with them?" he asked.

"Yes, muzzled," I said, not hiding the fact that his position angered me. "However, he did not warn his superior about me."

Con snarl-grinned. "Why did you return?"

I touched the sword and said, "The ancient one suggested I ask you to teach me about your wind."

My sorcerer uncle turned and surveyed the purposeful activity around him. It was already mid-morning and everyone seemed busy settling into the new place.

"One useful thing my sire taught me, without realising it, was the advantage of an alternate village site," he said. "At least I have not needed to move three times every cycle of seasons. Here we are well away from the old village. I owe you for your help so I will teach you that magic – but not here."

I let Con take me 'elsewhere' and we arrived in a place that was arid and almost barren.

"This was my sire's land," he explained. "It is very slowly regaining life. By tradition, and my own decree, it now belongs to you – as the one who finally defeated him."

I looked around and felt the aura, but only faintly. "Has no other tribe tried to claim it?" I asked.

"It's lifeless," Con growled. "My sire dragged all the life from it when he fled. I said at that time I would cede it to whoever found him and killed him. It kept all the ambitious landless sorcerers from challenging me."

"That I will keep in mind," I said, wondering if there was a benefit to claiming this land.

"For now, it will do to learn in," Con Ansuni told me. "I do not intend to create a big disturbance in the aura, nor do I need to. Watch… learn."

I felt a faint stirring in the aura, like a zephyr blowing around me. Not far from me, dust began to swirl and rise in a tight circular shape. I imagined that tornadoes or hurricanes might be like this, only much bigger. In my mind, I heard Con Ansuni chanting. It was a monotonous drone and the words had no meaning that I could understand. I guessed it was a means by which he focussed his concentration. As he continued, I felt he was drawing on the aura from some distance away.

"Once established," Con told me, "it requires little attention to keep it going." He showed me what the little foot high whirlwind could do. "This much I learnt by watching my sire. How to handle it and survive it, I learnt from a Traeger."

He showed me how to take control of it, once he had slowed its spin. He taught me the ritual to speed it up and slow it down, and how to direct it with my mind. When I had mastered those things, he explained how to make it larger, but in this place there was not enough power to make it much bigger than it was.

"Often a small wind can be more deadly," Con told me, as he shrunk the wind to a few inches. "The power of the wind in a small space is stronger than if the wind was man height or larger."

He allowed his wind to slow and stop. "Now you form the wind."

Before I had fully mastered it, he formed and freed a second whirlwind and shrunk it into a small but vicious tornado. He sent this at me.

Part of my mind kept my attempt spinning and the rest considered this unexpected and, I thought, unfair threat. I was aware that this second wind was warping the aura because I felt like an animal with its hackles raised. In the same way, I knew that I did not dare let this other wind touch me. I could not tell from his expression if Con Ansuni intended me harm or not.

I had very little time to think of a way to wrest control of the other whirlwind. I kept watching it, and saw Con gesture and direct it into a patch of struggling weeds. They were shredded by it and I imagined that it could blast the flesh from my bones and grind the bones to dust. I spun around as my uncle moved it behind me.

As it came directly at me, I instinctively flung my wind at it. Mine deflected his away from me, but that was all. Con immediately sent his wind back toward mine and merged the two.

I did sense a start of surprise from him. He had expected his wind to speed up, but it had actually slowed. Now I had only one thing to concentrate on and a few seconds to think, even as the wind was coming back at me.

The sense of the warped aura was stronger – if I didn't finish this soon, Traegers would be drawn here. It finally occurred to me that Con must still be drawing power from somewhere, since the land here had little to spare. If I could find that place where the aura was being drained…

I was on the verge of a revelation, the understanding of how to use this unnatural wind and the place in the aura that was out of balance. How could I bring them together, warp and imbalance, to mutual extinction? I only needed to wrest control of it for a moment…

For a distraction, I formed an illusion of a ring of Traegers around us. It deceived Con Ansuni, but only for an instant. It was enough, and I felt the warped aura being sucked away – but not to where I thought it would go.

Con approached and punched me on the shoulder. "Never take your mind off a sorcerer," he warned me. "A fact I should remind myself of. You cast your illusion well, but I know not all Traegers look alike. How did you make the wind vanish? Uncontrolled, it is dangerous."

I felt it fair to exchange the gift of his knowledge with the secret of mine.

"Empathy," I told him. "Empathy to the natural aura. You warped nature to form your wind. It caused an imbalance elsewhere. I intended to bring the two together, except the imbalance is still where I sensed it. I don't know where the energy went."

Con considered my words. "I see what you mean. I know where I stole the energy from. There is kind of a null area there – not that I care if Sorcerer Verdisian figures it out or not. The area will recover as ambient energy is drawn there."

Then Con stopped looking thoughtful and stared at me. "It went here."

"Huh?" I said, confused.

"Your idea was to send the energy back to where there was less. This land was totally drained by my sire – this land sucked it up."

It made sense, and it was certainly something useful to remember. If I ever needed a place to 'sink' a lot of power…

In that moment of thought, Con Ansuni formed a slower, bigger, whirlwind that circled us both. "What would you do now?" he challenged. "The faster the wind, the more deadly it is."

I already knew that, and I soon realised that if this wind was controlled by one outside, it could be moved on me from any direction and I could not possibly outrun it.

"Fix it in place," I said first.

"Do it."

In my mind, I pictured the wind staying in one place – but the wind was strong and straining to break free, and I was tiring. I sensed the energy around me and dared not touch it. I felt the ground trembling and suddenly laughed, imagining the energy going into the ground. The wind slowed to a playful dust eddy.

"There are other solutions," Con Ansuni told me, but I wasn't listening.

I felt the faintest brush of a thought in my mind – fleeting, there and not there. Jenha! It held the essence of calm, while also rousing an intense yearning to be with him. I knew this wasn't an invitation, but a warning. It was all that my mentor and former lover could do for me. The Kumatan were hunting me again.

"Go!" I told Con Ansuni.

He took on a listening pose and the rest of the wind stilled instantly. We both heard the thunder of horses' hooves. Con walked and vanished. I touched Larcia's sword and felt myself pulled. I walked in that direction.

On the third step, the arid desert of Stak's land changed to lush vegetation in a valley between mountains. I sensed the great power in the aura of the mountains. I breathed it in, filling myself with a reserve of energy. No doubt the sorcerer who claimed this land would soon be aware of my presence.

The first sign of that was the baying of a pack of dogs on a hunt. The prey, I guessed, was me. Running away from them would be both futile and a sign of weakness. I turned towards the sound and waited. The odd-looking dogs, more like hyenas, stopped and growled nastily at me. Some edged around to circle me.

"So," I said aloud. "The sorcerer who is irritating your minds wants me to wait here, does he? The coward would do better to face me himself. I have no liking for hurting innocent animals, but it won't stop me."

What I did do was to project peace to their minds and tried to give them a sense of 'I'm not dangerous and I'm not food'. The animals stopped snarling, but I guessed it had only worked because the mind of the sorcerer who had purposed them was elsewhere. Nearby, the aura was being disturbed. I wondered what trap was being laid for me. The dogs opened up a gap in their circle, and those on the opposite side slunk towards me.

"Ok," I said aloud again. "I have to go that way, do I? The little coward must have his games."

In this manner, I was herded to the edge of the valley where a sheer bluff rose from the valley floor. Once a river must have flowed here and cut the rock away. Once here, I was herded north until I reached a narrow cleft in the rock. The dog creatures raced around to cut me off from going further north.

All during the long walk, and it had to have been several miles, I had been sensing the sorcerer working with the aura. What I sensed now was the tension of a trap about to be sprung. I concentrated on reading the aura around me and had the feeling of 'wrongness' overlaying the natural aura of the mountain. A faint change in that was all the warning I got.

The sorcerer was powerful, but he could not drop a mountain on me. He could scarcely affect the surface of the mountain. A small pebble rattled down and hit me on the head, and then a second hit me. The surface of the mountain was beginning to move.

The sorcerer withdrew his mind from the mountain and waited. I sent a sense of terror to the dog creatures, and that sent them racing away out of danger. I felt the ground tremble, as more rock began to slide. The sorcerer had started it, but now the rock was obeying natural laws. It would be a waste of energy to bind the loose rubble back to the surface. It would slip again as soon as my concentration wavered. I judged my changes of outrunning the slide as very good, but I would win no challenges by running away.

Having recently mastered the devil wind, I formed it now so that it was close around me. As the loose rocks gained momentum, I used the released energy to speed up the circling wind. This was energy the sorcerer would not realise I was using.

The edge of my whirling wind was about an arm's length from my face. Having seen Con Ansuni's wind, I had confidence that nothing solid would pass that barrier.

The first small rocks reached it and were deflected away to hit the walls of the cleft, making sounds like a volley of gunfire. The larger rocks reached it and, judging by the darkening colour of the wind, they were being ground to dust as they slid down the wall of wind.

The rocks seemed to slide down for an indeterminate time. Finally the only sounds were of dust, dirt and gravel settling around me. Now I slowed the wind and used the released energy to bind the walls of the perfectly round space I found myself in. I looked up to the sky along the curved wall that reached well above my head. If I had done nothing, I would have been stoned to death. If I had only thought to form a protective bubble around me, I would have been l buried alive within it and eventually run out of air. This was an improvement on both.

I sensed the sorcerer approaching, like an itch growing in intensity. He was in no hurry, as he was savouring his victory. I had time to prove him wrong. I studied the wall around me, marvelling at how the rocks had been polished in the curve, matching the wind barrier. Between the smooth sections of rock were rough cracks – as good as a ladder. I wasted no more time in beginning to climb up, so I would be on the surface before the sorcerer realised I was not dead and tried something else. My head reached the surface as the sorcerer, following my scent, was almost at the hole.

"You cannot kill me that way, Jacek," I told him in his stunned moment of seeing me alive – my use of his secret name telling him I had won. He bowed his head to me for a very brief moment, then turned and walked back to his tribe without saying a word.

Elation filled me, even as I started coughing in the settling dust. I needed a drink. Food and drink would be better. I had eaten nothing for over two days, and only had some sips from Con Ansuni's river earlier today. My thirst, now I was aware of it, was becoming a torment – but there wasn't a river nearby, and I knew I would not be given time to find one. The sword was becoming active again.

With a sigh and a wish for a drink, I walked three steps across the newly filled rock cleft and its unstable rubble and into a sandy, dry riverbed. I felt like laughing at the irony. I had been thinking of a river so I could drink. This one looked as dry as a desert. Still, there was an avenue of trees along the banks and that might mean there was still water there if I could dig down to it. I went looking for some short, thick branches to dig with. I had never seen this done and had only heard about it, so I let instinct guide me to where the river had cut into the bank, under an overhanging tree. I began to dig. I was not used to such work, but I wasn't about to give up, even if I didn't seem to be making progress.

The thought occurred to me that the local sorcerer might be trying to keep the water from me. I considered using the aura to help me, but that was likely to be a candle flame in the dark to the sorcerer. Gradually, my hole became wide enough to be deep enough for me to feel the first seeping of moisture.

At the same time, the hair on my neck began to prickle. It was a sensation I was beginning to identify as sorcery at work. If I was to be ready to answer the next challenge, I needed a drink. I risked calling on the aura to bring the water up into the hole. I did not know if my improvised ritual worked or the aura of Korvu was answering my need, but enough water bubbled up for me to drink my fill. The water tasted wonderful and seemed to give me new energy, and I sensed I would need that soon.

The prickling on my neck was intensifying. I could smell Atapi, but could see no one.

"Invisibility." I thought. "Or illusion." I stood perfectly still, and surrounded myself with the aura of Korvu. I should be invisible.

Something hit me on my right arm. It was a painful blow that broke my concentration. I still couldn't see who or what had hit me, and I was trying to sense the warping of the air around the sorcerer's position. I glanced down, looking for footprints – none.

Not invisibility then, so – illusion? If it were illusion, the creature would have to concentrate to maintain it. I began a peculiar humming, without any rhythm or regular tempo. It would irritate the sorcerer's concentration. I heard the devil laugh just before he struck at me again. This time, though, I heard the hiss of the air as his staff swung at me. I turned, twisting instinctively, and grabbed. My hands closed on his staff and I yanked hard, taking it from him.

Larcia's golden sword began to vibrate. With one hand, I reached for it, while my unseen opponent grabbed his staff back off me. Instinct alone controlled my sense of the other's presence. My eyes, ears and nose were giving me no clues. I could feel every place where his staff hit or prodded me. I raised the sword; its point was always just ahead of my instinctive knowledge of the sorcerer's position. I used it in a rapid slashing movement. For a brief instant, I saw him, then he vanished. My thoughts whirled rapidly, trying to deduce what that meant.

Not illusion, not invisibility, and it couldn't be hypnosis. Another idea occurred to me – hallucination. But instead of my seeing things that weren't there, I was not seeing things that were. A kind of reverse hallucination.

There must have been something in the water I had dug from the river, and a simple mental suggestion had done the rest. I had seen that brief glimpse, because I knew the sword would cut through illusion.

Two solutions occurred to me – a counter suggestion to my own mind, which would require intense concentration to maintain, or to concentrate on metabolising the hallucinogen at a rapid rate. I chose my second option. Meanwhile, instinct was all I had. Instinct linked to empathy – a concept that male Atapi sorcerers did not understand.

Instead of merely defending myself, I chose to attack. My only weapon was the sword. My adversary would see it as a blindingly bright object. When I thrust it at him, the sword seemed to know exactly where to aim. I assume the sorcerer avoided my strokes, but I could not see how well. I just knew I hadn't touched him. I had the advantage of knowing that the sword was not a physical weapon in the same sense as his wooden staff.

It seemed that if he had thought he'd have the advantage over me in a one sided fight, he was learning differently. I had no intention of being bashed to death by a cowardly sorcerer who wouldn't show himself. I said as much aloud, and instinctively brought the sword around and up. I felt it contact something solid but it was not jerked out of my grip. Instead, I sensed anger, and I turned slowly following the direction that the sword was pointing.

"Abomination… female vermin…"

I was beginning to hear his voice. "I've heard all that before, you coward," I said. "Show yourself and make this a fair fight."

He laughed, the sound coming from the direction in which the sword pointed. I suddenly lunged forward and heard him scuffling backwards. "You are no challenge," the sorcerer taunted.

I didn't reply to that. He was welcome to keep underestimating me, but it was stalemate. He was keeping out of the reach of the sword, and I had no way to defeat him without seeing him.

The sorcerer began an offbeat chant, but I couldn't tell what he was trying to do. I was beginning to smell him and to see a hazy outline of him. I put a grin on my face and decided that it was time for me to spin an illusion of my own, now that I could see his reaction.

I slowed my movements, and made jabbing and slashing motions with the sword as if tiring both physically and from his inaction. Now I could see the smirk-snarl on his face as he watched my futile actions. I wanted him to start thinking that I thought he had gone away. I lowered the sword and made more 'coward' remarks, plus some choice epithets I had learnt from Stak's warriors.

He had enough self-control or overconfidence to ignore the comments. He was watching me, and while I still faced him, he probably wouldn't move. I had already decided on the illusion I intended to cast and now I had to prepare. I began to inch around, listen, move again and listen. He rushed at me as soon as I was side on to him, but I was ready. He swung his staff at me, level with my head, aiming to bash me unconscious. I side stepped, twisted and grabbed the staff from him again. In that instant, I went perfectly still and drew the aura around me, becoming invisible. He turned around, looking to see where I had gone. What he saw was an illusion of me running circles around him. He timed a leap to land on the illusory figure, and I walked three steps to land on his wings and used his staff in a bludgeon blow.

I remained kneeling on his back while he lay unconscious. My sight and other senses were nearly back to normal. I had my first really close look at the wings of a sorcerer when they weren't also trying to smother me. They were too bat-like for my own preference.

I waited for him to wake up, with his name humming in my head. This one would no longer consider me weak – I couldn't change the 'female' bit. When he hadn't roused after five minutes, I climbed off him and nudged him with my foot. I was beginning to think that I did not know my own strength. With the aura to call on, I was easily as strong as this sorcerer.

I grew tired of waiting; I touched the sorcerer's forehead and drew on the aura to heal him. When I felt him stir, I withdrew my hand and stood up. His eyes opened and he snarled at me. I laughed and tossed the staff down to him.

"I return your staff, Birok. It is a noble weapon indeed."

As he began to push himself up, his hand felt the bruise on his skull and his manner changed.

"Even the Old One cannot heal those who I strike with this staff," Birok accused me. "How can it be that you struck me with this, and I still live?"

"You lived, because I did not wish you dead," I told him. I wasn't going to try to explain empathy to him.

"Do you claim my lands? My tribe?" Birok demanded.

"No," I said truthfully. "I ask only your support and loyalty."

"Do you wish to raise yourself above the Old One?"

"Only if he cannot see that I have knowledge that will help strengthen all the tribes. How else could I, a female, overcome experienced sorcerers?"

"How indeed," Birok snarled. "I will support your ideas if they make sense." He turned his back to me, walked three steps, leapt into the air and flew into an illusion.

Once he had gone, and I let the aura slip back into the soil, I felt weary. It would be better if I could regain my own strength for a time. I found a sheltered spot in the dry riverbed and curled up. While I was still on Birok's land, I should be safe. I slept.

With Jenha Mosellan's help, Eamon saw his brother was made comfortable in his private quarters. Koenig would be alone in his bed, since his current favourite was indisposed.

"We will wait without," Eamon told the medic, who would stay beside the High Minister to watch him during the evening and night.

Jenha followed Eamon to the outer room of the suite and accepted the gesture to be seated, but waited until after the Kimh lord had seated himself.

"What do you see in the Atapi that the rest of us don't?" Eamon asked Jenha.

"Lord, if I may speak freely?"

Eamon nodded.

"I think that many of us forget that, just as all Kumatan are not alike, all Atapi are not alike." Jenha carefully did not refer to the Kimh. "Most of what is known is about the deeds of the sorcerers. Do you know much of the lesser Atapi? The females, children, warriors and healers?"

"You have a point, Jenha," Eamon admitted. "Go on."

"When I was young," Jenha said slowly, "Stacion Ansuni captured me and my sister. I think you could guess what sort of things he planned to do with two Traeger's children. It was Con Ansuni, his sister Jai, and another young female that helped us escape. Stacion tried again for my sister using some trinket of hers. The two females helped her again. Jai walked her back here. I was grateful to her, even though my father was suspicious of her reasons."

Jenha did not want to mention any more, but Eamon was an experienced Kimh counsellor, and he encouraged Jenha to talk of his friendship with the two young Atapi. These were things Jenha had never shared with any other Traeger or counsellor. He told him everything he knew about the younger Con Ansuni and his sister.

Eamon considered what Jenha said. "I think I would like to talk more with you on this subject. Your friendship, unorthodox as it is, is truly in keeping with the Nuath. If it urges us to cherish those of other worlds, who are different to us, should we treat those of our world with any less respect? What are your thoughts on Con Ansuni's actions?"

Jenha worded his answer carefully. "Would I be correct in saying that, until this recent event, there was never any incident to draw attention to him?"

"That was my observation," Eamon agreed.

"Then I would wonder what provoked him," Jenha said. "If Jai Cassidy spoke the truth, and I believe she did, the earlier incident of the murder of children would not have endeared those aliens to him. For the rest, we only know one version of the events."

"Surely those amazing visual records tell the facts?" Eamon proposed.

"Do you understand the technology that made them?" Jenha asked carefully, not provokingly. "I have seen such things before, on Earth. I won't say I understand how the images are preserved, but I know that the record can be changed – the human term was 'edited' – to remove unwanted pictures. It is possible that we only saw the parts that supported one side of a story."

"That is a serious accusation, Jenha. The Selkrit are allies of our world, and Auglan is a Galactic Councillor," Eamon warned.

"In the interests of honesty," Jenha spoke with a little more emotion, "I believe it is as wrong to assume that these new allies can do no wrong, as it is to assume the Atapi are fully at fault. We prejudge the Atapi based on the actions of past sorcerers. Until now, no ill was attributed to Con Ansuni, yet there are those ready to blame him without hesitation. Just because we know no ill of our new allies, we are ready to trust their word on everything. And Jai Cassidy is being judged because her grand sire was evil. No one here knows her as I do."

Eamon sensed the rising emotion in the younger man. "Repeat the third mantra of calming, Jenha," he directed.

When Jenha had regained control of himself, Eamon went on. "We will talk of her another time. Tell me how you decided there might be poison in my brother's food."

Jenha took a breath and said, "He was behaving uncharacteristically. A long time ago, I was taught a means to sense what is natural. I felt something was wrong with the High Minister, and it was like nothing I had sensed before."

Eamon thought, but could not recall any technique that Jenha could be referring to. He made a reasoned guess. "So it is possible to learn useful things from the Atapi?"

Jenha stiffened. "Yes, some are very sensitive to the aura of Korvu and what is natural."

"Is Con Ansuni one?" Eamon asked.

"To a degree," Jenha admitted. "Their healers are most sensitive."

"The females?" Eamon asked for the sake of clarity.

Jenha nodded.

Once again, Eamon was thoughtful. "Jai Ansuni?"

Jenha nodded again.

"I think there is a lot more that we should talk about," Eamon told Jenha. "Later, though. It is my thought that you should come with me to see Traeger Absolom. I would be interested in your opinion."

"I am at your service, Lord," Jenha said formally.

"We will go now. My brother seems well enough and should recover with rest and quiet. Come."

As Jenha accompanied the Kimh Elder, he wondered what Eamon thought of his admissions. Other Kimh counsellors thought his beliefs aberrant and wanted him to put them aside.

"Absolom is being kept here," Eamon told Jenha as they reached a room not too far from the High Minister's suite. "My brother wishes to learn the truth of his injuries. When they brought him here, every passive alarm was set off. He reeked of Atapi sorcery. Can you wonder that we believe they were responsible for harming him?"

The medic sitting with Absolom rose and bowed to Eamon.

"I have asked Jenha Mosellan to examine him," Eamon explained, and he gestured for Jenha to proceed. The medic took himself from the room.

Once again, Eamon noticed Jenha's eyes change and, in the dim light, they seemed to glow.

Jenha looked over Absolom and could sense-feel his injuries. He sensed the "Atapi sorcery" that others had claimed, but unlike the others, he felt nothing wrong about it. Looking around, he found the neat pile of Absolom's clothes, washed and folded on a table, and a small pile of his personal objects. He picked up a layered stone from the pile, felt how it was polished smooth and warm. He knew from his memory, what it was and guessed how Absolom had come to have it on him. What he did not know was how Jai Cassidy had come to have it.

"You recognise that," Eamon asked, coming to stand next to Jenha. The comment was a tacit request to explain.

"Yes, I have one like it. It is a healing stone," Jenha explained. It wasn't the full truth, which was that the stone was a power relic, which stored the power of the aura. The power was used for healing, but could be used for other things too.

"Atapi?"

"Yes. The one I had was made by Jai Ansuni, and given to me at a time when I had been poisoned by an asp. Without it, I would have died from the venom. This is the same type of stone."

"Really?" Eamon allowed his voice to betray surprise. "Is this stone depleted now?"

"Not fully, but it has been made quiescent."

"Do you think it was used to injure Absolom?"

"No," Jenha said firmly.

Eamon accepted that. "Tell me how you read events."

"Absolom would have been dead if he had not been in that cave. If the Atapi intended his death, they would have made certain of it."

"What if the Atapi just wanted him out of the way?" Eamon suggested.

"There are ways to do that without almost killing him," Jenha countered.

"Perhaps," Eamon allowed. "Still, we must hope Absolom recovers and can tell us what happened. Do you know why he still sleeps?"

"He may have gone into a healing trance," Jenha suggested. "If he knew he was badly hurt, and there was no way to summon help. In that cave, he would have healed, albeit slowly. And there are no Atapi bindings on him."

A knock on the outer door stilled all further conversation. Eamon called permission to enter, and Jenha slipped the Atapi stone in his pocket for safekeeping.

"Lord Eamon, your nephew wishes to speak to you," the medic announced.

Eamon went out of Absolom's room and saw Kaer and a Kumatan medic. Both bowed the ritual greeting.

"Lord Uncle," Kaer greeted, "I have discovered that both my father and the Lady Deandra entertained traders this afternoon. I took the authority to remove what remained of some off world delicacies. Healer Lan has found traces of unidentified substances in some of the items."

Jenha kept his face controlled when Eamon glanced at him. A hand gesture from the Kimh gave him permission to examine what the servant held. The servant was an Atapi, changed into Kumatan form, but Jenha did not betray the fact. He had the servant move to the table in this outer room and place the tray there. He removed the cover and held his hand over each of the different dainties. His eyes did not look at the appearance of the item, but rather he was sense-seeing the aura they emitted. This was another thing that Jai Ansuni had taught him, a long time ago, on a different world.

Eamon and Kaer waited for his report. "I agree with Healer Lan's assessment," Jenha said respectfully. "What I sense of their intent is for these things to be eaten and they would disrupt the higher brain function of the eater. Each has only a minute amount of the disruptive agent."

"The intent?" Eamon queried, echoing the words Jenha had used.

"Yes, Lord," Jenha confirmed, turning to face the Kimh Lord as was properly respectful.

"Are you saying that the traders wished the High Minister ill?" Eamon asked.

"I am making no accusations, but we should question the traders. Off-world food may contain substances harmful to us, but not to other races. The traders may be innocent of ill intent. These dainties may have become tainted somehow. All I can say is there was a sense of 'purpose' and 'intent' about these foods."

Jenha caught the glance of the servant, who met his eyes and then turned to cover the tray once more. If the woman was an Atapi healer, as he suspected, she agreed with him.

"What is being done to locate the traders?" Eamon asked.

Kaer merely said, "My brother has that in hand and he has increased the guards around my father."

"Send word to Malachi that I request extra guards on Absolom too," Eamon directed.

Kaer nodded, gestured to the healer and the servant that they could leave.

"Mosellan, is there anything else you can do for Absolom?"

"No, Lord. The healers have done all they can. He simply needs time to heal."

"Good. We will leave him to sleep," Eamon decided briskly. "We would all benefit from considering the third section of the Nuath and repeating the fourth mantra of focus."

Jenha was glad his face was averted from Eamon. From the corner of his eye, he saw Kaer stiffen. He wondered at that. Did Kaer sense the implied warning and rebuke in the selection of a meditation theme? The third section of the Nuath was on 'obedience to the truth'. Jenha refrained from feeling in his pocket for the healing stone.

CHAPTER 26 – Jai Cassidy – POV

Sometime later, as I slept into the early morning, I rolled out of my snug hole and across to the far side of the riverbed. I woke, but like being in the thrall of a nightmare, I couldn't move, not even to try to outrun the luminous wall of water coming at me along the riverbed.

It came like a tidal wave, picked me up and rolled me over and over. It tossed me onto rocks and tree branches, all the while pushing me down river at a tremendous rate. My mind went blank until I woke in the middle of the river, clinging to a tree branch and trying to cough up water.

If I could have become a fish, I might have fought the current, but I could not change shape. I was at the mercy of the water, and it was dragging on me, trying to suck me away from the tree, leeching energy from me. The taste of the water I coughed up told me that this was no natural flood. It tasted like the seawater on Earth.

More than one sorcerer had to be behind this flash flood. It proved the point I had made to Cotek that strength lay in cooperation. Trouble was – there was only one of me.

I guessed that at least three sorcerers were involved in this piece of vile sorcery. One of them could never have warped the aura enough to bring this quantity of seawater up the river. I assumed that the water was flowing downstream now – but I was by no means certain. I couldn't see how this volume of water could be picked up as a mass, and dumped upstream. I thought it would be easier to herd it upriver from the sea, and that would still require constant attention. Once they released it, it would require less effort to control.

My arms were losing strength from cold as well as the current. I tried to draw from the aura – usually strong in running water – but I could not abide the touch of the warped aura of this torrent. I felt my grip going and held my breath, wishing intently to stay conscious, stay limp and, if I had to, to breathe shallowly when my head was free of water. I did not want to drown.

The tumbling, churning, rolling disorientation resumed, until I was slammed into the trunk of a huge, long dead tree. It was so immense and broad that the water had to flow around it. It had died, fallen into the river and become a natural dam. Its roots were still more buried than exposed. I grabbed for one thick upright bough and felt a surge of unwarped aura. It gave me the strength to climb further from the water and for a time, I simply watched the waters surging around the tree. I was too tired even to think.

"Child!" a sharp mental voice poked my mind back to awareness. "What those sorcerers plan must not be permitted."

"I don't want to die," I agreed. My mind was still slow.

"If you are too weak, I must use another," Larcia mentally slapped me. "Look!"

Larcia sent my mind another bird's-view. I saw what seemed at first to be four people herding a flock of sheep. I felt another flick of energy cross my mind. Then I identified the sheep as a milling cauldron of water, and the four herders were Atapi sorcerers. In the centre of the 'flock' was a large dead tree and I was the ant on it.

"Look further," Larcia demanded.

Approaching the pent up water, on the left flank, was an army of mounted Kumatan. In the distance, not that far away really, was a town. I exclaimed in horror as I took in the overall situation.

First, the slope and direction of the riverbed was towards the town, which was situated on the fertile flood plain. When the sorcerers released the water, it would drown the men and the horses, flood the plain and the town, and poison the fertile land with salt. And they would give me, as a gift, to their enemies. I was to take the blame for all the evil results. Such an outcome was more than worth putting aside mutual antipathy, for the four sorcerers to work together.

I had to do something, but what?

I felt the morning sun, hot on my back – drying me. I thought of it evaporating the water, but that was too slow. I drew a wind to me, and pictured it circling around the four sorcerers and their controlled water. With their concentration on the water, I hoped they would not sense it. I gradually increased the speed of the wind and drew it closer.

When the sorcerers sensed the wind, they released the water, but it was in my control now. They tried to fly above the water that was spreading to fill the area within the wind. The Atapi do not like water, and these were trapped within my wind, being flung around, soaked and in danger of wing damage. I was bringing the wind into a tighter spiral, and this was picking the water up and forcing it higher to form clouds.

The Kumatan soldiers had seen the whirlwind, and stopped some distance away to watch. One of them was sent back to the town – no doubt to summon a Traeger. These Kumatan would have no doubt that the wind was Atapi sorcery. Even the most insensitive Kumatan child must surely be feeling the perturbations in the aura.

In the centre of the wind, I lay watching the clouds form above. They were becoming blacker and blacker with the moisture I was keeping there. Once the water had evaporated, the warped aura was purified, and I could use it. I was not yet ready to let it rain. I concentrated the heat within the wind, to speed up the evaporation, and tried not to think of my skin being burned as well.

When the air that was low in the whirlwind was almost dry, I began to slow the wind. I wanted to move the centre of the wind onto the riverbank where there was an area of scoured rock. Since I had too little energy to get to the bank and keep the wind centred on me, I had to slow it enough so it wouldn't shred me, but still be fast enough to keep the four unconscious Atapi from flopping onto the ground or into the water and keep the white dust from settling out.

As the wind slowed over the rock, the sorcerers fell – more gently than I felt they deserved. The white dust, purified salt, settled into a neat round pile on the rock.

After that, I was limp and exhausted. I could not force myself to do anything more – not even draw on the aura. I still had the 'bird view' in my mind, so I was aware that the Kumatan soldiers were warily approaching the pile of white salt and the still forms of the four sorcerers. They knew at once the nature of the Atapi – since only sorcerers had wings and tails. No time was wasted binding arms and legs, immobilising the wings and drawing some kind of dark hood over the heads of each figure. Only then did they go to examine the white pile.

"It tastes like salt," one reported.

"Sorcery-made," a second said in disgust.

"Look around," the leader directed, pointing to a small group of soldiers. "I don't know what these Atapi scum were doing, so be careful."

Larcia tried to make me move so that I would not be taken by the soldiers. She knew what Kumatan liked to do to Atapi sorcerers.

"I have to rest," I thought at her. "The Kumatan won't kill me."

"I cannot sense you in their places," she warned me.

"I have escaped them before. I can again," I claimed. "Besides, I cannot leave those sorcerers in their control."

"They deserve to die! They give the Atapi the name of vile despoilers," Larcia hissed.

"If I can save them now," I thought carefully, "perhaps they will learn there is a better way. Besides, their tribes will be defenceless without them, and I cannot take control of four tribes either."

"I do not like it," Larcia told my mind, but it was too late. I had been seen, and two soldiers were stepping carefully around branches of the tree to get me.

Even if these strange Kumatan knew of me, I doubted they would recognise me. I was battered and bruised, and all exposed areas of skin were sunburned. My clothes, already thin from long wear, were in tatters. The pitiful remains of my shoes had been dragged from my feet.

While I pretended to be nearly dead, I was lifted and gently carried back to the bank. From the comments I heard passing between the soldiers, I knew they thought me Kumatan, even though my hair was black and the Kumatan usually had blond or light brown hair. I was placed on soft ground and covered with a blanket. A soldier was told to stay with me, and others were to watch the sorcerers until a Traeger arrived.

Even though they were effectively immobilised, the aura still reached the four sorcerers and they began to heal. Their names, however, were in my mind, but I was not yet ready to reveal my victory over them. I had to wait until they awoke, and they could suffer a bit longer than that so they might realise the folly of provoking the Kumatan by doing major sorcery so close to a Kumatan town.

For my part, I was relieved to be left alone, as I was now actively drawing on the aura to return energy to my exhausted body. As I lay there, I felt Farcine trying to reach me and I allowed the contact.

The attempt on the life of the High Minister left me unmoved, except for the implied implication that Atapi were involved. I warned Farcine to be careful, and to pass that warning on to all of those who served in the palace. She told me that were now also guarding Traeger Absolom and I agreed that was wise.

The matter of Auglan and the beetles made me want to laugh out loud. I had not met the man, but he oversaw those aliens who had trespassed on Atapi lands. To the human part of me, he was just as guilty – particularly if he condoned the actions of his fellows.

Then the significance of Teregan's actions occurred to me. The whelp had a talent for sorcery, and he needed to be trained to use the aura properly. How could I do that? I couldn't, not when I was still fighting for my place in the sorcerer's rankings.

"Farcine, watch that whelp of yours." I sensed she knew what I meant. "He needs training…"

"For now, he is still in awe of me as Elder Mother," Farcine chuckled. "And the Elder Warrior is training him. Have you a solution?"

I thought of Con Ansuni, but I didn't know if he would train a whelp of another tribe. I didn't know if Atapi tradition allowed it. My intention to change Atapi traditions couldn't be done yet. For now, I had to follow them.

"In the time he has free from learning to be a warrior, teach him healing," I said.

I felt Farcine considering my suggestion. Healing had always been 'females work', but it also made use of the aura in a way that was closer to what was natural.

"Yes, Jai-devil, that is a wise idea. I will tell Teregan of your decree."

I let the contact drop away. The four sorcerers were rousing and finding themselves restrained and helpless. It was an insult to their huge egos. I flicked a malicious laugh through their minds, sending them from anger to fury. I wondered if they were too incensed to sense Traegers approaching; they were certainly struggling fiercely to try to get free.

By the time the Traegers rode up with their extra Kumatan guards, I was feeling back to full strength, but I pretended to be asleep. I listened to the original group of soldiers reporting to the Traegers, and stirred only slightly when one Traeger examined me.

"Have any of you a spare tunic?" the Traeger asked as he tucked the blanket back around me. "This poor woman is scarcely decent." I heard a murmured reply.

The Traeger moved away. I know he had reacted to the reek of Atapi about me and felt the salt in my hair. He was probably convinced I was the innocent victim of Atapi sorcery. I knew that my mixed blood was not obvious.

Further away, a second Traeger was examining the pile of salt.

"It is untainted by sorcery," I heard him state. "Have your men collect it before the rain begins and washes it into the river or poisons the land."

That had been my remaining concern, and the reason that I was still holding a binding on the clouds above me. I had no doubt that the Traegers were sensing that binding because, when I peeped through my slightly open eyelids, I saw the guards frequently glancing skywards.

I decided that fear was distracting them from realising that the Atapi who had shepherded the flood were not also responsible for the whirlwind that had caused them to be caught. Surely, if the sorcerers intended a salt-water flood, they wouldn't purify the salt into a neat pile. Perhaps they thought another sorcerer was around, but because I was female, it could not be me.

"Put those prisoners over horses," the Traeger who had examined me ordered. "They have trespassed onto Kumatan lands and must answer for their transgression. Take them to the holding room at the guard citadel. We will need to send word to the Kimh."

Guards moved to obey, and muffled curses indicated that the frantic sorcerers were not going to be compliant. I watched as the Traeger, identified by his civilian attire, strode over to the captives, and spoke a warning in Atapi. They were to come quietly or be immobilised. He had one of the rod-like weapons out, and was slapping it against his palm for emphasis. The sorcerers stopped struggling. Wise of them, I thought.

I heard I was to be put up on a horse in front of one of the Traegers, so when the two guards came for me, I decided to 'rouse'. It was only when they began to help me to my feet that I realised that I hadn't completely recovered. I had been okay lying down, but the upward movement of my upper body triggered both a vile headache and nausea. I rolled away from the guards, pushed up onto my knees and brought up a lot of salty water. A guard passed me a flask of pure water to rinse my mouth, and then the two of them helped me to my feet. With their continued help, I walked slowly to the horse and the already mounted Traeger. The horse was fidgeting nervously, reacting to the tension in the air. My headache grew worse as I kept control of the clouds until the salt had been collected.

I was handed up onto the Traeger's horse and placed in front of the man. He used one hand to steady me and to tuck the blanket around me.

The other Traeger was already mounted, and he glanced around and then gave the order to ride. I noticed, in a brief glance, that the pile of salt was down to a scraping on the rock. With relief, I broke the binding on the cloud and fat, heavy drops began to fall. This area of semi-arid country would bloom in a few days' time. Would the Kumatan appreciate the example of pure Atapi sorcery – in tune with nature?

The rain soon became a torrential downpour, and I sensed, as we rode, that the sorcerers were becoming more sullen. I knew they hated being wet. The blanket around me was soon sodden but the rain was refreshing me and rinsing the salt from my hair.

My headache had receded when there was a brilliant flash of lightning, and an instantaneous crack of deafening thunder. The horses tossed their heads, eyes wide with terror, and their riders had to fight to control them.

While I had not expected thunder and lightning, it did not strike me as strange. I was used to seeing dark clouds like this at back on Earth, accompanied by an electrical storm. It was only when I reached out to try to diffuse the clouds over a wider area that I began to sense more Atapi sorcery. I felt tension building, and the horses did, too. The Traeger behind me was murmuring to himself, and I tried to look around in the dim light. I had begun to smell Atapi, very strongly. The Kumatan guards were closing in around the Traegers and the prisoners.

In my mind, I began a chant to reveal enemies. I didn't need to chant aloud or make extravagant gestures to perform such a simple ritual. My headache had returned, and that was making it harder for me to concentrate, but I kept trying.

Lightning struck the ground, just missing one of the guards in the outer ring. All the horses were galvanised into a faster gallop. My concentration was broken, and I realised that the lightning was the work of an Atapi sorcerer. I should have guessed that the other sorcerers would not want to let four of their number be made captive and possibly killed. The tribes were too few.

A sudden idea caused me to start creating a bubble of protection, but before I could complete it, the next bolt of lightning sizzled in front of me, and lasted for longer than lightning usually did. The horse screamed in terror and pain, as its front legs burned in the intense heat and light energy. It reared again in agony and I was thrown off onto the Traeger. I whispered an entreaty to Larcia, and felt the residual energy go to ground through the sword and back into the aura.

The horse was mindless with pain. I stood up, ignoring the rain pouring down my face and the pain in my right leg, and reached for its reins. I projected peace and numbness, and the other rearing terrified horses quietened. The one I held was beyond help and even using the aura I was barely holding him.

I glanced at the unconscious Traeger, recalling his weapon, the immobiliser. With one hand, I reached over to where he lay unconscious, and felt for it. When it was in my hand, I looked it over and could not see how to operate it. I tossed it aside, and felt for another weapon. This time a found a knife, wickedly sharp, and with a twelve inch blade. With this, I quickly ended the horse's pain and the danger its hooves had been to the fallen Traeger. It had been too injured for me to try to heal without using a lot of energy. Other actions were more urgent. I had to protect myself, heal the burns from the lightning and protect the unconscious Traeger. So I formed the bubble of protection over the Traeger, damped the increasing agony in my leg and invoked a ritual of clear sight to see what was happening around me.

Through the heavy rain, I saw Kumatan guards fighting like frenzied berserkers in a circle around me and the captive sorcerers. The second Traeger was part of the defence. I knew by the smell that a horde of battle roused Atapi warriors were fighting to break the circle. I didn't try to figure out what 'nowhere' they had materialised from. I knew very well another Atapi sorcerer was around. He would not leave until the four prisoners were free. Whether he would stick around after that to try to kill me was moot.

Keeping low, I moved between the trembling horses to the ones with the four prisoners. I used the Traeger's knife to cut the bindings holding them on the horses, and then their wrist and ankle restraints.

"Conik, Narok, Zetuk, Ghomic," I said softly in Atapi. I didn't want to be overheard. "I have survived your challenge. Walk into illusion and go free. Take your tribesmen with you."

"Come with us," Narok invited, as he pulled off the black hood and snarled at the rain.

"I have business here. I will heal their Traeger, and prove that not all sorcery is evil."

"Fool," he taunted me, as the four of them stood and walked three steps and vanished.

I hurried back to the Traeger as more lightning lit he sky. Before I reached him, another bolt landed between us, drew all the breath out of me and seared my left side. I fell to the ground and drew desperately on the aura to keep myself conscious. I could not heal myself or the Traeger if I wasn't.

As I drew breath into my lungs, I felt the pain within. I was in a bad way, and moving would make things worse, but my injuries were painful, not critical. I crawled on my belly to the Traeger and touched him. He was more damaged than I was, and on the verge of death. The protective bubble of power had gone, but it had saved him from further damage and certain death. If I was to help the man, I needed to do what I could before my own strength ran out, and before the other Kumatan realised that I had released the prisoners.

Contact with the soil and aura of Korvu kept me conscious, and perhaps healed me a little. The rain was cool on my own burns, but every movement was agony, and I felt on the verge of blacking out. I dared not, and I prayed to Larcia that the sorcerer would throw no more lightning at me, for I did not think I could survive another.

I touched the sword beside me and felt a flow of energy. I should have used it to heal myself, but I knew the Traeger needed it more, and it would prove my sorcery was not being used for harm. I forced myself to my knees and touched the Traeger's chest and thought of his breathing, and began my healing there. Even concentrating on that, I was aware that the Atapi were retreating. Once they were gone, the Kumatan would come back here.

I heard the shouts as they discovered the prisoners gone, felt the alarm of one as he looked at me. I realised then that I was still clutching the Traeger's knife, and he thought I meant the man harm. I froze that guard mid-stride and threw the knife away from me.

The aura flowed from the sword to my hand, and I felt the Traegers's life signs stabilise, even as some of my own injuries were beginning to heal. I moved on to detect the worst of the Traeger's other injuries, focussed on them and felt the healing begin.

More shouts came when the frozen guard was noticed, with an angry voice demanding, "What in the frozen hells are you doing?"

I'd ran out of time. I had no energy to spare to answer, but I was the only conscious entity (excluding the horses) in the circle of guards. Had I viewed the scene as he saw it, I might have formed the same conclusions. The prisoners had been cut free, and I was the only one who could have done it and there was a knife not far from me.

In truth, I had freed them, but he only surmised it. Based on that, though, I had to be an Atapi partisan, and therefore, I must be trying to kill the Traeger. I couldn't move to dodge the force whip, even if I had seen it coming. It caught me on the back, neck and right cheek. The jolt knocked me down onto the Traeger and rough hands dragged me off and threw me onto the muddy ground. I wasn't unconscious, but only because I was full of the aura. I might as well have been, because I was no longer capable of movement. I needed minutes to overcome the stun effect, but in moments the guard had bound me more securely than the sorcerers had been.

Still, while I was touching the dirt, I could draw on the aura and did so.

"Is that necessary?" the second Traeger asked as he examined the fallen one.

"Sir, I don't know who or what this woman is, but the prisoners were cut free and I doubt it was by Traeger Petri. Either she is one of those devils in disguise, or one of ours who will do anything to help them," the guard justified himself.

The guard I had frozen was able to move again, and he walked unsteadily in my direction.

"Captain," he said in a voice that shook a bit. "I saw the woman crawling towards Traeger Petri with a knife. I am sure she was the one that spelled me. There was no one else around and the prisoners were gone."

The Traeger looked again at me, without expression.

"We need to get Petri out of the rain and back to town. Get some shelter erected and a stretcher made. Move him very gently. At least this rain will have helped to cool his burns, but much more will give him a chill."

I was aware of activity around me, and while I wasn't kicked, mud thrown up from the feet of the guards spattered over me, and some fell in my eyes. I heard the Traeger speaking softly, as if to himself, and I realised he was somehow talking to other Traegers who were some distance away. He was requesting help. When he finished his odd communication, he turned his attention to me.

"Who are you?" he asked as he looked down at me.

I tried to form words, but my throat was painful and swelling where the force whip had struck. It was hard enough to breathe. When I didn't answer, he realised that I couldn't, and his questions turned contemplative.

"Why did you, you who was almost killed by those Atapi devils, free them?"

He seemed to be considering his question and then muttered something in a low voice. I felt a wave of energy wash over me and I drank it in.

"So this is your natural shape. You aren't another of those vile devils," he murmured.

The guards were muttering amongst themselves. "Traitor," one said, loud enough to be heard over the rain.

"Is it an Atapi?" another asked.

"No, fool! Or it would have changed back by now," another voice spoke.

"We should kill it," another suggested.

"No," the Traeger quelled the discussion. "We cannot say if she was forced to help them, or chose to. We will take her back to be examined."

"I won't have it on my horse," I heard. Followed by a chorus of, "Nor I."

"We could drag it," was another suggestion.

I suspected the Traeger was ambivalent about me too. No doubt, I was outside his experience, but if he was a Traeger, trained to deal with Atapi sorcerers, he shouldn't consider me a problem.

"I have summoned help," the Traeger stated. "Once Petri is safely away, I will deal with this woman."

He leant down and touched something to my wrist. I felt something snake around it and suddenly my sense of the aura vanished.

A shiver, not caused by the rain, shook me. I had the sense that this Traeger was suppressing anger, and the desire to take his anger out on me. I didn't need to probe his mind to sense the reason. He was fully aware of what the four sorcerers had intended, and he'd had them prisoner – now they were gone. Another sorcerer, or perhaps one of those freed, had attacked the group and his friend Petri was critically injured. I had, he believed, deprived him of the culprits. He gave no thought to the meaning of the neat pile of salt.

His thoughts were turning towards me being as bad as the sorcerers and the need to find out what I knew by any means possible, including torture. How his view of the Nuath would justify that, though, I didn't know.

Being helpless in his control did not appeal to me. There was only one Traeger I trusted, and he was… muzzled. So my options were down to one.

"Kaer! Help me!" I thought desperately.

"Jai!" I felt startled surprise. "Where are you?"

I sent a vivid mental picture of the scene I saw.

"I will be there in moments," his thought came, and I sensed an implacable note to it.

Before I could wonder if Jenha would be with him, he arrived, his back to me, with an unfamiliar Traeger.

Kaer turned immediately, noted the bindings on me, but not my condition. He spoke to the Traeger who had 'walked' him here. "I want a full report of that happened here."

He had the start of his answer from the Traeger waiting with Petri, but halted the report when the help summoned for Traeger Petri arrived.

"See to Traeger Petri," Kaer insisted. "The rest of your report can wait until I get to the town."

The healer who was examining Petri spoke urgently. He had seen how bad Petri was, and wanted him back at the palace immediately. Two Traegers lifted the stretcher and took Petri, the healer and themselves back across planes.

Kaer turned to the Traeger who had come with him. "Fosbok, return to the palace and bring Subni-traeger Mosellan back here."

Fosbok bowed and voiced a protest. "Lord Kaer, what of yourself?" He was torn between obeying the command, and his traditional duty.

"Traeger Fosbok, as you can see the prisoner is immobilised and will be no threat. I doubt that the Atapi will return here now that the sorcerers have escaped. I believe they dislike being out in rain like this. If they should return, the guards are still here, and you will not be long on your errand."

At a gesture from the hovering Guard Captain, his men moved in closer to protect Kaer. Fosbok took the three steps to cross planes to the palace.

"Lord?" the Guard Captain spoke tentatively.

"Captain," Kaer acknowledged. "What can you tell me of what happened here?"

He began by telling of the odd flood that they came to investigate, mentioned the whirlwind, and finding the four sorcerers and the pile of salt, and me on the tree in the riverbed. What he mentioned was the same as the Traeger had said. He went on to mention the storm, the lightning, and what had happened during the fight with the Atapi.

"I have riders out scouting this area. We have no idea in which direction the Atapi retreated. And this rain… it is very localised. A mile from here in every direction, it stops suddenly. It has to be devil rain."

Kaer turned his face into the rain, and said, "It is untainted. Go on."

"That's pretty much it, Sir," the captain finished.

"I will require statements from all your riders, as well as yourself when you are back in the town," Kaer directed. "I will need to give a complete report to the High Minister."

"Yes, Sir," the Captain agreed, and accepted Kaer's dismissal. He moved off and told the guards nearest to stay alert.

Kaer looked down at me again. His expression almost seemed like disappointment.

"When you side with Atapi vermin, you will be treated as one of them," Kaer said without sympathy.

I couldn't talk back to him, but I could think at him. "Be as damn close-minded as the rest of your kind," I thought with no show of respect. "You would have had more trouble than a hundred Traegers could handle if I hadn't freed them. Besides, I beat their damn challenge and I wanted them to know it!"

Kaer was not impressed. "We have agreements with the Atapi. Those sorcerers broke them deliberately and should answer for their actions. You freeing them will be held against you."

"My very existence is being held against me," I snapped back. I was in no mood for politeness, since the pain of my injuries was returning with a vengeance even a torturer would appreciate.

"It seems that those sorcerers were intending to flood this area with salt water," Kaer said stonily.

"And how is that my fault, except that they did it with me in the middle of the flood? And if I somehow survived, I was to be handed to you like a wrapped present to take the blame?" I retorted. "Every damn one of you is missing the point. It didn't happen! This area won't be salt poisoned, the rain is untainted and this area will bloom. The salt from the water was purified and collected before the rain; the water was evaporated to form the clouds. Those bastards failed!"

"What about this storm that almost killed Traeger Petri, and might still be the cause of his death?" Kaer accused.

"A mistake," I thought at him, and then realised I should have phrased it differently.

Kaer told me what he thought of my mistake. Finally I had a chance to defend my words.

"My mistake was for not realising I was facing five sorcerers and not four. He knew what I'd done to those others, and he was aiming his lightning at me. Killing Traegers would be a bonus. He brought in all the Atapi warriors, and intended to free the prisoners, except I got in first. Had I not, more Kumatan would have died."

He picked up on my thought of needing to free them to prove my victory over them. Kaer stared out into the rain for a perceptible time. "Why do you insist on provoking them?" he asked me less sharply.

"They are provoking me," I retorted in his mind.

I sensed in that next moment that Traeger Fosbok had returned, for I felt the presence of Jenha. I could move my head just the slight amount I needed to see him, clad in the plain brown robes, and bowing to Kaer. How I hated seeing him in such a menial position – because of me.

Jenha ignored me until Kaer spoke, but I knew he was aware of me. I chose to look away, hoping to make it easier for him.

Kaer spoke impersonally. "The prisoner is to be taken to the secured room in the palace. As you have experience with her mixed blood, you will know what to expect."

Jenha nodded. When Kaer added nothing else, he came over to me. He didn't try to make eye contact with me, but he did examine me first. I saw the faint change in his expression.

"Lord Kaer," he said, respectfully requesting the attention of his superior.

"Yes," Kaer responded, breaking off from giving directions to Fosbok.

"My Lord, Jai Cassidy requires the attention of a healer." Jenha's tone sounded impersonal.

Kaer finished directing Fosbok and came over. "What is the problem?"

I listened to Jenha's summation and it pretty well agreed with my own. If I had felt like being polite, I might have told them that I was healing slowly, using the energy stored in Larcia's sword.

"No mention was made of injuries," Kaer remarked.

"Of course not," I retorted mentally, and both he and Jenha heard me. "I'm an Atapi sympathiser. Beneath contempt, beneath consideration."

"That is not the truth," Kaer rebuked me. "You deserve as much consideration as any living creature."

I sent a picture of the four trussed up sorcerers and then a picture of what I imagined I looked like. Kaer made no return comment, and I couldn't tell whether he had any sympathy for me. It probably didn't matter; he had to obey his rigid minded elders.

"Bring her to the town," Kaer directed Jenha. "The guard have a holding room we can use, and the healers can look at her there. Meanwhile, I must find out exactly what went on here."

I didn't volunteer to tell him everything, since whatever I said would probably convict me. I didn't waste energy to mentally ask if the restraints could be removed. That would have been a waste of time as well.

Instead of cursing myself for being caught, I considered the positives. Being kept in Kumatan custody meant that the lightning-making Atapi sorcerer would have to wait to try to finish me. I needed time to heal if I was to outsmart him.

Kaer finally spoke again, just before two guards came with a stretcher for me to be carried on.

"You will be given a chance to speak to the Council and to justify your chosen actions."

"Yeah!" I acknowledged. I didn't add, "They won't understand."

Jenha lifted me, very gently, onto the litter. He sensed the extra pain he caused and wordlessly reinforced the pain damping I had begun. I managed to meet his eyes briefly to signal my appreciation of that kindness. I also felt his pity for me, that one who was dear to him had to be treated so poorly. I let a thought trickle to Jenha. "It is not only the Atapi that need to change."

He did not acknowledge that thought, pretending he had not heard it. I knew, though, that his mind was more open than most of his kind, possibly because of the years he had spent on Earth, seeing different ways.

The twisting blackness of crossing planes seemed to send a chill into all of my burns. When we arrived, I instantly sensed that there were a lot of people around. Kaer and Fosbok had crossed with us, and as Jenha was directed to the holding room by the stretcher bearing guards, I heard Kaer giving orders to recall all the guards from near the river.

In the holding room, the stretcher was placed onto the rough bed, and the guards retreated outside the barred wall. Jenha waited with me for the healer to come, but we were told he was still treating Petri and would come when he could. When he did arrive, the healer obviously guessed I was a prisoner from my location, but just as obviously had not been told what I was supposed to be.

"Are these restraints necessary?" he queried, before he even started to check me over.

Jenha used his initiative to remove the band on my wrist, and to gesture to one of the guards to release the other bindings. He kept one hand on me to warn me about trying to escape – not that I was capable of doing any such thing. I was relieved, however, that I could vaguely sense the aura now. I also realised that Jenha was still feeding me a trickle of healing energy. I hoped no one would notice. I tried to guess how long I would need to heal, using that trickle of energy. A day at least, two would be better.

The healer seemed more resigned than eager to treat me. He began to cut off the borrowed tunic and the tattered rags beneath it. His nose wrinkled at the combined smell of unwashed human and burnt flesh.

Into Jenha's mind I inserted a request. "Ask him how Traeger Petri is."

Jenha asked it aloud, without looking at me.

"Bad. Very bad, but he will heal with time and rest," the healer began. "However, I did not receive a detailed report of the accident."

"Lightning grounded just in front of us. The horse threw us," I told Jenha. He passed it on to the healer.

"Lightning," he echoed. "That explains the burns. I wonder if that is the cause of the breathing pain."

"Yes," I thought at Jenha. "It was like the air was sucked out and fire sucked in."

When Jenha had repeated that, the healer suddenly looked at me directly. "Are you in contact with this patient?" he asked Jenha.

"I am," Jenha admitted. "The swelling on her neck and face is due to a force whip reaction. That is why she cannot talk. If you are able to reduce that, she WILL help you to elicit her injuries."

He didn't need to use that damn 'command' tone on me!

"I have been instructed to ensure that she can speak to the council as soon as possible," said the healer. "I cannot see that being possible for quite a few days. This patient is in a worse condition than Traeger Petri, and there are some anomalies in her anatomy."

How the hell could that healer tell that just from looking at me?

Jenha answered smoothly, "Jai Cassidy is a hybrid of Human and Atapi, and she was born off world. That is why the High Minister wishes to talk to her."

I sensed that the healer was re-evaluating me. Before he began to class me with the Atapi, Jenha added, "The Atapi sorcerer who sent the lightning attack was trying to remove her."

That changed his attitude completely. He now considered me just as important at Traeger Petrie. With a trickle of thought, I warned Jenha, "Hadn't you better stop twisting the truth about me? They already think less of you than you deserve."

"I have said enough," Jenha thought back. "And I have told no lies."

"Only that bit about lightning man trying to remove me. I made that up. He was trying to free the other four. I was a bonus, and Petrie was a bonus."

Jenha's stance did not change. He watched as the healer cleaned my wounds, gently rubbed a salve on the force whip swelling and another into the burns. When he had finished, I no longer needed to damp the pain from my injuries.

The healer then poured liquid from a flask into a mug and handed it to Jenha, while he helped me to sit up. I was told to drink, but I could not swallow easily. The healer produced a spoon and fed me the liquid a little at a time. It eased the fire inside me, making breathing easier. It must have had other properties, because I began to feel as if my mind was drifting. The last thing I recalled hearing was the healer asking if I needed to be trussed up again.

I felt Jenha's mind checking my condition – I was not quite unconscious, and too weak to move.

"They may remain off for a time," he said. "They will need to be replaced when she is moved to the palace. I will remain here."

I had just enough will left to tap into the aura and purpose it to heal me, before I gave up the attempt to stay conscious. With Jenha there, I felt safe.

Koenig sat back in the comfortable chair in his suite and considered the reports Malachi had given him. It was late afternoon, but little of importance had occurred, and his son had handled the duty of his proxy without trouble. He wished there had been something that needed his attention, for his mind insisted on going back to the previous evening, and the reason for the intense counselling sessions he'd endured since waking that morning. His Counsellor, an elderly uncle, had shown him how his control of self and mind had been eroded by the substance in the alien sweets. The cause had angered him, but time spent in meditation and quiet talking had helped him regain control. Tomorrow, he would be allowed back at his duties.

As a sign of his improved health, the healer was no longer in constant attendance. Instead, he had left medication for him, to take every four hours. In fact, it was almost time for one of those silently efficient servants to bring him wine to take away the taste of the tart liquid medicine.

He wished Lady Deandra was allowed to attend him, but he had heard of her indisposition and loss of composure, and was no longer sure he wished to be associated with her.

Koenig reached out his hand and found the filled wine glass and his medicine. The servants had come and gone without his notice. He appreciated their discretion; he had not wanted to be disturbed.

He rose and walked around his suite for a while, wanting to keep his mind occupied, but not feeling like reading. Instead, he decided to retire early. As expected, his bed was turned down ready and his night robe placed neatly on the foot of the bed. Even then he was restless and went to the window and opened up the clear panels to let in the evening breeze. It felt refreshing after a day kept confined to his suite.

While he stood there, he looked down and watched the night guards going out to patrol the palace grounds. His son, Malachi, acting High Minister in his absence, had increased the guards and even placed some in the passage outside his door.

"I'll end that nonsense tomorrow," he vowed. "The traders will be long gone by now."

He knew Malachi had given orders for the traders to be traced and their wares checked. The traders were to be warned that their items were incompatible with Korvu physiology. He did not believe that the traders intended ill. There had been traders visiting Korvu for the past two generations and none had ever given trouble. Korvu had benefitted from the exchange of cultures. It would be a pity to have to ban the delectable alien delicacies.

Leaving the window open, Koenig went and exchanged his day clothes for his night robes and climbed into his bed. He was reluctant to admit how tired he really was.

Some hours later, the healer came to check on him and was admitted by the vigilant guards. They were all surprised by the presence of the two white clad servants in the outer chamber.

"What are you doing here?" one guard challenged.

"We were sent to be of help to the High Minister," one said quietly.

"I must remember to thank the servant master for his thoughtfulness," the healer remarked.

The same servant spoke again, respectfully. "Healer, the High Minister is sleeping. Should we close his window? It will be cold before morning."

"It should be no harm to keep it open. The fresh air will be good for him."

The two servants moved back to one corner and let the healer enter Koenig's sleeping chamber. The healer did not disturb the sleeping High Minister, just listened to his even breathing and retreated. He did not notice two shadowy figures standing either side of the window, guarding the High Minister.

Back in the outer chamber, the healer spoke to the servants.

"If he sleeps at the mid of night, do not disturb him for his medicine. If he wakes after that you may give it to him, but delay the following doses."

One servant bowed in acknowledgement and the healer and guards retreated. When all was quiet, the two servants moved like wraiths into the inner chamber and stayed flanking the door. All were now visible, but at the slightest sound, they would fade back into shadows.

Three assassins had crept onto the grounds in the early hours of the previous morning, and spent the day scouting the palace and grounds in the guise of busy servants, walking briskly from place to place. When they had confirmed the location of their target, they each found a place of concealment and planned their attack.

These creatures were professional killers; highly skilled, highly paid. To them, this would be an easy night's work. The locals were unsophisticated, predictable and would be easy to avoid or overcome.

In the depth of the night they moved like ghosts, avoiding the guards and scaling the palace walls like spiders. On the roof, they moved by crawling on their stomachs so as not to make a silhouette against the clear night sky. They each stopped above a predetermined window, and watched the ground for a time before preparing to enter by the windows. There were guards below, but they never looked up to see the dark ropes uncoiling from the roof or the dark shapes climbing down and hanging briefly beside each window. They made no sound, and now they waited until the first of them entered and went to take out the guards in the passage and retreat back to the roof to watch for any signs of alarm.

The other two, finding one of the windows invitingly opened, entered through it. They stopped, listening to the gentle snores of their victim and letting their eyes adjust to the deeper darkness in the room. When they were ready, one touched the other with two fingers spread in a 'v' – their signal for 'ready'. One took from a pocket a can of an aerosol spray, and began to move to one side of the bed. The other went to the other side, ready to grab and hold the victim silent until the deadly spray did its work. Both had dark fabric covering their nose and mouth.

Before they reached the bed, two dark, unyielding figures materialised in front of them and hissed a warning.

"Come no further. We guard this one. You do not belong here."

The words were spoken in the traders' tongue, as that language was more widely understood than Kumatan. The intruders stopped, taking in the unexpected obstacle. They had not expected to meet resistance, but they were not unprepared.

"Move aside or you will die, too," one warned through their muffling folds of cloth.

"Come closer at your own risk," invited soft voices from beyond the first two.

The intruders could now make out two dark shapes perching lightly on the end of the High Minister's bed. They both glanced around in the darkness to see if more surprises lurked. Two to one odds were nothing. They now had different weapons in their hands.

"You are lizard-men," one intruder spoke in amazement. "His kind hate you."

"We know," the soft voice said calmly. "But his kind can ensure that your kind and those who sent you will leave this world."

The intruders sprang in perfect unison but the defenders were as quick to block them.

Koenig woke suddenly, and felt the weight near his feet. He heard the whispered words and took a moment to understand them. He drew his feet up and edged out of bed, aware of the scuffle of feet on the far side, and the skidding away of two metal weapons. He rang the bell beside his bed to summon servants. He didn't know who was fighting who, but he had heard 'lizard-men' and that was enough. He ran for the door and went through his outer chamber to the passage. In the dull lighting there he saw the two guards on the floor, apparently asleep. He yelled loudly, forgetting decorum and releasing his anger at having Atapi invading his private chamber.

More guards raced in answer to his yells, and with the first two, he re-entered his rooms. He explained quickly what he had seen and heard. The next two checked the fallen men, found they were dead and quickly followed the High Minister.

The guards lit the room with their portable lights, and saw two servants clad in white tunics standing over two prone figures in close fitting black suits. Someone lit the main room lights.

"Lizard men?" the senior guard snapped at the servants. He was looking at the unconscious figures.

"No, Guardsman. Lizard-women!"

"Have you killed them?" Koenig asked, not taking in the truth of the servant's words.

"No, High Minister," the second servant answered. "Although it was tempting. They intended your death."

"The Atapi would not dare!" Koenig almost snarled.

The two servants gave that comment no response. One of the guards leant over and pulled the face covering from the two assassins.

"These are no kind of being that I have seen before," the guard said.

"Atapi sorcerers can change shape," Koenig reminded the guards, and they belatedly drew weapons to cover the intruders. "Get a Traeger in here – one that can identify these devils. I will have them taught a lesson they won't forget."

"Have your Traegers question them and test the spray in their pockets," one of the servants spoke out. Both had moved back from the intruders, but neither had stopped watching them.

"Put restraints on them before they wake up, you fools," Koenig ordered.

The suggestion was readily obeyed, and then the guards started acting like the professionals they were meant to be, searching the clothing of the intruders. They found hidden pockets and hidden weapons sheathes and an array of weapons and instruments of death, including two odd metal containers. Many of the items were unfamiliar, but their purpose was easy to deduce.

The truth began to dawn on the guards. "These prisoners are not Atapi," one stated.

Koenig turned to the two servants as Traeger Solomon arrived. "Lizard women!" Koenig accused.

Neither of the Atapi females betrayed fear at his accusation.

Solomon took in the scene and assumed that the High Minister was referring to the two captives lying on the floor. He spoke words, and let his power wash over the men.

"Those two," Koenig pointed to the females, who looked like Kumatan servants. "What do you see?"

Solomon didn't question why Koenig had asked that. He repeated his earlier words, and the two humanoid servants changed back to being Atapi females.

The guards and Traeger Solomon backed back a pace and weapons were quickly drawn and aimed at the females. Neither moved.

"I would like to know how Atapi entered my rooms," Koenig stressed his words, and the guards knew there would be trouble and punishment for anyone involved or who was negligent.

"We entered by the door, High Minister, but only to serve you. Those others entered by the window, from the roof," the older of the two females spoke calmly.

One of the guards was sent to investigate the claim, and he found the thin strong rope dangling outside.

"How did you know they were coming?" Koenig demanded. "Why did you stop them? Surely the Atapi have no special concern for me."

"We did not know they were coming, High Minister, but it was our purpose to protect you. The nearness of those vermin was like an itch on our skin. Alien and unpleasant."

Koenig stared at the Atapi females with growing unease. He had thought female, no threat, and these females were not armed, but they had still overcome two intended assassins.

"Solomon, I have no further need to be served by these…" he bit off the impolite term in his mind. "Nor do I wish them to speak of this matter. I have questions to ask them, in the morning. See to their… comfort… immediately."

The two females bowed respectfully to Koenig, and walked tall and straight, a step in front of the Traeger. In spite of the polite words, they knew that Koenig meant for them to be prisoners. They were neither cowed, nor fearful; they had obeyed Jai-devil and the High Minister was safe. And he had no idea that two more Atapi females still guarded him.

Koenig forgot the females as soon as they were out of sight. To the guards, he ordered, "Take these prisoners to the lowest cellar and ensure they cannot escape. I am not convinced that they were not in league with the Atapi. And I want a full investigation of how they got near enough to kill me."

He had meant the females, too, but the guards assumed he meant the assassins. Belatedly, Koenig admitted to himself that the Atapi females had stopped these men killing him. He didn't want to think how close he had come to death.

"High Minister," the senior guard ventured. "The Atapi never deal with traders or off-worlders."

"Nonsense," Koenig retorted. "That hybrid Jai Cassidy is both alien and from off-world, and those females are hers. She is dealing too much with the Atapi."

The guards only knew the name, not all the facts about the hybrid, so they said little.

"Go on, remove that trash," Koenig insisted.

Each prisoner was slung over the shoulder of a guard and two more guards accompanied these as they went down to the cells in the cellar, which were meant for storing foodstuff, not people.

Koenig followed the group as far as his outer chamber where six more guards stood watchful and alert. His brother, Eamon, entered just after the prisoners were taken out.

"Guardsmen Tedlan and Boro are dead, brother," Eamon told Koenig. "They were strangled by a narrow band of some very strong material."

Privately, Koenig thought they must have been asleep on watch to have been attacked without warning. "Atapi work?" he stated more than asked.

"No, this is like nothing I have heard of before. Solomon has seen nothing like this either," Eamon remarked.

"Why would someone try to kill me?" Koenig demanded, forgetting the presence of the guards.

"Who indeed?" Eamon questioned. "I think you should come back to my suite for the rest of the night. Let the servants deal with your room."

"Have Solomon deal with it," Koenig directed.

"It is not a Traeger's job, Brother," Eamon said softly.

"I want to be sure there will be no surprises in there when I go back," Koenig said. "I want no unsupervised servants in my private quarters, and I particularly want to know how Atapi females came to be my personal servants."

Eamon looked surprised; he had not known about Atapi servants. "I don't know," he admitted. "But it seems you owe your life to them."

Koenig growled; he didn't want to be grateful to them. He changed the subject. "I want those intruders identified. Ask Auglan – he might have heard of that type of creatures. If he doesn't, he can ask the Galactic Council about them."

"I heard that the Councillor has been indisposed today," Eamon said quietly.

"Are there any other Galactic representatives we can talk to? They are the biggest interfering busybodies that I know of." Koenig resented their claim that they had the right to sit in on Korvu Council business.

"Not at present," Eamon considered. "A message arrived late this evening. It advises us to expect a delegation from the Galactic Council."

"For once they will be welcome," Koenig growled. "We can get them to remove those unpleasant creatures from Korvu."

Eamon murmured his agreement.

CHAPTER 28 – Auglan - POV

Councillor Auglan was relieved to be feeling better. His reaction to the bite of the revolting beetle had abated, and he finally felt like eating and that he might retain the food.

He was disgruntled because he had not had a reply to his message to the Galactic Council, even though he knew they carefully considered such accusations as he had made before acting. Still, he had believed his standing was more than sufficient, and his word trusted enough, to cause a quick hearing – though after the past day, when nothing he ate or drank remained in him, it was probably just as well that he did not have to talk to the Galactic Council in person. His presentation was not dignified, not at all.

In his ground floor guest suite, well away from the Royal Suites of the local nobility, he was out of touch with the reaction to his threat. He wondered, too, if the fool, Koenig, had recovered from his indisposition.

The local healer had given him a potion to drink, and apologised in advance because he did not know if it would help such an esteemed visitor. Auglan had taken one dose, immediately lost it, and not bothered with the rest of the supplied doses.

At least the local peasants were scrupulous in bringing him the messages relayed from his ship, the one circling in high orbit above Korvu. He was sure the locals knew every word of the messages, but he would pretend he didn't think that. They were a ruse, anyway. He would advise the locals that he had sent sixty of his men back to the ship for the duration of the retreat. The other twenty of the total he had admitted to having on the planet were in other rooms in this wing of the palace, enjoying the so called benefits of this fourth rate palace.

That satisfied that officious son of Koenig. What the locals didn't know was that one of those overt messages contained a hidden one, and that one filled him with glee. It confirmed that the people of this backward planet would be mourning their High Minister come morning.

Auglan decided it was time to prepare his proof of non-involvement. He sat in his chair and rang the bell provided for him and a quiet servant entered.

"Please ask the healer to attend me," Auglan feigned politeness, and continued weakness.

"Yes, Lord," the servant answered softly, keeping her eyes demurely downcast. "Is that all you require, Lord?"

"Yes, yes, go!" Auglan stood as soon as the servant left the room, and turned up all the lights. Memories of those beetles haunted him and he wanted to be sure that none were in is room. The unfamiliar sounds of this alien place seemed to sound like the rubbing of their wings, and he still seemed to be able to smell their acrid stench.

While he waited for the healer, he looked into the few wardrobes and the other hidden corners, glad for the austerity of the room. He found nothing and tried to tell himself that the dark shadows seen only out of the corners of his eyes, were a residual effect of the bite.

When the healer arrived, Auglan was seated again and the lights dimmed to suit an invalid.

"How can I help you, Lord?" the healer asked.

"I hardly slept last night, and I am very tired but do not feel like I can sleep," Auglan began. "Have you a potion that might help me?"

The healer nodded and delved into his pouch of medicines. When he again began to apologise for his lack of knowledge about Selkrit physiology, Auglan tightened his lips and decided to interrupt.

"Good Healer, the Selkrit are tough. True, this might not work, but be assured, it will not harm me," he claimed.

Well, he thought to himself, it wouldn't. He was only going to pretend to take it.

"I will come back in several hours to check on you," the healer promised.

Auglan managed to make his thanks sound genuine. It would be proof of his presence in his room all night, just as his many demands during the day had proved he'd been here. At least he had been able to send his messages from the spaceport. He had made no secret of them, and if anyone at that hick spaceport had translated them, they would seem to be passing on the orders arising from the High Minister's decree. What they wouldn't detect was the microburst message he'd sent with them.

With his presence in his room confirmed, Auglan washed the sleeping potion down the waste pipe from the small hand basin, opened the window slightly and settled into his bed. He lay awake with his ears straining for the sounds of an uproar – sure there would be shouting if the High Minister was found dead. He didn't expect to see or hear the assassins he had paid for – they were meant to be the best in the galaxy.

All his ears kept hearing was the little rustling noises that would stop for a while and then start again. Then there were high pitched whining of night insects… and he would start to smell that beetle smell, even though he had thoroughly cleansed himself, had his clothes taken away and new ones provided.

In spite of his intentions to stay awake, he did sleep. He woke when the healer came in, though he feigned deep sleep. He then drifted back into sleep without seeing the white clad servant watching him from near one wall.

Koenig did not return to sleep, even in the peace of his brother's rooms. As soon as the day showed traces of dawn, he dressed in borrowed clothes and strode to his office. The guards from the passage followed him wordlessly. After the previous night, he no longer objected to their presence.

His office was deserted, and looked just as he had left it. A glance at his desk told him that Malachi had been there in his absence. He sat down in his leather-upholstered chair and reached for the folder on the left of his desk. He glanced through the paper sheets and saw they were the reports that Malachi had summarised for him last evening. He put that folder back and took the one on his right, which should be his upcoming appointments.

He looked at the day's list and there was a mention of a request for an audience from Galactic Ambassador Quenten. It was followed by a brief resume of his origin and status, which was not unusual – however, the reason for his visit was not given.

The day's schedule was not full, but did also include a reminder to talk to the servants. Yes, that would be his first priority.

He closed that folder and took the one in front of him. It would be a new report that came in late last night. Perhaps something had been learnt from the assassins?

He opened it and recognised Kaer's precise writing, and wondered when he had delivered it. He began reading. His face suffused to purple and he clutched a stoppered inkwell, only barely restraining himself from throwing it. The incompetent fools had let four sorcerer-devils escape! They had them incapacitated and they let them escape!

Koenig controlled his breathing by mentally repeating the first three mantra's for calm. He was ready to begin reading again when there was a knock on his door.

"Enter," he called out, since his assistant was not in the outer part of the office. Caseon was never an early riser.

Kaer entered, bowed a greeting and spoke informally. "Father, I heard about last night. Are you well?"

Koenig did not intend to admit that he still felt uneasy about the attempt on his life. "Of course, the would-be assassins were overcome and are contained."

Kaer's face paled in shock. "Assassins? Who sent them and why?"

"We don't know yet. The creatures did not want to talk," Koenig spoke calmly. "Fortuitously, a Galactic Ambassador will be arriving soon. I have it in mind to ask him to deal with them."

"What of Councillor Auglan? Could he help us?" Kaer asked.

"I have been advised that he has been indisposed this past day. I did not feel it right to bother him." He did not say he was pleased the obnoxious Councillor had been ill.

Kaer hid a measure of relief. Had Jai's paranoia affected him? "Is it also true that two Atapi females saved you?"

Koenig's head snapped up. "Two of the females were in my room and I want to know why. As for saving me – they merely provided a distraction until I summoned guards. You have reminded me of the need to question them. Please summon Traeger Solomon at once."

Kaer nodded automatically and withdrew. He needed a moment to collect his thoughts. He had gone to his father, since he knew he was up and in his office, to follow up on his report. He had seen his father was reading it, but obviously had had not got far into it. He was prepared for a contentious meeting on that subject.

Now he had to consider that his father had learnt of the Atapi servants. It seemed that they had indeed protected his father as they had promised Jai Cassidy. Would his father suspect there were others? He suppressed his concern about his father's reaction if he found out that he, Kaer, knew about them and kept quiet.

Malachi saw Kaer after he had given a servant the message to give Solomon.

"Has Father heard your news?" Malachi greeted, too cheerfully for that early hour.

"Not yet. He was still reading my report," Kaer said, not responding to his brother's good humour. "He sent me to get Solomon. I surmise he has two Atapi females in seclusion and intends to talk to them this morning."

"What Atapi females?" Malachi sobered.

Kaer realised that his brother didn't know and related what he had heard. He omitted to mention that he had heard it from his own servants.

"I heard about the assassins," Malachi admitted. "They were caught and taken downstairs to be held. There was no mention of Atapi females."

Kaer shrugged slightly. "Where are you off to in a rush?" he asked to change the subject.

Malachi grinned. "We received word, late last night, of another Galactic Councillor arriving. I am to go and meet him and show him all due respect."

"Father mentioned that. He thought to hand those assassins over to him," Kaer remarked neutrally. "He mentioned Auglan was indisposed."

"Indeed. I heard it was a nasty reaction to something at the spaceport," Malachi said gravely. "I am not surprised. It is such an odorous place."

Malachi departed with a guard escort as Solomon hurried into view. His normally impeccable robes were slightly askew, as if he had dressed in a hurry. He quickly rubbed a hand over his hair as he approached.

"Lord Kaer?" he asked. "You required me?"

"My father wishes your attendance, Traeger Solomon," Kaer said impersonally. He strode off and forced Solomon into a fast trot to keep up with him.

They entered the High Minister's office to see Koenig and the Master of Servants talking. Caseon had arrived, but was standing to one side listening.

"If you didn't send them, why were they there?" Koenig was asking forcefully.

"Sir, the last two I sent had your evening medicine."

Koenig gritted his teeth. He couldn't even be sure that the two who had been Atapi were the same ones as he had seen earlier. They were so self-effacing and discreet, that he never paid attention to them.

"I want you to come with me when I speak to them," Koenig insisted. "Solomon, Kaer, I require you as well."

Koenig strode out of the room. The guards in the passage flanked him and the others fell into position behind him. They walked from the palace to a separate building that housed the Kumatan guards and servants.

The lesser-ranked people bowed low when they saw him, and stayed that way until he'd passed. All wondered at his presence. Some had heard rumours of two servants caught in his room who had been detained. No one knew what they had done, but all feared the anger of the Kimh, particularly the anger of the High Minister.

Neither Tisla nor Limia betrayed fear when the Kumatan guards came for them. Both had not changed back into Kumatan shape. Solomon had done something to prevent that.

When taken into the presence of the High Minister, they both bowed to him in the exact degree of respect that his rank merited. They bowed slightly to the Master of Servants, slightly more to Kaer and more so to a third person that entered after Solomon. They ignored the Traeger.

Solomon was aware that the last bow was not to him, and turned. "What are you doing here?" he demanded, drawing everyone's attention.

Koenig's face tightened when he saw the old Atapi female, attired like a Kumatan, moving around to face him.

"I am Farcine, Eldest Mother of the tribe of Jai-devil. I am here to represent these two of my daughters – as is my right according to Kimh and Kumatan law."

Only the servant master made a sound, as if he was about to protest, but had thought again.

"Very well," Koenig agreed, unable to think of a legal reason to send her off. He returned his gaze to the younger Atapi females.

"Who sent you to my rooms last night?" Koenig demanded. "Master Paradine did not."

"No, High Minister, that is true. We went there to protect you," Tisla admitted. She was the older of the two.

"Who sent you?" Koenig repeated his question.

Farcine spoke up. "I did, at the request of Jai-devil."

Koenig glared at her, his face tightening at hearing Jai Cassidy mentioned. "What other mischief did you plan?"

"No mischief, High Minister," Farcine insisted, ignoring the obvious discourtesy. "Jai-devil expressed concern for your continued wellbeing."

"How many more of you are acting as servants?" Koenig demanded.

Farcine chose to misinterpret that. "Two others spell Limia and Tisla. I serve Lord Kaer as a nurse for his ward."

Koenig gave Kaer a venomous glance, auguring a 'talk' later, and then returned his attention to the Atapi females. He was grateful for their actions, but the thought of having Atapi close to him made his skin crawl.

"I no longer require your services," he managed to sound polite. He met the eyes of all three females. "I want all of you, including the others you mentioned, to return to your enclave. If any of you step back into the palace, you will be punished. Any Atapi that sets foot into my palace will be punished."

None of the females responded to his instruction. Instead they just continued to meet his eyes.

"How many of you can change shape like sorcerers?"

Koenig stared at Farcine, but the old woman did not look cowed.

"High Minister, it is a natural skill. Before your Traeger rescued us and returned us to our home, we had to learn to protect ourselves on that distant world."

That notion was not well received by Koenig. "Solomon, did you know this was possible?"

"No, High Minister. I have never heard of such a thing."

Koenig continued to glare at Farcine, but the old woman still didn't react. If he could have read her mind, he would have learnt that, to her, he was nothing to fear when compared to an angry sorcerer.

"From the conclusion of the next Council session," Koenig spoke slowly, emphasising his decision, "there will be a ruling that any Atapi found out of their natural shape will be punished. Please tell all of your tribe of this decision, and of the penalties for entering the palace or Kumatan buildings."

Farcine bowed respectfully, her face betraying nothing of her personal reaction. She did not protest at the unfairness of his decision. Fair was never a word to describe the interactions of the Kimh and Kumatan with the Atapi.

"I am sorry that our service displeased you," Farcine said in a soft voice. ""We felt we owed you for bringing us home and granting us your protection."

Both Koenig and Solomon bristled at this invidious reminder that they were obliged to protect these Atapi, and couldn't send them away.

"How can you claim such a thing?" Solomon demanded. He was not one of the Traegers that had gone to Earth to return the Kumatan and these Atapi.

Farcine bowed slightly to him. "Slave master, it is like this – once we believed that our leader, Stacion Ansuni, would keep us safe and the Kumatan and their rulers would kill us on sight. So when the Kumatan rode into our village, on that distant world, and began grabbing male, females and children, we were afraid for our lives. Yet it was they who saved us – and those who had, we thought, escaped a dreadful fate died by the hand of Stacion's warriors. They killed even the tiny whelps. They were not given the choice of life and serving Jai-devil, as we were."

In a deep corner of Koenig's mind, he wished that those Kumatan, no doubt acting on Mosellan's orders, had not bothered. Then his conscience told him that he might be dead or badly injured if things had gone that way. He was angry at how these Atapi had tricked him. Farcine added, "Jai-devil told us she could not protect us, but should we serve you well we would be protected. She was wise, for until now that has been so."

Koenig resented that invidious reminder and subtle rebuke. He recalled how he appreciated the unobtrusive service, but now he knew what those servants were.

"You are free to return to your enclave," Koenig told the females, his expression controlled. "Solomon will escort you back. "Master Paradine, you may return to your duties," he then directed, and nodded at the man's bow of obedience.

Kaer saw his father's face set into one of displeasure and spoke quickly. "This is no place to discuss important matters, Father. And I have important matters to bring to your attention."

Koenig glanced around at the stoic faced guards. "You are correct. We will continue our discussion in my office." He strode out and let the others trot after him to catch up.

Halfway back to the palace, Koenig noted a group of people approaching from another direction. He recognised Malachi leading the group, walking next to a man in a black robe over a dark grey one-piece suit. The stranger wore a medallion that glinted in the sun. Koenig recognised the sun insignia of the Galactic Council. Following immediately behind Malachi and the Ambassador were two more figures, clad in black form fitting uniforms, and carrying a black and silver helmet. Koenig almost missed a step. Those two were Enforcers – the law control arm of the Galactic Council. He had heard of them, and really had not wanted to see any. He assumed, however, that they were present as guards for the Ambassador, and were exactly what he needed. He would request their assistance to question those assassins. He had heard they had ways to get the truth from anyone. Surely, they could discover who sent them.

Malachi spotted his father but did not draw attention to him. Koenig was dressed in borrowed clothes, and was not suitably attired for an important meeting. These visitors had not revealed to him the nature of their business, saying only that they must speak to the High Minister himself.

"Without meaning disrespect, Ambassador," Malachi said smoothly. "I will see you to an anteroom and provide refreshments. My father is expecting you, but we had some unpleasant events last night and my father has been attending to the outcomes."

"Oh, is there anything that I may assist him with?" the newcomer invited.

Malachi waited a moment to reply, as if considering. "There may well be, but it will be up to my father to ask if he chooses."

The Ambassador accepted that placidly.

Lord Eamon was waiting in the room to which Malachi led his guests. He acted as host by introducing his uncle, but then added, "I will advise my father of your arrival. I am sure he will be here as soon as he can."

Malachi slipped from the room just in time to intercept his father.

"Father, you cannot go in there looking like you are. You need to change into your official robes. I still have not managed to elicit their purpose, but I sense it is a serious one indeed."

Koenig nodded, and turned towards his suite. He stopped when he entered his bedroom, because the wall hangings and floor mats had been stripped away, and his bed was bare of mattress, bedding and enclosing drapes and the window was exposed.

Malachi ignored the barren state of the room and went directly to one of the closets, and took out a set of his father's most impressive formal robes. He turned back to see his father still staring at the room.

"Uncle Eamon ordered all the hangings, draperies and so on to be removed, in case anything unpleasant was left in here." That possibility had not occurred to Koenig. "Where are your servant's father?" Malachi asked, looking around.

"I dismissed them," Koenig said flatly. "Help me into these. I cannot be lacking in courtesy and respect to these visitors."

Malachi did as he was bid and did not complain at having to do the work of servants. Without seeming to, he hurried his father back to where the important guests were waiting. He noted when he returned that three of his brothers were talking to the ambassador – or, rather,

Caseon and Debenen were. Kaer was standing to one side. All three were dressed in their most formal robes.

Malachi drew everyone's attention when he entered and loudly announced his father. Lord Eamon came over to Koenig, escorted him to where the guests were standing and introduced each to the other. Caseon and Debenen moved politely back next to Kaer.

Eamon spoke conversationally, "I had not realised the distinction between a Galactic Councillor and a Galactic Ambassador. Our guest, Ambassador Quenten, explained that Councillors are selected by member worlds to represent their people on the Galactic Council. Ambassadors are representatives of the Council as a whole."

Koenig understood the distinction, and wondered anew what these guests wanted. "You will wish to discuss your business," he suggested.

"Yes, indeed," Quenten agreed. "Though I understand there might be a matter I could help you with. If I surmise correctly, something to do with unfortunate events of this night past?"

Malachi met his Father's gaze, the gesture giving him permission to speak. He gave the alien guests a terse report of the assassination attempt and the capture of the two aliens.

"Assassins!" Quenten exclaimed. "Centurion Bellus would be most interested to see these men you caught."

"High Minister Koenig, I am indeed interested in those you captured. They are still alive?"

"Last I saw, they were unconscious, but alive," Koenig confirmed, delighted in this outcome.

Bellus seemed excited. "Paid assassins usually have a means of killing themselves if captured. They usually choose not to be interrogated."

"It would have suited me if they had," Koenig said truthfully. "Do you have a means to make them talk? I would like to know who sent them."

"Naturally you would," Quenten agreed. "However, I don't hold out any hope. Few of these vile creatures talk and those few knew only their target, and nothing of the originator of their mission. Centurion Bellus, my business may wait until you have dealt with these criminals."

The centurion bowed. "High Minister, do you wish to be present while they are interrogated?"

Koenig shuddered. "No, I only wish to know their answers." He did gesture to Malachi to go with the two centurions.

Ambassador Quenten waited with Koenig, exchanging polite conversation until they both became aware of a disturbance. Kumatan guards opened the door of the room where Koenig and Quenten waited. The dark clad assassins, with their alien features exposed, were being held by the Centurions. Their frenzied struggles were of no avail.

"Ambassador, these are from the assassin's guild, without doubt. Could we have permission to land our shuttle in the grounds here? I have no wish to risk these escaping."

Koenig agreed quickly, shivering at the sight of the two assassins, now he could see them clearly. He listened as Bellus's fellow centurion took out a small metal device and spoke into it.

"Are these two listed in our data base?" Quenten asked Bellus.

"Do you wish me to check now, Sir?"

"If you would," Quenten directed.

This time, Bellus took out a device whilst still holding his prisoner, and held it to the prisoner's hand. The man jerked and intensified his attempts to get free.

Bellus ignored his prisoner's terrified struggles and studied a bright area on his device. He tossed the device to his companion, who repeated the procedure on the other prisoner. The other centurion made a report, speaking in an alien language. Bellus added words of his own.

"High Minister, we are in your debt. The Enforcers have been trying to capture these men for a long time," Quenten told Koenig.

A loud sound from outside heralded the arrival of the Enforcer's shuttle. Koenig followed the centurions outside and was fascinated by the small spacecraft. This was nothing like the fire spewing trader ships.

"We will secure them on our ship and return," Bellus promised.

Koenig waited for the shuttle to lift off and slip into upward flight, before returning inside.

Auglan woke late the following day and was annoyed that he had. He listened, but all within his room was quiet. Very little sound ever came in from the passage. Pushing aside the bed coverings, he walked to the partly opened window and looked out. What activity he could see seemed normal and unhurried. He watched for a while before deciding to ring for a servant to bring him food.

As he turned around, he caught sight of an object on the table next to the bed. He felt himself go pale and shaky. He recognised the object as a garrotte, and it was stained with red blood. As a message, it told him that his hired assassins had been in his room while he slept. Was this a token of a job completed? If so, why? It was more of a warning. The usual token was an iridescent disk.

He was suddenly no longer hungry. He returned to his bed and cowered under the covers. He roused from his unpleasant thoughts on hearing a shuttle land.

Hoping to see a Galactic Council shuttle, he moved quickly from the bed, and was rewarded. He began to chuckle with undisguised glee until he saw the two Galactic Council Enforcers dragging two struggling black-clad figures towards the shuttle.

He saw the strutting fool, Koenig, walking with a man in Ambassadorial black, and the high fool's offspring forming a guard around him.

Auglan felt a shiver of terror. If Koenig was still alive, and the assassins had been captured, who had left the garrotte in his room? He spun around, intending to take the garrotte and destroy it. It was gone!

He cursed. "There must be another assassin, still free," he babbled to himself. "Do they blame me for their failure? No! They couldn't know it was he who ordered the killing…they didn't …"

Hidden from the Selkrit's sight by a trick of Atapi sorcery, the unseen servant smiled at the effect of her trick. This arrogant alien was guilty. That was clear enough. Now he would be looking over his shoulder, fearing the third assassin would be coming after him. No one would be able to tell him otherwise. No one but Atapi knew that third assassin had died before being able to free his fellows, and his remains would never be found.

Kaer gratefully slipped away when his father dismissed Caseon, Debenen and himself. He wished he could get more sleep, but he knew that wouldn't be possible. As soon as his father finished talking to the new Galactic representative, if not before, Koenig would send for him to explain his report. Despite that, he went back to his suite, and closed himself in his office room to think.

Aniki saw him and slipped in with a drink for him. He rose and came to embrace her, finding comfort in her nearness.

"Teresa told us that your father dismissed Farcine," Aniki said. "What could she have done that he disproved of?"

Kaer drew his wife to the couch and had her sit next to him. "As I see it, she did nothing wrong, except tell him the truth." Kaer tried not to sound critical of his father.

"What truth?" Aniki asked, bewildered.

"That she is Atapi," Kaer said quietly. He felt Aniki tense in his embrace.

"Dear one, would I allow her here if I thought she would harm us?" Kaer reassured her. "She has served us well and Mikha is learning respect for us."

Aniki shivered. "I was taught to think of them as barbarians, but she has taught me so much. She is like my esteemed grandmother. Is it all wrong?"

"Does it feel wrong?" Kaer asked gently.

"No," Aniki admitted. "I really like her. So does Ellhi. Does that mean Teresa is Atapi too? And must she go as well?"

Kaer kissed the top of Aniki's head. "Yes, she is Atapi but Father is not aware of her," Kaer said carefully.

"Will he be angry with you?" Aniki asked, worried for him.

Kaer shrugged, indifferently. He didn't want to consider that, or say anything that might be implied as criticism of his father. Aniki was still in awe of her father-in-law.

"Warn Teresa to be discreet. It would be better for her to stay mostly in the suite," Kaer advised.

"I wouldn't want to lose her," Aniki said bravely.

Kaer sensed the fear she was trying to hide. "I trust Jai Cassidy. She will never be like the devil-sorcerers in the stories, and her tribe will follow her direction."

Kaer thought he had mentally prepared himself to face his father. When the expected summons came, he answered without delay. It was not because he was eager to finish his report, but so as not to anger his father further. He knocked on the High Minister's office door, and heard Caseon invite him in.

From his brother's guarded expression, he guessed his father was already angry about something.

"Go in, he's waiting for you," Caseon gestured.

Kaer moved to the inner door and pushed it open.

"What has happened, Father?" he asked, full of concern once he saw his father's flushed face. He didn't want his father to have another seizure.

Koenig looked to be considering what he was going to say.

"You might as well know," Koenig growled. "You are indirectly involved already. I have been served with a 'notice of investigation'. Even though I have never thought it necessary to be part of the Galactic Council – they gave themselves the arrogant right to come here and tell me how I should rule this world."

"Surely if you are not part of that, they have no say…" Kaer began to object.

Koenig took a mouthful of ruby wine and savoured it a full minute before answering.

"I have been told that I, personally, have been accused of deliberately breaking trust with the Selkrit by not ensuring the Atapi are controlled. It is my fault, they say, that the massacres of the Selkrit occurred."

Kaer protested. "You are not responsible for the actions of the Atapi, especially when the Selkrit went where we did not authorise. Are they trying to tell us to exterminate the Atapi like vermin?"

Koenig growled. "You have obviously developed a soft spot for them, but no, they did not go that far. Instead, they have given me a list of matters they wish to look into, as impartial investigators. I must follow their procedures or face financial penalties." He waved off the rest of the explanation. "The Ambassador and his two Enforcer guards have gone off to talk to Auglan. And I have sent Malachi off with Eamon to talk to our law-defenders. I insisted that this Ambassador discusses the Nuath with the Elder Councillors. At least the man agreed to the need to understand our philosophy."

"That is a point in their favour," Kaer ventured. "I have heard they aim to be fair and impartial."

"And I wish the Atapi to hell and damnation," Koenig exploded.

Kaer wished his uncle was there to counsel his father. He feared his father's mind was under too much stress. If he could not keep himself calm, the Council might move to remove him from office. He didn't want that, because it would mean that his ever cheerful oldest brother would become High Minister, and Malachi was not all that much older than he was himself. They needed someone with years of experience to see Korvu through this matter.

Koenig finally took his attention back to Kaer's report.

"And it did not help me, to read here, that you had four sorcerers in your grasp and they got away."

"Father, they were already gone before I was summoned." Kaer forced himself to stay calm.

"And why were you called?" Koenig demanded.

"Read my report, Father. It is all in there."

Kaer hoped his father's mood would improve when he knew that Jai Cassidy was secluded in the special shielded room in the palace. He had doubts, though, about whether Jai Cassidy would be better off.

CHAPTER 32 – Jai Cassidy – POV

I awoke to silence and the sense that I was missing a part of me. Before opening my eyes, I tried to sense where I was. My last memory was of the holding room in the guard citadel in some town, and Jenha removing the restraints the other Traeger had put on me. Yes, I was able to move a little. I opened one eye and studied the room. I was no longer in that primitive holding room. This room had walls that looked padded. I guessed, if I spoke, the walls would swallow my voice.

A figure, a Kumatan guard judging by his bluish grey coveralls and aimed weapon, came and stood over me. He must have seen my slight movements, but I had not sensed him until then.

"Awake?"

I didn't try to answer. I felt like I had no energy at all.

The man grunted, and then went on to say, "You won't be able to try any tricks in here, you little freak. Nor can your Atapi friends help you. And if you think a little runt like you can take me on – you will be immobilised before you reach me."

"Bastard," I thought weakly, and then I turned my face from him and my attention inward to see how I was healing.

Not fast enough I realised, and only then translated the guard's words. I couldn't try any tricks in here. What he meant was that this room was so heavily shielded that I was completely cut off from the aura – and without that, I could not heal. I moved my hand, relieved to still feel Larcia's sword, hidden under an illusion. I didn't feel the energy buzzing in it, and for a moment feared that the room sucked all the life energy from within it.

Then I decided it wasn't that. What healing I had done whilst in this room had used that stored energy, and now that store was almost depleted. I was still far from functional and, from the state of my throat, still unable to eat – which was the only other way I knew to restore my energy. Without even a trickle of energy, I would die – simply because just breathing required energy.

I didn't want to die, and whilst my mind spun in helpless circles of denial and anger, part of it recalled a ritual that might help. I forced my mind to calm. Three times I spoke the words, and imaged the actions that were supposedly needed. It didn't seem to be working until I noticed my eyesight greying out, and my breathing and heartbeat slowing. I felt like I was hovering on the brink of death, and I could have chosen to step over that metaphysical line. However, I was too angry to let everyone off that easy, and too stubborn to give in – or give up.

In that strange hovering place, I wasn't really asleep and the pain in my body was a far off thing. My mind wandered, but no further than the walls of the room. I could see that my body lay on a bed of some kind, and two guards sat at a makeshift table playing cards. Each glanced frequently in my direction, but were otherwise intent on their game.

After a while, the guards changed.

"Woke up for a bit," one of the card players reported. "Just for a minute or two."

One of the new guards approached my body and studied it. He had a weapon ready in one hand, but he reached out gingerly with the other as if he thought I might suddenly jump on him. He touched my chest, and when that got no reaction, he placed the palm of his hand there for a while before moving it to my mouth to feel if I was breathing.

"Get a healer here," that one ordered. "I don't think your prisoner is breathing, and I wouldn't want to be in your shoes if she is dead."

The fuss would have been amusing if I had the energy to care. The first healer to arrive tried jolting me back to awareness with a device that sent a shock through me. My body simply absorbed the energy like it was water poured on dry sand. The healer felt my chest.

"I felt a beat," I heard him say. I wondered why they were so frantic to have me alive.

The healer jolted me again, and my mind seemed to be being pulled back into my body. I resisted that, and sent the energy into the worst of my injuries.

Something of this must have been obvious to the healer. "This woman's burns are healing before my eyes." A guard came over and looked where the healer was looking.

The healer demanded, "Get a Traeger here immediately."

"What's the big deal?" one of the now off-duty guards asked, as his duty partner raced off to obey the request. "This room is supposed to stop a full-sized Atapi sorcerer. What chance does this runt have to do anything?"

The healer didn't answer him. He was feeling my chest again, and let out a breath when he felt the series of long spaced heartbeats.

Jenha led the Traeger into the room. From the way his chest heaved, he had sprinted to get here. He pushed the healer aside and made his own examination. He even pushed up my eyelids and looked at my eyes. I felt the tension in his touch ease off.

"She is alive," he announced. "Barely. I want warmed blankets in here and four braziers with coal fires."

He spoke with all the authority of his previous position, and was like the Jenha I had first met.

I should have been prepared for his next move. He placed a hand on my forehead and I began to feel his mind. "Jai Cassidy, you WILL come back to your body!"

I resisted. I couldn't seem to remember why I didn't want to be in my body, yet in his touch I felt him sending his own energy into me and with it that familiar craving I had for him.

"You're not playing fair," my mind tried to yell at him. I felt a mental slap, and I forced my mind back into the scene of the room, where warm blankets were being piled on me. I could not feel my body, or the warmth.

"What is wrong with her?" Traeger Fosbok asked. "What sorcerer's trick is she using?"

"Not a sorcerer's trick," Jenha corrected. "No sorcerer would put himself in such a helpless position. This is probably one of her human tricks. Atapi, when wounded, heal much faster than we do. In most, it is a passive process, but some can draw on the aura to speed up the process. Jai Cassidy can do that normally."

"So why isn't she? Or is she tricking us?" Fosbok demanded.

"She cannot, because this room is totally shielded from the aura of Korvu," Jenha pointed out, though Fosbok should have thought of it.

"I know that!" Fosbok snapped. "So sorcerers can't use their sorcery to escape."

"Well, Jai Cassidy is well on the way to escaping into death," Jenha said flatly. "I was told that Petri had her on his horse when they were struck by lightning. Do you know how he is doing?"

Fosbok admitted. "I have not heard how he is since I returned late last night."

The healer spoke up. "He is seriously ill, and lucky to be alive."

"He is alive because Jai Cassidy protected him from the worst of the burns, and grounded most of the power in the lightning. She used energy she could have used to heal herself, to save Petri's life," Jenha explained.

"Why didn't she heal herself too?" Fosbok countered.

"Because she was immobilised before she could," Jenha spoke carefully, without accusing anyone. "Since then, she has not been close to the aura or able to draw on it."

"We have been doing everything here to keep her healing," Fosbok challenged. "I was told she woke briefly during the last watch."

"It hasn't been enough," Jenha stated. "If she can't eat or use the aura, what energy she has is needed for breathing. I think she has slowed her breathing and heart rate to conserve energy. Any reserve she had is depleted, but if she keeps this up, she will die from being too cold."

I understood then the reason for the hot blankets and the ambient heat, and realised that my mind was being affected by the state of my body. Heat, I realised, was energy – different from the aura. If it was in touch with me I was able to absorb it, but not if my mind was… elsewhere.

The braziers were brought in and lit – the air in that room became very hot. The guards moved to the open door where they could feel the cooler air from the passage. The healer checked me again and seemed relieved that my heart rate and breathing were returning to normal. Then he felt the blankets. "The blankets are icy cold."

"More hot blankets," Jenha ordered.

The guard nearest the door was only too pleased for an errand out in the cooler air.

Once more, Jenha touched me. My mind tried to skitter away from his. He was chanting something, and I felt myself being dragged remorselessly back into my body.

It wasn't fair! Jenha was using Traeger tricks on me – ones like he had used to tame the wild child I had been, and ones I still did not know how to counter. Why did he insist that I come back to where I would be worse than a caged bird?

He sensed the thought and once again, he mentally slapped my mind to get my attention. Then he spoke aloud, "Because, Jai Cassidy, you haven't finished what you started!"

"Mosellan! You forget your place!" A voice of implacable authority made everyone tense up.

The man who strode into the room was dressed in rich fabrics of purple and white. He looked around, noticing everything. "What is the meaning of this? Fosbok, did you authorise all this?"

"I authorised it," Jenha admitted calmly. I felt him sending energy into me, and also sensed the tight control he had on his mind. I realised that I must be very close to my body.

"You have no authority, Mosellan!" the man said coldly. I decided I disliked him intensely. "Step away from her, now!"

Jenha obeyed, his head held high but the man glared at him as if he had done something unforgivable.

"Healer, what is happening here?"

From the deep bow the healer gave the obnoxious man, I deduced he was someone important. He reported to the newcomer how he had found me, how the jolts had started my burns healing, and how the heat was bringing my life signs back to normal.

"I want to see this for myself," the man demanded.

"Yes, High Minister," the healer agreed. He came and lifted the blankets from me, and pulled aside the light clothing I now had on.

"What's this?" the High Minister demanded, pointing to the sword lying next to me. He reached out to take it, and Jenha moved forward and spoke, "Don't, High Minister!"

"Silence!" Koenig roared, and Jenha stepped back.

Koenig took the dull grey metal blade from my side and immediately felt the heat drawn from his hands. He dropped it. He gave Jenha a withering stare, but the former Traeger met his gaze without any sign of apology or guilt.

"That artefact enabled this hybrid to escape. Are you intending to allow her to repeat the action, Mosellan?"

"No, High Minister," Jenha answered, staring back at Koenig.

I sensed this High Minister person was angry at Jenha, but I could not see why.

"Were you aware of the sword, Fosbok?" Koenig demanded.

"No, High Minister. Subni-traeger Mosellan knew what needed to be done."

"I see…" Koenig said, not thoughtfully, but with deliberation.

Another voice drew my attention to the doorway.

"Father, the artefact is normally hidden by an illusion or some kind of invisibility ritual. It only glowed when Jai touched it," Kaer said stiffly from over there.

Koenig shot Kaer a venomous look, and looked back to Fosbok. "Are you capable of neutralising this object, Fosbok?"

The Traeger chanted softly and reached for the sword that had fallen back to where it had been.

"Protect your hands," Jenha advised.

"Mosellan, will you be silent? I have had more than enough of your lack of respect," Koenig warned.

Fosbok took Jenha's advice and took the sword with his hand swathed in a cloth he took from his pocket. It gave several flickers of glowing energy that drew everyone's eyes, and returned to dull grey.

In that moment, when no eyes were on me, I was suddenly jolted back into my body, and I was staring up at the ceiling. Something felt wrong, and I realised it was that my connection to Larcia through the sword was gone.

I tried to reach out to get the sword back, but I had no energy.

"Take that artefact and put it in a secured, shielded safe-box," Koenig directed Fosbok. "Two guards, go with him."

"No," I tried to say, but all I managed was a croak just loud enough to attract the attention of the one I now knew to be the High Minister. I didn't need empathy to sense that he hated me.

"Healer, do we need all this anymore?" Koenig asked, sounding perfectly reasonable now.

"High Minister, the heat has helped my patient. She was almost dead."

"I doubt that," Koenig contested briskly. "Douse those braziers. This hybrid is more dangerous than a sorcerer. I have no doubt it was tricking all of you in an attempt to escape."

"High Minister, the injuries were not faked," the healer protested.

"Irrelevant, Atapi heal quickly." Koenig countered. "Jai Cassidy is conscious, able to speak, and if she chooses not to eat or drink you are to ensure she does. I intend to have her questioned, and for that, she is almost well enough. There is no need to hurry the rest of the healing, or she will simply find a way to escape. I suggest, Mosellan, you apply restraints to this hybrid before she causes more harm."

Jenha seemed wooden as he obeyed. His eyes did not meet mine, and his mind was shielded. I wanted to wipe the face of the High Minister with my fists for his treatment of him.

I think Jenha sensed my resentful reaction, or saw my fists trying to clench. The look he gave me was reminiscent of our first clash of wills. It seemed to say, 'don't worry about me, consider yourself.'

I looked away, still full of resentment.

The High Minister thought he had won. He ordered the guards to clear all non-essential equipment from the room and stay out in the passage, told the healer to ensure I had nourishment, and turned his back on me in a gesture of considering me a threat no longer.

Only Jenha and Kaer remained in the room with the High Minister and myself. I understood why Kaer had been so quiet and remote when the High Minister addressed him. "Kaer, take Mosellan to the Training Master. Tell him I have authorised level two physical chastisement – for showing disrespect to me, disobeying instructions, disregarding vowed promises and attempting rituals for which he was not authorised."

"Father," Kaer protested. "He did what was required to heal Jai Cassidy enough to answer questions."

"Be thankful that I do not authorise the same for you, Kaer," Koenig warned. "You will go and present yourself to the Chief Counsellor and request a room for solitary meditation – I think a full day will enable you to re-find yourself. Advise the Training Master that Mosellan will benefit from a similar period of solitary meditation. Go!"

"Bastard," I said distinctly.

The High Minister turned back to me. "I could order a similar lesson for you, hybrid. You have caused too much trouble already."

Koenig turned and strode from the room.

With the target of my anger out of sight, I tried to force myself to be calm. That was a mistake, because I then began to feel anew all the banished pain, and I was too weak to damp it again.

The bastard of a High Minister need not fear that I might escape right now, because I couldn't – but I would, I vowed. I owed him nothing.

When I let myself think of how he had treated Jenha, my eyes filled with tears. Even Kaer didn't deserve his censure. The worst thing was it was probably my fault, and Jenha had reminded me that I hadn't finished what I had started. I would have to escape, and when I did, Kaer and Jenha would probably be blamed. And I would be hunted like a criminal.

I feebly banged my fist on the bed, and felt the metal of the band around my wrist. I cursed creatively in Earth English. These bands were not like the slave bands that the Atapi had put on me, and I did not know how these ones worked. I banged my fist again, and this time I heard a faint clank. I repeated the action to be sure and this time I felt around for the cause.

My palm closed around a smooth pebble and I didn't have to look at it to know what it was. The feeling of missing something vanished and I felt the aura passively filling me, healing me.

The healer returned later with food for me. He asked me if I could eat soup. I considered my throat, and although the swelling had gone down, I wasn't sure I could swallow.

"Could you help me sit up?" I asked quietly and politely.

"You will have to do it yourself," he told me, but not without sympathy. "I am not allowed to help you."

I thought it was more likely that he didn't dare feed me like a baby in case I snapped at him like an alligator.

"I can't do it by myself," I admitted, resigned.

The healer had what he needed to force feed me, and I really didn't think he wished me ill. He did his job with gentle efficiency, and I endured the indignity of having a tube forced down my throat, the soup forced down the tube to my stomach. When the healer left, I couldn't stop the tears.

If those damn sorcerers could see me now, they'd laugh themselves to death. I could hope!

Kaer did not have to stay once he had passed on Koenig's order to the Training Master. He noticed that the old Traeger stiffened at the order, and hoped his own face had stayed impassive. Many decades of obedience to the Kimh, and to the High Minister, made the bow automatic. The Training Master turned to give directions to two other trainers.

Outwardly, Jenha looked calm, but Kaer sensed that was far from the truth. At this moment, he wondered how the former Traeger managed it. His own anger at his father's injustice was like a simmering volcano. True, Jenha had betrayed disrespect for the High Minister, but he had been strongly provoked.

The instructors took charge of Jenha and led him to the assembly area, where he was told to disrobe and kneel on the ground. Only then did Kaer recall that the punishment for Traegers in training was normally witnessed by all. That would be a further humiliation for one who did not deserve it. It was just as well that the High Minister, who ordered this, felt himself above needing to see the order carried out.

Kaer saw the instructors preparing to inflict the chastisement and realised they were deliberately ignoring tradition. He had no intention of calling attention to their tacit disobedience, or those venerable old Kumatan would in turn be punished.

He forced himself to watch, to be there as moral support. He felt himself twitch as each stroke of the cane lashed the kneeling man. Jenha made no sound, though his face contorted with the pain. At the end of twenty strokes, Jenha did not move – could not move. Kaer strode over to him, arriving before the instructors who would normally take the chastised to a place for solitary reflection.

"My Lord, let us tend him," one bowed and insisted.

"No, I will tend him," Kaer said firmly. He did let one of the instructor's support Jenha's other side and help him to his feet.

They walked slowly to the cubicles set aside for solitary meditation. In the one they entered, a bowl of water and a towel waited on a wooden table. Kaer and the instructor helped Jenha to a low pallet, and without their support, he collapsed back to his knees. Kaer went and brought the water closer and began to sponge Jenha's back.

"This is not your task, Kaer," Jenha said very softly. "You do not have to do this."

Kaer knew he meant that it was not fit that a member of the Kimh show concern for one of lower rank. He said nothing, because he couldn't guarantee that his voice would not betray him. Jenha sighed at his persistence, wincing involuntarily.

"Your father is under a lot of stress," Jenha said, still softly.

"That is not an acceptable reason," Kaer said in a sharp undertone.

"No," Jenha said with a sigh. "Thank you for your kindness."

If the instructors wondered at his unexpected actions, they said nothing as Kaer left to present himself to the Elder Counsellor. When he arrived, it was apparent that he was expected. The expression on the Elder's face was of disapproval. His delay in arriving had been noted, but he didn't care. Nor did he care if they sensed his anger as he went into the room they assigned him.

Even the room added to his anger. It had a carpeted floor, thick curtains to block out light and drafts from outside, a comfortable chair and a proper bed. All Jenha had been allowed was a hard mattress on the bare wood floor, a hard wooden chair and nothing to stop anyone passing from seeing into the room.

Oh, this room was austere by Kimh standards, but it was more comfortable than what Jenha must endure. It was just as well that the Elder Counsellor did not speak to him – Kaer felt himself almost bereft of ordinary politeness. On the table in his room were wine, water, bread and cheese. Jenha had only water and dry biscuits.

Kaer had never really appreciated the difference between the Kimh and their servers, the Kumatan. In his mind now was the belief that Jenha Mosellan was more worthy of respect than his own father and that notion would not be considered anything other than aberrant. As his father and as High Minister – Kaer owed his father respect.

He vaguely heard the door close behind him, but he simply stood inside the door and stared at the floor. His door would not be locked, but he knew that would not be true of Jenha's.

So many thoughts went through his head, building to the pile of injustices he had accepted until now. Every one of them was forcing its way to his attention. Petty things like how his brother, Malachi, had looked at him with a mixture of pity and contempt. Resentment at being publically and forcefully reminded of his duty, and to be told to control himself, or have control enforced. As Kimh, no one should treat him that way – but his father had.

His father was surely borderline irrational, and no one seemed to be aware of it. Oh, he was saying the right things, but not doing them. He was saying one thing and meaning another. Kaer recalled the times when he had held his tongue, not daring to provoke his father. Finally it had been too much. Years of obedience to his elders – and now this. From now on, the Counsellors would be watching him, and would intervene at the slightest hint of unacceptable behaviour. His judgement, his objectivity, his loyalty would always be in question.

"Auglan is a most ungrateful guest," Koenig remarked frankly to his brother in a private conversation in his office. "We have offered him a free and luxurious place to stay, and the same for his people. He will not lose out in the benefits due for the task. So what is his hurry? We will deal with the Atapi and all will be well."

Eamon sighed. The medicines from the healers were effective in calming his brother, but Koenig was forgetting important points. Fortunately, the Galactic Ambassador was happy to collect reports and views from all relevant sources and was off doing that. He had accepted that the stress reaction Koenig had displayed was the result of the attempted assassination.

"Let us not forget that his people went into areas we did not sanction," Eamon reminded his brother.

Koenig waved that aside. "My understanding of the Ambassador's words is that he does not sanction races that commit such atrocities as Auglan showed us. The perpetrators of such actions are arrested, tried in the Galactic Court, and exiled to a world where they cannot continue such acts. It is more civilised than just executing them."

Eamon thought to himself that the Kimh Council must debate that option before granting the Enforcers permission to move on the Atapi. He felt disquiet about letting off-worlders have free run on Korvu, just as various reports of Selkrit activities bothered him. He could not justify his vague concerns. Auglan and his people seemed to be adhering to the agreement and being innocent victims of the Atapi.

Malachi announced himself and entered his father's private rooms.

"Father, I am to advise you that Ambassador Quenten has accepted the invitation to discuss the Nuath with our Elder Counsellors and Centurion Bellus requests permission to interview Jai Cassidy."

Eamon noticed how the mere mention of the hybrid's name, shattered the effect of Koenig's medicine.

"Advise him that I require to be present when he sees the hybrid, as will a Traeger, and it will depend on the healer's report."

Koenig sounded like himself, but Eamon felt disquiet. "When you have done that, Malachi, talk to the healer and find out when he will allow questions. I will advise the Centurion of a time when I have that information."

Malachi departed and sometime later, a servant brought in a written request from Centurion Bellus, for an audience with the High Minister. Koenig read it and scribbled an affirmative, but made no movement to leave his chair.

"It would be better for you to receive him in your office," Eamon suggested.

"Very well," Koenig agreed, as if his mind needed telling what to do.

Eamon instructed the servant to return to the Centurion. He advised him that the High Minister would see him shortly, and to have the man wait in the anteroom to the High Minister's office.

Something prodded my shoulder and I awoke immediately. I had automatically tensed, ready to react, but I could still not move.

"The healer tells us you are able to speak," the man spoke to me. He was obviously a Traeger from the quality of his clothes.

"So?" I responded, not caring to be polite.

"High Minister Koenig and Centurion Bellus have questions for you."

"So?" I repeated. I had no idea who the second person was.

The Traeger looked away from me. "Healer, is this prisoner able to sit up?"

"Only for short periods, Traeger Solomon," the healer advised. "However, I can place a slanted board behind her to raise her for a short time."

"Do so!" another voice barked impatiently.

The healer was gentle – he no longer saw me as a threat and, to him, I wasn't. In turn, I was glad to be able to see the people who had entered.

Him! So that man was the High Minister – the one that had humiliated Jenha and Kaer. The being standing beside him looked to be a completely different species to any I had seen before. He had an odd cast to his features – most notably the eyebrows slanting up from centre of his forehead. He also had short black hair and a narrow moustache. He wore a black suit that clung to his body, shiny black boots that came to just below the knee, gauntlets and gloves in the same shiny substance, and carried a black helmet that would cover his whole head. Around his waist was a utility harness with pouches, and places for weapons.

"What are you?" I asked, looking at this stranger. I was curious and, since I had not met him before, not hostile. My hostility was being reserved for Koenig, who looked insulted by my ignoring him. Well, I didn't owe him anything – he didn't rule me.

The man in black inclined his head and announced, "I am Centurion Bellus, Lead Enforcer of the Orlek Federation and representative of the Galactic Federation." He walked to within polite conversational distance, but far enough away to seem unthreatening. His voice seemed odd, almost like it was a recording, but it took me a while to realise that I was hearing him in Earth English.

"I have no idea what you are talking about," I replied in my own language, as a test to see if the understanding went both ways.

"We are investigating a complaint regarding the Atapi," the Centurion went on, not explaining what right he had to ask about such things, "in regard to their massacre of Selkrit citizens."

He was trying to blame the Atapi for something, I understood, and I wondered if this was Koenig's idea. What were Selkrit citizens?

The Centurion went on. "You were identified at the site of one such atrocity. You are required to answer questions."

"And if I don't?" I asked mildly, sounding this stranger out.

"It is required," Bellus stated formally.

"Why you?" I asked. I'd figured the Selkrit must be the blue-blooded aliens, but why was this other kind of alien on Korvu.

"We are enforcers of peace, truth and Galactic Law," Bellus told me.

More damn idealists, I thought sourly.

"No," I said then. If Koenig was using these enforcers to get at the Atapi, I wasn't buying it.

"I did warn you that this human would be unco-operative," Koenig said evenly, but his face was trying not to smile in anticipation. "Traeger Solomon, would you invoke…"

"No need, High Minister," Bellus interrupted, supremely confident. He walked right up to me and lifted my hand.

I tried to pull it away, but all my strength energy was directed at healing myself internally. He must have felt my muscles trembling from weakness. His fingers forced mine to open from around the stone Jenha had slipped to me. I wondered if he felt the energy in it. He closed my fingers back around it, and then withdrew a short metallic tube. He held it to the top of my wrist and I felt a prick, like an injection.

"What was that for?" I demanded, as he released me.

My question was ignored as the Enforcer drew a flattish metallic box out of a pouch at his waist. When he inserted the tube into one end, the top of the box began to glow. He studied this.

"This one has no match on our data base," he said in Kumatan, glancing at Koenig. I had no idea what he meant.

"Of course not," Koenig said impatiently. "This hybrid came from Earth. I was told that world was still closed. You would have had no reason to go there."

"Ah, yes." Bellus seemed to recall something. "That was where that heinous devil-sorcerer fled. I heard that problem was successfully resolved. That was impressive, High Minister. I believe that the human population was never aware of your intrusion. I would like to meet the

Traeger who managed that. He would be valuable in understanding this child.”

I saw the flush of deep purple rising in Koenig’s cheeks, and that made me more favourably inclined towards the Centurion.

“Jenha Mosellan is involved with other important matters,” Koenig advised, stiffly.

“Later then,” Bellus agreed amiably. “As I think it would be better to wait until this child has recovered further before questioning her.”

I glanced at Koenig and caught his look of annoyance. He made no comment, and that made me wonder if the Centurion had power to overrule the leader of Korvu.

Centurion Bellus turned his attention back to me, and spoke again in English. I wondered at how he could speak English if his kind had never been there.

“Child, refusing to answer the questions of a Galactic Enforcer is not an option. We are authorised to use whatever method is necessary to obtain the truth. If you have done nothing wrong, you have nothing to fear from us.”

“I don’t believe that,” I said, seeing a flaw in his statement. “I don’t think I have done anything wrong, but they,” I nodded at Koenig, “think I have.”

Bellus nodded. “Be assured, child, we endeavour to learn the full facts, with and without emotional and cultural colouration and prejudice.”

I looked at him and challenged, “Who gives you the right to interfere with other worlds’ peoples?” What I really wanted to decide was whether I could get him on my side.

“Galactic Law allows intervention when the people of one world interfere with those of another in an unacceptable way. You could ask us to intercede for you if you wish to return to Earth.”

That was an unexpected thought, and I glanced at Koenig again, but as Bellus was speaking in English, the High Minister was only looking mildly annoyed.

I looked back at the Centurion, and after a moment’s consideration, told him, “No, I don’t want to go back.”

There was a faint change in the Centurion’s expression and I guess my answer might have surprised him. I had answered him in English, but now switched back to Kumatan. “I want to be left alone.”

Bellus spoke again in English, allowing us a private conversation. “You are reconciled to this prison?”

"No, but being here has a useful side effect," I told him.

"Protection whilst you heal," Bellus suggested intuitively.

"Yeah!" I admitted, then dared to ask, "Are you really talking to everybody?"

"Yes, that is what we must do."

"What have you heard about me?" I asked, and wondered if he would tell me.

He consented to answer, and I heard pretty much what I expected. I was a wild, unpredictable and dangerous being.

"Are you?" Bellus challenged me.

"Only if these well-meaning, closed-minded idealists try to stop me doing what I must do," I issued a warning of my own. "I don't want to tell that bastard High Minister anything. He dislikes me for no good reason, and he won't listen to me or try to understand me."

"Have you any advocates here?" Bellus asked in English.

"Yes, his son Kaer, and Jenha Mosellan – except he is having both of them punished for helping me."

Bellus nodded, and switched back to Kumatan. "I will be back to speak to you. Remember and consider we will have the truth."

I turned and stared at the wall until my guests had gone, and tried to hide under the coverings when the medic lowered me again. Very soon, I would have to get out of this shielded prison – but I would have to do it in a way that wouldn't have my only friends punished again.

As my guests left, Koenig was demanding a translation of what Bellus and I had said in English. None of his business, I thought, and was amused when Bellus only said he was enforcing the lesson of answering questions.

He had done that, not so much in words, but merely by the way Koenig had subsided around him. Yet, while I tentatively felt I could trust the Enforcer, I controlled a shiver. The Enforcer could easily walk over me if I resisted him.

CHAPTER 35 - Kaer and Jenha - POV

Exactly one day after Kaer had entered, the door to the cubicle was opened. The Elder Counsellor entered and looked around. He saw the water and wine was untouched, the bread dried on the plate, the bed unused, and the chair unoccupied.

Kaer, sitting on the floor with his back to the wall, watched him from his position between the bed and the wall. The Elder turned slowly, a frown on his face. His thoughts were clear – no Kimh would disobey his elders and walk out of enforced meditation.

Kaer wondered what they would have done if he had. He really didn't want to talk to the Elder, because even though the time to himself had been a boon, his mind was not settled.

"Lord Kaer, what are you doing sitting on the floor?" Torren rebuked him.

"My choice, Elder," Kaer said calmly. He did not add, "My father thinks me worthless."

No matter what he said, Kaer knew he was not yet free to go. He would still have to endure counselling, until the Elder satisfied himself of Kaer's mental equilibrium, and return to orthodox behaviour. He would be expected to reveal all his thoughts, and endure lectures on how he was wrong and how he must think in such circumstances.

Kaer had no intention of telling this inflexible elder what he was truly thinking. He would be sent into seclusion, not allowed contact with his family until his aberrant behaviour and thoughts were rectified. So he would pretend to be mortified that the danger to his father had caused his loss of control, and tell them all they wanted to hear. He'd hope they didn't suspect the alien ideas that Jai Cassidy had provoked in him – how she had made him see his world in a different way – and found his people lacking.

Tense, controlled and pale, Kaer met Jenha Mosellan as he, in turn, was released by the counsellors. For a brief moment, their eyes met, and Jenha betrayed surprise.

"How may I serve you, Lord Kaer?" Jenha asked respectfully, and his voice was calm and correctly modulated.

Contrasting himself with this supposed inferior, Kaer felt he was lacking something. "Walk with me," Kaer said tersely.

Jenha bowed correctly to his social superior and fell into step beside the younger man.

After moving away from the House of Contemplation, Kaer asked, "How can you be so calm?"

Jenha sensed that there were several levels to the simple question.

"I am not, always," Jenha said softly. "It is not easy to know a truth and be unable to act on it. One must sometimes be patient and let time reveal the truth to all."

"But how many people will be hurt, or die, while we wait?" Kaer asked, not quite pleadingly. "My father is not rational, but as High Minister, we must obey him without question."

"That is not precisely true," Jenha corrected gently. "Your father is not a dictator. He must still abide by the majority rule of the Council, and the Council does not act precipitously."

"That's true," Kaer agreed, some of his inner tension easing. "But how can I do my duty as advocate for Jai Cassidy if they only see her as Atapi and dangerous?"

"I know she is more than that," Jenha admitted, not presuming to speak for both of them. "I think your father was gifted with great wisdom when he insisted she be brought here, though I do not think he appreciates it."

"It is not her doing that the Atapi are rising against us and the alien visitors," Kaer insisted quietly.

"In part, it is," Jenha pointed out. "She intends to teach the Atapi a new way of thinking. Change will be no easier for them than it is for us. Old prejudices are difficult to change. We are a very sheltered people."

"I cannot see how she can succeed," Kaer admitted. "We might have brought her here to be killed."

"On her own world, she was well on the way to that fate anyway. I think I taught her a better way. She saw the need to change the Atapi, and I can only conceive it is because of lessons learnt by the people of Earth."

"You learnt from them, too," Kaer marvelled.

"Yes, I did. I can see the need for us to change and to be open to new and provocative ideas. Perhaps the new Traegers will share my view."

"Isn't that a dangerous course of action?" Kaer warned.

Jenha sidestepped the question. "The Nuath would have us embrace the differences in peoples from other worlds. Jai Cassidy and the people of Earth fit that qualification. But why would the Nuath preclude embracing the differences between the different races on our own world?"

"Why not indeed," Kaer considered. "Then why do all my elders detest the Atapi?"

"Because their minds are closed. They need to be stimulated by new experiences, as you have been…"

"By Jai Cassidy," Kaer felt a faint smile on his face.

"If you keep your mind open," Jenha felt he could advise, "you see the truth, and if you accept that the Nuath is a guide, the two can be reconciled."

Kaer felt that Jenha was hinting at something important, but he could not quite grasp what he meant.

"You of the Kimh see the Nuath one way – perhaps I see it differently," Jenha hinted further. "No doubt, if we teach her, Jai Cassidy would see it differently to both of us. We are guided by the experience of our elders, but new experiences of our own could let us see it anew. In such a way, young Traegers are trained. As we grow and experience more of life, we adjust how we react and understand various aspects of the Nuath."

"I understand," Kaer finally realised, and his residual tension and anger left him. "I do have a right to my own beliefs if I can integrate them into the Nuath."

Jenha said no more on that subject. Instead he suggested, "You have no need to escort me, Lord. And a need to reassure your family."

"If my father has not arbitrarily disrupted it," Kaer replied without thought.

"My Lord," Jenha murmured in a mildly warning tone.

Kaer began to recite a calming mantra in his mind. His newfound peace was still fragile. "Your point has been made, my friend."

"I am honoured," Jenha murmured.

"My new view of the Nuath tells me to accept offered wisdom, no matter the source," Kaer said, keeping his face neutral.

Before they parted company just outside the palace, a servant approached them.

"Lord Kaer, Subni-traeger Mosellan, you are requested to present yourselves to Lord Eamon immediately."

Kaer thanked the messenger and continued into the palace. He wondered what the summons meant and sincerely hoped it was not for a follow-up telling off from his father. He was so intent on that fear that he did not notice the black personal shuttle parked in the palace courtyard until Jenha subtly indicated it.

"The symbols on the shuttle indicate that it is a Galactic Federation shuttle. I would like to know their purpose here."

Kaer glanced up and saw what Jenha referred to. "So would I," he admitted freely. He wondered how his father was taking the presence of Galactic representatives and hoped he would be distracted from yesterday's matters.

Lord Eamon received them in the High Minister's office, and his expression was grave as he looked up at them from behind Koenig's desk. He was flanked by two black-clad humanoids. Jenha recognised the Galactic Federation insignia on the tabards worn by the strangers, though Kaer did not.

"Kaer, these beings are Centurion Bellus and Centurion Terr of the Galactic Federation Compliance Arm. They are here with Ambassador Quenten to investigate complaints from the Selkrit concerning the Atapi treatment of Selkrit citizens. We are required to co-operate with them in all ways possible."

Kaer nodded. "Lord Uncle, are you acting for my father?"

Eamon didn't claim that position. "The High Minister and Lord Malachi are with the Galactic Ambassador. However, under Galactic Law 17, sub-section 3, the ruling body of this world is suspended until the current investigation is completed. They have appointed me as interim administrator."

Kaer put aside his reaction to that and spoke to the Centurions. "How may I assist you?"

Centurion Bellus answered politely, "I would welcome the chance to discuss certain matters with you, in private. My sub-ordinate has questions for Subni-traeger Mosellan – also to be discussed in private."

Eamon responded to Kaer's glance, and provided the explanation, "They seek the truth, unbiased by emotion or history. I am sure you can help supply that."

Kaer felt he was being warned, and having come so recently from an intensive session of counselling, was afraid of speaking to anyone.

Jenha addressed the lower ranked Centurion. "I have been told never to fear telling what is truth. I will be pleased to assist you."

Kaer steadied, hearing Jenha's advice, but he was still unsure until his uncle rose and addressed the Centurions.

"You may use this office, Commander Bellus. I will show your colleague to a small room nearby that he may use."

Only then did Kaer realise the warning was actually well meant advice, and Eamon trusted him to speak fairly when not overseen.

Bellus tactfully did not presume to take the High Minister's seat. Instead he gestured Kaer to one of the other chairs and took one close by. He studied Koenig's youngest son for a time before speaking.

"I am told that your father ordered you to be punished for helping the Earth child," Bellus began and saw immediately that he had achieved a strong reaction.

Kaer, taught from a young age to be truthful, answered reluctantly. "There were other things besides that."

"Will you tell me?" Bellus encouraged.

"It is a subject I would rather not discuss," Kaer said truthfully. "Is there a need?"

"I would not ask without a reason," Bellus countered.

Taking a deep breath, Kaer said, "I permitted Atapi to be servants in the palace. One has served me well as nurse for my foster son, and two others served my father and foiled the assassins that tried to kill him. I also protested his decision to punish Jenha Mosellan in public."

Kaer wondered if this Enforcer would find his 'crimes' as heinous as his father had.

Bellus considered what he had heard in the context of his previous knowledge. "I can see how he might have felt betrayed for having Atapi here. I have heard they are no friends of your people. But I find it honourable to stand up for what you think is right."

"I dishonoured my father," Kaer told him.

"Are you resentful of his action?" Bellus asked.

"I have gone past that," Kaer said, feeling this session would be as bad as counselling.

"The Earth-child claims you as her advocate," Bellus provoked. "What can you tell me about her? What do you think of her?"

"About Jai Cassidy, I am ambivalent," Kaer admitted truthfully. "She is an influence disruptive to peace and serenity."

"So I surmise," Bellus agreed.

Kaer went on, "I was appointed to be her advocate when she was brought into our jurisdiction on Earth. As such, I try to be fair to her and to Korvu. She is not endeared to my kin because her human ways are unsettling and disruptive of peace. Nor is her idea of honour comprehensible to us. My elders expected obedience of her, and that is not a natural inclination for her – even amongst her human kin. She obeyed, as long as it suited her, and then she broke her promise to stay in our custody. But in her favour, she did so to bring back two Kumatan stuck in the human plane. She was correct in saying that it was better for her to go to get them than have a Traeger go. Also in her favour was the fact that she returned."

Kaer went on to speak of the effect Jai Cassidy was having on his people.

"Your father evinces strong reactions to her," Bellus suggested.

"I think he fears that she will become like her Atapi grandsire. He committed too many atrocities to be forgiven."

"And you?" Bellus probed.

"I believe that she is not like the Atapi we know," Kaer said. "Her tribe obey her, and they have served us well."

Bellus was silent for a time. "Your foster son is her child," Bellus stated.

"Yes," Kaer admitted.

"I think that shows her trust in you," Bellus approved.

"I believe she intended Jenha to raise him, as Mikha is also his son. But I was appointed the child's guardian, and I am supposed to ensure his Atapi blood never surfaces." Kaer volunteered this as a statement, not a criticism of his father's instructions.

Bellus turned his attention to other subjects and Kaer felt himself appreciate talking to such an uncritical audience. In turn, he was totally honest about his feelings, and separated what he knew personally from what he had only heard about.

It seemed that the Enforcer's main interest was in the events between Atapi and Selkrit, but Jai Cassidy was another sort of alien, and a provocative one.

"Do you think Jai Cassidy can effect a change in the Atapi?" Bellus asked after an hour of questions.

"I want to think so, but I am afraid for her. However, Jenha knows her best."

The first question Centurion Terr asked Jenha also concerned his mindset after being punished on the High Minister's order. He did so to establish any bias for or against any of the races involved in the affairs of Korvu.

"Even the strongest of us can be provoked beyond control," Jenha said calmly. "I did fail in my duty of respect to the High Minister, and to my promise of behaviour in my new position."

The Centurion withheld judgement on whether he agreed or not with the reason for the punishment. It was not his place to judge a culture, but to understand how people interacted in its context.

"What about your subservient position now you are back on your own world?"

"I am not so full of ambition that I am insulted," Jenha said serenely. "I was still not fully trained when I accompanied my father in pursuit of Stacion Ansuni. Then it was deemed acceptable for my father and a second Traeger to complete my training."

"I have heard that you achieved the downfall of that asocial creature – and maintained the innocence of the human people."

Jenha smiled wryly. "I cannot claim credit for Stacion's death."

"It is said that Jai Cassidy killed him," Terr stated.

"Yes, she was found with the knife, and was the instrument of his death, but I believe that some power used her, and that Stacion was so arrogant as to think her no threat."

"I will explore that idea with you later," Terr said. "Tell me about Jai Cassidy."

Jenha complied truthfully, omitting no pertinent detail, from the time he first met her, but stopping before mentioning his intimate relationship with her.

"It seems obvious that she had no love for the Atapi, nor they for her. Is that why you adopted her?" Terr asked.

"In part," Jenha admitted. "Part of my duty was to protect the humans from the Atapi."

"She is part Atapi," Terr stated, asking for confirmation.

"Yes, but she was raised as a human," Jenha pointed out.

"There was another reason?" Terr probed.

"Yes," Jenha admitted, reluctant to speak of something even to these strangers who would not repeat this conversation. "This is something I do not wish spread to my colleagues or superiors, but I took Jai Cassidy under my protection for the sake of a very brave woman, one who I considered a friend."

Haltingly at first, Jenha spoke of his friendship with Jai Ansuni and her brother Con Ansuni. He went on to tell how Jai Ansuni had gone with Stacion, and tried to limit his abhorrent rituals.

"She vowed that if Con could not kill him, she would. But she could not get close enough to him, and he was too well protected. On Earth, where he could not draw on the aura, he used the energy released during sexual acts and death and all kinds of perverted rituals, to add to his energy and power. Jai Ansuni would not touch that power, and could not call on the aura of that distant world, either. She only had her own innate energy and power. She had to flee from the Atapi place because Stacion realised what she intended. She chose to change, to bind herself into human form and have a child by a human. That child inherited her power and her potential, something Stacion never saw until Jai Cassidy used it against him. Jai Ansuni knew she would die birthing her child, but the child held all her hope. I think in the moment of dying, she sent her essence into an artefact she left for her child."

"I find it honourable," Terr said approvingly. "How do you reconcile your relationship with the Earth child, who is little older than your son?"

That was a question that the Kimh counsellors still discussed with him. Jenha tried to be honest and not care what this stranger thought. If Terr had heard enough of the people of Korvu, he would have learnt of the cross-species mating taboo. The Kimh abhorred the thought of mating with Atapi, but to him, Jai was not.

"I will not justify that with the reason that I was told to mate with her. That is the truth, but not all. I could not have done so if it were not for the fact that her mind and mine joined as well. I knew of that connection as soon as I had met her, but at first, she had to prove herself. And I would not have done so merely in the hope that I would engender a child, and she would die birthing it. I did not believe that would happen. I sincerely care for Jai Cassidy, but now, I am no longer able to acknowledge those feelings."

"Do you agree that your trust of Jai Cassidy is wrong?" Terr asked.

"No, she is honourable," Jenha said firmly. He realised that the Centurion was trying to provoke him, but it was impersonal – a means to understand him.

Finally, Terr spoke bluntly. "You become Traeger when your father died. Some here say you are not to be trusted because you do not hate all Atapi for what they did to your father."

Jenha had already decided that from the thrust of many counselling sessions. "I quite freely admit to hating Stacion Ansuni to a point just short of losing control," Jenha admitted, betraying a hint of that passion. "I was quite determined to finish off my father's work to destroy him. I did not, ever, hate all Atapi for Stacion's deeds, and I was willing to grant a second chance to any of his warriors caught obeying his orders."

"How did your father die?" Terr suddenly demanded.

Jenha had spoken of this so often now that it no longer raised anger in his mind. "Stacion Ansuni killed him," he said calmly.

"He was a powerful Traeger, was he not?" Terr stated. "What happened?"

"As I said before, even the strongest can be provoked too far."

"Go on…" Terr insisted.

"When we followed Stacion to Earth, my sister insisted on coming. She did not remain with the Kumatan colony, but moved widely amongst the humans. She worked with her friend, Jai Ansuni (who changed shape to seem human) to undo some of Stacion's harm. We would not see her for long periods of time. It angered my father, for he loved her and feared for her. Suzi insisted that, as his daughter, it was her duty to do her part. He would forgive her when she came home – until the next argument – then she went off again."

Jenha paused; this part was still raw, even after two decades.

"Then she came home pregnant with the child of a human. She had unrepentantly fallen in love with the man, and had ignored all the teaching that cross species mating was abhorrent. The argument that time was worse than any other and she fled back to Jai Ansuni. My father took his anger, at her and himself, out on seeking and controlling Stacion and his warriors and he must have come close enough to cause Stacion alarm.

"In retaliation, because of a chance meeting with her and Jai – Stacion had his revenge on my father."

Terr did not urge Jenha to continue, but waited quietly.

Finally, Jenha went on. "There was a war on Earth at that time, subtly incited by Stacion, who gathered death energies for his own use. Father was blocking him where he could and was working for peace. Stacion killed my sister, tortured her first and made it seem like she was blown up by a bomb. We never knew what happened to the child she had delivered a few days before, but Jai Ansuni told me the child was dead."

Terr looked pale, but asked, "And you bear no ill will to the Atapi?"

"Stacion is dead; his tribe had no choice under his rule. I chose to round up as many as I could, to save them. I am questioned for that choice too, but I do not regret it. When Stacion died, his warriors were compelled to kill all his tribe – males, females and children – knowing that I would be forever haunted by their death."

"I can find no dishonour there," Terr admitted. "But you were stripped of your rank and sent to be retrained."

Jenha smiled gently. "I spent many years on Earth and still had much to learn about my home world. They need to be sure that my exposure to such a tumultuous culture has not damaged me."

As they spoke, Jenha felt he was also teaching this younger Centurion a new way of looking at things. He expected that this young one and his colleague would compare his views with Kaer's and those of all the others they spoke to, and he hoped they would find the truth.

He had yet to decide what their interest was in Jai Cassidy – when much of their concern was in the alien Selkrit and the Atapi. Still, the more they knew, the better their chance was of finding the truth. He hoped he was pointing the way for them to understand the Atapi as he did.

"Do you think she can change the Atapi?" Terr asked.

"I think she was created for that purpose," Jenha said. "And she had survived challenges from nine sorcerers since her son was born, less than two weeks ago, and four more just before she was brought here. There are only seven more that she needs to win against."

Terr had not revealed much of his thoughts, but Jenha hoped they would not support the desire of the Kimh to keep Jai imprisoned. It would be much better for her to change the Atapi attitudes, than for the tribes to be decimated or uprooted to another world.

CHAPTER 36 – Jai Cassidy – POV

I was well enough now to be prowling the too small room. Traegers escorted guards in when they provided food for me. Their posturing with poised weapons half amused and half annoyed me. Soon they would provoke me too far. There were things I needed to be doing. I had to get out…

Two Traegers entered with their usual lack of warning. One placed a pile of clothing on the table near the door.

"You are required to dress appropriately and be ready for questioning in one hour."

I ignored their 'action ready' stance and walked over to the table to examine the clothing – Kumatan style women's clothes – servant's clothes.

"These are not appropriate," I told them, challenging them calmly. "I am not Kumatan. I am human. I will not answer questions from an inferior position."

With a commendable degree of control, the speaker asked, "What is suitable?"

Since this young Traeger pup was polite, so was I. "Lady Ellhi Mosellan is familiar with human preferences. I am sure she will be gracious enough to help you."

The Traegers gestured me back and departed.

That little battle of wills invigorated me. I was surprised that they had not opposed my suggestion – but, as I had noticed, those two were very young. I was contemplating ignoring them on their return, but that plan was thwarted. More people than just two entered, and one gave an unmistakable child's cry. I spun around and saw Ellhi and Jahni, and Ellhi was carrying my son.

The two Traegers had closed the door after my visitors and were politely staying just beside the door.

Ellhi handed Mikha to me and I felt his joy at being near me. I could not speak; such was the emotion filling me.

"Jai? Are you well?" Janhi asked. I could only nod, as I feasted my eyes on the child I had borne.

"Slave bands?" Ellhi queried softly as she dared to give me a hug.

"Yeah, I'm dangerous, remember," I retorted softly, trying to appear unconcerned. "It is not going to stop me."

Mikha snuggled in to me, and I regretted having to give him up.

"We needed three nurses for him," Ellhi confided. "The High Minister would not let Farcine stay, but Teresa is still with us."

"How did he find out?" I asked quietly.

"Two of your tribe saved the High Minister from assassins. He had the females confined, and Farcine went to speak for them."

Ellhi did not verbalise her censure of the High Minister. She didn't need to.

"Ungrateful bastard," I said. "Is that another reason why he had Jenha and Kaer punished?"

"I did not know," Ellhi said with concern. "I am not allowed to see him. I have only seen him once, when Mikha first arrived. But Lord Kaer was looking most unwell last evening. He would not even talk to Aniki."

"I am surprised that they let you come to see me," I said. "Though I am not complaining. All three of you look well. I hope they haven't tried to turn you against me."

"I will not let them," Jahni said fiercely, glaring at the Traegers. "They tried to tell me that Atapi are wild and uncivilised. I told them you were human and you had saved my life."

Ellhi added, "They officially dissolved our triumvir – declared it unlawful. But they cannot change how I feel about you."

"I hope that will not change, but do not jeopardise yourself for me. There are things I must do that won't endear me to the Kimh or Kumatan."

"They asked me about you," Jahni said. "I had to tell them everything. Lord Kaer told me I must."

"You did right, Jahni," I assured him. "Never be afraid to tell the truth. I am not afraid of anything you might have said. You are staying with Lord Kaer?"

"Yes, so I am with Mikha. Lord Kaer is kind to me, but very strict." Jahni told me.

"I don't think you need to be afraid of him. I think he will be fair to you and treat you well. Just remember that Korvu is a lot different to Earth and you have much to learn about life here."

"We are not to stay here long," Ellhi warned me. "Please be sure that Mikha will be well loved, and you won't object to this lot of clothes." She grinned wickedly when the guards could not see her.

The Traeger who had spoken on the first visit announced the High Minister. I handed Mikha back to Ellhi and realised that Jahni had gone almost rigidly tense. He was staring at Koenig as if he were a snake. I wondered what had caused that reaction. I waited silently to find out the purpose of this visit.

Koenig gestured for Ellhi to pass Mikha to him and my hackles rose. Mikha immediately began to wriggle, and being wrapped so tightly, unable to get free – he began to scream. I began to move forward, but the angle of the Traeger's weapons rose to be aimed at me.

"I wanted to assure you that your son was being well cared for. I have removed the unhealthy Atapi influence from him. He will be raised as a Kimh and this unseemly behaviour will not be permitted."

I saw Jahni begin to open his mouth to speak with childish candour – but Koenig looked at him and he gulped and stayed silent.

Mikha's screams were leaving Koenig unmoved, but that was not the case for everyone else in the room. I was growing angry, dangerously angry.

Into the pandemonium, Kaer strode, and for an instant, his face showed anger equal to my own. Koenig handed Mikha back to Ellhi, but my son was beyond reasonable. I was not allowed to go to him.

"Father, why are you here?" Kaer asked politely. He plucked Mikha from Ellhi and my son instantly quietened.

"I was letting Mikha visit his mother – proving that she is not a fit influence on him."

They hadn't gagged me. "He was quiet until you held him… High Minister," I said bluntly.

"He has no respect for authority," Koenig told me. "If my son cannot teach him that, I will find someone who can."

"My son is less than a month old," I said, not hiding my anger. "And you will notice that just as he knew you were a snake, he quietened instantly for Kaer."

Kaer quietly dismissed Ellhi and Jahni, passing Mikha to Ellhi and sending them back to his suite. Jahni sent me a fearful glance as he left.

"Father, the rest of the council is assembling in the Council Room," Kaer advised, his voice carefully neutral.

"As the council is in abeyance, at the demand of the Galactic Ambassador, I am not needed there," Koenig growled, still looking daggers at me. He may not have understood my word 'snake' which I had said in English, but he knew I had not been polite.

"You are still the High Minister, Father," Kaer said. "Our people still look to you for an example."

The prod to his pride worked. The spoilt brat, verging on a tantrum, controlled himself.

"Ensure Jai Cassidy understands the expected rules of behaviour," was his parting shot as he strode out the door.

I watched Kaer's face and tried to determine what he was thinking. "What's got into him?" I asked, settling my own anger.

"We are not here to discuss my father," Kaer told me stonily.

I sobered, not as interested in annoying Kaer as I had been in annoying his father. "Can I ask what he meant by the Council being in abeyance?" I didn't think he would answer.

"Galactic Ambassador Quenten issued a notice of investigation on the council. Until that is resolved, our ruling body is under the control of the Galactic Federation."

"Why?" I asked.

"The Selkrit Ambassador sent a formal complaint about the Atapi massacring his people. He holds my father responsible."

"That... is utter rubbish," I blurted. I wasn't concerned about Koenig here. "The Kimh don't rule the Atapi... and those blue aliens were trespassing."

"It does not give the Atapi the right to kill intruders on sight," Kaer insisted.

"But..." I began to protest.

"Jai – I am not here to argue law or politics with you. You know nothing of our ways," Kaer said flatly. That felt like a rebuke and I had never taken kindly to them. "I am to prepare you to go before the council."

"Oh that! What do they want? To condemn me for living?"

Kaer ignored that. "It will be Ambassador Quenten who will lead the questioning. I advise you to consider him with respect. He holds wider power than my father usually does. He could recommend that you be taken off this world."

I must have betrayed fear then. "Can they just up and take anyone?"

"Normally, no. However, if the person is a criminal, who has committed crimes against other races, other worlds, they have the right. They usually do not interfere with purely local treatment of criminals. You, however, were not born on Korvu, and are not considered as subject to local law."

He forestalled my attempt to comment. "Do not assume that means you can do what you please here with impunity. Any adverse acts you commit here, anything that jeopardises the wellbeing of a race on this world, can fall under their jurisdiction."

"I'm not a criminal, so what do they think they have against me?"

"Your presence here has provoked the Atapi to the greatest degree since before Stacion Ansuni fled. It has been alleged that you are part of the cause of the Atapi atrocities on the Selkrit."

"I'm not!" I protested forcefully, feeling my fists clench.

Kaer leant forward and touched my hands, implying that I needed to calm myself. It was too much to take in.

"They can't be trying to pin all that stuff on me?" I was incredulous.

"The Centurions, under Ambassador Quenten, are here to investigate all allegations and make a ruling. This is your chance to speak up."

"What if they decide the sorcerers are criminals?" I said aghast. "Could they take them away?"

Kaer nodded, reluctant to confirm it.

Anger truly burned then. "That shall not be!" I said, staring at Kaer. "The Atapi would die out without the sorcerers, and the sorcerers would die away from Korvu – they are bound to the land."

"Stacion didn't," Kaer reminded me.

"He was disgraced – his binding to his land broken," I said. "And I don't think you would like the details of how he survived."

"Are you prepared to defend the Atapi?" Kaer asked me.

"Yes!"

"The Centurions say they want to talk to the Atapi sorcerers," Kaer told me.

"So?" I asked.

"Attempts to talk to them so far have been ignored," Kaer explained.

"Surely that shows they aren't out for war on you," I proposed.

"Some say they are afraid," Kaer said. "That they are guilty and have fled."

"Perhaps they don't expect a fair hearing," I retorted. I did not understand the anger in me – nor, if I wanted to be truthful, my driving urge to protect them.

"The Galactic Enforcers are impartial. If they will not be received by the Atapi – they will forfeit the right to defend themselves."

I sat down, feeling suddenly weak. The enormity of it all overwhelmed me. "The Atapi are already dying out. And it's wrong…" I couldn't voice why I knew that. It was an absolute, irrefutable surety.

Kaer was silent for a while. I wondered who would benefit from the removal or death of the Atapi – but I couldn't think further that that Koenig was trying to destroy me, and lay all the blame on me.

"Jai?"

I looked up.

"Think before you speak – I know you are angry, but anger will gain you nothing. Remember the lessons Jenha taught you. He is a wise man."

I knew Kaer was right.

He went on. "You will need to be dressed better than you are and be ready in a quarter of an hour."

Kaer left me alone to dress, and I was relieved to have decent clothes again. My mind, though, wasn't still. I knew I had to try talking to the sorcerers and explain things to them, and get them to tell their side of the story to the Enforcers. To do that, I would have to get away. I couldn't just go with them in tow. I would have to convince them. I may have defeated the challenges of thirteen of them, but I had no right to dictate to them how they ruled their lands. Not yet – but I would, I vowed.

The decision to act came suddenly with the smell of fresh hot air through an open door. I was out of the shielded room, being walked between two Traegers to the council room. One of the Centurions strode along behind me, but I disregarded him.

The breeze, just a waft of it, brought with it the mind of Larcia and a rush of information, like a year's supply of weekly massages, arriving all at once. The sense of urgency I had felt once I had recovered fell on me in full strength. I could not stay here. I had to leave. I could not talk to the council because they would never believe me.

"I must," I told the mental voice. "I have to convince these others that Atapi are not to be blamed. I must not let them take them away…"

"Child, you cannot stay! You cannot go in front of that council and pledge to control the Atapi. Not until you have passed the last challenge. Even then, you have much to learn about us. You must win the last challenges before you can hope to reason with the sorcerers. They are all being provoked beyond reason by unknown enemies."

"Don't you see?" I thought back desperately. "I'm the only one here who cares – who can defend them."

"They will never listen, never agree to let you go. They have banded you and will keep you prisoner."

"Trust me," I pleaded. "I can handle these people."

"How?"

"The other aliens, the newcomers. I can apply to them for sanctuary. I am not from Korvu – they will listen to me."

Larcia had no conception of a galactic federation, and I knew too little to explain. I just saw a means to get free… if the Kimh tried to stop me.

Of course, I had no conception of the overall situation – only the conviction that I was right, and everyone else was wrong. I thought I knew enough.

I continued walking, planning my speech to the council – in which I would tell them what I thought and convince them to let me go and finish what I intended to do. Larcia had other ideas. Even as I felt the return of the sword to my side, I felt her pull on me, like she had done to send me to the various sorcerers' lands. The pull was not affected by the bands I wore – for it wasn't me drawing on the aura.

The effect was to yank me from within the circle of guards, and move me towards the door – only there, I encountered a solid seeming wall, right in the doorway.

I slammed into it. My mind felt Larcia's outrage, and desperation.

"I'll find a way out," I promised her. "Trust me!"

The Traegers reached me in seconds. Solomon lifted me like I was a puppy and told me, gravely, "Ignorant child. There is a shield on this palace so that no Atapi will pollute this palace. It also works to keep the likes of you in."

Before I could think to defend myself, he clasped both my wrists and touched the two slave bands together. They held fast where they touched.

Then the Centurion stood before me.

"Refusing to answer questions is a sign of guilt," he told me. "This is your only warning. If you do not proceed calmly and co-operate, you will be taken into Galactic custody and held in confinement."

"That wasn't my doing," I protested, but looking at his face I knew he could not believe it.

For the rest of the way to the Council Room, I was held by the Centurion. He had a grip like an iron ring.

Somehow, my mind could not function, except passively. The mental paralysis ended when I was released, and I found myself facing a richly dressed stranger. I studied the face and decided that he was probably the same race as the Enforcer – Orlek, was it?

If it was the same race, he was dressed quite differently. He didn't have the form-fitting outfit of the Centurions – instead he had leggings of saffron satin, with an ankle-length coat. It looked like a jacket where it fit to his upper body, and then it fell like a cape and this was in crimson satin. It was cut to enhance his fine physique.

I realised he was talking to me when a question was sharply repeated. I drew my attention off his clothing and onto his voice.

"Oh! Ah! Um – my name is Jai Cassidy," I finally answered.

The man in the eye-blinding colour asked then, "What is your planet of birth?"

"Earth, of course. Didn't they tell you that?"

"Do you have any kin here?" was the next senseless question.

"I have a son," I said, wondering what importance these questions had to the matter.

The next half dozen questions were equally senseless, but I answered patiently enough because I remembered Kaer's advice and the all too recent warning. That and the needs of the Atapi, and my being the only one who would speak for them.

As if he sensed my irritation, the questioner spoke to me. "You have been warned once. You will receive no more warnings. Have you had the repercussions explained to you?"

"Yes," I agreed, meekly.

The Ambassador explained the nature of the question session. He seemed to be phrasing his words according to some obscure protocol.

He finished by saying, "If you tell the truth, you have nothing to fear."

I did not believe that at all, and decided to answer without volunteering extra information.

After saying his piece, the Ambassador returned to sit behind the Council bench and let Centurion Bellus ask the questions. I wasn't offered the option to sit.

"Jai Cassidy, you were identified at the scene of an atrocity committed by the Atapi. Please tell this council how you got to be there."

"Huh?" I blurted in confusion. "Could you please be more specific? I am under the impression that many people here think all Atapi activity is atrocious."

Since I wasn't being obviously belligerent, Bellus complied. He described what had happened at the alien camp when Con had destroyed the helicopter machine. It was so close to the truth that I wondered how he had learnt of it.

"Can I ask how you came to know that?" I asked, warily.

"There is a film of it," Bellus said, or rather, he called it something else but that is what he meant. He didn't identify the source.

"Hmm, very well," I said as I ordered my thoughts. "I was on Con Ansuni's lands because I was intending to convince him that the Atapi needed to change the way they are."

"This meeting was friendly?" Bellus queried.

"Not completely, but at least he wasn't trying to kill me," I told him.

"You were helping him?" Bellus suggested.

"Are you kidding? He told me he didn't need my help. He was called away and he told me to stay in the village – I didn't."

Without adding too much detail, I told them that I had been in a position to observe the events before that – when two aliens had attacked Con Ansuni and he had taken action.

"He made them helpless," Bellus accused. "So his warriors could kill them."

"That's how you view it," I told him. "I believe he was concerned that no more of the children of his tribe would be hunted, butchered and eaten by members of that race."

I heard mutters of disbelief and disgust from amongst the Kimh, but Quenten did not accuse me of lying.

I went on. "At the camp of the aliens, I had one of Con's warriors with me, and he threw vines over the helicopter so it couldn't take off. We didn't know anyone was in there. When it couldn't lift, and the engine started, it twisted around, and began to spew bullets everywhere."

Bellus remarked, "It is not surprising that the alien began shooting after what happened at the canyon."

I stared at him and bit back on a sarcastic remark. "Perhaps," I tried to sound as if I agreed. "But if you are adding up rights and wrongs here – those blue aliens were trespassing on Con Ansuni's land, their kind had butchered two children, they were illegally prospecting, they attacked Con without provocation and Con was doing his duty to his tribe in protecting them. And those bullets could have killed the whole tribe, not just two criminals."

The Kimh were muttering to themselves, but I didn't try to hear which story they favoured.

"Why were those aliens there in the first place?" I asked pointedly. "I would like to speak to the person who told you of this, and I would like to see that film."

I turned and eyed Ambassador Quenten when I asked that. He studied me and nodded, and called for a break while the equipment was set up. I studied all the people in the room and saw only Kimh – except for two Enforcers and the Ambassador. I didn't count the half dozen Traegers all watching me.

I wasn't the only one watching that film with fascination. Most of the Kimh sitting in the seats facing the bench leant forward to watch the tiny moving figures in the pictures projected on the screen. Those that didn't, like Koenig, I assumed had seen it already.

I knew within two minutes that the film had gaps in it.

"Is this Korvu technology?" I asked, looking to Kaer for an answer. He was sitting not too far from where I stood.

He shook his head in a way reminiscent of humans. I wondered who had taught him that.

"Your words do not match what is recorded here," Quenten told me in a tone that was not yet an accusation.

I had my answer ready for that. "You say you can tell if I was lying," I challenged him. "Was I?"

He didn't answer, just watched me, and forced me to speak by that silence.

"I told you the truth and I have seen films before – on Earth. I know they can be edited to show only part of a story. That film jumps several times. That is where parts were cut out."

Quenten and the Centurions betrayed nothing of their thoughts. The Kimh were a different matter. My accusation that the film was edited shocked them, as if I had accused them of lying.

After that, the session degraded into an inquisition. After the Centurion had finished trying to make me vilify Con Ansuni, he asked me about my business with the other sorcerers. I repeated my reasons, namely to get them to change their ways, but that did not satisfy them.

"Since you have been here," a Kimh commented, "the Atapi have been more agitated than they have been for over twenty years."

I turned on that smugly sure speaker and said, "Your kind didn't have to bring me here. But since you did, I can see that your dealings with the Atapi border on prejudice and unfair simply because you all hate them and are terrified of them."

"So, you are stirring them up against us?" that Kimh accused.

I turned to that speaker and demanded, "Are you prepared to listen or must you keep on making false accusations based on paranoia?"

That Kimh turned an interesting shade of purple, but subsided at a gesture from Quenten.

"If you have something relevant to say, Jai Cassidy, by all means tell us," Quenten directed me.

"I am intending to change the Atapi," I said in a very rational voice. "I know how they once were, and if the tribes are to grow in number, rather than dying out, they must relearn ancient ways," I began, and there was a loud murmur of disbelief that I could know such a thing – being human, and only on Korvu for a short time. I went on, speaking louder. "However to do that, I have to challenge the sorcerers and win. Then I might have a chance to convince them that they need to change."

I glanced around the room, seeing only eyes that betrayed – probably disbelief in my sanity. I also noticed another figure sitting right at the back that hadn't been there earlier.

"So, they are resisting change," Quenten suggested.

"I haven't got that far yet! At best I have their attention – not cooperation."

Questions continued to be asked of me by Centurion Bellus about my connections to and interactions with the Atapi – including the matter of releasing the four Atapi devils. I didn't think that was any business of the Galactic Enforcers.

Finally, Bellus asked, "Do you have anything else you would like to say to this council?"

Exactly the invitation I wanted. "Yes. You self-important types need to realise that the Atapi are as important to Korvu as the Kimh and the Kumatan – they should be the defenders of Korvu since they are in tune with the aura and what is natural. Yet every one of you is only willing to think bad of them, and refuse to recognise that the aliens you are dealing with may not be as truthful and honest, as you are."

There was more of the subdued muttering that I knew was disagreement with my words. Once again, I raised my voice and spoke over them. "If you and those aliens succeed in destroying or relocating the Atapi devils – your protection will die, and you gullible fools will be robbed blind. I am intending to put an end to the acrimony between Kimh and Atapi by removing them to where you and your pet Traegers can't find them, and teaching them the old ways.

"How can you ensure this?" Koenig demanded. "Will you take responsibility for all the Atapi?"

I knew what he was implying and wasn't having it.

"I haven't finished what I must do yet," I told him directly. "It isn't lawful to make me personally responsible for them. Especially their past deeds. I will promise to show them a different way. I have power like the sorcerers do, but I use it differently because I have empathy. I have to work with the aura of Korvu. I don't warp it."

Quenten tried to get me to explain 'the aura' and I am sure I didn't do well. I don't know how he thought of how I 'crossed planes' either. He seemed to see the distinction between what I used sorcery for and what the sorcerers did – I healed, prevented a flood with salt water, and generally defended myself.

When I finished speaking, Quenten studied me for a long period of time – I simply stared back at him. "I am satisfied that you have co-operated honestly and fully," he told me, and I relaxed a little.

"So – am I free to go?" I demanded.

Quenten looked at Koenig, but I had taken enough of Koenig's paranoia.

"Sir?" I interrupted Quenten's musing. "I was told you are the one in charge at the moment. It would be your decision. I don't believe I have done anything criminal and therefore don't deserve to be incarcerated any further."

Quenten spoke sternly, "On certain matters, I must abide by the laws and edicts of the local ruling body – with respect to local citizens."

It did not seem to be too dangerous a thing to say, "I am not a citizen of Korvu – I believe I can claim the aegis of the Galactic Federation. As such, I will abide the recommendation you make – based on what you have heard."

Koenig looked about to explode.

Quenten considered me for a moment longer. "I have heard nothing to indicate that you are too dangerous to be loose," he said carefully. "However, I have no way to judge your sorcery power. What do you offer as a sign of your future intent?"

That was easy. "Before I was caught and incapacitated, I was trying to heal Traeger Petri. I am willing to continue that task."

I glanced at my audience and dared them to object. The Kimh next to Koenig was whispering to him.

Quenten agreed. "Yes, that would be acceptable. You may go to the healers and do what you can. The Korvu council may send observers with you."

"With respect," I relied to Quenten. "My healing will be more efficient if Traeger Petri could be taken out into the garden. I will need to draw on the aura to help me and I can't feel it inside here."

"I protest," Koenig finally blurted, standing up. "Petri is seriously ill and should not be moved."

"Then you want me to fail," I retorted.

Traeger Solomon approached Lord Eamon and spoke quietly, and then Eamon addressed Quenten.

"It appears that Jai Cassidy is correct in her contention that the aura is stronger in the garden."

Quenten issued the edict, and Centurion Bellus walked up beside me and held my arm.

"I am interested to see this healing," he commented, but I couldn't tell what he thought he would see.

Only when we had confirmation that Petri was in the garden was I allowed to leave the Council Room. Most of the Kimh Lords left first, Koenig and Eamon stayed, as did Traeger Solomon.

Having got my way to this point, I told Quenten that I would need the 'slave bands' removed.

"They stop me using the aura," I told him.

All the while I was healing Traeger Petri, my mind was considering how to get away. The bands were off, as ordered by the Galactic Ambassador, so at least Kaer would not be blamed if I left – and I was outside the barrier that had stopped me before. This was probably my only chance.

Where should I go? I knew they were after Con Ansuni – I had to warn him and tell him had to talk to the Enforcers or be assumed guilty. At least Quenten knew how he had been provoked. I know the Kimh didn't believe that, but the Enforcers were prepared to consider causes too. They had a way of making one tell the truth – so they would know he wasn't lying.

I cringed a bit as I thought that. I had told the Enforcer more than I had intended, and probably alienated all the Kimh, too. They knew I had no intention of forgetting sorcery. I had promised I would take the Atapi somewhere they would not interfere with Kumatan or Kimh anymore. Then I had to admit I couldn't do it yet.

The two Enforcers were standing quite close, watching me and talking to the Ambassador. Traeger Solomon was not taking his eyes off me, possibly fearing I would harm Petri. The only person with his attention elsewhere was the healer who was staring, mouth agape, at the visibly healing wounds and burns on his patient.

When I sensed that I had done all I could for Petri, I glanced at the healer. "He'll need to sleep," I told him. "But that's all I can do."

I only needed three steps, I told myself. If I acted meek and docile, Solomon wouldn't act.

I stood up, and began to walk towards the Enforcers. "What now?" I asked, sounding resigned. The Council still insisted I stay in their control; the Ambassador hadn't given a clear decision, and I couldn't guess what he was thinking. In a side-glance, I noted that Solomon was staring down at Traeger Petri.

Koenig spoke sharply to Solomon, telling him to restrain me.

"No!" I objected. "I requested the aegis of the Galactic Federation."

Koenig's face looked like a ripe plum – had he ignored me when I had said about that? I met the eyes of Ambassador Quenten, and after a moment, he nodded. "Bellus," was all he said, and I didn't know whether I was free to go or not.

The Centurion made no move to come to me, merely watching as I moved closer. I began to visualise the village area of Con Ansuni's tribe.

Had Solomon seen my face then, he might have reacted. If the Enforcers noticed my face go blank, they said nothing. I don't think they understood the concept of 'crossing planes'. All the same, I eyed the enforcers as I moved forward until just before I acted, and my back prickled with the thought that Solomon might immobilise me.

I heard a cry of warning from Solomon. He might have sensed me drawing on the aura, but he would have seen my body wavering on that second step, but by then it was too late.

I had formed the image of Con's village in my mind, but when I arrived I remembered that he had moved from there. I called his name and he arrived quickly, but he was angry.

"I have no time for you," he snarled. "My land is overrun with vile feral beasts. Arrows and spears can't touch them. They are fast and deadly – two of my old warriors were torn to pieces. Only magic can kill them."

"Con, the Kumatan want to talk to you," I tried to tell him.

"I don't want to see them – they are haunting my boundaries, they've intruded even here. Look at the hoof prints of their horses."

"I don't think they are doing this," I said. "Those blue aliens are trying to discredit you – make the Galactic Enforcers destroy you or relocate you. You have to talk to the Enforcers, tell your side of things or they will assume you guilty."

"I am guilty," Con snarled. "I killed those vermin. And I have never heard of Enforcers, so if they are newcomers, they probably released these beasts on us. I will have no part of them."

Con flew up and vanished. I heard a weird howling that raised my hackles. The beast that charged at me was like nothing I had seen before. I sensed nothing from it except malice. Since retreat was called for, I pictured the Rock of Arkor and ran the three steps.

I ran into Larcia's cave as if that mindless feral beast was still after me. The pounding of blood in my ears began to subside and only then did I hear Larcia's voice.

"Daughter, you must talk to the Old One," she told me.

"I know! I've got to convince him to talk to the Enforcers," I thought back as I dropped to sit on the floor of the cave.

"That can wait! The sorcerers are going mad – they will destroy themselves. They are provoking the Kumatan beyond sanity."

"What? What's happening?"

"Two of them have ridden off their land with their warriors – and attacked or besieged a Kumatan town. Two tribes attacked Kumatan on their borders and are fighting them on their land."

"They are being provoked," I swore. "Not by Kumatan or Kimh. It's those blue aliens doing this."

Larcia hissed. "Why? How?"

"I reckon they found metal ore, or something on Con's land, and possibly elsewhere, too. They want to mine it – take it away. Con won't let them – no doubt the others won't either."

"Then they must die," Larcia hissed.

"Every sorcerer agrees with that, but their methods are more than many Kumatan, the Kimh and those Enforcer types can stomach."

"Weaklings," Larcia hissed again.

I didn't want her to think me weak, but, "Their methods make me sick, too," I told her, and I went on quickly. "Mainly because I grew up as a human and they see things a different way, but that isn't the point. The Atapi are meant to be the defenders of Korvu, or so my mother's teaching said. If the other races were like us, they wouldn't need us."

There was silence in my head for a while. "Yes," the mental voice said more quietly.

I ventured a thought. "The blue aliens have effectively muzzled the Kimh and Kumatan by reporting the Atapi atrocities to the Galactic Federation. As a result, they sent Enforcers here to investigate. While they are here, the Kimh do not rule."

I felt Larcia hiss again – but I knew she had no conception of 'Galactic Federation' or 'Enforcers'.

"I know that they are more aliens but I think they have the means to find the truth," I said.

When Larcia said nothing, I went on. "At the moment, it looks like the Atapi are killing those aliens unprovoked, as though we are a race of murderers and we should be killed or relocated. The Kimh haven't been convinced yet, but they are half way to agreeing. I told them what I knew of the aliens, but the Kimh do not believe the aliens are not sticking to the word of the agreement they signed. The aliens have all kinds of innocent-sounding excuses for being in the wrong place."

Larcia hissed again, angry and impotent to act.

"That's why I have to convince the Old One to tell the other sorcerers to talk to the enforcers calmly, and share what they saw of the aliens. So far, attempts by the Kumatan to talk to the sorcerers by the agreed methods have been ignored."

Larcia stopped hissing in my mind and seemed to be thinking. "All the sorcerers are agitated."

"I'm getting blamed for that!" I muttered.

I sat for a long time before Larcia's mind touched mine again.

"It has been so long," Larcia told me. "So much has changed. So many sorcerers' names to recall. Those you challenged, I can recall and find now. I cannot yet extend my sense of the aura to the others' lands. What scared you so, daughter?"

I tried to explain the thing that I had seen so briefly, and told her what Con had described and I had sensed.

"Evil, unnatural – yes. I feel flashes of evil everywhere. More in some places – no wonder my sons are reacting and are too busy to talk."

"Con said only magic stops them. I didn't have time to ask how. Atapi weapons don't affect them, so the outer covering must be tough. It's not alive, so it must be some mechanical thing – designed to kill. I wonder how it chooses victims."

"Smell, body heat…" Larcia suggested.

"Movement," came to my mind. "Possibly things we don't know. Those aliens have helicopters, and had to have come here by some means – spaceships. Their machines must be far beyond any I saw on Earth. Korvu has nothing like them."

"They must not succeed, those vile aliens," Larcia told me.

"On that, my Queen, I totally agree." At that moment I had a sense of de-ja-vu from the time I decided Old Lammond on Earth was going to 'get it'. "There will be a way," I vowed. "Those aliens might have convinced the Kimh they are totally trustworthy, but I know better. I am not constrained by that Nuath of theirs – and those aliens don't know how sneaky and devious a human can be."

I sensed wordless approval from Larcia.

"Can you give me that bird's view of Con's land?" I asked politely in my mind. "I want to study those feral beasts."

As before, I was hovering and watching Con as he hunted for more of the beasts.

"Con Ansuni?" I thought. "May I share your mind on this hunt?"

"I have no time for distractions! Watch if you must," was his snarled reply.

I did for a while before asking a question. "Do fire and water harm them?"

"No!"

"Dropping them from a height?" I asked again.

"For moments only!"

"Cold?" I suggested.

He hadn't thought of that!

"They don't stay still long enough," he snarled.

"Do they head for fires?" I tried.

"No, why would they?"

"Do they kill animals?"

"Not hoppers, but why don't you see if they want to kill you?"

I ignored that suggestion. "Can they climb?" I persisted.

"No!"

"Dig out of a pile of dirt?"

I got a flicker of disgust for that. He considered it a stupid idea.

"Ok, are they active at night?"

Con didn't know that. "I have no time for these questions. Have you a way to rid me of these creatures?"

I was about to admit that I didn't when an idea occurred to me.

"Dig a deep pit and lure them into it," I said.

I sensed Con considering the idea with approval. His mind then became busy, and I withdrew mine.

"Daughter, speak to Jacek," Larcia directed abruptly. My bird's view changed to the land of the sorcerer who had tried to bury me.

He, too, was fighting the feral beasts, but he had Kumatan and a Kimh on his border. Like Con, he was too busy to talk to them, and I caught him flicking a feral beast in their direction. He had decided that his problems had come from them.

I watched the beast. The horses of the Kumatan saw the sudden arrival of the unfamiliar creature and were not quite rearing – but moving and prancing in place. The creature seemed stunned for a bit, but then it began moving as if sniffing for prey. It was ignoring the horses until it got to the one bearing the Kimh, and then it attacked the horse, causing it to scream in pain and thrash around. The Traeger grabbed the Kimh from the rearing horse and I think saved his life. The man had to be strong, for he was holding the Kimh to the side of his horse, which was sent galloping away.

The beast, I noticed, was not affected by the Kumatan weapons either and was now racing after the fleeing Traeger. The galloping horse stopped once it was well ahead of the beast, and the Traeger took the Kimh Lord across planes, leaving the horse. The horse saw the beast coming for it and began to gallop, but now the beast did not follow.

"Jacek!" I thought to that sorcerer.

"What?" he snarled back. "I have no time for you! The humanoids have gone too far – sending these beasts in to kill us."

"Jacek, it wasn't them. There are blue blooded aliens who did this."

"I have heard of them but they have not been here. Kumatan have. This is my business, not yours."

"It is not just your tribe affected," I told him. "But those things can't climb – you could dump them down that hole I climbed from."

"And put you with it?" he snarled, and blocked me from his mind.

I slumped back against the cave wall and thought about what I had seen. That beast had ignored the horses nearest it and gone for a specific one – the one bearing the Kimh Lord.

"Those things are not alive," I said aloud. "Why did it choose that horse? It looks as if it knew that killing a Kimh on the Atapi border would really make the Atapi seem guilty."

Really, even killing Kumatan would do that. "Larcia? Are horses native to Korvu?"

"No, they came many generations ago. Traders brought them."

My mind was teasing at an idea. I recalled the scene of the beast attacking the horse. It had not seemed strange that the horse bled red. Atapi had purple blood… yet it had come racing at me. I was part Atapi, but I had red blood… Ah, but Con had been there, and just left…

"It's attracted by heat, movement and Atapi blood," I said aloud, sure I was right. "Are you sure you can't send me to the Old One?"

"Not yet," Larcia admitted.

"How are you sending me around?" I thought to ask.

"An ancient ritual," Larcia told me, but I had the sense of something complex, incomprehensible.

"Okay," I muttered, thinking. "What about lightning man? I have unfinished business with him."

"His magic has touched you… yes," Larcia agreed.

"When I am finished with him, I will insist he takes me to the Old One."

I sensed a stir in the aura and knew Larcia was doing something.

Auglan spoke quietly to the aide who had delivered messages to him. He sat in his shuttle, now parked in a secluded canyon well away from the spaceport.

"Send messages to the site managers that we need to increase production," Auglan directed the younger Selkrit. "The council here is tied up and won't be able to do anything to stop us. Then tell the ship captain to implement the second stage of the instructions I gave him. Tell him to be very careful. Is he sure that there is only the one Galactic Ship?"

The aide nodded.

"Yes? Good. The Enforcers are wasting time trying to talk to these lizard men, but they won't face up – not surprising given all the little annoyances they are dealing with. Too bad the Enforcers expect obedience." Auglan chuckled, as did his aide.

"Oh, and tell him to send down the prisoners on punishment detail. They can work at the power station site. We must appear to be filling our part of the deal."

Auglan dismissed the aide, who went off to carry out his instructions. His revised plans were proceeding as he wanted.

He sat back and thought about the Council session that morning. He had arrived late, hoping to see this dangerous Atapi prisoner. It had been difficult not to laugh out loud. A female child – dangerous? How gullible could anyone be? And all the pale-faced humanoids were agitated because she had escaped! It was obvious that the Enforcers had allowed it. He would bet a thousand credits they had a tracer on her – and the child thought itself so clever just because it had mastered that creepy appear-disappear trick of the lizards.

And those lizards, since they were too dumb to talk to the Enforcers, were being treated by the Galactic Ambassador as guilty and hostile.

The local idiots still insisted that they could deal with them and Galactic interference was not required. Well, his ship captain would start phase two, and those lizards would be really riled up and convinced that the Kumatan were behind their troubles. He'd have some of those recalcitrant sub-ordinates of his killed in typically barbaric fashion. Get the lizards off their land and into Kumatan towns, making them fair game for the locals. Then he would spread some anti-inhibitor vapour over the Atapi lands. After that, one spark would have them fighting berserkers, killing each other and any Kumatan.

Auglan laughed and laughed. That know-all child thought she could control those sorcerers. Did the Enforcers really believe that? Unlikely. They were probably using her as bait – since the sorcerers seemed to hone in on her. If the gossip was true, that child had bested fifteen of the creepy lizard sorcerers already. If a mere girl child had beaten them, the lizards couldn't be very smart. Well, no matter, she was useful as a distraction or an inflammatory agent.

So once the Atapi were rounded up, Auglan thought ahead, he would build a power station or two whilst having his secret crews mining the rich deposits of metals on those Atapi lands. Odd that the best deposits were all on lands infested by the lizards.

A tickling on Auglan's spine caused him to turn around suddenly. He thought he saw a hint of movement out of the edge of his eye, and he felt as if he were being watched. And that awful smell…

Lord Eamon sat back in his brother's official chair and listened to reports from distant towns through the mind links of the Traegers. Solomon finished reporting on the attack on Lord Fessin's horse.

"The Lord was unhurt, thanks to Traeger Massant's quick reactions. He says he has never seen an animal act like that. He says the sorcerer flung it at them. Surely we need to take the Atapi to task for this insult?"

"Solomon, you know we cannot at this time," Eamon said, keeping his voice level. "The Enforcers are looking into these matters."

The Traeger's face took on a hard look. "They do not know the Atapi as we do, Lord."

"Which may prove to be the fairest way to proceed," Eamon advised. "What was the outcome in Halfstone Town? I understand the Atapi had it besieged."

Solomon recalled, "They broke into one of the outlying storehouses, Lord. Then they ran off."

"Was anything taken from the store house?" Eamon asked.

"It seems so, Lord. It was mainly used to store furs and skins. According to the keeper there, a large number of both were missing."

"And the Atapi ran off with them?"

"They must have," Solomon said at once.

"Facts, Solomon," Eamon reminded him.

"That detail was not mentioned," Solomon amended. "However, two Kumatan townsmen were found murdered inside the building. Both had been knifed."

Eamon merely nodded. "I will pass these events onto Ambassador Quenten. Was there more?"

"Not that I have heard, Lord," Solomon finished.

Eamon dismissed Solomon and called for a servant. He wrote a quick message in neat script and had the servant take it to the Galactic Ambassador.

Ambassador Quenten greeted Eamon and Koenig, and invited them into the main room of the suite assigned to him – a suite that was the equivalent in luxury as that of Koenig's own.

"You wished to speak to me," he invited, gesturing to them to sit. When they had, he sat as well.

"Yes, Ambassador. We have received some reports that you may not be aware of," Eamon spoke quietly.

"Proceed," Quenten directed, and he listened intently to the details of the two incidents.

"Thank you for telling me this," he acknowledged gravely. "Halfstone Town – could you show me where it is on this map you provided?"

Eamon obliged, standing and walking to the wall where a large map was inked onto a plain white fabric. He noted the glyphs already inked on the map – one was on the town of Halfstone.

Quenten pointed to it and explained, "My ship is in geosynchronous orbit, so it stays above one point on your world. I have had my crew observing the lands you advised me were Atapi occupied. This town and five others have reportedly suffered similar incidents. In each case, Kumatan died."

Eamon paled, and Koenig, silent until now, banged a fist on a low table.

"Ambassador, I must insist that you let us deal with the Atapi. They do not like off-worlders and will not respect you. They do, however, respect the power of our slave masters."

"That may be the case, Lord Koenig," Quenten agreed, calmly. "But they will come to respect the authority of our Enforcers. In these instances, I allowed the local garrisons of Kumatan Guards to deal with the incursions, since your agreements of non-interference only holds when the Atapi do not venture off their lands. In these cases, the incidents did not involve off-worlders. I considered these events were matters for local enforcement."

"What was the result, Ambassador?" Koenig asked, intently.

"The Atapi – a large number – outran the guards," Quenten told them.

"You are allowing them to get away with murder." Koenig thumped the table again. "They will think they can do it again and again."

Quenten did not rebuke the High Minister. Instead he asked, "How often do the Atapi arbitrarily raid Kumatan towns?"

Koenig stared at Quenten as if the question had stunned him. Eamon answered. "In the past generation, since we made the agreements of non-interference – never."

Quenten nodded. "I find it unusual that six identical raids occurred within hours of each other – when you have told me that Atapi sorcerers do not even cooperate between themselves. Please be assured that we are not condoning these incidents. I have requested a full squad of Enforcers to be shuttled down from my ship and a concerted effort will be made to interview the leaders of each tribe."

"Please accept the aid of our Traegers if you require translators," Eamon offered.

"That is generous of you," Quenten thanked them. "There was another more serious incident this day. Centurion Bellus has just returned from your Becton Province. The Selkrit, I understand, are constructing a power station there for you."

Koenig nodded.

"Our initial report was of Atapi stalking the site. When Bellus arrived, he found all but one of the builders and engineers dead – brutally so. On this alone, we have sufficient evidence to indict the Atapi leader, and others, under Galactic Law 113, sections one to twenty."

He briefly explained that law referred to interference in an agreed project, by or to an alien race.

"Since the sorcerers have so far ignored the offer to state their case with us – they are in default of Galactic Law 3, sections 1-5. We will be within our charter to apprehend the tribal leaders and have them questioned."

Eamon felt compelled to speak up. "I do not believe that the Atapi can conceive of a Galactic Federation. Even to us, you were only a trader's tale until recently. Will you consider that in your dealings with them?"

Quenten nodded. "I have noted that point. Was there another matter?"

Koenig gestured for Eamon to speak.

"Many of the Councillors have expressed their concern to me on one particular matter. It appears to be a united view that it would be wrong to remove Atapi sorcerers from Korvu."

"We do have that authority," Quenten reminded them. "May I hear your reasons?"

"From consideration of the example of Stacion Ansuni. He took his tribe to Earth, and when he could not use the aura there, he learnt to harness power from death and various depraved practices. I would not wish other sorcerers to learn this without Traegers to control them."

"I appreciate your concern," Quenten told them. "I understand that Jai Cassidy is related to that renegade sorcerer."

Koenig nodded. "She has power, and even if it is only a fraction of Stacion's she could become a dangerous menace. I am concerned by how easily she tricked you – accepting your protection to escape ours, and then eschewing it."

"I deemed it an acceptable risk, High Minister," Quenten explained, quite unruffled. "The Earth child thinks she is free and unobserved. In fact, she is neither. We have a tracer and bio-monitor on her and at need we can quickly locate her for retrieval or continue to monitor her activities."

"Ah…" Koenig sighed. "Then you know where she is."

Quenten nodded. "Indeed. Do you have a particular reason to want to know?"

Koenig merely remarked, "Only to be sure my people are not suffering because of her."

"As I told you earlier, there is insufficient evidence to indicate she was an intentional party to any atrocities. And I accept the healing of your Traeger as a gesture of good faith. However, there is no reason to withhold the information – when she left here, she showed up briefly on the land associated with Con Ansuni, but did not stay long enough for us to triangulate her position exactly. We only had one shot from her monitor that showed a winged Atapi. She vanished from there and reappeared near that giant monolith you tell me is sacred to the Atapi. I am amazed at how she did that."

"Atapi sorcerers and Traegers can walk across planes," Eamon explained. "If you wish, I can arrange a demonstration for you. It is quite safe. It is another reason for doubting the Federation's ability to restrict the movements of our sorcerers."

"Again, your offer is generous," Quenten said politely, but he personally did not wish to try what seemed like teleportation. "At last report, Jai Cassidy is still somewhere around that rock, but no other sorcerers have appeared there."

"So, you are using her as bait for the sorcerers," Koenig approved of that.

"It is our duty to apprehend Galactic criminals," Quenten stated, then thought to ask, "May I ask an opinion of you?"

Koenig and Eamon both nodded.

"I find myself uncertain of one point. Jai Cassidy stated that she could take the Atapi somewhere they would never be found and where they would leave Kimh and Kumatan alone. Do you think it possible that she believes she could take them back to her planet – Earth?"

"No," Eamon stated immediately. He noted that his brother turned an odd shade of grey. "Stacion only took half of his tribe with him and completely drained his land to do it. It took six Traegers, working in stages, to bring the Kumatan colonists back here."

"What else might she have meant?" Quenten asked.

Koenig's colour was returning to normal as he said, "Only moving them elsewhere on Korvu. There is a lot of unexplored land on other continents. It would be an acceptable option. However, I cannot see her convincing the Old One of anything like that. Really, I think that child is trying to scare us – youthful bravado."

"Yes, it does sound like that," Quenten agreed thoughtfully, but he didn't share his thoughts with his guests. He had seen a lot of the galaxy and seen many inexplicable things.

At that point, Centurion Bellus entered and spoke quietly to the Ambassador in his own language.

"High Minister, you offered a demonstration of 'crossing planes'. Bellus is willing to accept that offer. Jai Cassidy has moved again onto Atapi lands."

Eamon rose and walked to the door, opening it to speak to a servant waiting just outside. The servant raced off and, a short time later, Solomon arrived.

He was instructed to take Bellus to the Atapi lands situated at the map coordinates Bellus supplied. Solomon checked the location as Quenten politely ended the meeting.

CHAPTER 40 - Jai Cassidy – POV

It was late in the day when Larcia 'found' the sorcerer who had sent the lightning at me. She showed me a picture, and gave me the bird's view of the area. I did not wish to meet any of the feral beasts. Besides, experience had made me cautious, and this sorcerer had not shown his face or even formally challenged me. I had survived his attack, barely, and I intended to challenge him at a time of my choosing.

"Daughter, your intention is not strictly honourable," Larcia warned me.

"He attacked me, without warning or a challenge or provocation," I pointed out. "I will issue a challenge. He cannot claim to have defeated me – I'm alive – and I am not petrified of him. He might have stolen control of my storm, but I healed the Traeger he injured and myself. So to be fair, I should have a chance to get him without warning."

Larcia said no more. I touched her sword and felt myself moved.

On the instant of arriving in the warm moist air of almost night, I drew on the aura to hide me and used empathy to sense if anyone was nearby. I turned slowly, and smelt cooking meat and smoke from a village nearby. While I waited, I let my eyes grow accustomed to the dusk. It seemed that the sorcerer had not yet become aware of me. If he had, he'd either have come at once or begun to warp the aura.

Where I stood was an open area and I began to have the irrational sense of being watched. Once more, I turned slowly around, this time scanning the edge of the tree line. I saw the leaves of a tree move, and a dark shape drop down. The figure, roughly man-like, moved into the trees, towards the camp. It was no more solid than a shadow.

Moments later, I saw a winged Atapi moving after it, sniffing the air. He stopped in the clearing, looked right past me, and went on. I let him have time to get ahead and moved after him.

The sorcerer moved into the centre of his tribe's evening gather – was welcomed – but he snarled at them all. He was still sniffing the air and looking everywhere. I sought for the shadow I had seen before – not an easy task in the flickering firelight. I whispered the words of a ritual, trying to discern more clearly the unnatural – the intruder.

A sharp exclamation from a female, suddenly turning around and calling, drew my attention. A similar call was made by another female six feet away. There! The shadow – and from the same direction the terrified thoughts of two very young whelps.

I forgot my intention to challenge the sorcerer, and moved to intercept the intruder. I wasn't completely invisible as I ran quietly after the shadow, moved into the trees so that I could pass him, then stopped just ahead of him on the trail. He saw the glowing sword appearing to hover in front of him, and had to stop when the sword seemed to aim itself at his chest.

Only then did I let him see me and I sensed his surprise. It was instantly replaced with intent when he dropped the whelps and drew a long knife and some other kind of weapon – two rocks on a leather thong.

He twirled the rocks, and released them so they flew at me. I raised my left arm and they wound around it and not my neck.

The whelps were cowering on the ground, whimpering. I told them to get behind me and they scrambled to obey. I invoked a bubble of protection around them, and me. That sorcery drew the attention of the sorcerer and he roared defiance into my mind. Then I felt him gather the aura, and saw him release a fire bolt at me. He could not see the shadow between us.

The fire bolt did not hit me; it sizzled all over my shield. The alien was lit up as if he was covered in luminous fungi. Whatever had hidden the intruder from view ceased to work. Now the sorcerer, who had flown to face me, saw the intruder and raised a fist.

"Don't kill it," I called out, but the fist felled the intruder.

"This is my land and you both are desecrating it," the sorcerer roared. "I will do as I please."

"I challenge you then," I said calmly. "I win, I have that carrion. You win, you can do what you like with it."

"Challenge!" the sorcerer roared. "I killed you!"

"Obviously not," I retorted. "And this is no place to discuss things with young whelps listening."

The sorcerer sent a message and two females raced to him. He gestured to the whelps and the females grabbed their respective offspring and raced away.

"You intrude on my land like this carrion," the sorcerer snarled.

"You said that already," I provoked him. "But I found that one sneaking around, and I didn't let him steal two of your tribe's children. That one intended you to rouse your warriors and follow him off your lands to where you would be vulnerable to the Kumatan."

The sorcerer yowled and flung forked lightning at me. Some I deflected back at him, making him dodge, and the rest I avoided. He flung more fire bolts at me in quick succession. I appeared to 'catch' one, and the rest were grounded through Larcia's sword. I was unharmed. The one hovering around my hand I flung back at him and it singed one of his wings. He screamed in pain and rage.

"Weakling," I taunted. "I survived worse than that, and healed the Traeger you almost killed. I don't forgive you for harming an innocent horse. I claim victory, Wyvek, and this carrion."

Wyvek glared at me. "How could you see that carrion?"

"Empathy," I told him. "It puts me closer to the aura. If you agree to listen to me, and the Old One – I will teach you."

His reply was a snarl. "Are there more?"

Since I still had that 'eyes on me' feeling, I said, "Possibly."

Wyvek went to the unconscious figure and tore at the black one-piece suit. It resisted his strength, so he drew out a knife and slashed at the intruder's arm. The metallic tang of the alien's blue blood filled the air.

"What is this? It is not Kumatan. Is it one of those Kimh?" Wyvek demanded.

"No, it is an alien. Other tribes have encountered them before."

"Did the Kumatan send them? Do they know these vermin are here? Tell me!"

"No, to both questions," I said. "The Kumatan know they exist, but not that they are moving by stealth on Atapi lands."

"They know them, that is enough. They are as guilty as this one," Wyvek decided.

"These aliens would like you to go and take your anger out on the Kumatan." I nudged the unconscious one with my toe. "They are trying to convince the Kimh that all Atapi must be exterminated. The Kimh are resisting the idea, so the leader of this carrion complained to the Galactic Council – people who have the right to arrest and relocate vile criminals. The carrion wants them to think Atapi are criminals."

Wyvek had no knowledge of other worlds or other races. I needed to explain the concepts to him, and as I did his rage increased.

"Why do you want this carrion?" Wyvek demanded.

"I have spoken to the Galactic Enforcers," I admitted. "They can't accuse those aliens without proof. This carrion is proof."

Wyvek snarl-grinned.

"They may wish to talk to you," I warned. "They have ways to ensure truth."

Wyvek didn't respond to that. Instead he asked, "How will I see more of these?"

"Take me to the Old One and I will tell you," I tried.

"No, he will not see you," Wyvek stated.

I sensed he believed that. I leant down and whispered a ritual that would keep my prisoner helpless.

As I did, I heard Wyvek howl in outrage. I stood and spun around. Behind me was Centurion Bellus and a Traeger.

"Go," I ordered Wyvek mentally. "I will deal with these and leave at once. Ask your healers about a ritual to locate bodily injuries. Perhaps you can adapt it to a wider area. Go!" He went, and the Traeger protested. Bellus simply eyed me speculatively.

"Impressive," Bellus commented, glancing at the prisoner.

"I don't need your approval," I told him. "Have a present." I used my foot to roll the prisoner closer to him.

Bellus glanced down and seemed to recognise what he saw.

"Obviously you have a way to find me," I accused Bellus in disgust at my previous innocence. "Could you hear any of what went on?"

"Yes," he admitted cautiously. "Though we saw very little – it was dark."

"Yeah, well, I saw this one sneaking around, but only as a shadow. He tried to take two very young whelps. I'm sure you will agree that would anger a sorcerer who cares for his tribe."

"How did you disable him?" Bellus asked. "And his invisibility shield."

"Oh that!" I said casually. "He got in the way of some lightning, and didn't move his head out of the way of a fist."

"You?" the Traeger asked, crouching down next to the prisoner.

"No. Once his suit stopped working the sorcerer could see where to hit."

"He's dead," the Traeger reported. "Poison."

"He wasn't," I insisted. Or maybe had he killed himself before I put the last ritual on him?

"I will make enquiries about this one," Bellus announced. "And ask why he was sneaking around on lands forbidden to his kind and when all his kind was supposedly recalled."

"Yeah, you do that," I agreed. "And if you don't mind the advice, I'd get away from here as soon as you can. You are not welcome here, and you might be mistaken for more of that kind." I pointed at the dead intruder.

"Is there more?" Bellus asked.

I shrugged. "The sorcerer has gone to look for any more."

"If he finds any, will he keep them alive?" Bellus asked.

I said nothing – it was more tactful than saying, "No."

He accepted that I didn't know for sure, picked up the body to sling it over his shoulder – and gestured for the Traeger to leave.

I felt the pull of the sword and resisted it for a moment. In my mind, I spoke the words of a ritual like which I had suggested to Wyvek. Now I could see, glowing brightly, the alien's knife, and the rocks and thong.

Once I had cut it, rocks and thong dropped away. I put it in a pocket of the clothes I wore. Even through fabric, it felt vile. The knife, I hooked through my fabric belt.

I drew on the aura to recharge my energy, and only then touched the sword and walked forward. Five more to go, I told myself. I realised then, that I should have mentioned the feral beasts to the Enforcer, but I was not going to talk aloud to whatever thing he had to trace me.

The two young traders, who led the horse team and wagon, eyed the Enforcer warily. They knew what he represented, but the existence of one waiting at their ship – on Korvu – made them apprehensive.

They gave each other a glance, then the elder one passed the reins to his younger brother and moved forward.

"I am Xander of the Aurlean Trading Clan. Were you requiring to speak to us?"

"Yes, Trader," Centurion Terr confirmed. "May we speak privately within your ship?"

The two traders exchanged looks again. "It would be courteous," the younger agreed, and Xander unlocked the ship and extended the ramp. His brother hitched the team to a protuberance just outside the door.

Once within, Enforcer Terr sat himself in one of the seats around a table in the 'reception' area. Neither of the young traders felt comfortable enough to follow his example.

"Have we done something wrong, Sir?" the younger blurted. "Sorry, I'm Kacen."

"No, I am here merely as a courtesy to the local nobility," Terr explained. "Did either of you visit the palace here a few days ago?" He saw both traders relax a bit.

"No, Sir," Xander said earnestly. "We have just come back from the north east route. Our first trip alone. It is our elders who deal with the local nobility."

Terr nodded. He judged that these two traders were telling the truth. "How may I contact your elders?"

"I could do that for you from here," Xander offered.

"In a moment," Terr agreed. "Have either of you encountered any of the Selkrit engineers that have contracted to work on Korvu?"

Xander moved one hand behind him and seemed edgy. "Yes."

"Where would that have been?" Terr asked casually, pretending he hadn't noticed Xander's action and reaction.

"Three, no, four days ride from here," Kacen estimated. He, too, was edgy about something.

Terr did not think these two youngsters were of importance to him, at least not directly.

"Were they their usual arrogant selves?" Terr asked, making it sound like an idle question.

"Yes," Xander agreed, looking at his feet.

Kacen blurted, "They would not accept that we must make a profit. When we said we could not lower the price more, they attacked us."

Kacen lifted his tunic and revealed a large bruise on his side.

"If your elders wish to make a formal complaint, we will listen," Terr advised. "Though it really is a minor matter. What goods were you trading?"

"Crafted tools, off world hand crafts…" Xander listed. "The villages out that way are quite poor. They are not interested in more exotic things and luxury things. We often traded for their own handcrafts."

Terr nodded. "Did you see any of the Atapi on your trip?"

"The lizards?" Kacen asked. "No. We were told to stay on the marked route, and that is well away from the Lizard lands."

"Wise," Terr agreed. "I have heard they are not interested in off world goods and traders. Yes, I will take up your offer of contact with your elders now – if you would be so kind?"

Xander called his father, the clan leader on Korvu, and explained why he was calling. He handed the radio communicator to Terr and moved back next to his brother.

Terr, after introducing himself, began by alerting the trader to the escalating unrest by the Atapi, and mentioning that they were also targeting the Selkrit engineers. Kacen and Xander heard their father agree that the Selkrit could be aggravating, and he had encountered quite a few on his trip.

The Terr got to the meat of his conversation. "Are you able to tell me which traders visited the palace here recently?"

"One was me," the voice on the communicator admitted. "How can I help you?"

"I would like you to return here, please," Terr requested.

There was a pause before the trader replied. "We are about three days out. If I leave my brother here and ride back, I'd need a day to two days to get back."

"That will be acceptable," Terr agreed. "Contact me on the main galactic frequency when you return."

Trader Wilden rode into the spaceport and went directly to his ship. His sons were there as he had requested. He unstrapped a bulky parcel from the horse's saddle, and hefted it in.

"Did that Enforcer tell you what he wanted?" Wilden asked.

"No, Father," Xander admitted.

Widen looked thoughtful. "I only took the off-world sweets to the palace. That Selkrit ambassador liked the liquorice ones. The High Minister and his consort – if that's who she was – liked the very sweet ones. While I change from these grimy travel clothes, will you go and tell that Enforcer I am back? I'd like to find out what the trouble is."

The young traders came back even before their father had finished cleaning up. They had Centurion Terr with them. Wilden threw his towel back into his cabin and invited Terr into his 'office', along with the still packed bundle.

"What is the problem, Centurion?" Wilden asked – gesturing to comfortable seats.

"Two people from the palace are reported to have had a reaction to some of the food stuffs you were showing them," Terr explained, without making it sound like an accusation.

"I see," Wilden acknowledged. "On the off-chance that might have been the problem, I brought the last of the sweets back. I have had similar goods here before, and had no reports of ill effects. Do you require them for checking?"

"Yes," Terr confirmed. "Could you tell me about your visit to the palace?"

Later Terr reported to Bellus and Quenten.

"Auglan saw the trader first, and he actually suggested what the High Minister might like, and no doubt expected him to return."

"No proof of interference?" Quenten asked.

Terr shook his head. "All the residual items were passed by the medics and Mosellan, the trainee Traeger."

"Nothing conclusive," Quenten summarised. "Did you notice anything else?"

"Notice? No. The trader was keen to keep his name clean and was very helpful. However, both he and his sons encountered Selkrit on their routes. I was under the impression that all had been recalled."

"So was I," Quenten noted. "Have you locations where they were seen?"

"Roughly," Terr admitted.

"I have requested more Centurions," Quenten announced. "We need to be able to be in more places. I also think we need to speak to Councillor Auglan."

"Now, Sir?" Terr asked.

"I suppose morning will do," Quenten decided.

CHAPTER 42 – Jai Cassidy – POV

I expected to arrive in darkness, but not to find a full-scale battle. The night's darkness was illuminated by blazing trees and in front of these I saw the silhouettes of Atapi fighting Kumatan. It seemed like the whole tribe was fighting for survival and the devil was raging with berserk fury – turning Kumatan soldiers into flaming torches.

The reek of death, the clashing of swords and other weapons, the pain of hundreds in agony, quickly got to my nerves. It took all my will to stay standing, and not to flee or collapse with the agony of those around me until I drew on the aura to give me calm.

Then I looked around. This battle was wrong. "This should not be," I said aloud.

Without conscious thought, I raised Larcia's sword and began mouthing ancient invocations that were voiced into my mind. I had chosen to side with the Atapi, but that did not mean I wanted Kumatan to die. Once I had hated and feared the Atapi. Now I knew why they must live.

A swirling mist floated up from the ground, the combatants' movements became sluggish, and then stilled to motionless. I relaxed, but the mist remained.

The sorcerer felt my magic and gave a howl of outrage and hatred. He was full of killing lust, but none of the statues could kill or be killed. He flew at me across the battlefield and dropped onto me, wrapping me in his wings. I felt myself beginning to burn. Struggling was useless. I used my own power to neutralise most of his – so only the clothes I wore burnt.

Something within me warned me of a new danger and the sorcerer shared that knowledge. He released me and spun around with a hiss. We were encircled by a ring of Enforcers and Traegers – they were walking around the statues and closing in.

I had forgotten that the Enforcers could track me. This was not the time to finish the challenge. I raised the sword – a tear in the fabric of this plane appeared.

"Go through," I told the sorcerer with a flick of a thought.

I sensed him about to refuse, not wanting to desert his tribe, and then he saw through the tear, the other side of the mist.

"It's a simple binding," I told him. "Touch your people and go."

He snarled at me, resenting that he was indebted to me. I lowered the sword when the sorcerer had gone. He wasn't far away, but now the mist hid him, and he was outside the circle of angry officials. I sensed the Atapi melting away – all but the dead or fallen.

As I glared back defiantly at the Traegers, I urged the aura to heal the fallen Atapi. I sensed them rise to a crouch and spring away at a run.

The sword was still gleaming golden – it lit the determined faces – all twelve of them. The six Traegers seemed to be of one mind – that I, who had helped a murdering sorcerer to escape, would return with them in his place. They were willing me to move forward.

I kept still. That moment of contact taught me the value of self-discipline. "This battle should not have happened," I said to the Traegers. "Neither side was in control of their actions."

"Why should we believe you?" one Traeger asked.

"Because I stopped the madness," I said. "Because there is a smell in the air that is vile."

"Burnt flesh," a Centurion called to me.

"That and a smoke that comes from nothing natural," I told that one. I saw two of the Traegers reacting to my suggestion.

"Yes," one said, and turned to the nearest Centurion. "Can you test the air?"

Each of the Centurions drew out a hand-held device and began to move slowly, holding their devices at various levels and aiming it in various directions. That they were moving towards me did not go unnoticed. I stood my ground.

"If you do not wish it to affect you as well," I suggested. "You should breathe through a fold of cloth."

My suggestion was acted on; the Traegers drew out cloth to hold to their noses, and the Centurions did something to make their heads become covered in a solid bubble shaped piece of armour.

The devices of the Centurions began to flash red and beep. Two of the centurions moved off towards the trees. When they returned, the smell of the sickly smoke was reducing.

"The woman spoke truly," one of those stated. "The smoke was caused by a proscribed device."

The lead Traeger demanded, "What happened here?" He glared at me.

"I don't know, but I intend to find out," I told him. "But you should be prepared for the Kumatan here to be violent. This mist will clear soon and they will be able to move once more."

I turned to walk off, but I was challenged by one of the Centurions.

"Where are you going, woman of Earth?"

"I have business here," I told him coldly. "The lot of you do not. Collect these victims and go."

"That is not acceptable," the Centurion told me, coming closer.

"Take it up with your boss, the Ambassador. He's into spying on private matters," I said sourly. How could I do what I must if they kept popping up at inconvenient times?

"I will accompany you," the same Centurion insisted.

"No," I said shaking my head. "I know you must have orders to interview the sorcerer who claims these lands, but now is not a good time. Both sides need to come down off battle pitch."

He did not seem willing to agree with me and the Traegers were eying me too. In my mind, I spoke the words of a ritual and when I finished, I turned and walked into the mist and none of them could follow me. They would be able to see my path by the glow of the sword as I went from one injured Kumatan to the next. I drew on the aura to heal those I could, at least enough so that some of these would not die. There was nothing I could do for the dead, and those who had been flaming torches when all had stilled. The latter I eased into death, for they were too injured to heal. The fires I doused with a surge of the aura.

From one of the dead Kumatan, I took a cape to cover the burnt tatters of my clothes. I checked that I still had the alien's knife and the thong weapon, and then I walked across planes to the tribe of the sorcerer I had helped to save.

The Atapi were mostly lying prone on the ground – exhausted from manic fighting and still out of breath from the desperate flight. The sorcerer strode towards me, far from happy.

"What do you know of this?" he demanded of me.

"Ask your healers what they can tell you," I told him. "All I know is that when I arrived and smelt the air, I knew that neither your warriors nor the Kumatan were behaving as they should."

"Why say you that?" I was asked, intently.

"The minds of the Kumatan were full of berserk fury – not calm and ordered as usual. Atapi warriors are normally very fierce, but I did not think you had female warriors. Something had affected your tribe folk and the townsfolk in the same way."

The sorcerer turned and looked at those lying on the ground and only then noticed that truth.

I went on. "It doesn't matter now what you did to anger the Kumatan, or they to anger you. It should have ended when you returned to your lands. Instead, someone caused a sickly smoke to cover all, and then it only needed a spark to ignite the battle." I drew out the stone and thong weapon of the aliens. "And I know who set this up."

The sorcerer turned his full attention on me. "This belongs to a race of blue-blooded aliens," I said. "Have you heard of them?" I received a snarl. "If you invoke the ritual used by healers to find the source of illness and poison – using this weapon to match the contagion – anything belonging to the aliens, or touched by the aliens, will glow."

I tossed the weapon at him and he caught it reflexively.

It didn't take a genius to know that the sorcerer was exhausted; though it wouldn't take him long to recover if he drew on the aura. Now was a good time to challenge him, but would it be fair?

"I will not press my challenge now," I told him. "You have to help your tribe and protect them. And I won't have you claim you were exhausted when I challenged."

"You are the coward," the sorcerer snarled at me, and the spat a glob of saliva into my face.

I wiped my face and advised, "Save your insults. I've heard them all before and they mean nothing. And save your curses for the cowardly blue aliens who skulk around like shadows. Beware they don't sneak up on you and steal your whelps to eat, or kill you in your sleep, as they have done elsewhere."

"I need no rest to take you on!" he claimed.

"Take me to the Old One and we can finish this later," I urged, thinking he would like to see the Old One finish me.

"No! He will not see you."

"Listen, fireman," I snapped. "Your people are safe here only as long as none of those blue aliens find them. Not one of your warriors are in a fit state to fight. Right now, they are easy meat. I know a way to take the Atapi to where no one, Kumatan or alien, can find them."

"How?" the sorcerer demanded.

"That – I will only tell to the Old One."

"He will not see you," was the repeated answer.

"He must! Atapi are dying, and being accused of actions that were provoked so they look like a race of murderers. Half those intruders I saved you from are Enforcers. They claim the right to take dangerous criminals and murderers to other worlds, away from the weak, law-abiding people. Would you want to be dragged from your land, your bond to it broken, and to be taken to where you cannot feel the aura?"

I could feel the mindless rage rising again in the sorcerer. I had not intended to provoke that. His hackles had risen when I called him 'fireman', even if he hadn't understood the word, he had taken it as an insult. Now, my warning was being taken as a threat and he seemed to want to silence the messenger – me. I tried to exude calm, but I sensed he wanted me dead.

"Let's make a deal, fireman," I said quickly. "You challenge me, and if I survive and learn your name, you will take me to the Old One. Do that and I will let you forget you owe me for saving your tribe and I will worry about making the Old One listen to me."

My apparent confidence enraged him beyond control. Without the slightest warning, he sprang at me and entrapped me with his wings once more. I knew struggling would be useless, and only entrap me further. I heard him make a demand of one of his tribe. I wondered what he was waiting for.

Something liquid was thrown on the parts of me that were not wrapped by his wings. Whatever it was, was oily and greasy, and would be over the sorcerer too. I was suddenly released, but as soon as I was, more of the liquid fell on me, and was as quickly ignited.

The flames erupted around me and the oil seemed to be burning furiously. I had not felt the heat yet, and had quickly muttered a ritual that would keep my skin cool. I was thinking that this was true fire, and surprised the sorcerer by dashing towards him and brushing the fire against him. I felt his alarm, and the brief cut off thought that the 'oil' would burn him too.

I laughed maliciously into his mind as I realised how he was trying to trick me. It was not the 'fire' that would burn me, but the oil itself when touched by some ritual. The ritual was tied to the illusion of fire. The burning I was beginning to feel was not from heat but from some corrosive agent, but I had a short advantage. Most of the greasy stuff was on the cape I wore, whilst the sorcerer was scarcely clad. He had to hide the pain he was feeling or lose points in this challenge. For a moment when he was busy reinforcing his pain resistance, I walked to the fire and took a burning stick from the fire and touched it to the oil on my clothing. Then, as the oil blazed up briefly, fiercely, I threw the stick at him.

"Good try, Hirok," I commented when the sorcerer had doused the real flames that destroyed the oil. "But I always fight the illusion of flames with real fire, and real fire doesn't hurt me. As for that oil, this cloak ensured I was not harmed. You really were not thinking."

Hirok gave a mighty bellow of an outraged howl and threw murderous glances at me – but that was all he did.

I soon saw why – two more sorcerers appeared behind him and strode forward. Hirok did not greet them, and did not react to their presence. That told me he was expecting them. I touched their minds, and knew they were here to take me to the Old One. They sprang at me as soon as they appeared, thinking to take me unexpectedly, grabbing me by my arms. I didn't struggle, since this was what I had wanted.

One of the new arrivals spoke to Hirok, and I heard them say, "Our enemies are taking prisoners from all of the tribes. They have broken their word. Keep moving, stay alive. The Old One has a plan."

Somehow, I had the feeling that I was part of his plan.

I allowed the sorcerers to walk me across planes to where the Old One was waiting. I had seen him in their minds as they focused on their destination. I did not know if this was his land, but the Old One sat on a throne that glittered gold in the light of fiery torches in the circle around him – each held by a warrior. We had arrived no more than two feet from him. I shook of the grip of my escorts, though they stayed close behind me and ready to grab if I tried to escape. I studied the Old One and then knelt down on one knee and bowed – it was an Atapi gesture of respect that Larcia had inserted into my mind.

"You mock me," the Old One snarled, rising from his seat. The two warriors behind his throne moved around it and watched.

I felt the blow coming, but did not pull away.

"I will teach you respect," the Old One snarled again, and seated himself back on his throne.

I stood up again and faced him, meeting his eyes that were every bit as hostile as those of my Atapi grandsire. He stared at me for a long time, but I did not quiver with fear. It wasn't that I was not afraid, but I dared not show weakness to this one.

"You have Stacion's arrogance," he told me. "You think that power is enough and clever tricks are all you need. But you are female and no female has the strength of mind to master sorcery. In the past, those that tried went mad. And wild ones, like you, without discipline, give the Atapi a bad name. Do you truly have the arrogance to defeat me? I will not be tricked by you!"

"I do not disagree with you that I lack discipline," I admitted. "But my inheritance of power does not come from Stak, but through my mother – from the Ancient One."

I used what I now knew to be Stacion Ansuni's secret name. My mother had known it, and now it had the effect of confirming my victory over him. I went on – deliberately – to say, "My mother was a daughter of one of your daughters."

I mentioned that deliberately, since I was in effect claiming kinship to him. The Old One now sensed he had a way to have power over me.

"You claim that you bore the Ancient One's sword. Do you still have it?" the Old One demanded.

I touched it and it glowed into visibility. I held it out to him, hilt first, as Larcia prompted me. The Old One stood and came towards me again. He tried to take the sword, but could not, even though I was not gripping it. He touched it and his face seemed to go very still. I could not sense what was going through his mind.

Finally he released it and murmured, "The Sword of Truth." After a moment, he spoke to me. "Female or no, you have the knowledge of a great power. I will have that from you."

His hand went to my face, covering it. I felt him forcing his mind on mine, but I blocked him by recalling a stream of mental trivia from Earth. Then I felt something flick his mind away. He visibly flinched and his expression betrayed anger. Moments later, I felt his fear.

"They dare," he hissed. "The Kumatan dare take my tribe…"

"I can take the Atapi where they will be safe, Old One," I said loudly, interrupting his thoughts.

"How?" he demanded. "How can a whelp like you know such a thing?"

"Stak knew it," I told him. That got his full attention, even if most of the time he denied Stacion had ever existed. "It was how he hid his tribe from the humans and Kumatan on Earth." I didn't intend to tell him that the Kumatan had used it, too.

"Tell me!" The Old One stared down at me from his superior height.

"I need to show you," I told the Old One. "And I will have to start from the Rock of Arkor."

"The Kumatan are there in force," one of my still unnamed escorts snarled.

"Not inside the rock," I countered. "In the cave where I hid from you. I can take you there. And this does not have to take long."

Quick as a striking snake, my two escorts and the Old One grabbed me. "Show us where!"

I allowed them into my mind enough to give them the visualisation. "We must go together, or you will not be allowed in that cave."

The three sorcerers took the opportunity to make their grip painfully tight, and to hustle me forward the three steps to Larcia's cave. The Old One snarled and turned around, holding me as he seemed to sense the power within this cave. He released me, until he noticed that the other two sorcerers were now like statues. I prised open their fingers to get loose. The Old One hissed when he looked down the tunnel to the entrance and spotted the Kumatan guards there in force.

"They cannot see in here," I assured him. "And whilst you can walk out of the cave, you will be unable to return."

It was a warning that he should not go out and try to kill those desecrating the sanctity of the Rock. The Old One seemed to draw his attention back to what he was sensing here in the cave. His anger dissipated to wariness.

"The aura is strong here, pure and untainted. What is here? How did you get to come here? You are not a sorcerer!"

I didn't hear his question. In my mind, Larcia was speaking. "Daughter, bring my son to me."

With polite respect, I bowed to the Old One. "Please, follow me."

I led him to the smaller cave at the back and spoke aloud, "I have brought him, my Queen."

The walls of the cave began to glow, and the altar became visible.

I felt a brief flick of Larcia's mind, and then nothing. From the Old One's face, I knew Larcia was speaking to him. He was incredulous, thinking it was a trick. He flicked a glance at me and hissed, but then the ghostly remains of the Ancient One became visible on the altar. He was drawn forward, but touched nothing.

I decided to sit while I waited for the silent conversation to finish. I could see the play of expressions on the Old One's face, the whole gamut from suspicion to belief. Finally, he turned his attention back to me and simply glared as if I was something unpleasant.

I guessed the reason from what Larcia said to me. "Daughter, show the Old One that which you know. Our people must go to safety. Then I command you to accept the training of the Old One."

I did not like that last part, but I promised. "Yes, my Queen."

The Old One strode back to the outer cave, as the glow from the walls dimmed to very faint. The other two devils stirred and glanced around, unaware that any time had passed.

"Show us!" all three demanded.

I bowed to the Old One, moved back and raised Larcia's sword until the hilt touched my forehead. Ignoring the mutterings of the sorcerers, I concentrated on the important facets of that other plane I sought.

On Earth, the two planes had existed in the same time stream, but the plane on which the Atapi and Kumatan colonies had existed on was not the one I had been born on. Stacion had enabled his warriors to cross between the two planes, and Jenha Mosellan had done the same for his guards. They were the only ones attuned to the two planes and able to cross between them. I had learnt how when I had broken Stacion's binding – although I had not realised it at the time. When I tried it again, my mother's box had been the key I had needed.

The plane I sought now would be like the one we existed in, but where neither Atapi, nor the humanoid races of Korvu existed. The plane where I had waited for Mikha to be born.

"Touch me and walk with me," I commanded, and again the three chose to grip me painfully, on shoulders and arm. They snarled dangerously as I seemed to be walking outside – right at the Kumatan. The snarls turned to snuffles of bewilderment, for on the third step, the scene was the same but the Kumatan were not there.

We emerged from the cave, and the sorcerers sniffed the air warily.

"This is not a trick," I told them. "We are still on Korvu – you can still feel the aura. This is Korvu as it would be without Kimh, Kumatan and, until now, Atapi. This land is untouched by any intelligent race." The two lesser sorcerers moved away, looking around.

I turned and pointed at the Rock and said quietly to the Old One who was still holding me. "There is the same cave where we were, only without the sorcery needed to protect the ancient one's altar. She does not lie on this plane."

"Go and check the truth of these claims," the Old One commanded. He kept hold of me, so I would not leave and abandon them here.

The two devils walked off at once, using landmarks to their lands. In a very short time, they returned, excited by what they had seen. "The land is lush and fertile," one said. "And animals are abundant."

"Hold this creature," the Old One ordered, and as soon as I was again being held, he walked elsewhere.

Some of his normal arrogance was gone when he returned. I sensed that the emptiness of this plane was unnerving him.

Once back in the cave, I went to where water trickled into a rock basin and took a drink. The three sorcerers were squatting in a tiny circle and discussing things, excluding me from their conversation. I wandered to the shelf alcove where, in the other plane, I had found artefacts left by mother. It was empty and the walls there unmarked by glyphs. There, out of sight of the three sorcerers, a glow formed, resolving into a golden crown. I recognised Larcia's crown, but did not sense her mind here. I reached to the crown, but my hand moved through it. I pondered what it meant.

Larcia must have sent it here, but it was not quite fully here. I stared at it. The large single sapphire set in it seemed more solid than the rest. I let my hand pass through the ethereal crown and cup the stone. It felt solid in my palm and came away from the crown.

Strange. The gem was the size of a sparrow's egg, and had been set in that crown countless years ago for a sorcerer queen.

The jewel, but not the crown, had followed me across planes. It was real in both planes. I had received it here, but it was native to the other plane. Then I knew what it was – it was a 'key' linking this plane and the real one. It was like the box my mother had made for me. I did not need such a key to get here – the sword had opened the way and enabled me to cross freely between planes. Then I laughed to myself. I could do it without the sword, but the sorcerers did not need to know that. I intended them to think that only I could open the way.

This jewel could be used by another to cross planes to here and back, but I did not intend to give it to any sorcerer. It was my son who would need it, when he was driven to find me to learn this part of his heritage. I quickly slipped the stone into one of the still intact pockets of my torn and burnt cape. I would keep it with me until I found a way to give it to Mikha.

I became aware that the Old One's conference had ended and the three sorcerers were walking purposefully toward me.

"Return us!" the Old One insisted. "This knowledge must be shared with all the tribes."

They gripped me again, but with less force, and I walked them back to Larcia's cave. The two lesser devils departed at once. I assumed to return to their tribes.

Again the Old One studied me. "The Ancient One opened my mind to much that has been forgotten. The Atapi are like itinerant beggars compared to what we once were. I can see that on that plane – we could grow strong again."

"Yes," I agreed.

"All the tribes must agree. The sorcerers will meet and you will learn of our decision. Now, get out of my sight before I feel I want to kill you. I have many of my tribe to rescue from the Kumatan and the arrogant off worlders. I have the urge for fresh spilled blood."

"You need to talk to them," I said quickly. "Tell them that it was not the Atapi that started this."

"And they will believe it? I think not." The Old One made a motion of throwing something away from him, and I found myself flung through the air to land hard on the ground.

"Foolish whelp," he said derisively. "Go!"

I went.

When I left the Old One, I was only thinking of how tired, hungry and filthy I was – not to mention thinking ruefully of the woeful state of my clothes. I'd had enough of sorcerers and fighting. I wanted a rest.

I was somewhat surprised to find myself near the palace – not far from the compound where my tribe lived.

"Daughter, you have spent little time with them," Larcia said in my mind. "They, too, must decide if they wish to cross planes."

"Do I dare, my Queen? When so many tribes are going mad, being raided unfairly? Those Enforcers must assume we are guilty – because the sorcerers won't talk to them."

"Do you truly believe these creatures will listen?" Larcia asked me.

"Yes, and I think that they are taking not prisoners, but hostages – to force the sorcerers to come to them. And I think that if they keep that up, the sorcerers will decide to act together in ways that will forever damn the Atapi race."

"Then we must get them away from here…" Larcia advised.

"No!" I disagreed with her. "Until all the innocents are redeemed and those blue blood aliens are exposed for the criminals they are – I will not leave, and the sorcerers should not, either. Those aliens fear us, want us out of the way. If they get their way, the Kimh and Kumatan will be next and all the treasures of this world will be plundered."

"You are right, daughter," Larcia thought at me after a period of consideration. "Those aliens have been here before…"

"We need to scare them away, so they will fear us so much they will think a thousand times before returning."

I fell silent, realising I needed to find out what had been happening from the view of the Kumatan, the Kimh and the Enforcers – but I did not feel up to facing them just now.

"Jai-devil?"

I looked around. "Farcine," I greeted.

"Why do you stand out here? All of us will be richer for your presence. Let us serve you."

Truth was I didn't know why I stood there, or why I didn't go straight in. They were my tribe, I was their 'devil' –but I didn't feel that I could make demands of them.

"I could do with a bath," I said, accepting the offer of service. "And food. And I don't suppose you know how I can get another set of clothes from Ellhi Mosellan?"

Farcine chuckled. "Now you begin to sound like a devil."

My arrival caused a stir amongst my tribe. They instinctively gathered around me, expressing their pleasure at my return. I felt their heartfelt respect for me; it wasn't quite love, but it filled a void inside me. Every one of them would fight to protect me, even the whelps. They all considered that I belonged to them.

I told the males that I wanted to talk to them after I had refreshed myself. I had important things to discuss with them. Farcine, acting as leader in my absence because of her rank as Eldest Mother, told them to ensure I wasn't disturbed.

Most of the females went off to prepare food, a drink and a bath for me. Another changed shape in front of me and asked what message I needed to send. I told her my request of Ellhi and she trotted off.

"We cannot enter the Palace since they have warded it," Farcine explained. "Some of us are still within and cannot leave – but we have our ways to keep in touch."

I nodded. "What else has been happening?"

Farcine really only had snippets of information and in most cases I did not know if they were related to what I wanted to know or not. But I listened as I ate the delicious, if unfamiliar, meal they prepared for me.

When the bath was ready, and I was surprised to see it – I slipped gratefully out of the cape and tattered rags. I did not forget to remove the alien items and the blue sapphire from the pockets and have them put out of casual reach.

The water, poured into a deep hammock of joined skins, was the perfect temperature, and I found myself relaxing from days and days of tension. Two of the females came up and began to wash me, doing as they would have for a male sorcerer devil – that is, on the odd occasions that the males deigned to bathe.

I was not used to such service, but I did not stop them. I was just too tired to care. When one began washing my hair – it was blissfully relaxing. Behind it all, an instinct for caution warned me not to become too relaxed. Too much was happening. When I was clean, I let the females dry me and wrap me in a warmed fur blanket and lead me to a wickedly comfortable chair where a cool drink was waiting on a low table made from a foot high slice of tree trunk. Two remained in case I desired anything else.

Farcine returned, escorting a visitor. I rose and went to greet Ellhi with a delight equal to hers in seeing me. I hugged her and felt her concern at how thin I looked and I sensed other things from her.

"Farcine," I said. "I'd like some absolutely private time, please."

The females melted away, and I drew Ellhi within the fur blanket. I felt her begin to cry, and I led her to a low bed that was within the room so we could sit together. I didn't need to ask why she cried. She needed to relieve her own build-up of tension. She had needed to be strong whilst her husband had been kept from her. She had needs that she could not fill. The powers here had arbitrarily dissolved the triumvir of Jenha, her and I, but they could not break the emotional binding between us. The idea of a three-way bond was alien by the standard of my world, but accepted here. I had been welcomed by both Ellhi and Jenha, learnt about love with a man and a woman. Ellhi's need woke an answering one in me and, in this place of the Atapi, no one would question what we chose to do.

We did not pull apart for a long time; just lay together under the blanket, talking. Ellhi told me what she had heard, relating to the things I needed to know, and I could not help but become angry.

"I'm sorry," Ellhi apologised. "I did not mean to make you angry."

"I'm not angry at you," I assured her, stroking her hair gently. "But I know now how the Kumatan see recent events, and I know how the Atapi see things. Each blames the other – both sides have been cleverly provoked, but I cannot prove it."

Finally, we both drew apart, knowing we could not make this time stretch any longer. I dressed in the clothes that Ellhi had brought for me, and she fixed up her own clothes. I walked her out as far as the gate in the compound fence. As I walked back, I considered what I needed to say to my warriors.

All the males gathered around me, down to the youngest trainee warriors. I told them how proud I was of them, and they all stood straighter. Then I gestured for them to sit in a semicircle around me.

"I need you all to be extra vigilant," I began. "Every other tribe is fighting Kumatan in the belief that they are the cause of mortal insults. I know this is not true, just as I know that the Atapi have not attacked them unprovoked. You are living in the shadow of the palace, and I want you to remember this."

I told them all I had encountered elsewhere, and when I finished, they were all snarling softly. I counted the grown males in front of me – only twenty-four.

"How far from here do you range?" I asked.

They all exuded amusement. The Eldest Warrior, old Ketali, told me, "ten miles" and I was impressed. They were keeping themselves fit and their hunting skills honed. I was equally sure that their fighting skills were not rusty either. Somehow, I was going to have to prove to the warriors of other tribes that my warriors were not 'neutered', and to other people that they all had discipline and honour.

For now, I wanted to try some sorcery and have them hunt for me. When I had told them what I intended, they all quivered in excitement. I drew on their nervous energy as I spoke the words of the ritual that would reveal traces of the aliens. When I felt the ritual had indeed worked, I sent out the full warriors with instructions to look for, and report, glowing tracks.

A half grown whelp tried to sneak out with them.

"Teregan!" I said sharply.

The whelp stopped, but did not look at me. He dropped his head, turned in my direction and bowed as if to a male sorcerer.

"Sit!"

Teregan sat, and seemed surprised when I went and sat in front of him.

"Am I in trouble, Jai devil?" he asked timidly, yet daringly.

"You will be, you precocious whelp, if you don't listen to me."

I had his attention. "If I was any kind of proper sorcerer, you would already be my apprentice. Do you understand what that would mean?"

Teregan's eyes went much wider than normal.

"I cannot train you yet, but I want you to be very careful about what you do. I heard about that business with the Councillor from Selkrit and you need to know how dangerous that was. My nasty human side was highly amused, but as an Atapi sorcerer, responsible for everyone in this tribe, I am telling you not to risk yourself like that again."

The whelp had no idea of his danger. "You were lucky that that alien did not realise you were Atapi. He may have killed you right then, or he might have captured you and dragged you to the Traegers, as proof of the devilry they claim Atapi are doing to them. The Traegers would have muzzled you permanently. And the Enforcers would feel justified in hunting out all Atapi and confining them to question them."

Teregan dropped his head further. "When he was bit, I treated him good," he said, and he launched into details of what he had done.

"You did as you should have," I interrupted the whelp's attempt at trying to earn my forgiveness. "But the need should not have arisen."

"But…" Teregan tried to argue.

"Hush! I have a question for you. Farcine has told me you have been having bad dreams these past few nights – can you tell me about them?"

"He's in them, that horrid alien - or ones like him. I hear them talking but it don't sound like our words," Teregan told me.

"Pity," I said aloud, wondering how I could use this surprising development. "Can you show me in your head what you saw?"

He tried, but it wasn't clear. Perhaps not surprising, as one tends to forget dreams quickly.

I did something then that I intended as a warning to Teregan. I took a knife, not the alien one but one supplied by Farcine who'd seemed to read my mind, grabbed Teregan's wrist and nicked his hand on the ball of his thumb. He jerked in surprise, but I held him firmly as I squeezed a drop of blood from the cut. Pulling his hand closer, I licked the cut and whispered a ritual to heal it.

He stared at me as if I had changed shape.

"I have just blooded you to me," I told him. "Now I can oversee what you do when I am not here."

Teregan hunched up guiltily. I held his chin and forced him to look at me. "Show me those images again."

The blooding ritual had worked, better than I had expected. The pictures were better than before, but the alien faces were still not clear enough to identify individuals. I concentrated on the surroundings.

"Do you recognise this place, Teregan?" I asked.

"I think, Jai-devil, that it is his metal cave that I saw at the spaceport."

I looked again, memorising details, so that if I had to I could walk there. I reinforced the same details in his mind, as a lesson in providing a reference to cross planes.

"Treat this as a lesson in sorcery. What I just did to you is similar to what you did when you sucked venom from the alien. You seem to have formed a link between you and him. It is called the sorcerer's over-mind. And it is the means by which a sorcerer can link to the minds of his tribe or an enemy."

Teregan's eyes began to gleam.

"I do not want you to use it on anyone else," I warned him, and I had used Command tone to enforce it. I didn't miss the flash of resentment as I went on. "When you next get these visions, I want you to memorise them. I want to know what that creature is up to. This is very important to me."

The resentment changed to pride. "At other times, I want you to keep learning the art of healing – even though it is considered female's work. The healers use the aura and must have discipline and persistence. These are basic skills that you need to master. When you are not busy with the healers, I want you to keep practicing with the warriors."

Teregan sighed, and I gestured him to go off. He scuttled away obediently in the belief that I would know if he wasn't.

Something drew me outside to look at the palace. The first thing I saw was the blue glow that looked like it completely encircled the compound, outside the fence. It was bright enough to outline the figure not far away.

"Jenha?" I whispered, and I walked the short distance to arrive close enough to embrace him. He drew back after a moment, and I accepted the wisdom of that. "Should you be here?" I asked. "I do not wish you to be punished because of me."

"You need not be the keeper of my conscience, Jai," he told me. "And perhaps the time has come for meekness to end. Now listen well…"

In terse statements he told me the situation on Korvu from the view of the Kumatan and the Enforcers. He mentioned that the Kimh had been stood down as rulers.

"The Enforcers are beginning to doubt the honesty of the Selkrit, but at the same time the Atapi uprisings are escalating and the Selkrit are demanding action. The Enforcers are watching you closely – and intend to make the sorcerers talk to them."

That bit I already knew. I told him, "The Atapi have been made to believe that the Kumatan have instigated the battles. The aliens have snuck onto their lands, stolen children and ridden off on horses while looking like Kumatan. The warriors chase them to the towns to bring back their children. Can you blame them for thinking the Kumatan guilty?"

"Nor for being angry," Jenha murmured.

I added, "The aliens wear suits that make them little more than shadows and they do other mischief. What else has caused the Enforcers to be thoughtful?"

"Reports from the trader clan of seeing Selkrit in many places – when all Selkrit were supposedly recalled."

"Do you know where?" I asked.

Jenha murmured a negative. "Would that you could make the aura reveal them."

That was an idea…

"I would rather make it scare them witless and shitless," I said softly. Another idea…

"Can you?" Jenha asked softly. "The male sorcerers can use the aura."

I hesitated, thinking only of how the sorcerers might warp it.

"Surely it can tell what is natural to Korvu," Jenha suggested obliquely.

"Yes," I agreed as a vague idea formed in my mind. "I doubt I could make all the sorcerers work together when their tribes are under attack."

"The Ancient One?" Jenha murmured. "If you invoked her name… perhaps."

"I will give it thought," I promised. "But it won't be immediate. I will be gone by morning and I still have three sorcerers to face."

"Only three," Jenha murmured, impressed.

"And the Old One has seen an alternate plane," I murmured. "They won't leave yet."

"Nor should they. We have been sent to take hostages."

"I know of that. Does Kaer know that you are here?"

"He did not see me go out."

Sensing his mild duplicity, I grinned – maybe I had corrupted him – just a little.

"Return I must," Jenha murmured. "Thank you for being kind to Ellhi. Your warriors are returning."

I looked towards the direction he had glanced, and when I looked back, he was gone. I sighed and went to hear the findings of my warriors.

Apart from learning how frequently the aliens had been moving around in the area that my Chief Warrior claimed as his range, I learnt little that was immediately useful. I dismissed all but Ketali, and two of the oldest warriors.

"As a sorcerer, I have much to learn," I admitted. They gave no reaction to that, so I went on. "There is something I should have done long ago. Do you know of the blooding ritual?"

They each nodded, betraying nothing.

"Would you be willing to partake of it now?" I asked.

Ketali spoke for all of them. "It is your prerogative, Jai-devil. Surely not for us to refuse."

"I hoped you wouldn't, because I wish to have access to your years of experience and wisdom."

"We would be honoured, Jai-devil," Ketali formally agreed. All three bowed their heads in lieu of a full bow.

"As am I," I admitted. It surely couldn't be easy for these warriors to stomach a young female sorcerer. Yet I sensed their utter willingness to do whatever I asked of them. They were snarl-grinning in eagerness, and it occurred to me that maybe I didn't have to do everything myself.

As I had done to Teregan, I did to these three stoic warriors. I tested the link and felt both stronger and wiser for the contact.

"It should work both ways," I said, more to myself. I thought at them and asked them to think back at me. I heard three different sounding mind voices calling my name. I grinned, and told the warriors they could return to their duties.

Before I left, I had one more thing I wanted to do. The four females who had served the High Minister with such efficiency sat with me and Farcine in a circle. These four were no longer working in the palace, but were still able to keep in touch with other Atapi females there. I listened to all they had learnt, and then to all the little things that were being done to annoy the Selkrit councillor, Auglan. I grinned devilishly.

"I have heard that the engineers that accepted Kimh hospitality have moved out," Farcine added.

I wondered if that was good or bad, and where they had gone.

When I could learn no more, I knew it was time to leave. I didn't want the Enforcers checking my whereabouts and coming here to hassle my tribe. I wasn't sure they could still find me now that I had completely changed my clothes.

I returned to the cave in the Rock of Arkor, simply for a safe place to think. Well, safe so long as I didn't walk out of the cave. For a while, watching the Kumatan outside the cave distracted me. I could not imagine what they were doing there – but they were not my current problem, which was to find a way to know where the Selkrit were sneaking around.

I felt Larcia in my mind, but she was not intruding. When I gave up on my fruitless thoughts, I heard her say, "The Old One believes he can duplicate what you did."

"Can he?" I asked, since I had no idea of how powerful or skilled he was.

"Not yet, I think, but in time he might learn. For now he thinks he must work from here, and with the Kumatan here he won't come."

"I did it from here because the aura is strong here. I have actually done it before – when I hid until Mikha was born," I admitted.

Larcia accepted that and said, "You have a question, daughter. Do not fear to ask it."

"I have come to think of you as a real, living being," I thought carefully. "But you said you were only alive in the aura."

"That is true," Larcia confirmed.

"How do you sense what is happening away from here?"

"Through those who invoke my name, or through those who have come to me here," Larcia explained.

"Sorcerers?" I asked.

"Yes. What are you thinking of, daughter?"

"A way to drive all of the blue blood aliens away," I began. "I heard that their master, Councillor Auglan, had recalled them all but traders have been seeing them in many remote places, as well as on lands held by Atapi."

"What have you in mind, daughter?"

"Is there a way to find them through the aura?" I asked. "And ways to make the aura reject them?"

Larcia fell silent in my mind. Finally she responded "Once I knew the lands of all the hundreds of sorcerers. So many of them are long dead, but my link to their lands should still remain."

After a long time, I heard her hiss in my mind. "Yes! I feel those fiends. They are like a rash."

"Can you tell me where they are?"

So much information came into my mind. Larcia could list the names of the sorcerers, from the first sorcerer to claim the land to the last, but that did not help me. I could not write down the names, and Larcia had no idea of maps.

I wondered how old the maps were in the palace. I knew the Selkrit Councillor had been extremely interested in some. And did the Traegers record the names of sorcerers and where they claimed?

"Is there a way to affect the area where they are?" I asked next.

"I have heard of instances," Larcia admitted. "But it has been so long. You could evoke the dreaming."

"What's that?"

"Think of what you wish to know, and sleep," Larcia directed. "That is the way your mother learnt... the way it has always been."

It was worth a try, I decided. I thought carefully of the sorts of things that might make life unpleasant for the aliens and, in spite of my doubts, I slept.

When I re-awoke, feeling ravenous, my head was full of rituals and snippets of rituals. I ignored hunger for a time and sorted through a myriad of ideas. Over the countless centuries, the sorcerers had devised many, many ways to annoy or weaken their enemies or perceived enemies. I discarded any idea that required the warping of the aura and finally settled on some weather rituals, some to rally insects, animals and birds to attack what was not natural, and a ritual of 'ill luck'. Each needed an alien artefact to target the spell, but I had one of their knives.

Larcia guided my working, for I had no training in performing long and complex rituals. How long I lay on the hard rock, setting all the rituals in motion, I didn't know, but it was just on dawn when I woke from the casting trance.

My stomach was in tight knots. I needed to eat. Larcia told me to go outside and I would find a white substance on the ground that would be both edible and filling. I knew what she referred to, as I had learnt of it when I had first arrived on Korvu. It was 'manna', the fruit of tiny spores that grew during the desert night and lasted only until the sun was full on them. They looked like balls of cotton, and tasted like nothing I had ever tasted before.

Before running out, I checked that the Kumatan were not close. I saw no one, but I guessed they'd returned to the palace last night, and if so would likely be back very soon. I had a very short time to have my fill.

As I knelt, greedily stuffing my mouth with the white substance and trying to stuff more in my pocket, I suddenly sensed I was no longer alone. I leapt up and spun around.

"Jenha!" I exclaimed in surprise. I quickly looked around, but he seemed to be alone.

He smiled at me, and crouched down to taste some of the manna too.

"You have no handler?" I commented, cautiously. I wanted to know why he was here.

"Oh, I do. But one who is not afraid that I will run off with the wild Atapi when I am not overseen," Jenha spoke with a trace of irony. "Ambassador Quenten, at least, believes in my ability and experience."

"About me?" I asked wryly.

"And other things," Jenha agreed. "He has doubts about the Selkrit. That one you caught on Atapi lands was some kind of wanted criminal."

"They all are," I said.

"Perhaps, young one, your help is needed to prove it."

"What?"

Jenha considered his words. "He is constrained – limited in what he can do here by the wording of the official request. Auglan has relinquished the blaming of all on the Kimh, but still insists that the Atapi pay for their crimes."

"Bastard," I blurted.

Jenha quietly rebuked me. "Anger is counter-productive. There is another way..."

"Go on," I invited, intrigued by the way Jenha was acting.

"You, being related to the Atapi – but not a citizen of Korvu – and I am told now under the aegis of the Galactic Federation, can request the Enforcers to investigate the Selkrit. But you must follow the correct protocol and you must be authorised by the Atapi."

Jenha was treading a path very, very close to 'unacceptable' by Kimh standards. Hell, even his talking to me would be unacceptable according to those old thick-heads. He wasn't blatantly stating what he meant – what he was suggesting that I do. But I knew him too well to doubt his meaning.

"I will see what I can do," I said. "The Old One was rather ill-tempered with me when I finally met him. I think he felt threatened and not inclined to speak to the Enforcers himself."

Jenha stood up, nodded once, and 'walked' away.

"Sneaky," I said aloud. I was pretty sure that what Jenha hadn't said was the Quenten would welcome an official request to check out the Selkrit. If that was true, maybe I could get some promises from him that I could use to bargain with the sorcerers.

CHAPTER 44 - Kimh - POV

The Kimh Council was summoned to convene in the assembly hall at the request of Ambassador Quenten. When the Kimh Elders arrived, High Minister Koenig was seated beside Quenten, a fact noted with relief by all Kimh.

"I believe you have all been advised of events over the last few days," Quenten addressed them. From the nods and serious faces, they had. "I greatly regret the loss of life and injury to many worthy Kumatan fighters. In future, I am instructing all Kumatan town guards to refrain from challenging or engaging Atapi if they are seen around their town."

There was a murmur of protest. Malachi rose to his feet to be recognised and asked to speak.

"Sir, surely that will increase the risk to innocent townsfolk."

Quenten was ready to answer that. "It may seem that way, but I do not believe it will prove to be so. Some evidence has come to light that the Atapi were provoked in such a way that they believed that Kumatan had ventured onto their land and attacked them."

Eamon rose. "You instructed some of the Kumatan to collect hostages."

"Yes," Quenten admitted. "Many of those were taken off Atapi land. However, those instances did not lead to open battle."

"If that is not what provoked them," Eamon asked, "what did?"

"A Selkrit infiltrator was captured on Atapi lands. Later, after a battle, we took air samples and these revealed traces of a banned substance that causes normally rational creatures to act like savages."

Koenig rose. "I cannot believe the Selkrit have a part in the Atapi barbarisms. They suffered at Atapi hands. Surely they would not provoke those savages any further."

Quenten accepted his comment and asked in turn, "Was this council aware that Selkrit teams have gone out to remote areas? I understood that all the engineers were ordered all their teams to return."

"I did make that order," Koenig agreed. "I was advised that most went back to their ship. The rest are housed here."

Eamon rose again. "Have you spoken to Councillor Auglan of this?"

"Yes," Quenten confirmed. "He tells me he has kept all his engineers out of Atapi occupied lands, but while waiting for permission to proceed he has sent more men to work on the first power station and a few others to prospect sites for future population expansion."

"The Councillor's forethought is commendable," Koenig stated. "He is keeping his people usefully occupied while we are constrained and unable to settle the Atapi problem."

Quenten did not react to the subtle rebuke to his ruling. Instead, he considered all the other little things that didn't add up. Most were circumstantial and not firm proof. If these people were so blind…

He had proved to his satisfaction that it was not Koenig, or the Kimh as a whole, who were responsible for the Atapi atrocities. That was ludicrous, and the Atapi did not recognise the right of the Kimh to rule them. On that basis, his reason for suspending the council no longer existed.

Councillor Auglan, who was not present at this meeting, had accepted that but still insisted that the Atapi be held accountable for their murderous actions. Quenten needed the cooperation of the Kimh Council for that – but he also really needed a mandate to investigate the Selkrit activities on Korvu, but he could not ask for it directly.

"The matter of the Atapi is still under investigation," Quenten went on. "As none of the tribal leaders have consented to talk to us, they have been classified as hostile; and I am authorised under Galactic Law to take necessary steps to correct that refusal. In that matter, I am in full charge. In all other matters, this Council has resumed full powers. I step down to equal rank with High Minister Koenig."

Quenten allowed Koenig to take up matters that were of local concern, and sat seeming to listen politely to matters that did not concern him. He was hoping that his instructions to his subordinates would be completed before the meeting ended, but not until all the idealistic Kimh had calmed down from thoughts of Atapi atrocities.

Koenig's indrawn breath as one of the other Kimh was speaking drew Quenten's attention to the rear door of the Council chamber. The movement of turning heads caused the speaker to finish quickly, as Jenha Mosellan and Jai Cassidy walked in, stopping five feet from the half circle bench seating the Elder Councillors, as protocol demanded.

"What is the meaning of this intrusion? Solomon! Have Mosellan removed from here!" Koenig demanded. He knew he had no say in the matter of the hybrid.

Quenten spoke softly. "I have requested his services. He will remain."

Koenig's face turned a darker shade, but he did not try to overrule Quenten. Solomon had moved to be beside the new comers, and stayed still. He had caught the subtle hand gesture from the High Minister.

I felt the undercurrents in the Council chamber, but with Jenha beside me and with permission to stay, they did not worry me. So I waited politely for the Council to allow me to speak. Since I was following protocol, they could not arbitrarily evict me. Finally, Koenig gave the signal I knew to look for.

"I wish to address the council," I said loudly enough for all to hear me. I bowed then to Koenig, and then to Quenten. Jenha was whispering to my mind the correct protocol. He was ignoring the glare from the High Minister.

I went on to say, "I have requested Jenha Mosellan as my advocate."

Off to one side, I saw vague movement and recognised Kaer stirring uneasily. I ignored him. Jenha was risking enough.

Quenten waved a signal at Koenig, and the High Minister subsided.

"He has only partial authority back," Jenha murmured. "Address yourself to the Ambassador."

"Ambassador Quenten, I am Jai Cassidy – born on Earth of human and Atapi parents. In this council, I asked for and was granted the aegis of the Galactic Federation."

Quenten nodded confirmation.

"May I speak before this council?" I asked formally.

I received a nod, and, "Proceed."

I took a deep breath. "I am here representing the tribes of the Atapi. To protest at the removal of Atapi tribespeople from their tribal land."

As I had predicted, Koenig protested. "This council did not authorise that!"

Ambassador Quenten, canny negotiator that he was, admitted, "Some of those removals were on my orders."

I sensed that he knew what I was leading up to. "Then, Sir, I insist on the release of those Atapi that are in your custody." 'Insist', Jenha had said, was not as unacceptable as 'demand'.

"I will be pleased to make the appropriate arrangements with the Atapi tribal leaders," Quenten said evenly.

Koenig tried to hide his smile behind his hand, thinking I was outclassed.

"And the rest, Sir?" I challenged Quenten.

Koenig spoke first. "I can attest that Kumatan were not authorised to intrude on Atapi lands except under the orders of Ambassador Quenten. Who do you claim this offence against?"

I looked at Koenig directly, and it seemed to make him uncomfortable. "I do not challenge Kimh or Kumatan with this matter. And as I am not a citizen of Korvu, I cannot compel you to act on my request." I turned to Quenten.

"Ambassador, as an alien to Korvu, but one related by ties of blood and kin, and under your aegis, I formally request an investigation into the activities of the Selkrit on this world. I have seen proof of their duplicity. They are acting in ways not sanctioned by their contract with the Kimh High Council. Some have committed atrocities towards the Atapi and others have intended to steal metal ores from Korvu, which they have no right to do."

I kept my face straight and appeared to ignore the agitated Councillors. It was like I had shaken a bee's nest – with everyone suddenly objecting to my accusation.

"Such a request is a breach of trust between the Kimh and our allies, the Selkrit." Koenig thumped the bench as he spoke to emphasise his point.

Quenten used the bell and silence fell.

"Jai Cassidy, have you been duly authorised to act on behalf of the Atapi?" he asked.

"Yes Sir, I am acting on the orders of the Old One," I claimed with fingers crossed behind by back. The Old One's curses had not exactly been 'formal words'.

I hoped Quenten still had ways to know I was telling the truth. He studied me for a moment longer than comfortable before speaking.

"Your request will be acted upon," Quenten told me. "Have you time to put this request in writing?"

"Yes, Ambassador," I confirmed.

"Very well. I will expect you for a meeting at the conclusion of this Council session."

I bowed to both Quenten and Koenig before withdrawing past the unamused faces of the Kimh.

Once outside the Council chamber, Jenha led me directly to the Ambassador's suite, and Centurion Terr admitted us. I had half-expected Koenig to have me intercepted. Only when the door was shut behind me did I realise that I was shaking. I didn't know if it was from tiredness, reaction, hysterics or laughter. Jenha's hand on my shoulder steadied me.

"You did well," he assured me. "You are the only one who could have made the request."

I gave a smothered snort. We both knew that the Kimh could have requested it if they were not so trustingly naive.

Jenha tacitly did not mention that. Instead, he said, "I was impressed that you convinced the Old One to let you act for them."

I did laugh then. "If you call, 'Bah! You are a fit one to consort with aliens. Tell them to stay away from us – if they will do as you say. Tell them to remove the blue trash – or we will' – as authorising me."

Jenha's face twitched, but I sobered. "But if I read those Kimh rightly, they now probably want to use my guts to hold up their socks," I said derisively.

"What?" Jenha asked, confused.

I was tempted to tease him. I felt I needed an outlet or I would have hysterics. "Didn't you ever hear that Earth saying about having one's guts for garters?"

He shook his head.

"Too bad! They will never like me after this – and I am not finished yet."

"At least you still have a sense of humour," Jenha commented.

"Yeah, but only just! Those Atapi sorcerers have none."

Jenha knew what I was referring to. "Will you be able to get the sorcerers to talk to the Enforcers?"

"I think I have a plan, but I may not be able to make it work yet. It will definitely not be well received. I showed the Old One the alternate plane, like I told you. He is definitely interested but until the Selkrit activities are stopped, the sorcerers can't and won't meet. In the meantime, I expect the Old One will try to reach that other plane by himself."

"Could he?" Jenha murmured.

I shook my head. "Not unless he embraces empathy and all it means. And I still have two more under him to teach a lesson to. Do you know if these Enforcers can still trace me?"

"We can ask," Jenha suggested.

While we waited for Quenten to arrive at the end of the council session, Jenha wrote out the formal wording of the request and I signed it. Then he insisted that I eat something.

Terr stayed to keep us company but he was neither talkative nor intrusive, and was more relaxed than normal. He changed back to formal when Quenten returned. He announced that we had the request written and signed.

"I will help, all I can," I offered to Quenten. "But I do have other things …"

"Of course," Quenten agreed amiably. I wondered if that was because he had what he wanted – or from remembering what I had said when he first questioned me. "Perhaps you could answer a question for me – about the Atapi?"

"If I can," I agreed cautiously. "I don't know everything about them."

"There have been some odd deaths in fairly remote places," Quenten said slowly, watching me. "Atapi have been blamed. What are your thoughts about this?"

My first thought was, "Deaths of Kumatan or Selkrit?"

"Both," Quenten told me. "The Kumatan had multiple blade wounds. The Selkrit had no obvious wounds, but the bodies were swollen all over."

I glanced down, then asked, "Where exactly were these instances?"

Quenten moved to a map he had pinned to a wall and pointed. All places were well away from Atapi occupied lands, which had been shaded over in yellow. I tried to overlay the mental map I had sensed from Larcia, but I had no feel for the relative scale.

"I don't think the Atapi would have been there," I said. The feeling was instinctive, I couldn't prove it. "I don't think the ordinary Atapi or warriors usually venture far off their own lands. The sorcerers might – for a specific reason, like going to Arkor or if they intend to challenge another of their kind. But I don't think they did. Lately they've been too busy with all the annoyances, like intruders and feral animals."

Quenten considered that, all the while staring at me. I wondered if he was trying to tell if I was lying or not.

Jenha added, quietly, "There is a point which this young one may not have learnt yet. Atapi sorcerers avoid – or, rather, shun – the lands of sorcerers whose tribes have died out. It seems to be some kind of primal superstition. The Selkrit would not know that."

I stopped myself blurting out, "Con didn't." Jenha gently squeezed my arm as if sensing that restraint.

"No, they probably wouldn't," Quenten agreed. "Are all these instances on former Atapi land?"

Jenha looked as Quenten pointed to the places again. He nodded. I looked too, but did not understand Kumatan writing.

"How old is this map?" I asked, recalling an idea I had before.

"Less than a generation," Jenha told me, after peering at some markings on the bottom edge.

"Do you have older maps – much older – with the names of Atapi devils on these shunned lands?" I pressed on.

"Why?" Jenha asked. "How would such a map help now?"

"I'm not sure. I have names – in my head. Larcia gave them to me…"

"Larcia?" Jenha exclaimed. "How could she be alive still?"

"She isn't alive like us – she lives in the aura – at Arkor," I tried to explain.

"I still do not understand that concept," Quenten admitted. "Perhaps you could explain." He looked at me, but I glanced at Jenha.

"Consider it the 'life energy' emitted by all living things, which sinks into the soil of our world to beget new life," Jenha murmured. "Those sensitive to it can use it in various ways – like healing."

"What I am trying to say," I persisted, "is that Larcia can feel where aliens are on those old Atapi lands. She can't give me map references, of course, only the names of the sorcerers that once claimed them."

Jenha murmured, "Can you write them?"

"You never taught me to write Kumatan – only speak it. I can give you names…"

"It may help," Jenha agreed.

Quenten passed him paper and writing tools. I closed my eyes to concentrate, and began reciting the list.

"Impressive," Quenten admitted when I had finished. "If we can link any of those to locations – I will send Enforcers to check them out. I have sent men to the locations of each death. Jenha, have you any knowledge of what might have killed the Selkrit?"

Jenha was about to say, "No," when I muttered, "Stench beetles?"

"How would you know about them, Jai?" he asked me in surprise.

"I was warned to avoid them," I admitted, then added innocently, "I heard what they could do to people."

"Yes, that is certainly a possibility," Jenha agreed, looking at me thoughtfully.

"Ambassador," I spoke quickly, to distract him from thinking what Jenha was not saying. "Perhaps you can tell me something. Many sorcerers are fighting and having to hunt some kind of feral beast." I described the thing as best I could. "I think they must be some kind of constructed animal. Have you heard of them?"

Quenten gave me that penetrating look of his before speaking. "Yes. Revolting things – used by creatures that don't care who they kill as long as it is an enemy. I had heard of one incident, when an Atapi tossed it at Kumatan. Were there other incidents?”

“I can’t say how many,” I said first. “But they are attacking Atapi on their land.” I didn’t mention that Larcia had allowed me to see Sorcerer Jacek toss a beast at Kumatan, only to have it chase the horse with the Kimh.

“That is a serious matter,” Quenten spoke gravely. “About the only thing that deactivates them is an electro-magnetic pulse.”

“A what?” I asked, hoping it was something I could use.

Quenten, when he looked at me again, realised I had no idea of what he meant. He rephrased his answer. “The Enforcers can neutralise the constructed beasts.”

“Not totally useful that,” I told him sarcastically. “Is there a weapon I could…?” I saw Quenten’s expression and muttered, “Never mind. Can the revolting things be killed in any other way?”

That made Quenten thoughtful. “Terr, have you heard of any other way?”

“They are sluggish when it is very cold,” Terr offered. “I could check our database. I recall that they have an on-off switch, but it is located behind the scissoring jaws and impossible to get at once activated.”

I didn’t think that information was immediately useful. “The sorcerers are managing to kill a few, but it takes a lot of power. I suggested to one to drop them in a deep pit.”

That got Quenten’s attention. “So far, I only have hearsay evidence that they are being used here. If I could recover some…”

I grinned. “You didn’t mention how they are sent after one sort of people, not others. They went for Atapi, not Kumatan.”

Quenten didn’t seem prepared to answer.

“Blood, isn’t it?” I suggested pointedly – though why it went after the Kimh too, I didn’t understand.

“Yes,” Quenten admitted. “On the jaws. But once targeted, it must be turned off before it can be re-targeted. We treat anyone who uses them with suspicion.”

“I don’t intend to get anywhere near the jaws on that thing. I might be safe, having human blood, but I don’t want to get between it and its target. Anyway – you still have a tracer on me, don’t you?”

“Indeed,” Quenten confirmed.

I grinned wryly. “I really need to get going if you have no further use for me.”

“I will find you when I do,” Quenten assured me.

Jenha walked with me, allowing me to pass through the shields around the palace without causing alarms. "What mischief are you up to, Jai?" he asked me in a very soft voice.

"Trust me," I suggested. "I'm just working on a way to locate the Selkrit – like you suggested."

"If a Traeger goes with the Enforcers, they will sense sorcery," Jenha warned.

I shook my head. My personal theory about that was that they would only sense it if I warped the aura. "Those lands are vast. A few Selkrit will be hard to find. I have ideas, but I also have a question. Do you know the nature of what binds a sorcerer to his land?"

Jenha shook his head, Earth style.

"You told Quenten that sorcerers avoid shunned land, but would they send warriors there?"

"I do not believe so. May I share your thoughts?"

"I haven't anything worth mentioning," I told him. He didn't need to know what I was up to. "Be careful, Jenha."

He smiled at me and watched me walk away.

CHAPTER 46 – Jai Cassidy – POV

I wanted to think, so when I left Jenha, I went to the land once held by Stacion Ansuni. Now, if I chose, it could be mine. It occurred to me then that the aliens might be here, operating unopposed.

My mind flicked through the images I had received from Jenha and before that, those left to me by my mother. One of them seemed to fit the place, except that in the image, this place was a thriving village with verdant fringes. It was not where Con Ansuni had taught me to master wind, and so I tried reaching for the aura. This time I felt a slow, sluggish, tentative reaction. Perhaps later I could do something to return the aura to this place.

For now, I had to accept the dry sandy soil of the narrow valley would remain barren. This had been a village though. On both sides of the village centre, there were sandstone cliffs with numerous dark cave openings. The area was wide enough to need to take ten minutes to run from cliff to cliff. At each end of the area, the cliffs sloped downward to land where crops might have grown or animals might have grazed. I had fleeting images of how this place had once looked – memories of my mother's memories. She had once lived here, known it intimately. I concentrated on those vague memories, hoping to make them clearer. Odd visions came to me of the barren land overlaid with green lushness. I let myself wander, idly, until I reached a cave that was somehow familiar. I had climbed up along paths cut into the cliff to reach this upper level and when I went in, I felt safe.

It would do for me to think in. I faced the entrance, sitting cross-legged and spent time going over the devious ways I had chosen to terrify an alien race of thieves and worse. I kept a watchful eye on the deserted village centre, in case the aliens came there. Stacion's lands were extensive, and there were many other village sites. I recalled Con's comments about moving frequently. I would need to check them all, and the lands in-between.

Night eventually neared, and it seemed to prove my instinct was keen. I spotted an alien group, walking single file, to a cave opposite my viewpoint. They were all carrying heavy sacks, and that caught my attention. I stood up and moved closer to the opening of the cave.

As night fell, and it grew darker, I began to see the orange glow of a fire in that other cave. I assumed the unwelcome intruders were setting in

308

for the night. When it became full dark, it would be a good time to spy on them.

I began to hear the hunting calls of the dog-like creatures Jacek had set on me. Immediately I thought to keep alert for sorcerer tricks, though I did not expect any other sorcerer to think I would be here, even if I could claim this land. So I edged along the rock edifice, using the continuation of the path that had led me to the cave, and finally came back to the floor of the valley. I needed to backtrack to get to the position of the cave the aliens were using, and then climb up to the second rank of caves.

A faint whiff of rotting meat was all the warning I had. My next step was onto ground that was no longer there. I had not seen any difference in the look of the ground, but I found myself slipping into a kind of pit and the source of the fetid smell.

Some odd knowledge told me that the roof of some underground caves must have collapsed. After cursing myself for falling, I decided the collapse had been deliberate. It smelt like a rubbish dump, and was probably where the aliens dumped their refuse. Considering the pile I landed in, they must have been here for quite a while. I rolled onto my side to get to my feet, and if it had not been for Larcia's sword, invisible but present, the steel jaws of an animal trap would have closed on my leg. As it was, I felt the metal scrape my skin and clamp onto the fabric of the trousers.

With only the briefest thought of wrecking another set of clothes, I used the alien's knife to slash the fabric and get free. Then I stood carefully, pressing on who knew what to push myself up. I numbed the stinging pain in my leg and looked around. Down in the pit, the night's darkness was total, but my vision was not like that of a normal human. I could see a faint glow from here and there in the rubbish as things rotted, liberating energy to the aura, yet I decided that this was not enough. I used a ritual I had learnt, but never tried before, to improve my vision further. I did not want to encounter another of those traps as I tried to find a way to walk or climb out. Now, I could see almost as well as by day.

I did briefly wonder why the traps were there until I heard the howl of the wild dogs, closer now, and realised they were attracted to the carrion here. I was sure of it when I heard the 'snap' of another trap and heard the dying howl of a canine. I sent a burst of terror/danger to the dog minds – I did not want any more of them to die.

Was this the alien's revenge or answer to the howling, prowling dogs around their camp?

I did find several openings in the wall, but each one was blocked by rubble a few feet in. I kept going until I found the dead canine – its blood was seeping into the sandy ground. A little beyond that, I saw the dog's trail and decided if the dogs could use it, I could.

I remembered climbing out of the pit, and turning to check my surroundings, and then a brilliant flash of light. My eyes were blinded by the glare, and I think I stumbled…

I woke up – tied to a pole by some material I had never felt before. I couldn't see anything because there was a dark hood over my face. The combination of annoyances was meant to incapacitate a sorcerer, I reflected, and I wondered if these aliens knew who I was and what I claimed to be.

"Jenha? Kaer?" I tried thinking to the minds of two that I trusted. Nothing. I wondered how that could be. "Larcia?" Still nothing.

I tried to move to test my bonds, but couldn't. Like when I had been immobilised before, I could feel but not move. I decided to check my own condition. First, the deep scratches on my thigh – they were almost healed and I sensed no infection. There was a tender spot on my spine that might be a bruise or a swelling – I wondered if it was the residual from a worse condition. My eyes, at least, seemed back to normal, but the vision ritual had worn off. In my head, I sensed more than felt, a faint vibration and all of me seemed to be tingling. I instinctively tried to call on the aura, but not only was it low – the residual traces felt vile.

My intention was to get free, and for that I needed energy. It occurred to me that what caused the tingling was energy of a sort, and perhaps I could use it as I had once used the heat-energy of warmed blankets. But how to use it was the real question. If I knew what they had done to me, or how the odd restraints worked, I would have an idea of how to focus.

I heard talking, but the voices were alien. Then the hood was snatched off and a metal-gloved hand forced my head up. I recognised the Selkrit Councillor and I would have spit in his face if I could. He spat in mine, getting muck in one of my eyes. It blurred and pained. I diverted a trickle of energy so that eye would water more than usual.

Auglan dropped his hand, then turned and spoke to those who brought him there. He seemed to be boasting about something, for his audience made weird noises that I took to be derisive laughter. He turned back to me and spoke in Kumatan. "My men want to know if your meat will be good to eat. I told them it would be better seasoned with pain and terror."

Of course, I could say nothing. Auglan seemed to smile at that. "And as soon as the effect of that handy Kumatan weapon wears off – I will begin. I am quite looking forward to it. And whatever mind tricks you used to convince those idiot Kimh that you are dangerous won't work on me."

I tried an illusion of snakes replacing my hair, like I had once seen in a book. He simply punched my face with his metal-covered hand.

"You – a female child – are no match for me."

I sent energy to fix my nose and stop it bleeding and then a trickle throughout me to counter the effect of the immobiliser. I had experienced that Kumatan weapon before and knew now what to do. I let anger give me a boost of strength. I wanted to lift my feet and kick him in the stomach, but only then realised that there were bindings around my knees and ankles, too.

In spite of my invidious position, and Auglan's claims to the contrary, he must be afraid of me. Why else did he apply all the restraints? And if he was afraid, it meant I had a chance to beat him.

"I will be back in a few hours to season tonight's meal," he said before leaving.

I had all my thoughts to myself, and every intention of making the most of the slight advantage of my being better long before he expected it.

When I began to feel the tingling return of sensation, I was able to move my head to look around. I was not enthused about potential weapons in this cave – it was practically empty of everything. My mind kept returning to what looked like a pile of rags near one wall. I wondered what it was, and drew in the only aura around to augment my sight. My sight improved, but I was filled with jittery energy. That too I recognised, but I chose to accept it, as it made the tingling sensation increase rapidly then die down. I could move again. It was a good use of such vile energy to destroy the effects of a vile weapon.

I caught a hint of movement, and my eyes returned to the pile of rags. "Hello?" I spoke tentatively in Kumatan. The movement stopped. On impulse, I repeated the greeting in Atapi. The pile slowly rolled over to look in my direction. "Can you help me?" I asked.

An old Atapi voice answered – full of pain, despair, and self-loathing. "They broke my legs and my sword."

"Who are you?" I asked. "I am Jai Cassidy, daughter of Jai Ansuni – did you know her?"

For a long moment the silence in the cave was absolute, then, "She is back? Is Stacion back?"

"No," I said gently. I hadn't missed the awe in his voice when he mentioned my mother, or the fear when he mentioned Stacion. "My mother is dead, and Stacion Ansuni is dead. I killed him."

I saw the pile of rags slowly inching towards me, until the old Atapi could look up at me. He had the form of a Kumatan, but the skin of Atapi. He was a male, and old. His hair had turned white, and his sight was obviously limited.

"May I touch you?" he asked.

"Yes," I said, and when he did, I directed healing energy from Larcia's sword into him. He felt it. Within a short time, he tried to stand and found he could.

"You are truly her child. I am Obaki, Warrior. I will serve you as I chose to serve your mother and Master Con."

I wasted no more thought on how he was here when I needed him. "Can you see how to release me?"

"There are no joins," Obaki told me, confused

"Never mind," I said, making it sound like it was not a major matter. "I will think of something. When did they catch you?"

The old warrior seemed embarrassed, or shamed. "Days ago, when I challenged their right to be here. I was too weak, but they did not kill me – I was not worth killing. Even Stacion did not kill me for failure."

"He was stupid. So are these aliens. Both underestimated a great warrior. You may get a chance to help me later. Don't let then realise that you have recovered. It will be to our advantage and I plan to scare this alien so much…"

We both heard noises and the canny old warrior moved back to the wall and stayed still.

"Well if it isn't the big brave Selkrit Councillor," I greeted him. "Who is so afraid of a small human female that he puts more restraints on her than a sorcerer needs?"

Since he felt secure, he merely smiled an ugly smile.

"By the way," I went on. "I like these restraints – electrical, aren't they? Did you know I can use that energy? To heal, to get strong, to protect myself?"

"You haven't got free yet," he taunted me, turning to take something from one of his men.

I had guessed correctly what he would do first, and when he began to beat me with a slat of some flexible material, it was my turn to grin at him.

"That tickles," I said, forcing a laugh.

He stopped and stared at me. I stared straight back.

"I told you," I began, as if talking to an idiot. "The power in these restraints I can use."

I didn't tell him what I had used it for – which was to make a bubble of protection around me that would move with me.

If my words hadn't angered him, his lack of success in hurting me did. He spoke a deliberate command to his men, and two of them came to release me. I tried to struggle from their grip, and couldn't. Auglan laughed at me – thinking I was vulnerable. Little did he know.

If I couldn't end this soon, I would be in trouble – I now only had the residual energy stored in Larcia's sword to draw on and my shield used energy.

When Auglan moved closer to me, I sent a sense of terror at him and an illusion of a multi-taloned, multi-mouthed imaginary beast. He took a step back before moving forward again. The illusion vanished before his disbelief. He returned to trying to beat me, and I kept casting illusions to the point where he totally ignored them. I had seemed to change into so many twisting, writhing shapes that when I braced my back against my two holders and kicked at Auglan's stomach – he never expected it.

I must have kicked harder than I thought, for Auglan doubled over in agony. He managed to gasp out a command and I was dragged back to the pole. This time, though, I was kicked behind my knees and pushed to the ground. When I was tied to the pole again, I was still kneeling and they used leather thongs.

Auglan walked stiffly from my sight. The two others followed.

Obaki opened his eyes, and they gleamed in the dark. "That was not an honourable blow, young one. Jai Ansuni would never have done that."

"I'm not my mother," I told the old Atapi. "And some of his men killed, butchered, cooked and ate two of Con Ansuni's whelps."

Obaki cursed, forgetting I was a female, then said, "Then it deserves to be kicked in the…"

I translated that as 'male bits'. While I hadn't intended that, and assumed such bits were lower, like in human men and Kumatan males, I was gleeful.

Perhaps I should have been afraid then, as I still wasn't free and Auglan would now be in a killing fury. I needed to escape, and trying to adjust the thickness of my arms didn't seem to work. The thongs were much too tight, and almost cutting off my circulation.

"Obaki, do you still have your sword?"

"It's broken."

"The edge of one bit might still cut the leather," I suggested. "And don't be neat. Cuts heal fast."

I was listening for Auglan to return, and Obaki had only just freed my hands when I heard the Selkrit muttering darkly. "Back, Obaki," I warned.

Auglan strode up to me. When he saw that my hands were free, fury congested his face, making it seem almost black. He grabbed me by the back of my head and slapped my face. I did not feel the full force of it, but enough to warn me that my protections were weakening.

"There's only one punishment suitable for you, abomination," he told me with an evil grin in his eyes.

"Go for it," I dared him. "Didn't you realise that those Enforcers can see what I am up to? Find where I am – they probably don't care what happens – but they are into checking you creeps out."

The Selkrit seemed pleased to disabuse me of that hope. "Look at your hand. That paint on it neutralises the tracer. You can't rely on them to help."

I mentally shrugged, and wondered why Auglan seemed to be disrobing. He took off his fancy robes and some kind of light protection – that hadn't protected him from my feet – and opened a slit in his long shirt. Then he walked quickly towards me, grabbed my head again and held it tightly to the area I had kicked. I thought he was trying to smother me. In the second I had to see anything, I could make out no detail, but then I felt my face forced into a spongy mass. I couldn't move my head and hardly breathe. My protective shield was weakening and something hard was trying to force its way into my mouth. Suddenly I knew what he was trying to do and struggled uselessly.

I didn't hear Obaki moving silently closer, only Auglan's harsh voice. "Your mind games won't help you. That old hermit is nearly dead."

Like a breath, I felt cold metal between my face and the blue pulp.

"Withdraw, alien scum, or I will make a female of you," Obaki stated with grim intent.

Auglan ground my face into his maleness even harder and was working himself into a state of sexual excitement. Then he screamed and released me.

Obaki wiped his broken sword on Auglan's robes, and then cut the bindings at my ankles. I was staring at the ground and the blue blood pumping from Auglan's injury.

"We should leave," Obaki directed, as I vomited on the cave floor.

"No, in a moment," I said. I didn't want Auglan dead yet, so I reached over and touched the bleeding blue mess, sending healing energy into it.

"Fool," Obaki rebuked me.

"If I let him die, I will be a murderer and the Enforcers will treat me no better than him."

"Enforcers! Aliens!" Obaki spat.

"Well, I need the Enforcers to think me innocent and for them to remove these creeps from Korvu."

When I had done as little as necessary to keep the creep alive, I had Obaki help me to redress him and lay him near the wall. Then I insisted on hiding the blood but not the missing bit. It would be delightful torment if he woke and saw one of the scavenger dogs take that missing piece.

"We can leave now," I told Obaki when I had managed to control myself. "I need to get outside so I can walk away from here."

"You should have let him die," Obaki stated.

"I still have a use for him. Farcine's whelp is able to link with his mind, and through that link, I hope to find all of his people."

"Farcine?" Obaki asked, suddenly attentive. "She is alive? My grandchild?"

"I will take you to her," I promised. Before I left, though, I took up the weapons we'd taken from Auglan's clothing. I threw a knife to Obaki, and he caught it deftly. For an old male, he was still a warrior.

It seemed to me that Auglan had not wanted his men to know what he intended. We crept to the cave opening and looked out. The nearest aliens were well away. I took Obaki's arm, drew what energy I could from the aura and walked forward.

I had pictured the Atapi compound at the palace and was moving forward when I heard Obaki's grunt of pain. On the second step, as I felt the twisting blackness, I also felt him slump beside me. He was dead. I paused in the blackness, full of grief for the valiant warrior. I could not take him to the palace because I felt he deserved peace to rest in. I changed my picture to the place where Mikha was born and imagined walking forward. I eased him down onto the ground.

"Cotek," I called with my mind.
"What?" came the annoyed response.
"Obaki is dead."

Con Ansuni arrived within moments and crouched down beside the old warrior. "What happened?"

I sketched the main points, stressing how he had saved my life twice.

"He was too old," Con told me, with his grief obvious. "For years he has lived alone, there on Stacion's old lands, waiting for my sister to return."

"He deserves a warrior's honour."

"Yes, I will see to it. Do you wish to be present?"

"I will be there in spirit – it is better I am not. If that creature dares to mention what I did…"

"And lose face? I cannot see it," Con snarled. "Besides, you healed him, did you not? Obaki did the rest and he is dead. Do not fear to say so. He would, I think, be willing to protect you again from beyond death, for my sister's sake."

I nodded. "I need to tell Farcine…"

Con nodded. "And you should clean that blue mess off you before it attracts scavengers and other interference."

I watched as Con lifted the body of the old warrior and walked away. Then I glanced at my clothes and wanted to be sick again – the smell of alien blood, among other things, was strong. I ran to the waterfall and dove into the pool there, where I tried to scrub my clothes and flesh clean.

"Larcia?" I finally felt human enough to call her.

"Where have you been?" she returned, and it sounded like she was worried about me. I let her see into my memories, rather than trying to talk of the recent events. It seemed then that she moved those memories to a more distant place.

"He will not underestimate you again, I think," Larcia warned. "You have indeed made a deadly enemy."

"If he learns to fear the Atapi, it will be worth it. I am only half Atapi. Your devil-sons are worse than me."

I was in no hurry to leave this place – it was peaceful and I was grateful for that. After a while, my mind lost its grip on the horror I had survived and began to tell me I was hungry. I stood up from under a tree, and began to look for the leaves of the edible plants that grew there. I finally concluded that all of the things the various sorcerers had tried to do to me had been relatively impersonal. I was an obstacle to be climbed over, and that was all. Not so with what Auglan had tried. He had decided to do that out of a perverted desire to debase, revile, degrade and humiliate me for revenge, because I wouldn't let him torture me. What he had done was meant to make me die, slowly and painfully. I had sensed that much from him.

"Child, you need to eat," Larcia prodded my mind again.

She was right. I didn't have time to indulge in hysterics. I didn't know when I would have to face up to two more sorcerers, and I still had to get them all to talk to the Enforcers and to find all of Auglan's so-called engineers.

I broke off a medium sized branch from a young tree and used it to dig up the edible roots. Then I used the art of stillness to catch a fish. Back amongst the trees, I found enough dead wood for a small cooking fire. I wrapped roots and gutted fish in broad leaves, then buried them under the fire. It was handy not needing matches to start a fire – a useful piece of sorcery. The thought made me realise how much a stranger I was from the child I had been on Earth. I didn't belong back there, as I did here.

As I waited for my meal to cook, I rested against a tall, wide tree and tried to ignore the residual emotions from my ordeal. Those emotions were tending towards anger, but were also mostly revulsion. At least, I was beginning to feel less tired.

My body jerked, and I woke from a doze. I tried to sense the cause, but I only heard silence. The idle chatter of the birds, the humming of insects had ceased. I let my mind sink into the aura. Yes! Beyond the trees – something unnatural – something warping the aura.

Mentally, I checked my weapons, bringing my knife into my hand even as I looked around. I moved to where a handy club sized branch lay, and broke of several small side branches. My food was forgotten as I began to hear a rabid snarling. Dogs? I wondered. These didn't sound like dogs, though. What could they be?

In all the time that I had stayed anywhere on Korvu, I hadn't encountered dangerous beasts – yet this sound was familiar.

In that instant, I recalled when I'd followed my brothers into the forest when they went hunting wild pigs. Then, as now, a huge brute of a beast, black with long tusks and sharp teeth, had burst out of the trees and come straight at me. It had been the only time I had ever thanked Henry, my oldest brother, for he had ridden up and yanked me out of the way. He wasn't here now, but there was the big tree I had been sitting against and I climbed it like a monkey. Now, below me, there was a herd of snarling pigs, smelling me and pawing at the tree roots.

Something had enraged them, I thought briefly, recalling Henry's rage once we were safe. He hadn't withheld his hand from my backside for scaring him. I had never thanked him again, until now. It made me realise that the creatures below me were acting more like a pack of dogs, and that the pig form was illusion from my own fears.

Testing that theory, I recalled when I had been afraid of the neighbour's bull terriers. The memory was vivid, only now, they did not terrify me. I had only been two years old then. Sure enough, the pack below changed to demented dogs.

"Enough of this," I thought, sending out an aura of peace until the animals moved around uneasily. Then I tossed illusions of fireballs down at them. The creatures fled, all but about half a dozen, that then changed into birds resembling magpies. In my mind I recalled how magpies defending their nests by diving at people. Sure enough, these came at me, but I sensed no life in them and ignored the illusions. I created an illusion of my own – me picking up an Earth-style crossbow. I had never touched a real one, and only seen them in pictures, but I doubt that the sorcerer, wherever he was, had seen one either. Since it was an illusion, I could shoot it as straight as I imagined from my perch in the tree.

The birds flew closer to each other and came to resemble an Atapi sorcerer. I watched that shape, even though I sensed the sorcerer was actually elsewhere. At any moment, he might slip into that shape. The sorcerer was trying to distract me, and his next try was to send a swarm of rodents at me from under some low bushes. They looked like big grey rats, but I guessed they were actually hoppers, and the ones that began to climb the tree were illusions.

I flung an illusion of fire around the tree, and the real creatures fled from it and the illusions vanished. Now I was angry. I objected to the terrorising of innocent animals, and I was not going to win this challenge unless I attacked back. I began by using empathy to locate the sorcerer, lightly linking to his sight. I could tell where he was from looking back at where I saw myself. I turned that way and raised my illusory weapon. When he moved, my aim followed him. I released an illusion of an arrow, guiding it with my will. I could tell by the change of view that the sorcerer had dropped to the ground. I still couldn't actually see him, but the sorcerer thought I could. He believed my arrow was real, and it could hurt him.

I laughed mentally, expressing my contempt of him. He retaliated by sending at me a swarm of angry bees. They reacted immediately to the aura of peace and hummed around me without trying to sting me. I diverted them back to where I sensed the sorcerer to be – at the same time, making them look to be increasing in size.

For an instant, the sorcerer was afraid. He could not just ignore the bees, for they were real. He had to reduce them to their normal size and dismiss them. While he did that, I dropped from the tree and began moving towards him, crossbow at a ready to fire position. His view of me rose abruptly, and I sensed he was trotting backwards.

All of a sudden, right in front of me, there appeared a creature out of nightmare – a fire-breathing, winged reptilian spider. It was fast – its eight legs were flexible and each pair seemed to have a different purpose. It could run on four, six or eight legs.

I was quite sure this creature did not exist normally, yet it wasn't wholly illusion. It didn't respond to empathy, and it had come from the direction I had last sensed the sorcerer. He could be in that illusion, waiting for me to get too close.

The creature had raced at me, but now seemed to have stopped. All I could sense from it was malice and a desire for blood. I edged backwards as it raised four snapping claws and tried to reach my face. A jet of flame erupted from its mouth. I sensed the heat and ducked to avoid it. I heard a noise behind me, and turned to see a replica of the beast behind me, moving slowly forward. I sensed the sorcerer in that direction, but nothing else. If he came close enough, he'd attack. I began to edge sideways, and a third creature appeared there, then a fourth on the other side. I would bet that those last two were true illusions. One walked over my dying fire and vanished. I quickly dived that way and picked up a flaming log. I held that in one hand and the crossbow in the other.

I was facing the sorcerer now and that seemed to please my opponent. If he hoped I would forget the creature behind me, though, he was wrong. Nor had I failed to notice that the creature was not closing in on me now. I was pretty sure I knew what kind of creature was carrying that illusion. What did concern me was how the sorcerer was able to use it. I could not be sure that it still preferred purple blood to red blood.

Keeping out of reach of the first fire-breathing monster, I raised my crossbow illusion and fired it at the second monster with just one hand. The creature reached up a leg and contemptuously grabbed the arrow illusion from the air, throwing it back at me. I believed I was seeing an illusion until I felt a knife dig into my left arm.

I heard a malicious laugh. I made the crossbow disappear, dropped the burning branch and drew out the knife. The tip was stained. I threw it back at the sorcerer with my right hand and heard a yelp. It had flown true. The monster behind me seemed to go berserk, seeming to be trying to get closer to me.

I grabbed the burning branch again and touched the beast with fire, destroying the illusion. One of the feral animal constructs was revealed – tethered by a vine. With its current exertions the vine would soon snap.

I turned and threw the branch at the illusion where the sorcerer stood. He was revealed with his wings spread, ready to leap. His malicious laugh flicked across my mind. "You haven't won yet, female," he told me. "You still have to defeat the creature, and survive the poison on the knife."

"Dishonourable, when you yourself can't defeat it," I claimed.

"I caught it," the sorcerer claimed. "I have repurposed it. If you refuse to fight it, I win."

"Repurposed it? Really?" I said, sceptical because I knew more about those constructs than he did.

I tested an idea and inched sideways as if turning to look at the beast. I didn't go far, but it was enough. The creature was eying the sorcerer, not me.

"Very well," I agreed. "I will fight it."

With a rapid slashing motion, I used my knife to slash the vine tether. The beast ignored me and charged the sorcerer. I looked up in time to see the sorcerer take a flying leap, wings working furiously to keep him hovering.

"Controlled, was it, Lyvok?" I commented mildly. I watched him hovering for a time, laughing. Then I strode to where the beast had stopped, waiting for its prey to drop.

I approached from behind it, picked it up by the back of its neck, keeping well clear of the scissoring jaws, and concentrated on intense cold. The jaw movement slowed and finally stilled. Then I found the red 'off' switch.

Lyvok returned to the ground. "How did you know to do that?" he demanded.

I didn't let him take the feral bot back. "From the Enforcers at the Palace. They have their uses. Fortunately, they know that Atapi don't deal with off-worlders, and the Kimh and Kumatan would never use such vile constructs. Oh, and these were purposed to kill Atapi, not humans. Purple blood, not red."

Lyvok considered my words, but snarled, "How do I kill them?" He came close and stood over me.

"Talk to the Enforcers and ask them," I told him calmly. "Tell them how the blue aliens sent them at you."

Lyvok snarled again. "I have better things to do." He flapped his wings and rose in front of me. He vanished, but not to leave immediately. After a while, I sensed he had gone.

I did not relax until the birds and insects resumed their normal sounds. Only then did I feel it safe to see if I could salvage my meal.

"Jai?" The tentative mind touch was Kaer. "Are you well?" he asked next.

Should I answer? I closed my eyes and thought back, "Well enough. Why?"

"We need to talk," he thought.

"What about?" I asked. I had a bad feeling about this communication. It got worse when Kaer asked another question without answering mine.

"Will you come here?"

"I'm not fit for polite company," I thought at him.

"I must insist," Kaer thought back at me.

Whatever they wanted me for, it sounded like big trouble. Odds were that unmanned Selkrit was behind it. Did I dare agree to see them? Would they believe me if I told them what that Selkrit had tried to do?

"Alright, but I won't go there," I agreed, reluctantly.

"Where are you, Jai?" Kaer asked, still politely, carefully.

"Where you collected Mikha."

I didn't go to meet my guests. I let them find me. Three of them – Jenha, Kaer and Centurion Bellus. The fact that Jenha had his mind tightly shielded from me was ominous. I stayed where I was, sitting under a tree. They stood in front of me, staring down.

"Have a present," I told Centurion Bellus as I rolled the deactivated bot in his direction.

"How did you deactivate it?" he asked without inflection, with his eyes studying me.

"Quenten told me how," I said, looking at Jenha. "I made it cold, stopped it moving and turned it off." I looked away. "So what is the dire emergency?"

Bellus walked closer and pulled me up. I winced since he used my sore arm, and it hadn't healed fully yet.

"I have a Galactic Federal Warrant for your apprehension," he told me.

I took in the meaning of his words and felt suddenly weak. "What? You can't be serious. What charge?" It didn't take much to guess.

"Inflicting intentional grievous harm to Councillor Auglan of Selkrit."

"Then I want to make a counter charge against him," I stated.

"You will have a chance to state your case when you are at the Galactic Judicial Hub."

This was the last thing I needed right now. "I made a promise to Ambassador Quenten that I haven't fulfilled," I told Bellus. "And I didn't damage Auglan – I healed him."

"That is not what he stated in his sworn statement," Bellus told me emotionlessly. He had no trace of friendliness in his voice.

"Did he say where this attack supposedly happened?" I asked, hoping to have a lever to get out of this trouble.

What I heard was absolute lies, but his men had all sworn that it was the truth. But surely they had ways to tell if they were telling the truth, or did they assume that since everyone said the same thing it was true?

Bellus had a device out and was pointing it at me. "You have had Auglan's blood on you," he told me, as if that proved everything.

I shrugged.

Jenha spoke then. "Jai, what happened?"

I did not want to remember. "By the sound of it, I have no rights now?" I said, but at that moment, I heard the bird noises go quiet again and I had a very shrewd idea of why. Bellus noted my distraction and held me more firmly.

"Why did you remove the tracer?" Bellus asked bluntly.

"I changed my clothes," I told him. It had been my first thought about where the tracer was. My mind was listening for the approach of the sorcerer. I noticed that Jenha was also looking around.

Kaer was looking at me, but also looking quite ill. I must have let something leak into my mind.

"Centurion Bellus," Kaer spoke to get his attention. "I think you should question Jai Cassidy now and hear what she says. Do you have with you the means to test for truth?"

"Yes. However that idea is most irregular. Traeger Mosellan, please take us back now."

Jenha, however, was not listening to the Centurion. He could sense the nearness of a sorcerer, and my twitchiness. He began speaking something I didn't understand, and it had an odd rhythm. I felt some kind of shield come up around us. Moments later, a shadow passed over us. I looked up and caught sight of a winged Atapi.

"Would he have seen us?" I asked Jenha, eyeing where the sorcerer had gone.

Jenha shook his head faintly and said softly, "No."

"Jai Cassidy," Bellus said loudly to get my attention.

I turned my head to stare at him. "Could you please ease your grip a little?" I asked with exaggerated politeness. "I have a knife wound there."

He didn't take the hint. "You will return with me," he insisted.

I took a deep breath and asked, "Was Auglan man enough to present his lies to you in person? Did you make sure he was telling the truth?"

"You are in no position to make demands," Bellus told me. "Now, I insist we leave."

"That sorcerer, the one that flew over, is after me," I told Bellus with no trace of deference. "He won't go away, and he will follow me wherever I am taken. Now, before you think that is an excellent way to catch a sorcerer, I advise you not to invite his attentions."

"Jenha," Kaer spoke in a low warning tone. "We should leave."

"Lord Kaer, you were correct. I think we need to know the truth now," Jenha spoke as if answering Kaer's earlier remark.

Bellus made an attempt to disagree and invoke his authority.

Jenha spoke against his request. "Centurion Bellus, it seems to me that justice is not being served if a Galactic Councillor may make accusations without proof, because of his rank, and those accused have no say."

"I'll talk at the palace," I decided abruptly. I had a good idea why Bellus was keen to leave this wide-open, isolated area. He was agoraphobic.

"Jai!" Jenha said sharply. "You will talk to us now."

I looked at him pleadingly. I didn't want him to know what had happened.

Bellus pulled down his visor and examined my hand. I tried to pull it free. He opened his visor again and asked, "Did you attack Councillor Auglan?" His gaze was intent and he still held my hand and arm.

I stared back and said, "No."

"Do you know what happened to him?" Bellus then asked.

I was still staring at him when I said, "Yes."

"Were you there when he was injured?"

"Yes."

"Where were you?"

Suddenly, the memory came back in vivid detail, and I wanted to be sick again.

"Perhaps we should let Jai tell us how she came to be there," Jenha suggested.

I knew I wasn't going to win. It was either tell the revolting truth, or be accused of it and taken who knew where and let Auglan have his way. It helped that Jenha must have read some of it in my mind and he had seen his own share of horrors – but Kaer was an innocent. It was too bad, I doubted he would go away – he'd have to hear it. This was the only way I would be allowed to finish the next to last challenge and convince the sorcerers to talk to the Enforcers.

Jenha took the hand Bellus released, though the latter still had my arm in his firm grip. I didn't look at any of them, and so I could pretend no one was listening. Stick to the facts, I told myself as I sketched a picture of what I had done after leaving Quenten and Jenha. I omitted the mind games I had played on Auglan. When I reached the part after Auglan had almost fully disrobed, I felt and shared Kaer's nausea and Bellus's utter disgust.

"Obaki warned him," I said. "Auglan ignored him as if he wasn't there and continued trying to…" I didn't have the words to describe what he was trying to do. I felt Jenha's hand spasm as I mentioned the old warrior by name. Before that I had simply said I had healed the old warrior's injuries. Bellus supplied the words I lacked, almost spitting them out. "Mouth mate."

Kaer turned away and I wondered if he was about to be sick. I spoke to his mind, "I am sorry you had to hear that. But I am okay; his… thing… couldn't get in. I was shielded."

I felt the effort he made to control himself. The rest of my mind heard Bellus explain, as tactfully as possible, what he had meant. He added, "The fluid ejected is often harmful to other species. The punishment for that crime is emasculation."

Now that the worst was over, I finished telling how I had stopped Auglan bleeding to death, and how Obaki and I had slipped away. Bellus had to ask where Obaki was now.

"Dead. He caught a weapon discharge, and saved me again."

Bellus closed his helmet, I assumed to consider all I had said, or perhaps he had a way to report to Quenten.

"Obaki," Jenha said the name reverently. "I knew Obaki a long time ago. My father had him as prisoner. Your mother gave him his pride back and, for her sake, he served the Kumatan and his people well. I had not known he was still alive."

"Con Ansuni took him away to perform the honour rites for a great warrior," I told him.

Bellus reopened his helmet. "I must still bring you in," he told me.

"No," I said, suddenly desperate, and tried to wrest my arm free. "Don't you see? If I am in custody, Auglan will have time to hide his tracks, the Atapi won't talk, and he will get away with everything. Two days – give me two days – and then, if I haven't convinced the Atapi to talk, I will come to the palace myself. I promise."

Bellus closed his helmet again.

"Have you thought this out carefully?" Jenha murmured. He saw me glance at the sky.

"I need that time," I said to him. "You know what I must do."

Bellus opened his visor again and asked, "What happened to your hand?" His question was sharp and I felt compelled to answer.

"I don't know. Auglan implied he had done something." The compulsion eased and I added, "Why does that matter?"

"I am authorised to grant you two days parole, on the condition that you voluntarily present yourself to us at the end of that time and you consent to wear a full tracking monitor system."

"Fine, whatever," I agreed rashly, hoping he would hurry up and do it so I could go.

Kaer, his mind under control again, addressed Bellus. "Did my father agree to this?"

"It was not his place to object. This is Galactic Federation business."

Kaer merely nodded.

Bellus removed a flat box from some hidden pocket of his uniform, even as he still held my arm. Since Jenha was still holding my hand, Bellus released me to open the box. From what Auglan had said, the last tracer must have been small enough to have been implanted in my hand, probably back when the Enforcer had first met me. I certainly had not noticed it there, and I was now expecting something similar. I was wrong.

The device that Bellus now held was the size of a small coin, and he held it to my throat. Once again there was a painful prick, and this time I immediately began to feel weird.

I must have passed out, for I woke with Jenha crouched beside me.

"You should be able to stand now," he told me.

"Not yet," I decided, judging my own state. "Was it meant to knock me out?"

Bellus answered. "It is a normal reaction."

I felt better and pushed myself up. I noticed Kaer looking away, seeming to have a hard expression. "Is Kaer mad at me?" I asked Jenha.

"No, young one. He has many things on his mind that you need not concern yourself with. Finish what you promised, and don't forget you only have two days."

I felt a vague sense of disquiet, but Jenha was right. There was a sorcerer looking for me. "You'd better go," I told him.

Once they had gone, I returned to sitting with my back to the tree. They intended to examine the cave I had mentioned on Stacion's former land. It would provide proof of a sort for my story. I wondered if I should move back to that deadened land, which was mine to claim. It would mean the sorcerer could not draw on the aura there, but then neither could I. The truth was, though, I did not know that place as well as I did here. This was as close to home territory as I had on Korvu. As far as the sorcerers were concerned, it was open territory and unclaimed.

Here would be the best place. I drew on the aura to fill me with energy, while staying alert for any signs of a sorcerer trying to warp it, or approach silently.

After an hour, I stood up and walked around, checking my few weapons for the umpteenth time. The linked throwing stones, a knife, and several solid branches were all I had. I added a walk to the river to get a drink before returning to my tree.

I repeated this pattern until evening and began to believe that the sorcerer had given up. I decided I should dig up more of the roots to eat. I didn't want to relight my fire and draw attention to myself.

As it began to grow dark, I watched the timid hoppers venture out to find food and to drink. Mostly they ignored me; some hopped close, sniffed and hopped off again. I was enjoying watching them, since I was currently not interested in hunting them.

One came right up to me. I didn't move, not wanting to frighten it. I reached out to it with my empathy and was startled when it seemed to spasm as if terrified. I started to reach out to it when the hopper disappeared and an Atapi sorcerer appeared there. Even before I could react, he flung something over me. I struggled, trying to get the clinging substance off me. I soon discovered that the more I struggled, the more it clung to me.

Cursing was no use. I had not sensed the sorcerer approaching me, so well had he blended into the aura. He had carefully hidden his intentions in the hopper's mind. He was the only one to use the natural aura to approach me.

It became harder and harder to breathe and as I listened to his chanting – I realised he was intending me to suffocate. I called on the aura and drew in air through the folds of the fabric. The sorcerer became aware of my counter magic and nudged me with his foot, making me roll over and entangle myself further. Then he lifted me, slung me over a shoulder and strode off. I couldn't struggle now, but I needed to know his intentions. I touched his mind and realised he was taking me to the river. I breathed in and out as deeply as possible in my current state, and then at the last moment as I felt myself being tossed I took and held a deep breath. I landed unceremoniously in the pool in front of the waterfall. Water replaced air in the folds of the fabric, and did not loosen the adhesion of the fabric. Desperately, I made the surface temperature of my body rise higher than I thought possible, and the water around me turned to steam as I rose back to the surface. I breathed in some of the hot moist air.

The sorcerer was aware of my efforts and laughed that infuriating laugh. It seemed I had erred again. The heat caused the fabric to soften and cling even more closely to me. I felt myself panic, and I did the only thing possible – began to think through the ritual for slowing down all my body functions, as I had done once before. I stopped heating my skin and allowed the chilly water to cool it. I continued the process until the moment just before losing consciousness, I invoked Larcia to protect me. The cooling process continued without my conscious control.

Sometime later, I seemed to wake and stand up. I looked around and saw my body lying at an awkward angle on the edge of the river. I was still aware of my body, in a distant part of my mind; it very cold, but not quite frozen. I needed to watch over it, keep control of it. The sorcerer came to retrieve it and I idly thought whether I still needed it. Yes, I decided – I must return to it. The sorcerers knew me in that shape and if I changed bodies, I would have to fight them all over again. I hovered close to my body, so when the sorcerer 'walked' with it, I was with him.

The sorcerer had arranged a meeting with the Old One, somewhere on land that was neutral territory between their respective tribal lands. The Old One had brought some of his tribe to wait on him but my captor ignored these extras - several warriors and six females. His mind was full of triumphant thoughts and the expectation of praise from the other sorcerers.

The sun had yet to set when the Old One greeted my captor. He watched as my shell was rolled towards his feet. Soon, I would have to prove that my captor had not won – but first I must free my body of its cocoon.

"It's dead," the sorcerer told the Old One.

"Did you learn its secret name?" the Old One asked. The younger sorcerer growled a negative.

The Old One made his own examination by pushing my shell with his foot, then rolling me back a few feet and resting his foot on me. I wondered if he was trying to sense a heartbeat or sign of breathing. I had the sense that he was not convinced of my death and was reserving judgement. Then he reached down for a fold of fabric, and slit it with his knife. He reached a hand in, felt the icy chill and withdrew it quickly. The younger sorcerer reached in with his hand, touched my body and felt energy being sucked from him. His hand seemed stuck to my shell until he wrenched it out. His mind was confused, as he had never felt anything so cold that it burned.

"I claim the reward," the young sorcerer demanded of the Old One.

"I'm not convinced," the Old One proclaimed. "Come back tomorrow."

With a hiss of anger, the younger sorcerer vanished.

The Old One circled my body three times, and then addressed the members of his tribe who were daring enough to venture close enough to see what lay at their master's feet.

"No one is to touch this meat. Any that do will answer to me."

I was left alone, watched from a distance, but not touched. Where the Old One had slashed the fabric, air was able to reach my nose. It gave me a phantom tickle that I could not scratch. I was reminded of the need to remove the fabric, but for a start, I returned to my unresponsive body to sense its condition.

Con Ansuni led his warriors, running fast after the galloping horses. Anger as hot and as fierce as any that had surged through his sire many years past surged through him. How dare the Kumatan invade his land, steal his children! Hadn't he always dealt respectfully with them?

"Litok!" he called with his mind again.

His son, the younger of his two apprentices, had been guarding the cavern where he had gathered all the whelps for safety. The feral creatures still infesting his land could not climb up the narrow rocky path. However, he had been unable to reach his son's mind since the moment the females had woken to find half the whelps missing.

He left his older apprentice, Deben, to watch over the tribe who had been instructed to keep to their holes and caves, and build barriers of rocks across the openings.

The horse tracks led through the wild, unclaimed forest, directly towards the nearest Kumatan town. Con left his warriors to track the horses and leapt up to fly ahead. He saw the dust cloud in the distance and flew closer. The riders wore hooded cloaks, some with the hood down, revealing the armoured head coverings of Kumatan soldiers and guards. He could not tell if they carried his children.

The horses entered the walled town and were out of his sight. Aware that he was off his land and in the open, Con dropped back to the ground and changed his shape so he would appear to be Kumatan. His clothes, though, would attract attention. He began to trot at the ground-devouring pace that all Atapi were capable of. He reached the town, entered the gate, and was immediately challenged by guards.

Fortunately, Con had learnt to speak Kumatan as a very young sorcerer. He also knew enough about Kumatan customs to claim, "I didn't stop to dress properly. Someone drove off a herd of my horses. They are my livelihood. I found tracks coming this way and followed them."

Since Atapi didn't breed horses and never made use of them, the guard was diverted. "Only ones that came in here were the guards' horses."

"I expect you know guards," Con said, controlling his anger. "But if you'd let me check the ear markings on those horses, I would be sure."

This guard, being bored with his duty, was convinced the man was eccentric rather than dangerous. He agreed to the odd request and led the way to the guard complex and the horse yards.

The horses were lathered with sweat and had just been left, still saddled. In spite of being nearly exhausted, they still reacted to the smell of Atapi – either that or Con's anger. They milled uneasily as he moved to each one, checking earmarks as a cover to sniffing each beast. He smelt horse sweat, a faint trace of Kumatan, and… the vile aliens. None of them smelt of Atapi. He had been tricked. In his mind, he roared at his warriors, "Go back!"

Con now ignored the agitated beasts and the guard, and strode from the yard. Something about him sent everyone backing away. He strode around the town, sniffing the air, searching for traces of his tribe's children. If they were here, afraid, terrified, he would have smelt their fear smell. They must be unconscious or Litok would have sensed him.

His mind was so full of fear, anger and worry that he ignored the awareness of beings following him until a breath of an unfamiliar smell reached his nostrils. He spun around, finding himself faced by a handful of beings in black covering, with heads that were covered in round opaque bubbles. They were carrying unfamiliar weapons. He turned back and found he was now circled.

"What is the meaning of this?" he demanded in Kumatan. "I have done nothing wrong."

"You will come with us," an odd sounding voice spoke in Atapi. "Please put down any weapons."

Con felt his hackles rise. These were yet more aliens, but were they the ones his sister's child had mentioned? Enforcers? Should he trust them?

He drew on the aura, preparing a ritual of stillness. These beings had done nothing to him – yet.

The next Kumatan voice warned him, "Try nothing, Atapi sorcerer. You have broken your word and ventured into Kumatan territory. You must answer for the transgression."

Con's anger surged. "Kumatan ventured onto my land and stole children from my tribe. It is you who transgressed. You will return them to me!"

The Traeger who had challenged him activated his weapon as Con threw a blast of power in a circle around him. The black figures all stumbled backwards, the Traeger was pushed over, but Con felt himself falling and could not move. He had never before felt the effects of the Kumatan immobiliser. It paralysed him, but his mind still raged and that showed in his eyes. He was not made docile, just temporarily helpless. He drew greedily on the aura, and drew power into himself. He expected that the Traeger would have him taken to the cursed palace of the Kimh. Let them! He was waiting for that. Long ago, he had considered this position and believed he had the answer to that.

The black figures were talking to the Traeger and pointing to something out of sight. The result was that two of those aliens held him under the shoulders and dragged him to an odd-looking metal cave. Con considered changing back to his natural form, not caring if these aliens were terrified or not – but decided that letting them think he was less powerful, humanoid, may be an advantage later.

For now he could do nothing but hide his terror at being inside this alien cave, full of alien smells and alien objects. To do that, he turned his attention to undoing the effects of the weapon, making his body heal faster than passively waiting. He kept his eyes fastened on the Traeger – to the point of making the man nervous. He took some malicious pleasure in that.

Con was beginning to regain movement as the shuttle landed. The Traeger was aware of his 'twitching' for he urged haste to get his prisoner into the shielded room in the palace. His immobiliser was ready in his hand.

The same two Enforcers moved to carry him. As soon as his feet touched the ground outside the metal cave, and he felt the aura, he changed back to his own form, spread his wings and leapt. The Enforcers, who had been holding him firmly, found themselves dangling, and gripped tighter.

Con couldn't get high enough to fly, but he was still desperate and angry. He realised he was attracting attention and more people were racing towards him. His struggles became more frenzied as he twisted and tried to dislodge the Enforcers. One of those lost his grip and fell the five feet to the ground. The Traeger was trying to get a clear shot at him, but Con now gripped the second Enforcer as a shield.

Tiring, Con decided to cast the ritual of stillness, and the people below him turned to statues. All but one. Con hissed and dropped the Enforcer, not caring if the alien was hurt, only wanting to get away.

The one Kumatan that was unaffected was running at him, calling something.

"Con! Con Ansuni!"

In the moment of his hesitation, a guard from the far side of his spell's effect threw a spear on a rope. It went over Con, but the trailing rope tangled his wings and he fell, landing heavily. The guard tried to follow his spear, but as soon as he moved forward three paces, he reached the boundary of Con's spell and stopped.

Con felt hands helping him, and looked at the Traeger that faced him. Anger, but not the desperation, died from his eyes.

"Jenha?" he asked softly.

Mosellan nodded. "It would be wiser if you did not struggle or try to flee."

"I cannot stay," Con hissed. "Some vile creatures, be it Kumatan or alien, have stolen children from my tribe. One is my son. I must find them! Let me go!"

"I can't, my friend," Jenha said with true regret. "I need you to talk to the Enforcers – not for my sake – but for your own and for all Atapi."

"Let me go!" He had shaken off the rope but not Jenha's grip on his arm. "You've become like your father!" Con hissed the insult.

"And I know you have not become like yours," Jenha replied calmly. "I will have people looking for your children. That I promise you."

"No," Con denied, and he began to struggle.

"Con, please. I know these people – listen to me." Jenha was aware that two senior Traegers were diffusing Con's ritual, and would not give a sorcerer any chance to escape or do further sorcery.

Con jerked free, leapt up, but immediately felt the pain from some weapon, and his wings stopped working. He fell heavily and was unable to resist when the Traegers snapped a slave band on each arm.

Quenten had woken at his usual early hour, with his ears assaulted by a high pitched sound. When he went to his window, the sound became louder. His first thought was that the noise was caused by some malfunctioning mechanical device, but he had seen very little technology on Korvu. Closing the window muted the noise, but did not block it out. It seemed to be inside his head.

Outside, he saw that the patrolling guards were constantly scanning the area to either side of their path and they had their weapons out. Kumatan servants scurried from their quarters, giving frequent glances towards the fenced off compound where the Atapi lived. From the window on the second level of the palace, Quenten could just see the top of the wooden huts above the nearest trees in the garden.

A knock at his door, in the secret rhythm used by the Enforcers, drew his attention.

"Come in," he called, and as he expected, Senior Centurion Bellus entered.

"Good Morning, Sir."

"It would be except for that awful noise. Do you know what is causing it?"

"No one that I spoke to seems to know."

Resolving to ask the High Minister or one of his aides for an answer, Quenten put the question aside. "Did the night crew have anything to report?"

"A communication from the garrison ship, Sir. They lost contact with Councillor Auglan's shuttle. He told us that he was returning to the Selkrit base ship but when he took off, it was in the direction of the latest Atapi atrocity. He reached there and disappeared from our scanners."

"Did they do an intensive scan for the tech elements in his shuttle?"

"They did, but not even a trace was detected."

"They are certain that he didn't go to his ship?" Quenten insisted.

"The Commander sent a drone to circle the ship, and they still have it hovering nearby. None of the Selkrit shuttles are docked to their base ship at the moment."

"What about inter-ship communications?'

"Some innocuous traffic from the surface to the ship, but the messages are too short for us to triangulate the origin."

"Tell them to do everything possible to locate Auglan's shuttle. Galactic Councillor or not, what he tried to do to Jai Cassidy is a heinous act. He must answer for that."

"The ship crew have promised to be particularly diligent."

"I hope that doesn't mean that they forget to watch the tracking signal on Jai Cassidy. What has she been up to?"

Now Bellus began to shuffle, rather than remaining at attention. "Initially, she was just moving around in the area where we left her. Near dusk, she was watching some hopping creatures come up to her. The observers had a brief glimpse of a large figure facing her – then we lost visuals."

"What about the other channels?" Quenten demanded.

"We heard some rather strange sounds, like animals, and some scuffling sounds. It is possible that she encountered that sorcerer that was hanging around there yesterday."

"What are you trying to avoid saying, Bellus?"

The Centurion reached into his pocket for a palm sized device and passed it to his superior. "The other signals were strange, Sir. I had the experts on the ship analyse the recording."

Quenten read the screen, and interpreted the data for himself. "Oxygen starvation, water, heat and then cold," he murmured. "Then nothing…and no termination signal. Perhaps letting her go was a mistake. She has found a way to remove it."

"I didn't think that was possible," Bellus murmured. "However, it is the only interpretation our specialists came up with."

"These Atapi can do inexplicable things," Quenten admitted. "However, this means that she has broken her promise to us. Inform all squads to be on the lookout for her. If she is seen, she is to be apprehended and brought in for questioning."

"Have you any other instructions, Sir?"

"Just keep on trying to locate any Selkrit settlements. All those engineers have to be somewhere if they are not on that base ship. If anything urgent comes up send a message. The local nobility have their council meeting this morning. I still must attend."

"Are you going to ask what the cause of that noise is, Sir?"

"I am interested in finding out how it is affecting the ruling class first, but yes. It is enough to give one a headache, or drive a person mad."

Arriving early in the Council Chamber, Quenten was in a position to observe the Kimh Elders as they entered the room. Most of them were, as the title suggested, of advanced age. Their normally serene expressions were now marred by frowns, and their faces were unusually pale.

High Minister Koenig strode into the room and went immediately to his seat, barely waiting for Quenten to arrive at the adjacent seat before sitting. He turned and gave the formal greeting of, "Pleasant day to you, Ambassador."

As Quenten voiced the formal reply, he saw that Koenig's eyes were dilated, and a faint sheen of sweat beaded his brow. His face, unlike that of the Elders, was flushed to a noticeable mauve. He didn't look well.

A white clad servant poured some of the ruby coloured wine into a glass, and then refilled it after Koenig had consumed the first measure in two gulps. Then the servant offered him some, and this time Quenten decided that he would accept. He wondered if the beverage was fermented, and if it would further dull the keening sound.

Outside noises did not usually intrude into the Council Chamber, but that was not the case that day. Quenten took a sip of the wine, and confirmed that it was strongly fermented, and allowed himself several cautious sips – even with that little, he felt the effect of the alcohol, and the blessed dulling of the noise.

His attendance at these sessions was to remind the local ruling body that he still had authority over them. He did not speak out on matters of purely local concern, but would when they overlapped with his mandated area of authority.

The day's topics were mundane, and most of his attention was taken by observing the body language of the Kimh Elders. They were stoic in tolerating the dreadful noise.

He felt his communicator vibrate, but did not move to pull it out and read the message. Part of his role was to blend in with the local nobility or rulers. On Korvu, there was nothing like his communicator. There was a very basic form of radio communications, ancient in design and prone to interference, and used only for emergencies when there were no Traegers around to pass messages mind-to-mind.

Koenig, however, was not so reserved when it came to being interrupted. His full attention had seemed to be on the current speaker, and his long winded diatribe relating to the importance of educating Kumatan children in remote regions, but when a messenger passed him a written message, he rang the small bell for silence.

His terse, "One moment, please, Elder," was barely polite.

Quenten saw Koenig's expression change from bland to excitement as he read the message. He then announced, without apology, "This

Council session is adjourned. We will continue hearing you petition in the next session."

The speaker gestured for permission to speak, and on receiving the nod to proceed said, "High Minister, this matter of which I speak is of great importance and it has been put off for over a month now."

Koenig rose, repeating, "This Council session is adjourned."

The Elders rose obediently, bowed towards Koenig and the other four with positions on the raised platform, and then began to file from the room.

Koenig was in a hurry to leave. He brushed past his brother, ignoring Eamon's murmured words of concern, but stopped when Quenten asked, "May I have a moment of your time before you leave?"

He saw Koenig's posture stiffen, as he turned to ask, "What is it that you wish?"

"Can you tell me the cause of that dreadful noise we have been hearing all morning?"

Koenig's expression tightened. "It is the Atapi who insist that Jai Cassidy is their leader. No doubt they are trying to annoy us. I will send a Trager to silence them."

Koenig didn't wait to hear if Quenten had more questions, nor even to conclude the conversation with the traditional pleasantries. Lord Eamon gave Quenten a slight bow before hurrying off after his brother.

Since arriving on Korvu, Quenten had learnt the regular protocol for official sessions of the Council, and adhered to them. By contrast, Koenig was behaving in quite an agitated fashion – perhaps that noise was affecting him adversely. It wasn't his place to judge, but before heading out himself, he checked the message he had received. He immediately activated the communicator and contacted Bellus.

"You say that one of our teams have capture Con Ansuni?" he demanded.

"Yes, Sir, he intruded into one of the Kumatan towns."

"Was there any trouble?"

"No, Sir. Those Traegers know how to handle the lizards. Our shuttle has just arrived and landed in the open area at the back of the palace. Where we landed to collect those assassins."

"Where are you now?"

"Watching, Sir. That sorcerer was not as docile as they thought. As soon as they brought him out, he did something – turned everyone close by into statues and tried to fly off."

"They didn't let him," Quenten demanded. Already on his way towards the door leading outside. There was no one around to see him trotting in such an undignified fashion, with a hand to his ear.

"He didn't get away, two of our squad had hold of him and he couldn't fly. One of the Traegers that was outside the area affected by the spell, found a way to bring him down. Mosellan is talking to him – calmed that lizard man right down."

A moment later, Bellus added, "Trouble, Sir. The High Minister has just arrived and he is in a right rage."

Quenten ran faster. He had observed enough to know of the antipathy that Koenig had for Mosellan. He could easily predict what would happen next. He needed Mosellan's understanding of the Atapi, and didn't want the Kumatan Traeger secluded again.

As he arrived on the scene, he was in time to hear, Koenig say, loudly, "Mosellan!" In that single word, was an order, a statement of censure and the verbal expression of near hatred.

The unusually pronounced strong emotion evident in the High Minister's behaviour, alarmed Quenten. He knew that the man had been ill recently, but he had seemed to have recovered – until today. Perhaps that noise was responsible, he thought, but then decided that it couldn't explain the intensity of the hatred. Nor did it explain the frown on Lord Eamon's face as he sent a servant off on some errand.

In movements that were the antithesis of Koenig's, Mosellan stood up, glanced once more at the now controlled Atapi sorcerer, and obeyed the implied command to attend the High Minister. Even with that example, Koenig did not modify his voice as he reprimanded the man who approached him.

"I require an explanation of why you were enabling a dangerous Atapi the chance to escape. Consorting with them is an act of treason."

Mosellan stood without a trace of subservience in his posture, and did not look away from the High Minister. Quenten was impressed when Mosellan addressed the man who out-ranked him, and had the right to command him. He delivered a valid rebuke when he said, "There is no law on Korvu preventing me from talking to anyone in a civil and courteous manner. If you wished cooperation from Con Ansuni, High Minister, you may have just ensured you will not have it."

Koenig's face turned a deep purple as his blood pressure rose with his anger. "Con Ansuni! I think, Mosellan, you have proved you are not fit to be a Traeger of any rank." He pointed to the two Traegers dragging the sorcerer towards the palace. "That is how you treat an Atapi like Con Ansuni."

"High Minister, you have been poorly informed." Jenha allowed no trace of any emotion to infuse his tone. He knew he was close to angering Koenig beyond reason, and had no wish to be chastised again. But there were more serious matters to be dealt with than the whims of a mentally delicate Koenig.

"In believing Con Ansuni to be dangerous?" Koenig growled.

Jenha didn't directly answer the question.

"Con Ansuni is not like his Sire. However, at this moment, I do not disagree he is dangerous as a result of the arbitrary manner in which he was treated."

Koenig now seemed to be too angry to speak. His brother had a hand on his arm and was speaking in an undertone, urging him to be calm. From the direction of the palace, his sons, Malachi and Kaer, were approaching at an undignified trot, following the winding paths.

Quenten decided that he needed to interfere before the High Minister did put Mosellan out of reach. At least, for a moment, Koenig's attention was distracted.

"Mosellan? If you are finished here, I require your translation services." Quenten smoothly gave a bow to Koenig, one that was a greeting to an equal, and explained," I intend to question that Atapi as soon as possible.

"Take Senior Traeger Solomon and another one with you. Mosellan's training is questionable."

"I thank you for your concern, High Minister, but I will be in no danger."

Mosellan paused as if expecting Koenig to counter the request but when nothing further was said, he obeyed Quenten's request.

"Come," Quenten directed, as he studied the Kumatan's manner. He did not seem to be angry, rather his expression was of concern for the High Minister.

"I am sorry you needed to witness that," Jenha murmured. "The High Minister is under much stress."

"I thought that it needed to be said," Quenten admitted. "However, after the treatment he received, do you think Con Ansuni will be willing to listen to us and answer questions?"

"I have told him that he should, although I expect that at the present, he is rightfully angry. He believes that Kumatan or the blue-blooded aliens have abducted twenty or more of the whelps belonging to his tribe. And here we are, preventing him from looking for them."

Jenha Mosellan did not accuse Quenten of taking the children, even though he knew that the Enforcers were taking selected Atapi hostages.

"If it isn't the Kumatan who have taken them, and I know my Enforcers have no such orders, then I fear that there is only one answer." Quenten kept striding towards the palace. "We lost trace of Auglan's shuttle out towards Con Ansuni's lands. That man is understandable furious with both Con Ansuni and Jai Cassidy. But to take revenge in this way, on children, only confirms the claims of that earth child. I will not permit that dishonoured Councillor to remain free."

When they reached the palace, Quenten let Jenha lead the way to the shielded cell room. When they entered, they stayed back near the door, allowing the two Traegers within to finish what they were doing.

"Setting extra protections," Jenha explained. "There will be a force wall between us and Con Ansuni."

"What is wrong with him?" Quenten asked, for his eyes had gone to the Atapi who seemed to be slumped on the floor as if simply dropped there.

"I can only assume that he wasn't taking captivity well. The slave bands that were applied outside, prevent him drawing on the aura, and trying any magic, but they do not prevent physical action. I believe that they have also immobilised him."

"When will we be able to question him? I want to do that as soon as possible."

"Ambassador, it will be at least this time tomorrow. In this room, and with the slave bands, Con Ansuni will be unable to draw upon the aura to heal. Without that advantage, the paralysis effects must wear off naturally."

"Do you agree that it was necessary to immobilise him? What about the children he seeks?" Quenten demanded.

"I will organise guards to seek the whelps, and request help from a Traeger. That is all I have the authority to do." Jenha's tone was regretful.

Traeger Solomon noticed the two figures standing by the door and came over. He gave his attention to Quenten.

"Subni- Traeger Mosellan is correct. You will not be able to question this sorcerer until tomorrow."

"And the immobiliser? Was that really necessary?"

"It is a humane weapon," Solomon stated. "It was necessary for us to bring this prisoner here."

"I have been told, that Con Ansuni was seeking children, abducted from his tribe, when he was apprehended. Will you do anything to help find them while he is here?" Quenten demanded.

Solomon's expression did not change when he said, "No Kumatan took children. He trespassed into a Kumatan town – violating the treaty we have with the Atapi."

"And if it were you, trying to find your own children when you believed they had somehow gone onto Atapi lands – what would you do?" The sharp question took Solomon by surprise. "If you thought Atapi had taken them?"

The momentary change in Solomon's expression betrayed his first thought, but the Senior Traeger did not admit that he would have gone in to punish the abductors.

"I see, Senior Traeger," Quenten rebuked mildly, but it was enough for Solomon's face to flush red. "I believe it was the Selkrit Leader, Auglan, who ordered or carried out the abductions – in a heinous act of revenge. Unless you are willing to condone the maltreatment of innocent children, then I request that you implement plans to locate them."

"Yes, Ambassador," Solomon agreed.

"And I wish to be advised as soon as Con Ansuni is able to answer questions."

"I will ensure that, and I will accompany you at that time," Solomon promised. He gestured to his young assistant and was about to go to the door when he stopped and bowed, for the door had opened and someone had entered.

Quenten turned around, caught Jenha also straightening from a bow, and greeted the newcomer.

"Were you looking for me, Dahl Malachi?"

"No, Sir. I simply require Subni-Traeger Mosellan to come with me."

Jenha murmured, "Do you still require my services, Sir?"

Quenten gestured a negative. "No, since I am unable to proceed here."

He wished he did have a logical reason to keep Mosellan around, but he did not have the right to monopolise him without one. No reaction showed on his face as Jenha left the room. He had no doubt that the

High Minister had ordered him into seclusion. As that was a local disposition, he had no authority to act. He waited for all the locals to leave the room before giving the sorcerer one last glance.

344

Kaer stood back as his eldest brother tried to convince their father to return to the palace quietly, and rest. However, Koenig was too angry. He stood his ground and did not try to modify his voice.

"I am withdrawing permission for Mosellan to assist the Ambassador; he is obviously unfit to be a Traeger. Malachi, have someone else take over his duties and have Mosellan placed in seclusion indefinitely."

Malachi gave his younger brother a resigned look, and in it was the implied suggestion: do what you can to calm him down or he will have another seizure.

Kaer was not in a mood to meekly agree with his father's command.

"Father, Mosellan is the best suited to help the Ambassador. We simply pull any Traegers from their current duties."

"I can, and I will!"

Koenig began to stride off, saying as he went, "I intend to be present when that sorcerer is questioned."

"Father, wait! I will summon your escort!" Kaer called after him. He spotted two palace guards and gestured them over. A servant came with them.

"I do not need an escort in the palace gardens," Koenig growled audibly. "At least not now when Mosellan can't release any dangerous beasts in here."

"Father, that is not worthy of you."

Koenig stopped striding and spun around to rage at his youngest son. "What of you? Since you have a totally inappropriate soft spot for Mosellan's pet Atapi, take a Traeger in there and make them stop that unholy keening. Well? Get going!"

Kaer glanced around, wondering where his uncle had gone, and was relieved to see him returning with a healer.

"Go, I said," Koenig roared. "The damn Atapi need to learn obedience, and they just can't go anywhere they please, do anything they like. If they won't stop that noise, I want them all forced into sleep."

Eamon reached his brother and spoke softly. The healer added his own quiet words. Both tried to lead the High Minister away, but Koenig shrugged them off and began to stride towards the palace. They followed closely, and the two guards had to trot to catch up.

Kaer remained where he was, unsettled by his father's abhorrent behaviour, and loss of control. He almost felt that way himself, because of the distracting and unpleasant keening. It had already given him a vile headache.

"Lord Kaer, may I serve you," a soft voice spoke from nearby. He turned and saw the white clad servant, and belatedly identified her as one of the Atapi females who still served in the palace. A brief moment of inappropriate amusement overcame him, but then he realised that this woman might indeed be able to help him.

"Leona," he greeted the woman neutrally. "Please tell me what the trouble is that makes your kinfolk emit that uncomfortable noise."

"We are simply… concerned," Leona told him. She did not elaborate.

"Can you tell them to stop it?" Kaer asked.

"We cannot help it," Leona said simply.

Kaer noted then that Leona's throat seemed to be vibrating. "Is there something that you wanted of me?" He was trying not to feel frustrated at her lack of explanation.

"Yes Lord. Was that Con Ansuni here?"

Kaer studied the woman and tried to recall all he knew of Atapi customs.

"You need not fear him," Kaer assured her. "He will not be allowed to harm you."

The servant bowed and moved away. Kaer took a calming breath and went in search of an idle Traeger – if he could find one. His brother had not been wrong in saying all were busy.

He thought, as he strode back to the palace, that it couldn't be the presence of Con Ansuni causing the Atapi to make the noise. The sorcerer had only just arrived, but the unnerving keening had been going on all day. Then a thought struck him. Could something have happened to Jai Cassidy? Had one of the sorcerers badly injured her? It was possible but in view of Quenten having a means to check her condition surely if she had been hurt, he would know. The idea crossed Kaer's mind to ask the Ambassador that question then he wondered if Farcine could tell him more.

CHAPTER 53 – Farcine POV

The Elder Warrior sent Teregan sprawling once again.

"Pay attention, young one," the warrior warned for the third time. "Next time, I will set you to smoothing rock, and slacking will give you a sore tail bone."

The young Atapi was trying to obey, but all day and much of the previous one he had felt angry, and did not know why. His mother, believing it was the contrariness of young males his age, had warned him to control it.

"I am trying," Teregan yelled at his teacher. He was angered by what he believed was an unfair punishment.

"A new hatched whelp could have bettered you then," the warrior claimed. "You have not been listening."

Teregan muttered something about mumbled orders, and quickly realised that the old warrior had very keen hearing. He was immediately grabbed by his scruff and felt his tailbone receive three hefty swats. When he began to howl in protest, he received three more. The old warrior put him down, grabbed one ear and dragged him back into the wooden cave.

Farcine made no comment when the warrior pushed her son onto his bed shelf.

"When the whelp is prepared to learn, I will have him back," the warrior stated and stalked from the room.

Farcine stared at her male whelp with a severe expression. Teregan had been about to protest his complaints, but he subsided and crawled into a corner because he was not able to sit down. When several hours had passed, she called him from the corner and asked him what he had done.

When he protested, "Nothing! I was trying, but I couldn't hear everything he mumbled…" she cut him off and wordlessly pointed to his bed. She ignored the miserable look on his face. Warriors and sorcerers had to be strong and he was too old to need to be reminded of that.

Teregan crept closer to the wall, deeper onto his bed shelf, when the Elder warrior returned later. He unashamedly listened to what the warrior said to his mother and was relieved when he was not mentioned. One of the Kimh wanted to talk to her. He didn't know much about that race, only that they ruled Korvu and were more important than the Kumatan. He curled himself into a tighter ball.

His mother spoke of the Kumatan as being reasonable beings, but the other whelps claimed that Kumatan took naughty whelps from their families. They had forgotten that Kumatan had saved them by taking them. Many had been taken from parents and the parents had not come here.

He didn't know about the Kimh, and it didn't take long for curiosity to overcome misery. Teregan crept out and moved to where he could see the visitor.

He wasn't one of the old glow faces, but he had seen this one around the palace when he was shaping a Kumatan Guard.

"Lord Kaer, how may I serve you?" Farcine greeted with a slight bow. The weird ululation was happening softly, even as she spoke. It seemed to be coming from the area of her throat.

"Lady Mosellan," Farcine then acknowledged the second visitor. "You are welcome here."

"Farcine, is it possible for you all to cease that… unusual noise?" Kaer asked bluntly. "It is affecting everyone in the palace."

The Elder Mother had accepted Kaer as 'friendly', but not friendly enough to tell Atapi secrets to.

"It is an instinctive action – we cannot help it," Farcine said. In truth, if she tried to stop it, she would be subject to severe stress.

Ellhi held out her hands to Farcine. "Is there anything wrong? Can we help?"

"No, my lady," Farcine said, glancing to Ellhi and then looking down. "We are just… concerned."

"What about? Is it Jai?" Ellhi tried to let Farcine know she was genuine in her wish to help.

Farcine would say nothing more. Her fears were not something to share outside the tribe.

Kaer tried to think of what else to try. "Do you think Jai Cassidy is dead?" He recalled the mention that Jai may have removed the new tracer. Maybe she hadn't.

The thrumming grew perceptively louder.

"This may not be my business," Kaer began. "But if she had died, would you know?"

Farcine looked at him, as if considering. "I don't know, Lord, but I knew when Stacion died."

"There is something that Jai has done before," Kaer revealed. "When she was hurt, she slowed her body to near death. Perhaps she has done that again."

The thrumming reduced.

"I think I would know if she died," Ellhi whispered.

Farcine knew what this Kumatan woman was to Jai-devil and her mind eased. It was because Stacion had mated to her that she knew he'd died. The thrumming died right down.

"But it has been so long since I have felt her in my mind," Farcine whispered.

"Do you want Kaer to speak to Jenha – have him come to you?" Ellhi asked softly.

"There is no need, lady," Farcine told her. Then she asked, "Is it true they have Con Ansuni a prisoner?"

"Yes," Kaer confirmed. "But he will not harm you."

"He would not," Farcine stated with confidence.

"That's right," Ellhi agreed. "His tribe are kin to you. Maybe you all could re-join his tribe?"

"We serve Jai-devil," Farcine stated unequivocally.

"Of course," Ellhi agreed, patting Farcine's hand, then releasing it. "Let us know if we can help you."

"Thank you, lady," Farcine agreed. She watched her guests leave and turned back to her work. A movement caught her attention where none should have been.

"Teregan!" she called, using her authority as Elder Mother.

Her whelp crept back off his bed and slunk towards her, expecting a blow and not trying to avoid it.

Farcine had a sudden idea, now that the tension of the past two days had eased. She knew her son was precocious, advanced for his age, and a potential sorcerer. Perhaps his behaviour of the past two days was because he had begun to sense the 'tribe-mind'. Perhaps he, like the Kumatan and Kimh, had been hearing the unvoiced worry of the adults.

"Why do you think you had trouble hearing Warrior Tarok today?" Farcine asked him.

"He was mumbling," Teregan claimed and his mother smacked his face.

"Respect your elders at all times," she reminded him. "Respect is not punished. Disrespect will be. Do you normally have trouble hearing him?"

"N… No."

"Then what was different today?"

Teregan considered that. If warrior Tarok was not the problem, he was.

"I had noise in my ears," he realised.

"Is it still there?" Farcine asked.

"No, Mother. It came and went, but stopped before your visitors came."

Farcine considered that it may not have been because of her own concerns. "Were you seeing things, too? Feeling things from that alien?"

Teregan dropped his head. "Yes."

"Show me."

Teregan's mind skittered away from some of the memories and Farcine soon realised why. Although she didn't know exactly what the vile creature was doing to Jai-devil, she understood the sensations her whelp had received but not yet understood. Then she saw a face she knew. Obaki! He had helped Jai-devil and… that vision ended. The next was full of fury and shame and the fact the alien had been violently ill. Farcine controlled her reaction – not shock or horror, but glee.

The anger simmered in her whelp's mind. It was that alien he was getting it from. Most of what she saw then was darkness, as if the alien was too ashamed to show his face. Then she saw a series of places that her whelp had memorised well.

"The anger you have been feeling these past two days is not yours," she told her whelp. "The alien did bad things to Jai-devil and Jai-devil punished him. So he is angry. I will teach you to recognise his emotions and keep them from affecting you – if you will listen."

"I will listen, Elder Mother," Teregan promised.

Before he had finished his breakfast. Quenten received word that Con Ansuni was awake and should be able to answer questions. Traeger Solomon was to meet him at the start of the next hour and accompany him to the shielded cell.

When they arrived, Quenten forestalled Solomon, "I would like to go in alone."

"Ambassador, that is most irregular."

"Do you fear that the protections you set up are flawed?" Quenten asked as if he were merely curious.

"No, Sir. It is just that I do not wish to take a chance with a personage of your importance."

"You may be assured that I will take no harm. I simply wish to observe this sorcerer before you enter. I understand that sorcerers are not friendly towards Traegers I wish to observe his reaction to me, a neutral party."

"I will allow you five minutes," Solomon compromised. He had orders from the High Minister to report on the questioning. However, he wouldn't miss much in that short time. As he would for any of the Kimh, he moved to open the door for the high-ranking visitor.

Quenten could have reminded the Traeger that he did not have to obey arbitrary rules, when operating within his mandated authority. However, this time it suited him to be able to compare the sorcerer's reaction to him with that towards the Traeger.

The door closing made a distinct whooshing sound, but the pacing Atapi ignored it. Or did that extra air shield dampen the sound? Quenten had time to study the unusual physique of the lizard man. He had never been so close to a sentient creature capable of flight.

After a couple of minutes he said, "Con Ansuni. I am Galactic Ambassador Quenten. I have questions for you."

The sorcerer turned, gave him a head to foot glance, and returned to pacing. Quenten felt he had been dismissed as of no importance.

"I have the authority to have you released if you answer my questions."

He had spoken in Kumatan, and he knew this sorcerer understood that language, but he got no reply.

"Do you know who I am?" he persisted.

Without turning to face him the Atapi growled, "Another alien who does not belong here. And if you can, as you claim, overrule the High Fool, then I have proof that his kind are all fools."

Quenten moved further into the room until the invisible wall stopped him. It was hard to judge what the sorcerer might be feeling, apart from the desire to be free.

"Your friend Jenha Mosellan has sent people to look for your children."

The snarl that came as a reply might have been the reaction to the entrance of the two Traegers. The whole feeling in the room changed. Where the sorcerer had been ignoring him, Con Ansuni glared at Solomon. The smooth, rounded brown features, morphed into an angry snarl, revealing the two rows of pointed white teeth that contrasted with the darker skin. A rustling of wings, as Con partially unfurled them, drew everyone's attention. Solomon didn't draw his weapon, but his hand hovered near it.

"Con Ansuni, you will answer our questions." Solomon's commanded the sorcerer.

Quenten kept his face composed, when Con Ansuni spat a glob of spittle directly towards the Senior Traeger. Had the mysterious wall not been there, the accuracy would have been remarkable. Instead the liquid seemed to stay suspended in the air for a moment, before beginning to run down towards the floor. From his own viewpoint, the elongated drop was still suspended in the air.

The gesture, intended to be disrespectful, incensed Solomon, but Quenten spoke first, conversationally, "This is a friendly talk, not an inquisition."

He saw the quick glance that the sorcerer gave him, before the Traeger once more became the focus of his attention. To him, it seemed obvious that Con Ansuni was baiting the Traeger. He wanted to know why.

"I would like to talk to you about the aliens that attacked your tribe," he kept his voice calm. "I wish to know everything they did."

Con, turned to glare at the Traegers as he answered. "They are dead – those creatures that treated my whelps as meat, and tried to steal that which is not theirs. They will learn to fear the Atapi, and the Kumatan who ride onto my lands and steal my whelps will also feel my fury."

Solomon reacted instantly. "We did not break our word. We stayed out of your lands. It is you who trespassed onto our lands."

"Short sighted fools," Con Ansuni snarled. He turned his back on his questioners. It seemed then that he began to hum in a staccato rhythm.

"You can't do any of your magic in here, Ansuni." Solomon's warning was ignored and the humming persisted.

Moments later, Quenten felt the hair on his neck wanting to stand straight out. The air in the room seemed electrified.

"That's impossible!" Solomon said to himself. He had his rod-like weapon out now, as had the younger Traeger, a lad named Octan.

Quenten saw Con Ansuni's intent expression. It wasn't the angry snarl – more of a snarl grin. He saw that both Traegers had gone pale in the face, and he would have suggested that they wanted to flee, but they stayed and had their immobilisers out.

Whatever was affecting them, was either only directed at them, or he, Quenten, was unaffected because he was alien.

The staccato hum ceased, and now the sorcerer began a high pitched ululation that was even more mind piercing that the Atapi wailing of the previous day.

Quenten wondered why the sorcerer was deliberately provoking the Traegers. Did he want them to use their weapons on him again? He considered that probable mechanism of the immobilisers, an oddly high tech device in a low tech culture. It fired an energy beam that paralysed the victim's central nervous system. A quick, painless way to stop a fellow creature. Would it even pass through that invisible wall of force? And how did they create that wall?

In a glance at the Traegers, Quenten saw the young one tensing his hand.

"Don't fire!" he shouted a warning, but it came too late. The energy beam reflected off the invisible wall – returning directly to the young Traeger. Octan slumped to the floor.

Solomon, realising what had happened, threatened, "When the Council meets to decide your punishment for transgressing on our lands, and this will also go against you."

Quenten took a weapon of his own from a hidden pocket, and watched the sorcerer. It was obvious that he had done something, but the 'attack' if it could be called that, had been directed at the Kumatan. However, the injury to the young Traeger had actually been self-inflicted.

Con Ansuni had snarl-grinned at the result, but all of a sudden, he turned his attention away from them, and seemed to be staring past them and through the enclosing wall. The cat-like tail that had been twitching like it was shooing flies, was now quite still.

Quenten began slapping his weapon into the palm of his hand, and moved to be in the direction of the sorcerer's gaze. The snarl grin was less pronounced now, even though Solomon was kneeling beside his assistant, still murmuring, "It shouldn't be possible."

The senior Traeger stood up and said, "I need to get Octan to the healers. You should leave now, Ambassador."

"You take him where you must, Solomon. When you have done that, please arrange food and drink for your prisoner. I will leave shortly."

Quenten continued to stare at Con Ansuni, still slapping the weapon into his palm. He didn't have to make threats to bolster his authority. Now, he knew this young sorcerer was resourceful and clever, and it seemed the Atapi knew to respect him, even if he had baited the Traegers.

"I still wish to ask you questions, but I will return when you have had time to consider my request. At that time, I will have answers. You will tell me what I want to know willingly, or I will have it from you unwilling. I have heard ill things of the Selkrit – those who transgressed on your land. If you co-operate, the truth will be revealed. If you do not, I can only assume that the Atapi are guilty of all the things the Selkrit claimed."

Quenten watched for a reaction, but the sorcerer could hide his reactions as well as he could himself. "I think you understand me, Con Ansuni."

Con snarled and turned his back.

After several minutes, Quenten decided to add, "Jai Cassidy spoke well of you. I believe she is related to you."

He heard the sorcerer making a low chanting sound and warned, "You will not provoke me as you did the young Traeger. I am not so naïve as to forget that blocking you from the aura makes you helpless. You should not waste your personal energy in annoying me."

Now Con turned back to face him, snarl-grinning. "I will not underestimate you, neither do I intend to be friends with you. All of you are keeping me here when I have whelps to find."

"They are being sought and I need information from you."

The rigid posture told Quenten that he would have no chance of getting so-operation just then. And truthfully, he did not blame the sorcerer for his anger.

"Jai Cassidy," he prompted, thinking that this sorcerer shared some of her belligerence.

Unexpectedly, he was answered.

"My womb-mates child has some very strange ideas. One of them is that I can trust your kind of alien. When considered with her intention to challenge anyone of importance, I can only assume that the idea is as foolish."

Quenten smiled. The Kumatan considered the Atapi to be uncivilised, and therefore both stupid and ruled by emotion. This Atapi was neither.

"Do you know where you foolish relative is now?" Quenten reminded himself to ask if she had been located.

"She has not irritated me since the day before yesterday," Con muttered. "She has a death wish."

His face formed into a snarl grin, as if he privately admired her persistence.

"Why do you say that?" Quenten asked, although he privately agreed.

Even as his mind wandered to the reactions he had had from various people to Jai Cassidy, he saw Con Ansuni's expression change. His body, which had eased its rigid stance, stiffened again. Now he seemed to be straining to hear something that was far away. A muscle began to vibrate in his throat, and the weird ululation began again.

"Perhaps we can help each other," Quenten proposed, but his words went unheard.

He continued to watch the strangely intent sorcerer for several minutes, and wished he understood more of this 'aura' that the Kumatan and Atapi seemed to treat as some almost visible form of energy.

This room was shielded against it, was meant to block telepathic communication, but Quenten felt sure that Con Ansuni was aware of some bad news – in spite of that.

"I'll return later," he promised the unheeding sorcerer. Now he left the cell, nodded to the guards outside, and began to walk towards the Kumatan living quarters to speak discuss the sorcerer's odd behaviour with Jenha Mosellan.

Two things struck him as he reached the garden at the back of the palace. The first was that the Atapi had resumed that unpleasant keening. He wondered if it had started at the same time that Con Ansuni had started acting strange, and whether the cause was the same. The second realisation was that Mosellan, most likely, was in seclusion – which might as well be a polite euphemism for high security solitary confinement. His mandate did not allow him to arbitrarily order Mosellan's release. So, when he saw Traeger Solomon returning, he walked to meet him.

"I wish you to take me to speak with Jenha Mosellan," he requested of the Traeger.

"I am sorry, Sir, Mosellan must remain in seclusion. The High Minister has so ordered it."

"Very well," Quenten feigned indifferent acceptance. "If I am required, I will be aboard my shuttle. You may go about your other duties."

Half way to the shuttle, where he'd hoped to be able to block out that keening sound, he wondered if he could approach Lord Eamon, or one of Koenig's sons, and have them intercede. Then he berated himself for cowardice. He should ask Koenig directly. Surely he would have calmed down by now? He would go and express his hopes that the High Minister had recovered…but later. He needed to talk to Bellus and get the latest reports.

His Senior Centurion was already in the shuttle, sitting back in a chair with his feet on a bulkhead. Quenten smiled faintly, and deliberately made more noise than usual to warn Bellus of his arrival. By the time he had traversed the short passage from the entry lock to the control section, the feet had disappeared from his narrow field of view and Bellus was standing at attention, waiting to greet him.

"Have you had word about Jai Cassidy?" Quenten asked about his main interest of the moment. "She promised to arrive in two days."

"She may still consider this the second day," Bellus suggested. "But no, we haven't seen anything from any of the signal modes."

"If we still have no contact by this evening, upgrade the 'locate and restrain' order to level 1."

"Yes, Sir."

"I can understand why that child irritates everyone she meets," Quenten admitted. "However, I will personally see to it that she learns to respect the Galactic Federation."

"How did your session go with the sorcerer?"

"I would have done better to have gone without those narrow minded Traegers. Con Ansuni is understandable furious, but oddly, he was not hostile towards me. He was able to provoke those Traegers like he was a master psychologist."

"So he wouldn't talk," Bellus intuited. "Do you want me to use the neuro-corticator to extract the information you want?"

"Not yet. I believe he will co-operate with us when it becomes clear it will be the only way he can go out and find his missing whelps. Our affairs have a distant second place to his current worries."

"Did you propose that?" Bellus asked.

"No, the time wasn't right. He wasn't hostile when I first went into the cell, but when the Traegers came in, you could see his hackles go up. I think that I will get you to go and see him later, when he has had time to calm down. Go alone, and don't make the mistake of thinking him any less intelligent that the Kimh or Kumatan."

"As you wish, Sir. However, are we certain that we can interfere in this?"

"I would rather not confront the High Minister about it. That man is mentally unstable. Our expanded mandate does require us to get the cooperation of the Atapi. If we can help him recover his children, we show our good intentions.

"Can we find them?" Bellus asked.

"I'd be willing to wager that Con Ansuni could. So when you do go to see him, send a transmission of sight and sound. I want to observe, see if I get any other ideas."

Bellus merely nodded. "That was not an unusual request. It meant that Quenten could, if he deemed it necessary, offer his insight and experience via the communications channel.

His father's private sitting room was not usually used for the business of ruling to be conducted, but this was how Koenig was interpreting the healer's insistence that he rest.

Kaer, as the youngest of his father's male children, was delegated to the task of note-taker. Meanwhile, Malachi, Deben and Caseon discussed various problems with him. So far, everything was routine administrative matters, long covered by Council edicts, and only needing official sanction.

His normally cheerful, never seeming to be serious eldest brother, Malachi, could have handled everything without trouble. Yet their father had insisted that with all the recent events on Korvu, the unsettled Atapi, the duplicitous Selkrit, and the damnable presence of the Galactic Ambassador – they needed to be handled by someone with years of experience.

Whenever Koenig tried to move the topic to any matter that needed to be presented to the full council, Malachi adroitly reminded him that he would soon be fit enough and could deal with it at the next council session. Put that way, it seemed that Koenig was happy enough to leave those matters until later.

The resumption of the dreadful keening was making all of them tense, and the sound had become more pronounced in the past half hour. So far, Koenig had made no mention of it, but that might have been because of something the healer had given him. Kaer wondered, in between taking notes, what had brought the keening on this time. He hoped his father would stay calm, and that his own headache would get no worse.

A knock at the door distracted them all. The guards outside had been given instructions to let no one in. Kaer rose and went to the door. When he had opened it a few inches, he saw Solomon, and decided it would be better for him to go out and see what the matter was.

"Lord, that sorcerer, Con Ansuni, somehow managed to injure Traeger Octan. This was while the Ambassador was trying to question him."

"Do you want me to mention this to my father?" Kaer asked, reluctant to let Solomon in to report this news. "He needs to stay calm right now."

"The High Minister requested me to report the outcome of the questioning session, Lord Kaer."

"Very well. Please wait here until you are called in."

Kaer hoped that his brief absence would be unnoticed, but he found that wasn't the case.

"Now that you have deigned to re-join us," Koenig spoke tartly. "Please record my decision regarding increasing the levy of recruits for the guard." From his bed, he waved to Malachi. "Tell him!"

With a faint hint of amusement, Malachi began. "We are to send letters to the guard posts in all areas. Yearly levies for recruits are to be increased by a quarter. And this number of recruits are to be sent here for training by the end of the next moon cycle."

Without reacting to the rebuke, Kaer returned to his task, and noticed that Malachi was pouring their father another glass of the light wine. While Koenig paused to drink it, Malachi wondered over.

"Who was at the door?" he asked softly.

Kaer murmured, "Solomon. Father told him to report on the question session with Con Ansuni."

Malachi pulled a face and managed to sound like his usual self. "Well, I guess we will have to bring him in. Did it go well?"

Kaer continued to write, as he said, "Not really. He said Ansuni managed to injure Traeger Octan."

"How?"

"I didn't ask."

Malachi glanced back at Koenig. "We've almost covered all the routine stuff. When that's done with, we'll have him in but you'd better slip out and have one of the guards go for the healer."

"What are you two talking about?" Koenig demanded from his relining position.

Malachi grimace was gone before he turned around to reply, "Solomon will be here to report once we finish all this routine business."

His tone was light and unconcerned, as if matters about Atapi sorcerers were relatively insignificant. This satisfied Koenig until another knock preceded entry by one of the guards. The man announced, "Galactic Ambassador Quenten is here, Sir."

"Pleasant day to you, High Minister Koenig," Quenten gave the traditional slight bow of greeting for one of equal rank.

With acceptable aplomb, allowing for the fact that he was only dressed in casual lounging robes, Koenig returned the greeting, "As I hope it is for you Ambassador."

Deben quickly vacated his chair and moved it into a position where the Ambassador could easily converse with Koenig.

"You went to see that Atapi sorcerer, I believe?" Koenig began, leaning forward to hear more.

"Yes, and I wish to request the assistance of Jenha Mosellan," Quenten began, only to have Koenig cut him off.

"Malachi, bring Solomon in here. I would like to hear his report first."

Kaer saw Malachi's shoulder shrug and obeyed the tacit order to, "Bring him in."

Once the Traeger had entered, Kaer whispered to the nearest guard, "Please fetch the healer that attends my father, and have him wait out here."

Solomon, after greeting the High Minister with a pronounced bow, launched into his report. His voice remained low and even, but even so, the tone of the report was acrimonious.

Kaer, thought privately that Solomon needed to work on his emotional control. It wasn't his place to say anything though. It needed to come from his father, or Malachi. However, he wanted to hear what the Traeger was saying since he heard, "…was injured."

He was as incredulous as his father and brothers, but held his tongue. Quenten was sitting placidly, a subtle example that his father should heed.

"If I may insert a comment," Quenten requested. "Con Ansuni did not injure the young man."

"Nonsense," Solomon snapped, before quickly recalling decorum. "Ambassador, I felt him working magic, just before…"

Quenten gestured him to silence. "I believe that he was using his personal energy to provoke you. Traeger Octan was injured because he aimed and activated his weapon at the sorcerer, and the energy reflected off your protective wall."

Kaer was in a position to notice Solomon's expression of hatred. And reflected that the Senior Traeger might also benefit from a period of quiet meditation. The House of Contemplation was built to block extraneous thoughts and sounds. However, Quenten's words did have the effect of reminding Solomon of his position.

"I did manage to exchange a few civil words, on a neutral topic, with Con Ansuni. And I will speak to him again, later. However, before then, there are points relating to the Atapi culture that I need to understand. That is why I require the services of Jenha Mosellan."

"Out of the question," Koenig snapped. He must remain in seclusion or his aberrant ideas will endanger us all. Solomon can tell you anything that you need to know."

Kaer decided that Quenten's abrupt silence was eloquent. The Ambassador revered the truth, uncluttered by emotion and prejudice. Solomon had demonstrated that on this matter, he lacked both. Perhaps to the point of a lack of knowledge of how the Atapi thought.

"Before I left that protected room," Quenten spoke thoughtfully. "I noticed Con Ansuni become very distracted. It was my thought that he was listening to something…perhaps from far away."

Solomon, once again the image of calm, replied to that. "The room is shielded to prevent sorcerers from communicating mind to mind, as well as to block the aura. I think Ansuni simply decide to ignore you."

"I see," Quenten remarked. "I think then, that I should not take up more of your time."

"We are finished here," Koenig decided. "Those tyrannical healers have restricted me to here, and my sons have work to do. Kaer, bring those notes over and I will initialise them."

"Have a pleasant day," Quenten murmured, following the tradition that Koenig was ignoring.

Kaer murmured, the expected reply quietly as he passed on his way to his father. He hoped that the Galactic Ambassador did not have the authority to oust an existing ruler for rudeness.

Solomon requested permission to withdraw, and reached Quenten by the door. "I am free if you require my assistance, Ambassador."

"Thank you, but I know you have many matters to oversee. How is young Octan?"

"The healers say he will be right by morning, Sir."

"With an appreciation of the need to avoid provocation," Quenten suggested. "I will send for you if I have need."

Malachi took each sheet after his father finished with them. When the ink was drying on the final page, Kaer carefully removed the small crystal flask of ink and stoppered it. Then he placed the ink and the pens in the rounded hollows of the portable desk that stood beside his father's couch.

Is there anything else that you require, Father," Kaer asked, being mindful of his duty to assist him.

"Yes, go and talk to those damned Atapi. Take a Traeger with you and knock them out this time. Do whatever you need to do to make them quiet. You fixed them before. Just do it again!"

"Father, the only Traegers available are trainees," Kaer reminded him respectfully.

"Then use one of them – the senior trainees should be able to do such a simple task."

"Yes, Father." Kaer decided not to argue the point.

Malachi followed him from the room, and once they had gone, the healer stepped in.

"Hope you can quieten things again, little brother. I am not in a hurry to take on Father's responsibilities."

Malachi was setting a fast pace along the passage, and Kaer had to hurry to keep up. "Nor am I in a hurry to have you do it."

"Tut, tut, do I hear some anger in your tone? Your success yesterday impressed me."

"I doubt that they will listen to me today. It was only because I took Ellhi Mosellan with me that they admitted me at all."

"So what was the problem yesterday?" Now that they were well away from their father's suite, Malachi slowed.

"I think it was uncertainty about the wellbeing of Jai Cassidy."

"Well they should expect trouble if that Earth child is out provoking sorcerers. Her luck won't hold for ever."

"Logic suggests that, but all I could discover yesterday was that Farcine, the Elder Mother, could no longer sense Jai in her mind."

"Could be any number of reasons for that," Malachi considered. "Doesn't the Ambassador have some way to find her?"

"He had some device to track her, but now he thinks that she removed it. I don't claim to understand how it is meant work, but he suggested that if the wearer died while having it on, it sends a certain message. Apparently, it didn't, it just stopped sending information."

"So what does that mean? She removed it and now has come off the worst against one of those sorcerers?"

"That is what I am afraid of. That the noise today is a death wail for Jai," Kaer admitted. "If that is the case, then the only person they might listen to is Jenha Mosellan."

"Perhaps so, but you will have to find another answer. You might have to get Solomon to…"

"No! That is not the answer. As far as Solomon is concerned at the moment, I do not trust his objectivity. Nor is this a task for an incompletely trained Traeger."

"I don't envy you," Malachi admitted. "You will have to do something or Father will be impossible to deal with."

"You don't have to tell me. And I cannot even ask the Ambassador to overrule him about Mosellan. If he had that power, he wouldn't have come asking Father if he could use him."

"Well, if you are really stuck, I will try again to change his mind," Malachi offered.

"He won't change his mind! And he'll just get mad at you too."

"You'd better get going then."

Kaer slowed his pace further once is brother had turned off to the administrative section of the palace. As he headed for the door leading out into the gardens at the back of the palace, he tried thinking at Jai Cassidy himself. Often, he could reach her mind, but this time her uniquely unruly mind was silent. It did not even seem like she heard him and was ignoring him. Maybe Ellhi Mosellan might be able to reach her? No, he wouldn't ask. She had said that she would feel it if Jai died. He hoped, that since she hadn't said so, that somehow Jai was still alive.

If that were the problem, then she would not be able to help anyway. Besides, she needed to help Aniki with Kelhi, Mikha and Jahni. He knew that Mikha had been most difficult whilst the keening had been occurring. He really should see how they were today, but he didn't have the time. In fact, he hadn't had much time to spend with them since Mikha had come to stay with him. Yesterday, he had arrived at his suite after they had all gone to sleep.

"I am going to have to go myself," Kaer murmured aloud, and he squared his shoulders and made an effort to review the first three mantras for calm.

He passed servants going about their tasks, all seemed to have a frown on their faces. He tried to make his own seem calm and serene. Though once he was outside, he gave up trying. The nearer he got to the Atapi compound, the worse his headache got. No one could doubt that this was the source of the wailing – the sound was deafening.

Yet when he arrived, and saw the open gate, he did not know what to do. Protocol required that he ask permission to enter, and normally there would be at least five of the males lounging around outside. He suspected that the overt idleness was a ruse, and they would be quick to block the entry of uninvited callers. What could he do if there was no one to ask?"

Again, he had to do something, so he put aside his dignity and called out, "Farcine! May I speak to you?"

He tried again, trying to make his voice into a bellow that would carry inside. After five minutes he stopped, his voice felt strained, and he doubted his loudest call could be heard at the fence – which was a mere arm's length away.

Should he just enter, and completely shatter courtesy? Break the agreed inviolacy of the Atapi compound? This small area was considered Atapi land and he had no right to enter uninvited. Should he do so, they would have the right to punish him as they chose.

Kaer recalled Jenha saying that sometimes, you had to act and do what was right. He didn't know if going in now was right, but…

He took a calming breath and walked through the gate, following the way that led to the room where Farcine had received him before. The old woman was amidst of a group of howling females. They did not even notice him. Whelps huddled around the walls, but when he tried to talk to them, they ran away. There were no adult, or near adult, males around.

Kaer withdrew. Something was wrong – badly wrong. These females would not stop until the problem was dealt with. With grim determination, he strode out of the compound and went to the House of Contemplation.

"I am here on the orders of the High Minister," Kaer told the Elder he recognised as Elder Deveron. "You are to release Jenha Mosellan into my aegis."

"You have a document?" Deveron asked.

"No, Elder, I do not. My father is badly affected by the grief-howling of the Atapi. Mosellan knows them and should be able to quieten them."

The Elder considered and then nodded. He walked off at a sedate pace.

Kaer refused to dwell on the lie he had told – well, half-lie. He had been ordered to quieten the Atapi. If he was challenged later, he would simply say he had done what was necessary. Having the Atapi made to sleep was not the answer. The howl would resume when they awoke and it would not solve the problem. If his father ordered him to be 'corrected' for this decision, Kaer would petition the council.

The House of Contemplation was made of thick stone and designed to be a haven of silence. Kaer could not hear the howling inside, but he could still feel it in his mind and that was odd.

Elder Deveron escorted Jenha to him, still at the sedate pace that was expected in the House. Kaer saw the strain and the whiteness of his friend's face. He made no comment. When they were outside, Jenha looked immediately towards the Atapi compound.

"Jai Cassidy has not returned?" he asked.

"No, and I cannot feel her mind. Can you?" Kaer asked.

Jenha slowed, his concentration elsewhere. "I cannot feel her mind either."

"Do you think she is dead? That the howling is for her?"

"I can't be sure," Jenha said after a moment of consideration.

They picked up their pace and continued to the Atapi compound. Kaer considered Jenha's reaction. Elder Deveron may have mentioned Kaer's reason for having him released, but Jenha's attention had been drawn to the Atapi as soon as they had begun to hear the howling again.

There were still no males around, and no one preventing them from entering. Jenha went in without hesitation, going unerringly to where the females huddled.

"I am here to help," Jenha said in Atapi. "What can I do, Elder Mother?"

The females moved apart. Farcine rose, her face full of grief, but she drew on the dignity of her rank to face him.

"Consort of Jai-devil," Farcine greeted. "I cannot talk to you. Tribe business is sacred."

"Is it Jai-devil?" Jenha asked gently. "Is she dead? I promised you protection. Nothing will change that."

"No, I don't think Jai is dead, but she won't answer me. Surely she would come…" Farcine almost wailed.

"Yes, if she could," Jenha murmured. "I don't think she is dead either. Could you not let me help you in her stead?"

Farcine was torn between obedience to tribal customs and her grief. She glanced at Kaer, and then away.

"My Lord," Jenha said correctly. "Perhaps you could wait, briefly, outside?"

Kaer nodded. He should not leave, but if it was the only way to learn of the problem, he would ignore protocol.

"Farcine, what is the problem?" Jenha asked gently. "I will not speak of everything you tell me, only the basic facts and only if I must."

Farcine waited for Kaer to be gone. "It is Teregan, my son. He is missing and I fear for him."

"Tell me," Jenha encouraged.

Slowly and with astute prompting, Jenha elicited the pertinent details from Farcine. The missing whelp was a potential sorcerer and had inadvertently formed a link with the Selkrit, Auglan. Farcine knew what that alien had tried to do to Jai-devil and feared what he would do to her son. She had revealed that Teregan was receiving emotions and visions from the alien, and she showed these visions to Jenha's mind. They were of places unfamiliar to Jenha, and what was probably the Selkrit shuttle.

"Last night," Farcine went on, "he came to me and said he had seen whelps, and the alien was hurting them and enjoying it. They were not from this tribe, so I said we could do nothing – their own sorcerer would help them. He was angry at that, but I made him promise to stay here."

"You think he ran off to try to find them?" Jenha suggested.

Farcine nodded. "I can't get images from him if I am not with him. But I know that the alien has him."

The thought of Auglan with Atapi whelps, children and babies, roused anger in Jenha.

"Where are your males? Out searching?" Jenha asked, and Farcine nodded.

Jenha thought quickly. "Did Jai blood Teregan to her?"

Farcine nodded again.

"Has she done it to all of you?"

"Just Teregan and the three oldest warriors."

"What you need to do, Farcine, is to keep trying to reach your whelp," Jenha advised. "Have the other females support you. Try it from outside where the aura is stronger – and invoke Larcia to help you."

Farcine's expression turned to determination.

"And tell those three warriors to keep trying to reach Jai-devil," Jenha finished.

"Lord Kaer suggested Jai-devil might be pretending to be dead," Farcine volunteered.

"Yes, I think that is possible, so you need to keep calling her. I will, too," Jenha promised. "I have some other ideas on how to find her, and there are already others trying to find the whelps. They are from Con Ansuni's tribe."

Farcine hissed. "They have him a prisoner!"

"Yes, but trust me," Jenha asked. "Do you have anything of Teregan's – something personal? A blood-stained garment would be best, or an unwashed garment, or some other personal object?"

"His knife," Farcine said at once. "He did not take it."

Jenha hid his first reaction to that. "Keep it safe – it might be needed," Jenha told her. "When I have spoken to some others, I will come back."

Jenha found Kaer waiting outside, relieved that the level of howling had decreased. "We need to talk to Ambassador Quenten," Jenha told Kaer. His mind was so full of concerns that he did not remember to use the correct courtesies for his friend.

Kaer did not comment. "What is the matter?"

Jenha summarized tersely. "I can't tell you all the details, but one of the whelps is missing," Jenha explained. "I have reason to believe he is with those Con Ansuni is seeking and that the Selkrit Councillor has them all."

Jenha noticed Kaer's slight tensing.

"We need to act quickly," Jenha told him. "For the sake of the young ones and to prove the kind of person that Selkrit is – or do you still believe in their honour?"

"My father…" Kaer began hesitantly. "Did not authorise…"

"Ah," Jenha exhaled. "My release."

Kaer gave a brief nod. "But you were the best one to help here."

Jenha raised the hood of the robe he wore – the kind that those in seclusion and meditation often wore.

"Do not be concerned for me," Jenha said calmly, hoping that Kaer would sense he had a plan to remain unnoticed by the High Minister. "My disposition was not widely announced, and of course you required the services of a Traeger."

"Father has already denied Quenten permission to use your skills," Kaer warned. "However, that was when the reason did not impinge on his mandate or when, in theory, any Traeger could help him."

"Yes, indeed, but now the matter concerns that unpleasant Councillor," Jenha murmured, so his voice did not carry further than his companion. "Now, I believe he will be able exert his authority. I should remain unscathed if we reach him quickly."

"Then we need to find out where he is so that we do not waste time looking everywhere."

"In that case, Lord Kaer, we should go to his shuttle. There is usually one of the centurions on duty there. If we request permission to speak to the Ambassador, and he is not there, they can tell us where he will be. Likely, he will choose to come to us."

"Yes," Kaer agreed. That solved his major concern, but it did not mean that they wouldn't encounter any of the Elders. If Jenha were seen with him, both of them would be taken to the House of Contemplation.

Ambassador Quenten sat in his shuttle while Centurion Bellus went to talk to the sorcerer. He had on a helmet, a more open version than that which was part of the Centurion armour. He had the advantage, of blocking all external noise, so that he could listen to the communication feed from other units.

The clear visor was now pulled down in front of his eyes, and it acted like a screen on which the visual from the tiny camera on Bellus's uniform showed what was in front of the Centurion. For now it was the path and the ornamental trees and bushes in the palace garden. Speech and other sounds were also transmitted, but as yet, the fragments of conversations from the people he passed were not important. He could if he wished, give Bellus orders through the earpiece/ microphone of the helmet.

He had suggested that Bellus not request to be accompanied, just to state that he had instructions to talk to the sorcerer. Bellus would be ready to counter any objection the door guards had. However, the ploy of acting as if you had all the authority needed, worked as it usually did, and the guards stayed outside.

Quenten was not surprised when Con Ansuni ignored Bellus's introduction. The sorcerer gave him that head to toe glance, and turned away as if the visitor was of no interest to him, and nothing he said would be of value. After seeing how this sorcerer had expertly provoked the Traegers, this was probably a ploy to test the latest visitor.

"Why do you let yourself be a stable sweeper for the Kimh?" Con Ansuni demanded.

Quenten allowed himself some amusement, as Bellus subvocalized, "What?"

The sorcerer's tail was twitching now, not as if he were really aggravated, but merely irritated by the intrusion.

Bellus chuckled, causing the sorcerer to turn around. "I don't think I can claim that. I have to obey Ambassador Quenten. He came here earlier. He is a lot more rational than the local leader, but twice as demanding."

The sorcerer snarl-grinned. "What do you want? You and your master are persistent, but I don't care to talk to you."

"Then perhaps, first off, you will listen?"

"Only if you can tell me how to get free of this cage. I have important things I need to do." Con Ansuni went back to pacing the confined space. Staring at different sections of the white fabric covered walls as if looking for a weakness in the protections.

As Bellus began to explain the concept of a Galactic Federation and Galactic Law, Quenten considered the behaviour of this sorcerer. For a creature that was understandable angry, he was behaving in a controlled manner. Yet the Traegers had warned him to expect berserk fury from any sorcerer that was apprehended. None of them had even hinted that they had a sense of humour, yet it seemed that Bellus's frank admission had amused him.

Bellus finished his spiel, but the only reaction that he got was, "What does that all mean to me? It is useless information."

"Will you answer questions?" Bellus tried.

Con Ansuni studied him as if he were an insect, and demanded, "Can you order the High Fool to release me?"

"I…no. My master might, but he needs to act within the constraints of the Galactic Council."

Quenten realised that little of the explanation had been comprehended by the Sorcerer. He subvocalized into his microphone, "Tell him that we need to know all he can tell us of the blue-blooded aliens so that we can act."

Bellus passed that on.

"Why should I do as you want? I am being treated like a wild beast – and none of you care that I have twenty whelps to find. You are keeping me here when those children were stolen by creatures riding Kumatan horses. Why don't you question them?"

"We need to know what you can tell us."

Con Ansuni began to growl, and his tail began to twitch faster. "You still want to talk when, for all I know, right now my whelps are being tortured, killed, butchered, or eaten. One is my son! How can I trust anyone who will allow that? If I answer your questions – will I be free to go? Or will you wipe the feet of the Kimh and keep me here until my whole tribe dies out?"

"Don't you want those blue-blooded aliens removed?"

"If they come onto my land, they die! I don't need more aliens interfering."

"If we help you find and rescue your children, will you answer our questions?" Bellus tried.

"How do I know I can trust you? The High Fool thinks those vile aliens can do no wrong. You are another kind of alien. If you can get me free of here, I will consider helping you – but only if Jenha Mosellan assures me that you can be trusted."

"I will ask for his help, but his people have placed him in seclusion."

The sharp white teeth appeared as Con snarl-hissed, "That is because he is a fair minded Kumatan, who does not see the Atapi as a race of murderers. That is why they muzzled him. The High Fool does not want to be fair to us. Now get out of here before I prove that their puny air-shield is no protection against an angry Atapi sorcerer."

Con spread his wings and stalked to the barrier. "Get out!"

Bellus didn't move – just stared back for long enough to prove he was not afraid, before leaving.

Back in his personal shuttle, Quenten tilted the visor up and removed it. As frustrating as things seemed, there would be a way to proceed. He could not bring himself to be angry with the sorcerer for not answering questions, and he did not want to force the answers from him. The procedure often disabled the subject for a period of days, and in this case, the lives of many innocents were at stake.

If only the sorcerer could have seen the value of answering the questions. He could have acted immediately, perhaps even ordered his release.

Bellus strode into the shuttle, his boots echoing on the metal floor. His jaunty bearing changed to a dejected slump when he didn't need to act for the locals.

"I'm sorry, Sir. That lizard man simply cannot see a wider view than his own tribe and lands."

"You did better than I expected," Quenten admitted. "He has no reason to love any alien."

"Not even Jai Cassidy," Bellus asked without thinking.

"He calls that young oath-breaker an irritation. And speaking of her, send Terr into see me while you take a break and eat."

If only he could find Jai Cassidy, Quenten thought. He had agreed to her outrageous demands because she had an 'in' with the parochial lizard folk – while at the same time, not being so backward and ignorant.

"Sir?" Centurion Terr greeted.

"What have you to report? Have you located Jai Cassidy?" Quenten demanded.

"There is still nothing of value coming through the tracking device."

"Might she be hiding out at that monolithic rock? It has blocked our signals before."

"I don't think so, Sir," Terr disagreed, "For all of the reasons you told me."

"What about the Selkrit encampments?" Quenten changed topics.

"We are doing everything we can, but this planet is huge and we don't know what they are after."

"No, that's true. Who have you got watching the screens at the moment?"

"Team two, Sir."

"Have them contact our ship – get them to look for vapour trails from the Selkrit shuttles. Even if they have developed some kind of cloaking for their ships, they can't hide the exhaust trail."

Terr went off but returned almost at once. "Sir, Lord Kaer wishes to talk to you."

"Send him in!" Quenten stood and straightened his tunic, trying to control the hope that suddenly sprang into his mind. His control nearly slipped when he saw the hooded figure, who had accompanied the High Ministers son, lower his head covering.

"You are… available… again?" he asked Jenha, carefully keeping the eagerness from his voice.

Kaer answered. "I had need of him to help with the Atapi, Ambassador. My father did not authorise his availability. However, we have knowledge that comes under your mandate and impacts upon Con Ansuni as well."

Quenten invited hid guests to sit, and when he had as well, he said, "Please explain."

Jenha repeated what he had told Kaer, but was then asked, "How did you obtain this information?"

"While not being a member of the tribe, they still consider me Jai Cassidy's consort. I promised not to reveal any more than the bare facts to any outsider. If I break that trust, they will reject me."

"I accept that. Tell me how I can use this information. If we are able to find these children, Con Ansuni will be in our debt."

Jenha spoke slowly. "Jai Cassidy would be able to find the whelp of her tribe. Do you have knowledge of her whereabouts?"

"No. She is in default of her oath to us. Do you think she is alive?"

Kaer murmured, "Ellhi does not think she is dead."

Quenten accepted that and said, "That human child has, I believe, removed the tracker. It is powered by the body's electrical impulses, so we have no way to find it, and she could be well away from it. If she is alive, and we find her, she will answer for that transgression."

He paused to see the reaction of his guests, but it seemed that they had more immediate concerns. "Is there an alternative?"

"Yes. " Jenha admitted, "One of the missing whelps is Con Ansuni's son."

"I recently learnt that," Quenten admitted. "Were the Traegers that captured him aware of it?"

"I do not believe he was given the chance to explain, or was listened to if he tried," Kaer felt compelled by honesty to admit. "It was enough to condemn him, just being within the Kumatan town."

"He was tricked!" Jenha said, disgust and anger warring in his voice.

"When he was found, he was checking the horses that had just ridden into the town," Kaer revealed.

"Surely he could have located his own child," Quenten suggested.

Jenha shook his head, "Ambassador, Atapi whelps are only still when they are asleep. They do not meekly accept being held. To take that many of them any distance would be difficult unless they had first been put to sleep. And if they were asleep – Con might not be able to sense them."

"Would they have been left unguarded?"

"Not with those revolting mechanical creatures loose," Jenha said at once. "The females would have been guarding them, and they should not be dismissed as fighters. They must have been overcome quickly, so they could not stop the abductors or raise an alarm until a long time later."

"That makes sense," Quenten agreed, nodding. "So, do you need me to authorise that sorcerer's removal from that peculiar room? How can I be assured that he will not immediately escape? He has not yet answered our questions and refuses to help unless he has your assurance. Why you?"

"I believe that he trusts me because when we were young, we were friends."

Quenten didn't seem to find that admission at all strange, although Kaer knew his elders would find the thought unsettling.

"If he is allowed to find his children, do you think he will talk freely to us and speak to his brethren on our behalf?"

"I will ask him to, and I think he will agree, but he would consider rescuing the whelps a priority, as would I."

"Come with me now," Quenten directed.

The guards outside the door of the shielded room had no hesitation in allowing the three of them to enter. Quenten led the way to indicate to the prisoner that he was in charge.

Con Ansuni stopped his angry pacing when he spotted the latest intruders and recognised Jenha Mosellan.

"What?" Con snapped.

"We think we know where your missing children are," Quenten said. "If we help you rescue them, will you answer my questions?"

Con looked at Jenha, who nodded and spoke quickly in Atapi – explaining what he had learnt. Then he looked at the other two. He seemed to dismiss Quenten, and concentrate his attention on Kaer.

"And this whelp? Is he one like the High Fool?"

Jenha guessed his concern. "Kaer understands the importance of finding your whelps. He has a child of his own and he is fostering Mikha." As he knew it would, that last statement had most force in persuading Con.

"Does the High Fool know what you are proposing?" Con asked, and snarl-grinned to see the young Kimh flush purple. "I thought not."

After a moment's silence, Con addressed Quenten. "I'll trade. I will not try to escape – yet! But if I find those honourless aliens – you had better remove them before I get near them."

Jenha knew that Con should not have admitted that, so he murmured a suggestion. "It would be wise to accept the company of the two enforcers – for now."

Con met Jenha's eyes in tacit agreement.

"What do we need to do now?" Quenten looked to Jenha for the answer.

"We need to go to the Atapi compound."

"Am I to be reviled yet again?" Con demanded.

Jenha said softly, "They are still kin to you and Farcine, the Elder Mother, has agreed to this."

"And that whelp who calls herself a sorceress?"

"Is missing."

"Dead?"

"We do not know, but even if not, I don't think she will object."

"She is ignorant! I would not let another sorcerer have free entry onto my land."

From the moment that Jenha murmured the phrases that took down the protective force screen, Kaer felt the impact of what he was doing. The personality of the sorcerer was immediately apparent, and seemed to be an elemental force. Until that moment, he could have called a halt to this course of action, and he felt it was the right action to take. However, his father would never forgive him for this.

He tried to look confident, assured, in command, but inside – he knew all that was a lie. As they walked the passages to the door leading outside, his eyes were flicking everywhere. He saw the servants take a glance at the procession, and duck out of sight. He expected one of them to run to tell his father, who would suddenly appear and revile him. If he did, his anger at what he would consider an unforgivable betrayal, would surely bring on a fatal seizure.

They emerged into the fresh air, and he saw Con Ansuni stand straighter as he sniffed the air. He also spotted one of the Elders, sedately walking towards the palace along one of the paths in this ordered garden. The figure glanced up from looking at the newly blooming flowers and stopped, before changing direction to come to the unusual group. Kaer felt the blood drain from his face.

"Kaer," Lord Eamon greeted, when he was in conversational distance of the group. He made no reference to his nephew's companions, but his interest was tacit in his mild greeting. "I believe you sanctioned this excursion?"

Eamon moved into place beside Kaer and invited, "Please, continue where you were going."

Sensing that this was not as friendly a confrontation as it seemed, the group stopped. Quenten stayed next to Con Ansuni, aware that the sorcerer was breathing deeply, and wondered if he was drawing on the invisible aura and likely to commit some sorcery. He watched the sorcerer, but also this interaction between uncle and nephew.

Jenha removed the cowl from his head and stepped up next to Kaer, accepting equal fault if blame was to be cast.

Kaer appreciated the gesture, for as he met his uncle's look, he felt himself trembling. He knew what his uncle must be thinking and tried to think of a way to phrase his reasons that wouldn't have him sent into eternal seclusion.

At first he didn't understand when Eamon merely said, "Your father is resting within the House of Seclusion, now that the howling has been reduced to a bearable level. I am impressed by your success. Did you find the cause?"

"I believe so, Uncle," Kaer said stiffly.

"And this procession?" Eamon implied the question.

Kaer drew a deep breath and spoke quietly, admitting what he had found out with Jenha's help and what was now intended.

"Worthy reasons," Eamon allowed. "When you locate those whelps, how will you get there? Will you release this sorcerer, Con Ansuni, or will you encourage Jenha Mosellan to break his vows again?"

Kaer flushed again. Neither option would reflect well on him.

Quenten, listening to the quiet exchange, inserted quickly, "I have Enforcer teams ready to move at a moment's notice."

"That is well if we can give them an exact location," Eamon nodded to Quenten. "However, we of Korvu do not have your technological ways to describe a location. I will place two Traegers at your service. Each can accompany two other people. Will you be sending Enforcers with them to witness what is found?"

"Yes, indeed, and your offer of Traeger assistance is most kind."

The procession did not start again immediately. Jenha moved back to Con Ansuni and asked, "Can you sense the mind of your son?"

"Not with these accursed slave bands on," Con growled.

Jenha unobtrusively murmured the controlling words that would remove the bands and allow Con to try again. This time Con snarled in frustration.

"It is like he is asleep."

"We still have hope," Jenha began in Kumatan, but switched to Atapi to continue. "Farcine's whelp is talented, and not yet an apprentice. Would you be willing to interfere in Jai's tribe, since no one can reach her either?"

Con replied, also in Atapi, "If they are blooded to her, I cannot interfere."

"The whelp is, and three warriors," Jenha murmured back. "Not the rest. And I believe they are still your kin."

"You did not learn all that from your sire," Con accused.

"No, I learnt it from your womb-mate."

Kaer asked, "Can he sense them?"

"No, we will need to go to Farcine. However, it would be best if the extra Traegers and the Enforcers, when they come, remain outside."

Quenten merely nodded, and for a moment, seemed to be talking to himself.

When the group moved off, towards the Atapi compound, Kaer noticed that Con Ansuni was now moving with even more vigour, strutting with the arrogance of one who was sure of his power. As soon as they were within sight of the gate, Kaer saw a whelp race inside, no doubt warning of their approach. Several females came to stand in the doorway. By the time they had entered and were approaching the door, Farcine had joined them, and come to stand in the fore of the group.

Jenha was now leading the group, and he introduced, "Eldest Mother, I am aware I am trespassing on the land of Jai Cassidy, with Lord Kaer whom you know. I would like to introduce you to Lord Eamon, uncle to Kaer, and Quenten, a representative from the Galactic Council."

Farcine glanced at the two new comers, but her attention quickly returned to Con Ansuni.

Jenha went on, politely, as if abetting a sorcerer to enter lands belonging to another was a routine courtesy.

"You know Con Ansuni, I believe, and I apologise for bringing him here without first asking permission. However, he is seeking his whelps and wishes to ask your assistance."

"Honoured relative, I am relieved by your offer of help," Farcine spoke with cautious welcome.

Con dipped his head at Farcine. "Elder Mother, Farcine," Con answered her quietly. "You were my sister's friend, and your son cared enough to help mine and the other whelps. In this we share a common need. I do not think Jai Cassidy will object, and I will be in her debt for this indulgence."

Farcine bowed, accepting his help.

"Do you have something belonging to your son?"

Farcine trotted across the room to take Teregan's knife and hand it to Con. Quenten, Kaer, Eamon and Jenha watched as Con first sniffed the knife and then licked the hilt. After that he began to chant a ritual, pausing a moment at the end, and then repeating it. After the third repetition, Con closed his eyes and looked inwards, letting sights and sounds impinge on his mind.

The ritual worked. He saw out of the eyes of another – one who was much shorter that he was. He was aware of the muted keening of frightened children, saw shadowy shapes, squirming together in a huddle. A young Atapi voice was talking to them, calming them. He saw his son, looking as though he were dead. They were in a dark place, lit only by a few odd greenish lights.

"Teregan?" he thought at Farcine's whelp. He sensed shock and fear.

"Ye… yes?"

"I am Con Ansuni. I need your help. Do you know where you are?"

"In… in something… like the blue alien's metal cave," Teregan thought back with a shiver.

"Is it moving?" Con asked.

"N… No."

"Are you alone?" Con asked next.

"No. There were two aliens here. They liked hurting us but I scared them away. They are sitting away from us – watching us."

Con considered what to do and then thought at Teregan, "I want you to repeat what I tell you, three times."

"Yes…"

Con patiently cued Teregan through a simple ritual, hoping the whelp had enough personal energy to make it work. "Look at the aliens – are they moving?"

Teregan waited a moment to be sure. "No."

Then Con directed the distant whelp to turn slowly around so that he could see the place where they were being held. "Well done, Teregan. Jai-devil will be proud of you. Help is coming. Do not be afraid."

Con opened his eyes, returning his attention to those around him. "I have the visual picture. Will those Traegers let me show them?"

Jenha spoke calmly. "Show me, and I will share it." Once he had the picture in his memory, the group went outside. Two enforcers in full armour and closed visors waited with the two Traegers. The latter were young, recently promoted to full rank. They bowed respectfully to the group and looked at Jenha with respect.

"There are two guards – perhaps less than normally active. I cannot be sure for how long," Jenha warned as he shared the mind picture with the two Traegers. "The effect may not last long, and there maybe others helping to guard the whelps."

Kaer sensed his uncle beside him as Quenten stepped forward to take charge of the remaining details. He was instructing his Enforcers. "Go with the Traegers, let them deal with the younglings. I want you to apprehend any of the Selkrit who are there and secure the shuttle they are being held in. If Councillor Auglan is there, treat him with respect, but ensure he returns here."

As the purposeful preparations were made, and first Jenha and Con Ansuni walked two steps and vanished, and then the two Traeger/Enforcer pairs, Quenten came over to speak to Lord Eamon.

Kaer heard him say, "I am very glad that I can leave this mission in the hands of those two keen young Enforcers. They don't seem to mind having their essences dragged into nothing space."

As Eamon reassured the other man of the safety of that mode of travel, Quenten flipped down the clear visor that had been resting on his head. He fiddled with one side of the head frame holding the visor and focussed his attention on something only he could see.

Eamon spoke after a moment. "I have seen some marvels since this visitor arrived – that are as much magic to me as our Traegers are to him."

Kaer didn't try to make a reply, he was still tense, expecting censure. However, his uncle's next words relaxed him.

"However, the greatest marvel of all, is this moment when Kimh, Kumatan, Atapi and alien are working together in harmony. I have seem no higher epitome of the expression of our Nuath."

All Kaer could think of to answer that was, "I hope my father can see it the same way."

As he touched Con's arm to make the transfer to the alien shuttle, Jenha sensed many things from Con Ansuni. First was a complete lack of distrust between them, and second that the sorcerer was drawing on the aura to replace the last of his depleted energy. They would both be ready for the unexpected, when they arrived. At that time – Jenha was quite willing to let Con be in charge.

Their sudden arrival frighted the mewling whelps even further, and Teregan, who was standing on guard, could not see the new arrivals clearly – only sense them. His mind betrayed the fact that he hadn't seen them arrive, and it was apparent to Jenha that he was on the verge of falling asleep on his feet.

"Be still," Con used mind speech to command all of his whelps. Then he snarled, "This is indeed one of the foul holes of those evil ones. It reeks of their vile stench."

Into the space behind them, the two pairs of Traeger/Enforcer arrived.

Con turned his attention to Teregan, who had moved back, until he was nearly stepping on the younger whelps.

"Is the evil one still here?"

"No…" Teregan's voice, like his whole body, was trembling. "Please…don't be angry…"

Jenha spoke over the timid voice, confirming, "We have missed him."

"He is fortunate. I would have continued slicing him into pieces from where Obaki left off." Con snarled as he looked around the dark space, seeming to see what he wanted easily enough.

Jenha observed that the Enforcers had found the paralysed guards and were applying restraints that glowed faintly in the darkness, and the young Traegers were awaiting directions, but also alert for others who might enter the shuttle. "Leave him to the Enforcers. When they finish with him, he will be truly humbled. We need to tend your youngsters."

Con turned his attention back to the trembling whelp trying to look defiantly at him.

"Well done, young warrior. I am Con Ansuni." Con reached out and touched Teregan's head, and sent him reassurance. "You have no need to be afraid of me, I am in your debt."

Teregan was still both rigid with fright and unable to speak.

"At this moment, my friend, I am very much reminded of your sire," Jenha murmured, hoping Con would understand. He sensed Con's anger draining away.

"What happened to Litok?" he asked in a much gentler voice.

Teregan found he could breathe again, now that this powerful sorcerer was no longer exuding rage that was reminiscent of Stacion, back on that other world.

"He…they beat him real bad. Just because he tried to protect the others," Teregan whispered.

Con went directly to where his son lay, gently pushing some of the tiny whelps out of his way. He ran his hand all over the prone body, very gently feeling for injuries.

Teregan quietly slumped onto the floor, trembling again, but this time from relief. Jenha moved to crouch beside him. Both watched as the tiny whelps came and clung to Con's legs.

"Jai-devil will be proud of you," Jenha murmured to Teregan.

"No, she will be angry. I disobeyed the Elder Mother, who guides us when she is away. I interfered with another tribe, and he is Con Ansuni, son of Stacion…"

"He is not angry with you, youngling, but with those who treated you harshly. Did you not hear him say he is in your debt?"

"No, he will punish me…"

"Young one, he is not like his sire. Did you ever see little whelps clinging to Stacion, as they do to Con?"

"No…and he never even acknowledged me!"

"Another major mistake that renegade made," Jenha dismissed the dead sorcerer. "Have you the energy to remain here a little longer? We would take the tiniest whelps first."

"Yes, I won't disappoint Jai-devil."

"Indeed. I have no fear of that."

Jenha stood again, and moved to Con. "Let me carry Litok. I think the young whelps would be more reassured by you."

Con nodded, plucking the whelps from his legs and letting them hold onto his arms and neck. Jenha gestured the two Traegers closer.

"Each of you, carry two whelps," Jenha directed, allowing Con to transfer them from himself. The Traegers immediately held them as if they were their own younger siblings. The eyes of the whelps were wide with fear, but when these strangers treated them gently, they snuggled into the offered safety.

Con picked up four more of the mewling whelps, and each stopped crying when he held them. "This is something that I had never thought to see," he murmured to Jenha, but looking at the Kumatan. "Have you been corrupting these new Traegers?"

Jenha made no admission, just said, "Let us take them to Farcine. She is a healer."

Jenha saw that he arrived at the same time as Con and the other Traegers, and within moments, Atapi females were running from the hut to take the whelps from the rescuers. Farcine came directly to him, and asked, "What happened to him?"

Con snarled, "All have been beaten, Litok worst of all." He allowed the four little whelps to be taken from him.

"Come, honoured one, bring Litok inside and I will tend to him."

"You honour me, Elder Mother. But first I must return for others."

"Go," Jenha murmured. "I will follow shortly." He glanced briefly at Kaer and Eamon, still standing near the compound gate, but neither made a comment when Con departed alone. Quenten still seemed to be staring at the inside of his visor.

He carried Litok inside and placed him where Farcine directed, onto a pile of soft furs. Then he too, returned to the shuttle.

Two more trips, and all of the Atapi whelps were safely away. Jenha helped Teregan back, having to support the exhausted whelp to even stand. He decided that the youngster would forgive him if he lifted him back inside.

Farcine looked up from where she sat beside Litok, and merely pointed to Teregan's bed shelf. Where Jenha lay the whelp and covered him with a fur, before going outside.

"The whelps and Farcine's son are all here," Jenha reported to Eamon and Kaer, with a smile of satisfaction on his face. "Con is with his son. Litok tried to protect the others and took the worst of the punishment – though all the little ones have been wantonly beaten."

Quenten flipped up his visor and asked, "Will Con Ansuni be free to talk now?"

"Allow him some minutes while Farcine invokes the healing. Con will be able to send more of the aura to help her," Jenha suggested.

Quenten accepted that, as his attention was caught by the emergence of the two young Traegers. Their expressions were not inscrutable as before, but full of wonder as they came to join the group. They both bowed to Jenha, while glancing to include the others present.

"I had not expected Atapi females to be so like our women," the first admitted.

The other said, "Those little ones, as strange as they look, snuggled into me as much as my own little son does. And they ran and clung to that sorcerer. I did not expect that."

Jenha murmured to the two young Traegers. "It is as I proposed, you are taught to hate, but the Nuath tells us to embrace the differences and in doing so, we often find the sameness."

They both drew themselves back into the stance of respect for a senior. "Are we still required here?" the first asked.

"No, you have both done well. Thank you for your assistance."

Eamon asked Quenten, "Has your device shown you the events at the shuttle?"

Jenha caught the faint surprised that the question gave the Ambassador. "Indeed. Two of the Selkrit have been taken from the shuttle, and will be taken to our ship in orbit. My Enforcers are currently downloading the shuttle's computer memory and we will then bring it up to the ship as well."

He stopped when he saw the expression on the elder Kimh Lord's face.

"I don't claim to understand your…technology," Eamon admitted freely. "Nor do I think that I need to. I am satisfied that this venture has also been a success for you."

"That it has been! I will soon know if the two prisoners have Galactic criminal records. However, I will not be finished here until I have spoken to that sorcerer. Once I have his cooperation, I will be fully satisfied. Mosellan, we will go and see him."

Eamon gestured for Jenha to go with Quenten, and stayed with Kaer.

At the door of the hut, where Quenten paused to take in the scene within, he murmured to Jenha, "You have opened my eyes, Mosellan. It is my duty to treat all races alike, but today, I have seen these strange lizard like women, in their own place, and they act like the women of my own race. Con Ansuni did not act as I was led to expect, either. Today I saw him as himself, acting as he would without supervision or coercion. He has given me a whole new view of the Atapi and the sorcerers."

Jenha inserted a warning. "Con Ansuni is unusual amongst sorcerers."

"What was it that you said to those young Traegers? That we are taught to hate? Was it because he and you met as children, without adults telling you how to think, that such friendship is possible?"

Rather than trying to expand on that statement, Jenha simply gave a brief nod. He then asked, "If you wish to talk to Con Ansuni, will you require my presence?"

"Can he leave what he is doing yet?"

"I can assist Farcine in his place, if you do not need me."

"Then, if you would be so kind. I am anxious to find the monster who ordered this atrocity. I believe that Con Ansuni can help me. He understands Kumatan perfectly well, and this is far from the first time I have needed to negotiate with hostile races. I think, though, that after this joint venture – understanding will come quickly."

Jenha nodded once more and moved off, walking amongst the females tending the injuries of the young whelps and avoiding the tumbling and trotting of the whelps of Jai's tribe. He went to Con's side and waited for him to notice him.

"My friend, Ambassador Quentin, wishes to come to an understanding with you. May I assist Farcine with Litok, while you talk?"

Con stood and looked at the alien that had organised his freedom – overruling the Kimh. "You trust that alien?"

"Yes, I do. He is a stranger, but he is capable of accepting all people and will listen to them. He is fair, unbiased and able to determine the truth so that justice can be done."

"Can he change the minds of the Kimh and Kumatan about the Atapi?" Con demanded.

"His role is not to be a dictator, Con, but if you listen to him, help him, then you and I might begin to change those ideas ingrained in the Atapi as well as Kumatan. And yes, maybe even the Kimh. Kaer shows promise…"

Con snarl-grinned softly. "I will hear what this alien has to say, I will promise nothing more."

Jenha watched Con walk towards Quenten, and then went to settle beside Litok. After a while, some awareness caused him to look up as Kaer and Eamon looked in from the doorway. He spared a moment of concern for Kaer, but Lord Eamon had proved to be flexible in his thinking. He had let Con help his whelps, accepting the rightness of the act. It would be good for Kaer to listen to him.

Turning his attention to Farcine, he murmured, "I had expected your males to have returned by now."

Her reply amused him. "They know that all is well here and that I do not need to deal with hot-blooded males who would take exception to Traegers, aliens, Kimh and invading sorcerers. They are out checking the lands around here to be sure that none of the blue aliens have dared to return. If they do find any, they will return with the indisposed trash. And I will deal with my transgression for all this when Jai-devil returns. Today has reminded me that I must not give up faith in my sorcerer."

Quenten walked next to Con Ansuni, going outside into the deepening darkness. "How much of what Centurion Bellus told you, do you understand?"

"What do I care of worlds that I will never see?" Con challenged. "Will they help protect my tribe? Feed my tribe? I do not grant the right of the Kimh to dictate what I may or may not do."

"Yet you have agreements with the Kumatan to stay off their land," Quenten began to explain his point, but Con growled.

"Nor do I recognise the right of any alien to tell me what I can do. Or claim the right to punish me for transgressions."

"That is not what I aim to do, Con Ansuni. What I was trying to explain is that you and your fellow sorcerers made an agreement with the other races on this world, for the mutual benefit of both sides. As a result, until the blue-blood aliens came, there was peace."

"I do not need you to kill those who infest my land."

"Merely killing a few will not solve the problem. I have the power to root out those who have found something of value on your lands, and who will send more and more of these monsters."

"How can you do that?" Con demanded.

"It is because I have powers that are not restricted to one area, or one world."

"What do you want of me?"

"I need to know every detail that you can tell me about those aliens. Their leader made claims of unprovoked attacks, unprovoked murders…no, please hear me out…I do not wish to believe their claims since these recent events prove that they are not to be trusted. However, I cannot act against them without proof. And I wish to hear how they angered you."

Con turned his head to study the alien who called himself a Galactic Ambassador. He felt that this humanoid, like Jenha Mosellan had promised, would listen and not be quick to condemn him. Though should he try, they were outside, his energies were refreshed, and he could draw on the aura to escape.

"The first I heard or saw of them was when they killed two whelps…"

As Con spoke, Quenten was both recording the conversation, and comparing this narrative with that of Jai Cassidy. Both were consistent, and told different parts of the story. He did not consider that he and Jai Cassidy had concocted and agreed to tell this story. The sorcerers were fiercely independent, and did not expect, or want, help from outsiders. Yet in this case, Jai Cassidy had given Con ideas about how to deal with the flying machines." He mentioned this to see what Con would say.

"That whelp thinks she knows everything, but her ideas worked, that time."

"Con Ansuni, will you allow me to send two of my centurions onto your land – under your supervision, to find and remove both Selkrit intruders and any of their feral constructs?"

"I do not allow even Kumatan onto my lands."

Quenten considered what else he could say and settled on, "Can we agree that we want rid of the aliens and their objects, and that I want live prisoners to question about their masters?"

He interpreted Con's growl as agreement. "How could you and I work together to achieve this?"

"I will deliver the trash to the border of my land."

"We have ways to make the stealthy intruders visible to sight," Quenten commented. "To work, we need to be within 100 arm's length of them. Could my centurions work with your warriors?"

"Your prey would see you, recognise you, and flee!"

"If your magic could not hide them, then my technology can," Quenten proposed. "Once we have located an intruder, we will neutralise them until they can be questioned. This will free you for other hunts. Did we not work well together, today?"

"Yes, then. We will do this – is that all you want of me?"

"The only other thing that I ask, is that when I approach the other tribal sorcerers, that you suggest to them the benefits of cooperation."

"I will not go onto the lands of another tribe," Con stated flatly.

"You are here," Quenten pointed out.

"I only dare because Jai Cassidy is not here. I am a trespasser as much as you are."

"Surely, if she has sensed you here, she would return immediately?" Quenten proposed.

"She knows nothing of what it means to be a sorcerer. Perhaps she has learnt to fear me and will return only when I have gone."

"Perhaps she provoked one sorcerer to many?"

Con snarl grinned. "Since she thinks she is immortal, maybe she did. However, I have no time for her. I must return my whelps to their mothers."

"And I thank you for our agreement."

Kaer and Eamon had entered the building with more hesitation. When they saw Quenten leading Con aside, Eamon said, "I do not think we are needed here. Walk with me, Kaer."

Kaer glanced at Jenha, who had taken Con's place beside the unconscious whelp. He mentally shrugged and followed his uncle back outside.

"You have opened my eyes," Eamon commented to his nephew. "The Atapi that I met today are not what I expected."

"Father met Farcine," Kaer said, controlling his resentment.

"Yes, we spoke of it. My brother felt that Atapi females did not know their place. What do you think of her?"

"She is a wise old woman," Kaer said without hesitation. "And I do not think we should expect her to be like our women."

"I agree it would be wrong to try." Eamon was thoughtful as he walked back towards the palace. "Con Ansuni is nothing like by brother portrayed him."

"Uncle, my father listened only to his name and assumed he was like his sire. Jenha has always said he was not. My father has given Con Ansuni no chance to be other than angry. He had children to find and he rightly feared for them. You saw them, you heard what the Traeger said – those little whelps had been beaten for no reason except fun."

"I noticed how the little whelps clung to Con Ansuni," Eamon agreed. "He knew them all by name, like they were his own. Do you think the other sorcerers are like that or could be like that?"

"I don't know, Uncle. How many of us have ever made the effort to get to know any Atapi? I admit I was shocked when Jenha admitted he and Con had been friends as children, but I think that has given him a much better view of the Atapi."

Uncle and nephew spoke for a while, putting aside 'traditional views'. When the conversation lapsed, Eamon told Kaer, "Go back and wait for Jenha. When he is finished here, take him to your suite. I am going to recommend to the council that he be reinstated as a full Traeger, though I do not want you to hint of that to him yet."

Kaer walked back into the Atapi compound, approaching he hut once again. Inside, he found that the rescued whelps had recovered from their shock. They were now climbing and crawling everywhere with the whelps of Jai's tribe. He watched from the door for a while, then went further inside and found Teregan sitting on the bed next to Litok, whilst watching his mother tend to the younger whelp.

"Will he recover?" Kaer asked Farcine, wondering where Jenha had gone.

"Atapi whelps are tough, Lord Kaer," Farcine assured him. "Jai-devil's consort has done what he can. We will let him rest. And I am finding it a pleasure to have so many little ones here."

Kaer tried to imagine being as unrestrained as the Atapi children. He had never been like that.

Farcine lifted a whelp that was trying to crawl onto her lap. "Tusi is almost asleep. Perhaps you could hold her for a while?"

Without thinking it odd, Kaer took the whelp that Farcine held out to him. It – she – snuggled into him like his own little daughter did. Farcine smiled sagely.

Kaer finally relinquished the child into the arms of a serene Atapi woman.

"Lord Kaer," she addressed him. "I am Bernea, Con's mate. Thank you for bringing Jenha to help us."

"I… was pleased to," Kaer said awkwardly. As Con's mate moved away, Jenha came silently up to him.

"My Lord, I am ready to return," Jenha murmured.

Kaer straightened, bringing his mind back to his duties. "Farcine told me you had done what you could for Litok."

"The child had no life-threatening injuries," Jenha assured him. "He will be well by morning, and young Teregan has been warned of the dangers of crossing planes."

Kaer caught the implication that Teregan was a young sorcerer, but did not choose to comment. "I am to have you stay with me, at Lord Eamon's instruction. Has the Ambassador finished with Con Ansuni?"

"Yes, and I would say that he was pleased with the outcome. He has gone back to the palace to oversee the removal of the Selkrit shuttle."

"And Con Ansuni? Is he as satisfied?"

"I believe so, particularly as the Ambassador has allowed his freedom. He is preparing a pass through from here to his lands so that the whelps can return."

"Today has been most instructive," Kaer admitted. "Now we must hope that the other sorcerers can be convinced to be equally helpful."

Neither Kaer nor Jenha referred to the promise that Jai Cassidy had made, or to their concerns that she was missing. For now, both were filled with the satisfaction that comes with doing something worthwhile.

Kaer wanted to savour it while he could, before his father could try to twist his actions into something improper. He intended, once they were in his own private space, to allow Jenha and Ellhi time together. His father had punished both of them for far too long.

The following day my captor returned, again insisting on his reward for defeating me. The Old One had already tested my 'shell' using the slit in the clinging fabric to feel the cold within. He was also interested in the feel of the fabric, which was, like my body, nearly frozen.

"It's dead meat," my captor insisted. "Nothing can stay that cold, for this long and be alive."

"It does not smell dead," the Old One stated.

"The meat is cold. Cold meat keeps longer."

"It is too cold," the logic continued. "And I have not wasted energy preserving it."

"Then it is unconscious if not dead," was the next protest. "None of us can hold a spell without being awake."

"No?" the Old One snarl-grinned. "What of our permanent pass throughs?"

The younger sorcerer did not have an answer for that. He growled in frustration.

"Come back tomorrow."

Another two days elapsed following the same pattern. On the third day, the Old One ordered my captor to 'unwrap the meat'.

I sent my mind back into my body once I had seen the Atapi equivalent of an arrogant smirk on my captor's face. He strutted back to me, leant down and pulled on the fabric where the old one had made the slit. As he did so, he reached for his knife to slash at the rest of the fabric. He stared, astounded, when the fabric disintegrated where his hand touched it.

Now that I was back in my body, I felt the hot sun on the fabric and the heat was spreading into my body. I drew on the aura now, to make a faint breeze. Flakes of the rotted fabric broke off and blew away. As the fabric disintegrated further, more heat reached my body and I drew on it greedily, allowing it to warm me from skin to core.

My captor was no longer so arrogant. I heard his thoughts. His spider silk fabric had never behaved like this before. Suspicious now, he poked me. His finger was a conduit to more energy, and my body needed to thaw - so I could conclude this challenge. The finger stayed on my skin as if stuck there. He pressed his other hand on my chest, trying to pull his finger free. His hand stuck too.

I could do nothing yet, not even open my eyes, but I could link my mind to my captor's. He glanced around, frantic for inspiration. His eyes saw, but ignored, the Old One who was now watching avidly from a gold embossed throne. My captor was too desperate to solve the problem and avoid being thought weak. The lesson of his stuck finger and hand had not yet sunk in, for he tried to overcome the problem by heating up his hands. It might have worked if my body was an ice block, instead, I absorbed all that extra heat energy from him. I was warming up at an increasing pace.

The process took another night and day. All during that time, the Old One watched impassively – doing nothing to help or interfere, while I had plenty of time to wonder why this sorcerer had not simply used his knife to kill me once I was helpless. I wondered what reward the Old One had offered for my death or defeat.

The younger sorcerer was on the verge of hypothermia when his name came into my mind. I whispered it into his ear, "Pywuk."

I released his hands and he collapsed into a heap. The Old One stood up and came over. He saw that my eyes were open and called to the females who had been tending him during his vigil.

I whispered quickly to Pywuk. "Draw on the aura, imagine it warming you."

He should be able to do it, since he had been able to hide so well in the aura. When the Old One turned back to consider us, we were both teetering to our feet. I was shivering, still feeling the cold.

The females approached warily. In their minds, I was a walking ghost that looked like a Kumatan. Yet the Old One had ordered them to tend to me. Two of the females helped me to stand upright, and helped me to walk over to where a third female was building up the fire. Another female wrapped a warm woven blanket around me, and I was lowered to the ground. Yet another of the females placed a wooden platter and a clay mug in front of me. Warmed hares milk and a savoury nutty smelling flatbread.

Five pairs of eyes watched me as I ate. The sorcery they had witnessed had no precedent – I had, in their eyes, come back from the dead.

I wasn't going to disabuse them of the idea, nor suggest that Pywuk also needed tending to. He had started this, and I had finished it. When I glanced back at where I had lain for four days, I saw him slinking away –

glancing back over his shoulder to where the Old One was again on his throne-like chair, studying me.

Once he got over his deep thoughts, I decided that he would be off after Pywuk, if that sorcerer had not succeeded in walking off the Old Ones land. It seemed he did not yet have the energy needed to cross planes to return to his own.

After seeing to my comfort – food, drink and clothing – the females took me to a small vacant cave, where a small fire burned low, and a pile of furs were heaped near it. I hadn't been able to eat much, since my stomach was cramping from days of eating nothing. The drink had gone down and I had felt my body absorbing it like my flesh was a sponge.

The females left the rest of the food within my reach, and brought in a skin filled with water. They left me alone, and I appreciated the solitude. Even more of a relief was that the Old One was leaving me alone. He probably didn't consider me a threat...at the moment, I wasn't.

Even though I had done nothing for four days – I was deathly tired, but I didn't want to sleep. My mind had just recalled the state of affairs before I had been captured. I had begged that Enforcer for two days in which to finish the last challenge and convince the Old One to speak to him. I had promised to return whether I had or not.

It had been five days! The Ambassador would have them hunting me now, convinced I was as much a criminal as that foul creature, Auglan.

I felt my throat – the tracer was still there. I wondered if it still worked. Surely, if it was, they would have found me by now. They had seemed most definite that I remained in their control. Perhaps they thought me dead, like Pywuk had.

I didn't want to think about the Enforcers, who would find out I was alive soon enough. I still had to argue with the sorcerers to get them to talk to Quenten's people. Thinking of that, I walked to the cave entrance. Two battle-scarred warriors guarded the cave I was now in. They watched outwards, but as soon as I stepped an inch outside, they turned with their weapons aimed at me. The message was clear. I was not to leave. With nothing else to do, I went back and continued eating. After that, I slept.

The prodding of my leg with the butt of a spear woke me. The warrior looking down at me gestured for me to get up and move outside.

The Old One waited there, and as soon as I reached him he grabbed my arm and walked forward.

I felt the twisting darkness between planes, and was not surprised when we emerged in the shadow of the Rock of Arkor. We were inside a circle of the other sorcerers. He released me, and went to sit on a rock outcrop as part of the circle. As well as the regard of the sorcerers, I felt Larcia welcoming me and filling me with warmth and energy. I felt fully alive again.

The Old One watched me as I glanced around the circle. "Show the rest of us the place of sanctuary."

Larcia echoed, "Let them come."

I considered what I needed to do, and said, "First, you need to build a cairn of stones. Outside of the cave yonder."

Pywuk challenged me immediately. "You didn't need that last time!"

I gave him a look that suggested he was an idiot. "I could invite the Kumatan back here to provide the needed contrast."

Pywuk subsided quickly and I heard a hiss from the Old One, who was not amused. He gestured for the lower ranked sorcerers to get busy. That courtesy amused me, but I went and pointed to where I wanted the cairn – where it would be visible from the entrance of Larcia's cave. When that was done, I allowed the males to see the opening. They were all so astounded by the sudden appearance of the cave that they headed inside before me to see what was there. Just as I entered, I thought I heard a high-pitched beep. Since it wasn't repeated, I decided my ears were playing tricks.

This time, Pywuk and Wyvek saw the cave, though the rear chamber was hidden. The Old One noted that fact as a warm breath of a whisper in my ear.

"A secret of high sorcery," I told him. "None of the others are ready to see it."

This appealed to the vanity of the Old One as I intended. It was obvious, though, that the others still sensed the strength of the aura here. I moved to the cave entrance and created the pass-through to the other plane.

As expected, they all expressed disbelief at it working, as I had made no sweeping gestures or long winded chants. I let the Old One remark, "The cairn is gone."

He went on to tell them that they could find their tribal lands on this plane by using the natural landmarks, but if they were not back in a short time they would be stuck here.

Pywuk and Wyvek went off again, though the Old One did not. He stayed and watched me as if I was not to be trusted.

Centurion Terr was staring at a blank screen as if his full attention was there. It wasn't. For the past five days, during his shift, he had seen nothing at all. Either the tracer on the human child had stopped working or she had removed it. The effect was the same. Full spectrum bio-tracers were not meant to be removed easily but somehow she must have done it.

His mind was jolted sharply by a friendly punch on his shoulder. He turned quickly, in time to stop a second one.

"What's all that gibberish on the screen?" Bellus asked. He had no need to be formal since there was only the two of them.

"Static," Terr said in a bored tone. "It comes and goes. I have it figured that the human child removed the tracer and dropped it somewhere. Either it is in the sun or some animal picked it up in its paw. I don't know why we still have to watch this."

"Orders," Bellus reminded him. "How long has it been going on?"

Terr checked the log. "Since yesterday."

The screen went completely blank again. "There is not even enough signal to locate the device to recover it."

"The damn signal was cutting in and out even when it was working properly," Bellus mused. "Like when that child does that teleportation thing, and when she is near that rock monolith. I wonder if there is something in that rock that blocks the signal."

"That's an idea," Terr said, his mind back to full alertness. He had a sudden inspiration. "I wonder if those Selkrit engineers know something."

"Jai Cassidy did seem to think the ones in that rock canyon had found something that really interested them," Bellus continued the thought.

"If this is not an idiot's idea," Terr proposed. "What value would such a thing have on the black market?"

"What indeed?" Bellus said sardonically. He didn't need to say 'mega-credits'. "Why don't you try sending the reset sequence to the tracer?"

"It was tried each shift for the past four days," Terr noted, but he acted on the suggestion. They waited several minutes but nothing changed. "Same lack of result!"

Bellus had another idea. "When that static or interference comes again – try it then."

"If you say so," Terr agreed. "So what are you doing?"

"Avoiding the Council meeting. I have no wish to be around that unsettled High Minister when he finds out that his prize prisoner was released. If he were the leader of Orlek, he'd have been removed a long time ago. The man is unstable."

"So that Sorcerer agreed to talk?" Terr asked out of interest. Since more Orleki Enforcers had arrived, he and Bellus had not been on constant duty.

"I believe so. The Ambassador seemed pleased about something, though he hasn't told me what was said. I know he sent a coded message to the Galactic Judicial Hub." Bellus did not need to guess that something serious was afoot.

After watching the black screen for a while longer, Bellus straightened. "I might just go and wait for the Ambassador in his suite, run our idea past him. He did ask himself why the Selkrit would risk harsh penalties."

"Go ahead," Terr said resigned. "I have another hour of this."

Ambassador Quenten was back in his suite, and had changed out of his formal garments, when Bellus found him.

"What is it, Centurion? More trouble?" He went and sat in his chair and waited for the answer.

"No, Sir, not trouble. I was doing a routine oversee of the tracking unit. It has been receiving odd interference and static during the past day. Were you aware of that?"

"Yes, I have been advised," Quenten said neutrally. "The general agreement is that the tracer was removed somehow."

"That was my feeling too, Sir, since the unit did not send the termination signal before it stopped working. However, an alternative idea occurred to Terr and myself. While we have been tracking that human child, she has found several places where the signal doesn't work. Like at that rock monolith."

Quenten was listening intently. "Go on…"

Bellus proposed the idea, "What if there is a mineral in those rocks that upsets the tracker signal?"

"That is too frightening an idea to ignore," Quenten admitted soberly. "We will need to collect some rock samples to have analysed. I think Con Ansuni may cooperate since the Selkrit seem to keep coming back to his land. And it might explain why the two Selkrit we have in custody have outstanding Galactic warrants."

Bellus looked intently at his superior and Quenten decided to confide some recent information. "We found a score of Atapi children in a Selkrit shuttle. The two guards were both wanted criminals. We had word that Councillor Auglan had been there."

"Word, Sir? From whom?" Bellus asked.

Quenten relaxed his face to smile wryly. "If I have it correctly, one of the Atapi whelps from the group living near the palace has a mind link to Auglan and can see what he sees. He saw these missing children and somehow found them. That was the cause of that demented howling."

"They spoke to you, Sir?" Bellus asked.

"No, they spoke to Mosellan. He must be the only non-Atapi on this world that understands them. Con Ansuni would speak to no one else, and as for cooperation, he was keen to do whatever was needed to get his tribe's children back. I think he found that young whelp's mind and a way to get to him."

"Teleporting?" Bellus asked. That had been a weird experience, but no worse than his first experience of free fall or zero gravity. "I wish I knew how those Atapi do that."

"That and a lot of other things," Quenten agreed. "There has to be a logical scientific rationale, because I do not believe in magic. A lot of it is probably mind gifts – they have been well documented, but I have never heard of people who could tap into the energy net of a planet."

"Nor have I," Bellus confirmed. He changed the subject. "You said the Councillor was not with the children?"

"No he wasn't, and I don't think the child had a reason to lie. Everything else he said was provable – he did find the children. And Auglan has not been here since that incident with Jai Cassidy. I took the opportunity to investigate his suite. It is quite empty, as are the rooms used by his people. I found some skin flakes in each of the rooms and I have sent them up to the ship for analysis. We will have a genetic scan run through the data banks."

"I see, Sir," Bellus answered. "Sir, do you mind if I ask – do you think the human child is dead?"

Quenten considered his answer. "It is possible, but I think not. More likely she is hiding amongst those rocks. I think she probably tried to remove the tracer, and considering the unexplained things those sorcerers can do, she may well have succeeded in disabling it."

"We tried sending the reset signal again without a response. I told Terr to try again next time we get static on the screen."

"An excellent notion," Quenten agreed. "Please arrange for a squad to be on standby and an escort of Traegers. I want you to lead the group and be ready to move on a moment's notice. If we get a location from that tracer, I want you there before that child has a chance to get away. Oh, and make sure Mosellan is part of your group."

"Are you expecting trouble, Sir?"

"No. I am hoping that Jai Cassidy is about to appear again. Surely she must think that we believe her dead by now. If that is her plan, I want to teach her to respect us. If it was coincidence and she is still intending to try to get the sorcerers to talk to us, as Mosellan believes, I want to precipitate those talks. Mosellan has implied that if they do agree to talk to her it will be near that monolith."

All the warning I had was a breath of a mind touch from Jenha. The feel of it put me in mind of how he had been before we left Earth, when he had been confident and in control.

The twenty sorcerers were discussing the pros and cons of disappearing en-masse to the alternate plane. I didn't choose to warn them that I was expecting company. All I could say to myself was that Jenha's timing was way off. I hadn't had a chance to bring up the 'get rid of the aliens' subject.

The Old One hissed angrily when he saw the ring of Enforcers and Traegers walk into view. I, who was sitting at his feet, heard him hiss, "I will not forgive you for this intrusion," as I stood up.

The other sorcerers turned their attention outward, forming a circle around the Old One and myself. The only one of those that was not twitching with the desire to kill the intruders was Con Ansuni. I wondered why, but he had not come near me since I had been fetched by the Old One.

I walked out of the circle to face Jenha and Centurion Bellus. I didn't bow to either of them, but I noticed from how he was dressed, that Jenha had been granted full Traeger rank again and I flicked a thought of gladness to his mind.

"Why are you here?" I demanded.

Bellus began to speak. "We need to speak to each of these tribal leaders, and you are in breach of your agreed word. You will be returning with us."

"Really?" I commented, then turned my back on him to address the Old One. "Those with the Traegers are Enforcers. I would not assume them weak and harmless. If you really wish those blue blood aliens away from here, they have the power to remove them. Since they have no ties to the Kimh or Kumatan, they do not have a bias against you."

"And the Slave masters?" the Old One hissed in my ear as he grabbed me roughly.

"You can trust Jenha Mosellan to be fair," I said.

The Old One spoke into my ear – an extremely rude and crude description of what Jenha was to me. He laughed maliciously as I blushed crimson.

I kept an eye on the intruders as the Old One considered them. Jenha and Bellus were coming closer to me as the sorcerers were still glaring at the uninvited arrivals.

"Back off!" I told Bellus in a tone betraying my intent. I wanted neither his protection nor for the sorcerers to think I had allowed him to get control of me. Both options would negate all I had been through in defeating all of the sorcerers bar the Old One.

Bellus began speaking to me in Earth English. I gave no indication of listening to it. I didn't need to know the penalties for not returning as I promised.

Instead, I interrupted him and spoke to Jenha. "Tell them what is needed and the benefits to them. And why they should help the Enforcers rather than disappearing off the face of Korvu like Stak hid his tribe from you."

Jenha very slightly inclined his head in my direction before giving the Old One a slight bow of respect – a greeting of equals.

"You mock me," the Old One snarled.

"That is not my intention," Jenha said smoothly. "My intention is to offer you assistance in removing the alien intruders and their rubbish from your lands, in exchange for each of you speaking truthfully of what you know of the aliens."

"I will not have slave masters on my land! They came and stole members of Atapi tribes and have no doubt tortured them to death."

Jenha did not react to the accusation. He spoke calmly. "Those you refer to, and others who were taken when they went close to Kumatan towns, are unharmed. Some were taken by the blue-blooded aliens – they made it look like our doing with the intention of provoking you to attack us, and for us to attack you. I am aware that many escaped, but I cannot say all did. I, for one, resent being manipulated into fighting unjustly."

Con Ansuni edged up to the other side of the Old One. "And I resent how those blue aliens stole twenty of my whelps and beat them like animals. Jenha Mosellan freed me from the captivity of the Kimh to rescue them and these Enforcers took charge of the beasts that had them."

"Probably let them go again when you weren't there," the Old One accused, trying to provoke Jenha and Bellus into anger.

"I think not," Con countered. "The stink of the alien's fear was most pleasurable."

"I'd prefer to treat them in my own way," the Old One snarled.

"Like cutting off their man bits," I said bluntly, not looking at, but aware of, the reactions of the males around me.

Bellus's face twitched, Jenha's expression hardened, and the Old One hissed, "I will not under-estimate you, human female."

Jenha mused aloud, "I don't think Jai Cassidy can claim all the credit. The old warrior, Obaki, took exception to the attempts of the alien leader to humiliate her. I am impressed by how she convinced the alien leader that Obaki was just an illusion."

The Old One's grip eased, as if he now thought me less dangerous. His snarl was laughter and his manner towards Jenha seemed less hostile.

"This female, who claims to be a sorceress, promises to take us where neither alien nor slave masters will find us. To a place where our tribes can grow strong again and multiply. We don't need your kind."

"There is merit in that choice," Jenha agreed thoughtfully. "It will give your people and mine time apart to let emotions settle. The blue aliens have much to answer for. There has been peace and respect between us for three decades before they came."

Traeger Solomon dared to approach – he was still senior Traeger. He noticeably tucked his weapon away, showing he trusted the Atapi. Jenha had not had his out at all.

"If you were to leave, what is there to stop you from coming back when we do not expect it?" Solomon asked.

I spoke the answer to that, "I understand your concerns, Traeger, but the knowledge needed to create the pass-through will be limited. There is no sense in the Atapi returning here like bad smells, for it will simply provoke you to find us. That is not the idea behind moving away. The break will be clean."

"I will accept that as a promise," Solomon nodded.

Jenha inclined his head to one side. "We are, however, concerned about removing the alien influence from Korvu. There are indications that the Selkrit are not simply improving Korvu in the way we required. They were not given permission to trespass on Atapi tribal lands. The Enforcers must discover the full truth before passing judgement. I believe that none of you would wish the Selkrit to escape just punishment because you did not tell what you know of them."

The sorcerers growled in general agreement when it was explained that way. I noticed that they were all getting edgy, feeling the need to return to their lands. None of them dared to remain away much longer.

"I will not have slave masters on my land," the Old One repeated his statement.

Solomon bowed slightly. "We will restrict our participation to escorting the Centurions to the agreed meeting places at your borders."

Now the Old One scrutinised the other intruders. They all wore strange black garments, slung with holders for odd weapons, and most wore the bubble-like head covering. Only Bellus had his face revealed.

"How do I know I can trust you?" the Old One demanded.

"What can you offer as a sign of good faith?" I interrupted

Bellus kept his face straight. "I am authorised to release and return all Atapi that are in our custody back to their own tribal lands."

I glanced at the Old One. He nodded, agreeable to that – but he had a question. "How do you intend to remove the blue trash from our lands? The snakes are like shadows and the beasts they brought are vile and insatiable."

Bellus had obviously been advised by Jenha.

"The mechanical beasts are susceptible to an EM pulse," he began, and then realised that the Atapi had no understanding of such science. "A weapon that interferes with the energy they run on."

The sorcerers murmured covetously. "You will provide them for us," the Old One demanded.

I hid a smile – I knew the Enforcers would not do that, so I proposed, "How close to the beasts do you need to be to make the weapon effective?"

Bellus was quick on the uptake. "Within two arm spans."

The sorcerers still wanted the weapon.

I said, casually, "I've seen those beasts. They're fast. If I were you, I wouldn't want to keep getting that close to those things."

"What are you meaning, female? That we are cowards?" the Old One hissed at me, and tweaked my arm.

"No," I shrugged. "That you are smart enough to let these aliens take the risks if they truly want your cooperation. It will prove their worth." I wasn't going to tell him that the beasts were targeted to Atapi blood.

Lyvok snarled at me. "You picked one up and killed it!"

Bellus glanced at me in surprise after Jenha had translated that for him.

"It wanted sorcerer meat, not female meat," I muttered. "How did you tie it up?"

"I stunned it," he said, and I knew even that much had taken a lot of power.

Bellus added, "We really need some active specimens to test the weapon settings on."

One of the sorcerers, Jacek, snarl-grinned. "I have a deep pit full of them." He turned the snarl-grin on me. "That was Jai-devil's idea. You can have all of them."

"That will be highly acceptable," Bellus agreed. He nodded at me, and said something to Jenha in a low voice.

Jenha relayed it to my mind. Bellus hoped to find traces on them to indicate the creature that purposed them.

"What about those infiltrators that look like shadows?" I asked pointedly. "Will the same weapon work on them?"

"The stealth suits may be affected the same way, but you need to know where to aim. A broader area weapon may be better," Bellus said as if making an admission.

"How would you know where to target?" I asked, trying to sound like I was trying to provoke him. "Atapi lands are vast."

Bellus didn't have an immediate answer. I did, but I was wondering if Wyvuk would speak up. He did.

"There is a ritual which enables us to show where unnatural traces are. I used it to find two infiltrators. Their protective illusions do not stand up to my lightnings. It works best when targeted using something of the aliens."

"I burnt all of their foul rubbish," one of the younger sorcerers snarled. Several others agreed. The rest said nothing, but I sensed they had destroyed all traces, too.

"Well, I have quite a lot of their rubbish. I hoped to use it to learn about them, but I have had no leisure of late. Whoever wants some can have some," Con Ansuni offered.

Jenha interceded once more. "I can see it is in the interest of all of us to finish this cleansing quickly." He glanced at me, reminding me that the aliens had also been around the compound housing my tribe.

Bellus bowed to the Old One. "Honoured Leader, may I offer the services of my Centurions to accompany you to apprehend the trespassers on your lands?"

"Only when my people are back, unharmed," he growled.

Bellus nodded.

"Your offer is most kind," I said, deciding to make a tactful suggestion. "But there is a point to be considered. I have used the ritual." I shrugged a shoulder at Wyvuk, since I didn't know his tribal name. "It may also detect traces of other alien types. It would be unwise for the Centurions to wander too widely."

Jenha had guessed my reasoning and asked, "How do you propose the Centurions do their part?"

"The ritual can be tied into the aura and become effective over the whole of each tribe's land. The warriors know their land and can track the traces. When they find an area that is glowing brightly, they can summon their leader and he can bring the Centurions. They can activate their weapon there, and wait for the infiltrators."

The sound I was now hearing from the Old One was very like a purr of satisfaction. I had no doubt that he resented an outsider coming onto his land and 'taking over' – now it seemed he would be in control.

In my mind, I felt Jenha's approval. "Well done, young one."

I thought back, "These sorcerers really need to get back to their lands – I wouldn't want to think what the beasts or infiltrators are doing in their absence."

Jenha aired this concern as if it had been his own. "Centurion Bellus, would your men be willing to split up – one to assist each leader? Then they can listen to the leaders speak of the aliens while the warriors are hunting."

All the sorcerers had been lulled into a cooperative mood, and I knew Larcia had been subtly influencing them, too. It was quickly organised – each sorcerer took one Traeger and one Centurion with him when he returned to his lands. While the sorcerers went off to check for dangers, the Traegers would arrange for the return of the tribes folk.

Bellus, Solomon, Jenha and I remained with the Old One.

Jenha turned to me and asked, "Don't you need to check your tribe's wellbeing, Jai Cassidy?"

The Old One gave a snort of derision. "Those within the cage are muzzled and neutered – no threat to anyone."

I knew he was trying to irritate me. "Not while they are within," I seemed to agree. "My warriors, few though they are, should not be underestimated, nor the females of my tribe."

The Old One snarled with amusement.

"The alien taint is very strong around the outside of what you call a cage," I noted. "Perhaps the aliens are studying my tribe, seeking weaknesses in other tribes."

"Then they do us a service," the Old One snarl-laughed.

"I said, don't underestimate my warriors as hunters, trackers or fighters – there are no alien traces within the compound and they have made sure that where they range is free of spies."

Jenha gave me a sharp look, but I simply met it and made no gesture of being in the wrong. He had known about the females working in the palace and kept silent. I did not expect him to betray my warriors, who had not been given permission to roam freely.

The Old One had also picked up my innuendo. "How did they find the shadows?"

I grinned. "The ritual that was mentioned. The spies glow like the full moon and they underestimated the skill of my hunters. These alien 'shadows' did not see their own shadows. They did not expect the tame Atapi to prod them into running to save their lives."

Jenha knew this last statement was an evasion of the truth – but not quite a lie.

I stared at the Old One, daring him to make further derogatory remarks about my warriors. Instead he snarl-grinned, liking the idea that had occurred to him about the prodding being at spear point and probably fatal.

As far as Jenha knew, no bodies had been found to indicate that the stealth suits were not impervious to spears.

Jenha then reminded me, "I believe the Enforcers wish to know how you deactivated that mechanical beast."

I sensed other reasons. All I said was, "So you are not the all-powerful avengers you think you are."

Bellus did not react to my slur on his ability. He turned to the Old One and said, "We are ready to accompany you to your lands and return those who look to you."

Jenha waited for the others to leave. "When you all go to that other plane, will your tribe be accepted? It is obvious to me how little they are regarded."

"I hope so," I said. "I guess you didn't think of that when you saved them." Then it occurred to me to ask, "You couldn't have known I was about to kill Stak when you began that snatch raid, could you?"

"No, indeed. It was my intention to weaken Stacion Ansuni by reducing his tribe. I am not sorry that I saved them."

"Yeah," I agreed. "Look, we can't stay here. Where do you want me? Or does that Ambassador want my hide?"

"You did promise two days," Jenha reminded me.

"Yeah, well, things happen."

"Yes, and there are things that need to be done. I think the Ambassador can wait a short while. You have a young problem to deal with."

I saw the picture he sent to my mind. "Teregan," I said.

Jenha nodded. "We will tend to that first."

Farcine was noticeably relieved to see me, but immediately threw herself at my feet, begging forgiveness. It embarrassed me that this wise old woman should so abase herself to me – I was a whelp not much older than her youngest son, and she was older than my mother.

I couldn't understand anything of what she was saying. "Elder Mother, I cannot hear you if you are talking to the floor. Whatever could you have done that was so heinous a crime? Please get up."

Jenha waited behind me, still as a shadow. No one else seemed to be around. When Farcine refused to get up, I sat down in front of her. "Please tell me what is upsetting you?"

I heard about Teregan going missing and how Farcine feared I was dead, and how she asked Con Ansuni for help and how he had found her son and his missing whelps.

Then Jenha added detail to the picture by admitting his part and what he had done.

I couldn't see what the big deal was. The important thing was that the whelps were safe. I was obviously missing some very important data on tribal or intertribal etiquette or why was Farcine feeling so guilty and upset?

"Farcine – I am not angry – really. I am glad Jenha was here to help you. His advice has always been good. Everything worked out – the children are safe, Con Ansuni is free, Jenha is reinstated, and I know I can trust you to care for the tribe when I am busy."

"You are most gracious, Jai-devil," Farcine thanked me.

"I'm no kind of damn devil," I said with disgust. For the first time in my life, I realised that I didn't know everything. "Jenha knows more about the Atapi than I do. And I am pleased that Con Ansuni feels he owes me a debt of gratitude – I need all the allies I can get."

Farcine straightened, hearing doubt in my voice. "Jai-devil, what is the matter?" Now she was back to sounding like the Elder Mother. "We are all proud to serve you."

"And I don't deserve any of you," I told her fiercely. "I am an impertinent whelp, not much older than your son. I hardly know anything about being Atapi – I am so abysmally ignorant."

"But Jai-devil, you have made us so much more than we were," Farcine told me. "We have more purpose than just hunting, foraging and raising whelps."

"Even that wasn't me," I told her. "Jenha and Ellhi taught you most of that…"

"It was your idea!" Farcine insisted.

"And I have hardly been around," I reminded her.

Jenha spoke softly. "Young One, your tribe is different because you are. A tribe often reflects the attitude of the sorcerer. You have proved that the Atapi can coexist peacefully with other races."

"Proved to who?" I growled. "Or have the Kimh and the other Traegers magically changed their minds about me?"

"Some have – it is a start," Jenha encouraged me. "Sometimes a slow change is better."

"Whatever," I brushed that aside, and returned my attention to Farcine. "I promised to take the Atapi away from the other races around here. I know how to do it, and when we go, all of you will come with me. But how can I subject you all to the sneers of the other tribes? The Old One calls you neutered and muzzled."

"Jai-devil – do you think of us that way?"

I looked at Farcine as if she were challenging me. "No! No way – of course I don't."

"Then all is well," Farcine said calmly. "We do not care what others think, if you are pleased with our obedience. Do you think we are ignorant of what those we serve think of us?"

I had to grin wryly, "I guess not. There is a certain male around here that has made his thoughts well known." I didn't mention Koenig by name or title, so Jenha could pretend ignorance.

"Jai-devil, we will abide by your decree in all things."

"I can't work that way," I told her. "There is so much I don't know. Jenha, do I need to see Quenten immediately? I really need to talk to everybody about… things. And it might be smarter if you do not seem to be taking on a role as tribal leader."

I felt Jenha brush my mind with his knowledge of my teasing warning, but the touch was as intimate as a caress.

"We will speak to Ambassador Quenten when you are done. I will wait without."

When Jenha had gone, I said, "Farcine, Elder Mother, I really need your advice."

"Ask what you need, Jai-devil."

"Your forgiveness for one," I began. "I put you all in danger. I know what I have to do, but I never thought... I mean, I was just too full of youthful arrogance, and more, to think I would fail when I challenged or was challenged by the other devils."

"You have won against them all?" Farcine dared to ask.

"All except the Old One, and how can I think to rule all the sorcerers better than he can? I've been lucky. All those other sorcerers assumed that I would do the sorts of things they would do. I won because I didn't."

"Daughter, you have Larcia's sword. Dos she not guide you?"

"So far, only to find my next victim – she said I must fight them by their own rules. And...I must let the Old One teach me..."

Farcine was silent, thinking on that. "You said you had much to learn about being Atapi..."

"And about sorcery. I know how a lot of things can be done, but my experience is limited. And now that the sorcerers have got to know me, if they challenge again, I might not be so lucky. That last one used my own tricks against me and almost succeeded in killing me."

"If the Old One agreed to teach you, he would protect you," Farcine advised me.

"Would it not mean I would be his apprentice?" I asked.

Farcine nodded slowly. "They know no other way. What are you afraid of?"

"For me – nothing much," that was bravado. "It is the rest of you. Teregan, for one. I can't train him – I don't know enough and if I must learn from the Old One, how can I protect all of you?"

"We could go with you." Farcine suggested.

"Not if it means his tribe ridicule you. They cannot conceive of the benefit of learning new ways. They think that your serving the Kimh is a weakness not a strength, and I would not like to put Teregan in his hands."

"No, it would undermine your authority as leader, to be placed at the same level. Have you another plan or must I accept Teregan only as a healer?"

"He needs training, I know that. I know how much trouble an undisciplined whelp with a sorcerer's talent can get into. I was one until Jenha took me in hand. And no, he wasn't the one I thought of – even though he would be a worthy mentor. I was thinking of asking Con Ansuni, but I don't know if is even something I dare ask – let alone know what it would imply and what others will think if I do."

Farcine was thoughtful once again. "I never heard of such a thing before," she admitted. "But I know that sorcerers consider their importance by the number of apprentices they have. They guard them jealously because they can use the power of their apprentices to augment their own. None would give one away."

"But if I did?" I insisted. "It would be better for Teregan to be taught by a male, I think."

Farcine nodded, becoming Teregan's mother for a moment. "A male who won't let him become like his sire – your grandsire. It is your decision, Jai-devil, but I would not object."

"Do you think Con would?" I asked.

"You must ask him, Jai-devil," Farcine advised. "He is close kin to you and his tribe are kin to us. Your consort suggested – if you had died – that we could be taken in by Con Ansuni because of the kin ties."

That relieved me – if Jenha, who knew Con Ansuni better than I did, thought it possible.

"Jai-devil, I cannot speak for everybody, but if you were to offer us the choice, I think all would still want to serve you. If you decided we should accept a new leader, we would."

I made a decision. "Farcine, get all the females back here. Is there still a barrier about the palace?"

"Ask your consort," Farcine suggested. "He is a wise one."

"Yes, I will do that. I will call all the warriors back and we will talk about it. Then I will decide and talk to Con Ansuni."

I rose then, and went to find Jenha to tell him I needed to speak to the females still working in the palace.

"Yes, the barrier is still there. I cannot remove it, but when you go in to speak to Ambassador Quenten, I will ensure you can speak to all you need to."

That would have to do. Then I spoke very softly and asked him about my idea.

"Young One, I think Con Ansuni would agree to reunite the two tribes back into one, if only for the sake of your mother. Are you sure that is what is best?"

"No, but I need to know the implications to all if I did."

I listened then to Jenha, who knew what I needed to know, without necessitating my fumbling questions.

Finally, I decided, "If he agrees, I will see whether he'll insist on blooding them all to him or not – or if he will take them in until I am free to act, then release any who wish to return to me."

"Surely you will need them," Jenha murmured.

Truth was – I really didn't know what to do with them, and it would be worse when I had to live like the full Atapi. The other truth was – for what I had to do – I felt I needed to be free to move from tribe to tribe. I couldn't do that if I was tied to a tribe of my own.

Jenha waited patiently with me until my tribe returned. We discussed many things, increasing my understanding of how Kimh and Kumatan viewed life compared to the nomadic Atapi. He did not ask about the outcome, or the details of my encounters with the sorcerers. It was as if he trusted me to do what I intended, and approved.

With Jenha as my escort, the warding on the palace did not cause alarms to ring, nor did the guards do more than observe carefully as we passed. Until then, I had forgotten the nature of my attire. Their intent gazes made me feel uncomfortable. I was wearing Atapi style clothes, and by Kumatan standards, they were scarcely decent.

However, it seemed that Jenha had already thought of that. When he led me to a small room on the lower level of the palace, Ellhi waited for me with a new set of clothes, warm water and cloths for a sketchy wash.

Jenha smiled as Ellhi embraced me and he said, quietly, "I will find out when Ambassador Quenten will be available. I will tell him that you need to make yourself presentable first."

He slipped out of the room before I could object. I would have liked to spend some private time with him.

Ellhi went and secured the door, and then began to help me out of my clothes. I objected when she began to wash me, her eyes full of concern at the new scars and bruises.

"I want to do this," Ellhi insisted. I sensed the rest of what she wanted and didn't disagree. By the time I was clean, I wanted the same, urgently.

When we rolled apart, we were both relieved and relaxed.

"It isn't fair," Ellhi told me. "Jenha says he must not acknowledge you, now that they've dissolved our triumvir. He said, though, at least you can share this much of us still."

I kissed Ellhi lightly, and said, "He is right. He has his proper rank back and you have him back. That makes me happy. Besides, they do not realise that a triumvir is not merely words of mutual consent. But Jenha knows that I have things I must do, and he must not distract me from them. My place is not among the Kumatan, but he wants to remind me of my humanity. And I want you to be happy."

"And you?" Ellhi asked me.

"I will be too busy," I said. "I'll be fine."

I would be, I insisted to myself, forcing away the sense of longing. I still felt the pull of Jenha when he was near me. Ellhi had eased it, for even with her, I felt I was with him, too. I knew Jenha had intended to make things easier for me.

We were both dressed and washed when a tentative knock on the door put our minds back onto business. Ellhi opened the door and a group of what seemed to be Kumatan servants entered. Ellhi slipped out.

"Jai-devil," Teresa greeted me. "Mikha is thriving."

I smiled. My son was another distraction, one more thing tying me to this plane.

"Will you be seeing him?" Teresa asked.

"I don't know. There is much I must do, and I need to talk to all of you." I gestured at the floor, and sat down. They sat in a group in front of me – eight Atapi females, looking like Kumatan.

I told them what I had told the rest of the tribe. "You each have a choice either of staying here and serving, coming with me as one of my tribe, or going to your kin in Con Ansuni's tribe – if he will have us. Farcine thinks he will."

They all agreed to abide by my decision, happy to stay serving me if I let them. All except one said they preferred to stay where I would be. Teresa was more thoughtful and I did not pry.

"You each have to choose what feels right to you – regardless of my recommendation. I will ensure you know what I decide after I have spoken to Con Ansuni."

It seemed that as soon as the females had left, Jenha was back to escort me to Ambassador Quenten. He was making use of a small room near Koenig's office. Just a space with chairs in a circle, and abstract patterned wall hangings.

I studied Quenten as I entered. He was dressed impeccably in his Ambassador's robes, but his body language was rigid and his expression severe. I simply met his gaze and stared back at him.

"Your pet Enforcers are out chasing spies with the Atapi sorcerers – happy?" I said first, going to a chair and flopping into it.

"Yes, indeed," Quenten agreed. "However, you were to return four days ago."

"Things happen," I said dismissively. "Anyway, I did what I said I would."

"I will leave things as that for now," Quenten decided. I had no trouble guessing that he found my attitude unacceptable. He followed my example and decided to sit. Jenha stayed standing, close to but not behind my chair and he had not said or thought any rebuke at me about my tone.

Quenten continued to speak after pausing to make his point. "Jenha Mosellan tells me that you might have a way to locate more Selkrit – those that are off Atapi lands. I would like to hear how this can be done. I understand that one of your younglings has a mind link to Auglan."

Since the Ambassador had stopped emphasising his authority, I stopped feeling I had to challenge him.

"Yes, and I heard that youngling helped find Con's missing whelps, so you know such a thing is possible. I did not have a chance to speak to Con when we were at the Rock or a chance to speak to Teregan. What exactly do you want?"

"I have instructions from the Galactic Judicial Hub to bring back all the Selkrit from here. I particularly want Councillor Auglan for questioning."

I looked at Jenha, and he said, "I believe that most of the pictures the young one is seeing are of the inside of his flying craft. There were several scenes, but none clear enough to use."

"Let me have some time with Teregan," I suggested. "There isn't a rush, is there? And most of your Enforcers are busy, aren't they?"

"True enough," Quenten agreed. "However, there is one area that is not being looked at."

"So?" I asked, not sure what importance that was to me.

"The land that was once Stacion Ansuni's," Jenha reminded me, and he must have felt my reaction to thinking of that place. "Is it not yours now?"

"I… I haven't decided to claim it," I managed to force out. In fact, I really did not want to go back there.

Jenha was aware of my reluctance and its cause. "Centurion Terr and I will go with you."

"If those aliens are smart they won't be in the same place – and none of us are hunters or trackers," I pointed out, hoping to delay the idea.

"Surely some of your warriors still know that land?" Jenha proposed.

That gave me ideas. "The older ones – three or four of them," I considered. "But will the High Minister let them out to help?"

"I will authorise it," Quenten said immediately. "This is something we can do now."

"We? Do you intend to come, too?" I was surprised. I had the distinct feeling that he did not wish to 'cross planes' in the manner that Jenha and I could.

"I do want that area checked as soon as possible, but I need to remain here to collect reports," Quenten explained.

Yeah, okay, I'll accept that, I thought with amusement.

I decided to try mind-touching Teregan. It worked very well and I was able to tell Quenten, "Auglan is still cowering in his metal cave. The Coward! Don't you have ways to find ships?"

"We haven't been able to find any of the Selkrit shuttles," Quenten admitted. "And that is a serious situation that I want to rectify."

I bet you do, I thought. "My warriors will meet us at the compound gate," I told Jenha.

"Centurion Terr will meet you there shortly," Quenten advised. Then he asked, as if it were an afterthought – "One question, Jai Cassidy. How did you deactivate the tracer?"

"I didn't think it was working anyway," I told him with a trace of resentment. "No one came to help me when that homicidal maniac tried to smother me and then drown me."

"Heat and cold?" Quenten asked then, telling me that his Enforcers had been aware that something was happening. I am still surprised that none of them had come running to make sure I wasn't going to escape them.

"I didn't deactivate it," I emphasised. "At least, not on purpose."

"What about that mechanical beast?" Quenten was really interested now.

I laughed. "One of those clever sorcerers managed to stun one – long enough to tether it. He hung an illusion on it to get me reacting to dangers that were head high while he hoped the beast would get me from below. He expected me to have to kill it before I could claim victory, even though he didn't know how to do it himself."

"But you did deactivate it," Quenten stated.

"Yeah."

The Ambassador glared at me. I let him wait for my answer. "Extreme cold stops it moving and then you can get to the off-button," I told him.

"How did you get near enough to catch it?" To say that Quenten was sceptical was an understatement.

I grinned maliciously. "It didn't want me – I don't have purple blood like Atapi and Kimh. It wasn't so hard to catch when it is trying to snap at a hovering Atapi sorcerer."

"What about the cold? How could you do that?"

I looked around, found an ink pen with a metal handle and held it between my hands. It didn't become as cold as the beast had, but I offered it to Quenten. He quickly dropped it.

"I can make my hands very hot or very cold," I said casually, smothering memories of Stak burning me that way.

Quenten reached out and took one of my hands – they were normal temperature again. "Repeat what you did with that pen."

While still looking at his face, I did as I was bid. His eye ridges contracted in surprise and I couldn't resist saying, "And I have nothing in my hand or up my sleeves."

Quenten, released my hand, and looked at me with an odd expression on his face. He seemed relieved when Centurion Terr arrived.

Terr came with us when we went out to the compound. On the way, Kaer intercepted us and spoke quietly to Jenha. All I heard was, "…another day."

Jenha hustled us on, and I had a question that I asked him, "Jenha, did the High Minister return your rank to you?"

He glanced my way. "The Council reinstated me."

I was getting better at hearing what was not spoken or thought. So the Council had, and Koenig had not. Interesting. Perhaps they had stuck Koenig in seclusion - for another day?

My four oldest warriors were eager to hunt and to return to their former home range. Jenha and I shared the work of transporting them, and Centurion Terr to Stacion Ansuni's withered land.

"This is a wasteland! What weapon did this?" Terr asked, shocked by what he saw.

"No weapon," Jenha explained. "Stacion Ansuni took all the life energy from his land when he fled. It is only just starting to recover."

Terr began looking at me as if I was dangerous. "I can't do that," I told him. "The very idea is vile."

He made an effort to regain his official demeanour and asked formally, "Then can you do that ritual for finding alien traces?"

Everyone looked at me expectantly. It felt strange to have an audience. This time, I deliberately spoke aloud and used the hand gestures as I repeated the ritual three times. My warriors, who did not seem to be worried by the near desert appearance of a once lush settlement, squinted into the bright sunlight and began seeing the glow of the alien taint. I could see them quivering to be set free to hunt.

I pointed to a cave. "Auglan was using that cave," I told my companions. "The others – that one." I moved the direction of my finger. "They came back from the west. Don't go near the caves to the south. There is a subsidence there that has been used as a rubbish dump and there are nasty animal traps around it."

Then I gestured and my warriors raced off at a fast trot towards the caves. Those were empty, as I had expected, and once the check was done my warriors disappeared at a ground-devouring lope towards the west.

Within a short time, I felt the touch of Ketali, the Eldest Warrior. They had found one of the Selkrit flying craft – one of the small helicopters hidden under a net of mottled colours. I received the picture of the location, shared it with Jenha and the three of us went there. Centurion Terr told us to stay back and he went to check it. He returned, reporting it empty and saying, "It will not go anywhere now."

The warriors went off again, still following the glowing tracks. I began to feel the sense of being watched, and realised that Jenha felt it too. He spoke to Terr as I looked around. This area was uneven ground, with gullies and small hills. I had no personal experience of this land, but my mother had and my eyes were drawn to look in a particular direction. I used a ritual my mother had once known to scan the scene in front of me.

"They have built some kind of lean-to tent by the stunted bushes, directly between here and the highest peak of the distant hills," I said.

Terr almost gaped at me, but Jenha nodded, seeing the picture in my mind. At that, Terr accepted my statement as fact, then did his own magic and became as much a shadow as the Selkrit infiltrators. To my sight, he glowed as much as the hidden Selkrit camp did while under my spell. It was easy for me to follow him as he walked directly to where I had specified.

I had begun to think of the Enforcers as merely fancily dressed civilians, but I soon saw otherwise. He reappeared to normal sight right at the lean-to, and I heard him call out a challenge. His head covering was down.

Three Selkrit charged at him, as another used a weapon to bathe the Enforcer in an energy glow. Terr ignored the energy, grabbed the closest Selkrit and quickly disarmed and immobilised him. The other two realised they were outclassed and turned to run. Terr ran after them. He aimed a weapon at one, making that one fall, and continued after the other, catching him and tackling him to the ground. He dragged both unconscious aliens back to the first and put restraints on all three. He left them there, and went into the tent, bringing out an assortment of things. We trotted to join him.

"Maps, records, communicators," he said. "And data storage modules. There are signs of twelve occupants. We should look for another of their flying machines as each only takes six."

After four hours, my warriors had found and disabled six more aliens and found where the aliens were mining. Terr collected samples of the ore.

All the immobilised aliens were hidden out of sight, taken by either Jenha or myself to a place near the helicopter.

Two of those I had moved had been terrified, the rest merely defiant. I studied the former, who were watching me with an odd expression. I decided that they recognised me, and I mentioned that to Terr, as we waited for signs of the remaining three aliens. He nudged those two prisoners and asked them where Auglan was. Neither, it seemed, had the ability to speak – they were too scared. I wondered who they were more afraid of – me or Auglan.

Jenha and I hid in a shallow cave, and I erased the signs of our presence by sweeping our footprints away by conjuring a breeze. Most of the energy needed had come from that stored in Larcia's sword. Terr stood outside, in what would have been full view except for him having that invisibility field about him. My warriors were still roaming further away from where we waited. Through them, I first heard the returning helicopter and warned Terr. When it approached the camp, it hovered as if suspicious of the darkness and lack of a fire. Terr drew a weapon and aimed it, but when the helicopter decided to land, he did his stealth act again.

The Selkrit fell one-by-one as they came out and only then did Terr became visible again. I recalled my warriors and waited with Jenha as Terr attended to his prisoners. The Enforcer must have had a means to talk to his fellows, because a huge flying machine came into view and landed in a clear area nearby. I stopped my jaw from dropping open. It was nothing like I had ever seen before, but Jenha seemed to accept it calmly. I watched as the two helicopters and all the prisoners were loaded into it.

Terr returned to join us, now with his bubble-like helmet open again. "A good day's work," he said with satisfaction.

"Were you expecting more trouble?" Jenha asked as Terr collected the loose things he had taken from the tent. "I am pleased that there was no blood shed."

"They were arrogant, and did not expect trouble," Terr said derisively. "I do not expect that all will be so easy to catch."

My four warriors trotted back to join us, and my opinion of Terr increased greatly because he praised them for their skill. I translated the words into Atapi and sensed their pride. I added my own praise and then asked, "Do you think you can teach the younger ones to hunt blue aliens?"

Four snarls confirmed that.

CHAPTER 65 – Jai Cassidy – POV

I spent that night with my tribe, using one of the beds that the Kumatan had provided. Most of the others preferred to use the fleece-filled mattresses on the floor. When I awake in the morning, I found myself surrounded by half a dozen of the smallest whelps. I had seen these same little ones sound asleep in the communal 'nursery' before I had gone to sleep.

There was no reason that I knew of to get up yet, so I enjoyed their presence until I heard whispers of concern – probably from the mothers of these unusually placid whelps. I thought at Farcine, rather than speak aloud.

"If you are worried, I have six guests in here."

The Eldest Mother entered quietly, followed by five other females. "Did you bespell them, Jai-devil?" she asked.

"I must have, but not on purpose," I said. "Do they not usually sleep this late?"

I felt their amusement at my ignorance. "You can leave them here if you want," I found myself offering. Actually, I was amazed at myself. Babies had never interested me before this – except for Mikha. But thought of my son reminded me of the gem in my pocket – the one I wanted Mikha to have – and I felt an urgent need to see him. Therefore I was not too bothered when the sleeping whelps were carefully lifted to be returned to their normal sleeping place.

Now that I was awake, I felt no desire to return to sleep, even though it was not yet daylight. The females offered me breakfast, and I was more than ready for that. While I ate in their company, I warned them that I wanted to invite Con Ansuni back to talk to him. They accepted the idea calmly enough. They had met him and he was unthreatening. When the Chief Warrior appeared, I told him, too. He knew Con Ansuni from his youth, and did not question my wisdom either.

I went and sat outside the building, on the ground facing the open gardens towards the East, rather than the Kimh palace.

I sent out my call. "Con Ansuni, I need to talk to you."

"Why?" was the instant and sharp reply. I ignored the hostile tone.

"I need your advice," I sent back calmly. "Will you be a guest here with my tribe?"

There was a mental silence so deep that I wondered if he intended to ignore me.

"You will excuse me if I say that you are too close to those whose hospitality is lacking," Con sent back. I thought I sensed a trace of amused condescension and curiosity. "I will come to a neutral place. Do you know of such, or we could go to the land you could claim?"

"Okay," I agreed, thinking. "But not to Stacion's land, even though it is clear of intruders." Instead, I sent him the picture of the place I had gone to await Mikha's birth. I pictured sunrise. "I will be bringing three warriors and Farcine."

Con sent a terse agreement, and I went to arrange for my meeting.

When it was only minutes before sunrise, I walked my group to that place I knew so well. Farcine had a carry skin with her. I was not surprised that Con had already arrived, and I guessed his warriors had scouted the area for traps or dangers.

Farcine began to set out what reminded me of a picnic, which her mind told me was a traditional politeness. Con and his three warriors approached me, as two females moved away from him to approach Farcine.

"Are you comfortable with this place?" I asked Con.

"It is a pleasant place," he said neutrally. "Though hardly neutral. You have already claimed it, I sense."

"Hardly," I objected. "Wasn't here all that long."

"Long enough to plant your marker." Con pointed to a mound of dirt, and I realised that something about that mound was pulling me to it.

My mind suddenly knew what was buried there and I didn't want to touch it. "Stacion's knife," I said aloud. "How did you know?"

"You are still abysmally ignorant," Con told me. "Why did you bury it?"

I decided not to tell him I hadn't. "I really don't want to have it on me."

"Maybe you are beginning to get wisdom," Cotek considered.

I was thinking how to bring up the subject that I had wanted to talk of when Farcine moved up to my elbow.

I glanced at her, and she took that as an invitation to speak for and invited Con to share refreshment with me.

We went to where the 'picnic' was set out. Once there, I recognised Bernea, the woman who had tended to me after Tesla's attack, and Cassia, who was now Con's younger mate.

Cassia gave Con a glance, and he nodded slightly. She came up to me and bowed in deep respect.

"I wanted to meet you again, Jai-devil," Cassia said shyly. "And to thank you. I am with egg to Con Ansuni."

I gave her a human style hug and told her I was happy for her. Bernea and Farcine were now standing side-by-side, ready for the traditional greeting ritual. Beyond the females, the two groups of three warriors were standing straight and battle ready, and eying each other.

Con had also noticed the signs of challenge. "Ketali, Yurok and Regulas all taught me to fight," Con said quietly. "Do we need them to guard our talk?"

"No. I brought my warriors to find out how your warriors would react to them, and I bought Farcine to be sure that I didn't totally shatter accepted behaviour for a meeting like this."

Con snarl-grinned. "There is no protocol for a discussion with an aggravating whelp who has claimed a tribe before proving her right."

I grinned right back, and gave Farcine the nod to do her part. Con was further amused when I choked on the potent drink. "You have yet to develop a taste for fermented hare's milk."

Maybe it was just as well that I could not speak my planned retort. Con used the moment to tell his warriors to relax, but keep alert. I gestured to my Chief Warrior, Ketali, to do the same.

The females moved away to allow us to talk.

"Do you really believe that you owe me a favour?" I asked first.

"My youngsters are safe again, and your tribe helped greatly – yes."

"I don't know if what I want to ask is wise, or acceptable, but…" Con waited for me to find the words to continue. "Do you believe that the Old One will agree to go to that other plane that I showed you?"

"He'll go," Con assured me. "We are all tired of the restrictions placed on us by Kimh and Kumatan. Whether they intend it or not, they are slowly killing us off. In that you are right."

I looked at Farcine, happily chatting to Bernea and Cassia, and the warriors already engaging in mock fights to test each other.

"What we discuss here is to stay secret between us," I told Con, trying for a stern look.

"Very well," he snarl-grinned his agreement.

"Larcia petitioned the Old One to train me," I said abruptly.

I sensed surprise, and possibly satisfaction in his reaction. "You would give him power over you." Con remarked.

"I'd have to, wouldn't I?"

"It is usually the way," Con said neutrally.

"That's what I thought," I nodded. "Once he agrees, and I am not sure yet that he will…"

"He will. He will want to control your power," Con assured me.

"Anyway, when I move the tribes, mine must be allowed to come, too, but the Old One considers them weak, neutered and muzzled. And that their serving the Kimh and Kumatan means they have been corrupted or something. I do not want him taking them as slaves."

"You mentioned a debt I owe you?" Con said then, and I wondered if he guessed my intention.

"Would you allow my tribe, who are kin to yours, to become part of yours?" I asked.

"That is not a simple request, Jai Cassidy. Do you truly understand what it would mean?"

"No. Beyond that I hope that with their kin they will be treated with respect, not contempt. If I am to be the Old One's apprentice, I cannot be there to protect them. And of all the sorcerers, only you could appreciate that serving one's enemies is not the sign of a moron, but a means to learn from and teach them that we deserve to be their equals."

"It will mean that you will have no tribe, Jai-devil. No power base, no one to serve you," Con explained.

"I am no kind of tribal devil – and ruling my own tribe is not what my mother created me for. I need to be accepted by all the tribes."

I sensed Con thinking, maybe remembering. "I will accept any that are willing. They are, as you say, kin."

There was another request I wanted to ask of him. "Teregan," I said abruptly. "I cannot train him. Will you take him as an apprentice?"

"You are a fool, Jai Cassidy," Con told me, not as an insult but as advice. "You give me as a gift what would usually be a valuable bargaining piece. What do you want in return?"

"My tribe…"

"Is also a gift. It is not unknown for apprentices to go to another tribe, but it is usually in exchange for another. It forms a binding of mutual cooperation."

"He is a whelp of your sire – talented. I want him to learn from you. I think he will soon be reluctant to take orders from a female."

"You may be correct – and I will ensure he does not underestimate you. You learnt from my sister, but so did I," Con warned me. "I will take him – on the condition that once the Old One releases you, you teach what you know to Litok, my son."

"I would be honoured," I said. Nothing had prepared me for that offer.

"He is talented too, but he is a gentle whelp and not suited to being a warrior," Con explained. "He would, I think, fight to save a life."

"I think, Con Ansuni, that you are a league above all the other sorcerers. You look at things differently."

"Don't you dare tell the Old One that," Con snarled.

"He will be busy enough with me," I growled back.

"I believe he will," Con agreed. "And I had best teach you a few manners or he will simply swat you for your absolute ignorance. My sister, the one who filled your head with idealistic sorcery, only knew some of how Stacion trained me, and what Stacion expected of me. Will you listen?"

I nodded.

"First though, I agree to accept all of your tribe who wish to serve me. I will not make them swear to me unless they choose. If, later, they wish to return to you, I will release them."

"Thank you." I had not expected him to be so generous.

"The Old One will want to leave soon, now that our lands are rid of intruders and vile creations," Con warned.

"I cannot leave yet," I stressed with some force. "There are many more of those blue aliens on lands no longer held by the Atapi. They need to be found or they will return to your lands when there is no one there to stop them. I can increase the respect those Enforcers have for the Atapi by helping them. I believe I have a way and I need Teregan for that. Is it true, though, that now you are bound to your land you cannot work on those old lands?"

"The old lands are shunned, we will not go there."

"Wasn't your land once shunned?" I asked.

"Impertinent whelp," Con snarled. "I am pleased I will not have the training of you. Yes, but the truth is that Stacion so weakened Loschak that when the aliens came, he was easy meat. I inherited his knife – he gave it to Jai, my womb mate, and she gave it to me."

I didn't quite follow his reasoning as to why he was entitled to it, but I didn't push the issue. I had the answer to one of the questions.

"Could your warriors hunt on those lands?"

"No."

"Could mine?"

Con considered that and answered fairly. "The young ones, born on your world, could, I think. The older ones were bound to Stacion's land, but I don't know. Stacion was disempowered; the binding to his land was broken."

"How would I tell?"

"They will feel weak," Con said. "It has been the way that limits warfare between the tribes to battles just between the sorcerers."

We sat talking for an hour before I felt the need to be returning to my tribe. Before we left, I invited my warriors and Farcine as well as Con's consorts and warriors to share the rest of the food and drink Farcine had brought. It sealed our agreements of mutual benefits.

My mind was full of useful advice. What was most important to me was the means by which I could hide my full power and energy from the Old One. It was something my mother had taught Con, and the only reason that Stacion had not drained him to the dregs, or to death.

I returned to the palace compound and found I had four guests. Janhi flew at me and hugged me. He had gained inches since he had returned. Beyond him, I saw Jenha smiling and Kaer holding Mikha – a struggling little bundle of energy. Jahni released me and let me take Mikha from Kaer.

"What are you all doing here?" I asked. I was pleased, but cautious. "Surely the High Minister does not approve?"

Kaer, now with his hands free, plucked up an Atapi whelp that was clinging to his leg. "My father, on the advice of the healers, is visiting the House of Contemplation. He will return later today," he said, not quite casually.

I took that to mean that Koenig did not know of this visit and would not find out.

Kaer went on, "Lord Eamon, who is acting as Regent, felt that Mikha should meet his distant kin."

"It seems that Jahni has made a friend, too," I noted, seeing that he had returned to playing some game with Teregan.

Mikha was snuggling into me, and I went over to Jenha. "Am I needed by the Enforcers?"

"Not yet," Jenha told me. "They are busy processing the captives taken yesterday and last night. Ambassador Quenten is very impressed – as am I – at the cooperation between Atapi, Kumatan and his men."

"So," I commented. "All the sorcerers behaved well."

Jenha smiled at me and I sensed his approval. "Did you expect less after the masterful way you handled them?"

"They are arrogant, self-centred, spoilt brats," I muttered. "It probably takes one to recognise it, but I wouldn't have wanted to guarantee it."

"You sell yourself short, young one," Jenha told me quietly.

"Then you must have taught me very well." He inclined his head briefly, acknowledging my thanks.

I went on to ask, "So why are you really here?"

"So that you can make your goodbyes without haste," Jenha said softly. "So that when you are alone, you will have fewer regrets about leaving those who love you. I don't want you to feel you are an abandoned orphan. I hope Ellhi reminded you of that."

"Yes," I said, finding it hard to say more. There was one goodbye I craved, but I could not indulge myself with Jenha as I had with Ellhi. I bent my head to kiss Mikha's curly black hair.

"You are making the right choice," Jenha told me, and I knew his words had meaning on several levels.

For the Atapi, by taking them away. For me, because I would never be fully accepted amongst Kimh or Kumatan. For him, although it hurt us both, to have chosen to break the binding between us. He had his rightful rank back again and I did not want to be the cause of further disgrace for him. I needed him as a friend to the Atapi and a voice of conciliation and good sense.

"Yeah," I agreed without enthusiasm.

Then he shattered my relaxed mood. "You have been requested to present yourself to the Council later this morning."

"What for?"

"I was not advised," Jenha admitted.

"Probably so they can accuse me of sorcery again, and forbid me to help the Atapi. Is that it? I told them what I intend to do and I haven't changed my mind." I felt angry.

"Young one," Jenha warned me. "If you maintain a placid demeanour, all will be well. Speak what you believe with the strength of your conviction."

The sudden anger was quelled. "Will I have you or Kaer as an advocate?"

Kaer answered that question, proving that he had been listening but tactfully staying silent. "Once you claimed the aegis of the Galactic

Federation, I was no longer required for that role. I will not be allowed to speak for you."

"What if I disavow that claim?"

"That would not be wise," Kaer advised, but he didn't explain. Instead, he said, "You would become subject to the Council once more."

Was that a tactful way of telling me that Kaer's elders still didn't trust me? At least I felt I knew where I stood with them.

"Okay," I said, though what I really meant was, "If that is how it is going to be."

I decided to pass Mikha to his father. My son wriggled and gave a growl of displeasure.

"Con Ansuni will allow those of my tribe, who wish it, to re-join his tribe," I told Jenha. "But I need to discuss things with Teregan before that. Do you mind?"

Jenha had his hands full with Mikha, so he only gestured me away. I didn't want him, or Kaer, listening to my little talk.

Jahni and Teregan stopped their game when I approached to come sit near them. "I am glad you both have become friends," I said to put them at ease, then asked about the game. It was unfamiliar to me, and was something Janhi was teaching Teregan. I let them talk. After a while, I nudged Teregan's mind to quieten his chatting.

"I have things to say to both of you that are important and do not need to be shared with anyone else. I need a solemn vow from each of you."

The two boys nodded.

"Teregan, I have asked Con Ansuni to train you in sorcery. I expect you to obey him and be an obedient apprentice. "

"Have I displeased you, Jai-devil?" Teregan was suddenly no longer cheeky.

"No," I assured him. "It is just that I still have a lot to learn, too. It would not be fair to you if I tried to teach you. I want you to be a powerful sorcerer one day, and at least you have met Con and his son, Litok – who is also his apprentice."

"Con Ansuni scares me," Teregan said, seeming to shrink into the floor.

"Do you good, you precocious whelp," I said firmly. "He might keep your concentration on your lessons. And Jahni feels the same about

Kaer, and does not seem to have suffered from having to learn from him.”

Teregan glanced from Jahni to Kaer and back. I sensed him thinking that he would prefer to learn from Con Ansuni.

“He treats me fairly,” Jahni admitted. “Though he still scares me. What did you need to say to me, Jai?”

I needed to choose my words carefully, and considered how I was going to phrase my request as I drew the blue gem from Larcia’s nebulous crown out of my pocket. Before beginning to speak, I checked to see what Jenha and Kaer were doing.

“When Mikha is older, he will want to seek me out. He will need a way to find me, but I am going where others can’t follow. There is a way, and it requires a kind of key to open the way. I have one, and I need you to keep it safe for Mikha. Will you?”

Jahni nodded. I sensed that Kaer and Jenha were still busy with a grumpy Mikha. I palmed the stone to Janhi and nodded for him to pocket it.

“You will need to learn how such a key works. Your father knows how, but it will not be a good idea for you to ask him, or Kaer.”

“You don’t want them, or anyone else, to know I have it,” Jahni said in a whisper. He had yet to learn the idea of tacit silence. I nodded quickly and began to talk of other things, gradually making my voice louder.

When I left the two youngsters, I saw that Kaer had swapped the Atapi whelp for Mikha, and a bemused Jenha was holding a wriggling Atapi whelp.

“Now you know where Mikha gets it from,” I teased Jenha. “I thought Traegers were a match for any Atapi?”

He smiled at that, and said, “We cannot stay longer. I will return when your presence is required. Will you be here?”

I nodded. “I am not intending to challenge the Old One, and Larcia is quiescent.”

Jenha called to Janhi and my four visitors departed. I gently called Larcia in my mind. I felt a brush of awareness, of approval, and that she was occupied elsewhere.

Jenha followed my angry stalking along the palace passageways. Behind him, two of the palace guards were 'escorting' me out. Just then, I didn't even think I could speak civilly to Jenha, and I had no desire to get him angry at me. He knew how to make me feel like a naughty child.

I had gone to face the council, dressed neatly in my version of Kumatan dress – another set of trousers and tunic made by Ellhi, only this time she had made them in a restful light green fabric. I had even made sure I had bathed and tidied my hair – things I had not been doing much of late.

And I had gone with the intention of taking Jenha's wise advice. I had tried to keep my temper, and tried very, very hard to be calm and reasonable. Even with Lord Eamon acting as Regent, and in charge of the Council session. I knew that he, at least, could think outside of their rigid, inflexible ethical code – that Nuath of theirs.

But I had lost it. Those rigid, inflexible damn…

The choice curse words I had used, ones I had learnt from Jenha's servants on Earth, still echoed in my mind. Saying them had earned me a warning, but someone had to shake them up, open their eyes, and shove some reason into their heads.

The Kimh Councillors had to accept that they had been royally conned by the Selkrit, who were little more than pirates. They had listened to Ambassador Quenten on the subject and, after that, they had been angry in their icily controlled fashion. That I could understand, but if the Kimh were always so reasonable, why wouldn't they listen to me?

Was it because anyone that was under thirty was, to them, still a child? Or was it because I was a human female with Atapi blood and had the appalling taste to be the grand-daughter of the worst Atapi sorcerer-devil in their history?

Despite ample proof of my good sorcery, they hadn't believed me when I told them of the Selkrit's trickery. They still didn't believe me, when I said they needed the Atapi and that I could get the sorcerers to work together and change their ways. Even the evidence of the sorcerers cooperating with the Enforcers to locate and capture Selkrit infiltrators was ignored. No, they'd rather believe Quenten had fixed that on his own.

The Council still resented and distrusted the Atapi. They could not – would not – see that they needed the Atapi. What if these aliens, more of their kind, came here again? And what if the Enforcers weren't here? Who would fight the aliens who could slip around unseen and land their ships unseen?

The aliens had weapons and machines, and things the Kimh had no conception of. Even I only had an inkling of such things, but only because I had grown up on Earth where they had some mechanical technology – much more than they had here on Korvu. Earth had electricity for lights, while Korvu still used candles and lamps. As I saw things, the Kimh were sheep – innocently ready to invite ravening wolves to dinner.

If I had to compare the two groups of stubborn, inflexible males, I think I would have to say that the Atapi had proved more willing to learn and change than the Kimh. The Atapi sorcerers, for the first time ever, had worked with an alien race, and had seen the damage that other alien race had done.

The Kimh were only now seeing the truth about the Selkrit. Could they not also consider that they might have been wrong about the Atapi?

In the end, I was warned that I was a disruptive influence to the peace of Korvu, and if I wished to live here, in peace, I had to learn to be more respectful. With that advice hanging in the air, I took a few deep breaths and told them that the Atapi should be their equals, not a race to be considered animals at worst and slaves at best.

There had been an outcry of objection and I had raised my voice to be heard over them, with Lord Eamon ringing a bell to try for silence.

"Why, then," I had asked then, "do the Traegers, who deal with the Atapi, have a title that translates as Slave-Master?"

The obedient Councillors said nothing to that, and let me finish. I told them that they didn't deserve Atapi concern – and that once I had taken the Atapi away, hell would freeze over before I brought them back.

The only thing that they all agreed with me about was the removal of the Atapi to where they could not interfere with the lives of the Kimh or Kumatan. One Councillor summed it up – "They will not be accepted back."

That was when the last vestiges of politeness had left me and when Lord Eamon invoked the 'disruptive behaviour' clause of their 'rules of meeting', ordering me to be evicted.

I assumed that Jenha, who had not been sitting near to me, had been sent after me.

Only now, aware of Jenha behind me, did I begin to think it odd that he, who had warned me to be calm, had said nothing. He had not even warned my mind, or sent a flick of mental disapproval – nothing.

"Why don't you say it?" I demanded of Jenha. "Tell me what an undisciplined, incorrigible brat I am?"

He still said nothing – neither to approve nor to disapprove of what I had done. After a few minutes of his silence, I demanded, "Do you want to totally reject me?"

That was how I was feeling. His mind was so tightly closed against me.

"No," he said, so softly that only I would hear.

I slowed my pace a bit, and let him catch up to me. I glanced at his face; it was completely calm and neutral. Without speaking, he seemed to be chiding me on my simmering anger. I sensed there was something he expected me to understand, but I was too hurt, angry and confused to think it out.

The palace guards left off following us when we had gone beyond the Council Precinct. I kept on walking until I was outside in the garden – the formal garden with its ordered plant beds and neat paths. It seemed to be symbolic of the minds of the Kimh.

Jenha still walked with me, still saying nothing and with his mind closed to mine. I became aware of Ellhi walking towards me and that Jenha had stopped. I stopped too, guessing that he had summoned Ellhi, perhaps hoping she could help me calm my mind.

Rather than accepting the implied offer, I turned abruptly and walked off at an angle to both of them. I walked off the implied 'right path' and went across the grass, and hopped over flowerbeds, finding amusement in my analogy by thinking of myself as following my own path.

Finally I chose to sit on a patch of grass, rather than the seat that was on the edge of it. I drew on the aura, letting it surround me and hide me. From where I sat, I could see Ellhi walk to Jenha, and both of them look in my direction before turning to walk together into the palace.

When I had worked out the worst of my anger and convinced myself that I didn't give a damn about the Kimh, I gradually calmed and let my mind drift back over the council meeting. I realised that it wasn't the reaction of the Kimh that had angered me – I had expected little else from them. I was angry because they had made it impossible for Jenha to be close to me, as he had once been. I was angry because it seemed that Jenha had closed himself off from me.

Now that I was calmer, I began to realise what Jenha had wanted me to understand. 'Tacit silence' – a concept that he and Kaer were good at – the sharing of the understanding of an idea, without using thoughts or words to do so.

Jenha could not have said the things that I had said and got away with it. What I had said needed saying, and I was not going to be staying around and having to live with the Kimh. Jenha had been acting with perfect decorum and 'correctness' as I knew he had to. For him to openly agree with me was unacceptable to the Kimh. For him to disagree openly would be dishonourable in his own eyes. To him it would be a lie – a perversion of truth. He knew what I intended, and he had told me it was the right thing to do. And it was. Both Kimh and Atapi needed time away from each other – to allow memories to fade and attitudes to change.

Perhaps, if the Atapi were needed back, sometime in the future, those few Kimh and Kumatan with vision would have provoked a change of attitude.

I thought on the idea and summarised my feelings. Pigs might fly, and the Atapi might walk on Korvu's moon before they did.

When I decided to re-join Jenha, I did so quietly. He gave me a searching look and I returned it with a wry shrug. His silence was no longer daunting, but more the silence of friends who didn't need to talk. I seemed to see his faint smile of approval. He began to walk in the direction of Ambassador Quenten's suite, and I went with him. Centurion Terr met us at the door, and ushered us into the small waiting room, as the Ambassador was not there. I went to the window to stare out into the garden while I waited. Jenha made himself comfortable in a chair, and watched me without talking to me. I appreciated the silence, since I was still trying to think about what else I could have said to the Kimh to change their minds. I was still a little angry with them.

Sometime later, someone else entered. I didn't bother turning to see who it was. The person came closer to me – I sensed that much – but then seemed to be waiting for me to acknowledge them. I didn't.

"Jai?" Kaer spoke softly.

"What?" I managed to ask politely, even if a bit abruptly. I finally turned to face him

Kaer was uncomfortable, betrayed the fact by the way he was gripping a roll of paper. "The council holds you to your promise of removing the

Atapi to where they will not interact with any other race, or the Kimh and Kumatan."

"Nice of them to approve," I said with heavy sarcasm. "Was there more?"

"Yes. They agreed to having you remove them as soon as possible."

I had been standing with my arms hanging by my side, but at that statement, I folded my arms across my chest and shuffled so my feet were slightly apart. "Stuff them," I said deliberately. "I haven't finished here yet, and I want this damn tracer off me before I go."

Kaer flushed slightly.

"You can tell them that for me," I told Kaer, knowing he wouldn't dare. I relented. "So why did you get the job of telling me this? I didn't think you were my advocate anymore."

"My Uncle, Lord Eamon, felt you would be…less difficult if I spoke to you. He felt that you respected me."

I gave him a dismissive glance from head to foot before asking, "What's the rest?"

"Once the Enforcers have left, you will be subject to the council again, unless you leave with them."

"I am not leaving, and I had figured that already," I told him.

Kaer's hands wrung the paper roll, creasing it. He was definitely uncomfortable. "Once you leave here, you will not be welcome back. Should you return, you will be placed in seclusion."

I thought to myself, "penned like a pet rabbit." I said, sourly, "And you agreed to it?"

"Until I am thirty, I have no council vote," Kaer said diffidently. "And it was not the time to dispute it."

That was probably the closest I would get to him admitting that he did not agree. I saw Jenha moving slightly in the chair as if easing into another more comfortable position. He still wasn't saying anything about my rudeness.

I took a breath and admitted, "Your uncle was right. I don't despise you and the council decision was no more than I expected. And I really don't care about those old fossils."

I think Kaer was relieved when Quenten arrived with both Bellus and Terr in his wake. He greeted each of us, but I didn't bother to respond. I ignored the scrutinising look he gave me.

"Lord Kaer, the council received my apologies?" Quenten asked.

"Yes, Ambassador. Lord Eamon was hoping for an update on yesterday's actions," Kaer spoke politely.

"I will have that prepared for him. I have been overseeing the processing of the fifty prisoners. They have all been taken to our ship, and their equipment has been confiscated for study, and the data storage in the helicopters is being downloaded for analysis."

Kaer nodded when Quenten finished. "Thank you, Ambassador." He made his exit with signs of relief.

Quenten turned his attention to me. "So you have made the Korvu ruling council eager to see the last of you."

"They'll be just as keen to see you leave, too," I predicted.

"Are you ready to gratify their wishes?" Quenten asked me.

"Yes, but none of those blue creeps had better get near me just now."

"I require them alive, Jai Cassidy," he warned me.

"How alive?" I tried to sound innocent, but from the way Quenten's face tightened, I had failed.

"In a state to answer questions," he specified. "Of those we apprehended yesterday, many have Galactic Warrants. Some were innocent scientists who had no idea who had actually hired them."

Jenha finally spoke to me. "We have had some success in locating land that had belonged to long dead sorcerers."

Quenten added, "We have the coordinates and a shuttle ready. As you said, the areas are vast. Have you a means to locate those we seek?"

"I think so. My warriors are experienced hunters, except I don't have the visual location to get there."

"The shuttle can take you," Quenten suggested.

"Okay," I agreed. I had never flown before, but surely it wasn't unlike the planes on Earth and they were safe enough. "Where is the shuttle?"

"Aloft. We can land it in any open area," Quenten said easily.

"I suggest the area behind the Atapi compound," Jenha spoke softly.

"The Enforcers are ready. I have someone listening to the ship-to-ship communications of the Selkrit," Quenten told me.

"Let me organise my warriors," I said.

I was tempted to just 'walk' from inside the palace to the compound, but I remembered the time that Larcia had tried to move me, and the barrier had stopped me. I wasn't in the mood for that, so I let Jenha escort me.

I told my chosen warriors to get ready for a long hunt, and I sensed their quivering eagerness.

"The Enforcers want the prisoners alive enough to answer questions," I told them, and from their snarl-grins I knew they understood that they didn't have to be totally gentle. I added, "We will be going to the hunting ground in their flying machines, which will be a new experience, even for me. However, it is quite safe and something no other warriors have done." They all growled approval.

I divided my warriors into four groups of six, each led by one of the oldest males, and each a mixture of young and old warriors. I caught Teregan before he slipped out to join one of the groups.

"You stay with me," I told him, and he obeyed.

While I waited for the males to return with their weapons, I spoke to Farcine. "Start packing everything into carry sacks so you can be ready to leave as soon as I get Con to come. It might be before I get back. Tell me when you are ready and I will organise for the ones at the palace to come back."

Jenha murmured, "Wait here, young one, and I will arrange that now."

He 'walked' back to the palace. Farcine said to me, "If Con comes and you are not back, I will remain to ensure the males have taken all their things." I gave her a wry grin.

The shuttle door closed with a metallic clang, and I had the sense of being closed in. My warriors, I noticed, had the look of captured wild dogs with their eyes wide with fright. They quivered, now with the restrained desire to flee.

Some of the Enforcers, calm and efficient, told us where to sit and explained how to strap in and the reason for it. They betrayed no sign of anxiety at having long pointed weapons loose in the craft. They simply suggested for the spears to be laid alongside the warriors' seats and held in place by their feet.

I had Teregan beside me, and he was so excited that he wouldn't sit still long enough to be secured. The threat to send him back to Farcine had the desired effect. While his antics and enthusiasm helped my warriors to relax, even he felt the odd sensation as we lifted straight up and looked a bit ill.

Once the craft was high enough and began to move at a constant height, I relaxed too, and sent the feeling to all of my tribe. I risked a glance out of a small window and decided I preferred not to see the land below looking so far down.

We landed after a seemingly long time, somewhere northeast of the palace. The coordinates that the pilot used meant nothing to me. I emerged before my warriors and looked around – immediately locating and memorising landmarks to help identify this place.

I called to Teregan when he bounced down the ramp to the ground. "Does this place look familiar to you?"

He took a glance around. "No, Jai-devil."

I pointed to a rock formation in the distance. "Think carefully. That may have been in the background."

"Nope," he said at once. Maybe it was the truth. He was looking at me as if waiting to be told something useful.

"Send me the picture of what you remember of that formation I pointed out," I directed him.

He considered for a moment, and I saw the picture come into my mind. It was clear and detailed.

"Very good," I told him, thinking that if Auglan had come here, he may not have seen the formation unless he was piloting the ship himself. He would also know exactly where the camp was, and would probably have the exact coordinates of it. We didn't, and wherever it was it would be hidden.

All of my warriors were now behind me and I sent off two groups to scout the area, looking for the signs of aliens. The other two groups were to wait, until some clue to the location of the camp was found. I had an idea of how I could find that, and I needed to be away from the Enforcer shuttle a bit so the alien taint of that did not distract my search. I took Teregan to a shaded place near an outcrop of rock, and sensed Jenha and Centurion Terr following me at a discreet distance. Well, they wouldn't see much for a bit.

Once we were both seated, I took both of Teregan's brown hands and allowed a part of my mind to watch his. Then, with another part of my mind I called to Larcia. When she answered me, I knew Teregan sensed her too, as his eyes widened.

"Daughter, you are on Wessuk's land. What you have started is in motion. Do you sense it?"

Since I was sitting on the ground, I let my mind sink into the aura like it was a still pool of water. Once there, I could feel the disturbance not far away. I turned my attention there, aware that Teregan had instinctively turned his head to look in that direction.

I smiled at what I found. The aliens were besieged by wild canines and overrun with beetles. I released Teregan, summoned the rest of my warriors and pointed to the direction they needed to go. Bellus strode over and demanded, "How far?"

I had to admit that I didn't know, but added, "When they get there, I will be able to get you there. Will your ship be able to follow?" He nodded tersely.

After about an hour, I knew my warriors had found the camp. I felt their contempt for the prey they had captured.

"How many?" I asked the mind of Ketali.

"Ten, Jai-devil. Two more were a week dead."

"Give me a picture!"

Ketali studied the scene in front of him and I shared it with Jenha. He took Bellus by the arm, and I took Teregan, and we 'walked' there. I expected what we saw, Bellus did not. I saw him jerk back, then put his helmet down and stride forward. Jenha felt no need to go closer, and Teregan was trying to control his reaction to the smell of decaying flesh. As an Atapi, being trained to be a warrior as well as a healer, this was a lesson that he needed, but I told him to stay with Jenha as I moved forward. I muttered a ritual that caused a breeze to blow from behind me, and force the stench away.

As Ketali had reported, two of the aliens were dead, and the beetles were swarming the wrapped bundles. Of the other ten, four were being held immobile at spear point, their weapons being held by a young warrior. Three were being guarded by the privy pit and three more were kneeling on the ground, retching. These three all had blue blood on their left hands.

Bellus must have spoken into his helmet communicator and summoned the shuttle. It arrived, and landed. During the process of loading the live prisoners and the two dead, I undid the purposing of the beetles and the prowling canines. Not all of either creature decided to move away, since the beetles were attracted to refuse and the canines were scavengers.

I stayed clear of the Enforcers as they went on to record the scene, then search the camp and surrounding area.

Jenha watched impassively, and I took time to teach Teregan the first mantra for calm, but he suddenly stopped heeding me. When I felt his mind, I knew he was having a vision from Auglan.

I gestured to the nearest warrior and whispered, "There is another one, somewhere in sight of the camp." As he set off at a trot, I told Jenha and he warned Terr. Teregan was getting the full brunt of Auglan's anger and hate. From the lack of visual detail, I knew he was still cowering in his shuttle. I wished I could understand what he was saying and said so when Bellus came over. He may not have understood how I was able to know what Auglan was doing, but when I repeated two or three distinctive sounds being made by Auglan, he was convinced I did indeed have a link to the creature. He sent a junior Centurion to the shuttle and he came back with a contraption of wire and plastic.

"This is a translator," Bellus told me as he fitted it over my head. He spoke some words in his own language, and I heard them in English. He suggested that it might help me understand what my mind was hearing. I listened, but had to admit it didn't help.

"Keep it on," he told me.

My warrior reappeared carrying an unconscious Selkrit and he dumped the creature at Bellus's feet. The Selkrit had a dark bruise on his forehead and a little finger missing from his left hand. The wound was oozing blood.

"How did you know about this one, Jai Cassidy, if you could not understand his speech?" Bellus asked.

I patted Teregan, and told him, "That prisoner was reporting to Auglan. I guessed it was the cause of Auglan's strong negative emotions."

Bellus seemed to stare at me, but then he nodded and returned to his work. My warriors gathered about me and waited. I heard them talking derisively of 'easy meat'.

We returned to the shuttle, sitting in the forward section whilst the prisoners were confined in a rear section. I was glad that I could not smell the two dead ones and did not bother to ask where they had been stowed. This time, when the shuttle lifted, my warriors were perfectly calm.

At the second location, my part was the same. I soon knew that bad weather and ill-luck were the problems besetting this camp. When I sent warriors off to find it, I nudged the weather pattern back to normal, which meant when we finally reached the place, the rain would have stopped.

My warriors quickly located the camp, which was in the direction that had been obscured by heavy rain. A short time later they reported finding the mine being worked by the Selkrit. At my direction, warriors circled the camp and the mine to watch for potential escapees. It seemed, though, that half of the estimated Selkrit at the camp were trying to dig some of their group out from a collapsed cavern.

When Bellus, Jenha, Teregan and I arrived we were unnoticed. I whispered to them what the oblivious Selkrit were doing.

The Enforcer ship arrived. Two of the diggers dropped their shovels and raced for a dense clump of trees. I knew they wouldn't escape. Six others saw the shuttle and ran for it. I understood their chatter, thanks to the translator. The Enforcers were like miraculous help.

I didn't listen to the whole story, but I heard that they had endured days and days of torrential rain, and something had been washed out and their workmates had fallen into some underground cave. Their efforts to dig the men out were obvious and ineffective.

"Leave them there," I suggested.

I shrugged when Bellus disagreed, and began to issue orders to his men.

I went over towards the subsidence, sensing the caves under the ground. I was trying to locate the old entrances, but it seemed they were all blocked. There were seven men trapped below, in various states of health and mental stability. All were huddled in one small alcove that was above the level of the rising water.

While I was relatively unobserved, I murmured the ritual for forming the whirlwind as Con had taught me. Then, as I had done on Jacek's land, I forced it to drill a hole from above. I sensed Jenha move up beside me as most of the surface men moved away. The Centurions, once they realised that the whirling wind was controlled, kept on digging. Those below were cowering in fear. All could hear the shrill scream of the wind.

Bellus watched the wind with a controlled expression. If I had to guess, he was stoically remaining calm while the hair on his head must have been trying to push his helmet off. Probably his fellows were doing the same. I had to give them credit for guts.

I had targeted the hole right over a pile of rubble in the cavern below. The trapped men were able to scramble out without too much trouble. Most of these, although relieved to escape, regretted it when they saw the Enforcers waiting for them.

My warriors returned with the two that had tried to run. They had them slung over their shoulders and both prisoners were missing a small left hand finger. I said nothing to draw attention to their collecting of trophies.

We all returned to the shuttles once the Enforcers were finished. I overheard that two of the helicopters had been found, and that each had been disabled and would be collected later. I had the distinct feeling that Centurion Bellus was very pleased.

While we had been waiting, I had Teregan fidgeting beside me. He was bored by his small part in this. Jenha had whispered a suggestion to me. So for the rest of the time, I was teaching Teregan the first mantra for concentration and having him practice it.

After off-loading all the prisoners at the space port – a place that really unnerved me – we went to yet another location. More aliens were captured in much the same way, since all were demoralised by days of unnerving attacks by birds and animals. My warriors were still talking of the 'easy meat'.

When we were finished at the fourth location, we were taken back to the palace compound, where I delivered Teregan to Farcine and Jenha took me to Kaer's suite.

"Isn't this tempting trouble?" I asked when I realised where Jenha had taken me.

"Today is a reflection day for the Kimh," he told me quietly. "They will all be quite occupied. I want to make sure you have a proper meal. You look as if you have been neglecting yourself lately."

I couldn't disagree with that. Jenha told me to sit down and he went into another room of the suite. He returned with Ellhi and Teresa, who was trying to hold onto Mikha. I was told that Aniki, Kaer's wife, was resting and little Kelhi was sleeping. I was presented with Mikha, who instantly quietened in my arms.

"Where is Jahni?" I asked.

Ellhi quickly explained, "He is with Kaer."

Teresa stayed close to me. "I will stay here, Jai-devil," she said quietly when I had finished asking questions. "All the others have returned to the compound. There is now a narrow way in and out." She glanced at Jenha and then back to me.

"What of your whelp?" I asked her, recalling that her son had just been weaned before Mikha had arrived.

"He will be well cared for," she assured me with confidence.

"It will be lonely here by yourself," I warned.

"But it will be interesting," she countered. "And Nikal says he will stay too."

I nodded. Nikal was her mate.

The food for me arrived promptly, and I wasted no time in eating it. Mikha tried to take tastes of it from me, although he was not yet ready for solid food. He stayed clinging to me with one small fist and I tried not to think of how hard it was going to be to leave him, even though I knew it was better for him to be here.

Just as I was about to leave, Kaer returned with Jahni in his shadow. Jenha's son came to me and gave me a hug, but obeyed Kaer when he directed him to go to bed. I no longer sensed strong resentment and was relieved that Jahni had accepted his place here. Ellhi replaced him in hugging me and during that brief time, I had the sense of a three-way embrace, but when I looked at Jenha, he was talking to Kaer. He stopped when I stepped up beside him.

We walked the long way back to the compound, giving ourselves a chance to talk.

"We have not located all the aliens," Jenha remarked. "Have you a way?"

"I'm working on it," I hedged.

"Is that why those we found were addled and slow?" Jenha asked casually.

"They can't expect to have everything their way. The aura rejects them."

We parted at the gate and I went to find Teregan.

I found him seated within a square of four warriors. He looked mutinous and I wondered what he had been doing. I left him there and sought Farcine to ask the question.

She made no excuses for him, and told me of his aberrant behaviour. The mildest of what he had been doing was kicking everything and speaking with unrestrained rudeness. He had earned himself a sore tailbone, and when that had not stopped him, Ketali had decreed he be minded by the guards.

The cause, I decided, had to be Teregan's mind link to Auglan. I replaced one of the warriors – the one facing Teregan – and seated myself at his level.

I took both of his hands and evoked the 'over mind' to see what his mind was receiving. If I had to describe it, I would have to say that Auglan had gone mad – and become incoherently, furiously angry. It was little wonder that Teregan was so overwhelmed.

Having me share his mind, and act as a barrier between his and the alien, calmed Teregan. I deepened my sensing of the link until I felt like I was Auglan. It was as if I was speaking the alien words and hearing in my mind the English translations.

The Selkrit leader was hearing reports from the scattered teams of miners, and every one of them was reporting dire things, a series of accidents or ill luck such as insects swarming their camp and work site, animals scavenging and destroying food stocks, or the weather being very cold, wet or windy.

Auglan was ranting at them, telling them to increase production. He would tolerate no excuses for failure. At the same time, he was thinking that he needed enough of the ore to make an obscene profit.

I wondered if I could influence Auglan's mind in this state, and set about trying. In feelings rather than words, I thought on the overwhelming need to personally visit every place, and whip any slackers.

In his state of fury, the idea appealed to him, but he shrunk back into the darkness, away from the communicator. He recalled his neutered state with fury, and the fear that the underlings would laugh at him. He had killed the few that knew the truth, but he was afraid they might have talked before they had been silenced. I inserted the idea of inflicting the same on any underling who even looked contemptuous, and that appeased his fury.

He thought of leaving at once, but I nudged his mind into first finishing all the calls so he could leave at daylight. The idea of waiting was difficult to enforce, so I thought on the idea of a drink he was craving and felt him go to get it. The potent beverage jolted him back to reason, with a recollection of someone paying him who would not accept excuses for any delay.

When Auglan had finished his calls, he was concerned by the lack of contact with three teams. The one team that did make contact left him seething with their report of Enforcer presence. His private thoughts revealed that he was afraid of the Enforcers. He recalled the angry words of his backer for bringing them, and his own extreme vexation that the idea had backfired on him.

The violent anger was rousing again, and I felt it beginning to affect me. I eased the link before it grew too strong.

With what I had sensed, it was no wonder that Teregan had reacted the way he did. He was still very young. I sat there and spoke the words for a ritual of calm, casting it on Teregan. It worked and I sensed the three guarding warriors beginning to relax.

"Take him to where I sleep," I told the warriors. Ketali lifted Teregan, who was exhausted by trying to control the roiling emotions he had shared. He fell asleep as soon as he was placed on a mattress next to my bed.

I was awake for a long time after my tribe had fallen asleep. Something nebulous was worrying my mind – a sense of danger. I checked Teregan – he was so deeply asleep that he would not be receiving anything from Auglan. Merely thinking of the disgraced Councillor intensified the feeling of danger. Did he know that all of his infiltrators were gone from Atapi lands? That all of his revolting mechanical beasts and other nasty traps were neutralised?

If he did, I had no hint of it.

But what if he did? His attempts to make the Atapi look guilty, and those to provoke the Kumatan, had failed. The feral beasts had been more of a nasty piece of revenge on the Atapi.

Revenge…yes, he was that sort. I shivered. He would have a very personal wish to have revenge on me. How would he do that? Would he know how to find me? What did he know about me?

Assume he knew too much, I told myself. Assume that he knew the tribe at the palace was mine.

He hadn't dared to send the feral bots in there – but the trail of alien had been bright around the fence. Could they not get in? Why?

As I lay on my bed, I allowed myself to sense the energies around me. Finally, I relaxed just a bit. There was a kind of shield over and around this compound. I tested it – more like tasted it. It was not that strong, and meant to keep out those with ill intent.

The palace nearby had a shield around it to keep out the Atapi – I tried to sense if that was all the shield did.

I suddenly thought of a truly dreadful possibility, and sat up on my bed.

"Jenha!" I put all the force I could into the mental call.

I felt his mind wake from sleep to instant alertness. I repeated my call.

"Jai?" he acknowledged, sensing the urgency.

Very quickly, I told him of my dire fear. "When you were on Earth, did you learn what bombs were?"

He had.

"This Auglan – he is furious about what we did today. He knows of the first raid, and he can't contact the other four camps. If he knows I was involved, when he already hates me, I think he will try to remove me."

Jenha didn't tell me I was paranoid. "That is a real possibility – also because he knows you are a partisan of the Atapi. He would also be angry with the tribe leaders who defeated his infiltrators. Do you think you should warn all the tribes?"

"Yes, they should be warned, but what if he decides to strike here where I am? Or even the palace – since his plans are dust?"

That thought had not occurred to Jenha. I explained my fear. "Will that shield that keeps Atapi out of the Palace protect against bombs?"

"No. Leave that with me. Can you guard your area?"

"We won't be here," I told him, and broke the contact.

I sprang off the bed and ran to shake Farcine awake. "Wake everyone, get ready to leave."

"Con Ansuni!" I thought as strongly as I could.

"Jai-devil?" His reply came instantly. Had he been wakeful too?

I sent to his mind my fears of what Auglan might do to the Atapi for thwarting him. How his infiltrators might have revealed the locations of the Atapi camps and how Auglan might use this knowledge to destroy the tribes.

He sent a snarl back. "His spies have not found us again."

That relieved me. "Can you warn the other sorcerers?" I felt his agreement and admitted, "I fear for those here. Can you bring them through to you now?"

"Yes," he decided. "We can open a pass-through – link to my mind."

I did so, strengthening the contact. Con had been here, so he could do it. I could not, for I had never seen his new village site.

An odd glow began to form in the doorway leading from the meeting room to my bedroom. Teregan had woken and was helping his mother pack things in carry sacks. Young females, each carrying two sleepy whelps, were coming into the room. Bundle-laden young warriors were amongst them.

"Con, I am sending females and whelps through with young warriors who can help with the females."

I felt him agree to the plan.

For each small group of females I sent through two warriors, choosing them by name. "Go through – you are expected and will be welcomed. Help with the females and whelps, and obey Con as you would me. He is kin to me and to you."

The procession moved quickly. I touched Larcia's sword to maintain my energy, which was being used up as I maintained the pass-through. As soon as I said, "That's it," the pass-through vanished.

"What is left?" I asked Farcine. Teregan stood beside her.

"Basic needs and food," she told me.

I turned to the ten remaining warriors. "We can't stay here. Is there a place nearby where we can go?"

Ketali bowed. "Yes, Jai-devil."

"Two of you go out and check the place. Everyone else bring the food, blankets and other things. We are moving out."

I grabbed my blanket and one of the food bundles. I had no personal things.

Morning came without my fears being realised. I hoped I was wrong. There were still more Selkrit to find, and I offered Farcine the choice to stay at this new camp or to come with us. She opted to stay and watch. I told her to keep away from the compound.

When Jenha came to find us, he offered to take Farcine into the palace. She chose to do this, knowing she would need to keep out of sight in Kaer's suite with Teresa.

Ambassador Quenten met us before we left for the day's hunt. He spoke to Bellus and Jenha, excluding me from the discussion. Finally, though, Jenha gestured me over.

"Your warning last night was timely," Jenha told me. "The Enforcer ship noted several explosions. All were on Atapi lands. Have you heard anything?"

"No, and I don't think Teregan has either. If Auglan arranged the explosions, it must have been when Teregan was asleep."

"Auglan is not his original name," Quenten told me. "There are five Galactic warrants on him under different names. He is very dangerous and we want him – urgently."

"I haven't finished with him," I said, daring Quenten to object. "Have you any idea how many more Selkrit are on Korvu?"

Quenten glanced at Bellus, who could give him no estimate.

"We now have an Enforcer crew on the Selkrit main ship," Bellus told me. "We have had no success yet in accessing the data banks there. We are hoping to find a list of all the personnel that came on the ship. Of course, some might be dead already, due to accidents or fights."

I decided I had a better idea than he did.

"There are at least seven more camps," I said.

"We only know of one more," Bellus remarked, giving me an intent look.

"I know, but I am hoping Auglan will reveal more," I said.

"How?" Quenten demanded.

"All I need is a picture," I said, and Jenha nodded. "He won't even realise I am getting it. He just has to get out of his shuttle to berate his teams. I think he is angry enough to overcome his shame of being half a man."

"I don't know what you have been doing Jai Cassidy, but deliberate interference with other races is frowned upon," Quenten reminded me.

There was no point in telling him that was exactly what he was doing, so I said, "Nobody in their right mind would leave Auglan loose longer than necessary. However, you want all the Selkrit, and he is my means to get them to you."

"Very well, I will accept that," Quenten desisted. "However, I do not want him escaping."

"If he takes off, I can't stop him. But if your people are in charge of his ship – where can he go? If he stays here, he will be found."

That provoked a reaction – Quenten spoke tersely to Bellus in his own language, forgetting or unaware that I still wore the translator. "Issue orders to all trader ships in the port to lift off."

Bellus bowed slightly and trotted into the shuttle.

Quenten withdrew into the palace and the hunters entered the shuttle to head to the last location that Quenten had discovered.

Whilst my warriors were tracking and scouting to find the camp, I sat with Teregan and helped to reinforce his state of calm. Auglan was active and, I hoped, moving to visit one of his illegal claims.

Teregan alerted me when he began to have visions of places outside the shuttle. I studied what I saw in his mind until I found a definite landmark.

"Yes," I hissed, and I shared the picture with Jenha.

We reached each subsequent camp to find Auglan had thoroughly scared his teams into ignoring petty discomforts, then angered them and left. Some of the personnel had been punished for things they had told him were not their fault.

The relatively innocent Selkrit were in shock, and the less innocent were angry. Many were more than willing to speak against Auglan if it meant the Enforcers would treat them better. The few who knew the most in each group kept quiet. They quickly realised that the Enforcers were not on the side of the Selkrit.

By the end of the day, I had more pictures than we could deal with. We went to five of the places and still had six more to go. As far as I could tell, Auglan was not aware that we had been to these places after he had left.

On the journey back to the palace with a full hold of prisoners, I sensed Teregan's rising anger. I was prepared for it, and held his arm in a firm grip. Jenha moved seats to be on Teregan's other side. To me it was evident that Auglan had arrived at one of the camps to find the men and mined ore gone, with evidence of our presence, both Atapi and Enforcers.

I concentrated on deepening the link, as I had last night. Auglan was in his shuttle. Either it was flying itself or the pilot was keeping well away from his passenger. Either way, Auglan was alone, and trying to reach the camps that had not answered the previous night. He called out an order for the pilot to go to one of those places. He was muttering to himself, and some of it was understandable. He was going to grab what he could and run. He wanted to 'fix' everyone on Korvu who had stopped him.

I didn't realise that the link to Auglan was affecting me until I felt Jenha's hand on my arm.

"The man is insane," I said with a shudder. "He plans to flee with what he can, but wants to destroy everyone who thwarted him."

Jenha released me when he sensed I was calmer. He went and spoke to Bellus before returning to his seat. Teregan was wide-eyed and looking like he did not want to be near me.

I heard Jenha speaking to my mind telling me, "You were almost buzzing with power."

I still felt that way when I left the shuttle, and it did not abate as I strode to my temporary camp.

CHAPTER 68 – Jai Cassidy – POV

Larcia roused in my mind as I sat eating fire-roasted hopper. Her anger matched mine – I felt the uproar from the Old One's land. Without stopping to think, I stood and tossed the half-eaten haunch of meat in the fire. I didn't need a picture to walk to; the pull of the agony of the injured Atapi was enough.

Whether it was caused by a bomb or some other weapon, the whole area was aflame and burning furiously. I felt the Old One working to quell the fire and I wasn't going to interfere with that. My concern was with the injured – the line of agonised bodies that had been pulled from the flames. I went to the first and began. All the while, as I was using the aura to heal what I could, I was aware of the Old One's volcanic anger. I didn't want him to notice me because, despite what I was doing, he would not appreciate me being there.

Some females ran up to help with the injured. At first thinking I was a stranger, they challenged me. When I turned, some of them recognised me and told the rest how they had seen me come back from near death. Now they hoped I could help their kinfolk do the same.

As I worked, I wondered how these twenty warriors had been in a position to be harmed. Surely Con had warned all the tribes.

The flames grew less intense and died to embers, with fresher air beginning to replace the smoke. The Old One strode around inside the burnt area, unmindful and unharmed by the extreme heat of the scorched ground.

I continued to work my way down the line of injured warriors until he grasped me by the back of my tunic and lifted me high enough to dangle. I really hated that.

"You are not welcome here!"

The Old One's female folk dared to protest. "Majestic One, she is healing these injured warriors faster than we could. And she is teaching us things that we had not known."

The sorcerer considered the injured and then me. "This will not make me a friend of yours, and it will not make me think better of you."

"I don't expect you to," I glared at him. "But I wouldn't think much of myself if I hadn't come."

Without another word, he lowered and released me, then stalked off. I had expected him to drop me, so perhaps he was a little grateful.

Just as I had done what I could for the last of the victims, and had finished tying the healing into the aura, I sensed the Old One standing behind me again. His anger was still simmering. I stood up to face him, and he punched me so I fell back onto my bottom.

"You knew of this!" he accused. "Con Ansuni said you warned him. How did you know?"

"I did not know," I said defensively. "But it seemed likely the bastard would strike somewhere. The leader of the blue aliens – the one who sent the intruders and creatures…"

"I will have his liver and grill it!" the Old One snarled. "Do you know where he is?"

"No. The coward is hiding from the Enforcers and anyone who might sneer at him for being a half-man."

"Then we will leave this plane now, tonight, before any more Atapi die."

"Your injured cannot be moved yet. I have tied the healing into the aura," I told him.

"You work sorcery on my land!" he roared.

"Healing! Females' magic, not sorcery," I said quickly, trying to crawl backwards away from him.

The Old One considered the distinction. "How can you know the mind of the evil one?"

"A talented whelp of my tribe tasted his blood. Through him, I can sense the blue alien's mind. With this thing the Enforcers use, I can understand his words."

The Old One growled, still angry.

I quickly went on, "He does not know I am using him to find the rest of his servants. When I have finished finding all of them, I will find him."

"I demand a piece of him," the Old One snarled.

"The Enforcers want him alive and able to answer questions. They want to know who put him up to coming here."

"And then what?"

I told him what I thought would happen to Auglan, including the fact that if Obaki had not made certain 'alterations' to him, Galactic judges would have ordered it be done anyway.

The Old one growled, but seemed less threatening to me. "When he is the only one left, you and I will hunt."

"All the sorcerers," I suggested. "One alien will not be easy to find."

"Yes, we will all hunt and you will be bait. He hates you enough to find you irresistible."

"If he is wise, he will not take the bait," I said, not liking the idea.

From the snarl-grin directed at me, the Old One did not think the alien would be wise.

"When we are rid of him, we will leave," he stated.

After visiting the last six alien camps that I knew of, I was glad to return to my temporary camp away from the palace. Teregan was my shadow, no longer fearing the power he sensed in me. He was more afraid of the visions he was receiving from Auglan. I wished I didn't need to force him to keep having them – however, he was my only link to that revolting creature.

My much-reduced tribe, except for one sentry, was asleep, and Teregan was not far off, when I sat and mentally evoked Larcia.

"Daughter, your warriors hunted well."

"I know. Do you think we got them all, except for one?"

"If any others are left, they will not survive on their own," Larcia promised. "Will you undo your rituals?"

I had unravelled most of the rituals, but not all. "Yes, I will. Not all aliens are bad for this world – me for example."

There was a vague sense of amusement from Larcia as I concentrated.

"Can you feel where that last alien is?" I asked, hoping it would be that easy. It wasn't. I sighed – it looked like I was going to have to be bait. I was not going to let him stay free.

Teregan was not quite asleep, so I turned my attention to what he might be sensing from Auglan. I evoked an image of the Selkrit and began to be aware of him. He was tired and his day had been very satisfying, having quenched his anger by punishing his weak underlings. His mind seemed to be calculating profits based on the camps he had been to. It had not yet occurred to him that more might have been raided.

I didn't try to provoke him into action, but after a while he began calling his camps. None answered him. He yelled for some subordinate, who arrived with wise promptness.

"Check the communicator," he ordered.

The man departed and returned, reporting that the communicator was functioning perfectly. Auglan tried calling several places again with the same lack of result. He then called his orbiting ship, and the reply came promptly. He asked for a report on the Enforcer ship and was gratified to hear that it was still in the same holding orbit, not doing anything suspicious.

Auglan then told the ship's officer to be ready to break orbit – he intended to leave soon. When asked if they needed to recall all groups, he merely said he would do that, but to send down the large shuttle in stealth mode.

I smiled to myself grimly, knowing the Enforcers were in charge of the orbiting ship. Should he flee, he would be caught, but I wanted him first.

Very carefully, I inserted into his mind a fleeting picture of me and sent the infuriating and malicious laugh that aggravated male sorcerers. Auglan thought it was a memory of his own and squashed it immediately. I waited a while and repeated it. He remembered I had been at one of the raided camps, and he suddenly had the thought that all his camps had been found. He felt terror then, for himself, and that was followed by a killing rage. I let him consider what he would like to do to me until I heard Teregan begin to whimper in fear – so instead I insinuated an idea of where Auglan could find me.

He thought immediately of the compound where he knew my tribe had been when he was last there. He brooded on the wisdom of trying to destroy it, as it was close to where one of the Enforcer shuttles was parked. He considered destroying that, too – but he knew more about the Enforcers than I did, and quickly decided that would be a bad, bad idea.

My preference for a confrontation was somewhere near the Rock of Arkor. Not only was I close to the protection of Larcia there, but all the sorcerers would meet there without recalling inter-tribe feuds. I wanted all the sorcerers to be utterly sure of the guilt of the Selkrit and the innocence of the Kumatan. After a while, I inserted a brief flash of a picture of the Rock into his mind. I felt him pounce on the idea and recall how the Kimh had said the area was sacred to the Atapi. He pictured blasting it to rubble.

I knew that with Larcia there, and the strength of the aura, the Rock would not be damaged.

That was enough, I decided. I shielded Teregan's mind, and he quickly fell into deep sleep. I hadn't finished, though. I mentally called Jenha, and found that he had not yet retired for the night. I sensed he was involved in something important. He let me know he would be free in a few moments.

I waited. I did not expect Auglan to act immediately, nor to be close to the palace and the Enforcer ship. When I felt Jenha's mind, it was a calm haven compared to that of the Selkrit's.

Without mentioning I had provoked the idea, I told Jenha what I has sensed from Auglan – from his intent to flee, to his intent to get me. I warned him that Auglan might decide to firebomb the compound or something.

"Do you want him to know that he failed to get you?" Jenha asked, startling me.

"You know me too well. Yes, though not blatantly. I thought perhaps that Bellus could report to the orbiting Enforcer ship in an easily broken code that I had left the compound and the place was empty. Perhaps he could also suggest they try to find me near the Rock of Arkor."

I sensed that Jenha was trying to deduce my next move. "Be careful," he warned me.

"I won't be alone."

"Enforcers?" Jenha queried.

"Only if they can't be seen. I'd prefer Bellus and Terr if given a choice. And only if they keep out of it."

"Your reason?"

"To convince the sorcerers that it wasn't the Kimh or Kumatan that have been attacking them."

"The Ambassador must know of this," Jenha warned.

"He would anyway, he still has that damn tracer on me," I agreed irritably. "Just tell him that Auglan will be in a condition to answer questions."

Jenha kept his mind controlled. If he suspected what I intended, he made no comment or admission. All he said was, "I will advise the Ambassador."

The expected attack came before dawn, waking all of us. Within minutes, I saw the Enforcer shuttle rising from the palace grounds and flying off. Our compound was now a blazing inferno. More than just the wooden buildings were burning. The palace beyond was illuminated by flames, but untouched. The same could not be said for a large area of the palace gardens.

While all attention would be on the fire, I called Con Ansuni. I gave him the image for my small camp, and he arrived quickly, immediately aware of the fire.

"Auglan is out to get me," I told him. "The rest of my warriors are ready to leave."

The three eldest warriors stepped forward and Ketali spoke for them. All bowed. "We will serve you Master Con, but our loyalty is first to Jai-devil."

"I will accept that," Con agreed, and then he turned his attention to my shadow.

"Teregan." I called the whelp forward. He was shy of the older sorcerer, even though they had met. "I want you to learn from Con Ansuni. I trust him to teach you well – to be a warrior and a sorcerer. I cannot do that – not yet."

"My mother…" Teregan ventured.

"She knows my will on this," I told him.

"But…"

"No buts. You will be training with Litok."

Con took Teregan by the arm as he opened the pass-through to his tribe. When the last of my warriors had gone, the pass-through vanished. I was alone.

There was no reason to stay there. I collected a few essentials – blankets, a pot, food, water-skin – and 'walked' to Arkor.

My new camp was a lean-to shelter up against the base of the Rock where I could easily slip into Larcia's cave. I fetched branches and leaves from elsewhere to make the roof and then threw one of my blankets over it. On top of all that, I tossed lots of sand. It was not perfectly camouflaged, but neither was it extremely obvious. I didn't want it to be too easy to find, as that might make Auglan suspicious. I wanted him to waste time looking for me.

I had given thought to what he might do when he found it – perhaps something sneaky, like landing out of sight and creeping up on me. He might try to bomb or burn me – but he would want to be sure I was there first.

However it went, I was ready. I had created a bubble of protection and shrunk it to be close to my skin. With so much energy around me to draw on, nothing would get through it. That gave me a sense of security that was ten times better than having twenty sorcerers nearby, hidden in the aura. I doubted if any of them would mourn me if Auglan killed me.

The Selkrit shuttle, if it came here, probably had a way to hide its presence – some kind of mechanical illusion. It might not make much noise either – their helicopters were very quiet compared to the one I had heard back on Earth. If I could hear it, but not see it, it wouldn't be surprising if I emerged from my shelter to look for it.

In fact, I sensed it long before I heard anything, and when it felt close, it seemed to be zig-zagging over the Rock. When the pilot spotted me, the noise seemed to hover a moment before the shuttle sped off.

Moments later, it came speeding in from the east, out of the sun, right at me. When it was close, it suddenly became visible. Bellus, hiding in the Enforcer's cloaked shuttle, had used his fancy weapon on it. I smiled maliciously.

The sound of the shuttle engine stopped, and the quiet was eerie. The shuttle kept gliding towards me, as two objects ejected into the air and began to float down on parachutes. The shuttle crashed into the Rock and exploded, sending burning wreckage down the side of the Rock and onto my shelter. I ran out of the way, staring at the wreck and my burning camp, seemingly unaware of the people approaching from above.

Both Auglan and his pilot landed behind me and I spun around. The Selkrit Councillor's expression was feral as he released his parachute with one hand and aimed a weapon at me with the other. The pilot was eyeing me with something more akin to confusion, as if wondering why Auglan was threatening me.

"Don't try to run anywhere, you little freak," I was warned. "You won't get five yards."

I simply glared back at Auglan and then glanced upward as if expecting help or more intruders. It was a move to let him spot the tracer embedded in my throat. I doubted that he would see the wire frame of the translator that was now able to transmit sound.

The second Selkrit was circling behind me, but I gave no sign that I knew that. When Auglan moved towards me, I moved back until the pilot caught me around the neck with a strong arm. As I tried to remove his arm, Auglan ran forward and squirted my neck with liquid from a tiny canister.

"So much for the tracer," Auglan snarled. "They won't have pinpointed you yet."

"I've been here since last night, creep," I told him.

"I stand by my comment. They can't locate you this close to this pile of stone."

"You can bet the farm that they do know," I retorted. "But this way, they won't know that I killed you."

The arm around my neck tightened, but I was only pretending to be afraid and helpless.

"What a laugh," Auglan sneered. "You can't go anywhere…"

His face turned to one of alarm when his pilot suddenly released me and collapsed to the ground. There was no one else in sight. Auglan still had his weapon aimed at me; still felt he had the upper hand.

I straightened and moved towards him. "You're next," I told him. "All your other stooges are in Enforcer custody and they will be here soon to get you. They know that you sent those feral beasts, and infiltrators, onto Atapi lands. Crimes, those are."

Auglan's anger was simmering. "I bombed your tribe," he told me.

"You bombed an empty compound," I corrected. "I donated my tribe to a worthy sorcerer, and my few remaining warriors were out hunting blue-blooded aliens."

"I didn't miss on the other tribes," he claimed.

"Liar! All the tribes moved after they hunted out your infiltrators and gave them to the Enforcers."

"I do not believe you. Those lizards won't go near the Enforcers."

"I changed their minds, and I also found the location of all your camps from your very own mind. You can check if you like. All the live prisoners caught by my warriors are missing little pieces – trophies you know."

The mention of 'missing pieces' enraged Auglan beyond reason.

"You," he spat. "You are meat." He sprang at me, only to be jerked up short

I smiled at him, and I knew it wasn't a nice smile. "Sorry to disappoint you."

Only then did Auglan see the ring of Atapi sorcerers as they emerged from the aura.

"It won't be me dying a thousand deaths this day," I told him maliciously. "And there will be no Enforcers around for you to bleat to, half man, even if you dared. You would have done better to have given yourself up to them."

He spat at me again. I moved my head to avoid the spittle. "I am glad you didn't. It would have been too easy. All they would have done is humiliate, discredit and exile you. We did save them the necessity of neutering you. They would have done that, you know. It is the punishment for what you tried to do to me."

"Why didn't they neuter you, you abomination?" Auglan struggled to get to me, but Con Ansuni had a very strong grip.

"Because it wasn't I who attacked you. I had healed Obaki, the old warrior. He took exception to what you tried to do to me. And you were warned."

Auglan spat again and tried to look around. He didn't have many escape options. His shuttle was wrecked and his pilot probably dead.

"What do you want?" Auglan demanded. "I can pay you whatever you like – if you let me go."

"I know what I would like, but I am not the one in charge here. I promised these sorcerers a chance for some Atapi retribution – on the creature that caused them so much irritation. And as you implied, Atapi don't like aliens."

"The Enforcers will come," Auglan yelled, forgetting that he had earlier claimed the opposite. "They will punish you all for this…"

"Really?" I interrupted. "They know what crimes you have committed here. They know how you made the Atapi and Kumatan attack each other. There are Galactic laws about that. The ones so ill-treated have a right to punish you."

I walked off and gestured to Inrak, the lowest ranked sorcerer. I turned my back and allowed him to begin. When Auglan began to scream like a dying hopper, I walked back to him.

"What a weakling you are, half man. When we finish here, the Enforcers can have you and everyone will know what a foul creature you are."

"Make him stop," Auglan begged.

Since Inrak was only giving him a beating, I was in no hurry to stop it. "We have only just started, creep."

When Inrak moved back, the Old One walked closer and suggested, "Stake the meat to the ground. It is beneath our dignity to hold him erect."

Two of the sorcerers carried out the suggestion, quickly and efficiently taking Auglan from Con and effecting the change in position.

The next lowest ranked sorcerer approached and again I walked away. Sastek knew how to summon ants from the ground and proceeded to do so. The ants naturally relished the source of meat as Sastek whispered insults at his victim. Auglan's screams took on a higher pitch. I let them continue until they got on my nerves. At my gesture, Sastek sent the ants back into the ground.

I had my suspicions, due to the fact that his screaming stopped as soon as the ants stopped biting. I went to stand over him. "You think that it's over, do you? Those little insects put poison in their meat to break it down. Within hours, your skin is going to bubble into blisters and begin to break down. Then you will know what agony is."

Every one of the sorcerers wanted a piece of Auglan, but they knew we were to keep him alive and they knew that Bellus was observing. They were enjoying this. I personally detested Auglan, but did not feel the same degree of antipathy for the men he had used. The innocent, well-intentioned scientists and engineers would fare best in the hands of the Enforcers. Most of the rest were criminals, lured by the promise of riches. Some were out and out psychopaths. If they had Galactic records, they would have death sentences at worst, or end up like Auglan at best.

After each sorcerer had finished his piece of revenge, I goaded Auglan with how helpless he was. I knew Bellus had questions for him, but I was not ready to ask them yet. At the present, nothing that Auglan was being subjected to was likely to be fatal – unless he died of fright. But I intended for Auglan to be a quivering wreck by the end of this, and preferring the Enforcers to the Atapi. I had learnt that part of the '1000 deaths' ritual was to make an endless mental loop – so that the victim relived each torture repeatedly.

By the time the fourth sorcerer was finished, I had had enough of the screaming. But it was only noise – I could tolerate that.

"I was lying you know," I told Auglan casually. "I can call the Enforcers here if I want to, but I don't."

"Liar," he screamed at me with foam flecking his mouth. "You don't dare. They would shoot you all for this."

"I would dare and I am not afraid of them. But you fixed the tracer – too bad."

I decided that I needed a bit more power over Auglan. I dipped the tip of one finger into a cut still oozing blood from the beating Inrak had given him. I touched it to my tongue. It tasted vile, but the mind link was instantaneous. I wondered if the other sorcerers should do this, too, as it would increase the effect of what I had planned. Perhaps.

To the fifth sorcerer, I whispered questions to ask the prisoner while he worked his punishment. I didn't expect Auglan to answer, but I hoped to get images and thoughts. The first question was why had he come here and what was he after?

My suspicions were confirmed. The screams were deliberate and he was trying mind games on me. That made tolerating his screams so much easier. Each of the next sorcerers whispered curses, insults and questions. Auglan maintained silence as far as the questions went, but his mind produced pictures. I described what I could understand to Bellus via the translator.

When it was his turn, Con Ansuni approached with deliberate intent. He had suffered from Auglan's scheming more than every other sorcerer except for the Old One. In those few moments, he reminded me of his unlamented sire, Stak. First, he slit open the Selkrit's remaining clothing, even the light armour under the shirt top. He exposed the Selkrit to the merciless hot sun of Korvu and the ring of hostile watchers. Then he made his hands hot enough to burn and placed them in all of Auglan's most sensitive places, branding him over and over with his hand prints. I felt that Con's deliberate actions were more terrifying than the actions of all who had preceded him. The others had been angry, as was Con, but my uncle had his anger controlled. This was more terrifying than Stak's malice when he had done this to me. This time, the screams were real.

I glanced over to where I knew Bellus was watching, and gestured him over. When Auglan stopped whimpering and looked at me, he saw Bellus, too.

"Arrest her," Auglan demanded. "You can see what she is doing to me."

"Jai Cassidy has done nothing to you," Bellus stated.

"Yet," I told Auglan's mind.

"I request your mercy." Auglan tried to claim the protection of the Galactic Council, as I had done.

"Knowing what I do of you, Fascian Naziere," said Bellus, using Auglan's original name deliberately, "I require a token of good faith."

Auglan took that to mean Bellus wanted a bribe, so offered him wealth.

The Enforcer ignored the offer and asked, "Who financed this plundering trip?"

The prisoner snapped his mouth shut.

I said in a deceptively mild tone, "I think I will let the rest of my friends try harder. He is less afraid of us and the Enforcers than his backer. I have some quite interesting ideas now."

"Continue," Bellus directed, walking back out of the way.

"Wait," Auglan shouted, to no avail. The next sorcerer moved closer as Con and I moved back.

After that, I suggested to Auglan, "Tell Bellus what he wants to know and he will stop this." I was quite sure he wouldn't give in to me. He didn't. He began cursing in his own language. It must have lost something in the translation, for I did not react as he expected.

"Get Bellus here," Auglan demanded.

"Talk and he will come," I countered.

Finally, only the Old One and I remained. All the other sorcerers had been sent back to prepare their tribes to leave.

It was my turn. I walked over to where the creature was staked to the ground, and stared at the fully exposed meat that was Auglan. He found the energy and the moisture to spit.

"Like what you see?" Auglan taunted. "Want more of it?"

I knew what he implied and suggested, "Slice by slice. I can make sure you don't die too quickly." My tone was deadly serious.

"Pack of cowards," Auglan snarled. "If I was free, I would neuter the lot of you."

The Old One came up behind me and whispered suggestively, "Are you going to take these insults, Jai-devil, after all he has done to you?"

I sensed that as much as the Old one was enjoying seeing Auglan suffer, he was intent on testing me. He slashed the bindings holding Auglan down and walked away contemptuously.

If I thought Auglan was beaten, I found out I was wrong. Those Selkrit must be tough. He rolled and pushed himself up, shook off the tatters of his clothes and faced me with blazing eyes of hate. I didn't dare back away, so I stood ready to react to his attack – assuming he could do more than glare.

"There is more than one way to punish a female," Auglan promised me. He began to describe them.

"Talk is cheap," I interrupted him. I forced a laugh as I looked him up and down dismissively. "You couldn't catch me if I chose to run, half man. And when it comes to torture, you are an amateur compared to Stacion Ansuni."

He sprang for my throat and pushed me over, straddling me. "I don't see the Centurion racing over to help you."

He was squeezing my neck as hard as he could. I felt some pressure, but my protection was holding.

"I don't need his help," I told him, and I attacked with the only weapon I could use at that moment – my mind. I had a direct link to him now. I didn't need to go through the mind of an innocent child, and he had no defences.

I hit him with my empathy, sending to him memories of all the pain and humiliation that I had endured, all the suffering of the Old One's injured tribesmen, and the anger of the sorcerers. With his vulnerable mind completely open, I dredged from his memories all of the horrid things he had done to females, all the crimes he had got away with. Then I made him feel all the tortures he had committed in the past, as well as all the ones just inflicted. He would feel the suffering of his victims repeatedly – as though they were being done to him.

His hands went limp, and his hideous bulk collapsed onto me. His depraved memories and his fear-stink sickened me.

This time, his pitiful, "Make them go away," was genuine, and it left me unmoved. I whispered to his mind how to stop it. "They will only go away when you confess each and every crime to the Enforcers. Until then you will experience them in a never-ending cycle. To end it all, you must answer, honestly and fully, every question the Enforcers put to you. And you know what? You won't be able to kill yourself."

The meat on me was a quivering wreck, just short of completely losing control of his bodily functions, only because I didn't want to wear it. I saw Centurion Bellus approaching. The Old One had done nothing yet. He arrived first, lifted the meat off me, and tossed it aside to land at the feet of the Enforcer. I pushed myself to my feet.

"What have you done to him, Jai Cassidy?" Bellus asked.

"You will find him ready to confess every real or fantasised crime he has ever committed."

"Please, please, take me away," Auglan whimpered. "I will tell you everything you want to know."

"Starting with your backer," I said, and told Bellus the name I had found in his mind.

The Old One spat in Auglan's face. "You let a young, human female get the better of you, vermin."

"You are to be commended," Bellus told me. "Your restraint is admirable."

"Get the damn tracer off me," I demanded, ignoring his commendation. "I did what I promised you. Now I have to finish what I promised the Kimh."

Bellus took on a listening pose. I assumed he was asking permission from Quenten. The Old One wasn't going away.

CHAPTER 69 – Jai Cassidy – POV

The alarm came into my mind as a mental scream. "Farcine!" I said, reaching to find out what was wrong. I felt nothing. I began to move, to walk back to the palace. The Old One stopped me.

"Wait here," Bellus told me. He hefted Auglan as if he were a child and strode to his now visible shuttle. He returned after a short time, and came up to me and forced my chin up. He placed a device over the tracer. A coin-sized piece of metal fell into his hand.

"You are free to go, Jai Cassidy. Our thanks." Bellus strode off.

I tried to shake the Old One off. My mind was still trying to reach for Farcine.

"Jai-devil," the Old One stated, but I hardly heard him. I was forming the visualisation of the palace garden. As I tried to walk forward, something like lightning flicked across my mind. Angered, I spun around, feeling then the grip on my arm and only thinking, "Who dared?"

The Old One's black eyes met mine. "I claim you, Jai-devil. You are mine."

"Of all the lousy timing…" part of my mind thought.

"Master," I bowed acknowledgement. I had promised Larcia that I would let him teach me.

"Where were you planning to go, Jai-devil?"

"Farcine… something happened…"

"She is no longer your concern," the Old One told me.

"But…"

The Old One hit me, a push in the face that sent me stumbling. He stopped me from falling completely, and released me when I was kneeling.

"If I want comments from you, I'll ask for them. Are you going to dispute my authority?"

I shook my head, but it wasn't a gesture he understood. "No," I said.

He hit me again. I was in a no-win situation. He pushed my head down to the ground with brown scaly-skinned foot.

"This is your place now," the Old One told me. "The lowest of my apprentices." He muttered an incantation and removed his foot. "Now, Jai-devil, you will maintain a vigil here until I return. Then you will open the way to the place of sanctuary. It would be wise to renew your energies. Will we be going from within the cave again?"

I didn't dare speak. He had asked a question, not told me to answer.

"Tell me what you intend?" the Old One invited.

I lifted my head, but stayed kneeling.

"Larcia's Cave is not for lesser eyes," I said. "I could make a pass-through from each tribe's land…"

"No."

"Or I can make one here where the power of the aura is strongest. I would use a portal made of two uprights and a cross beam over the top. Something is needed for the lesser Atapi to see where to go."

The Old One considered. "That is acceptable. Wait here, Jai-devil."

It was an order I dared not disobey. "Yes, Master."

I stayed where I was, still kneeling. When I was alone, I invoked Larcia.

"Daughter," she said in my mind.

"Larcia, could you look out for Farcine? Something has happened to her."

"She has invoked my name, but if she is within the Kimh palace, I cannot sense her."

I had hoped otherwise, but I had to accept that.

It worried me that I could not reach her mind. I did not know if she were dead or unconscious. I kept trying to reach Jenha as well, but I sensed nothing from him either.

From the changing shadows, I knew several hours had past. I finally felt the mind of Farcine, and it was full of pain. Involuntarily I stood up, then had to force myself to stay.

"Jai-devil," the Old One spoke. "The portal will be erected soon – are you ready?"

"Please, I have to go…"

"No!"

I felt the Old One grip my arm and then bite it. He licked the blood and I felt the force of his mind. I still struggled in his grip.

"I have claimed you, Jai-devil," the Old One reminded me. "You will not go back to the place of the thin skins."

"But Farcine – the High Minister is torturing her. She does not deserve that!" I rebelled.

"Did you not claim to have the concern for the welfare of all Atapi? One old female is nothing if all the tribes die out. Only you can open the way from here to the safe place. Do it now!"

I stood staring at him.

I was aware of Con Ansuni approaching. He bowed to the Old One, who was still glaring at me. He asked permission to speak to me.

"I know about the Elder Mother," Con told me and I turned to look at him. "You can do nothing for her. Let Jenha do what is needed. He promised her protection, did he not?"

"Koenig is mad!" I turned my anguish on him.

"Farcine is kin to me, too. I know she would not thank you for risking yourself for her. It is what the mad one wants – to make you come. Let those who are staying be with her."

"Who?" I drooped in the Old One's grip.

"Teresa and three old warriors," Con told me.

"And the rest of the neutered ones?" the Old One demanded.

"Most are young, born elsewhere. I will retrain them. The females have their uses, and the whelps will be trained properly. All are kin to me and not blooded to Jai-devil."

I felt a mental flick from the Old One for stupidity. "Jai-devil has a lot to learn," he said aloud. "Bah! Worthless you are! I will kill you within a week." He threw me down to the ground and stood over me.

I felt tears of helpless frustration running down my cheeks.

"Jai-devil, you will open the pass-through as soon as the portal is completed."

The Old One stalked off, but Con remained.

"If he did not want something of you, Jai-devil, you would not still be alive. It is only because he is the Old One that he will take you on."

"Larcia spoke to him. He felt her power in me and wants it."

"It is as I told you," Con agreed. "Jai-devil, trust Jenha. You must not go back because, if you do, you will not return. You must be with us. You told me that for the Atapi to regain their rightful place as equals of Kimh and Kumatan, it must be on this plane. If you are not with us, helping us grow strong, how can we return?"

"The Old One has the power to do it," I admitted.

"Are you sure? You said we should not return merely to have our revenge on other races, but when the need is sufficient to earn our place."

I then felt Larcia confirm the rightness of that. She promised that the sacrifice of those staying behind would be remembered forever in the Rock of Arkor.

"How did you get to know me so well?" I asked Con.

"I knew your mother," he said quietly. "You are worthy of her."

I stopped resisting and climbed to my feet. I gave him a slight bow of respect and turned to follow the Old One, resolving to accept whatever punishment this behaviour warranted. I wished I could have reached out to Jenha to ask him to help Farcine, but since the moment that the Old One had tasted my blood, I had been unable to reach him. I felt bereft, as if Jenha had died.

From my position as the Old One's shadow, I watched all the tribes assembling. Every lesser Atapi – male, female and whelp – were carrying things they wanted to bring, or things not replaceable in a new virgin country.

The Old One's throne-like chair had been brought to the Rock. When he sat there, I sat at his feet.

As soon as all the tribes had arrived, he stood.

"Begin, Jai-devil."

I scrambled to my feet and followed the Old One to the newly erected portal. He watched as I created the pass-through – watched and learned. I did it differently to the Atapi sorcerers, but then I had learnt from Jenha.

The instant the pass-through was open, he sent his tribe through in the charge of his older apprentices.

"Go at once to the land of our tribe. Use the same landmarks. Take the tribe there."

I figured that he wanted to keep an eye on me.

Twenty tribes, and all their belongings, took a while to pass through the narrow opening. Holding the pass-through open was draining, but I'd used the most power opening it. At least I could use the aura from the Rock to help me.

During this time, I considered that the Old One's apprentices would be busy for a very long time. I did not know if any of them could open a pass-through, but if they couldn't, they would have to 'walk' all the tribe's folk there.

The day was well-advanced when the last sorcerer followed his tribe through. The Old One went next and called me through. As soon as I was through, the pass-through collapsed, and I wanted to do the same. I had to draw on the aura to get the strength to walk. The Old One took me to his land.

The scene we arrived to was one of frenetic activity. The village was being made to resemble the one they had just left. Hunters were returning with meat for a feast. The females were preparing roots and plants.

Five apprentice sorcerers presented themselves as soon as the Old One sat in the throne chair. I stayed standing.

"Milben, Vidor, Banus, Lixmar, Saneel." As the Old One named each, they bowed faintly. "Jai-devil," he said, introducing me to the others. He seemed amused by the odd looks they gave me. I was too tired to care – but I glared back, daring them to try anything.

"Sit, Jai-devil," he pointed to the ground right of his feet. He waved at his apprentices, and they seated themselves on either side of the Old One.

I merely listened while the Old One questioned his apprentices about things that meant nothing to me. In fact, I was almost asleep until the smell of cooked food roused me.

The females served food to the Old One first, and then to his surprise, they served me. As the newest apprentice, I should have ranked after the others. The server told the old One that as I had saved twenty warriors, and delivered the tribe from the yoke of the Kimh, I was due the honour.

My fellow apprentices grumbled, but I ignored them. I was ravenous.

The meal was truly a feast, and afterwards, when all could relax, the tribe seemed to be in an unusual mood. I decided they were celebrating. I had never seen such behaviour before, and it was heartening. The young sorcerers went and joined in some kind of dancing, and they all had young females flocking around them.

I felt myself wanting to nod off again, but when the Old One rose, I forced myself up. He told me to follow him, and we left the gathering. He led the way to a cave, already prepared. He pointed to a sleeping mat over near one wall, away from the others. I teetered over to it and was past ready to crawl onto it and sleep.

CHAPTER 70 – Jai Cassidy – POV

Noises from outside the Old One's lair woke me. I looked around. Light was coming from the entrance to the cave, lighting up the interior. I could see where the other five apprentices and the Old One had slept. The bed pads were haphazardly arranged.

Since I had a rather urgent natural need, I rose and went to find the females, asking the question of where I could go. A young female showed me the way.

On my return, I went by the cook fires and asked about breakfast, which I seemed to have slept through. I received a hunk of crude grain bread and a mug of water.

The noise that had awoken me was still at the same level, and I went to see the cause. Two young warriors were having a wrestling contest, while The Old One watched intently.

I didn't know what was expected of me, and since my master was occupied, I entertained the idea of crossing back to the other plane. Just a very quick visit to be sure Farcine was all right. A quick flit to the Rock of Arkor, and then to the other plane and the palace… I could be back before anyone missed me.

The picture was in my mind and I was taking the first step when I walked into Milben, the oldest apprentice sorcerer.

"Going somewhere?"

"Not really," I lied. "Am I meant to be somewhere?"

"Our master wants you. He doesn't like being kept waiting."

"Fine, I'll go see what he wants, then."

Milben stepped aside, but followed me.

I walked up to the Old One and waited to be noticed. He took his eyes from the wrestling warriors and I bowed a greeting. Before I could straighten up, he took control of my body, and I felt his mind in mine.

"I thought so," the Old One said to me. He flicked a gesture with his tail, and Milben trotted off.

I had the absolute conviction that he knew what I had thought of doing. He released my muscles.

"Come with me," I was told.

We went back to the Old One's lair, where the untidy mess was now tidy. He pointed to a spot in the middle of the cleared rock floor. "Sit there!"

I sat, and he stood over me and glared down. "I will tell you this only once, Jai-devil. Female you might be, but I agreed to train you, and you will be treated no differently to my other apprentices. You are an ignorant whelp, and you will learn."

"Yes Master," I agreed, sounding meek. He punched my face.

"You will not say 'yes master' with your voice and not your mind," he warned me. "Remember, I blooded you to me. Do you know what that means?"

"Some, Master," I admitted. "You can oversee what I am thinking."

"Then remember this. I do not trust you. I can and I will know what you are thinking at any time of any day. Should you have continued with your intention, I would have been angry and you would have been wise not to come back."

Many things came into my mind, but I quelled them all and made my mind a blank. The Old One seemed satisfied that he had made his point.

"All of the tribe's sorcerers and their apprentices are to meet tonight at Arkor. You will be there, but you will say nothing unless I permit you."

"Yes, Master." This time I meant the agreement.

"Until then, you will train with Musani to prove to me that you have the strength to be a sorcerer."

"Thank you, Master," I told him, hoping I could go soon. I'm sure the Old One sensed it.

"Musani won't take nonsense from anyone — whelp, warrior or female. Now get!"

I went.

Musani eyed me, without emotion. He set me against whelps much younger than I was, and swatted me if I gave my young opponents any advantage. He gradually increased the skill of my opponents, giving me just enough time between each opponent to get my breath back. I discovered that I liked wrestling with these Atapi whelps — at least until I began to be paired with males that were much my age.

They had rules for these matches, though some were obscure — I received some swats for a foul move and I didn't know what I did wrong. Some of the older whelps received hard swats from Musani and others were sent off to do some sort of punishment chore.

My turn came again and I faced a whelp that was older than I was, and this one was an arrogant one.

"Why do you insist on looking like a verminous, weak-skinned Kumatan she-dog?" he greeted me.

"I like this shape," I replied mildly. "Makes my opponents underestimate me." I wasn't going to say that I couldn't change it.

It made this one think he could prove me wrong. He pulled a really nasty move, and it really hurt. He grabbed my front and lower woman parts and squeezed. Then he threw me to the ground. Before he had time to stand over me and crow at my weakness, though, my reflex action had him tripping over my leg, almost falling on me and finding his own delicate parts squeezed as hard.

Musani lifted my opponent, swatted him and tossed him aside. He lifted me by the scruff of the neck and gave me an extra hard swat before dropping me. When I showed no sign of wanting to stand up again, he nudged me with his scaly foot and said, "You will show me that defensive move, Jai-devil."

He didn't sound like he would take 'no' for an answer. A tiny part of my mind was amused by being in a position to teach this Chief Warrior. Another part groaned; my previous opponent was now snarl-grinning at me.

I had never tried to teach that move to a male, and hadn't taught it to a female either – few would be game to use it.

The next ten minutes were spent with me trying to receive the minimum number of kicks, swats and wrenched limbs. At first, I was hesitant about my task, since I did not want to hurt the Chief Warrior. He swatted me for not trying. Finally, he succeeded in making me angry enough to go full strength against him. I know I managed several on-target kicks, but the warrior betrayed no pain. He used the same tactic that the whelp had, so I would react as I had done then and he could try to figure a defence against it.

"Do all human females fight like this?" Musani asked me during one wrestle.

"No," I told him. "But I am not a proper female of any species."

After tossing me yet again, Musani gave me a rest while he went and checked the other trainee warriors and their older opponents. I used the opportunity to try to draw on the aura, though I was finding it harder than normal to do. Still, it was enough to keep me going, or I would not have lasted the three hours of physical activity.

My last young opponent, having recovered from my attention and Musani's swat, crawled over to me.

He hissed, and warned me, "You won't catch me like that again."

"Well, male whelps can learn something from a verminous female," I insulted him. "Don't worry, if try your foul tricks on me again, I have other ways to fix you."

"You don't know when to stop, do you?" he said with distain. "Females can't be warriors or sorcerers."

"You'll see," I promised him.

Musani returned and sent me running from the clearing where we were practicing, to a distant landmark and back. After that, I would be allowed to have food. Since I was already ravenous it was good incentive, but even so I was passed by every other trainee warrior.

I arrived back last. The others all snarl-laughed at me, since they had ensured that little of the food provided was left. I took what scraps remained and made no comment. I was still hungry when I left the eating clearing to go to the privy pit.

In this village, the privy pit was at the back of one of the communal caves at the far end of the village. When I had gone there earlier in the morning, I had discovered that it was situated over an underground river, and had many natural holes in the rock floor to squat over. However, even in the few hours since my earlier visit, some of the male artisans had built low rock walls around the bigger holes that were almost seats. I decided that when they finished, this place would be better than the outhouse on my father's farm back on Earth – even if there was no "ladies' and 'gents' separation.

I assumed that the work being done here was to make this place like its equivalent on the other plane. However, whether that would include a way to have water in here to wash hands in, or something to wipe with, I would have to wait and see. If they didn't, maybe I would suggest it to the artisans.

For now at least, I could go to the lake, a little way out from the village. I'd seen women and young male whelps bringing skins of water from there.

I had more than one reason to go there. First was to wash my hands, as I had been forced to make a habit before I left my father's farm. The second was to find a place where I could bathe. After the intense exercise this morning, and the run before eating, I felt both dusty and sweaty and felt I deserved a quick dip in the lake to clean up and cool down. I didn't even bother undressing.

Several half grown male whelps, not yet old enough to start warrior training, were there filling waterskins. My antics amused them, since Atapi males rarely wash. I was no stranger to their reaction – the 'only morons needed to be washed' comments. But, they could snarl-grin all they liked – I felt gloriously refreshed.

Two of them followed me back to the village and were still laughing and making rude comments when I preceded them into the eating clearing. I had the nasty idea of giving them both a bath next time I found them at the lake.

However, vicarious revenge came almost immediately. One of the Elder Mothers that organised the food for the village, hard their comments, and boxed their ears. She told them that I was not some kind of captured Kumatan slave, but the Old One's newest apprentice. The look of fear they gave me was delicious to observe, as was the decision that these two foolish whelps would have to spend the next moon cycle renovating a cave for me.

From their reaction as they slunk away – some moments of snarling at each other – I decided that their punishment was going to be hard labour.

Once the whelps were out of sight, the Elder Mother gestured to me.

"Come with me, I have more for you to eat."

My stomach instantly growled in anticipation.

"You come any time you are hungry," she invited, before she disappeared into a hut built of mud and branches. She returned with a bundle wrapped in woven fronds. "Those young warriors are too full of themselves. We heard them plan to eat your share, so we only put out plain food for them. We saved this for you."

The Elder Mother opened the bundle and urged, "Eat."

I didn't argue, and wolfed down the savoury meat that was wrapped in coarse bread. "Thank you," I said sincerely, belatedly recognising one of the healers I had met when I'd helped the tribe.

The woman merely smiled back at me and retreated.

I went and re-joined Musani for the afternoon, and he sent me off with an old warrior to learn hunting skills. I sensed the dislike of my new mentor, who did not think it was a woman's place to hunt. He probably didn't think me capable of being quiet and stealthy, and wouldn't allow me to try my human skills. Nor did I have any weapons. Yet, I found his attitude strange, for in Con Ansuni's tribe, the women both hunt for small game and foraged for roots and grains.

He put me in a clump of bushes and told me to stay there. While he went off, I found some roundish rocks and waited in case a hopper or some other small game came into my view. I wasn't expecting it, since I knew how wary animals were on Earth. What I hadn't allowed for was the fact that until yesterday, no large predators had lived on this plane. When my mentor returned for me, I had two squirrel-like rodents and a hopper – all killed by first being stunned by a rock, and finished off by strangulation.

A closed expression on the warrior's face was the only reaction I got. When I returned to the camp, I was glad I hadn't been expected to skin and prepare the carcasses for cooking. That was female's work, and although I had learnt how it was done, I always made a messy job of it.

Milben was sent to fetch me once I had cleaned myself up again after the long afternoon walking and sitting in the hot sun. He found me coming from the river, and made similar derogatory comments about bathing as the youngsters had. I returned his pleasantries with, "That's so you won't smell me when I creep up on you."

Milben growled and told me to hurry, as the Old One was waiting.

My Master was leaning back in his throne chair, watching me approach. I almost felt the eyes prodding me.

"I hear you have some unusual fighting skills," he said, freezing my muscles when I was within speaking distance of him. "Who taught you, Jai-devil?"

"I watched Stak's warriors and whelps when I was meant to be learning to be petrified of the Kumatan."

"His warriors did not teach that move, I think."

"No, Master. I learnt that off my human brothers." I met the gaze of the Old One, almost daring him to disbelieve me.

I hoped that I had done well that day, and that was why I wasn't greeted by scathing remarks. While the afternoon had been boring, I felt that during the morning I had been punished for every little irritation that I had given the Old One, intended or not.

"Remember the lesson, Jai-devil," my master advised me, proving he was still watching my mind.

"I will, Master," I said truthfully, and I felt my muscles released. That was another lesson, learning he could do that to me.

I stayed quiet while eating the meal provided for me, listening to the Old One quizzing the older apprentices about rituals they had been performing that day. From what they said, I knew they had been placing protection spells around the village and a wider area. I had no intention of questioning why I had been told to stay in the camp. I had already guessed that.

My fellow apprentices were currently of the opinion that because I was a female, and some kind of alien, that I couldn't possibly do more than basic sorcery. However, they were all smart enough not to question the fact that I was now their equal and would be taught with them. I wondered if they knew their master could listen to their thoughts. If they didn't, I wasn't going to tell them. Nor was I going to tell them that I could pick up on their thoughts as well.

Milben and Vidor, the two eldest, were planning to make things difficult for me because they thought I was somehow their master's favourite. They saw the Old One keeping me close to him as favouritism, not that I wasn't trusted. Both of them were much older that I was, and taller. Both had wings that were almost fully formed.

After the meal, my Master told me to stay in his large cave. He took his other apprentices away, without enlightening me of where. That meant I had nothing to do until the time we would go to Arkor. At least, sitting near the throne chair, I was able to draw on more of the aura, using Larcia's hidden sword as a conduit. Directly, my ability to re-energise myself was limited and I was sure the Old One was doing that. But Larcia's sword passively collected energy from around about, and the Old One was full of power and energy, as was his throne, which was some kind of power relic.

I doubted that letting me stay there was a kind gesture, so that I could recover from my strenuous day, but I was glad that I could. Whatever was going to occur later at the Rock of Arkor, might well go on for hours. With the cave empty, I could let myself doze off for a while, with the confidence that I would wake when the other apprentices arrived back. The Old One might move silently, but Milben and the others had yet to see the need.

Sure enough, the babble of Milben and Vidor woke me, and I quickly stood up and walked to meet them. They only had moments in which to grab a drink before the Old One took us all to Arkor.

The Old One had a plain 'throne' at the Rock of Arkor. It was placed near to the cave that was equivalent to Larcia's cave back on the other plane. He sat there, and told me to sit to the left of his feet – as usual.

Behind us, the other five apprentices formed an arc, with eight warriors in another arc further back.

While I sat and waited, I was filling my mind with human trivia, deliberately recalling things from Earth. After a while of this, I saw the Old One turn his attention from watching me to his other apprentices. He paid no attention to the stream of arrivals until representatives from all the tribes had arrived. Then, he gave me a sharp jab with his foot to get me to pay attention.

Some sort of signal must have been given, for the sorcerers from all the other tribes came up to the Old One, with their apprentices, in order of their rank, and had a number of their warriors deposit odd shaped, wrapped bundles at his feet. When all had done so, the sorcerers squatted in a semi-circle in front of the throne chair. The warriors and apprentices from each tribe sat behind their sorcerer. I saw Teregan wriggle to where he had a better view from behind Con Ansuni. He snarl grinned at me, but I didn't try to return one of my own. Too many eyes were on me as it was. The scene made me think of a king receiving gifts from his subjects. I squashed the idea that I felt like the king's concubine, before it was a fully formed thought.

The Old One leant forward to talk to those closest to him. "You have all reported your lands to be lush and fertile, untroubled by enemies. I too have found this plane to be superior, with good hunting and verdant vegetation. Jai-devil did as she promised. Our enemies cannot follow us here."

The combined growl from the sorcerers was one of approval.

"This night we create our place here – make our link to the aura – the place to train the young sorcerers who will be our future. Here where no people have been except Atapi, the land is open to the taking. Even lands once shunned on the other plane can be taken once more."

That decision caused comment, but the Old One seemed not to notice.

"Jai-devil, collect these things and follow."

I turned to him and said coldly, "I am not your slave, Old One."

His face didn't change. "No, you are a sorceress that I have agreed to train. Bring what you can carry." He told his other apprentices and the other sorcerers to bring the rest. The warriors were not invited.

As I moved to follow the Old One, I saw one of my warriors. He gave me a brief bow of greeting. The Old One caught the movement and as he stared at the warrior, his eyes went to the fringe of trophies at the warrior's waist. They were, I realised, the little fingers of as many aliens.

The Old One stopped in front of the warrior, and said, "Impressive." He glanced at me and back to the warrior.

I wished I could figure out his thoughts – so I thought at the Old One, "They were never neutered. They were brave to choose to live, not die, and they have served the Atapi well in matching my desire to rid Korvu of those blue aliens."

"I will remember that, Jai-devil," the Old One said aloud. "It seems that being led by a female did not make them weak. I will not be fooled into thinking you are."

"You'd better believe it," I thought.

The Old One led the way to a large open cave on the side of the Rock. Inside was a natural stone chair, and he went to sit on it. He directed those holding bundles to open them. He inspected each offering and then sent them to be stored in one of the smaller niches around the cavern. Woods, furs, crude metals, gemstones and some types of plants – I had no idea of the significance of the items. Saneel, the youngest of the Old One's apprentices, took enjoyment in telling me that they would be used in various rituals.

Once again, I was told to sit by the Old One's feet – within arm's reach, I decided wryly. The sorcerers reformed the half circle around him.

"We are beginning a new era away from those who would see us die out. Once the tribes numbered in the hundreds, now we are only twenty," the Old One announced, holding everyone's attention. "Not all of that was due to the slave-masters and their masters. Some was due to feuds and fighting between tribes. There is no need for that any more. This land is ours and there is space for everybody. I will act against any tribe that wars on another."

That ultimatum pleased me. A few other ideas flitted through my mind, only to vanish when the Old One spoke again.

"To be able to expand and grow more numerous, we need more full sorcerers," he continued. "To achieve that, all the apprentices from all the tribes will come here to learn from all the tribal sorcerers."

My mind recalled 'the dreaming' I had done on the other plane and how the learning of past sorcerers was inscribed on the Rock. We did not have that here. Much knowledge might be lost.

As if echoing my thought, the Old One made the same point. "We cannot afford to hoard secrets. All knowledge, no matter the source, will be shared."

I felt the Old One nudge me with his foot as he allowed murmuring amongst the sorcerers. I knew it would be hard for all of them to share secrets. The Old One placed his scaly hand around the back of my neck and I shivered.

"Teach us to move between planes, Jai-devil."

I felt, then, not only the compulsion of the Old One but also the combined will of the other avidly listening sorcerers. To counter it, I needed every iota of stubborn human determination that I possessed.

"No," I managed to say, and the pressure became a force of anger.

"Speak your mind, Jai-devil," the Old One invited, and I knew my logic had to be faultless.

"It is not something that I know how to teach," I began and that was true enough. "It is essentially the same as how you all got from your new lands to here. Instead of just memorising landmarks, you need to feel the difference between the two places. But I don't think teaching you to do it is a good idea."

The slightest tightening of the Old One's hand warned me that he did not like to be opposed.

"If I could teach you all – every one of you would, at some time, be tempted to go back. Whether it is to perform some barbaric ritual on the Kumatan, or liberate some luxury things from them. I know each of you have excellent memories and much reason to hate the Kimh and Kumatan."

The consensus of the comments was, "With reason."

I went on. "The Kimh dislike Atapi – they also believe it is with reason. The only way to let memories fade is to make a complete break. Right now, they will know we have gone. They don't know where, and are probably scouring the whole planet to be sure this is not one of my tricks. Eventually they will relax because there is no sign of us, and that will make them very happy."

There were growls of anger. I went on quickly. "We know better."

Inrak growled. "The slave masters won't give up."

"No, because if they did – they would be out of a cushy job," I said tartly. "I think I know enough of the Kumatan to say that if there is no sign of us, and no sign of our activities, they will be content. Hasn't that been the case for the last decade or so until those aliens stirred things up?"

The growls now sounded more like grumbles.

"If you go back, and are seen, those others won't relax and feel safe. Koenig will drive them to greater lengths to find us. At least two Traegers who went to Earth know how Stak hid his colony."

Mentioning his name was a mistake. I felt the hand of the Old One spasm, and squeeze my neck.

I forced myself to keep speaking. "If any of us keep returning, they will recall and use that ability. I trust Jenha Mosellan not to try to find us unless ordered by the Kimh. The other I cannot speak for."

Then came the reaction to my mentioning of Jenha. The knowledge that he and I shared a child had spread, and the revulsion at the idea of such a hybrid was intense. The sorcerers recalled that I was a similar abomination.

"Get over it!" I thought sharply. "I exist and I can teach you other things."

"And how do we stop you returning to your…?" Pywuk didn't tone his words down when referring to Jenha. English doesn't have a translation, but consider it more disgusting than 'male whore'.

"I am pledged here," I defended myself. "I know how important it is to stay here."

"Pledged?" Wyvek hissed. "With none, save the Old One, with the power to stop you, and you with too many ties to the old place?"

"I promised the Ancient One, Larcia, I would accept the teaching of the Old One."

Most of the sorcerers considered Larcia a myth. Con Ansuni spoke to me then.

"Can you sense her on this plane?"

"No, but that changes nothing," I claimed.

"How?" Con demanded.

"I brought you here safely. If I was going to jeopardise that, I wouldn't have bothered."

"You could bring us here and go, leaving us with no way back," Wyvek hissed.

"How would any of you lose if that was my intent?" I asked the question, but none of them answered.

Then Con asked, "You told me that Atapi should be equals of Kumatan and Kimh. How can we be that if we are stranded here?"

"I have no intention of stranding us here."

Con persisted. "What if others like those aliens return there again, without us to hunt them out? Will this plane be affected?"

I didn't have an answer for that.

"Jai-devil?" the Old One drew my attention. "Where were you going to go earlier today?" He knew very well, but he wanted me to admit to it.

"I had thought of going back for the sake of the five of my tribe that stayed there."

I didn't like the sound of the low snarls. The other sorcerers did no more than that. I was the Old One's apprentice and he had the right to deal with me. I was still feeling the effects of his lesson, and I now knew he hadn't finished with me. His scathing words had another purpose besides humiliating me.

He began by reminding me that it was not safe for me to return because I had achieved a state of animosity with the High Minister of the Kimh. He reminded me that I would be trapped if the Traegers banded me and they would not let me trick them into removing them.

When he'd finished insulting my intelligence and painting a dire picture, I wanted to shrink into the rock. However, he was not finished. His hand reached down and grabbed my wrist and, before I had even started to think of resisting, he snapped a band of metal around it. I felt my awareness of the aura subsiding.

I was instantly angry at the unfairness of the action and of the public humiliation, but I fumed in silence, quite sure the Old One was aware of it.

Mentally, he told me, "You exaggerate your importance." It was like a slap.

He was right. Everything he said to me, was effectively true for the sorcerer-devils. However, seeming to humiliate me, was a way to say it to all without alienating every one of them.

The Old One was now delivering a new edict. "We will return to the old way of training apprentices. Once, all apprentices were banded." He held up my wrist to show what he meant. "This means that they learn to fully utilise their own innate power before becoming lax and using the aura. Wearing these bands also teaches discipline. Those apprentices without bands will come here."

There was some amusement in watching the reluctance of many of the older apprentices. I was proud to see Teregan stride forward proudly and bow to the Old One. He accepted the band as a symbol of his new status. I didn't dare think at him, but smiled when only he would see.

The Old One's other apprentices didn't need to come forward. I hadn't noticed bands on them when I had seen them during the evening meal, so they must have been given them while I was resting. They were not resenting them as much as I was, but then I knew the power I could wield without them.

Then it occurred to me that Jenha did not draw on the aura as the Atapi did. I also knew how powerful he was. The thought consoled me. Then I remembered that I had been banded on Earth and had got free. In the next instant, something like lightning flicked through my mind and suddenly, I could not remember how I done it.

"Attend!" the Old One said loudly. "We will all take part in building the protections on this cavern."

That meant the apprentices, too, and I was as excited as all the others were. If nothing else, I was determined to do my part well. I noticed Teregan, keeping close to Litok, and paying strict attention to Con, and I did the same to my Master.

That night was the start of a hectic routine – nights of learning, days of sleeping and learning about tribe management. The full sorcerers took turns in teaching rituals to the apprentices. For the most part, the sorcerers ignored the detail of my gender, but they enjoyed seeing me in the inferior position. They had not forgotten that I had won against them by trickery.

Most of the other apprentices either ignored me or, when no one was watching, tried to anger me or disrupt my concentration in order to earn me a reprimand. By accident, I learnt a way to return the favour. It earned me a few blows at first, but once I had convinced everyone that sneezing was something that humans couldn't stop and the more one tried the louder it came out… I had frequent revenge. Since the Atapi had no equivalent reflex, they couldn't disprove my claim. So when I sneezed, timing my 'reflex' to occur at a critical time in a ritual, the annoying apprentices were in turn reprimanded for their lack of concentration. I didn't feel at all guilty about it. After all, a sorcerer fighting to protect his tribe for instance, would need to be able to complete it even when there were distractions all around. It might be the difference between life and death one day.

Teregan never tried to get me in trouble, and he usually kept away from me. He was another target for the more experienced apprentices. When I could do so unobserved, I taught him things that the others still didn't know, and enjoyed the outcome when the bullies were confounded.

As a very new apprentice, I knew I had a lot to learn. Older apprentices would brag about their skills with one another. I didn't. I learnt quietly, practiced in private and moved on. None of the others had any idea how fast I was learning or how much I already knew.

Several cycles of seasons passed. I survived.

CHAPTER 71 – Jai Cassidy – POV

Dawn was still a long way off and I, who had been learning rituals for weather manipulation all night, was deeply asleep when awoken by someone shaking me.

Even an apprentice devil had some privileges. I spoke angrily at the one who had disturbed me until I felt the fear coming from the very young Atapi male that had woken me. It wasn't just my annoyance that scared him, but something else as well.

"What is wrong?" I asked the whelp.

"Mumon ill, she-devil. You come? Heal her?"

I never considered refusing.

Since I usually slept in whatever I had been wearing – because I was usually too exhausted to do more than collapse on my bed after a night of instruction – I had little to prepare. I just grabbed a cape to wrap around me, and let the whelp lead me out of the tiny cave I now called my own.

He took me to one of the larger natural caves – which was a relief. Many Atapi preferred underground holes and they made me very uncomfortable.

The cavern was full of females. No males were present and my guide departed as soon as his task was done. I let my eyes adjust to the lamp-lit dimness. I didn't need light to guide me to the one who needed me. Her pain was like a magnet, drawing me to her.

The source was an egg-heavy female, who was squatting and panting heavily – trying to lay the egg. Between the panting breaths, she begged me to help her. I knelt down next to her, but I had no idea what I could do.

"Has she had this problem before?" I asked the two closest of the hovering females.

"Yes, twice," one told me.

The other added, "But she has also laid two healthy males – Banus who is being trained by the Old One, and another who will be trained in a few more years."

"The eggs that gave her trouble – what were they?" I asked.

Neither female answered.

"Did those eggs hatch?" I tried.

"No."

"Do you know if they would have been male or female?"

The two females became distressed. It didn't seem like they wanted to talk about it. I wondered if there was some Atapi superstition about talking about the dead.

"Never mind," I muttered. Somehow, I had to find out what was wrong and try to help the woman.

At least the band on my wrist did not restrict my empathy. I used it to try to 'become' the woman before me. In the trance-like state I had to get past the aura of pain, so I touched the woman and eased her agony – and then went deeper.

I really had no idea of Atapi anatomy, and wondered if I would recognise the problem if I saw it. It felt like the egg was ready to be laid. I couldn't sense any physical reason for why it wouldn't drop.

Curious, I went even deeper – into the life within the egg. It was strong and healthy – a female and an empath. It felt like me.

I withdrew a level. In a distant part of my mind, I had the nagging sense of having the answer just out of reach.

The ripple of a contraction drew my attention to the muscles that were trying to push the egg out and the barrier that should be opening. The female screamed again in pain. With my hands, I felt around the opening where I could feel the crown of the egg. I used my power to relax the muscles there.

Another contraction and I sensed the still soft-shelled egg being distorted. The life within was being squashed, causing pain to the unborn whelp. The barrier was beginning to open. I concentrated my attention there and the egg began to emerge.

So total was my concentration, that I did not sense the approach of the Old One – or the wariness of the other females. I felt the flick of lightning through my mind and this time I found myself thrown across the cavern. I didn't lose consciousness, but my concentration was broken and I had to gasp to regain my breath. The female screamed in pain.

The Old One was angry and his anger filled the cavern with a palpable aura. It forced all the females back against the walls. The anger was directed at me and I couldn't understand the cause of it. I was trying to help the labouring female.

I could understand him being annoyed at being woken, since he would have had as little sleep as I, but why had he woken?

Then I swore. Even after three years as his apprentice, he still didn't trust me. He must have an internal alarm to tell him if one of his apprentices was using power. I was angry now, too. I was feeling the female's pain and he was not letting me help.

"Leave here, Jai-devil." He was now standing over me, glaring down.

"Master, I can't leave this woman in pain. I can help her."

"Leave! If this one cannot survive, she is weak and useless," the Old One snapped. He was angered further by my refusal to obey.

"Master, she is Banus's mother, and has another whelp that will be sorcerer-trained. This eggling is strong and healthy. We don't have enough talented male children – dare we let the potential mother of more die? We need more females like her if the tribes are to grow and prosper."

I felt the force of the Old One's glare and another flick of lightning across my mind. It gave me a headache and my awareness of the other woman faded. I felt the Old One's awareness touch the woman, enter her and depart.

"Save the woman, Jai-devil," the Old One said coldly and he stalked out of the cavern. I didn't doubt that a small part of his awareness was still with me.

I crawled back to the woman and returned my awareness to her. The contractions were continuing, increasing in intensity and frequency. I checked the eggling again and recoiled in shock. Now there was nothing there. The eggling was dead.

I watched in shock as the distorted egg began to emerge. I was now able to help the barrier open further, but still not enough. The intense contractions forced the egg out, and left the woman weak and bleeding. Both were relatively minor problems. I stopped the bleeding and shared some of my own strength with the woman. She struggled to stand up.

"Thank you for coming, she-devil," the woman said to me. Her breathing had eased and her pain was gone.

"The egg will not hatch," I told her. I was miserable because I had failed to save it.

"It was the will of the Ancient One," the woman accepted the news calmly.

"No!" I told her. "Of the Old One perhaps, not the Ancient One."

I felt a moment of blending. The woman was trying to share her calm acceptance with me. I stared at her in surprise. This woman had empathy! Vague, formless, distant – but there. Again, I had that elusive feeling of an answer just out of reach.

The moment ended. Without further words, I strode out and returned to my sleeping place to think. I didn't expect to be able to return to sleep. I would have an accounting to give to the Old One about my actions, my refusal to obey him immediately, and my disrespectful thoughts. He had punished his other apprentices for less. I knew he would summon me as soon as he had finished greeting the sun in the morning, and I was not looking forward to it.

I did doze off, though, slipping into curiously symbolic dream – of ribbons winding about a female baby Atapi. I thought of it as the eggling I had tried to save. It should have lived. It was healthy and an empath – like me. Ribbons wound around me – unwinding. Then, in my dream, was the lightning striking the child, and striking me. The same theme repeated over and over.

I awoke suddenly. The answer was within my grasp. The Old One had struck the eggling causing it to die – because of the empathy. Was it possible that he recognised it? No. No, I was sure he couldn't.

It seemed that the eggling had to die – because it was female and an empath. Why? The mother wanted it to live and must have known what it was, yet she hadn't been able to lay the egg. She had laid males without trouble.

Ribbons? Winding, binding… that was it! A binding against laying female empaths. But how and why?

The mother had empathy – untrained and suppressed. She had known what her child was – and so the binding had acted. Perhaps that female's mother had not known.

Inside my head, the instinctive knowledge of the cycle of the day told me dawn wasn't far off. I wanted to talk to the Old One and ask him questions about my dream, what he had done and why. The knowledge was important to the Atapi race. I would have to make him listen with logic and patience and discipline. I must.

As I rose to go to him, I recalled the inevitable accounting I would need to give the Old One. He would be within his rights to punish me for the disobedience and disrespect. I didn't think it right for me to be punished for trying to help ease another's pain – but he had not sanctioned that use of power, so again, it was disobedience.

Well, I couldn't get out of it, but I felt I had a valid point of disagreement. Therefore, I wouldn't cower, hide, and have to be found and dragged to the Old One. I would be waiting just outside his cave, ready for him.

I had no doubt that he knew I was there and decided to keep me waiting. However, I controlled my apprehension while I awaited his pleasure – so to speak. My thoughts were on the startling revelation of my dream, but I didn't know how much of those thoughts my Master would understand since I was thinking in my native Earth English. If he only understood the pictures, he might think I was thinking human trivia.

A shadow blocked my view of the just risen sun. I looked up and saw Musani.

"Jai-devil, you are to attend the Old One," the Chief warrior told me.

I scrambled up from the little heap I had made of myself and followed him. I didn't want him to think I was scared or reluctant. In truth I was both – my heart was pounding and I could hear the blood throbbing in my ears.

When I entered, I was immediately conscious of the Old One sitting on his wooden throne. I approached him to the accepted distance and bowed low, not straightening until he told me so. It felt like an hour later.

He didn't ask me to explain. I should have obeyed him without question. All he did was summarise my 'sins' and that was for the benefit of the other five apprentices – six if you counted little Raski, tagging along after Saneel.

They were all standing back against one wall. Milben and Vidor, the two eldest, were probably glad to see me in trouble. They had finally realised that I wasn't as ignorant as they imagined. Both of them were well trained in obedience, and I doubted they had ever had an original sorcerous idea in their heads. It hadn't stopped them trying to make me fail. Saneel was probably trembling. He had not been in big trouble yet, and little Raski had no idea what was going on. Banus and Lixmar, the other two, were in trouble more often for making stupid mistakes. I was the one that kept asking annoyingly apt questions.

So I was to be the day's lesson and in this I was treated no differently to any other rebellious apprentice, with Musani applying the beating with stoic impersonality. When the Old One realised that I had withdrawn my awareness from my body, he mercilessly drew it back and ordered an extra five strokes. Somewhere during that, I lost consciousness.

I awoke in a heap on the rock floor. No one had done anything to help me and no one would. The pain I felt now was part of the lesson. I must learn to be indifferent to it if I insisted on earning it by disobedience. I didn't even feel that I had the strength to dull it, and didn't dare try to use the aura stored in Larcia's sword or I would probably be beaten again.

When I finally had room in my mind to consider my surroundings, I realised I was still curled up at the Old One's feet, where I had fallen. The other apprentices had gone. I looked up at my Master and saw his neutral expression. I took that to mean he felt I had been punished appropriately. Stifling groans of pain, I crawled closer to the Old One, forced myself to my knees and bowed my head. I apologised for my 'sins' and asked his forgiveness.

He was surprised, and I had a brief sense of his surface thoughts. No apprentice so recently punished had ever volunteered an apology. He considered that I continued to do surprising things – probably because of my alien blood.

"Why do you apologise, Jai-devil?" he asked neutrally. "You have been punished. The matter ends there."

"No," I disagreed, speaking with difficultly because even breathing was painful. "I failed to give you the respect you deserve, Master. I don't obey you out of fear, but out of respect for you personally and your wisdom, knowledge and experience. What I fear more than punishment is the thought that I might have lost your good opinion of me."

I didn't know if he understood what I meant, but I think he sensed my sincerity. I felt his hand on my shoulder. "You wanted to talk to me Jai-devil?"

I nodded.

"Sit then," he invited, pointing to a position close to his throne. He watched as I moved into a more comfortable position. I tried not to wince too much. As it was, I needed some minutes to settle the pain again so that I could think.

"I need to talk and I need to understand. I hope you won't get angry with me again, because I am not sure I can explain things very well."

"Take your time, Jai-devil."

"In all the time I was fighting all your devils with sorcery, which is alien to one born on Earth, I never felt alien. Using that power came naturally to me. It felt so right," I began, pausing to try to order my thoughts. "I could have got those Enforcers to take me back to Earth, but I didn't. I chose to stay here to help the Atapi race. It felt right for me to do that. But now, I am feeling alien and out of place. It is probably the difference between how I was taught to think as a human, compared to how I would think if I was raised Atapi."

"Last night – tell me why you felt so strongly," the Old One invited.

I nodded, and began. "Once I felt that woman's pain, I was compelled to help her, just like I knew I had to fight your devils. To me, it was the right thing to do. It came naturally to me; it was even more natural than the rituals you are teaching me."

I sensed the change in his manner by the tightening of his grip.

"Master, I am not trying to anger you," I said quickly. "But I have to tell you certain things about me that I wouldn't let you find out before."

I felt his mind trying to read my memories, but my mind at that moment was too alien for him to succeed. As he made to withdraw, I grabbed his hand and although he stiffened, his presence remained.

Forcing myself to relax, I formed images, drawn out of my memories, so he could understand. My eyes were closed in concentration.

I scanned my earliest memories very quickly. Most of them only showed humans. I went more slowly when I came to my first meetings with Atapi and Kumatan. When I came to my encounters with Stacion Ansuni, my Master's mind betrayed great interest. The recollection of when I absorbed the aura of the metal box my mother had left me, the words I heard then echoed clearly in my head – except they were in English, not Atapi, which the Old One could not understand.

His grip became painful, but I continued reviewing my life up until the time I came to Korvu and 'escaped' from Jenha.

"What did it say? The box you read?" The demand was urgent, imperative.

I closed my eyes and remembered the words again, speaking the Atapi translation aloud. When I had finished, the Old One muttered to himself, "What sort of vile creation have I agreed to teach?"

"Perhaps I deserve that description," I said carefully. "But you seem to have forgotten what Larcia gave me." I let the sword glow into visibility. I think he had almost forgotten it still stayed with me. "I don't think she would have supported my intentions without good cause. She is wise beyond mortality. Will you let me propose things without becoming angry?"

"Speak, Jai-devil." The voice wasn't friendly, but he would listen.

"Larcia gave me the sword. I didn't want it, but when I thought I had left it behind on her altar, I found it beside me. It follows me as if it was sheathed on my belt. I know it is not a weapon and you called it the

Sword of Truth. With it, she named me her successor – but I am not that yet."

"No," the Old One agreed.

"I think you must accept that sorcery is not limited to males. Larcia was called she-devil and she was the mother of all the tribes. I think I have proved I have the power for sorcery, and when I am no longer your apprentice, I will use that power differently to the way I am being trained now."

"Tell me!"

"I work best with the aura of Korvu, not against it. So much power is lost, wasted, in the process of warping nature to your will. I find it hard to cause hurt to another living creature, or to feel their hurt without trying to ease it. I think, too, that I have a greater sensitivity to it – even than you do."

"You think too much of yourself."

"Perhaps," I agreed. "But at Arkor, the land hid me, protected me. I think it would do the same for you if you were fully in tune with it. Once the whole Atapi race was attuned to the aura, and then the Atapi were strong, healthy and plentiful with lots of sorcerers to protect the people."

"I am aware of our small numbers, Jai-devil. What do you see as a solution?"

"Do you agree that the strength of the Atapi is based on the power of the sorcerers?" I asked.

The Old One nodded briefly.

"With empathy, the power of the devils would be much greater," I suggested.

"Teach me!"

"Empathy can't be trained into people; they must be born with it."

"Then it is of no use. What has this got to do with your attitude last night?"

"I learnt something important last night."

"Speak then!"

"I believe that the reason that so few talented males are born is because there are so few females with empathy to bear them."

"Are you offering your services, Jai-devil?"

I blushed, knowing the 'service' he meant. I ignored his comment. I had seen enough to know that Atapi male bits were incompatible with my human female parts, and I couldn't see him learning to shape a human male.

I went on, "That woman last night has whelped two talented male children, yet she cannot drop eggs with live females inside. That eggling was female. It was a strong, healthy empath. I felt her. I think the mother had empathy too, but it had been stifled and gone unrecognised. After leaving her, I dreamed the answer."

"Then tell me, Jai-devil, before I grow bored."

That was a warning that his tolerance was growing thin. I got to the point.

"There is a subconscious binding on the females, so that if they recognise that their egg contains a female with empathy, they will subconsciously prevent it being born alive. And it will happen even if she really wants the eggling. So even without your interference…"

I felt his hand move from my shoulder, and didn't try to avoid the stinging slap on my face. Once again, I hadn't thought before revealing disrespect.

"Even without my interference," he stressed the word, "it would have died. She would have killed it, and possibly herself. I saved her for you, Jai-devil."

"I know that now, Master," I said contritely. "I might have saved the eggling, but I can't be sure. Anyway, I can do nothing for it now, but wonder how it was that the mother survived birth herself."

"What was your conclusion, Jai-devil?"

"That her own mother could not have been aware of her child's empathy. Do you know why there would be a binding preventing female empaths? Are male sorcerers afraid that such females might be stronger than them?"

The Old One's hand moved swiftly and slapped me again. I cursed my habit of saying what I thought, and stared at the ground.

"Perhaps if they were all as infuriating as you, Jai-devil, it was to do the Atapi race a great service," the Old One snarled.

"Master, I'm sorry…"

The Old One held my mouth shut. "There may be some truth in what you said," he admitted, surprising me. "But I was not aware of such a binding."

"Can you sense the empathy in me?" I asked.

"No, only your power. I sensed nothing from the eggling."

"Did you look for it?"

"I had no reason to. I have known of instances like that before. I knew the egg would not be laid with the eggling alive. I saved the female to breed more talented males."

"Master, I thank you for that. May I have permission, in future, to try to save such egglings? Larcia has burdened me with the task of strengthening the Atapi race. This is the only way I have thought of so far. If I can save talented females to breed sorcerers and female empaths to support them – then we can become more fertile and viable again."

"You will do nothing until I first consider the matter. And I will not train other sorceresses like you."

"I would train them in healing and empathy," I said quickly. "Not sorcery. There is something in me that rejects the rituals of sorcery and I think it is in the nature of empathy. I don't think that any fully Atapi female would wish to be a sorceress – your culture is against it."

My Master was thoughtful. "You claim, Jai-devil, that it is hard for you to inflict hurt or pain. Yet I saw in your mind, you kill the nameless one."

"He needed killing," I said flatly, thinking of how he had totally pissed me off. "But it wasn't me – I held the knife, but some essence of my mother was with me, speaking some ritual of disempowerment."

"You see, Jai-devil, it is sometimes necessary to kill. Could you do it?"

"If there was a very good reason…"

"Could you?" the Old One was demanding the truth.

"No." I whispered the admission.

"Then you must learn," he stated.

I shuddered, but I had promised to learn all he could teach me. I had to be a leader and fighter as well as a healer and teacher. In fact, the memory of the blue aliens and thought of them returning still haunted me. If they remembered me, they would try to kill me. I might have to kill to save my own life.

With nothing more to say, I sat quietly, looking at the ground and held in place by the Old One's grip on my shoulder. He was considering my words, and I had no wish to distract him from those thoughts.

He sat in silent meditation for a long time. I was becoming stiff and cramped. Finally, he stood up. "Do not leave here, Jai-devil," he instructed and he walked three steps forward to elsewhere.

In the two days he was gone, I had plenty of time for my own thoughts, but came no closer to figuring out how to break the binding I had sensed. I had, however, come to other conclusions.

One was that my tongue had run off without me thinking again. In my passionate intent to sell empathy to the Old One, I had revealed how I was vulnerable. I had not learnt to block off my awareness to the pain of others. I wondered, too, if this was a reason why Larcia had made me learn the barbaric rituals from the Old One.

When my Master returned, I was wandering around his lair and trying to quell my grumbling belly. While he was away, no one had dared to enter, and I had been told to stay within. Fortunately, I had found a source of water.

He made no sound when he returned, but I sensed the aura of power around him. He had to have been visiting the Rock of Arkor. I was drawn to him like a moth to a flame.

"Master," I greeted him with a bow. He walked to his throne and sat.

"Sit, Jai-devil," he said, pointing to the place by his feet. "I have thought about all you have told me. Your words have merit and they offer hope. In spite of what I think of you, this matter is more important. I will let you do as you suggest but only under my control."

"Yes, Master," I promised, careful to squash my elation. He sensed it anyway and warned me.

"I will not tolerate further disobedience from you, Jai-devil. To ensure that, you will remain by me at all times."

I sighed. "Yes, Master, as you wish." What was I in for now? I expected the older apprentices to think he had made me his favourite and despise me for it.

I became the Old One's shadow, except when I had to attend an urgent natural function. Even then, I didn't feel alone.

After a few days, my Master seemed convinced of my compliance. He then issued an order for every female of breeding age and not currently with egg to attend an audience with him. The tribe's Elder Mother, Malvina, introduced them one by one.

I sat at my Master's feet, a place where everyone was becoming used to seeing me. I pretended to be disinterested, yet I was open to each woman – reaching out with my empathy for any trace of an answering spark.

The Old One made no secret about his intention to take multiple mates with the intention of breeding more sorcerers. Most of the females were flattered by his attention and hoping he might honour them. Some were shameless in trying to get his attention. I stopped listening as it made me feel nauseated. In addition, as that amused my Master, his talk grew more blatantly suggestive.

Five females in over two hundred had some touch of empathy, and in each, it was only a trace. These were the chosen ones and he had them brought to his lair. This was a privilege of his rank as tribe's sorcerer. He could take whichever female he chose for as long as he wanted, even if they were already mated. I knew this, having found out during my visit to Con's tribe – but it still disgusted me.

What I hadn't expected was to have to be present when my Master coupled with each of them in turn. The proceedings made me physically sick, but my discomfort was ignored. My part was to tell my Master if the female had become with egg on that night.

Three did, and these were allowed to return to their normal routine. The other two were young females, just into breeding age, and had to remain with the Old One until they too became with egg. I was relieved that my Master did not suggest trying to couple with me.

This process went on, and I found that sitting just inside the cave entrance was one place where I didn't have to watch the Old One doing his duty with the last of his chosen mates. Not that I wasn't fully aware of everything anyway. This last female was becoming shy of the idea of mating with the Old One, and he was getting more than mildly angry. I had the idea that this young female had already chosen her preferred mate and was only waiting until her chosen earned the privilege of taking a mate, to state her preference.

I had no way to warn her that her reluctance would not be appreciated. If I tried, or even admitted that I agreed with her notions, I would be deemed to be in the wrong, too.

Thinking this, I was aware of a shadow slipping into the entrance of the cave. I scrambled to my feet and jumped out in front of it.

"Hey! No one is permitted within," I said in my best sharp sorcerer's voice.

"Out of my way, you unnatural freak. Jessilia is here. She's mine and I intend to get her."

The young warrior tried to push past me but, even banded, I was stronger. "Are you intending to challenge the Old One?" I demanded, hoping he would come to his senses. He spat in my face and attempted to push past me.

I grabbed his arm and twisted. Even though I knew I was hurting him, he made no sound.

"Jessilia and I have sworn to each other. She promised herself to only me."

"Have you mated yet?" I asked. They would both be punished if they had.

"No," he snarled. "I have just this day been permitted to take a mate."

Even though I disagreed, I said calmly, "The Old One has chosen her. It is an honour. It is his right to choose whom he wishes and should she bear him a talented male, she will gain much prestige."

The young hot-head did not wish to listen.

"Let me go, you obnoxious scavenger," he went on, his voice getting louder. When he tried to twist free, he found out I was not a weak and submissive female. I kept hold of his arm and pressed his face into the dust, with my foot on his back.

"You will wait here until my master is ready to see you," I told him.

He turned his head and continued to revile my supposed ancestry and me. He had no idea of my true lineage.

"You would benefit from learning manners," I told him mildly. "And a more respectful attitude." If it were not for his belligerence, I might have spoken in his favour – since I whole-heartedly agreed with his grievance.

Since I was concentrating on keeping a warrior subdued, one who resented being bettered by a female, my mind was off the activity within. I was not aware of the Old One behind me until he leant over my shoulder and took the warrior by the back of his neck. I released him and moved aside. The Old One lifted the tall warrior and dangled him off the ground. It was as though he'd picked up a puppy, and the warrior knew it, even though he tried to appear stoic and resolute.

The Old One's anger was so hot, I expected the young warrior to be charred by his glare alone. My face was hot enough trying not to see the Old One's magnificent physique and nakedness.

"Hannatic." He identified the warrior and set him down hard.

As soon as he did, the fool dived towards where Jessilia was quietly howling. The reaction was swift and vicious. The Old One reached out, jerked Hannatic back and, in almost the same movement, bit his neck. The young warrior collapsed without a struggle.

My Master turned his attention on me. With what I was sensing, I wished myself elsewhere. However, I looked back at him and stayed still.

He was angry at being interrupted by the young fool and by being thwarted by the girl.

"Come," was all he said.

I followed reluctantly. I saw the young female cowering in a corner between a rock outcrop and a small log table, uttering muted howls. Her distress drew me and I went and squatted in front of her. In my mind, the Old One was telling me to insist she did her duty to the tribe.

I would rather have told him, "Don't do it if she isn't willing," but he wouldn't take that from me any more than he was going to take this girl's refusal.

"Jessilia, you have been honoured by the Old One. It is your duty to bear him a child that has a high chance of having sorcerer potential," I told her.

She didn't answer me and I tried to sense her reasons. "This isn't the first time you and he have mated, so what is the problem?"

"What has he done to Hannatic?" she hissed at me.

"Nothing yet. The young fool must answer for invading the Old One's privacy."

"I promised myself to him only," she hissed. "He won't want me now. Why did the Old One want me?"

"It is his choice," I told her, as I sensed my Master getting angrier.

"Come, woman," he ordered. I sensed the power of the compulsion he put on the girl. She stood and walked to him, but every fibre of her being was full of revulsion, guilt and fear.

"This young fool deserves that other," the Old One said aloud, "if I don't neuter him."

Jessilia seemed petrified.

"Once you are with egg, I am finished with you," the Old One told her savagely. "Now I will have you. Jai-devil, hold her."

I went behind her and hugged her. I let her sense my concern and desire to ease her fears. I thought of my own first experience with a male, the emotions and sensations of that encounter, and the intense pleasure. The girl began to respond and closed her eyes.

We were both standing and I was wide open to Jessilia when the Old One entered her. I felt like the one being coupled with. Pain ripped through me, as well as the girl. My Master was not being gentle and considerate. I quickly superimposed the memory of intense pleasure. The girl forgot her reluctance and begged for more. My Master took her from me, and I withdrew my awareness before she picked up on the overwhelming nausea rising in me. I ran to the furthest extremity of the cave and threw up. I squatted there, fighting for control of myself until the Old One approached.

"You will get nowhere being so squeamish. This was your idea, Jai-devil," my Master told me without pity. "You must now deal with the one who insulted you." He had no sympathy for my feelings and only contempt for my weakness.

"I bear him no grudge, Master," I managed to say.

"Perhaps, but I do," he said harshly. "He challenged my will as leader of this tribe. Would you prefer I punished him for this crime?" There seemed to be an unspoken inference of, "And you as well?"

"No, Master, you are correct. I warned him that he needed to learn respect."

I stood up and faced him. He drew a metal cylinder from the robes he had donned after finishing with Jessilia. He tossed it to me.

I examined it. It was a force whip and usually only used by sorcerers. The Old One impressed on my mind the means to operate it and wield it, along with a reminder of his lack of tolerance. I did not want to do this, and he knew it.

My feet walked me out of the cave, towards the spot where a conscious Hannatic, now stripped of his warrior's tabard, was being held by two of the tribal Elders. One of them was talking softly to him. They saw me approach, but Hannatic had his back to me. I stopped, knowing the exact distance I needed to be from the one I was to punish.

I activated the weapon and lashed the disgraced warrior. I shared his pain and almost dropped the weapon.

"Again," came the implacable mental command. I obeyed. "Again… again… again."

Even with the Old One demanding it, I could do no more. I dropped the weapon and fought to control my emotions and revulsion. I had to keep standing, and I had to control my stomach, or lose any respect I had as an apprentice sorcerer. To betray weakness now was to lose all I had gained so far.

Hannatic was led away, his teeth clenched on a wad of rag and his back on fire. I shared it all, and I could not show it.

In this extreme of my tortured empathy, I felt a barrier slip into place as if I had turned off the memory of what I had just done. My awareness of Hannatic's pain receded and I gulped deep breaths in relief.

"You have learnt an important lesson, Jai-devil," the Old One said with no anger left in his tone. "Pick up the weapon and come with me. I feel the need to eat."

I leant over woodenly, forcing myself to pick up the weapon I had dropped and to wipe the dust off it. Feeling like it was something rotten and decayed, I passed it back to my Master. As for eating, I was sure I could not.

My newly formed barrier was being tested but I held onto it. The lesson had been necessary – no lesser provocation would have achieved the result. I needed to become harder. But I would not let the Old One harden me into the sort of barbarian my Atapi grandsire had been. My human upbringing would prevent that.

To my surprise, I found I could eat – and I was in fact ravenous. In addition, for once, my Master's expression as he watched me was neutral, not hostile.

"I have decided not to neuter that young fool," the Old One told me, with a snarl-grin. "I am feeling kind-hearted."

Kind-hearted. I didn't trust kind-hearted. Alternatively, was it because he had enjoyed tormenting me, too?

"Of course, he must start over to prove himself ready for a mate."

"What of the girl?" I dared to ask.

"When she has whelped, I will ensure the whelp is raised by another. I will not risk a sorcerer being raised by a fool."

"I agree with you, Master," I told him.

"Well that you do, Jai-devil. It seems that you might be beginning to learn wisdom."

Was that a compliment?

The Old One continued. "I was beginning to think that I needed to use the force whip to get some into you."

The first had been a compliment, but the next comment had been to make sure I didn't get a swelled head. I realised then that my lessons so far could have been harsher. My Master snarl-grinned at my discomfort. He liked keeping me afraid of him.

"As a reward, I will set up a challenge between you and Milben," my master decided. "Don't be too lenient on him."

"No, Master," I agreed, with suppressed enthusiasm. This would be a chance to get back at that bully and release a great deal of suppressed aggravation. I had no doubt that he had been aware of the friction between his oldest apprentice and myself. I had put up with it, not certain if it was a way I was being tested.

Somehow, though, I was beginning to see that my Master often had more than one reason for his instructions.

Once all chosen females were with egg, my Master released me from constant attendance on him. My days reverted to the routine of learning rituals at night, sleeping late, and assisting with the day-to-day duties of the tribe – taking turns to be at the side of the Old One.

Often that meant being present when a tribe member was punished for breaking one of the rules. Some of the rules were incomprehensible to me. I had not been told to use the force whip again, and indeed, that was only for major infractions. Even so, without the mental barrier, I would have felt all the pain, and I was in no position to change the laws of the tribe.

My mastery of the basic and more complex rituals was progressing. Some rituals I only needed to see once and I knew what to do. The hardest part of some of these was performing the stylised and, to me, unnecessary actions with the chants. To be considered competent, I had to have both parts exactly right.

Since I had won the challenge with Milben, he was treating me with more respect, and paying more attention to the dull, mundane aspects of ruling a tribe.

Those aspects were as interesting to me as the lessons on sorcery. I still had a lot to learn about the Atapi culture and why they did things a certain way. As an alien, my view was different and many things still made no sense to me.

I had lost track of the days since I had come to this plane – having been kept too busy to care. Now, it was my duty to keep track, as I had the extra duty of monitoring the progress of the females bearing the Old One's future offspring during the five months the eggs enlarged within them.

Each day, I visited the five females in the company of the Elder Mother. I made my own assessment, and then accepted the opinion of the old female. In this way, she taught me about Atapi physiology and reproduction. In my few hours of free time, I asked the Elder Mother to teach me the herbal remedies, and other healing that could be done without sorcery.

The females were still confused about my ambiguous position, but they began to respect me after I had detected early signs of infection, illness, or injuries going septic, before they did. After a while, they accepted me into their 'healing circle' and I learnt more of this 'female magic'. They all dismissed this magic as 'of no great importance' and trivial compared to the sorcerer's skill. The same tacit lie I had heard from the females of Stak's tribe, back on Earth.

They gave me an intent stare as if daring me to disagree. I did, but not aloud and not in my mind. I simply said, "Small magic, applied correctly, can do much. Healing is an important skill."

The females had nodded, satisfied with my discretion.

I was summoned when egg-heavy females reached their time. If I was free, I went with the Elder Mother to watch and learn how the process should proceed. Sometimes things went wrong, and I watched what the Mothers did. However, none of them had an answer for the times when the ancient binding acted.

One of the five special females was the one I had helped earlier. She was bearing another female. This time I hoped it would drop safely. The other female eggling was Jessilia's and the Old One had said, contemptuously, that she did not deserve a male child. These two of the five worried me most, but they were the ones I had most contact with.

Jessilia was in the care of the Eldest Mother, on the orders of the Old One. The girl had received a scathing lecture on her duty to the tribe, her undeserved honour of mating with the Old One and bearing a whelp of his. She was not permitted to see Hannatic, and was made to be thankful to me. She knew I had been the one to punish her beloved, but she fervently believed that had I not, Hannatic would have been neutered.

When I spoke to her, I reinforced the required attitude, and she was thinking of me as a friend. I needed the trust and rapport of those two females if I was to help them. The other three females had male egglings and I did not expect trouble with those.

When the time neared for the first of these five eggs to drop, I requested permission of the Old One to have the females moved to a cave in the Rock of Arkor. I explained that I would need to draw on the aura to help me, and it was strongest there. I added that I might need to have the slave bands removed at the time. He agreed to move the females, but gave no answer to the other request.

My awareness of the aura, while strongest at Arkor, was still limited. One thing I knew, though, was that when I was there, Larcia's sword recharged and I could draw on that was power at need.

Unusually, because males were seldom present at layings, the Old One spent time with the females due to drop his offspring. He kept back out of the way, while I was assisting the Elder Mothers to tend the labouring female. I allowed myself to sense the whole process, which at the laying stage was similar to human birth.

The first two females dropped their eggs easily, a day apart. It gave me a chance to learn what the females needed to do to tend the egg for the month before the whelp hatched.

The third female, the one I had helped unsuccessfully before, started her labour while I was off with the other apprentices, learning a particularly onerous and distasteful ritual. I would have left immediately, but since I hadn't been excused from the teaching sessions, I was jerked back and made to start the whole ritual and finish it. When I rushed it, I was made to repeat it. My growl of impatience was kept firmly in my mind, as I knew the discipline of the exercise had to be maintained.

When I was permitted to go to the female, labour was well advanced, but not yet at the point where the trouble had started last time. I sent a helper for water and washed my hands as well as I could. Then I began to massage the muscles around the barrier. In my mind, I pictured what must happen and went into rapport with the woman. So closely were we linked, that the actions of the woman's muscles were mirrored in mine. I pictured the barrier opening, helped it to open, and thinking into the other woman that this egg was mind-blind – but it was not enough. I was feeling the barrier start to resist the passage of the egg. My best was not good enough.

The sense of desperation grew in me, and when I was about to give up, the Old One approached and briefly touched the slave bands. They fell open and dropped unheeded.

With relief, I felt the aura filling me and I used it greedily, using it to force my will on this process of birth. I sensed the Old One in my mind, overseeing a process he had never considered before. I kept my concentration on the muscles that were slowly relaxing, and the egg that was slowly emerging with much pain to the mother. I was doing all I could to protect the eggling.

"Ah!" I felt the exclamation in my mind. I felt a snap – like a rubber band breaking. The egg suddenly dropped onto the soft furs. For this woman, at least, the binding had been broken.

The other females took over now, and I picked up the discarded slave bands and edged out of the group. I went back to where the Old One watched. The aura was giving me a feeling of elation, but it ceased abruptly when the bands were closed on my wrists again.

I sighed, but quietly. "Thank you, Master," I said, indicating the bands. "My power alone was not enough."

"Come away from here." The Old One took a grip on my shoulder and I allowed him to walk me elsewhere.

We arrived outside his lair, and I was urged inside. He released me and called to the nearest females to bring him drink and food.

When sat in his throne chair, he said, "You were right about the binding. It is a very old magic. Older than I am. I could not tell what its original intent was."

"I felt you recognise it, Master, and you did something…"

"Yes."

The Old One seemed to be studying me. "You know the sorcerer's over-mind, I think?"

"Yes, Master. I can feel when you are in my mind."

"You have used it?"

"On several of my tribe, yes."

I felt, then, the Old One pressing on my mind. I saw a picture. "Examine it."

The image was in energy colours and although I knew he was trying to teach me something, I didn't know what.

After a while, I admitted, "Master, I'm baffled. I don't know what you expect me to see."

The picture vanished. "Sit," he ordered me, and I sat as usual near his feet. "Do you know of the sorcerer's sight?"

"Not exactly," I had to admit.

"That ritual we used to see the alien traces invokes it."

"That's females' magic, used by healers," I dismissed it with a flick of mental impatience.

"You need not try to pretend, Jai-devil. I am aware of what those old females do and if they confine it to healing – I don't choose to make an issue of it."

"Yes, then," I said meekly, and he cuffed me for he knew I wasn't being meek.

"I will teach you the ritual I used to release the woman. You and no one else."

I bowed, accepting the honour. Next moment, I felt the knowledge forced on my mind.

"When the next egg drops, use the sight to observe the process. Compare it to what I showed you. If you are indeed perceptive, you will see where you need to focus the ritual."

"Is that all there is, Master?"

"No, you need to be doing whatever you were doing to protect the egg and relax the mother. You slowed the action of the binding enough for me to recognise it."

"You will let me do this when Jessilia's time comes?"

"Yes, Jai-devil. You may try it on that little fool – since I have no further use for her."

"What aren't you telling me, Master?" I was full of sudden suspicion.

He snarl-grinned at me. "You must be precise in the focus of that ritual. If you are wrong, you could neuter or kill the woman."

"Are you hoping I will, Master?"

He side-stepped the question. "I expect perfection of all my apprentices," he said with a growl. "However, if you do not measure up in this case, there is no great loss. You may practice the over-mind on her, but no one else."

"I understand, Master. May I return to the females?"

"Get out of my sight," the Old One growled. The period of mutual purpose was finished.

I did as the Old One directed as the third male egg dropped. I studied the energy picture with the one given to my mind. Only then did I see what he had seen. When I compared the memory picture to the sense of 'inside' the woman – I realised why I needed to be careful.

When Jessilia began the process of laying her egg, the Old One came for me. He told me he would be observing my skill. He removed the slave bands and moved back out of the way. This time he had no intention of intervening.

In the back of my mind I sensed his irritation at the howling and complaining of Jessilia. None of the other females, even the other young one, had been so… weak-minded.

"Jai-devil, make the pain stop," Jessilia demanded.

I was spared having to answer when the Elder Mother cuffed her. "If you had been practicing the exercises I taught you, this would be easier for you. Evelon had no such trouble."

"But it hurts!" Jessilia kept on.

I stood up from where I had been massaging the barrier. The pain that I had been dampening for her reached a crescendo and she screamed. I let her experience a minute of it and it only took that long for her to black out.

"Hold her in position," I directed two of the older females. "Keep her still. I might be able to do something now."

The process of labour slowed whilst she was unconscious. I was able to use the sorcerer's sight to see where I needed to focus the ritual. On the same instant that I broke the binding, Jessilia woke up and tried to struggle.

The females held her, speaking soothingly, and I caught the egg as it dropped. I held it as the females began to tend to the splits in the barrier. This was a bigger egg than any of the others had been and the eggling was healthy, strong and female. The empathy was unmistakable.

I would have stayed to help heal Jessilia once the Elder Mother had taken the egg from me, but the Old One was already snapping on the bands and pulling me away. He exuded satisfaction. I wished I knew why, but he didn't enlighten me. Instead, I considered the positives – I had broken the binding, the egg was alive and my Master was pleased with me. He took me back to the tribe's land and let me alone. For once, I had nothing to do.

Jessilia and the remaining females returned the following day, brought along by the Old One and Milben. I went to where the Elder Mothers lived, and the Eldest Mother drew me aside. She spoke in an area reserved for private talks.

"I don't think Jessilia will have more eggs," she told me.

I had a very strong feeling that I knew the reason for the Old One's smugness. He didn't want a foolish female like her to have more eggs.

"The ritual I performed carried some risk," I admitted. "When she woke up and moved… I am probably to blame."

There was no censure in the Elder Mother's manner. "Could the same ritual work for those who would be better off bearing no more eggs?"

That got my mind working. I recalled the picture – the energy image – and where I had aimed and where the image had jumped as Jessilia had woken.

"Yes," I confirmed.

The Elder Mother nodded with a faint smile. "It might even work on males?" she suggested hopefully.

I shivered. "Please don't even think that. I don't need some males getting ideas."

Her hand covered mine. Quickly, I asked a question that was not quite on the same subject. "Since you can remember, have you noticed a reduction in the number of whelps born? Or the number of eggs laid that don't hatch?"

She considered. "It does seem that there are fewer hatchings now," she agreed. "But surely you now know how to change that?"

"Only some," I told her. "Can you tell me – of the eggs that don't hatch – were many distorted like that one I tried to help first?"

"Not that many. One or two a year."

"How many others?"

"Ten, twelve."

I had my own estimate of the live births from seeing the whelps around the tribe. It came out as too many stillborn egglings.

"Do you have any idea why?" I asked her. I was trying to recall something I had heard of back on Earth.

"An idea, but nothing that can be changed," she admitted.

"Tell me, Elder Mother," I asked, just as I felt the Old One in my mind.

Her eyes betrayed awareness of a similar sensation.

"The problem the females have… in breeding… might be due to the sameness of their diet. The males now might be able to go further to collect a variety of herbs that could not be found where we were."

I realised the old female was implying that the tribe needed to have new blood.

"Herbs? I don't know how to identify many of them," I said, thinking of my ignorance. The Elder Mother took the hint to go into boring detail. The sense of having the listener in my mind retreated.

"Inbreeding?" I asked quickly. I saw a nod in reply.

She explained, "Sorcerers are jealous of their bloodlines – they don't like the idea of males from other tribes stealing their females, or getting them with egg. They expect the stolen females would be made to betray their birth tribe, or the whelp to be able to be used as a spy. They are afraid other sorcerers will come to challenge them or steal their tribe."

"I will think on it – for the new tribes."

I had hoped my small cave was inviolate, but I found I was wrong. When I came back from washing myself and my clothes in the river, I found the Old One waiting for me. I saw him and stopped, thinking quickly to recall if I had done anything that might have annoyed him.

He was amused by my paranoia.

"All that washing in the river is the sign of a disturbed mind," he told me.

"Humans like to be clean, Master," I replied calmly. I knew what Atapi males thought of bathing.

He snarl-grinned at me and went on. "I have decided that you are a depressing influence on my other apprentices. You are not to attend lessons again until I say so."

"Okay," I agreed warily. I felt he was playing with me. "Have I displeased you, Master?"

"Apart from being a human female who knows too much sorcery… No."

I wished he would get to the point.

"I am giving you to Con Ansuni for a time. He has sent a magnificent gift to me for the privilege."

"Master, what does he expect of me?"

"He heard what you did for me and requires the same service. Do well, and he will reward you. I believe he knows how to shape a Traeger – perhaps he will mate with you."

"Even if that were possible, it would be a waste of time. Besides, he's my uncle! It is stupid to breed that close."

The Old One rose and approached me. "Are you implying I am stupid?" he challenged me with a snarl.

Very quickly, I said, "No, Master. I meant, I would be stupid if I did it. When am I to go?"

"Now!"

When we met Con Ansuni at the Rock of Arkor, he made suitably derogatory comments about me in the Old One's hearing, but I could read his mind and knew it was for show. He was the only one of my teachers to praise my skill.

I said nothing, and thought only of my reluctance to leave my Master until I arrived on Con's land. He took me at once to where he had recreated his altar to Larcia.

"This area is shielded," he told me. "I doubt if the Old One can oversee your mind in here. Elsewhere, he might be able to. So sit. Bernea will bring refreshments in shortly."

I chose a fur-covered cushion and dared a question. "Will the Old One be suspicious if he can't reach my mind?"

"I will tell him that I keep my private quarters shielded for privacy," Con told me. "And he will ask. You have grown powerful, Jai-devil. You could almost challenge him."

"Surely not!" I protested.

"Is he reluctant to let you out of his sight or control?"

"He has always been like that. I have to watch everything I think or say," I told him.

"Perhaps. In this place, though, you are free to say or think what you wish. But for now, tell me how you selected his mates."

Con listened intently to how I had come to have my revelation, and what I had done since then.

"That is a longer term solution," Con growled. "I need more male whelps to be warriors."

"I had another idea, based on what the Elder Mothers thought," I admitted. "I haven't felt it was the right time to broach it to the Old One since I was in no mood to make him angry."

Con snarl-grinned. "Tell me."

"It is likely that the tribes are becoming too inbred," I told him.

"Explain."

"Breeding within too small a group. I remember hearing something when I was growing up – about children being born with really freaky problems. There we are not allowed to mate brother and sister, and cousins are not much better."

"Cousins?"

"Sort of like Litok and Deben to me."

Con thought on that.

I dared a question. "I got the impression that you sorcerers were as ready to fight each other as to fight Kumatan…"

"Some hot-heads," Con agreed. "My sire was like that – he stole my mother from the Old One. But I understand your point. There has not been much new blood put into any tribe. We have had no wish to dilute our own lines or breed a traitor. If you were to suggest a solution, what would it be?"

"I am not saying you should raid other tribes for females. You could, perhaps, arrange trades of adolescent or pre-adolescent females between tribes so they can mate warriors and breed strong whelps."

Then I had another idea. "And when the next new sorcerers go off to start a new tribe – I'm not sure how that is done – but if they take not only some of their own tribe, but volunteers from other tribes, once they are blooded to the sorcerer – they become the new bloodline. That is not something I would suggest for existing tribes."

"Very wise," Con agreed. "Perhaps I could broach some of those ideas to the Old One for you."

"You are welcome. He will be pleased to think and tell me that I don't have all the ideas."

Bernea and Cassia arrived with refreshments. Con's younger mate was again with egg. Her first by Con had been a male. I allowed myself to sense this one. It was female.

"That is another reason why I wanted you here." He was aware of my thought. "I had not encountered the problem. Bernea only had male whelps and only two were talented."

I nodded and asked, "How is Teregan? He doesn't come near me when training with the others."

"He is itching to see you, Jai-devil," Bernea told me. "As for avoiding you, it is because a late starting whelp has much to catch up on as well as keeping up with others his age. He did not want to embarrass you."

"He wouldn't. More likely those other bratty whelps will try to anger him by belittling me."

"Teregan is learning to control his temper," Bernea assured me.

Con commented then, "He is keen to learn. Now, could you tell Bernea what you told me?"

I did, and I saw Cassia turn pale.

"I can insist she stay as long as needed," Con assured his younger mate.

Though I had promised not to tell anyone else the ritual I'd used, I found myself telling Con. I knew he would not betray me. No other sorcerer would receive this confidence. He could possibly do as I had done, if he was not squeamish about the birth process.

The females in Con's tribe treated me like a minor goddess. Many of them had once been part of my small tribe, but it seemed that word of my growing skills at sorcery and healing had spread to all the rest. I was amused by it, since I didn't consider myself as such. I spent my time with them when I was not 'attending' Con in the cavern where he had Larcia's image. At least he did not make me be present for the mating, only to check the female later to see if she had conceived.

When I was in that cavern, and I was not being overheard, I had the freedom to think on many things that I dare not think around the Old One. The most provocative idea was about how to remove the slave bands.

I'd also had questions from a lot of females who were concerned about being unable to conceive a whelp. In Atapi society, for the males, monogamy was by choice, not law. It was an issue that went unaddressed, because if the first mate of a warrior was barren, he took another when permitted. He was satisfied if only one mate produced whelps.

My mind produced ideas, provocative ones, like if the female didn't conceive for one mate – assign her to another. It might work, but it would not be popular, and if I were the female, I would object. Still, I raised the idea with Con so he could consider if it was legal by the tribe's laws. I also discussed the problem with the Elder Mothers of Con's tribe in case they knew of herbs that might help.

As a last resort, I could 'attend' at the matings of females who had whelps, and those who seemed barren. Perhaps I could sense a reason for the failure to conceive. I would only do this if both partners agreed. Trouble was, many were desperate enough to agree. Con simply snarl-grinned at me.

I had not thought to look with sorcerer-sight when the Old One had coupled successfully, so I had no comparison for these unsuccessful tries. Con's solution was to have me attend when he mated with the next three of his eight new mates.

There was no blatant conclusion for me to draw. Either the male seed couldn't go the distance or the woman blocked it. Con accepted the answer and ordered his healers to look for herbs to give the males, to 'strengthen' them. Sorcerers, I heard, were naturally more potent.

After Cassia dropped her egg, and three other of his temporary mates had also laid eggs with the female eggling alive and healthy, Con returned me to the Old One via the Rock of Arkor. Con's gifts of thanks to me were not objects that others would value. The obvious gifts were clothing made for me by his tribe's females, many of whom knew me well. They were in the style I preferred, but in Atapi materials. The gift that was not obvious, but valuable to me, was the teaching of ways to block the Old One from knowing everything I thought. Con had also taught me how to make a metal box similar to the one my mother had given me.

While the two sorcerers met, they compared the success of the trial. Con then proposed some of the other ideas I had given him. The Old One did make approving comments about the suggestions and belittled me for not thinking of them. I simply smiled to myself and commended Con for his cleverness.

The idea of moving females from one tribe to another was a provocative one. Con already agreed with the idea, but the Old One was not keen. He quizzed me on my thoughts and I told him that I couldn't see why the females should have to be dragged from their families and friends. Con looked suspiciously at me for saying the opposite to what I had told him, but he hid a smile when my Master changed his mind. Before they parted, they agreed to swap three young unmated females from each tribe to the other.

The Old One did agree to put all the ideas to all the sorcerers, and to the oldest apprentices who might soon be able to start their own tribes. While the tribal sorcerers agreed to try herbs to increase fertility and potency, none of them wanted to swap females, but a few were cautiously in favour of having volunteers to go to form new tribes. I had a very good idea that they thought they might have an influence on the new tribe that way.

Nothing would change quickly, I knew. That Con and the Old One were trying the ideas was a start.

I did not speak at the meeting, but I did listen to how the Old One was managing the other sorcerers. It would be useful to know in the future. Patience for now was necessary. If my plans were so far confined to two tribes, so be it. If the ideas worked, that would be a powerful incentive for others to try it. As it was, until I had mastered all the rituals and became a full sorcerer-devil myself, I was bound to one tribe – and my Master was not in a hurry to graduate me from apprentice.

My routine returned to normal, with the addition of meetings to work on ways to increase the tribes. I heard that all six of the swapped females were with egg, and that sounded like a good beginning, but I wanted to be sure it was not coincidence.

The training I was undertaking became more abhorrent to me. The rituals were those that needed to warp the aura. This was extremely unpleasant, and I had to force myself to perform them. The sorcerers wanted to find fault with me and my skill, but my control of my emotions and my power had been hard won and no one sensed my distaste, not even my Master. For that, I thanked Con's gift of teaching me the mind tricks – ways by which, even with the sorcerer's overmind, my Master would not know all of what I was thinking.

I often consoled myself with the knowledge that once I was free of the slave bands – a full sorcerer – I would not need to use the aura warping rituals.

The thought of wanting to defeat the Old One began to grow within me, and I remembered Con saying I could. I had to be careful when I considered that idea, even using Con's mind tricks – choosing times when my Master was busy, and preferably away from the village.

Being subservient to the Old One was beginning to irritate me. I sensed impatience within me, and an urgent need to return to the other plane. In the moments between finishing training and falling asleep, I kept thinking of those I had left behind. It seemed they were calling for me – insistently. Some of this must have been apparent to the Old One, for he had started watching me as if preparing to pounce. If it weren't for the slave bands, I would go. I was growing desperate to be rid of them.

CHAPTER 74 – Jai Cassidy – POV

Suddenly the need to go crystallised within me. I was teaching basic skills to some young whelps but, in that instant, they all began to back away from me and run to their mothers. I watched them go and turned to see the Old One materialising in front of me. We looked at each other, both knowing the inevitable showdown was imminent.

Some unknown emotion was rising in me and making me reckless. "I challenge you Master, and when I win, you will free me to go where I must."

"If I win, Jai-devil, you will be mine to do with as I please."

I was barely aware that every other Atapi had disappeared into their caves or holes. They all knew better than to be around during a battle of sorcery.

The Old One was already throwing taunts at me. I didn't grow angry. He degraded my heritage, my ability and my sanity enough to make a full-blooded Atapi livid with fury. Calling me a half breed and an illegitimate monstrosity and so on didn't worry me, though. I was what I was. I wasn't ashamed of my human blood, or my appearance. What it all came down to was that I could happily have done without my Atapi blood – though the same taunts might have angered me had they come from a human friend.

On the other hand, I knew how to irritate Atapi males, and in particular how to make my Master angry. Normally it would not be wise to denigrate his power, and call him an old fool whose time was over, but this was a mind game and I did not believe the lies I was speaking.

During this preliminary exchange of insults, we were both taking stock of each other. I did not think that the Old One would underestimate me, and I knew he was powerful. He began to circle me slowly as he spoke his insults and we eyed each other. Then he began a low chant that began to gain in tempo. I felt his power stirring. He had the advantage of being able to call on the aura, but I had the power stored in Larcia's sword.

I knew that in this challenge it would be folly to stand still, and I began to run around the Old One chanting a ritual of my own. I had almost completed a third circle around him when he realised what I was doing. He forgot his own ritual and flicked his mental lightning across my mind. I had not expected such a basic binding ritual to succeed, but it had achieved the purpose of spoiling his intent. I laughed gleefully, even though my mind knew I could not let the Old One land any debilitating physical blows either. This battle would be proceeding too quickly for me to heal myself, especially without being able to use the aura.

The initial skirmishing lasted three hours, and most of the time I was merely defending myself. Sometimes I flicked mental lightning across his mind, and at other times I began a ritual that seemed serious enough that my Master's concentration was drawn from his own ritual.

He gradually realised that I did not have to chant to attain the power needed for a ritual – particularly simple ones like causing him to trip or stumble. Another useful trick was hiding in an illusion of invisibility. It took him a little while to sense where to target his next attack.

The Old One was hundreds of years old, and still in his prime. He used every trick he had learnt from countless encounters with other hostile sorcerers, and some he invented on the spot, even some I had used previously to good effect. It took all my skill, all my concentration and all my luck, to save myself from his attacks.

I would not say we were evenly matched in skill, because I knew we were not. I also knew that it was the weaknesses that the Old One derided me for, which were actually my strengths. He taunted me for my instinctive and undisciplined approach to sorcery, but those instincts kept me one step ahead of him.

Without conscious thought, I knew what his almost unintelligible mumblings were meant to achieve, or how he wanted to position me to receive an attack. Then I would move randomly out of the pattern being formed. It was instinct that told me when to push through attacks of my own.

Once he surrounded me with illusions of himself, seven of them, all circling me. It was instinct that told me which was the real image, and when he attacked, his knife drew sparks from Larcia's sword.

After that, I learnt that the Old One had telekinetic powers. He wrenched Larcia's sword away from me and flung it behind a circular wall of force. He came at me again with his knife, but I had seen his trick and knew I could do it too, so his knife flew from him and joined Larcia's sword behind the force wall.

"Touché," I thought to myself. Losing the sword was not a critical loss – it wasn't a physical weapon and the power that had been stored in it had been depleted during the battle, keeping me standing despite the blows I had taken. We were both tiring, but I was desperate to succeed because the call on my mind from the other plane was getting stronger.

I had to force my mind from it when the Old One sent two star blades at me. These five pointed metal pieces were thrown like the round discs I had played with as a child on Earth. I retaliated with five illusions of the same blades, all flying on random courses. He thought they were real until one passed harmlessly through his, and he laughed, thinking he had me.

What he didn't realise, though, was that in the brief respite, I had created as many tiny wind whirls that were equally deadly. These I juggled, throwing them at him and bringing them back to me. More by luck than intent, two of the whirls knocked his blades to the ground. The Old One was prepared, though – he replaced the fallen blades with wind blades formed from finely honed wind. One came at me before I was aware of them and sliced a deep gash on my arm. I wasted energy that I couldn't spare to cauterise the wound and more to create a close fitting bubble of protection. The Old One crowed his victory.

I closed my eyes to concentrate on the positions of those blades, and worked an impromptu ritual to superimpose an illusion on each of the wind blades. To the Old One and any other viewer, they now looked like the multi-coloured flying boards of my memory. He saw that I was not looking, and chose that moment to attack me physically. He hit me hard with his body and threw me to the ground. I felt the sharp edge of a rock in my back and the fierce grip of the Old One's hands around my throat. I fought him, but he was strong. His wind blades were still circling, erratically now. I knew they were still dangerous, but the Old One seemed to think I had made them harmless, and was ignoring them and thinking I was using power to neutralise them.

I had no energy to spare to talk, so I let him read my thoughts, as one of the blades was coming at us both. He rolled free, seeing the vision in his mind. The blade missed him, and bounced off my protection. Angered, the Old One spoke words that neutralised my protection and more that caused pain where his hands touched. I sensed his thoughts, which were full of killing lust. Any trace of common purpose had fled from his mind. As I began to black out, I retaliated with the only thing that made me different to male sorcerers.

Without the empathy within me, I would not have survived past the opening skirmish. It was the only thing that had saved me. Now, I opened part of my mind to the Old One and he, sensing victory, attacked mentally. But he did not realise that I had learnt to hide part of my mind from him and had force-built the barriers around the hidden part. I risked all on the belief that his barriers would not be as strong as mine, and in all the time I had been with him, I had never tried to force his.

Without empathy, he would not be so sensitive, would not need such barriers as the ones I had built at such cost. Inside my mind all my anger, frustration, suppressed memories of pain, humiliation and desperation were building up. I dropped my barriers and directed this onslaught at the vulnerable and open mind of the Old One. It was like breaching a dam – all control was gone with the last of my energy and the last of my breath.

The Old One could not stand the force of the onslaught. His hands stopped pressing on my throat, and I gulped in a huge breath. My neck hurt, and my chest hurt, but my vision returned. I kept up the mental attack because I had not won yet; I did not know his secret name. I wriggled free from under the Old One, and he was unable to stop me. He was still fighting against the mental pain, fighting to stand up and prove his strength. He got as far as his knees, even though he was gripping his head with his hands.

I did not let up until I realised that I was receiving the Old One's very thoughts, memories and pain. In that instant, he gave up and the backlash of his pain nearly finished me. I fought to rebuild my barriers and breathed as deeply as I could in relief.

I had won the battle and in my mind was the Old One's secret name. He was Arclak, and my mother had been his granddaughter. The laugh that filled me bordered on hysteria, and I pulled myself together. I had very little time before Arclak recovered, very little time to study the slave bands before he muddled my mind again.

Even if he was conscious, I would not ask the Old One to remove the slave bands. This was the last test I must pass to be free of his control and a fully-fledged she-devil. Once, I had known how to be free.

I used my empathy to sense the nature of the slave bands. They were made of metal, but they had never felt like a part of me or of the natural order. They seemed to be half way to somewhere else. I repeated that thought slowly – 'half way to somewhere else' – it sounded like nonsense, but was it?

For a while longer, I studied the metal. It had been treated by some ritual... that was it! It was out of phase with the plane I existed on. It would be in phase with the nowhere region between planes, and that was why it did not enable me to draw on the aura. The answer was suddenly plain to me. All I needed to do was attune myself to the bands – accept them as they were and become like them. My surroundings faded and became tenuous as I was drawn into that region between planes, where Stak had once trapped me. Once there, I snapped the bands open and felt the aura of Korvu drawing me back.

There was no reason why I could not have done this sooner, except that the Old One had made me forget and never given me a chance to think it through or remember.

As I felt Larcia's sword return to me, the force of the call from the other plane grew to unbearable intensity. I wanted nothing more than to go immediately, but I fought with myself. The Old One was unconscious, collapsed in a heap and defenceless. I wasn't in much better state, but now I was able to draw on the aura.

When I was strong enough, I stood and lifted the Old One and walked him to his lair. In this state, he would be no match for any challenge and I did not want him dead or disgraced. Nor did I want to leave him in the undignified heap in the middle of the tribe's common ground. It had never been my intention to have him humiliated publicly.

Once in his lair, I laid the Old One on his sleeping mat, and allowed my energy to flow into him and heal him. The tribe needed its leader well and active. When I felt he was about to wake, I moved away and began to walk away.

"She-devil!"

His voice was weak, but I turned back to him. "Master?"

"You could have killed me, She-devil, if you had been unbanded."

"That was never my intention, Master."

"Master no more," the Old One told me. "You know my name?"

"Yes, Master. I read it in your mind."

"Say it!"

"Arclak."

"I expected your anger, and your challenge, She-devil. You could have left me and gone. Why did you stay when I feel you are drawn elsewhere?"

"I would not leave you defenceless and open to ridicule from whelps who think they know everything."

Arclak forced a snarl. "I never expected such gentleness from the one who defeated me."

"It does not make me weak, Master."

"No, I can see that. What did you do?"

"I fought you with empathy." I probed him and realised that I had opened that same sensitivity within him.

"I felt you open my mind, and I felt you healing me."

"Yes," I agreed. "You will probably feel the aura more strongly now, and be able to draw on it to heal quickly."

He looked at me with new respect.

"You are free to go, She-devil," Arclak told me. "Will you be returning?"

"Of course, Master. My life is here now."

"As I said, I am no longer your Master. What do you intend? To return and take my tribe?"

I squatted so that he did not need to look up at me. "No, Master. I intend what I have said all along. I will work to make the Atapi strong and plentiful again. After this though, can you and I work together? I really need your knowledge and experience and your help to get the other sorcerers to cooperate."

He snarl grinned and waved me away. "Go where you must, and when you return we will talk."

Rising again, I looked down for a moment and then bowed deeply in respect to him. Then I straightened, turned and walked three steps vanishing from his sight. I saw the cave fade and the Rock of Arkor appear   in   front   of   me.

CHAPTER 75 – Jai Cassidy – POV

I walked into what I thought of as Larcia's cave, even though I did not feel her presence on this plane. When I continued through to the inner chamber, I saw on the rock altar not the ghostly crown I had seen before, but a fully visible gold crown.

Did that mean that Larcia had sensed my victory here? The crown was mine to take – solid and real – not that I knew what to do with it. I took it anyway and walked with it to the matching cave in the 'real' plane of Korvu.

The difference, slight though it was physically, was obvious to my empathy. The presence of Larcia seemed so strong. I went to the altar where her body had lain – it was no longer there.

"My Queen?" I spoke aloud.

There was no immediate answer in my mind. I felt immense grief. So much still remained that I wanted to learn from her. I had her crown and her sword, was her successor, but I didn't feel ready.

In many ways, though, on consideration, I was more prepared for and suited for the times now than she was. Larcia had been as good as dead for more than a thousand years.

Her aura here was still strong, and her wisdom, knowledge and memories would still be within the aura. I could still tap into them when I needed help – couldn't I? I touched the aura briefly with a question, then cleared my mind. I felt the dreaming start. The power was still there. Reluctantly I broke the flow of power, and the full impact of the summons that had called me back came at me again.

My preference would have been to clean up first, but the call was too strong. I relaxed and let the powerful compulsion draw me across planes.

I arrived inside the Kimh palace. My surprise at that was drowned out by the violent clamour of alarm bells. It pained my ears as I turned around expecting to find myself in danger. I did not recognise the room, but I saw the people and knew them all. Jenha, Ellhi, Jahni and… I sensed Mikha and knew at once he was desperately ill.

Before I could move to go to my son, the thundering of booted feet became audible above the clamour. The door of the room burst open and guards burst in with weapons ready. I held a hand out in their direction and muttered a ritual that was effectively, "Stay there and don't fire at me."

The look in Jenha's eyes made me realise what a splendidly barbaric and dishevelled figure I must be. I strode across the room to greet him and realised that I had grown taller in the past four years. My bow to Jenha was of equal degree to that which I gave Arclak.

"Mikha – where is he?" I demanded urgently.

Jenha glanced at the guards. "Stand down," he told them and he stared at them until all weapons were lowered.

The leader of the guard group spoke into a communicator device attached to his jacket. The alarm bell noise ceased. Only then did Jenha move, and he took my arm to lead me into a side room. I saw the small bed, and an unfamiliar Kumatan sitting on the far side of it. He put down a book and rose to eye me distastefully. I ignored him, my eyes were on my son and I knelt down to hug him.

"What are you doing? Who are you? My patient is very ill and must be allowed to rest."

Jenha silenced him by saying, "Jai is Mikha's mother."

My son was so thin and frail. His eyes opened at my touch and recognition was instantaneous. He threw his arms around me and pulled himself out of bed. In seconds, he was clinging to me. I opened myself to his illness and felt it dragging the life from him. He was burning hot. Some of my own strength flowed into him, returning colour to his pale face.

I asked the healer, "What is it that ails him?"

The man did not acknowledge my question, and I bit back a snarl of anger.

"We have been doing everything possible for him, Jai," Janhi told me from near the door. I glanced at him. He was taller and older than the youngster I remembered. "But nothing we have tried seems to help him. Lots of people here have been sick, even the Kimh."

I sensed some sadness in Jahni's mind, but I was concerned only for Mikha.

Jenha dismissed the healer, who went out giving me a look of loathing. "He has been suffering from fever, weakness, nausea…" Jenha told me all the symptoms.

"Where are Teresa and Farcine? Did you ask them if they knew a remedy?" I demanded.

Jenha glanced away and then said calmly, "They are both in seclusion. I am not able to speak to them."

I felt anger rising in me and I growled softly. Mikha whimpered in my arms.

"Can you help Mikha?" Ellhi asked me. She, too, had followed me into the room.

"That is why I was called, I think."

"Called? By whom?" Jenha asked, turning back to me.

"I called her," a new voice spoke from behind me and I turned, recognising Kaer's voice but wondering at the pain and intense grief that he was emitting.

"Lord," Jenha greeted softly. I sensed his concern and sympathy for Kaer and I wondered what had happened.

"No, Jenha, I have not lost all my sense. I simply did what you, Ellhi and Jahni have been trying to do this past month."

"Your father…" Jenha began, as if in warning.

"Is, at the moment, cowering in the protection of four Traegers, who will I trust, keep him well away from here," Kaer said without his usual politeness.

"The guards reported the location of the Atapi intruder?" Jenha queried.

"Of course," Kaer confirmed. He turned to me. "Can you help Mikha?"

"Yes, but can I also help you in any way?"

"No Jai, it is too late for that. Help Mikha. I will give you any help you need."

"I'm sorry, Kaer. I came as soon as I could."

"You owe me no apology, Jai."

I studied Kaer with all my senses. "Lord Kaer, who died?"

He didn't answer, nor did Jenha when I glanced his way. Mentally, I shrugged.

"I will need to work in the garden, like last time."

"Come then," Kaer commanded.

I followed him, carrying Mikha, and I sensed Jenha following. He told Ellhi and Jahni to stay behind. The guards in the outer room stiffened when I reappeared.

"We will be going into the side garden," Kaer told the guard leader. "Your men may follow us."

I kept close behind Kaer as he strode along the passage, ordering servants out of the way. Most servants took one look at me and fled anyway. At various points along the way, fresh sets of alarm bells began to clamour. At each point, Kaer ordered the noise silenced.

A second group of guards blocked the way to the garden.

"Move aside," Kaer ordered. They did not.

"Lord, we have orders to apprehend the Atapi intruder."

"Whose orders?" Kaer demanded.

"The High Minister, Lord."

"I am countermanding that. I will attend to the problem. You are dismissed."

"With respect, Lord, the whole palace is aware of the Atapi stench…"

I moved up beside Kaer and said calmly, "Then go off and arrange me a bath so that I can smell like a human. If the word of a Kimh Lord and the presence of a Traeger is not enough for you…"

My gaze alone sent the man a few steps backwards. Jenha moved between the guard and me.

"Your aura is powerful," Jenha commented very quietly.

It wasn't surprising, since I had just finished battling the Old One. I damped my power a bit.

We continued unhindered to the centre of the little ornamental garden. The guards spread out into a circle around us as I put Mikha down gently onto the soft grass. "Lay still, Mikha my son," I told him. "Jenha, if you would take one of Mikha's hands and one of mine…" I completed the circle of power by holding Mikha's other hand.

There were two reasons for this. One was to make it look as if Jenha was overseeing the healing. The other was that he could add his skill to mine. Mikha was his son as well.

I was already full of the aura, and so I only had to attune myself to it. Then I let my empathy attune me to my son. The aura had welcomed Mikha when he was born, and now I asked it to direct my skill to make him better. Soon I felt my son's relief when the endless ache of his muscles eased. Then, I drew on Jenha's knowledge of Kumatan and my mixed blood, and directed my healing energy to overcome the virus that was spreading unchecked through my son's body. A vague bluish green glow encased him and, as he healed, it faded to invisible. Mikha fell asleep.

For my own comfort, I kept hold of Jenha's hand, past the time when the healing had finished. "He will still be very weak," I said quietly. "I have seen something like this before. You must tend him carefully or another infection might start. There is an herbal brew that the Atapi make to strengthen those weakened by illness. It requires a small amount of healing magic to give it its greatest healing potency."

"Can you tell me the ingredients, Jai-devil?" Jenha asked.

"Yes, and I will make the first lot," I promised. "Farcine and Teresa are both healers – they can make more when needed."

"That may not be possible, Jai-devil," Jenha told me.

"Make it possible," I whispered forcibly.

Jenha considered for a moment. "Would this medicine help the Kimh and Kumatan?"

"It would do no harm," I assured him, then added to needle him. "Atapi healers can heal others, too. You told me that my mother helped humans."

I saw a very faint smile on Jenha's face. "Perhaps your healers will wish to return with you. How then would your elixir be prepared?"

"I could teach you, but Farcine would be a better instructor. I have had little time to study healing. What of my three warriors?"

"Well, and training young Traegers," was his straight-faced answer. "I will speak to them, but I think they will stay if the others must, or choose to."

I dropped Jenha's hand and checked Mikha's forehead. His skin was already much cooler.

"Is that healer I met your choice?" I asked. Jenha understood that I meant, "Do you think he is the best one to tend to Mikha?"

"Healer Rosti has also fallen ill, as have many other Kimh healers. Healer Gauss took over from Rosti."

"Jahni said that the Kimh have suffered from this disease, too," I recalled, speaking softly.

"Yes," Jenha said softly. "Kaer lost Aniki, his wife, and their baby son. His daughter, Kelhi, has been with her cousins and is still well."

"We can return Mikha to his bed," I said, changing the topic. "Will I then be allowed to prepare the tonic I mentioned? I can make enough so we can share some with Healer Rosti. He can feel for himself if it is effective."

"Indeed," Jenha agreed.

"If it is, do you think he would welcome two apprentices who are skilled at making it?"

"No healer likes to lose patients," Jenha commented, not acknowledging that he realised my devious intention. "I will ensure you are permitted in the healers' still room."

I nodded and lifted Mikha once more into my arms. He didn't stir. Kaer came forward from where he had been watching and led us back to his suite. On the return walk, I noticed that I was no longer setting off the Atapi-intruder alarms. Was it, I wondered, because I had reduced the excess energy I had arrived with, or because they had been turned off?

Jenha spoke to Kaer and explained what I needed to do. He merely nodded, but at this need to act, he pushed his grief aside for a time.

Ellhi helped me settle Mikha, and suggested that I refresh myself before going out again. I agreed, and left Jahni sitting with his brother.

"You do smell Atapi," Ellhi admitted. "And I do have some more suitable garments for you."

I did smile at that, and gave her a hug of gratitude – holding her longer than mere thanks warranted. Then, after leading me to the bathing room in Kaer's suite, she took my Atapi clothes and promised to have them cleaned.

"Just the cloak," I suggested. "The rest has seen hard wear. I can soon get more of that style made."

Once clean and smelling of the fragrant soap the Kimh preferred, I dressed and went to sit with Mikha and Jahni until Kaer returned. With no one to tell him not to, Janhi stood and came to give me a hug. He had indeed grown in the past four years. He was almost at my increased height.

"You look well," I told Jahni.

"I am, Jai," he said. "I am being taught with the Kimh children, as well as by the guards. I hope to be a guard officer someday."

"Are you happy doing that?"

He nodded. He asked then, "Will Mik be well now?"

"With care, yes." I repeated what I had told his father, and what I hoped to do.

"Will it help the Kimh, too?" Jahni asked then. From him, the question surprised me.

"It could… why?"

He answered with another question. "What if they aren't sick yet? Will it help them resist the sickness?"

I nodded. "It could."

Jahni sighed with relief. "Lord Kaer and Kelhi should have it. My guardian seems to want to get sick, as if he would not care if he died too."

"Do you think your father is aware of that idea?"

Jahni gave a human style shrug. "It isn't my place to suggest such things. Lord Kaer is Kimh."

"Well, I am a tactless human," I said, intending to mention the idea to Jenha.

"It is Jai Cassidy, isn't it? She is here, setting off all the intruder alarms. And you are protecting her?" Koenig ranted at his youngest son. "You disappoint me. Do you not recall that there is an outstanding apprehension order on her?"

"Father, such an order is totally unjust. She has done nothing to harm the Kimh, or the Kumatan. She has done as she promised and kept the Atapi away."

"But she did not stay away!" Koenig continued to accuse his son. He began to list his accusations against Jai Cassidy, but Kaer cut him short.

"With due respect, Father, you are not the entire council, and I intend to petition them to drop those unjust charges they placed against her."

Kaer knew his father was getting angry, and didn't care.

"If you do, I will have words with the counsellors on your behalf."

"Jai Cassidy came here because I called her. She came to help her son and, unless you are trying to say that you would rather Mikha died too, I intend to ensure she departs safely. You can call off the guard detail. I will guarantee her good intentions if you need such assurance."

Koenig opened his mouth to speak, and then closed it.

Kaer didn't need to hear that his father would hold him to his guarantee. He knew that Jai Cassidy would not start trouble while she was visiting, unless strongly provoked.

"No," Koenig finally answered, coldly. "The guards will remain. Not everyone is as unquestioningly trusting as you are."

"Very well then, Father," Kaer bowed and turned to leave.

Koenig called out as he was about to leave. "You will ensure that the hybrid faces the council tomorrow."

"I will ask her to attend," Kaer turned back to give his answer. "She will not come unless Mikha has recovered sufficiently. Even though she overcame the infection, he is very weak. I have Healer Rosti's permission for Jai to prepare an herbal elixir for Mikha."

"You had no authority to arrange that," Koenig spoke sharply.

"Father," Kaer managed to sound calm. "You are treating Jai Cassidy as if you expect her to murder us all in our sleep. I think that attitude is really beneath you."

Koenig's face started to turn a deeper purple shade. Before he spoke again, Kaer went on. "I came to advise you that the Council have called an emergency session. Your presence is required."

"What is the reason?" Koenig demanded.

Kaer chose to remain silent. His father would find out who called the session soon enough and he would not give him any pre-warning of the topics since he was in such an unreceptive mood. The full council, he hoped, would consider his requests from a less biased viewpoint.

"Ten minutes, Father," Kaer said, and he turned and walked out without the politeness of requesting permission to leave.

Jenha moved up beside him as he strode back to his suite to change into more formal robes.

"Rosti was unable to speak to me," Jenha murmured.

"Convenient," Kaer remarked. "No one will be able to question him as to why he gave permission for Jai to make her elixir."

"Lord?" Jenha asked warningly.

"It is the right thing to do. We both know it."

"And the council?" Jenha implied a range of questions.

"Will be meeting shortly, at my request," Kaer told him. "Leave them to me. See if Jai can help Rosti with her elixir. If it works for him, it should work for others."

Jenha understood. "Yes, Lord Kaer."

With the guards believing I was still within Kaer's suite and my presence no longer setting off alarms wherever I went, Jenha took me to the room where the medicinal herbs were stored. The Kumatan healer in charge of this room accepted my presence with Jenha.

I set to work, able to recall the lesson I'd had from the Elder Mothers of Con's tribe. The preparation took time and the healer was taking notes. The final step needed the touch of magic, and since I used power stored within me, I did not set off an alarm. When I explained what I had done for the healer's benefit, his face paled in fear.

While I decocted my brew into two small bottles, Jenha calmed the man. Then I tasted a spoonful of the mixture in plain view of the healer to prove it was not poison. I also did not want to fall ill of the sickness. Jenha suggested the healer try it himself, but the man resisted the idea.

"If I cared so little for the people here, why would I bother to do this?" I tried to reason with the healer. "I will prove to you that it works by giving twice daily doses to my son. At least he will thank me for making him well."

Jenha led me out and along various passages. As we walked, he spoke. "Healer Rosti collapsed and was brought here. Do you think you can help him?"

"With or without active healing?" I asked.

"He will recognise active healing, and your tonic should relieve his discomfort. I believe he will appreciate a fellow healer, even if you are alien."

"I will do what I can for him, Jenha, because he is your choice to tend to our son."

Rosti lay sleeping and he looked like a very old man. I took one of his hands very gently, and let my mind tell me his symptoms. I began my helping by easing his laboured breathing and went on from there. For this healing I was using my own power and that stored in Larcia's sword. I would not be able to do as much for him as I had for Mikha. I hoped it would be enough.

With my eyes closed, I did not realise that Rosti had woken up until I released his hands.

"Thank you," his hoarse voice spoke. I opened my eyes and he said, "You have great skill. How is it that I don't know you?"

I let Jenha answer.

"Atapi? I thought they had all disappeared." His tone was more of wonder than of anger.

"They have," I admitted. "I came back to help Mikha, and when I knew others were sick, I felt compelled to help. Not many will let me, I think."

"Did you help the boy?"

I smiled at the healer and told him how I had left my son. Then I added, "I have made him a tonic, but if you are willing to try it, it might help you too. There is enough for both of you. I tasted it, and it is not unpleasant. It should relieve symptoms and strengthen the body to fight the infection. You only need a small spoonful twice a day."

Rosti tried it and, because of the magic step in its making, the tonic was fast acting.

"Can we make more of that?" Rosti demanded urgently.

"The healer in charge of the herb store has the method and ingredients," Jenha told him. "But to be fully potent it requires a touch of Atapi healing magic."

That caused Rosti to turn an odd shade of purplish pink. Then he said, "It works and it is effective. How much can you make?"

I shook my head. "I won't be staying. Once Mikha is improving, I must leave."

"You can't leave," Rosti said in alarm.

"I'm not welcome here, Healer Rosti. The council does not like me, and if I do not go, they will place me in eternal seclusion because I won't ever start seeing things the way they do. I will be taking the two Atapi female healers with me, since your council decided to imprison them for no good reason."

Rosti was grateful to me, and I hoped the seed I planted would grow into an ally to help me have Teresa and Farcine freed. If they were freed and wanted to leave, I would teach Jenha how to activate the elixir. If they still decided to stay, and allowed to stay free, Jenha would not have to use Atapi style sorcery.

"Could the Atapi females do the activation step?" Rosti asked.

"Yes. Farcine knows more of healing than I do. Even Teresa knows more."

"Would they be willing to help me heal the sick here?" Rosti sounded eager and respectful.

"We must ask them."

"Oh!" The problem with his idea occurred to Rosti. "I would not be allowed to bring Atapi with me."

I murmured softly, "Both have learnt to shape Kumatan – tactful, you know."

Mikha slept again after I had given him some of the elixir. After that, I was content to sit next to the bed. Jenha sat opposite and seemed to be studying me. I was fighting off the inappropriate surge of desire that I always felt when I was near him. I don't think he was aware of the effect he was having on me. I thought through a ritual that the females had taught me to reduce lust in randy warriors. It worked as well on me.

"I challenged the Old One and won," I told Jenha to make him realise that I was not the person he knew anymore. "I have full sorcerer-devil rank now."

His sudden stillness told me that he understood; I must be forever out of his reach.

"Well done, young one," he commended.

"I had to challenge him to come back here," I explained. "And I must go back."

"I understand," Jenha said softly. "Though I believe you will need to speak to the council – to reassure the nervous ones."

Nervous? Pig-headed more likely, or paranoid.

"Not until I am sure Mikha will be well," I told him firmly. I then considered what Jahni had said about Kaer.

"How much of a slave are you to the Kimh and how much a friend to Kaer?"

"We are not slaves, Jai," Jenha murmured. "We serve the Kimh as privileged commoners might serve the royals on your world of Earth."

"Fine. What about the rest of the question?"

"Kaer and I are not merely Lord and servant, but friends."

I sensed it was deeper than that, but not in an intimate way.

"Is he okay?" I put the question to Jenha. "And don't give me that 'it's none of your business' look. He might be doing a good job of feigning typical Kimh inscrutability to you, but not to my senses."

After some moments, Jenha merely said, "He is grieving. Aniki and his son died not yet a week ago."

"That's what I sensed, but there is also a sort of uncaring attitude about him and that worries me."

"He will be fine," Jenha tried to assure me. "He will do what is right."

"So where is he now?"

"He is speaking to the council on your behalf. More than that, I cannot say. He wanted me to have time with you."

I grimaced. That was probably a tactful way of saying 'minding me'. Or did he intend something rash and he wanted Jenha out of it? My empathy was telling me that the latter was as true as the former.

"I think I need to talk to him," I decided. "How is his little girl?"

"Kelhi is fine. She is staying with her cousins and aunt," Jenha assured me.

I wasn't reassured. To me it meant that it was one less concern if he said something unforgivable and the council enforced seclusion on him. If he did that, my concern was for Mikha.

"If Kaer needs a period of solitude, to heal from his grief," I tried to ask tactfully, "who will care for Mikha?"

My son was my main concern, but I didn't want Kaer to be punished for speaking up for me again.

"Ellhi tends to Mikha and Kelhi," Jenha told me.

"What if the council appoints a less suitable guardian for him?" I asked bluntly.

Jenha understood all the subtle nuances of my question. "I will not let them," he vowed, meeting my eyes with an implacable gaze. I nodded.

When I heard noises from the outer room, I stood up.

"Stay with Mikha," I suggested to Jenha.

"Perhaps you should wait to go out," Jenha countered.

"Probably, but if you are sensing what I am, Jenha, you know he needs help. I think a volatile human can understand him better just now. Trust me!"

He said no more to try to dissuade me.

I moved quietly, and Kaer did not hear me approach. I spoke his name softly and received no response. He felt to me like wire coiled so tightly it might spring apart at any time. His posture was almost rigid.

"I wanted to thank you for caring so much for Mikha. He thinks of you as a father."

He heard me, for I sensed a flicker of, "He is a son to me."

Then he said, with anger tightly controlled, "I have lost my wife and my son and they want to take my foster son from me, too."

I grew angry on his behalf. "Thank you for speaking for me today, especially when you have so much on your mind."

"It was the right thing to do! You are a stranger here," Kaer's voice was almost a hiss.

I dared to touch his arm, and in that contact sensed what the council had said of me. They said I had been here long enough, but implying that I personally had done too much that they would not condone. They'd also implied that I had proved to be too Atapi, and Atapi were not worth defending.

"So, I have been here long enough not to merit the courtesy due to strangers?" I mused softly. "Have they made me a naturalised citizen then? Do the lesser ranks here deserve no advocate? On Earth I would be entitled to a lawyer."

Still without looking at me, Kaer spoke. His tone was formal, but some of his rigidity had eased enough for him to speak. "I won some concessions for you. Farcine and Teresa will be released and must leave when you do."

I considered that, and thought my snide retort in Earth English.

"Thank you," I said. "And?"

"You will be allowed to leave here – provided you never return."

"Smart of them not to want to keep me around," I said blandly. "Can I talk to Farcine and Teresa?"

"No."

I did not ask him about my three warriors who were still here. If Kaer knew of them, they were still a tacit secret.

"For your victories on my behalf, I am sincerely grateful," I told Kaer. "But if these concessions were victories, why are you still angry? Is it because they want to take Mikha from you?"

"That suggestion is in abeyance for now," Kaer said, but his mind betrayed the truth. In tones that sounded sincere and concerned, his father, the High Minister, had implied that his son's grief was still strong and he should be given time to deal with it.

Kaer had sensed more, and I shared it. He had been specifically disbarred from being my advocate, and so speaking out for me today was extreme disobedience at best, treason at worst. Implied with this was the suggestion that grief had turned his mind and he needed a great deal of counselling. He had protested that grief was not an excuse to avoid doing what was right and just.

Personally, I decided that grief had destroyed his patience for the convoluted dance of words that the Kimh indulged in to skirt a direct accusation. To me, a human, I found what he had said acceptable. Koenig took it as a personal attack. If I was asked, I would say that Koenig was ultrasensitive to the subject of me – which I knew – and whilst he'd hoodwinked the council into thinking him sane, he wasn't.

However, it had happened that during Koenig's spiel of politely phrased scathing remarks, he had collapsed and was unable to speak.

In Kaer's mind, in spite of the discord between them, there was very real concern for his father and guilt for provoking him. He had not been allowed to go and help his father, but been held back by the presence of two guards.

Another of the councillors had stepped into the role of council leader.

I did not know if Kaer was aware of how much I was receiving from him, but he spoke again at that point.

"Elder Neilly has made it official. I am not your advocate. If you wish another to act for you, you will have to request it."

Since I did not think they intended to advise me of that option, they probably hoped I wouldn't. Even if I did ask, I was sure they would still not let Kaer act for me.

Kaer's mind soon betrayed the rest of Elder Neilly's words, and I was angrier than ever on Kaer's behalf. The Elder had publically and officially reprimanded Kaer for his actions, words, and behaviour in the council towards the High Minister, his father.

He didn't deserve that.

"If I were you," I said quietly. "I'd be chucking things at the nearest hard surface."

In my mind, knowing Kaer could sense them, I pictured throwing glasses and plates at a wall, and having them shatter into confetti-sized pieces.

As I was doing this, I noticed Jenha emerging from Mikha's room. He stopped near the door and simply watched. Since he made no move to interfere, I kept thinking of images.

Where my hand rested on Kaer's arm, I felt some of his muscles relax. Perhaps my novel form of therapy was working. The Kimh may not encourage that form of anger release, but… well, I was human!

I hadn't finished. In my mind, I was venting a tirade of my own, but thinking in English, which Kaer did not understand. From seeing Jenha's slightly raised brows, though, perhaps he did. I had enough unflattering things to say about the council and what I thought they could do with themselves to keep me going for ten minutes. I included pictures of the less provocative ideas so that Kaer would get the gist of my comments. Like 'pig-headed' councillors. The worst I pictured was the councillors grovelling before me.

About then, I felt the weight of Kaer's hand on mine. "Enough, thank you."

I sensed that his anger was down to a manageable level. "A novel form of therapy," Kaer remarked. "Is that how all humans deal with anger?"

"No, and I know better than to throw breakables. But my reaction depended on who had angered me and how."

"Really?" Kaer murmured.

"I put treacle in my brother's boots once, and left them outside overnight."

I sensed Kaer's puzzlement.

"Sticky sweet stuff. The nasty biting ants love it," I explained.

The notion of such a nasty trick shocked Kaer.

"I discovered that Henry didn't share my father's aversion to hitting women."

Kaer would never even consider hitting someone in anger, or any of the other ideas I had projected to his mind. If he now indulged in a little 'Kimh are better than humans' thinking just then – I was glad.

It raised his self-esteem back up to where it belonged and not where that sanctimonious Elder had sent it, which was down near where their thoughts about Atapi and human were.

"You did what you believed right," I told him bluntly. "That is not necessarily what everyone else thinks is right. Sometimes, plain speaking is needed. I cannot see that you have done anything to be ashamed of."

Kaer didn't comment on that. He only said, "You wanted to talk?"

I waited for him to sit down, and I made use of another chair. After five years of sitting on the ground or squatting – this was luxury.

"Why did you think I would come?" I asked, referring to his admission that he had called me.

"Mikha is your son," was his answer. He had his thoughts under control again, for I could no longer sense them. At that moment, with his stillness and control, he reminded me in some way of the Old One.

"You couldn't have known I could come," I said. "But I thank you."

"You are different, Jai," Kaer remarked and he waited for me to speak.

"Not really," I shrugged.

Jenha spoke quietly from across the room. "She is now a full devil."

Kaer seemed to twitch for an instant.

"Well, yes I am. To be able to come back here, I had to challenge the Old One."

Jenha added, "He is the most powerful of the sorcerers and the nearest they have to a leader."

"That isn't important here," I said quickly, knowing the idea made Kaer uncomfortable. "I came for Mikha's sake. I have helped Jenha break the hold of the illness and made an elixir to help him regain his strength and fight the infection. I think you and Kelhi should have some, too — before either of you get sick. Healer Rosti has tried the elixir and found it effective."

"Really?" Kaer commented.

"He was a bit taken aback that I had to use some Atapi healing magic to activate it to full potency."

Kaer took on that tenseness that I guessed hid undiplomatic thoughts.

"I do not think I have the right to ask you if you could make more elixir — for others," Kaer said.

"Is that because you think I won't do it, or because your kin will flay you for suggesting it?" I asked. "I won't be around, since they want me to go."

"Jai!" Kaer said sharply. "I don't want to beg, but my father is now ill with this sickness."

"Sorry!" I said immediately. "I showed the healer from the herb room how to make it. He can make as much as he likes. If he brings it to me, I'll do the magic on it while I am here."

Kaer glanced at Jenha, who'd seemed to sense his order for he left the room at a fast walk.

"Do you intend to tell your father where the elixir comes from?"

Kaer didn't answer. I did. "I thought not. He'd probably accuse you of trying to poison him. Let Rosti give it to him, he can attest to its effect." I gave a rude chuckle.

Obviously, having obtained my cooperation to help his father, Kaer did not want to discuss that subject anymore.

"What are you intentions now, She-devil?" Kaer asked politely.

"Right now or long term?"

"Both."

I knew Kaer wanted honesty, but he might not get all of the truth. "I hope to stay long enough to be sure of Mikha's recovery. Jenha mentioned something about reassuring the council…"

"Tomorrow. They have requested your presence," Kaer told me.

"I want Teresa and Farcine freed, and I will leave. So what does the council want to accuse me of now?"

Kaer ignored my sarcasm. "I do not know. My father ordered you to attend."

I gave a quiet snort of derision, and pushed that concern aside for the immediate moment. "Long term – I intend to return to the Atapi and work with all the tribes to make them grow in size, and teach them to respect the other races on Korvu."

"Will you ever bring them back?" Kaer asked.

"No, of course not! I'm only allowed to leave if I never come back, or so they told you," I said in a neutral tone that hid my true thoughts.

Kaer reached over and touched my hand. He spoke to my mind. "The truth, Jai."

"I came because you called. I care little for your kin, but if they cannot accept that the Atapi saved them from the worst intended depredations of those blue aliens, then they do not deserve my concern."

"Those aliens are gone. The Enforcers have them in their control. The leaders were executed… they will not return."

"Kaer, you really are a sweet innocent. Maybe those particular ones won't return, but there was something here that they wanted badly and they expected it to be valuable, to pay all the lesser beings they brought here and make the leaders filthy rich. Others may come. The rest of the universe will not be like the Kimh. Will I return? Why should I? I won't be welcome – but maybe I will, if someone I trust calls me."

Jenha returned accompanied by three guards, who saw me and straightened. I felt their recognition, but in their current role they could not show it. Kaer paid them no attention, and I couldn't decide if he knew what they were or not.

"I will not be allowed to call you again," Kaer said without inflection.

"That isn't a problem for me," I told him carefully. "I have enough of a life's work tending the Atapi as I was created to do. Your relatives believe in their own wisdom. They don't need me."

"What do you know of us?" Kaer asked, challenging me.

"Maybe I don't know much about them, except how they have treated me. They have judged me – not on my own actions, but on those of generations of Atapi who lived before I was born. They have no right to judge me, because they have made no attempt to understand the cultures and forces that made me what I am. I am a she-devil, Larcia's chosen successor. I am human by birth and early rearing. I have the power of a devil sorcerer, but I don't have to use it as others do. Even after four years, I still don't fully understand the Atapi. All I can do from now on is to proceed as I believe to be right."

"I do understand that," Kaer admitted. "And I think your comments are correct. I don't know how to change the minds of my kin."

"One thing I know. Yelling at them won't work; it will just make them more inflexible. You have to be sneakier,"

I advised. "You have to pick away at their beliefs so that they don't realise you are doing it. Jenha is good at that! You could provoke them with questions or different views. I have heard references to your Nuath, and how it is like the human's Bible in terms of living by its words. The way I see it, everyone could understand those words in different ways. But you could tell me of it, and perhaps it would help me provoke you kinfolk less."

And perhaps it wouldn't, I said very softly to myself.

"I can recite the words," Kaer offered after a short silence. "We learn it as children and recite it from memory. You are right about it – there have been many books from learned men on the interpretation of the Nuath."

Kaer took a moment to gather himself, and then began to recite the Nuath. His voice was calm, expressionless, and I listened intently – willing my mind to store it all. Unexpectedly, I heard echoes from my memory coming from what I knew of the Atapi Devil Lore. In a distant part of my mind, I believed they had to have had a common origin.

When Kaer finished, I broke the ensuing silence with, "Do the Kimh often form close friendships with the Kumatan?"

Kaer glanced briefly at the quiet Jenha. "No, we generally only deal with the Traegers who are closest to us in attitudes and ideals. We generally work with whichever Traeger is available. My father only works with the senior Traeger. Kumatan Traegers have talents that the Kimh do not. Our races blend together, but are wholly separate."

"Do any Kimh do hands-on work?" I asked.

"Sometimes," Kaer explained. "The Kimh have always been the ruling class, but we need to Kumatan to survive."

Jenha rephrased that in terms of what I knew on Earth.

"The Kimh are like the kings and queens on Earth. Traegers are like the lesser nobility, and the other Kumatan are the commoners."

"And the Atapi?" I challenged Kaer. I knew what my mother believed, and Jenha had agreed with her.

"Jenha tells me that, in the history archives, the Atapi were once equal to the Kimh and Kumatan," Kaer said in a tone that seemed to indicate the notion was uncomfortable. Did he know what I was leading up to?

"That being the case," I said, "how can you kind reconcile the part of the Nuath that relates to treating other races with respect, with their way of treating the Atapi as vermin?"

Kaer twitched in his seat. "There are degrees of agreement with that attitude, but it seems that the Atapi do not respect the sanctity of other races."

"I will agree that some do not, or rather did not," I allowed. "But I argue that the other races involved in friction were not always blameless. It is still plain to me that the Atapi are judged as a race by the actions of a tiny few – and because of that, those who were innocent now feel they have no reason to respect other races."

Kaer sat still and I said nothing more. I allowed him the courtesy of choosing not to speak against his kinfolk. I thought it might be interesting to challenge the council on that same point. I changed the subject.

"Have you ever heard of the Atapi Devil Lore?"

Kaer simply said, "No."

I glanced at Jenha and he shook his head Earth-style.

"I had to learn this as part of my training, and I didn't learn it as a coherent whole, but piece by piece. It, too, can be interpreted in various ways. Would you be surprised to learn that it is very similar to your Nuath?"

Kaer leaned forward, and Jenha moved closer to listen. When I had finished sharing all I knew, they were both quiet and thoughtful. Did it occur to either of them that for such similar beliefs to exist in two different races there must have been a common origin? I watched them both considering what I had told them, and when it seemed they would be that way for a while, I returned to sit beside Mikha in the inner room.

After a while, Jenha came in.

"I want to talk to Farcine," I told him. "I know you said it is not possible, but I am not a good little Kimh or Kumatan woman."

"No," Jenha agreed softly. "However, you do not want to be taken there."

He was right about that.

"How have Teresa and Farcine been treated?"

"No worse than I was during my period of seclusion," he assured me. His mind recalled a picture of the entrance hall.

I didn't think highly of his treatment there at all. My mind conjured tiny cell-like rooms and times with counsellors. My mind pictured the idea of 'walking' in there and out again.

"It is not done!" Jenha told my mind.

I smiled and kept my intention to myself. If it had never been done, I thought, they would not expect me to do it.

That evening, a servant brought in a makeshift bed for me to sleep on. I didn't sleep. When all was quiet, I 'walked' out of the room and into the House of Contemplation. I quickly went to a corner and invoked an illusion of invisibility.

"Farcine?" I thought, picturing the Elder Mother as I had last seen her.

I sensed surprise. "Jai-devil?"

"Yes! Picture where you are!"

Moments later, both Farcine and Teresa were hugging me. The younger Atapi woman was in a bad state. Farcine, although much too thin, was coping better.

"I can take you both with me when I leave."

Hearing that, Teresa babbled her relief. Farcine had other concerns. "If we are all gone, Jai-devil, what of your son?"

"He will have his father and brother," I told her.

"Is that what you really want?" Farcine asked me.

"I don't want undeserving people imprisoned here because of me. They won't let you stay, except in here."

Farcine gave me a faint smile. "If I wanted to stay, Jai-devil, what would you do?"

"I would tell you what a foolish old woman you had become." I was only half jesting.

"These Kimh and Kumatan – they only see what they expect to see," Farcine said slyly. Wasn't that exactly what I had thought before coming to them? Farcine continued. "Until I told them who I was, they had no idea. How could you make them think I had gone?"

An idea occurred to me and I grinned broadly. "You are a wicked old woman!"

Teresa held my arm tightly. "What of the three warriors?"

"They are still unsuspected. I have offered them the choice to stay or go. They will abide my instructions. What is your choice, Teresa?"

"I want to go, away from here," she said, seeing the chance to be free.

Farcine added, "I want to stay. For you and for your son."

"You honour me," I told her.

She merely smiled and asked, "What is your plan, Jai-devil?"

I decided that she had no regrets about her choice. "Should you stay, you will be giving up your identity as an Atapi and you may never have the chance to return to us."

"I am an old woman. My life has been full, and here new things are still stimulating my mind. It is my choice, as it was the choice of my grandsire, Obaki. I will serve the Kumatan as he did, and perhaps help build understanding between them and us."

"I wanted you to be sure. Ketali and Yokin will stay if you do. Nikal wants to do as Teresa wishes. My thought was that I have Nikal change shape to resemble you. You, in turn, will have to modify the Kumatan shape you take on and adopt a different name. They expect me to leave with two females and, this way that is what they will see."

"And then what, Jai-devil? How will I get to stay close to Mikha?" Farcine asked.

"I will ask Jenha to introduce you as a Kumatan with healing skills. At this time, they have an urgent need for healers due to an outbreak of a dreadful sickness. It responds well to that herb brew I learnt from you. There is a healer here who would accept your help – but for his sake, you would need to be bound in Kumatan shape."

I explained what I knew of the situation, including the fact that the High Minister, who was responsible for imprisoning her, was ill of the fever.

"If I am bound in that form, would they know what I was? Would I set off the alarms?" Farcine wanted to know.

"I think not. My warriors move freely and do not set off alarms. Now that I am not buzzing with power, I'm no longer setting them off."

"How will I explain my healing power?" Farcine asked me.

"Females' magic," I said promptly. "If that is not enough, imply you were a Traeger's illegitimate offspring. They can't all be paragons of virtue like the Kimh like to think they are."

Farcine chuckled. "Can you do the sorcery needed?"

"Not yet," I admitted. "Jenha can do it. I know he did it to Lancho, back on Earth. That was so my people did not see him turn lizard when he died. And I think, though he has never said so, that he bound my mother in human form so she could conceive me.”

“Jai Ansuni was the bravest of us. She would be proud of you. When must I be ready?”

“Shortly. I will bring Nikal and take you away,” I said.

Teresa, who had been listening, began to grow agitated at the thought of Farcine going away.

“Nikal will be here for you,” I told her.

She stood up straighter. “Must he stay looking like a woman?”

“Only for a short time,” I promised. “And you, brave one, will not be here much longer. As soon as I am sure my son is recovering, I will be going. I have no wish to stretch the hospitality of the Kimh any further. They want me to talk to them tomorrow, but I do not think they will like what I have to say.”

By morning, my plan was in place. Jenha took two warriors and Farcine with him, having left word that he was going to seek more healers to help with the epidemic. In fact, he would find a secluded place where he could perform the complex working to bind the three in the shape of Kumatan. When he returned, he would introduce Farcine as the healer, Anna, from some distant town.

As far as the Elders in the House of Contemplation were concerned, Farcine was still there. As far as the guard leader knew, Nikal had been summoned by his family.

I had time only for a short nap, waking with a much improved Mikha climbing over me. He knew me, even though I had not been around much since he was a baby. He was so excited that he began clinging to me as well as wriggling like an eel. That time together was precious, and I wanted to remember it.

My concern for needing to leave him eased when Kaer entered the room. Mikha ran to him with equal eagerness and bounced up to hug him, too. With Mikha clinging around his neck, Kaer had some trouble explaining why he had come.

“The Council will be convening shortly,” he managed to say. “You will need to prepare yourself. I should also mention that there is a Galactic ambassador and several off-world representatives on Korvu at this time. All will be present at the meeting.”

“Because of me?” I asked.

“In part,” he admitted.

“What about your father?”

"I do not know. It will depend on whether the medicine you made helps him."

542

Kaer escorted me to the Conference Room, although I found I remembered the way. When we arrived, we were announced by the Kumatan acting as herald. He announced me as, "Jai Cassidy, Atapi ambassador."

Tactfully, I omitted to mention the she-devil rank I held. My presence was unnerving enough to the Kimh as it was. They, like Kaer, could probably sense the difference in me.

We separated once we were in the chamber. Kaer moved to one side where he chose a seat. An usher led me forward, and I concentrated on emitting meekness. I saw High Minister Koenig in the position of honour; he was still looking rather ill. He finally turned his attention to me, and stopped glaring at his youngest son. I stopped moving when I was the appropriate distance from the Council bench for one addressing them. As protocol demanded, I bowed respectfully and waited to be invited to speak.

"My respects, High Minister, members of the Council." I spoke the words demanded by protocol, and in the correct tone. "I have come at your request, and I am honoured by your recognition of me as a citizen of Korvu. As I understand that I no longer require an advocate, I wish to formally thank Lord Kaer for his courtesy to me."

It was all perfectly polite and absolutely proper; the High Minister, currently turning an interesting shade of deep purple, could only nod acceptance of my words. However, it was Lord Eamon, Koenig's brother, who spoke the required response. He was not exactly thanking me for coming, just acknowledging my presence in the correct formal manner. I nodded, accepting his reply – in much the same way Koenig had a few minutes before.

"How may I assist this council?" I asked, giving them a slight bow.

"You mock us!" Koenig accused, speaking loudly.

I guarded my expression and said calmly, "High Minister, that was not my intention when I asked about the proper protocol for council meetings."

That was true, but it was also true that I was hiding amusement at how irritating being polite could be.

"However, if I could have your permission to speak plainly…"

I implied the question, and Koenig looked at me as if he'd like me removed. Once again, Lord Eamon answered.

"You may speak freely, according to the rules of this council. Please begin by explaining why you returned here."

"Certainly," I agreed. "I returned because my son was ill."

"Your son!" Koenig objected. "The child you abandoned is a ward of the Kimh. You forfeited your rights regarding your child when you took up outlawed Atapi sorcery."

"With respect, High Minister," I began my reply and hid my anger. "I did not abandon Mikha. I sent him, with his brother, back to his father and his father's wife. That does not mean I am no longer his biological mother. I did not expect the Kimh to take an interest in his wellbeing, and I am honoured that they did. It was my choice that he learn of his Kumatan heritage from his father. I was not of the belief that the Kimh have the right to abduct children from their rightful parents. However, I am not ungrateful that Mikha has formed a loving attachment to Lord Kaer. Having Atapi blood is not an easy thing. Lord Kaer is a haven of peace for him."

"Your presence is a disruption of peace, Jai Cassidy," the High Minister accused. "The child is better off away from you."

"I disagree, High Minister. I am the only person on Korvu who shares the other part of his heritage – human and Atapi. If he is better off without me, how is it that I arrived to find him dying from an illness that no Kimh or Kumatan medic could cure? How is it, then, that I could heal him and make him strong again?"

"Using sorcery," Koenig countered.

I counted to ten before replying. "Is healing the same as sorcery?"

Before anyone decided to comment on that, I began to quote a section of their Nuath about those that do good by whatever means being considered favourably for that action.

Koenig managed to turn an even deeper shade of purple and seemed to be speechless. He knew that I was deliberately provoking him. I could have added the tacit lie told by the Atapi healers, that this magic was 'of no great importance' and trivial compared to the sorcerer's skill. I knew differently.

"Yes, I healed my son. I used the aura of Korvu to help me. I do not believe that was an evil act and I would do no less for anyone else I could help – be he Kimh, Kumatan or an alien visitor to Korvu. Even you, High Minister, if you were willing to accept it."

"I do not need any help from you, Jai Cassidy," Koenig stated coldly.

I allowed a trace of my amusement to show. "Then I am pleased that you are recovering, High Minister. I had heard you were ill. You may be sure that I do not inflict healing on unwilling patients."

My eyes flicked to Lord Eamon. He knew I had provided the elixir that had helped Koenig. Odds on, the High Minister didn't know that. So would the healers stop giving Koenig the elixir, now he had stated that he did not want my help? A nice little dilemma, that!

I decided to take control of things before they could bring up any more specious arguments and accusations.

"High Minister, I would like to assure the Council that I have done what I promised four years ago. The Atapi are not about to return just because I came to help my son. Frankly, why should they? Where they are now, they are free of the disapproving existence of the Kimh and Kumatan. They have all the land they need to range freely and the tribes are growing stronger."

One of the Elders on the Council bench challenged me. "Where are the Atapi now?"

"Respected Elder, I am unable to answer that. I can take you there, but I cannot give you directions to get there."

The babble of disbelief that began then was only quietened when I reminded them of the way Traegers moved from place to place.

"What is there to stop the Atapi returning?" That question came from the audience. I turned around and saw the Galactic Ambassador standing.

"I am the only one who can do that," I told him. "None of the other sorcerers can."

"Just where did you take them?" Koenig demanded. "Wherever it is, they know their places here well enough to walk to."

I was not going to try to explain the 'here but not here' idea. If Kaer guessed it, he was saying nothing. Instead I stated, "They are far enough away that they will not bother the Kimh or Kumatan, and will not in turn be bothered by you. As I have already stated, I cannot explain how to get there."

Lord Eamon gestured to the audience, and I turned, seeing that another entity had risen to be recognised and allowed to speak. This was an elderly woman, a rarity in the council meetings.

"Jai Cassidy, I am Theona, matriarch of the Jeldar trading clan. My people have had firsthand knowledge of the Atapi torture. I understand the females of the Atapi are subservient to the men. How can you, a female, control the male devils? They consider themselves supreme."

This woman demanded truth, and I turned to face her. "I can because I am what I am." For certain, the rest of the audience would not like what I was about to say. "You are no stranger to power, Lady Theona. Nor am I. I overcame the challenges of all the sorcerer-devils, except the Old One. He trained me, but to return here to help my son, I had to challenge him and win."

The expected murmur of alarm began and I saw the Kumatan guards moving closer. One of them was leaving, no doubt to summon a Traeger. With a glance back at Koenig, I went on. "I am a sorceress and she-devil in my own right. The other sorcerers have been forced to accept me and will obey me because I hold in my mind their secret names of power."

"Then, She-devil, you are the most dangerous Atapi proponent," Theona challenged. "What can you say to make me believe you will not practice the barbaric rites like the others?"

Instantly there was a loud babble that was only silenced when Koenig rang the bell.

"I would like an answer to that," Koenig insisted. He was staring at me with eyes glittering with some strong emotion – it felt like hate.

I turned my back on him and spoke to Theona Jeldar. "I am, first and foremost, an empath. I cannot inflict pain without also feeling it." That wasn't strictly true, but…

"And I am a protector of life, not a warp maker. With empathy, I can tune into the natural aura of this planet. It is the source of my power. None of the male devils has empathy and by working with the aura, my power is stronger than theirs."

Theona nodded. She was satisfied with my answer.

Slowly, I turned around and took in the ambience of the chamber. The Kimh were looking ill. They now knew they had an Atapi devil in their midst. It didn't take much effort to guess what they were thinking.

When they finally worked up the courage to speak, their questions proved my guesses were right. The questioners were still embodying me with personal responsibility for all the crimes of all the Atapi devils, since the start of recorded history. I gave a shrill whistle and the room went quiet.

With due respect to the Elders, I quoted another section of their Nuath – the part about judging each person by their own actions, not those of others.

"I have been on Korvu less than five years," I reminded them. "Anything the Atapi did before then is of no connection to me. Four years ago, I did what I promised and took the Atapi away. In all that time, have any Atapi been seen? Has any Atapi sorcery been seen or sensed? No! I kept my promise – judge me on that."

One of the Kimh began to bring up the 'torture' of Auglan, the unlamented Selkrit who had posed as a Galactic Councillor. I avoided answering that by asking a question of the currently present Galactic Ambassador, hoping he would be as fair minded as Quenten had been. "Has this council been advised of the crimes of the Selkrit known as Auglan?"

"How is that important?" Koenig demanded. "We were told he was tried and sentenced by Galactic Law – not by a lynch mob."

"We did not kill him," I told Koenig. I directed my attention to the Ambassador, and asked, "Would you be permitted to enlighten them?"

My sense of the Ambassador was proved. He was not biased against me and he did as I suggested. He began to list Auglan's crimes, but he was not allowed to continue for long before Lord Eamon requested him to stop.

The Ambassador changed his topic. "The information that the Atapi encouraged from the Selkrit calling himself Auglan, was required by the Enforcers to determine his fit punishment. He was executed by order of the Galactic Council.

While the Kimh were digesting that shocking information, I spoke again. "You should be thanking the Atapi for protecting you from the worst of those aliens' depredations." The bench of Elders might just as well have been a brick wall. "And you cannot be sure that others, as bad or worse, won't come in the future."

The Galactic Councillor used the shocked silence to speak up. "High Minister, Jai Cassidy is correct. That is why I urge you to become a member world of the Galactic Federation. We can provide protection."

Further babble broke out. I whispered to the Ambassador who had walked up next to me. "They won't, you know."

He nodded agreement. I appreciated his subtle gesture of support.

Koenig silenced the room again. He waited until it was quiet enough to hear one's own breathing before rising to speak.

"Jai Cassidy, this council has decreed that you and the remaining Atapi females will be allowed to leave and return to the tribes. Should you, or any Atapi, return to the occupied lands around here, you or they will be placed in seclusion."

"So I heard," I spoke in a clear voice, and amiably enough – since I was still out-witting him. "My parting advice to all of you is some wisdom I learnt from the Atapi Old One, some quotes from the Atapi Devil Lore… and I expect the courtesy of being listened to."

Trained politeness resulted in all the Elders, including Koenig, becoming quieter. It didn't stop all the murmuring or erase the looks of faint distaste on many of the faces. I wondered if they expected me to say things that were intolerable and offensive. I began before any of them thought to object.

"No one tribe, one gender, or one age group has the advantage of perfect judgement. Learning, training and experience bring wisdom. Having an open mind will reveal the truth.

No male of female is born superior to another. Tradition provides role guidance, but all should work within their own skills, ability and nature.

Why should all tribes and races, males and females, to be identical copies of each other? What would be the point? How would new ideas be spawned? How would unforeseen difficulties be overcome?

Action and reaction are equal and opposite. When you persecute people, you rouse them to be strong and they will react according to their nature.

Strength lies in differences, not similarities. It is only when all tribes, all races, work together that true unity is achieved. When we spill sweat, not blood."

There was utter silence when I finished, and into that silence I said, "I have heard of this happening, here on Korvu – Atapi, alien, Kumatan and Kimh – embracing their differences, finding the similarities. But since everyone here wants to persist in ignoring such precious moments, it will be a frigid day in Earth's hell before I come back to help any Kimh or Kumatan."

All the Elders vented their disagreement, rejecting my apparent twisting of the words they lived by. Koenig tried to regain control of the Council and order me detained, but the voices in the chamber were too loud, even for the bell.

I walked out before he could have me secluded for treason. Kaer made to rise and follow me, but I spoke to his mind. "Don't. I'm going. Be good to Mikha, please."

As for the rest of the Kimh, I hope their Nuath haunted them, the hypocrites.

I strode back to Kaer's suite to say my goodbyes and to insist on having Teresa and 'Farcine' released. Jenha, somehow, knew when I left the Council chamber and intercepted me. As we walked back, he deflected the guards. I am sure he sensed my mood, but he made no comment on it.

"Anna is safely with the healer," he told me. "The other two are waiting in Kaer's suite. You should not stay much longer."

"Thank you, Jenha. For everything. What I said to the Council does not apply to you. If you need my aid, you will not need to beg – it is yours without question."

"Thank you, Jai-devil. Be well."

He left me at the door of Kaer's suite. The guards there were used to me and let me in.

My abrupt departure from the Council would win me no favours from the Kimh. When I had left before, they had warned that I would be secluded if I returned. I was sure Koenig would consider that, particularly in the light of my admissions that only I could bring the Atapi back. No way would I let him capture and control me.

Therefore, I chose to heed Jenha's warning and went at once to Mikha's room. On the way, I glanced at Teresa and her disguised mate, and smiled at the two very efficient looking Kumatan guards. They saluted me as if I was their superior in the guards.

I slipped into the room, and saw Jahni sitting beside the bed reading to Mikha. Neither noticed me for a moment and I wanted to impress that scene into my memory. Janhi sensed me and turned. Mikha scrambled from his blankets and held his arms out to me. I moved close and let him climb into my arms. I sat on the bed and buried my face in his head of tight black curls. Janhi moved to sit beside me and I freed one arm to hug him, too.

From my son, I sensed unconditional love. From Jahni, I received uncritical, deep friendship and respect.

Jenha's elder son had done as he promised me, and taught Mikha to love me. I had no way to thank him, except to give him my trust.

From a pocket in my new clothes, I brought out a small box. It was the thickness of my little finger and the size of my palm. "Do you still have the jewel I gave you?"

He nodded. "I still don't understand how to use it," he admitted in a whisper.

"There is still time," I assured him softly. "This box is another such key. I made it on the other plane, and I give it to you on this one. It is for Mikha, so he can find me."

"I will keep it safe, Jai. I promise. Can you tell me how to use it?"

I considered quickly. "You will need to learn to walk across planes like Traegers do."

"They won't teach me that," Jahni said sourly.

"You have the power in you," I told him. Then I gave him a very brief outline of how it was done. "I think, if you … um… accidently… try it, say from one side of the room to the other, and your father sees… he will be obliged to teach you properly."

I warned him of the danger of getting stuck half way in the black nothingness, then repeated to him the advice Jenha had given me. Jahni was listening avidly. "I will teach Mikha when he is older."

"Only if no one else will," I suggested. "To find me, Mikha must hold the box, and think of me as he walks the steps. That is all."

"Could I use it?" Jahni asked.

"Yes, but I do not advise it," I told him firmly. "And do not tell anyone what it is. Part of the box is a message recorded for Mikha. No one else will be able to see or hear it. Nor will he, until or unless his Atapi heritage surfaces. When that occurs, he will be driven to seek me out."

"I won't tell," Janhi promised.

I returned my attention to the clinging limpet who was my son, and wondered if he would remember what I told him today. "Mikha, my little warrior, my life is not here and yours must be. I can only be a mother to you in spirit, but you will always be the secret joy in my heart. Listen now, and remember always. I love you, but I want you to learn all that Jenha, your father, and Kaer, your guardian, can teach you. Obey them in all things."

Mikha buried his head on my chest and clung tighter. "In my heart I am human, and that is what I want you to be. But I am also Atapi and my two halves are not always in harmony. I know you will not have an easy time either. One day, your Atapi blood will cause you unrest. Then you will be welcome to come and seek me out."

He would understand one day, but now, at only four years old, all he knew was that I was leaving him again.

"Stay with me," he demanded, and repeated it over and over, each time getting louder.

Ellhi Mosellan rushed into the room. She hadn't expected to see me, and she tried to pry Mikha from me.

"You need to leave, Jai," she warned me, urgently. I didn't have to ask why.

"I know," I admitted as I tried to erect a barrier in my mind.

I could deal with the entire Atapi race, but I could not deal with my son by blocking him out of my mind. But that was what I had to do, and Mikha sensed it as a rejection. His screams turned to anger. This, I realised, must have been what my father and foster mother had been forced to deal with, many times. Such strength of will.

It was into this a scene of chaos that Jenha and Kaer arrived. Jenha succeeded in taking Mikha into his arms, but he could not stop the screams that battered my physical ears and my emotional barrier. He sensed the barrier and the emotion it masked in my eyes.

"I have given you a devil's child," I told Jenha.

"He will forgive you," Jenha assured me. "He is a loving child. But you must go. The Council has pronounced sentence on you, and have ordered that you go into seclusion. They are on the way to the House of Contemplation to secure the Atapi females. When they find they have gone, they will come here."

Kaer took Mikha and spoke quietly to him. The screaming subsided. I was grateful to him, the man who had had the early rearing of my son.

I lowered my barriers, seeking my son's mind. Inadvertently, I touched Kaer's – controlled, unruffled. I sensed the genuine concern he had for Mikha. I relaxed, knowing that Mikha found Kaer a haven of peace. When he took Mikha from the room, I took a moment to embrace Jenha, Ellhi and Jahni in turn.

"Your son will be well, Jai, and I hope you, too, will find peace," Jenha told me.

"I have found my purpose," I said. "That will have to do. Please don't let Mikha forget me. Teach him about the Atapi – their good qualities and what drives them. Don't let them teach him to hate them. I know you and Kaer will teach him to master their influence."

"Are you sure no one will find you?" Jahni asked me.

"Yes. We are still on Korvu, just… not here."

I saw Jenha nod, understanding. He could follow me to that other plane if he chose, but he would not lead others to me just for revenge for past wrongs.

"One day you might need the Atapi," I said to both father and son. "The Atapi will be ready. But I have to go. Is the barrier still up?"

Jenha shook his head. I understood. I strode out to the other room, gestured to Teresa and Nikal, and 'walked' the three of us elsewhere.

Jahni followed Jai out of Mikha's room and saw her vanish from sight. He straightened and tried to shrug off his regret at her departure. He heard in his mind the final whispered words that Jai had said to him. "Do not fight Kaer. He is not your enemy."

It reminded him of the box sitting heavily in his pocket. He took leave of his father and went across to his own room, intending to hide the box.

He was startled to find Kaer sitting in his chair, waiting for him. He forced himself to hide his irritation. Kaer was still his guardian, even though his father was once again a full Traeger. He had not got over his resentment that the guardianship had not ended with his father's promotion. It seemed that the Kimh still wanted him to be a Traeger, even though the prestige of that role seemed to have less and less meaning for him.

"My Lord." He managed to speak the ritual greeting.

"Show me what Jai gave you," Kaer asked.

Jahni wanted to lie and say, "She gave me nothing," but he could not look into those calm, implacable eyes and utter the words. Neither did he want to betray Jai's trust. He stood unmoving, torn in two ways. Kaer waited patiently for his answer.

"I cannot give it to you," Jahni said finally. "I promised Jai that I would keep it in trust for Mikha."

"Need I remind you that I am Mikha's guardian," Kaer said relentlessly. "And yours?"

Jahni tried to stare back, but had to drop his eyes.

"That object has set off every sensor in the palace," Kaer said.

"But… she must have had it when she arrived," Jahni stammered. "Days ago – why now?"

He was only just aware of the muted alarm klaxons. "Her leaving must have…"

"That is not the intruder alarm," Kaer told his ward. "No doubt she intended to confuse the guards. Once they know that Jai Cassidy is gone, and the sensors are still aware of the object, they will search."

Janhi felt rooted to the floor with indecision.

Kaer went on, "The Council sent guards to apprehend Jai Cassidy. If they find the object in your possession, you will be charged with abetting her departure. The object will be confiscated and destroyed. You will be required to attend the counsellors and undergo a period of solitary meditation. Is that what you want?"

Logic – cold and inescapable.

Unhappily, Jahni reached into his pocket. "Mikha will need it," his voice held a plea.

"Mikha will not be Atapi," Kaer said bluntly.

"He is Jai's son. She said his Atapi heritage will surface," Jahni told his guardian. The box was in his hand.

"Mikha will learn self-control and self-discipline. He will, with the right training, overcome that heritage."

"You are wrong, my Lord," Jahni dared to argue. He was barely holding onto his own self-control and anger.

Kaer held out his hand for the metal box. Jahni placed it carefully on the small table, out of his guardian's reach, and turned to walk out of the room – ignoring the protocol of asking permission to leave.

"Jahni!"

Janhi stopped, but did not turn to face his guardian. He did not want Kaer to see how close he was to losing control. "With your permission, my Lord, I would like to leave." His voice was not quite steady.

"Why?" Kaer asked sharply, annoyed at the boy's rudeness. Protocol demanded that the lesser ranks did not turn their backs on the Kimh unless they were dismissed. Jahni knew better.

Thinking quickly, Jahni knew he could not just say he wanted to be alone to think. His guardian's tone told him he was in deep trouble. He turned and bowed. "My apologies, Lord Kaer. I have need of some solitary meditation and wished to find somewhere suitable."

"You may stay here," Kaer said, less severely. "When you are ready, you will bring that object and anything else Jai gave you to me."

Jahni nodded and stood aside to let Kaer leave the room. He felt no relief when he was alone. There would be words later about his rudeness. Plenty had been said when Kaer first became his guardian. He thought, resentfully, that most of his friends had little to do with the Kimh. He felt he had too damn much. Right then, he felt like indulging in some uncontrolled behaviour, like kicking something. A full on physical work out would have helped, but Kaer's "you may stay here," was more in the nature of 'you will stay here'. Meditation it would have to be.

Before he settled, there was a knock at his door. His father entered upon invitation. Jahni guessed that Kaer had sent him.

"Do you mind if I join you?" Jenha asked his son and received a quiet answer.

"I guess not." He gestured to the cleared centre of his room, and sat down on the floor, allowing his father to sit close enough for them to clasp hands, and to begin the preliminary relaxation exercises. They both went into a light trance, in which they were able to speak mind to mind.

"You would benefit from the training I had," Jenha merely stated as fact.

"It would not be honourable to be trained so when I have no intention of taking the Traeger's Oath," Jahni stated. "And you have not insisted before this – why now?"

"I am not insisting, I am merely saying it would help you at times such as this," Jenha calmed him. "You have a great deal of talent. There are other ways of using it for the good of others."

"The good of whom?" Jahni responded. His mental voice was almost sullen. "Before we came here, when you were on Earth, the position of Traeger meant something. You made decisions, were doing important things. Here the Traegers seem to be little more than flunkeys for the Kimh."

"Is that all you think I am?" Jenha asked.

"Father! I know you are more than that. But here, unless circumstances are extreme, you can't move without the Kimh saying so. It seems the new Traegers are still being trained in the same inflexible way and with the same intolerance to the Atapi. Even the title is snobbery. Slave masters! If that isn't saying the Atapi are inferior people, what is? I can't change those attitudes as a Traeger, but I might as a private citizen."

"What is it you think Traegers ought to become?" Jenha encouraged his son to talk.

"They should understand the Atapi as a race of people – appreciate their values, their intelligence and their culture. Not simply condemn them for past deeds. Sure, the Kumatan are not so perfect in our relations with them. We can't force our culture on them, any more than we would accept if we were forced to adopt theirs. They are different to us, but that doesn't mean we can't co-exist. The strengths and weakness of our race can complement those of the Atapi. Jai taught me a lot about them, and about this world. The Atapi know it intimately, we only know it second hand. We are missing so much by sending them away."

"I have had more chance than most to learn about the Atapi," Jenha admitted. "Even I am guilty of expecting barbaric deeds from any and all of them. I knew Con Ansuni and his sister Jai Ansuni, when I was young and neither were like their sire. Yet I still expect ill deeds from other Atapi."

"Jai Cassidy has never been like the tales of Atapi sorcerers," Jahni insisted.

"No, indeed," Jenha murmured. "When I saw her first, with you, her heritage was obvious, although she wasn't aware of it. I could not interfere then, even though her mixed blood had already caused her to reject her human kin. Events proved she had honour, and even though she had no reason to love the Atapi, since they only wanted her dead, she in turn did not want all of them to die. It seems to me to be an example of how Kumatan and Atapi can learn to accept each other."

"Lord Kaer said that Mikha will never be Atapi," Jahni admitted to the point that was the core of his discontent. "He says that with training and discipline, his Atapi heritage will never surface. Jai says it will be inevitable."

"Perhaps it is only you and I who can understand that mixed heritage," Jenha told his son. "We have lived with her, know her. She wants Mikha to be human at heart, and so she entrusted his rearing to us…"

"But the Kimh took him away…" Jahni interrupted, only to see his father's gesture for silence.

"The discipline and training that Lord Kaer can give him will help him," Jenha stressed. "Remember the times that Lord Kaer could calm him when we could not? Mikha will need to be able to find within himself a haven of peace. Kaer cannot teach him about the Atapi, so it is our responsibility to teach him to love his Atapi heritage, so that when it surfaces it will not tear him apart. He will have Jai's power, and mine. He must learn from this young age to use it wisely. In future years, he will be our only link to Jai and the Atapi."

"But you…"

"Now, yes, I could find her if I needed to, because I understand how she has hidden the Atapi. But as time passes, my connection to her will weaken."

"Jai left me something for Mikha." Jahni let his resentment show. "I promised to keep it safe, so when he needed to find her, he could. Lord Kaer will not let me honour my pledge to her. I have to take it to him, but if I do, how will my brother seek Jai?"

"Kaer is not as closed-minded as you fear. He, too, has had a glimpse of Jai's worth – yet he must act as he is expected to do. Let him safeguard what Jai gave you. He will not have them destroyed. When Mikha needs them, there will be a way to get them."

Jahni shook his head. "If his father learns of them, he will insist they be destroyed."

"Jai warned the Council that a time might come when they will need the Atapi. I do not think Kaer will forget that. She told us she would come if we needed her," Jenha assured his son. He still sensed resentment in his son, and decided to offer some advice. "There will be times when we have to go against the Kimh. If we are always resisting them about little things, when the matter is of vital importance, they will not heed us. Flow with them for now, and have faith in Lord Kaer."

Finally, Jahni nodded.

Jenha rose and said quietly, "Meditate in peace, my son."

Jahni remained in the position of meditation after his father had left. He thought over what they had discussed, and things that Jai had told him during that time long ago when they were waiting for Mikha's birth. His own inherited power was not that different from hers, and she had taught him how to find the silence at the heart of all living things. He sought that place now, and was reminded of how Kaer had helped him when he had first come to the palace. He had been kind, even if he had also been a very terrifying person. He thought of how Jai and Kaer were together, and realised that Jai trusted Kaer, even though his father was set against her. If Jai trusted him with Mikha, could he do less with Jai's gift to her son?

The peace that he sought settled into his mind and he held onto it as he prepared himself to face his guardian.

During the past four years, he had never voluntarily sought out his guardian. Even now, it felt like an ordeal since he knew he would probably be sent for some sessions of counselling. He had been rude to his guardian, and deserved censure.

Yet Lord Kaer had protected him from the attentions of the High Minister in the past. That must mean he was less rigid in his thinking… perhaps he would understand how he felt in needing to keep a promise. Maybe, it would be better for Kaer to keep the box and the blue jewel.

No one was in the outer room of the suite when he emerged from his room and crossed to the room Kaer used as an office or retreat. He knocked softly on the door and heard the invitation to enter. His guardian was sitting in his chair reading from some papers, and looking relaxed.

He put the papers aside and gestured to a chair, but waited for Jahni to speak first. When his ward seemed unable to start, he suggested quietly, "I'd like to understand what is bothering you."

Keeping the image of peace in his mind, Jahni was able to talk to his guardian about why he was upset. Kaer listened without interrupting, and when Jahni had finished, they gently discussed the matter.

Jahni left, still feeling the peace within him and having a closer rapport with his guardian.

Teresa and Nikal looked around in awe as they arrived at the Rock of Arkor. Both were edgy as they knew the Rock was sacred and usually only sorcerers went there.

"No one will challenge you here," I assured them. "I want you to wait here. There is something I must do before we leave."

To them, it would seem that I walked into solid rock as I went into Larcia's cave.

"Larcia?" I spoke aloud.

Even though her remains were gone, I sensed her in the aura.

"Daughter?" was the response. "You have grown powerful. What do you wish of me?"

"To know that you are still here. I cannot sense you on the other plane."

"You can always return," she assured me.

"I know, my Queen. But I am thinking of the new sorcerers who might want to evoke the dreaming. I do not want them to be able to cross planes back to here at whim. You sent your crown to me there – can you not reach there?"

There was silence in my mind. Finally her answer came. "I think, perhaps, when you are there, I might be able to reach and allow others to dream from the cave there."

"What of others – if they invoke your name?" I asked.

"The connection might grow stronger over time. I can teach you how to record the new lore on the rock there."

It was my turn to think. At first I thought it better to keep all the recorded knowledge together. Ideally I would want the new learning recorded in both places, so that when we returned to the other plane, it would be there for us. Then I thought that the new learning, using the aura and not warping it, should be readily available to sorcerers in training.

"How does the dreaming work?" I asked.

"Work? It just is."

I tried to rephrase my question. "Did all the devils record their new learning in one specific place?"

"No, they simply found a place to inscribe what they would. Once done, it is reachable from every part of the Rock."

"I must find out, if I write to the Rock on the other plane, if you can read it here," I thought to Larcia.

"You could make a pass-through to here," Larcia suggested. "And have this cave sealed."

"I will think on it," I said. "Could you tell me how they record knowledge?"

Letting Larcia into my mind to teach me took my mind off having to leave Mikha again. I couldn't dwell on the pain of leaving him. I needed to look to the future. I needed to be Atapi.

As I considered the lesson, I felt Larcia become distant.

"Yes," she said in my mind. "I can sense that other cave. The Old One is there."

I wondered why, but I could learn the reason soon enough. It was time to collect Teresa and Nikal and return to the new place.

Crossing planes without using a pass-through was a new experience for Teresa and her mate. I held onto them and sensed their fear on the second step. When we again saw land around us, Nikal's face was stoic, and Teresa breathed deeply to calm herself. They both looked around, and I gave them time to sense the subtle differences.

"The little cairn of rocks is gone and there is a cave behind us now," Nikal observed.

"Yes. This plane is like the other, but only Atapi have ever been here. If you have recovered, I will take you to Con Ansuni where the others now live."

"No," Teresa said firmly.

I stared at her, but didn't grow angry. "Jai-devil," she began.

Nikal corrected her. "She-devil."

Teresa's eyes widened in awe and fear. "My pardon, She-devil," she said as she bowed low. Nikal copied her.

"Enough," I said mildly. "What did you want to tell me?"

"We want to stay with you, Jai, I mean She-devil. Both of us. Can we? Please?"

"Uh…" I was surprised. I wasn't expecting this. Having helpers would be useful, but I wasn't used to the idea. "If that is what you want, I would be honoured to have you as my helpers – though how you would be accepted by the Old One's tribe, I don't know."

"We will manage," Nikal stated. He seemed confident.

"Let me know if there is trouble you can't handle. I have rank enough now to knock heads," I offered.

"You are most kind, She-devil," Teresa murmured.

"In that case, you will need to wait around here for a bit. There is something I must do… in private."

They both bowed, agreeing to my request, and then walked off to a discreet distance.

I stood a while longer, outside of the cave, absorbing the aura. Larcia had been correct – the Old One was within. I could sense his frustration. The messages and knowledge in the aura was like static in his mind – tantalisingly out of reach.

He was not aware of me as I walked into the cave because I had blended my essence into the aura. With his eyes closed, he would not sense me. He sat facing the altar, and I walked to take a positon between him and it, facing him.

"Why are you here, Arclak?" I asked softly, speaking to his mind.

His eyes opened and he was surprised to see me. He was also relieved, but he stifled that emotion.

"I came seeking wisdom." His voice betrayed nothing. "Have you found that the aura has changed? I cannot dream here."

"It is in part because Larcia rests on the other plane, and so far all the knowledge is recorded on the other plane," I told him.

"You did not consider that before you had your grand plan," Arclak growled at me.

"No," I admitted, earning a snarl. "However, I have given the problem some thought, and I think you and I can link the two planes so we can again access the knowledge we need."

I could feel Larcia in my mind, but Arclak could not.

"I seem to be hearing voices, just too far away to understand," he said, confirming what I had sensed.

"When you invoke the dreaming, what do you do?" I asked.

"I dream," he growled.

This was frustrating – how could I explain what I needed to know? "Is it something you usually need to teach the young sorcerers?"

He gave me a look that should have cleaved me in two. I wondered if he would answer, but after a period of thought, he did.

"Some find it easy," he said neutrally. "Others must be taught to focus. There is a chant."

He spoke it to me and I repeated it in my mind – sensing its effect.

"Is it the most arrogant apprentices that find it hard?" I asked then.

After more thought, Arclak said, "Yes." He felt like he expected me to call him arrogant.

"That makes sense." An idea was beginning to emerge in my mind. I let Larcia's sword and crown become visible. The latter had settled on my head and I removed it.

Before Arclak began to do more than ooze resentment and resistance to the idea that I ruled him, I spoke quickly.

"Didn't know what use this damned thing could be – but I have an idea."

The Old One snarl-laughed. "Had you tried to act like the Kimh High Minister and claimed power over me – I would quickly have proved I was a match for you, She-devil."

"I will not underestimate my teacher and if I ever start acting like the one you mentioned, I would deserve to have my tail kicked."

"I am glad that we agree. What did you think of?"

"Do you know what a 'key' is?" I asked. What I referred to was crossing planes using an object.

"Only as a Kumatan object for securing chains," he said to me. "I sense your meaning is different."

"Yes and no." My intended explanation suddenly changed. "I would call it a way of bringing two places, planes, closer together."

"And this would do what?" Arclak demanded.

"It would make it possible to reach all the knowledge stored in the aura on the other plane."

"I know of no ritual to do that," Arclak growled.

"There has never been a need," I agreed. "The first time I crossed planes – like between this one and the old plane – I used a key. Something that was native to one plane, but I received in the other. This crown is such a thing. It was made on the old plane and I received it here."

I passed the crown to Arclak and suggested that he try to reach the aura of the old plane whilst holding it.

He did not tell me what it was that he wished to know and I did not ask. While he held the crown, my mind was full of the sense of not being ready to take Larcia's place. I began to sense the memories of another, and something rattled on the floor, taking my mind from them.

"It does not work!" Arclak snarled.

The crown that he had thrown across the cavern reappeared in my hands. I studied it as in my mind I asked Larcia for help. The answer came to me, but I wondered if Arclak trusted me enough to let me teach him.

"You have the skills to do this," I told him carefully. I did not want to seem to be calling him ignorant. "I know what the problem is, and it is my fault you are having trouble now."

He snarled at me again. "Explain, She-devil!"

"To read the knowledge in the aura requires empathy," I began. "All sorcerers must have this, or they cannot use the aura. When you were training me, it was like the way warriors are trained and I think they learn to block this sense. I can only think that when you invoke the dreaming, and sleep, the sense is not blocked, and you can sink in to the aura and learn what you need."

"You are trying my patience, She-devil. How is this your fault?"

"From when I fought you with empathy," I explained. Arclak snarled, not liking this reminder of his defeat. I went on. "Master, because of me, your empathic sense is wide open. You are blocking everything you are receiving from it and that is also blocking you from the aura. Let me help you with that."

"I am not your Master at this. Teach me the secret of empathy, She-devil!"

"Do whatever you do to attune yourself to the aura," I told him and composed myself to do the same. This lesson would be easier done mind to mind but he was suspicious and wary of my intentions. I tried to send to him the sense that I meant him no ill, but he resisted this since he was more used to having to watch his own back from the challenges of younger sorcerers.

He had to trust me. I reached out and gently held his hands. He tensed until he realised I intended no more than that slight touch. When he relaxed, I told him, "Come into my mind."

My inner thoughts were tightly shielded as I waited for the impact of his mind. I knew the strength of his mind from when I was his apprentice. Arclak tried to take advantage of me, and to control my mind. My barriers held, but then he had helped to strengthen and temper them. I did not react, or try to retaliate or force my mind on his. Instead, I waited and finally felt his respect and readiness to cooperate. Only then did I begin because to teach him about empathy, I needed to be wide open to him.

Into my mind again came the old memories – from Larcia, who was at the time a young Atapi empath. A crisis threatened the Atapi at that time and she had reached into the aura of Korvu searching for an answer that would save her people. Memories of how the young Larcia had discovered what to do, but felt she was not strong enough to do it. Then we heard the memory of the voice that had spoken to her then, reassuring her. An unfamiliar word came into my mind – Arclak translated it as 'mother of the land'. We both felt that mind telling us to use the wisdom within the aura to learn, and the wisdom within self to guide. This was the primary tenet of Atapi Devil Lore.

Thus I showed Arclak, mind to mind, how I had built layers of shielding on my mind so that my empathy no longer overwhelmed me. I could selectively lower barriers when I needed to feel the sickness of a patient, or so I could heal, or sense the emotions of others. When I wanted to sneak around, I was tightly shielded and hidden in the aura so no one could sense me.

Arclak withdrew from my mind, but I kept a light link to his as he tried again to reach the aura of that other plane. I knew he succeeded, for I heard Larcia welcoming him and asking him what he needed. He did not know exactly what he needed, so he filled his mind with images of what concerned him. I interpreted them and they paralleled concerns of my own.

While I had been gone, he had determined that his oldest apprentice, Milben, and another apprentice were ready to be tested. The nature of the testing was clear in his mind; the thoroughness of the process was enlightening. My challenging of the Old One had short cut the process. Both apprentices had done well. In the past, the next step required spending a night in meditation at the base of the Rock of Arkor – for their secret name to come to them. For these two, this had not happened. The fate of these two apprentices was in limbo. The Old One had to decide their fate.

I let images from the other plane flow through my mind, flicking rapidly, until they slowed. I realised I was seeing Arclak's memory of his younger self as he relived the moment when the aura named him. I knew then that Larcia had named him. I let the images continue unheeded as I realised that this role would now be mine. I wondered what Larcia had looked for in the devils she named. Not all devils were named. The new images in my mind concentrated on the succession of candidates and I sought for the common factors that separated those that were named and those who slept at the foot of the rock and never woke.

To me, only a few Atapi stood out as distinct individuals, but in the memory of Larcia's life, she could see each Atapi as an individual and recognise tribal ethnic likenesses. Each new devil could trace his line of descent from one of the five great tribes, each begun by one of Larcia's five sorcerer sons. The names Larcia granted the new devils indicated the tribe that formed the major part of their heritage.

"She-devil?" Arclak interrupted the flow of memories, and I opened my physical eyes and dropped Arclak's hands.

He was waiting for me to accept my new role, but I had an imperative question.

"How will your successor be chosen?"

"If I die, the next oldest surviving devil will assume the role of Old One."

"And?"

Arclak snarl-grinned. "He must survive the challenges of any younger ambitious devils to prove his fitness to rule."

"What if the Old One becomes too old to rule wisely?" I asked.

"Then the Old One would be challenged, and lose."

I had learnt to respect Arclak, and in turn had won his respect. We could work together for the benefit of the tribes. My former Master was already a thousand years old, but he should still live for a long time with my subtle support. When the time came to choose a successor, I would have a role in that, I promised myself.

"The two candidates that concern you are the first of a new era of sorcerers, Arclak," I said solemnly. "They must undergo one final test." In my mind, I knew what that had to be. "I will seal this cavern as it is on the other plane. Then, when you and the other sorcerers have tested each apprentice, I will join them in their vigil. I will teach them about empathy and how to become attuned to the aura. Then I will leave them to their meditations. When they can find their way into this cavern, they will be named. It will seem to be as it has always been."

"Then it will be you who judges us all!" Arclak challenged.

I did not answer immediately, but sat still as I recited the ritual to seal off the cavern.

"Each of you was judged by the power within the aura – the spirit of Larcia. Not all that were tested received a name. I know why some failed."

"Tell me, She-devil," Arclak asked me.

I spoke a word in the old Atapi language. It meant 'Ancient Father' and it was a term of great respect.

"Ancient Father – what I speak of now must remain a secret between you and me. Of all Atapi, only you and I know that Larcia was more than just an ancient legend. She was a focus for the aura of Korvu. You alone know that I have become the new focus – although not in the same way as Larcia. However, I am young and have not had thousands of years to gain wisdom. I must draw on the wisdom of Larcia as I gain wisdom of my own. She will guide me in learning the true heart of each apprentice."

I shifted position slightly to ease stiff muscles and to retain an image of one who is not godlike.

"I have told you where my life's work lies, and to carry it out, I must work with all the tribes. All the tribal sorcerer-devils respect you because you are the Old One. I need them to respect me, too, but not to fear me or revere me as some almost deity. I have to be approachable."

"You are still a female," Arclak stated. "But that you have full devil status will set you apart."

"I understand that. May we come to an understanding?"

He considered me for a long moment. "What are you asking?"

"That I might take a place beside you as leader but, by my choice, be seen as slightly inferior to you in rank."

I saw Arclak begin to snarl-grin. "However, you must not forget that I can, if I choose, enforce my will. I will only do that, though, if the reason is imperative. I still have much to learn, and I hope much you can learn from me. I hope you will listen and consider what I tell you when I feel I must have a say in the decisions you make."

"I will listen, She-devil," Arclak promised.

As confirmation, I simply nodded and returned to the problem concerning Arclak.

"The moon is still full. Have the two who were tested back here tonight."

Arclak rose, bowed his head to me a mere fraction, and walked from the cave – disappearing back to his tribal lands.

When he had gone, I stood with a fluid grace honed by the years of practicing the squatting position. One could not stand as quickly from the human style of sitting cross-legged on the ground. When I drew the crown and sword back to visibility, I felt the aura easing the vague aches and stiffness. The sword stayed at its place by my side, but I took the crown in my hands and placed it on the stone altar – the replica of the one where Larcia's remains had been on the other plane.

My fingers felt the rock, hard and rough, but when the crown touched it, it seemed to move subtly to cushion it.

That was the final clue I needed for what I had decided to do. For the next hour, I worked at forming the altar into an extension of the crown, and creating a new focus where the aura of the old plane and the new plane touched. Then I linked the outer cavern into the focus, so that I could once again hide this inner cavern from all others.

Success was obvious to me as the sense of Larcia grew stronger.

"You have wrought well, daughter." The sense of Larcia filled my mind. "Now as you look after the new tribes and land, I will continue to watch here."

"I had hoped that would be so," I admitted. "There are some of the other races who believe in you, too."

Before I left to return to my place with Arclak's tribe, I had some more sorcery to perform. When I was finished in there, the outer cavern would be the new dreaming place. However, I did not want to have to be there whenever a sorcerer wanted to invoke the dreaming, and I did not want just anyone to be able to enter.

For the existing sorcerers, I created a semi-permanent pass-through from a noticeable rock formation outside the cave, to within the outer cavern. It would only require a minor ritual to activate and I would teach the sorcerers that ritual.

That meant that when they wanted to invoke the dreaming, or bring in an apprentice to learn the dreaming, they could. As an afterthought, I added a second ritual that would be activated when the pass-through was active. This one would make the walls glow whenever someone was within.

I intended that the new sorcerers would not need to use that way in. For them, I would teach them about empathy and open it in them. If they could attune themselves to the aura, they would be able to see the cave opening and physically walk into the outer cavern. Knowing how the first of the new sorcerer apprentices had been trained, I expected them to find this difficult – opening their minds to the aura would feel a lot like being vulnerable. If they could get over that, they would feel the immense power available to them, and crave it. But in opening their empathy, they would find it most unpleasant to warp the aura as their Elders were used to doing. In future, I intended to have a part in training the newer apprentices so that the empathy became a natural part of them.

What it would mean that night was that if the two would-be sorcerers accepted the constraints of empathy, they would find the way into the cave to dream – and would learn their secret name. It would be their final test.

I would not attempt to open empathy in the existing sorcerers, as I had in the Old One, because they were hardened to warping the aura. Other than that, and except for Con Ansuni, they would never trust me enough to let my mind into theirs. Con might just be able to find the opening for himself.

For now, that was enough. However, in the future, I had it in mind to have a similar pass-through for the females who were healers. I would allow them to enter the inner cave so they too might share the knowledge recorded there.

I walked out of the cave and mentally called to Teresa and Nikal. They had walked some distance away, and I sensed they had been celebrating their new freedom by forming a new life. Within minutes, they were trotting up to me.

"I'll take you back with me now," I told them. "You will be able to stay in my little cave tonight. Once I have returned and changed into more suitable clothing, I will be returning here."

Both accepted my statement and moved close to me.

My return to the tribe of the Old One caused a ripple of excitement. Everyone who approached greeted me with a bow of respect. I had not realised that my new status was so obvious, and remarked as much to Teresa and Nikal.

"You are too modest, Jai-devil," Teresa said with a faint laugh.

The Eldest Mother hurried over to see me, a smile filling her face. I introduced Teresa and Nikal to her, and added that they had chosen to serve me and merited respect. She sent one of the hovering whelps to fetch Musani when Nikal asked to meet the Old One's chief warrior.

After that, with all the females eager to serve me, I asked only that food for three be brought to my cave, along with basic necessities for Teresa and Nikal.

I shooed the whelps away and directed Teresa to my cave. "This will be your place until you settle into the village and make a place for yourself," I offered. "We'll work out duties and other details tomorrow."

With that I went to my sleeping alcove and discovered that someone had replaced the sleeping furs with new ones, and left me new robes of finely dyed fur – a pleasant shade of green that I had not previously seen used by the Atapi. On closer inspection, I was overcome with delight. Whoever had made them knew that I did not share the male sorcerers' preference for minimal clothing, and had observed my preferred style of dress. These were not like the simple tunic frocks of the Atapi females, but a kind of sleeveless tunic that fell down over leggings. Each section was trimmed with white fur.

It was a gift worthy of a sorcerer, and I wondered who had arranged it and who had made them. It was exactly what I needed to show my rank and give me the confidence for my first acts as a sorceress.

CHAPTER 81 – Jai Cassidy – POV

When I went back to the Rock that night, I sensed the two almost-devils wandering in a state of unease not far away. I 'walked' to meet them, arriving in front of them as if I had just walked out of solid rock.

Milben stared at me; his initial snarl of derision was changed to one of respect. He saw that I had indeed become a full devil. I wondered if he knew I had defeated his sire. He had not been around when I had challenged the Old One and I had not wanted Arclak to be seen as defeated.

I read in their minds that they knew they had to find a cave – and their failure was weighing on their minds.

"Why are you here, Jai-devil?" the one I knew of as Dorsim demanded. He was Wyvek's apprentice. "Are you here to gloat?"

At the same moment, Milben commented, "I thought my sire had killed you or banished you."

"No, I challenged him, and survived," I stated.

"You received your secret name?" Milben demanded intently. I merely smiled, and they took that as an affirmative. He seemed to visibly shrink, as his defiant arrogance deflated.

I drew Larcia's sword from under its veil of illusion. It emitted a soft golden glow, enough so that the two males saw that I was indeed un-banded and I in turn saw that they had mastered the bands, too.

"How did you find the cave, Jai-devil?" Milben demanded, almost pleadingly.

"That is why I am here. You have been taught by all the other sorcerers, except me. You are the first of the new era of sorcery. I have knowledge that you will need and I will teach you the secret way into the cave. Will you listen to me?"

"Teach us, Jai-devil," they both asked with desperate desire.

In the hours that followed, I opened a channel of empathy in both of these young males. As I did, I examined them using my empathy against the standards Larcia had set. Then I set about teaching them to become more aware of the aura of Korvu, and gave them the sense of the power they could use if they were in tune with it. I taught them to shield their minds, as I had taught the Old One. As Sorcerer Devils, there would be times when they had to be hard, and could not be distracted by the emotions of others.

After I had told them enough, I repeated the details of the challenge they must achieve to receive their secret name.

"You must use what I have taught you and fully attune yourself to the aura. If you can do this, you will see the cave and be able to enter it. If you cannot, your eyes will never see the cave. When you are within, allow your mind to fill with that which you most desire. When you sleep, you will invoke the dreaming. If you are worthy, you will discover your secret name."

They stayed sitting cross-legged, facing the Rock, thinking over what I had taught them, and of the glimpse of my own power I had revealed to them. Neither saw me go. I would wait for them to enter the outer cavern, but I would be within the inner cave where they would not see me. I did not want them to know that their secret names would come from me.

Already I was sure that both would succeed, but it would take time. Both were greedy for the power I showed them, but they were also sure of their own excellence. Their earlier uncertainty had gone, but now they would have to make the deliberate choice to give up their control of their own power and become vulnerable. Only then would they be in tune with the aura.

Later, they would decide how to use their power – either in its natural form, or to warp it to their purpose. I believed that once the new sorcerers had sensed the source of greatest power they would pursue it. I would not teach any of this to the older sorcerer-devils – those that had led their tribes for decades. They had not, and probably would not, accept the restraints of empathy. Too many years of performing barbaric rituals had made them impervious to it. The new sorcerers would not have the reason or as much opportunity to practice those barbaric rituals and would turn their minds to other aspects of sorcery. When they became sorcerer-devils, with tribes of their own, I had hopes that the tribes they established would be strong and fertile.

When the first of the two would-be devils walked into the cavern, I was not surprised that it was Milben. As a rival for the Old One's approval, he knew more of what I had been capable of. However, Dorsim arrived soon after, and both adopted poses of meditation. I let my mind enter each of theirs in turn, and tracing their ancestries in the aura, found names for them – Andtrik and Yancek.

Such a simple thing – a secret name – but what a change! They had been full of themselves, outwardly, but still unsure deep down. Now they became assured, confident, and arrogant full sorcerer-devils.

With my mind, I watched them walk across planes and back to their tribes. I felt within myself a similar confidence now I had begun my life's work.

Unlike those males, I did not need a secret name to open my power. It was enough to know that I was who and what I was – Jai Cassidy – daughter of Matthew Cassidy and Jai Ansuni. My Atapi heritage could be traced back to Larcia; my destiny was just beginning.

The End

Other novels by Margaret Gregory

Atapi Sorceress Series - THE WILD ONE

Sixteen year old Jai Cassidy thought she was finally free of her family until
she is discovered by her other relatives…the ones that aren't human.
Jai uses her natural perversity and cunning to escape their control, but
catapults herself into the middle of a deadly feud between two alien races.

The Tymorean Trust Book 1 - POWER RISING

The Tymorean Trust -
When peace rules Tymorea - Peace reigns in the universe.
Chosen to be the Advocates of the mystical and incorporeal Guardians of
Peace, twins Tymos and Kryslie must first learn to control and use the
power rising in them - or it will destroy them. On Tymorea, only the ruling
Triumvirate Governors are powerful enough to guide the strong-willed
alien-bred twins until they have mastered their power.

The Tymorean Trust Book 2 - GREAT ONES

The peace of the Guardian Planet, Tymorea, is in deadly peril. War there
will create ripples of unrest and destruction throughout the settled
universe. Tymos and Kryslie, still adolescents, have barely mastered their
power and Llaimos is still less than a year old, but they are the three chosen
to be Advocates of the mystical Guardians of Peace, to safeguard the
Tymorean Trust.

The Tymorean Trust Book 3 - THE RETURN TO EARTH

Even before the war on Tymorea, the Elders foresaw that Great Ones
Tymos and Kryslie would have an imperative mission on Earth.
But as the Tymoreans prepare to build an Earthbase to support them, they
discover that specifications for two vital protective shields are missing.
Now, nearly a century later, Tymos and Kryslie must find his work and
build the generator before the base is found.

The Tymorean Trust Book 4 – <u>EARTH MISSION</u>

Just before their graduation from the prestigious WSRA Washington University, Tymos and Kryslie Ward deliberately disappear.
The Great Ones have foreseen the capture and death of the new Tymorean missionaries and discovered that the leader of the Eastern Imperium plans to undermine the United World Nations. Tymos and Kryslie must protect their kin and prevent a potentially devastating world war.

The Third Generation Series – <u>WANDA: FROM BAD TO WORSE</u>

If she was going to die young, like her mother, Gwen Willard was determined to die rich and she had very few years to do it. Her first step was to leave home.
She met Hooch, who taught her some exciting and illegal skills. She was the Dracos lucky mascot until she came to the attention of the police.
Then her uncanny knack for predicting trouble, warned her to flee to the city and change her name.
Life wasn't easy. She was 15, had little money and no regular job, but her new skills came in handy. Then she crossed the path of an evil and unscrupulous man and she didn't want him to have his way.